ASTEROIDS:

IT'S NOT JUST A GAME ANYMORE . . .

Carialle cornered wide around two sides of a rock ten times her size, then hugged in close behind a flattened sphere of an asteroid, searching for a ravine or a cave she could duck into. One of the intruders was waiting. Carialle grimly vectored away at as sharp an angle as she could.

A red light, infinitesimally small, bloomed on the pursuer's hull.

"Brace!" Carialle cried out as the energy bolt struck her.

The blast tore through her shields as if through cellophane. Painful heat ran along her sensors, which then mercifully died. Damage control monitors showed her an elongated oval tear in her dorsal hull. Emergency systems kicked into operation at once.

"How bad is it?" Keff asked the air.

"Hull breach, minor. Already being fixed," Carialle said shortly.

Keff slammed his fist down on the RECORD button to send a message to Central Worlds. "Mayday. This is the CK-963. We are under attack by three vessels, origin unknown. If we are unable to escape, send fleet ships to the Cridi system at once. We have already taken damage. I repeat, we are under attack—uh-oh! Cari, they're shooting again!"

"I'm moving, I'm moving!" Carialle exclaimed. The ship zigzagged, but there was no way to dodge another blast. "Our shields aren't meant to take this," she cried. . . .

BOOKS IN THIS SERIES

THE SHIP ERRANT

JODY LYNN NYE

THE SHIP ERRANT

A Baen Books Original

Baen Publishing Enterprises
P.O. Box 1403
Riverdale, NY 10471

ISBN: 0-671-87854-9

Cover art by Stephen Hickman

First paperback printing, December 1997

Distributed by Simon & Schuster
1230 Avenue of the Americas
New York, NY 10020

Library of Congress Catalog Number: 96-27743

Typeset by Windhaven Press, Auburn, NH
Printed in the United States of America

To Val and Rick
with love

Preface

To: Dr. Sennet Maxwell-Corey
Inspector General
Central Worlds Administration

From: Commander Lavon Muller-Danes
Alien Outreach Department

A transmission has been received by this office from
RNJ-599, known locally as Ozran, requesting transportation of representatives of its government to its
homeworld.

I have before me your memo asking me to inform
you if such an eventuality arose. While the CK-963
brain/brawn team is, to say the least, unorthodox in its
methods, it is effective. Furthermore, they did discover
the "globe-frogs," as they call the aliens, and they speak
the local language, which none of our other personnel do. Though the CK-963 would not have been my
personal choice to undertake this mission, I bow to
pressures from above that dictate we should not antag-
onize the Ozranians in any way, lest that jeopardize
future cooperation.

Furthermore, the Ozranians have particularly requested
that the same scoutship team convey them to their
homeworld. Unfortunately, due to discovery of the Ryxi
species a few months later, and the press of budget and

1

time considerations since then, the Ozran file was placed at the bottom of Alien Outreach's agenda. As a result, no secondary contact team had been dispatched to the colony world to make further contact with the amphibioid population as was originally planned. The Ozranians prefer to deal only with humans who are familiar to them, and insist on Carialle and Keff.

I gave orders that the team be pulled from its current assignment. It was a routine courier mission that did not specifically call for the talents of a brainship, and has been reassigned to another available crew.

In reply to your insistence that we immediately remove CK-963 from the Ozran return mission I am taking the opportunity to acquaint you with the details of the original mission. In view of the outstanding success of the first contact, it is AOD's opinion that there is no apparent need to take this action. While I have reviewed the voluminous file you forwarded, there is no event among the forty-six incidents listed that would warrant an immediate recall of the brain/brawn team. If at some future date you produce evidence of instability on a level as to interfere with the mission, we will then follow your recommendation and replace the CK-963 with the group of experts now being assembled for the follow-up mission to Ozran. Those specialists should be on the station designated SSS-900-C within a month. I have simplified the technical material so as to make it understandable by the members of your department.

AOD Mission CK-963 5458.89 OZ0001

Initial observation two years ago of indigenous life on planet RNJ-599 revealed that there were two, possibly three, species of tool-using beings resident there. All three groups were soft-skinned, bilaterally symmetrical upright bipeds. Two of them, very humanoid in appearance, had skin colors in the beige to dark-brown range. One group of these appeared more intelligent and advanced than the others. Their manipulative extremities had five digits, arranged as a human's would be, with four fingers and an opposable thumb. They used a sophisticated system of power manipulation that was so advanced in its technology that it could be used to make the user fly, teleport solid objects, or even change the weather. The second species of humanoid bipeds had only four digits on each manipulative extremity, and had hairy pelts. These beings served as the first group's trainable workforce. The Ozran "mages and magesses" (gender specific reference) had an extremely complex social hierarchy, and used without comprehension the scientific technology they possessed.

Because it was so easy to use by beings with a high level of telepathy, certain "mage(sse)s" were able to access an amulet's power more readily than others, hence the stratification of society. Because it was easier to use the conductor units than to accomplish a task by hand, over time the humans pushed the gigantic generator almost to destruction. By the time Keff and Carialle landed, the system was disintegrating dangerously, and Ozran society was in a downward spiral.

The third species, observed only casually, was a race of much smaller bipeds with skins in the green part of the spectrum. These lived a marginal existence in the meager swamps and marshlands of the arid continents.

Further observation revealed that both of the larger species were of the same race, and not native to Ozran. In fact, they *were* human beings. The four-fingered hands of the workforce were not the result of mutation, but mutilation. These mages and magesses mutilated the others to prevent the system being used by anyone not considered to belong to the intellectual elite.

The servitors were kept tractable with the use of drugs by the five-fingered controllers.

Upon investigation, the humans proved to be a colony of the Central Worlds, who had landed on Ozran ten centuries ago. Ancient records of the initial overfly of the planet showed it to be a plum for settlers, with a fortunate climate, arable land and potable water, nitrox-mix atmosphere, suitably balanced gravity, moons to produce tides, and generally non-toxic plant life. Over time, they entirely lost contact with the Colonization Department. These humans had not invented the power system, but rather had inherited it from a race that had temporarily inhabited the planet. It was this unknown race of aliens that had stolen the power system from its inventors. They passed it on to the human settlers, then died out without telling them its source.

The contact team discovered that the creators of the fabulous power control system turned out to be the small, green creatures (called by the scout team "globe-frogs"), also found not to be native to Ozran. The humans had dismissed the globe-frogs as mere swamp animals, failing to observe the signs of intelligence and civilization the beings displayed. It took special intervention by the brainship team to restore the technology to its inventors before the neglect of centuries caused a planetary cataclysm. Access to the power conductor units was sharply restricted, although not entirely removed from use by the mages and magesses. Before the team left they saw the beginnings of an attempt to establish a system of government shared equally by humans and globe-frogs.

This amphibioid species, while not indigenous to Ozran, is of unusual interest to many sections of the Central Worlds government, not the least of which is this one. Such interest centers mainly around this scientific breakthrough reported by the initial contact team: the device which makes possible the remote manipulation of matter. Empirical observation suggests that those humans who use it have inbred a tendency toward telempathy which is necessary to operate the system. Science Research seems to think that it is possible to develop a variation of the power amulet that will allow anyone to make use of the Ozranian generators. As a result, we are all anxious to cooperate in any way the Ozrans require, to retain access to this important scientific breakthrough. Other departments that have requested more information are Science Research, Linguistics, and Economic Development.

The location of the Cridi (globe-frog) homeworld has been pinpointed as closely as possible by Exploration's astronavigators. Assisted by Carialle, who also translated the globe-frogs' extant charts, a program was designed to roll back celestial movement to where the stars lay a thousand years ago, approximately the time the globe-frogs lost touch with their homeworld. Two possibilities have emerged: two dwarf yellow stars in binary combination. The CK-963 team is to try the nearer star first.

We have complied as promptly as possible with the amphibioids' request for the CK-963 to escort them to their homeworld. Central Worlds Administration pictures the globe-frogs as partners not only on the colony world of Ozran, but in the greater task of exploring the universe at large. We regret that the preliminary diplomatic and fact-finding mission to the globe-frogs' homeworld of Cridi also failed to materialize, but it is now too late either for regrets or a hasty dispatch of seasoned ambassadors. We are having to settle for Carialle and Keff going in cold.

I would like to assure you that both Carialle and Keff have been thoroughly briefed on the importance of this assignment, and have been cautioned under penalty to keep the contact on an absolutely professional level.

I again thank you for your interest in this department's function, and suggest that since we have come to terms with the immutable situation you should do so as well. I feel it is unwise to anticipate failure.

Sincerely,

Lavon Muller-Danes, Commander
Alien Outreach

Chapter 1

En Route to the Cridi System

"What say you, good Sir Frog?" Keff asked, peering over the head of the small, green, bipedal amphibioid at the pieces of the three-dimensional puzzle spinning in midair at the entrance of the great hall of Castle Aaargh. The green being glanced up at him. He gestured toward the conundrum then flicked the tip of his unnaturally long forefinger against his knobby temple.

"Not difficult," Tall Eyebrow signed. Swiftly, he pointed from one piece to another, indicating which edges fit against one another. As he made each match, the pieces flew together until there was only one object spinning before them. Keff studied it.

"The Mask of Mulhavey," he said, awed.

"What is this Mask of Mulhavey?" the globe-frog asked, combining sign language with the unfamiliar Standard words voiced in the high-pitched peep of his kind. "Is this an important artifact in your culture?"

"Just a pretend artifact, TE," Keff said, as a quick aside. "Carialle made it up for the game. Stay with it."

"Ah, make-believe." Tall Eyebrow nodded, and threw a self-deprecating gesture toward his host. "Forgive me. I forget this is but Myths and Legends." His signs grew more theatrical, in imitation of the human male. "What does this mean?"

7

"I know not, my lord," Keff said, replying in both frog sign language and Standard. "Perhaps if we looked through the eyeholes we would see a wonder."

"He's altogether too good at theoretical and combination spatial relations," Carialle said over the central room speaker as the two "adventurers" bent to see through the apertures of her creation. They made a curious picture. The man, of medium height for a human, had a broad chest, muscular arms and legs. He was dressed in a garment that reached to mid-thigh, not unlike a medieval tunic, over trousers and boots. His usual gentle countenance wore a watchful, inquiring scowl. Around his waist, a sword belt held a glow-tipped epee ready to hand. His companion stood less than a meter high, had shiny green skin, a short, narrow body and beady black eyes. His hands and feet were almost as large as those of the human beside him, the fingers of almost equal length to one another. He wore a beret, a short cape, and a belt around his small middle, its buckle a large, gold boss with five indentations in it that looked made for the fingertips to slide into.

"Better than I am, my lady," Keff laughed, shaking his head. "I give up, TE. You tell me what you think we need to do with it."

The game they were playing was Myths and Legends. Among the grounders, who occupied the safe and settled planets, it was a children's game. Keff had learned it in primary school, and had introduced it to his brain partner, Carialle, as a means of occupying the infinitely long intervals of space travel. To Keff it gave life a certain special meaning, to accomplish points of honor, to lay successes at the feet of his Lady Fair. He was a born knight errant. His private aim, ever since he had been a child, had been to *do good*, a goal that had gotten him into more than a few playground fights with schoolmates who lacked his natural devotion to the greater concept of truth. To Carialle, it provided an outlet for the creative bent that was so often lacking in the technical jobs given to shellpeople, even brainships. And it was fun. Over time, it had simply worked its way into their everyday lifestyle, to the despair of the Exploration arm of Central Worlds. To Exploration and Alien Outreach, Keff's globe-frog playmate was Tall Eyebrow, ambassador and representative from a shared colony world known to the humans who lived there as Ozran. To the knight and his lady, he was also occasionally the Frog Prince.

Tall Eyebrow gestured to Keff to look through the eyeholes. Carialle was amused when her brawn had to crouch down on the floor to put his head at the same level as the globe-frog's.

"It should have taken longer for him to solve that jigsaw," she said. "I'm going to have to make the puzzles harder. These little chappies have surprisingly deep minds. I am continually having to reevaluate my judgement of their ability to learn."

"Well, you've already surpassed my understanding, Cari," Keff said cheerfully, rising from his haunches with his hands on his thighs. He turned toward the titanium pillar that contained and protected her physical body, and winked. The two years that had passed since they had first met the globe-frogs had lightened a few more hairs on his curly head, and possibly slowed down his reactions by milliseconds, but hadn't taken a whit off his boundless good nature or enthusiasm. His muscle tone continued to be excellent, Carialle was pleased to note, and the bright blue eyes in his mild, bull-like face were clear and alert. Respiration and pulse, up a little, but that had to do with excitement over the game rather than exertion. He stretched his arms out and rotated his broad torso from side to side to ease his back. "Actually, I'm enjoying being TE's sidekick, if I allow the truth to be known. After adventuring on my own for so many years, a change is nice."

"I, too, am enjoying it," Tall Eyebrow signed quickly. "Too much reality for so long, to strive without fear is high fun."

Keff grinned. "Well, that's why we do it— Yoicks!"

Carialle had chosen that moment to activate the next peril in the ongoing game. The human jumped back as the holographic "stone wall" beside them slid back to reveal four villains, armed with chains and machetes. He felt for the light-tipped sword at his side, and was soon engaged in healthy battle with his computer-generated adversaries.

The enemy was only a holograph, but Carialle made them look utterly real, using a combination of projective cameras like the ones that drove her navigation screentank. The setting, complete with cobwebs and rats, could have been any pre-industrial village, instead of the cabin of a sophisticated starship. The brain behind it was as clever as the swordplay of the villain facing him.

Completely into his part once again, Keff slashed his blade overhand and thwacked the scarred villain in the arm. The man dropped his guard, giving Keff a chance to fling himself forward with a thrust to quarte. The glowing cursor went home, and the villain collapsed to the floor with a wail. Keff threw back his head with a feral laugh. "Come on! Who's next? Together we cannot be beaten!" Another adversary stepped forward over the body of his fallen chief, saber flashing in the candlelight.

The globe-frog emitted an alarmed squeak. "What are those?" he signed, pointing at the sparks, like fireflies, that poured out of the dark hall after the human villains.

"Some foul, unknown peril," Keff called over his shoulder, not taking time to sign. "Catch them!"

The sparks flitted all over the room. Keff ducked a squadron of the small glows, then skillfully parried a chop from one of the hoods wielding a machete.

The globe-frog took a moment, translating Standard human language to his own, then his small brow rose in comprehension. He bounded up to clap his hand against the wall next to Keff's head, trapping a "firefly."

"That's one," Carialle said. "Fifteen to go."

"You're letting them get away!" Keff cried. He was cornered between two of the foe, who stood tossing their weapons from hand to hand. One of them feinted, and Keff parried, sweating. Tall Eyebrow ran toward another elusive spark.

"I will assist!" cried Small Spot. He was the more impetuous of the two aides who had accompanied Tall Eyebrow from Ozran. Small Spot, in spite of his diminutive sounding name, was large, as the amphibioids went. The "spot" was a lighter greenish patch in the center of his forehead. Unlike most of his species, his hide had a smooth color all over but for that. He sprang up from where he had been sitting on Keff's weight bench to aid his prince. The fingers of one hand slid into the five long grooves of his power amulet, and he rose five meters in the air to capture a "firefly" that had slipped Tall Eyebrow's grasp.

He floated down from the ceiling, looking sheepishly at his empty palm. He glanced up at the others shyly.

"I forget, there is nothing there to touch."

His companion, Long Hand, an older and more cautious female, perched out of the way of the action on the console, emitting the high-pitched creaking that meant one of their species was laughing. Small Spot returned to his place, skinny knees bent to show embarrassment.

"I do not understand human games," he admitted, small face set in a self-deprecatory grimace. "It is one more cultural oddity to which we must adapt."

"Relax, Small Spot," Carialle said. She made the image of a globe-frog appear on the wall at their level, and addressed him in sign. "There's no disgrace in being fooled by a good illusion. One of my better ones, I must say."

"She . . . gets . . . better . . . all the time," Keff panted, dancing away from an enemy whose skill matched his own.

"I had not been observing properly," Small Spot said.

In shame, he flapped one of his big flat hands away from his face, not looking at her simulacrum. To distract him, Carialle showed him a different hologram, a piece of technological schematic she had adapted from her observation of the Core of Ozran, the gigantic power complex that supplied the amphibioids' amulets. The mechanism connected each user to the Core by means of high frequency transmission. For the journey to the globe-frogs' homeworld, Carialle had installed a similar but much smaller system to serve their needs while they were aboard. Their delicate skins needed to be kept moist. With the amulets they could maintain an electrostatic charge that clothed them with a film of water all over except the palms of their hands and the soles of their feet. It put a tremendous strain on her engines, but she and Keff felt it was necessary to allow them to have freedom of movement and so not everything on this ground-breaking trip would be strange. It was enough that they were the first of their kind to leave their planet for the first time in a thousand years. Carialle felt it was her duty to put the nervous amphibioids at their ease.

"Maybe you can help me," she said to Small Spot. "I felt another odd surge, another sonic feedback, when you used your amulet just now. If I've adjusted the receptors correctly you should be able to draw power from my engines without this much signal noise. I think the problem comes from here." A portion of the diagram enlarged, bulging out from the rest as if under a magnifying glass.

"Let me see," Small Spot signed, gesturing it closer,

clearly grateful for the chance to save face. Long Hand bounded down from the console with leggy grace, and trotted over to help. In no time at all, the two were signing away energetically over the faulty circuit diagram. At the other end of the room, Keff and Tall Eyebrow had moved on to the next part of the game, where they had to figure out the mystery that the Mask of Mulhavey was concealing, in spite of other pretend perils that occasionally distracted them. Tall Eyebrow grinned as Carialle responded to his questions, showing some of the hidden map and key as he answered each one correctly. Though make-believe was an unfamiliar concept to his species, Tall Eyebrow was embracing it as if he'd been brought up to it. In fact, the small aliens had adapted with remarkable speed to space travel, too.

The amphibioids, whom Keff and Carialle had dubbed "globe-frogs," for their mode of transportation (clear plastic bubbles partly filled with water) and their resemblance to Earth amphibians, had a very flexible outlook indeed. To ascend as they had from a marginal, swamp-bound existence where computer technology and particle science were taught in theory on clay tablets for lack of equipment in the lonely dream that one day they'd be able to use their handed-down education, to an equal partnership with technically capable but theoretically ignorant humans was a certifiable miracle. To then bring their shared planet forward centuries in only two Standard years was a more than respectable achievement. A human autocracy had been replaced by a republic governed by representatives of both races, human and globe-frog. When conditions had improved to a point where Tall Eyebrow and his conclave decided that the combined society would prosper without constant supervision, they sent a message to the Central Worlds, and asked for transportation to their native planet, Cridi, particularly requesting the CK-963 as their escort.

The team had been called home with a message coded urgent. They were briefed and rebriefed and re-rebriefed as to what to say and how to behave to the homeworld amphibioids. Carialle knew they weren't Alien Outreach Department's favorite team. The upper brass considered them too odd, too idiosyncratic to be good representatives of humanity and the Central Worlds. Still, it had been the CK-963, and not a more traditional team, that had discovered and reinstated the globe-frogs, and it was the CK-963 who must convey the visiting party from Ozran to Cridi. Carialle preferred to call their peculiarity "imagination" rather than "idiosyncracy," but looking at it from the perspective of people who ate pureed mush of unreconstructed proteins and carbs for lunch lest they be troubled by form, color, and texture, she supposed she and Keff must be as strange as . . . well, another alien race.

Several departments of CW had carefully examined all the tapes Keff and Carialle had made, and they wanted the power control technology. The team had warned that a high level of telepathic ability was necessary to operate it, and that unlimited use was destructive to the environment, but all the brass could see was effortless, remote manipulation of solid objects. Credit balances of high digits followed by endless zeroes danced before their eyes. Whatever obstacles needed to be overcome would be examined after the power control system was in their hands. Surely the Central Worlds had much they could offer in exchange. Carialle and Keff were to bend over backward and whistle if that was what was needed to ensure diplomatic ties with this fully mature, space-ready race of intelligent beings. Nothing must come between humanity and the Cridi, and the Cridi's wonderful scientific advances. The diplomatic arm warned the team to behave themselves, and put dozens of strictures upon them, punishable by fines and penalties too horrible to name. The brass weren't going to be best pleased that the "Odd Couple" had polluted the minds of the visiting party of frogs, teaching them their fantasy game to while away the long voyages. The slack cut for the CK-963 because of their big discovery would only go so far. Silly folderol would not be tolerated.

Carialle didn't care, and she knew Keff didn't, either. All they wanted was the opportunity to revisit Ozran, and they got it. They had been amazed at the difference after only a two-year absence. The almost-desert world of Ozran had become lush. Verdant cropland burgeoned, thousands of young trees sprouted, and the skies rained, rained, rained. Keff had found it dreary, but all Ozrans, shades of green and brown alike, stared up at the gray thunderclouds with expressions of bliss. It all depended upon your outlook, Carialle thought.

Tall Eyebrow had succeeded in trapping all the dragonflies, and Keff was out of swordsmen to kill, so Carialle slowly shifted the holographic view forward, engulfing them in the darkness of "the great hall."

"Great suns, the lights are disappearing," Keff complained. Worried cheeps erupted from the two globefrogs at the far side of the cabin, whose sole light source now was the hovering circuit diagram.

"Mulhavey," a tiny voice peeped.

Carialle smiled to herself. Tall Eyebrow had amazing powers of observation. On infrared, she watched his skinny form lope towards the spinning mask. He bent to look through it. It allowed you to see in the dark. He followed the floating hologram, grabbing Keff on the way, to three doors concealed behind a tapestry at the end of the room.

"Bend down," TE chirped in Standard, since his sign language was useless in the dark. He prodded Keff to look through the eyeholes at the three doors. They started a low discussion about which door to choose. Carialle left them to it, and made a crosscheck of her systems, and took a look at the long-range monitors. Hmm, number three engine was running a trifle too hot. She damped down the carburetion filter until all five engines were running in harmony.

Tall Eyebrow and his people had been out of touch with their homeworld, ever since the advent of the second alien race. Carialle reviewed the combination sign the Ozran globe-frogs had for these others, one hand with two fingers pointed downward like legs, but with the knees facing backward, and the other stretching the eyelids of one eye wide. No verbal name existed. The Crook-knees learned how the power system worked, commandeered all the power units in one single lightning grab, then moved their population base into the mountains, far out of reach of the Cridi. Without their devices, the globe-frogs were helpless. They couldn't range far from water, and had grown too dependent upon using the amulets to know how to survive without them. But a thousand years of subsistence living had taught them everything there was to know about making use of natural resources. Vulnerable to every hazard and large animal on the planet, sensitive to the atmosphere, and deprived of even basic luxuries they were forced to use the only resource left to them: their intellect. They lived virtually without waste, made use of all available resources, and appreciated every benefit that came their way. Carialle thought that such an admirable attitude would be a better import for the Central Worlds than the amulets.

The adventurers in her cabin passed through the correct doorway, and found themselves in a torchlit corridor, which in normal use was the passageway that led to Keff's quarters, the spare cabin, and the lift down to the storage bay. TE, letting the mask hologram float off, put his hand up flat to his face with the three middle fingers bunched together, and the long pinkie and almost equally long thumb slightly apart from the others so his round black eyes could peep through. It was his symbol for Carialle, "the One Who Watches From Behind the Wall."

"Yes?" Carialle asked at once.

"We have succeeded to the next stage. Food and water now?" the globe-frog asked, his small face plaintive.

"How thoughtless of me! Keff, you can go on for days without sustenance, and I have my own feeding systems, of course. Certainly, TE!" To keep within the context of the game, she had a floating globe appear that led the two adventurers toward the food synthesizer at the end of the cabin near the weight bench and the other two globe-frogs.

"I'd have just left the castle and gone to find a pub," Keff said apologetically. "Sorry, TE. You're not familiar with the conventions."

The hatch opened to disgorge in succession a bowl of succulent marsh greens, a glass of water, a glass of beer, some amorphous proteins shaped like Ozran grubs, and a plate containing one of Keff's favorite set lunches. Traveling with the globe-frogs was good not only for Keff, but for her as well. She had a chance to stretch her synthesizer's repertoire.

"There is not a strong enough resistor here," Small Spot said, pointing to the schematic. Carialle, distracted from her musings, noted his correction, tested it, found it good, and directed her internal mechanisms to make the adjustment.

"All right, try floating again," she instructed Small Spot. Obediently, the amphibioid put his fingertips into the niches on his amulet and took to the air.

But monitoring the game, meals, and the schematic took only a small portion of Carialle's attention. She had an oil painting in process, a globe-frog paddling its way across the dusty fields of Ozran, the way they were when she and Keff had first seen them, two years earlier. The canvas was meant to be a gift to the new joint government, to remind them of what they had left behind them. Her custom painting equipment took up as much space at one end of the cabin as Keff's exerciser did at the other. Critically, she examined each pixel she had done so far of the special microfiber-cell canvas, and with the greatest of care, flooded ten more cells of the thin, porous surface with medium green, and five with dark green, creating a minute stripe and highlight along a globe-frog's back. The result looked like a brush-stroke with a very fine sable brush, exactly as she wanted it to. She ought to be finished with the painting by the time they returned to Ozran. Carialle also gave her own hardware a good going over, to make certain the boffins in the repair bay at SSS-900-C, the last space station they had visited, hadn't left any screws untightened when they had examined her innards to install a ton of new memory. It appeared nothing had shaken loose since her last diagnostic. Their friend Simeon, the shellperson station manager, ran a tight ship. But Carialle liked to look after her own innards.

It was a wonder that the human race hadn't met the amphibioid race at least in passing. The coordinates that TE had given Carialle for his homeworld weren't far from P-sector, where Carialle herself had traveled many years before. Had no bored scientist with a radio-digital telescope ever swung it toward that system and picked up the traces of RF transmission? There could be a thousand explanations for failing to spot Cridi, but the result was, Carialle thought smugly, that she and Keff would be the first to meet the frogs, and the credit would be all theirs. Score two for the screwball crew, Carialle thought, her attention passing lightly over a cluster of unused memory cells. Alien Outreach didn't want a byte of possibly useful information about humankind's newest neighbor sacrificed for lack of space. They'd loaded her with new chips and controllers along every available circuit. Carialle felt that if she coughed she would rattle.

She scanned space around her. P-sector had only begun to be opened up in the last thirty years or so by exploration teams. It contained numerous spatial anomalies that frightened commercial shippers as much as it intrigued them as to what salable wonders might lie upon some of those as yet undiscovered planets circling the only just charted stars. When she herself had visited part of P-sector years ago, it was in the course of an investigation, with her first brawn, Fanine Takajima-Morrow, the mission had ended disastrously. A bomb planted by saboteurs in Carialle's fuel tank exploded, killing Fanine Takajima-Morrow, and leaving Carialle floating derelict, to wait weeks for rescue. She had survived, only narrowly avoiding the madness that haunts sensory deprivation.

It was right near here, in fact. Something long buried in her memory nudged her that she was passing within a few hundred thousand klicks of the exact spot. She did not even need to check the coordinates to know that that was true—how could she not have taken that into her calculations when she was planning the course to the Cridi system? Her thought processes must have been taken up with other things.

Still, her navigation program must have observed details about their route. Undoubtedly, her subconscious had told her she had old business to deal with, and steered her this way. Keff would have warned her to avoid the spot, if he had known. Bad luck, or some other softshell notion. But she wasn't superstitious— shellpeople weren't. Luck had little bearing on their situations. Considerable thought went into every facet of their lives, from pre-natal survival to the last hookup in their shells. Carialle's own disability had been diag- nosed while she was still in her mother's womb, and she had been enshelled at once to save her life. So why did she feel, as they said in the old saw Keff had once dug up in his linguistical research, as if a goose had walked over her grave? Could there be leftover psychic vibration in a place where a trauma had occurred? That had to be a myth, and yet she began to experience the anxieties she had suffered when she was marooned here. These—yes, these were the last stars she had seen before the bomb in her fuel tank exploded, destroying her first ship and killing Fanine. Adrenaline surged through her system. Frozen, Carialle felt panic rise, not stopping it as it turned her nerves to barbed wire. It could happen again! Frantically, she ran a safety check on the fuel mix in her tanks, measuring carbon levels, looking for the telltales that might indicate the presence of foreign substances.

"Cari!"

A millisecond passed before she recognized the voice, and responded.

"Keff?"

"Cari, what happened? The game holos are gone. Why did you fire off a message probe? What's wrong?"

That question brought her immediately back to the present. The cabin had indeed lost its veneer of medieval neglect. Keff and Tall Eyebrow stood in the center of the plain, enamel-painted room looking incongruous in tunics and swordbelts. Keff stared at her pillar.

"Are you all right?"

"What message probe?" she demanded, then checked her own telemetry. Sure enough, one of her small emergency rockets was streaking away into endless night, following a vector that would take it toward their last point of contact with the Central Worlds. Carialle searched the chips which supplied her with hard drive storage, found nothing, and extended the search to her other components.

"I didn't do that on purpose," Carialle said, crossly. "It must have been a malfunction caused by a bad connection. Darn it, and I was certain they'd checked everything in dry-dock!" Frantically she traced the circuits leading back from the controller in the rocket port.

"No, wait . . . Somebody planted a post-hypnotic suggestion on me."

Keff shook his head. "You can't be hypnotized, Cari."

"It's the shellperson equivalent," Carialle said, her voice becoming crisp and cold. "Programming has been inserted into my circuits to respond to certain stimuli under certain very precise conditions, with the result you have just observed. There are microfilaments inserted into my nutrient storage tanks. They are probably there to monitor unusual demand for brain chemicals and carbos in a combination that approximates paranoid hysteria with pseudo-psychotic overtones, a condition that I admit I submitted to momentarily just now."

"Who?" Keff asked, his face setting into a grim mask.

"Who do you think?" Carialle countered. "Who's been trying to Section-Eight me for the last twenty years? Who thinks I'm a flying emotional time bomb who should be relegated to controlling traffic on a Central Worlds ground station? Maxwell-Corey, of course. That afterburning, fardling collection of random neural firings Inspector General!"

"Are you sure?" Keff asked.

"Who else would Rube-Goldberg me without my knowledge?" Her blood pressure rose, so she adjusted slightly her intake of saline and gave herself five micrograms of a mood leveler. The panic attack had left behind its debris of epinephrines and excess gastric acids that were fast disappearing down the blood-cleansing apparatus. "He doesn't trust me. He never has."

"This is harassment," Keff said, all his protective tendencies coming out at once. "We should report it to SPRIM and MM." SPRIM was the Society for the Protection of the Rights of Intelligent Minorities, and

MM, Mutant Minorities, two agencies that spoke up
on behalf of shellpeople who ran into difficulties with
unshelled bureaucracy. Dr. Sennet Maxwell-Corey, a
psychiatrist by training and a nuisance by avocation,
was a particular bugbear to both of them, but he had
a special animus toward Carialle. He had never been
convinced she had recovered from being marooned.
The fact that she and Keff took a lighthearted view
toward the naming of the indigenous species they
encountered on their missions for Exploration, and their
devotion to playing Myths and Legends, made her
sanity all the more suspect to the unimaginative bureaucrat.

"I am composing something scathing right now,"
Carialle said, "while I destroy the implant with extreme
prejudice." Her self-repair facilities, micromachines of
various designs, crawled along the electronic neural
extenders and yanked the filaments out of her tanks
and filled in the drillmarks. Others traced down the
filaments to the control boxes carefully hidden in
deadware like the bottom of her waste tanks.

"Don't send the message without my input," Keff
insisted. He got up from his chair and paced back and
forth in front of her pillar. "I have something to say
about imperiling my partner's well-being. And I want
to tell them just what I think of his big-brotherism."
He smacked one fist into the other palm. Tall Eyebrow and the other two globe-frogs jumped away from
him. He was sorry to frighten them, but he was
unspeakably angry.

"Why did it happen?" he asked, stopping short and
looking up into her nearest camera eye.

"We're in P-sector," Carialle said flatly.

Keff's eyes went wide. He knew all about her history, and always had been extremely supportive in
helping her heal from her traumatic experience. "Are
we . . . there?"

"Yes."

Keff noticed the emergency lights on the console board, and went to shut off the alarms. "Are you all right now?"

"Yes." Carialle's voice was thin with anger. "Damn him! I passed my last six psych tests, two of them—*two!*—since our trip to Ozran. I feel *violated*. There's a message box in my memory, with all kinds of circumventions to make certain I couldn't detect it. Planted among the microdiodes at the same time as the uninitialized chips. Nowhere near the new stuff, which the wily bastard knew would be the first things I'd suspect. It's a custom job, too . . . "

Keff interrupted. "But why would you have reacted like that? Why would you have set it off at all?"

"I know every inch of this parsec," Carialle said unhappily. "I spent an eternity here, Keff. Not that far from here is where my fuel tanks blew up. There." A holoview of the sector appeared, with their path indicated in blue. A red X blossomed at a distance from their present location and floated toward them, crossing the blue line and passing toward a cluster of stars to their starboard stern. She squared up their current location on the tank, and Keff looked at it solemnly. "I was disabled here for weeks. And just for a moment, I was reliving that experience. I was *counting*, counting the seconds to keep from going insane. Then I remember feeling those footsteps on my hull, feeling those hands dismembering my components, stripping what they must have thought was a wreck, and hearing myself screaming. 'Who are you?'" she wailed.

Keff shuddered and covered his ears. "But it's been almost twenty years, Cari."

"You know what my memory is capable of. The sensation is as clear and intense as if it was just this minute for me! I was desperately afraid those unknowns would break open my shell and leave me to die in space. I was helpless! It affected me so deeply that no matter how well I think I am, subconsciously I have never gotten over it. I never found out who was performing salvage on my skin. The headshrinkers still don't believe that there was anyone there. M-C still must think I had a psychotic episode, dreamed the whole thing. That's why he's has been dogging me all these years. He's been so sure I would flip out. And he made doubly sure I would launch a message probe to him if ever I did, so he could drag me out of my ship and lock me in a padded room. I wonder what else is buried in there," she added bitterly.

"Nothing," Keff said, firmly. "He's not that imaginative. There won't even be a backup mechanism in case that failed. Look, Lady Fair." Sheathing his light sword, he stepped forward to plant both palms earnestly on her pillar. He looked up at the nearest camera eye. "When this is over, we'll find an independent, trustworthy memory doctor and have you scoped for other intruders. I'll stay there the whole time, if you want. I promise."

"I thank you for your courtesy, good Sir Knight."

The lady's face appeared and smiled at him, but the image wavered slightly. Carialle's heart wasn't in it. Keff's insides twisted with sympathy.

"We'll find those bastards one day," he promised her.

"Game is ended?" Tall Eyebrow piped up from behind him. "Enjoy games. Interruptedness?" The little alien stood in the passage opening, looking disappointed. Keff gave his forgotten playmate a rueful grin.

"Sorry, TE," Keff said. He moved away from the pillar, but kept an eye on it, wishing there was something he could do for her.

"I apologize," Carialle said contritely. "I didn't mean to let everything drop. Computer malfunction. Minor. It won't happen again." In a moment, the castle corridor rose around Keff again, and a three-dimensional letter puzzle appeared between them. Tall Eyebrow happily waddled over to it. As he moved his finger through the image of each two- or three-letter piece, it enunciated its sound. Some of them were syllables, and some were just noises, thrown in by Carialle for fun. With a delighted chuckle, the globe-frog began to construct Standard words out of the assorted noises, touching them again and again.

"Ook." "Hind." "Honk!" "Eeuu." "Be." "Aaa-OOO-ga!" "Be." "Loo." Ding!" "Ook." "Loo-ook," emerged from the audible babble as Tall Eyebrow found a match. Keff grinned.

"When all this is over, let's go find the parasites who were hacking you up, Cari," Keff said, making use of the sublingual implant in his jaw so the others couldn't hear him. "What with the bonuses from Ozran still in the bank, and the booty from this trip, we can afford to take even a year off."

"I hope the answers are still there to find," Carialle said in his aural implant.

"Look-be-hind-you," Tall Eyebrow spelled out aloud. "Look behind you," he signed suddenly to Keff. He spun in a circle, clutching his amulet in his long fingers.

"He's good," Carialle said. "Twenty-eight seconds, and it's not his native language."

More villains began to pour into the newly reconstructed great hall. Some were humans, brandishing weapons at Keff. Some were waist-high foes, snarling as they sought to surround Tall Eyebrow. Keff drew his sword, then hesitated, blade in midair. TE stood, gazing curiously at Keff, wondering why the man wasn't charging. The brawn looked at him, feeling as if he had seen them just now for the first time.

"I just had a horrible thought," Keff said, subvocally to Carialle. "What if it was TE's people, the Cridi, who were the ones stealing your components?"

"Don't think it hasn't occurred to me," Carialle said,

her voice crisp in his ear. "I hope not. I'm going to be watching them like a bank guard every minute. But I so hope not."

"I hope not, too. I wouldn't be able to behave the same towards them if they almost killed you, inadvertently or not."

"I refuse to theorize in advance of the facts, as someone once said," Carialle stated firmly. "Right now the important thing is to get TE and his party safely to Cridi. When this is over, we'll go and find out the truth."

"When you will and where you will, my lady," Keff said, swallowing his concern. His partner was under control again. If he pushed for more details he might risk making her relive her ordeal. He raised his sword before his face in salute and, with a gallant bow toward her holographic image, charged into the fray.

"Well, come on, TE!" he shouted at the surprised globe-frog. "You're on the threshold of your first big battle. Hop to it!"

Chapter 2

A few days later, Carialle interrupted the game and darkened the room to fill all the walls with views from her external sensors. The bright yellow-white, blue-white, and dull red dots of stars glimmered into view. Subtly, a white grid of low intensity divided the blackness into cubes.

"Gentleman and amphibians," she announced brightly. "Best visuals coming up. You see overhead on Y-vector the border between Sectors P and R. Imaginary, of course, visible only on benchmarking programs, but enhanced for your viewing pleasure. Beside us to starboard is a pentary of five stars known to Central Worlds as The Ring, a source of infernal radio interference to all space travelers hereabout. Below and to port, other constellations, brought in at *treee*mendous expense to the management. No shoving, please move along in an orderly fashion. And the entity ahead of us, frogs and sir, is star PLE-329-JK5, half of a binary otherwise known as your home system. And there, in that spot," she highlighted a single, dim yellow dot, two-thirds of the way around the ecliptic from them, "is your first real view of the planet Cridi. Welcome home, my friends."

"Hallelu!" Keff carolled, picking up datasheets and throwing them in the air.

Tall Eyebrow and Long Hand did a joyous dance together in midair around Keff's head. Small Spot bounded lightly from weight bench to wall to console and to Carialle's rack of paintings and back again, narrowly missing everyone else. They were all laughing in their shrill voices.

"How long until we make planetfall, Cari?" Keff called. He couldn't force himself to stop grinning. The corners of his mouth stayed glued up near his ears. He slapped his small friends on the back and shook their hands.

"A while yet," Carialle said. "I'm dumping velocity so I can drop into orbit at under 1,000 kilometers per hour. In the meantime, take a good look, folks. We made it."

The globe-frogs peeped and chirped to one another in high excitement, gesturing frantically at the holographic display.

"It is different from Ozran," Long Hand signed. "Orbit much wider. Cold?"

"Not recorded. We shall cope," Small Spot said. "See how warm the sun is! How lovely gold red."

"Who shall we meet?"

"Who indeed?"

Tall Eyebrow looked up at Keff in despair.

"What shall we say to one another? How different will we be from them?" he signed. "How will we interact?"

"Well," Carialle said, thoughtfully, "you've had a very small and limited gene pool to work with for ten centuries. I wouldn't be surprised if there hasn't been the beginnings of genetic shift, but it's unlikely to make any real difference. At worst you might need artificial assistance to interbreed with the majority population. We could offer Central Worlds' expertise in that department. Our scientists have no trouble fitting tab A into slot B, particularly with our knowledge of the confluent species that resembles yours in our biosphere. On the other hand, if you're just worried about your past experiences differing, I'd suggest you just be yourselves. They won't be expecting identical lines of development."

"Carialle!" Keff said in exasperation. Once a scientist, always a scientist. He turned to the aliens. "They'll just be glad to see you, TE."

"I do not know," Tall Eyebrow said, seeming dazed, staring at the tank. "It was not real until now."

"Well, it certainly is real," Keff said. He spotted an artifact ahead of them in the holoview. Its surface was too smooth to be natural. "What's that, Cari? Tracking stations? Signal beacon?"

"A little of each, I'd say. I'm getting a scan from it. Lots of subspace transmissions. I am recording them and attempting to translate."

"Feed it to me when you get something, please."

Keff sat down in the crash seat before the console and stared at the screen. He drummed his fingers on the console and tapped his toes in anticipation, feeling perfectly happy. This was a bonus, on top of the payoff for finding the civilizations on Ozran. To be able to observe an anthropological phenomenon heretofore unknown in human history: the first meeting of two different groups of the same race, divided for over a millenium. The linguistic diversity alone would provide him with the material for at least one blockbuster academic paper. Tall Eyebrow waddled over and hopped up to perch on the chair arm to watch with him.

"Anything yet?" Keff asked Carialle. "How about particle scans? How much activity is their spaceport seeing?"

"Patience, please. All I am seeing out there is a little debris, and some very old ion trails," Carialle said. The screen lit up with an overlay of green dust streaks that were scattered and stretched by the orbits of the planets in between. "I'd say no one's come through here in a long while."

"Always underfunded," Tall Eyebrow offered, with his hands turned slightly upward to show apology. "It is in the records. Resources small offered. Metal scarce. Volunteer work never enough, raw materials always short. Mission to Ozran one of three major projects to be funded in ten revolutions around the sun when my many-times ancestors had prepared for the journey to Ozran."

"Bureaucracy never changes anywhere," said Keff, sympathetically. Then he sat up straighter. "You don't mean you have memos dating from a thousand years back?"

"For every day," said the Frog Prince, with a satisfied gesture. "In all our troubles, that was never neglected. We have brought them with us for the perusal of the Cridi government."

Keff felt his jaw drop. The globe-frogs had loaded only a few containers into the cargo hold, and most had contained gifts. "In those little boxes you have a thousand years of records?"

"Communication system is kept frugally," Tall Eyebrow signed.

"I'm impressed with your systems," Carialle said.

"So am I," Keff said, with a whistle, promising himself a good rootle through the boxes when they were offloaded. "Talk about microstorage."

"Aha," Carialle announced. "It's sensed us. I'm receiving a hail from the orbiters."

She ran the data patterns through digital analysis, dividing the sum of on/not-on pulses by a range of prime numbers, formulae and logarithms, until she came up with a coherent 1028-unit wide digital signal. It wasn't a computer program, but a video transmission of an amphibioid wearing a glittering silver collar.

"Take a look at this," she said, and relayed it to the cabin screens. Keff was fascinated, but the three Ozranian globe-frogs were dumb with amazement.

"Not much obvious genetic difference, Cari," Keff said, staring at the image, looking at every detail. "Thank goodness for that."

The camera was centered on the Cridi's hands, rather than its face, which remained expressionless and still, staring at the video pickup with fixed, black eyes. The long hands snapped out signs in a quick sequence, then repeated it over and over again.

"I can read that. 'Identify yourself,'" Keff translated. "'Do not proceed further.'"

"There's a spoken language, too," Carialle said. "Transmitted on either sideband of each copy of this signal on every frequency I tune into: wide band, narrow band, microwave, datasquirt, even a form of tight-beam. Very thorough. They want to make certain you don't miss it. Very musical, too. Listen." She put the sound over the cabin speakers. A pattern of peeps, creaks, chirps, and trills repeated over and over again. Keff squinted with concentration as he listened to the rhythmic squeaking.

"I bet it says exactly the same thing as the hand-jive." Keff's eyes gleamed. "Record it, please, Cari, and run it through the IT."

Keff's Intentional Translator program had been of assistance in learning the Cridi's sign language back on Ozran. He was constantly updating the system, which theoretically contained full grammar and vocabulary for every alien language that the Central Worlds had yet discovered. The program functioned with indifferent success most of the time. It rarely provided them with the key to an alien language *when* an explorer needed it. More often, someone found a key first, then used IT to build up a translation system from collected data. The IT was still full of bugs, Carialle thought cynically, but Keff never seemed to be bothered by them. Still, he *had* been improving its interpretation of the Cridi signs.

"Ah," Tall Eyebrow signed, his black eyes shining, "the language of science! We have all but forgone its use in the arid atmosphere of Ozran. The waters and the globes prevent sound from carrying, and we have had no amulets to broadcast it, so we let it drop except infrequently, in conclave."

"Interesting cultural redundancy," said Keff.

"Not at all. It makes sense for a technologically advanced race to develop some kind of oral language," Carialle said, thoughtfully. "Having to manipulate starship controls while signing home to mission control seemed to me like a difficult combination."

"But they had created remote power control," Keff protested.

Carialle's voice was sugared with sweet and insufferable reason. "What did they do before the amulets came along?"

"Sign is older," Long Hand explained, waving her hands for attention and interrupting the argument. "It was our first true trait of civilization. The small voice," here her hands went to her throat, and indicated diminuition with a finger and thumb, "does not carry as well as long sight. It came useful when science reached us, but not during our earliest years. Silence was essential to hunting together in the earliest days. We have good eyes and poorer ears. The wild food animals had good ears, but bad eyes. We must show silently to one another our intent. To us it meant survival."

"To which condition we were reduced on Ozran," put in Tall Eyebrow. "It has been so many generations since we did anything but survive. I am glad to see in the last year we have not forgotten how to think, how to invent with our hands. I shall not be ashamed to face my ancestors' other descendants." But the Frog Prince looked nervous all the same.

"But can you translate it?" Keff asked, almost

bouncing with excitement. He gestured toward the
screen where the silver-torqued amphibioid was still
signing his message.

"If it has not changed since the mission to settle
Ozran," Tall Eyebrow signed, "we may be able to." His
hand waggled sideways to show uncertainty.

"This is a job for my all-purpose, handy dandy translating program." Keff flew to his console and opened
the file. He sat listening avidly to the excerpt, keying
in notes.

"But that trick never works," Carialle protested.

"Sure it does," Keff said with high good humor,
purposefully ignoring her insult. "Especially, because
this time I can cheat. I have a native speaker with me.
TE, will you tell me what each of these sounds means?"
He touched a control. "I'll slow it down, and you tell
me where each phrase starts and stops, and then translate it for me."

"If I can," TE signed nervously. He slid his hand into
his amulet to hover at the human's eye level.

They went through the recorded message together.
Keff listened with his teeth clenched as the slowed-
down chirrups grated through the speakers like chains
being dragged up a gravel road. At the Frog Prince's
signal, he tapped a computer key, designating the end
of a word or phrase.

"It seems to be linear," he said to Carialle. "The IT
is already beginning to crossmatch similarities between
phrases on the tape. Multiple overlay of meaning
beyond tense or gender would be more difficult to
distinguish. Now, TE, what do they mean?"

Tall Eyebrow tried to translate each phrase into sign
for them. He listened carefully, signing to Keff to replay
each several times.

"The first is formula for diminishing forward velocity
to zero, or 'halt,'" he said, holding up a skinny palm.
"These next four I do not know. Some familiarity, but

not enough. The first three are in command tense, but with certainty I cannot tell you their meanings."

"So there has been some linguistic shift," Keff said, nodding to Carialle's Lady Fair image on the wall. "It moves a lot faster than genetic or geographic alterations. Your ancestors might have used a more complex, extended phrase to mean whatever these do."

The globe-frog nodded, and tilted his head again to listen to the tape. "This is X=N, 'identify.' Three unknowns. This is the formula for no forward motion, 'not-proceed,' a command. More unknowns." Keff watched the small aliens hopefully as the tape ran out.

"Well, that's enough to go on," Carialle said. "It's very much what I comprehended from the visual portion of the signal. 'Stop, tell us who you are before you proceed.' Precisely what you'd expect from one of our own security beacons."

"Expressed entirely in mathematical concepts," Keff said. "Very interesting. TE, will you sing me the numerical sequence, and all the variables for IT?"

"With pleasure," the amphibioid said, still bobbing lightly on the air, "but what to do now about message heard?"

"Well, then, we reply as best we can," Keff said. "TE, do you want to do the honors?" He made way before the communications console, and courteously bowed the globe-frog into his own chair. "It's your home."

"I do not know what to do," the small alien said, looking up at Keff uncertainly. "What does one say to one's cousins after a thousand years?"

"Take one step at a time," Keff said. "Tell them who you are, where you're coming from, and ask permission to land. Mention us as your friends and allies. We don't want to have to explain anything more complicated than that at these long-distance rates. I'll stand behind you so they can see me. We'll answer their other questions when we arrive."

Following Keff's instructions, Tall Eyebrow made a brief translation. Carialle could see on close magnification that the small green male's hands were trembling, but his signing was perfectly clear and precise as he identified himself. The long part, the explanation of his people's long absence from Cridi, he alluded to with some quick symbols and a few chirps, mentioning Keff and Carialle as their rescuers and allies. At the end, he asked for instructions.

"Good, TE, good," Keff said soothingly, patting the globe-frog on the shoulder as soon as the camera went off. Tall Eyebrow's shoulders collapsed inward with relief. His two companions crowded in to comfort him.

"It is difficult," he signed.

"Good job. It's going to be a big day for you," Carialle said, signing through her globe-frog image. "That was just fine."

"And now, what?" Tall Eyebrow asked, stepping out into the air from Keff's chair, which was a meter too high for him.

"And now, we wait," Keff said, reclaiming his seat and throwing himself back with his hands behind his head. "Remember, they said, 'halt and not-proceed.' In the meantime you can sing me the symbols for each number, sign, and modifier."

They didn't have long to wait. Within a few hours, Carialle picked up a new transmission from the beacon. A harried-looking frog, not the silver-torqued one, appeared with a new message, which consisted of a single, short trill, and the screen went blank.

"What was that?" Carialle asked, replaying the transmission. "Welcome? Go away?"

Tall Eyebrow's hands flew. "It means 'proceed to the second planet from the sun, listen on this frequency for beacon, and follow in great-circle, equatorial orbit for landing procedure.' It would seem procedure does not change.'"

"That little ding-a-lingle meant all that?" Keff laughed.

"No stranger than the 'beep-a, beep-a'," Carialle imitated the communication-line busy signal, "which means, 'the party to whom you wished to speak is engaged on the line. Please disconnect and try again later.'"

"True," Keff said, his eyebrows raised in amusement.

"It is an abbreviation," TE acknowledged. "Such a sign is phonetically recorded in our archives. I am surprised to hear that it really does sound like it is written."

"It's a pity you didn't continue the use of your verbal language on Ozran," Carialle said. "Humans are geared toward spoken dialects. The mages might have realized sooner that you were sentient."

"Things might have gone faster with us, too," Keff agreed. "My IT program is geared more toward aural reception and translation."

"Yet inside our globes," Tall Eyebrow said gravely, "no one could have heard us cry out."

The second planet from the sun, behind a scorched clay rock and an insignificant asteroid belt where an unstable planet used to be, was large and beautiful and wet. As she swept into orbit above the equator, Carialle read her spectroanalysis monitors and discovered high relative humidity, due to a respectably thick and variable cloud cover in a nitrogen/oxygen atmosphere.

"I'll have mold galore, and possibly rust in my drawers when I lift off."

"Don't worry, lady," Keff said, cheerfully. "If TE's cousins have the magic technology, they can keep you as dry as you want."

"Oh, I want, I want," Carialle said. "That's one

application of the technology I would look forward to using."

Within minutes, Carialle had picked up the signal from the landing beacon on the largest landmass in the planetary-northern hemisphere. She oriented herself to it, following a great circular route that would pass directly over it.

Beneath them, peeping through the cloud cover, half a dozen small continents floated on the surface of a vast, blue-green ocean. Small, blue ice caps appeared, then fell off to either side of the globe as Carialle descended. As the clouds parted, they could see how very green the low-lying lands were. Small Spot and Long Hand looked positively awed. They had never imagined the existence of so much water. Hazel-brown islands dotted the seas like freckles. Carialle opened megachip memory to record every detail and gave full visuals to those in the control room.

There was some minor particulate matter in the atmosphere, probably a sign of industrial activity, that created a beautiful sunset half a world behind them. She caught the occasional sunspark as tiny airborne craft speeding below her reflected the yellow star's light. The whole scene reminded her of any one of hundreds of the Central Worlds, but everything was in such small scale compared to those in a human settlement. Her sensors told her that the flyers were only a meter square by less than two meters in length.

"How could we not have known they were here?" she wondered aloud.

Keff, never moving his eyes from the screen, shook his head slowly from side to side and clicked his tongue in agreement.

"This is the race, all right," Keff said, happily.

The partners' dream had always been to discover a sentient race equal to humanity in technological advancement and social development. There was no doubt about the well-established civilization below them, and their guests were living proof of the culture's prowess in space exploration.

The globe-frogs became agitated as the ship neared the stratosphere. Carialle picked up signals that were almost certainly what was arousing their senses.

"Take a look at the readings for the enormous power source down there," she told Keff. "Much larger than the Core of Ozran. The frequency hash is even greater. I'm reading controller codes in tiny bandwidths that I doubt could sustain what's necessary for one of the older amulets. Your machines will undoubtedly need tuning," she told Tall Eyebrow.

"It is true," he said, placing his long fingers on his belt buckle. "I can feel the great power source, but I cannot focus in on it to draw from it. My amulet frequency is already in use here."

"Well, you can stay on my engines for the time being," Carialle said. "Our hosts should give you a guest frequency when we land."

"But where *are* we going to land?" Keff asked. "The instructions didn't give a location."

As if in answer, the ship shuddered. Carialle felt a forcefield surround her firmly, but gently, like a velvet envelope. She tried to accelerate out of its grasp, but it was everywhere. It swept her out of her orbital path and rerouted her, drawing her into a side-to-side sine-curve path that led toward the surface. Her passengers were thrown off their feet. The surprised globe-frogs missed slamming into the wall only by swift use of their amulets. Keff, without technological assistance, was knocked to the floor. He grabbed for the base of the control chair as he slid towards the bulkhead, and hoisted himself up toward the seat. The three hovering amphibioids looked down at him sympathetically.

"That's why," Carialle said simply. "They're going to put us down on the landing pad themselves. *Damn* it!

I hate being manhandled—I mean, froghandled, when I'm perfectly capable of doing this myself."

"Do you mean you didn't make that course adjustment?" Keff asked, hauling himself up to his feet by grasping the arms of his crash couch. He sat down and pulled the impact straps around his body.

"Look, ma, no hands!" Carialle said, feeling somewhat bitter, but at the same time admiring the expertise and technology required to take over her landing. "You know I don't drive that badly. They've taken complete control of my vector and speed. I could shut off my engines right now and probably land very nicely, thank you, but I don't trust strangers that easily."

"They're holding us like an egg," Keff said, looking at the exterior pressure monitors. "It doesn't hurt, does it?"

"No," Carialle admitted, with the sound she used for a sigh. "However much I despise it, I have to admit they're doing a competent job. The Cridi are light-years beyond the skills of the mages of Ozran. It's more like a pillow than pincers. Chaumel the Silver and the other mages could only pin me down with their controllers. They couldn't catch me in flight."

"Lucky for us," Keff said, with a nod.

"And for us," Tall Eyebrow added, staring at the screen that monitored the continents over which they were flying. "Else we would not be returning home now."

"I'm shutting down thrusters," Carialle informed them.

At the same time the force was guiding her downward through the troposphere, Carialle had the sense she was being probed. The "mind" penetrated her hull, through her shielding, into and around her engines, her memory banks, the cabins and cargo hold, and into the shell which held her body. She stilled all life support activity except for respiration, wondering if she would be interfered with by curious technicians, but the touch passed on and out of her ship. She forced her circulatory system to excrete the unnecessary adrenaline produced by her anxiety, and added nutrients and serotonin from her protein and carbohydrate tanks. She disliked being out of control of her functions, but at least this time she could see everything and, to a minor extent, move herself slightly in the soft, invisible grasp.

"I will not panic," she told herself firmly. "I will not panic. I am in control. I can veer upward out of here at any time. I can. I *can*."

Of all the softshells in her cabin, only Keff was unaware of the scan. The frogs, whether through latent telempathic sensitivity or the offices of their amulets, knew someone was examining them. Tall Eyebrow put his hand to his face with his fingers parted: a question to her.

"Yes, I feel it," she said, verbally and with sign through her frog image. "We're being given the look-see to find out who we really are."

"We come in peace," Tall Eyebrow said, worriedly.

"They must know that," Carialle commented, "or they could have dashed us all over the scenery by now."

"They may still," said Long Hand, cynically. "Are they waiting until we are over a certain point to pull us down?"

The velvet envelope absorbed the inertia as it slowed Carialle's velocity down to about a third. Gradually, she dumped more speed as her course destination became more evident. The northern continent appeared over the rim of the planet. The ship was whisked over jungles and rivers and a network of small cities, all looming larger and larger as they dropped. Carialle focused in tightly on the terrain, judging by the angle of descent and speed where the invisible hand would eventually set them down. The datafile she'd gathered of Cridi geography during her spiral told her that ahead on the eastern edge was a broad, flat plain. Most likely the spaceport lay there.

Traveling at only a few thousand kilometers per hour Carialle had time to record more detail of the land below as well as speculate on the welcoming committee. Most definitely the Cridi held all the reins on access and communication. Keff was looking forward to airing his sign language and the smatterings he'd already picked up of cheeps and twitters. Carialle just hoped that she wouldn't have to face one of her worst fears: seeing parts of her original hull being used by humanity's newest allies as chip and dip trays.

The land dished upward into low, rounded, green-backed mountain ranges as a broad river valley spread out beneath her. Carialle's aesthetic sense was pleased by the cities she could see now in greater detail, integrated fully with the rainforests that covered most of the continent. Blue and bronze-metal skyscrapers poked up through clumps of trees that were like giant date palms. Tributaries that eventually led to the great river wound among residential areas, passing under innumerable small bridges. Much of the broad, green plains were uninhabited. Carialle guessed that the Cridi preferred to live in a jungle environment, and leave the open spaces to the ruminants. It was all unimaginably pretty.

"Brace yourselves!" Carialle announced, feeling the restraint around her tighten. Tall Eyebrow and his two companions buckled themselves into the second crash couch, their staring eyes grim as the ship seemed to skim right over the tops of the trees. Carialle widened the view out to give them an accurate picture of their descent. They were actually still hundreds of kilometers above the ground.

Now she could see a landing strip appearing in the extreme range of her sensors. The huge, open field was lined with rows of low buildings. Ragged heaps of undifferentiated junk, half-grown over with vegetation, lay at the edges of the field, but two nearly complete spacecraft stood proudly on the wide, green plain. Perfect miniatures, the graceful spires measured about a sixth of Carialle's height.

"Not much current use," Keff commented. "I guess what Tall Eyebrow said about sparse government funding holds true even ten centuries later."

Their speed lessened again, this time sharply. The passengers surged forward in their crash seats. Keff clutched the arms of his couch and ground his molars together. Forward propulsion was down to a few hundred kilometers per minute, then a few tens, then diminished entirely. Keff had an uncomfortable feeling of weightlessness for a moment.

"I'm upending," Carialle said. And she began to drop. Keff felt his heart slide upward to his throat. He gulped. The frogs, lifted momentarily upward against their straps, exchanged nervous glances among themselves, but none made a sound. The ship fell like a stone.

"If they drop us now, we're scattered components," Carialle said. "I couldn't ignite to full burners in time to save us."

Groaning against the gravity-force upthrust, Keff huddled back in his impact couch against the thrust, his heart racing.

"The question of the day," Carialle said in Keff's ear, her voice sounding sharp with panic regardless of her calm choice of words. "Would a culture with a technology this advanced be reduced to performing manual salvage on a space-marooned hulk?"

"Doubt it," Keff gritted, trying to keep his stomach from forcing its way up his throat and out of his mouth. His heart was in the way, and they'd all come out at once. He tried to sound definite. "Hope not." He closed his eyes and clutched harder, his fingers denting the upholstery of his crash couch, hoping the chair wouldn't have to live up to its name.

The red-painted ship descended gracelessly from high atmosphere onto the junk-strewn Thelerian plain. It landed with a boom that echoed into the surrounding mountains like a bark of divine laughter and sent yellow dust swirling up toward the hot, golden-white sun. Thunderstorm and Sunset waited until the roar of the engines died away, then approached the cylindrical tower.

"Almost a temple," Sunset said, unable to keep the awe out of his voice. He was very young. Thunderstorm smiled, his bifurcated upper lip parting to show the upper row of his fiercely pointed teeth.

"But the godhead is served by strange priests, Sunset," he warned. "Remember that."

A final deafening blast of fire spread out from under the tail of the red ship, making Sunset jump, then the engines shut down. Heat haze spread out from the hull, obscuring the tall cylinder in a shimmer. A tongue-shaped portion of the ship's wall separated and swung down on hinges until the tip touched the ground. A ramp, Sunset thought, trying out the human's word in his mind. Figures appeared in the opening. Sunset would have run ahead to meet the descending aliens, but Thunderstorm rattled a wingtip at him.

"With dignity, youngster!"

Chastened, Sunset dropped behind to follow his elder. Three upright figures walked down the ramp. Two of them stopped a half dozen body-lengths short, but the tallest one came up within a single length.

"Greetings, honored ones," Thunderstorm said. He bowed low, then introduced himself, his assistants, and Sunset. "As always, we are pleased to have you here, Fisman. To what do we owe the pleasure?"

So these were humans! Sunset thought, very excited.

The tallest alien, whose V-shaped torso lacked mammary protuberances, meaning that it was a male, grinned, meaning the corners of its mouth lifted, but the lip did not part in the center. What hair it had was mixed black and white. Its bare face was a narrow wedge, point down. Its mouth showed flat, white teeth like those of a rodent. He wore a smooth, slightly shiny tunic over thin covers that concealed his abdomen and limbs. Around his neck was a chain bearing many strange devices, among them a curly piece of metal with a sharpened point mounted at a perpendicular angle on a short stick, a bulbous construction mainly consisting of white glass with a shiny gray metal screw-shaped end, and a rectangular plate with characters on it in the human tongue. Sunset leaned a little closer to read it, and jumped back when the tall male made an impatient sign with his manipulative extremity—his *hand*.

"It's Bisman, damn it, Thunder, but after all these years I ought to know you still can't say your b's. Sunset, glad to meet you. This is Mirina and Zonzalo Don, brother and sister. My partner and her younger sibling. We bring you more parts, Thunder. Is this the apprentice you promised us?"

"Yes, sir."

The younger male approached only a few paces and looked down at Sunset haughtily. "Does he know his stuff?" Zonzalo asked.

Thunderstorm nudged Sunset forward.

He answered in the biped's language, carefully rehearsed for this moment. "I've memorized every component in the manuals. I know how to repair each one according to its rite. I obey orders."

"Very good," Mirina said, with a smile for Sunset. She was slightly wider in frame than her brother, and she had the proper protuberances, both front and side, of a human female. Sunset was glad. He'd been afraid he wouldn't be able to tell, and Thunderstorm had been firm about the etiquette of addressing humans correctly.

"Thank you, ma'am," Sunset said, which won him another smile from Mirina. Sunset noticed with a shock that the human had eyes of two colors arranged concentrically, with the pupil a *round dot* in the center. How incredibly strange. Yet, her eyes were the color of loamy soil: a warm, light brown, with a black ring separating the tan from the white; and her teeth, though flat, were very white. Sunset ducked his head to keep from staring. Humans were not so unattractive after all, even though they lacked proper haunches, tails, and wings.

"Has he taken the Oath?" the younger male asked.

He had. Thunderstorm had adminstered it himself. Sunset remembered all the grand-sounding phrases. They came to his mind as he stood, waiting as his elders discussed him over his head: obedience, silence, competence, humility, striving towards perfection in all things, and always keeping oriented to the Center of Thelerie.

"Yes," he piped up, realizing that Zonzalo expected him to say something.

"Do you know what it means to be a member of the Melange?" Bisman asked Sunset, for the first time looking him square in the eyes. That strange round stare was disconcerting. The younger Thelerie nodded several times to recover himself.

"I do. Humans and Thelerie together form the basis of trust. Since we are different, we may blend together only those things sacred and invisible such as trust and knowledge. But in that partnership we are indissoluble, and must remain loyal to one another throughout all time. Where our travels may lead us is a test of that trust."

It was practically quoting the Manuals, but the human didn't seem to mind. He nodded, bobbing his small round head up and down.

"Good. Well, there's no time like the present. Come on, lad," Bisman said.

"Now?"

Bisman glanced at Thunderstorm with an expression that Sunset could not translate. "Yes, now. We haven't got all day. My people are ready to unload and go as soon as we're refueled. Do you want a chance to serve, or not?"

"Of course I do," Sunset said, realizing he had made a mistake. "I am eager to serve. My skills are ready, and my center is sure."

That must have been the appropriate response, because the adults turned away from him then and chatted low among themselves. Bisman tapped himself on the manipulative extremity and spoke into his wrist. From the red ship, a crew of bipeds emerged. Part of the hull peeled away to reveal a huge storage bay full of containers.

At Thunderstorm's signal, many Thelerie came forward with the heavy lifting equipment they brought from the capital city. The human crew unloaded all the goods onto the pad, well away from where the fire would lick out and consume them when it departed. The cargo consisted of spaceship parts, and Sunset recognized all of them. Only the largest one, which had to be hoisted by derrick onto a flat car, he had never seen except in the manuals. It was a primary space drive, probably the first one on Thelerie in many years. Each one was numbered, he had been told, in over a hundred places, on each of its many components. So interested was he that he didn't hear the final transaction between the elders, Thunderstorm on behalf of the Thelerie, and Bisman, the spokeshuman.

"Come on, lad," Bisman said, coming over to tap Sunset on the wingjoint above his vestigial hand. "As a member of the Melange you've got to prove yourself now. This is your quest. We're looking at another opportunity to build onto your people's space fleet, but it takes time to get to where we're going to get more parts. Can't spend time jawing." He looked at the Thelerie and their wide faces. "You've got plenty of that."

It seemed to be a joke. At least, all the humans laughed. Sunset attempted to emulate the grin, keeping the centers of his lip together. He followed his new captains toward the ship. Sunset stared at it in fascination, seeing the joints of each part interlocked with the ones on every side. And within, the components working together in harmony like . . . like the Melange. All was as he had studied for the last three years.

On the side of the great, red ship were hieroglyphs of the human tongue. Sunset couldn't quite make out all of them, but he recognized the word "Central." He extended his wingtip to Thunderstorm, to ask him what they were, and touched no one. Startled, he looked back over his shoulder to see his elder standing at the side of the field, not moving. Sunset opened his great wings and glided back. It was almost the last time he'd be able to do that for a while, so he enjoyed the sensation of air under his pinions.

"Come on," he urged his mentor.

"I am not coming, youngster," Thunderstorm said, with a shake of his great head.

"Why not?"

The older Thelerie reared back onto his muscular haunches and touched Sunset with a foreclaw. "My reiving days are over, lad. Go with good grace. Come back with honor."

Chapter 3

"In ten, everybody. Ten, nine, eight . . ."

When Carialle's tailfins touched the ground, the passengers and Keff felt hardly a bump.

" . . . Two, one. Welcome to Cridi. And thank you for flying Air Carialle. Please wait until the captain has turned off the 'fasten seatbelts' sign before debarking."

Keff, who had been worried about her mental state when the Cridi took control of their flight path, was relieved at her flippancy. He took off his crash straps and stretched.

"Completely painless," Keff said to Tall Eyebrow, who timidly followed his host's lead. "No wonder your people have such a successful space program. No chance of breakup on reentry."

"No chance of missing the launch pad, either," Carialle said, activating one of her exterior cameras and tilting it downward. She had landed exactly in the middle of a round pavement surrounded by a pattern of lights laid out on the ground like a snowflake, illumination marching inward from the points.

Tall Eyebrow saluted Carialle for the safe landing.

"None of my doing, TE," she said. She noticed that his thin hands were still shaking, and made her frog image appear on the wall opposite him.

"Don't worry," she signed to him. "They'll be glad to see you."

"If only I can be certain," the Frog Prince signed back. He shook his head, a gesture of uncertainty that his people shared with humans.

"Here comes security," Keff said. "The party's beginning."

The first sight Keff had of the inhabitants of Tall Eyebrow's homeworld was the tops of helmeted and visored heads sticking out of an open vehicle that was plainly meant as field security. The flattened, molded, bulbous shape of the craft would force any missile, from thrown rocks to laser beams, to bounce upward or outward away from it. If there was anything aloft that looked more like the ancient myth of the flying saucer, Keff had yet to see it. How appropriate when the inhabitants were, verily, little green men. The thin pipes protruding from sockets in the vehicle's upper shell had to be weapons. He couldn't focus quickly enough on the moving craft to estimate whether the pipes shot solid projectiles or some other deterrent.

"I wish we could tell them we're unarmed," Keff said worriedly.

"They know," Carialle said, feeling the light sensation fluttering over all her sensors once more, this time lingering at the ends of her neural synapses. "We're being scanned again. Whew! That was thorough. Good thing I'm not ticklish. They probably also know your age, your shoe size, and how much you weigh."

"If they can do that, then why the heavy armament?" Keff wondered.

Through her audio monitors Carialle also received the frequency signatures of half a dozen frog devices, plus the quasi-telepathic communications that the system both required and made possible. Since the messages were in high-pitched cheeps and arpeggios, she couldn't understand until the IT got more data on

the language of Cridi science, but at least she understood the drill. It was carried out on every planet, spaceport and asteroid in the civilized galaxy.

"Trust, but verify," Carialle replied.

Another burst of high-pitched music issued from the
speakers, a mathematical sequence that Tall Eyebrow
quickly translated for them.

"Sigma is greater than zero. X equals zero. Y equals
zero. XY equals infinity."

"Very interesting," Carialle said. "To the rest of us
folks, it means, 'Come to a stop; don't move; don't
attempt to lift off. Any efforts will result in disinte-
gration into uncountable particles.' Not that I can move.
They've got me held as tightly as a fly in amber."

The frustration in her voice was not lost on Keff.
"Give them a moment to get to know us, Cari. We
haven't sent out a herald yet."

Carialle's Lady Fair image appeared on the wall beside him and made a face. Keff grinned.

The security vehicle made one more sweep, zooming close to Carialle's dorsal hull, then there was a hash
of static as several controller-based broadcasts collided
in mid-frequency. Tall Eyebrow looked at Keff and
shook his head. He couldn't translate any of that, either.
IT's vocabulary base gathered dozens of new syllables
and put them on a hold in the datastream.

From the buildings at the field's edge, a party of
frogs emerged and began to make their way across the
field. Instead of walking, they glided a few centimeters over most of the beautiful, green sward. Suspicious, Carialle did a scan of her own.

"Do you realize that these landing pads are almost
the only dry land in sight?" she said, showing them a
map of her soundings. "That bright verdure covers
either mud or marsh, depending on where you step."

"I bet only the poor folks on this planet live on dry
land," Keff said. "Water is riches around here."

"Then everyone's rich," Carialle said.

The welcoming committee came within half a kilometer and stopped. Keff counted eight frogs he would classify as dignitaries, and twice that many who were hangers-on, aides, and, to judge by the number of devices hovering in the air near them, reporters. Around them and the ship, the hovering security vehicles described slow circles. The three Ozranians stared at the images of their long-lost cousins, hands flying as they speculated on relationships.

"They are just like us," Long Hand said, with great interest.

"That's as far as they're going to come to meet us. You three had better make an appearance," Keff said.

"If . . . " Long Hand said, hands twitching nervously. She held onto her usual composure. "If they do not disapprove our coming."

"You won't know until you try," Carialle said, trying to lighten the situation. "But I know that our government would be thrilled beyond words to rediscover a long-lost colony. Go on."

At once, all three started to make a hasty toilette. Tall Eyebrow divested himself of his beret, sword belt, and cape. Small Spot checked his immaculate hide for dust or smudges. Long Hand dashed for the sonic shower and cleaned herself all over. They resumed their controller units on elastic belts around their chests. Tall Eyebrow already had his on from the game. Keff thought that they did it more for moral support than for use. Once out of the range of Carialle's engines, the ancient amulets would be of little use, even for keeping the skin of water around their bodies. The leader must have sensed Keff's thoughts, for even as he was fitting his long fingers into the five depressions on the bronzed surface of what once had been a lady's belt buckle, he gave a nervous smile.

"For luck only," he signed, crossing his two first

fingers, "since they cannot work here. We must go without globes as well as the protective slip of water. I will return to our people's birthplace standing tall and with dignity, ignoring inconvenience and discomfort."

Small Spot looked unhappy about his leader's last statement, but he too stood tall, and strode with what dignity he had toward the airlock.

"If we can do it without losing our pride," Long Hand said, more practically, "I will ask our cousins how to adapt the amulets to their system."

Carialle opened a tiny panel in her outer hull. A balloon pump took a fifteen cubic centimeter sample of the oxygen, which she ran through a barrage of tests for gas density, humidity, and chemical impurities. It confirmed what she had already guessed.

"The atmosphere's safe for all of you," she said. "Good, healthy nitrox mix, few harmful impurities, apart from a trace of predictable industrial pollution. More particulates than you three are used to, but not bad. If you want breathing filters, just ask."

Tall Eyebrow signed a polite refusal. He stared straight ahead of him as Keff moved to the controls for the airlock.

Keff stayed behind and out of sight as the ramp lowered and grounded with a squish. The Ozranians hung back a moment, reluctant to leave the surroundings that were, if not home, then safe and familiar.

"Go on," Keff urged them. "I'll be right behind you."

The amphibioids looked out across the field. Keff tried to picture himself in their place, to be the first to bridge the gap of a thousand years' silence, and was overwhelmed by the urgency of explaining, the enormity of understanding. Keff realized he had forgotten to breathe for a moment. Their feelings must have been shared by the party of dignitaries. The small party of dignitaries had pushed forward ahead of the crowd, and were looking expectantly at the ship's hatch. There was no perceptible physical difference between them and the three Ozran-born Cridi. Seeing no movement, the party surged forward again.

"It's your turn," Keff said, straightening up. "Are you ready?"

"No," Tall Eyebrow signed, "but, yes. Come."

With dignity, the small alien turned and walked out of the main cabin. Long Hand and Small Spot followed his example, straightening their spines and tilting their heads slightly upward. Together, they marched through the corridor and into the airlock. Carialle slid the inner door shut, and the outer door open.

Keff, right behind them in the shadows, heard shrill cheers as the crowd caught the first glimpse of the three Ozranians in the starship's airlock. In silhouette against the bright daylight outside, Keff could see Tall Eyebrow's knees begin to tremble. Small Spot, overwhelmed by the sound, edged backward until he bumped into Keff's legs.

"You can do it," he urged them. "Go on. Take that one last step. Just march forward. Count to a hundred. Don't think about anything but the numbers. Go on."

"One," TE counted out loud in Standard. "Two, three, four . . . " The other two marched behind them, out of the airlock, down the ramp, and into the sunshine. The crowd went wild, throwing flowers and sheaves of green plants into the air. Keff stayed behind to watch. He counted their footsteps. A hundred paces took the three visitors about half the way to the party of dignitaries on the edge of the field. There they hesitated, and the Cridi government officials took their cue at once. Dignified but clearly excited, they glided across the swampy ground, to alight in front of Tall Eyebrow and his companions.

"Go get 'em, frogs! Yeah!" he whispered.

"I'm all choked up," Carialle said in his ear.

Keff squinted, bringing the magnifying lens in his left eye to full telescopy, and listened to Carialle's amplified audio. He could see the expressions on the faces of the dignitaries: bemusement, kindness, curiosity, but no hostility. The globe-frogs had come home.

"Who are you?" signed the leader of the Cridi delegation, an elderly male whose once-smooth skin wrinkled into a million tiny folds around his wide mouth. A narrow cape of ornately braided strips hung to the ground from the nape of his neck. It was held there by a hammered bronze band that stretched across the top of his back and sprouted into filigree coils over his shoulders. "Where do you come from? We have seen the message sent to the beacon, and we do not know what to think."

Another Cridi, a slender female wearing a slim silver torc with matching bracelets and anklets piped an enthusiastic, "B equals B," and signed, "We agree! Since we received your transmission, all has been a flurry of excitement. Where do you come from?"

Tall Eyebrow identified himself and his companions. "We return to you from a colony world known as Ozran." The final name emerged as a buzz and a honk.

"Ozran?" one self-important frog repeated, bellying up to stand before the landing party. Of all the Cridi present, he was the largest: broad, round, and tall. His yellow green skin was mottled, reflecting a choleric nature. "What is this name *Ozran*?" he peeped indignantly. "Not a Cridi name." Keff chuckled to himself. It wasn't easy for a whistle to sound dignified.

"Big Voice is impatient, but he asks a question all of the Conclave have," said the elder. He brushed the palm of one hand lightly over the other and touched a delicate fingertip to his chest. "I am Smooth Hand," he said.

"In our ancestors' records our world is designated

as Sky Clear." Tall Eyebrow executed two symbols quickly, and vocalized a long, complex trill. Keff's aural implant barked out a long string of numbers punctuated with signs and symbols. He recognized the resultant formula as spatial coordinates, though naturally not those used by the Central Worlds.

Without changing expression the self-important frog leaned back on his heels and waved a single finger. One of the aides came running up to the leaders with a flat board to show them his notation. The eight leaders gathered around, emitting exclamations of disbelief and amazement. The aide moved back into the crowd, signing in an apparent aside to a friend. Everyone within range observed the gist of his statement, and passed it on. Word went around, catching fire within the group, until everyone was speculating about the data on the screen.

"How is this possible?" the senior Cridi said, looking up from the small board with delight. "We thought that colony had died. It was mourned many hundreds of years past. So many of our world's offshoots have failed, we thought that Sky Clear was just one more."

"We lost touch with Cridi through no fault of our own," Tall Eyebrow said. "It is a story of treachery, survival and, lastly, friendship, with beings like Keff." He turned to look expectantly back at the ship.

"My cue," Keff said, pulling down his tunic hem to make certain it was straight.

"I should say so," Carialle said. "Final subvocal check, please."

"If the folks back at SSS-900-C could see me now," Keff pronounced, into his oral implant as he stepped out into the airlock and walked down the ramp.

"You'd be the handsome prince from the fairy tale," Carialle said, amused. "Don't let anyone kiss you, or you'll turn back into a frog, too. Watch your step."

❖   ❖   ❖

The high humidity of the air outside slapped him in the face like a wet fish. Keff felt almost as if he were walking through a curtain of water, and highly unsavory swamp water at that. *Phew*. What he'd imagined looked like smooth, rolling fields was a level and endless pool of watery mud with petal-like plants growing on top, giving only an impression of solidity. He'd go floundering if he chanced to step off the solid base of the landing pad. No wonder nothing was ever built out on these open spaces. The atmosphere was breathable and flavored with smelly esters from abundant plant decay. Good photosynthesis action, that meant, resulting in the cyclic exchange of carbon dioxide. No wonder their explorers had chosen Ozran. The Cridi wanted the same things humans did in a colony. The xenobiologists were going to have a picnic here. As long as they didn't spread their cloth out on the green.

Keff moved slowly and cautiously, holding his hands away from his body to show that he was harmless, but there was no way to lessen the impact of his appearance on the crowd. As soon as they saw him, some of the Cridi scattered and ran away, shrieking. The rest stood rigid, staring and pointing, rows upon rows of pairs of beady black eyes, and long, green digits like accusatory asparagus.

He raised his arms to his waist to sign, "We come in peace."

His hands fluttered through the motions, then froze in the air by his belly. He tugged, trying to free himself from the invisible force. Nothing doing. The shock of his appearance had delayed security's reaction, but they were in command again. Cridi amulet power surrounded him with a rock-hard shell of invisible force, clamping him in place and forcing his arms down against his sides. He gasped, but not because of the jungle heat. The forcefield was just a little too tight around his chest. If it closed down any harder, he'd pass out. Giddily, he wondered if he would remain erect.

A host of helmeted frogs all but materialized at his side, preparing to defend against him should he move at all—as if he could.

"TE, tell them I'm your friend!" Keff gritted, willing his lips to move. Black spots danced in front of his eyes at the strain.

He wasn't sure if he could be heard over the screaming, but TE was a superlative lip reader. The Ozranian turned to sign at his hosts.

"Release him! Please!" Tall Eyebrow said, making energetic gestures at the eight leaders. "These are my friends, and the representatives of a great government, here to be our friends." He trotted back across the field and placed himself between Keff and the guards. "You must not treat them like animals or enemies."

The members of the conclave peered at Keff from a safe distance and Keff could feel his restraints ease off slightly. The youngest one took a step forward, thought better of it, and retreated to the far side of the solid platform. Smooth Hand, he of the ribbon cape, tilted his head to one side.

"Well, they are strange to us," he said, apologetically. "So large. Such an odd color in the face. And there is another one onboard the ship. Why will it not come out and show itself?"

"Because she cannot," TE said, emphasizing the feminine pronoun. "She lives within the walls, and never moves. Keff and Carialle are my friends and have been our defenders on the colony world of Ozran."

"Sky Clear!" the self-important one corrected him imperiously. "Why have you changed the name?"

"It is the name by which the joined colony of people like Keff and our own race is known," Long Hand added. "Humans live on the world with us."

"When the homeworld lost touch with Sky Clear

there were none but Cridi there," Smooth Hand said, referring to the data pad, which was held for him by a female in a red cloak.

"It would take long to explain by hand," TE said, looking back at his own aides. "We have archives to give you."

Small Spot, smiting himself in the head to show abashment for his forgetfulness, ran back into the ship to get the boxes of records.

Carialle, guessing what he wanted, had thoughtfully rolled out one of her small servo drones, and the excited globe-frog loaded the boxes aboard its flat back. The boxy robot followed him out to the waiting crowd, trundling stoutly over the soggy ground.

"We present to you the complete records for the life of our colony," Tall Eyebrow signed proudly. He stood back from the drone and allowed some of the guards to remove the boxes from its platform. Carialle recalled her robot, ordering it to spin its treads at the bottom of the ramp to avoid trudging mud over her decks.

"A magnificent gift," said the female in silver bangles. She pried open one of the containers and lifted out one of the tightly wound spools of plastic inside. "Unlooked-for treasure. It will make interesting reading. Scholars will vie for the honor of transcribing."

The elder statesman held up his hands to get the attention of the whole crowd. "We welcome you home, cousins, and look forward to writing joint history from now on," said Smooth Hand. "Perhaps together we will discover the well-being of other lost children of Cridi."

The old one stretched out his arms toward Tall Eyebrow, palms out. The Ozranian stepped forward, and laid his large hands against those of the elder. The crowd cheered again, and surrounded the three travelers. The senior Cridi beckoned.

"We all have much to discuss. But come, you are our honored guests. You shall have the finest accommodations, sample the best foods, visit sites of our history and of our future." He put an arm around Tall Eyebrow's back and led him toward the spaceport buildings surrounded by the chirping horde. Suddenly he looked back, an afterthought occurring to him. "Oh, bring the giant, too."

A guard waved his hand, and Keff stumbled forward.

"Depot in range," said Glashton, the pilot, over his shoulder. "I'm keeping that string of asteroids between us and their sensors."

"Good." Mirina Don paced back and forth behind the pilots' couches, peering at the computer construction of the asteroid-bound repair facility. Old, but well-supplied, if their scout's report was anything to go by. And they'd recently had a delivery that interested the Melange. "Notify Bisman."

The young Thelerie in the co-pilot's seat threw off his straps and arose, prepared to run aft. Mirina caught him by a wing-joint and turned him back. "No, Sunset. Use the intercom."

"Yes, madam," he said, his slit-like pupils wide. He scrambled back into his padded couch and reached out one skinny wing-hand to activate the communications channel, at the same time keeping track of the ship's progress. He lay rather than sat in the couch, his mighty haunches curled up behind, leaving free clawed fore-legs and wing-fingers so that his head was between two agile pairs of hands. The boffins told her that with their long eyes they could watch both sets at once. He glanced back at her eagerly. "He is on his way."

Mirina shook her head. So young. So heartbreakingly anxious to please. Some of the Thelerie never got over their initial awe of humans, never stopped seeing them as benevolent gods, whose bidding must be done no matter how perilous. Not even after their first missions, when the humans proved themselves to be thieves and pirates. The Thelerie just kept on trusting them, even against the evidence. Their ethical culture told them that a person was what he said he was, even if he wasn't. That made them jam for the dishonest beings in the galaxy like the Melange.

Mirina felt responsible for all the Thelerie they enrolled. She suffered nightmares when one of them got injured or killed, and still dreamed about the first time she had had to take the body of an apprentice back to its homeworld. As guilty as she was, the alien family didn't blame her. They trusted humans, not realizing that they were as mortal as Thelerie, with no special powers to save anyone, or any special wisdom to keep them from falling into danger. They thought everything humans did was wonderful. It never occurred to them that the ships the humans flew were old, cobbled together out of spare parts and baling wire. They never saw that the couches had been mended a dozen times, nor that the equipment in the control room came from a dozen different derelict ships, and failed as often as it worked.

She'd once been told by a suitor that she had fine eyes. The mirror in her cramped little cabin let her know that the strain of the last years had put a hard quality into them that frightened her, and would have put off that long-gone beau. That tough shell protected what was left of her soul, because business was business. The presence of the Thelerie was essential to the success of her venture. There'd have been far more bloodshed, and much more loss of life if she couldn't rely upon their unique talent. Even to herself she admitted that she minimized the danger in every way possible. She didn't want anyone else to die. Anyone.

"Close in," she said, leaning over Glashton's shoulder. "Plot us in, staying as close to the asteroids as possible till the last minute. I don't want them to have time to push the panic button. Can you see the parts depot?"

"Aye, sir."

Bisman came striding up. He had on an armored pressure suit, the helmet held under one arm. His grizzled hair was hidden under the protective hood, and his sharp, dark eyes were calm.

"Boarding party ready," he said shortly.

"Stand by," Mirina said, turning back to the viewtank. "How long to the drop?"

Sunset ran through one of those instantaneous mental calculations that seemed so effortless for his people.

"Eight minutes, madam."

"Don't call me madam," Mirina snapped, yanked back with annoyance from her planning.

"Sorry again," he said, contritely. "Thunderstorm told me always to use titles of respect."

Mirina felt the corners of her mouth start to turn upward in an unwilling smile. "My name will do. Thank you. Stand by."

"At least he isn't calling you 'holy one,' any more," her brother called from the engineer's seat, where he was waiting to operate the airlock and grapple controls.

Sunset glanced up at the human male, then hastily ducked his head. Bisman smirked at the young Thelerie, his narrow jaws drawn upward. Mirina glared at her co-leader.

"Isn't anyone else here thinking of business?"

"On my way," he said, fending off the evil eye with an uplifted hand.

"Wait a minute, Aldon," Mirina said, as he turned to go. "Remember, just grab those containers and go. No killing."

"That's the idea, lady," he said, offhandedly, holding his helmet up over his head and shaking it to free the hanging tabs. "Strike hard so they don't know where you're coming from, then move out. But I'm not going to stand helpless and let them tickle me. My people will use self-defense as needed." Mirina moved to place herself in his path.

"Disarm and disable only. Those are my orders. Just take the stuff and go!"

He paid no attention as he clamped the headpiece into place. The seals whistled a diminishing scale as he sidestepped her and stalked away down the corridor toward the airlock.

Mirina stared after him, feeling fury rising fit to choke her. There wasn't time to lecture him again, and she was beginning to feel like she was losing control of him. *She'd* turned this operation around into a profit-making enterprise. He and his miserable little group had only three pathetically archaic ships when she met him eight years ago. Now they had sixty, and more under construction. *She'd* been confirmed as the leader by a majority of the vote. But there were some people who couldn't take direction from anyone, especially not from a former government spacer like her. Bisman had been raiding for thirty years, had started under his father, who'd owned the original three ships. Anyone who'd survived that long deserved respect, just for sheer longevity, but damn it, it was bad for crew morale to have him defy her every single order. She snatched up her remote communications headset and clamped it down on her head.

Zonzalo sat in the engineer's seat snickering. Mirina rounded on him.

"What are you laughing at? You couldn't survive in a planetside shopping center."

"Hey," he held up helpless hands. "I didn't say anything. It just reminds me of Mom and Dad, how you two carry on."

"I suppose I asked for that," Mirina said, feeling her cheeks burn. "But I want him to remember what I say."

"It won't help," Zonzalo said. "It never does. I don't know why you keep trying."

Mirina shook her head. She and Bisman had had an affair when she first shipped with them eight Standard years before. He was twenty years older than she. She was attracted by his maturity, by his long, lean looks, daredevil attitude, and hard-driving determination. He liked her clear-sighted organizational bent, and he complimented her on her figure, saying he liked a curvy armful. They'd broken off the physical side of their relationship when they found they couldn't work together *and* be lovers. *He* thought she was compulsive. *She* hated his collections of little knickknacks and his untidy way of thinking. *He'd* said she was too bossy. *She'd* known his recklessness would get them all killed. At almost any cost Mirina wanted to stay in space, but serving under a hot dog who thought he was Jean Lafitte or Xak Milliane Ya was just out of her price range. Bisman was too casual about killing. Mirina wasn't a complete innocent. She had been involved with, or rather felt responsible for, the death of one so dear to her she'd never recovered from it. Mirina never wanted to feel like that again, but she was exposed to the possibility over and over every time their ship went reiving. So, at risk of having Bisman mutiny and strand her and Zonzalo somewhere out of frustration, she kept on his back about safety and minimum use of force.

"You are just like my teacher, Thunderstorm," Sunset said, in his resonant voice, glancing up as his four hands performed his tasks. "He tells and tells, but I make my mistakes all the same."

Zonzalo laughed. He'd become friends with the Thelerie, partly because they were the youngest beings on board and partly because he thought Sunset's innocent pronouncements hilarious.

"She is just exactly like a thunderstorm in space, isn't she?" Zonzalo said. "Uh-oh, the clouds are moving toward me." Mirina advanced upon him and glared down. Zonzalo pretended to cower, his shoulders hunched. Mirina swatted him lightly across the back.

"Act like adults," she snapped. "In case you weren't listening, some of our spacers are going down there. Their safety depends on you, too. Pay attention to your boards." The two young males exchanged humorous glances, then concentrated on their screens.

"Approach final. Attacking speed," Glashton said, not looking up from his console. "Grapples away!"

On the main tank, the background of stars shimmered as the forcefields locked onto five points surrounding the space station. The engines filled the ship with the scream of abused metal as the reiver dumped velocity, using the grapple anchors to halt forward momentum. On external camera, Mirina watched as the flexible white tube shot outward from the side of her ship to cover the airlock of the repair port and sucked closed. Bulbous-headed shadows inside it— Bisman's raiders in armor—bounded downward. There was an actinic flash, from which everyone in the cockpit automatically shielded his or her eyes, then Glashton switched video and audio input to a suit-mounted cam on the uniform of one of the raiders.

The crew plunged ahead into the darkness of the landing bay. Narrow beams of light slashed through the black tunnel, picking out steel-riveted walls, signs and directions etched in enamel next to huge louvered doors and at intersections. Two raiders found a communications circuit box and blasted it with slugs and energy weapons. That should have cut off external communications, but it also caused the inhabitants of the station to take notice. Sirens wailed in the distance. Blurred figures, bleached white by the raiders' searchlights, cannoned into view, weapons leveled. Bisman's people were ready. Mirina watched arms being raised, saw the spark of muzzle-flash. The defenders fell, arms splayed. A few of the raiders ran forward to collect their guns.

Bisman's voice barked hoarsely. "They'll only be out for about twenty minutes. Find the control room. Find the lights! Move it!"

Mirina held her breath as the camera eye followed the bobbing forms deeper into the repair facility. Someone found the control for the lights. The white blurs coalesced into armored backs and armloads of equipment. The siren's discordance chewed away at her nerves until she was tapping her foot with impatience, mentally urging Bisman to hurry and get out of there.

The louvered doors flapped up one by one, revealing empty bays. Suddenly, a door rolled up, and the hoped-for containers were right in front of the video pickup. The inventory numbers for ion-drive engine parts were printed on the side and top of each case. Zonzalo and Glashton cheered. Mirina pointed at the corral of heavy-loaders in the foreground of the screen, and snapped an order into the headset mike. Bisman had seen them, too. His hand appeared in the lens, making an "OK" symbol.

"All right, children, start loading 'em up!" The triumph in Bisman's voice came through the plasteel bubble helmet. Mirina felt smug, too. Even if they only sold half and kept the rest for running repairs and trade with the Thelerie, those engine parts should bring in enough to keep her fleet in space for another six months, at least.

"Hold it! Drop your weapons!" A commanding voice boomed out of the walls. The raiders looked around. His arms held up from the elbows, Mirina's videocarrier turned slowly to face a squad of guards in dark blue uniforms. At their head was a tall, thin woman with silver hair. Her tunic was trimmed with more silver, including rows of medal flashes. From the confident manner with which she held her long-barreled slugthrower, Mirina guessed that some of the medals were for marksmanship. Some of Bisman's crew began to comply, bending over to set their guns on the ground. The raiders were outnumbered at least two to one. Mirina bit her lip. She dreaded what would surely follow.

"Slowly . . . " the woman said, in a calm voice. "Slowly. Good. Now, hands above your heads."

"Now!" Bisman shouted. As one, the raiders dropped flat on the floor. The screen went blank. "Fire!" Mirina could tell by the sounds, they were spraying the defenders with energy bolts. Shouts, then screams erupted, followed by the noise of scuffling. Individual cries rose above the noise.

"What's happening?" Zonzalo asked. He had joined his sister to hang over the viewscreen. Mirina felt her blood drain away toward her feet. She swayed a little.

"It's all going wrong," she said, and turned to Glashton. "Shake 'em up. Give Bisman and the others a chance to get out."

The pilot nodded sharply, the muscles in his jaw twitching. He clawed at a series of controls, activating their secret weapon, the Slime Ball. The ship shuddered under their feet as it lit thrusters and pulled against the grapples. Always steering outward, so the return motion wouldn't yank the asteroid into their hull, Glashton zigzagged from one thruster to another.

The effect as seen on the screen was frightening. The raider wearing the camera was now lying on his back. The ceiling shook, and the giant plates seemed to rub against one another. Mirina wondered if they would crack apart and fall.

The crates of parts were vibrating, too, with every thrust of the ship. Inside their padding, the components were undoubtedly safe from impact damage even if they fell over, but if one landed on a human, there was nothing left to do but hold the funeral.

While those in the ship had suffered a temporary loss of visuals, Bisman and his crew had regained their weapons. Between surges, the raiders managed to round up most of the defenders. A few blue-shirts lay, heads a-loll, on the floor; unconscious, Mirina hoped. Bisman and two of the others, kneeling, held the rest at gunpoint while the raiders mounted heavy-loaders and lifted stacks of the valuable crates. The stationmaster made one attempt to protest. Bisman nodded to one of his gunners, who ratcheted her weapon to a higher setting, and with one sweep slagged the metal floor in front of the silver-haired woman. The others gasped as the woman nearly stumbled forward into the red-hot mass. She stopped protesting, her hands in the air, but her eyes flashed hatred at Bisman. The loaders trundled out of the storeroom.

Zonzalo ran to his station to open the cargo bay to receive the coming crates. He cackled to himself over each load as it passed the cameras.

"Thruster modules," he said over his shoulder to the others. "Energy reburner pods! My God, do you know what those are worth? One new fuel tank, two, three— too bad there aren't a few more."

"They'll all put oxygen in the tanks," Mirina said distantly. She was watching Bisman, worrying whether he would make some violent gesture at the end to keep the defenders from following. Glashton spoke over the helmet communication link, letting the raiders know that the violent jerking was over. The ship still swayed lightly from side to side from inertia, but everyone could stand up again.

"Mi— Mirina, do not those boxes belong to the humans of the station-asteroid?"

"They did," Mirina said tersely. "Now they are ours. We need them more. Your people need them to keep your space program running. Those humans would have refused to give them to us. This was the only way." But she had the picture in her mind of the uniformed men and women on the floor. Something about the ragdoll quality of the way they lay shouted at her that they were not unconscious, but dead. Bisman had overdone it again. Instead of a simple snatch and grab, they had more murders on their souls, not to mention their growing rap sheets in the Central Worlds computer bank.

Glashton, responding to a triumphant cry from Zonzalo that the last of the heavy-loaders was on board and the raiding crew with it, sealed airlocks and blasted away. He gave an OK to Mirina, who yanked off her headset and squeezed herself with difficulty between the pilots' couches against the thrust of the engines. Her flesh flattened against her bones, and she shut her eyes.

God, who'd ever have thought I'd come to this? she mused, wriggling her body down farther to avoid somersaulting out into the corridor. *Fairhaired child of the corps, ace pilot, partner of . . . Damn it, stop thinking of him!* She turned her concentration to the star tank, drilling the hologram with her gaze. The star, around which the asteroid circled, shrank swiftly until it was another undistinguished dot of light on the scope. Just like all the other stars around which orbited facilities, planets, and ships they'd robbed for goods to keep them going.

"Shall I not go out there some day on a gathering mission?" Sunset asked Mirina, once they were clear of the heliopause.

"No," she said shortly, pulling her attention away from the star tank. "Never. You must be kept safe in the ship."

"But . . ."

"But nothing," Mirina interrupted him. She leveled a finger at his weird, striped eyes. "You don't understand your place in the schematic. You're the backup we count on in case of emergency. If we lose every system but drives and life support, you can get us home

again, even if our navicomp is a slagged ruin. You're
the last line of defense we have. I'm not letting you
go out there and risk your neck, not when thirty other
lives are depending on you."

"Oh." The young Thelerie pulled himself up, looking important and nervous and proud all at the same
time. Mirina bit her tongue at having to tell him a lie,
since sooner or later he'd meet up with others of his
race who had joined the raiding parties after they'd
apprenticed on the navigation board. But he was too
young now. He'd be a liability to himself and the raiding crew.

"My center is sure," he told her.

"Good," Mirina sighed. "Keep it that way."

Bisman handed his way into the control room. His
armored suit, now dusty, bore the black streak of a laser
shot that impacted over the sternum and skidded
upward toward his left ear. He grinned triumphantly.

"A megacredit run, at least," he crowed.

"Is everyone back on board?" Mirina asked.

"Yeah. Simborne and Mdeng bought it. They're
cooling in the cargo bay with the containers."

"How many injured?"

"Not too many," Bisman said, offhandedly. "Fewer
than the blue-shirts, that's for sure."

"How many?" Mirina asked, and she knew he knew
she wasn't asking for the list of wounded. Bisman
pursed his lips and shrugged. "How many?"

"Five? Six or seven at the most."

"What?" she gasped. "What were you doing? Why
did there have to be casualties?"

Sunset glanced up, then hurriedly ducked his head
behind his wing to avoid the leader's glare. He was
shocked at how angry she was.

"But you wanted those parts," Bisman complained.
"They wouldn't give them up. What were we supposed
to do?"

"That electroshock weapon of yours has more than one setting, doesn't it?" Mirina asked nastily, stepping up to the big male. Bisman retreated a pace out of surprise.

"He was going to pull an alarm! I had to stop him, quick! Damn, I'm tired of your jawing, Miri. We're partners, right? I make some of the decisions, right?"

Mirina's brown-in-white eyes filled with water—tears—and she said huskily, "I had a partner once. He died. I don't want to hear about partners. We're *co-leaders*. They owe us the stuff, *right*?" she said, mocking him. "They owe us, but they don't owe us their lives."

What she said made sense to Sunset, but Bisman appeared ready to disagree with her. Humans' flat faces were full of emotion, easy to read. Bisman's cheeks turned red, and his eyes stood out. Sunset thought for a moment he would strike Mirina, but he clenched his hands and left the room. Mirina's round face was set. She stared after the male, then closed her eyes. Sunset could see a slight vibration shake her body.

"There's enough in this shipment, Miri," Zonzalo spoke up softly from his station. "We could settle down somewhere on our share. CW would never find us. How about the nice place we stopped before we were on Base Fifteen the last time? We're heading back that way. We could scope out a place, buy some land?"

"No," Mirina said, opening her eyes. "I can't *settle*. I hate being groundbound. I prefer to be out here, in the blackness, away from people."

Sunset spread the shoulder pinions of his wings in acknowledgement. He had caught her many times just staring out into the void, communing. Space spoke to her in a way he had always believed it did to the blessed ones. That was no doubt why she was so cross when he interrupted her. Zonzalo was easier to befriend. Mirina turned suddenly to him, and the young Thelerie jumped, wondering if she could read his thoughts.

"Which way's your world, Sunset?" she asked. Without hesitation, he pointed toward his Center, and she sighted along his wing-finger.

"We count on you, you know that," she said, wearily. Sunset nodded. "Good. Go take a rest."

"You should, too, ma— Mirina." Then he dropped on all fours and hurried out of the control room, surprised by his own boldness. The woman stared after him.

Zonzalo waved at his sister, and pointed at a light on his control board.

"Message coming in," he said. Mirina stood over his shoulder and watched the brief transmission.

"Route it to Bisman," she said at once. "He has to hear this."

The co-leader was in the control room almost at once.

"A ship penetrated the other P-sector system near Base Eight? We have to send word to have the others destroy it!"

"We can't," Mirina said. "It's landed on the second planet. It's protected. Listen to this all the way through." She signalled to Zonzalo to play it back again.

"The reptiles," Bisman said, exasperated. "The Slime. Damn it, I thought we had them bottled." He recorded a return message to their base. "Keep an eye out. If anything else happens, take appropriate action and notify us at once. *Appropriate* action," he repeated, with heavy emphasis, and one eye on Mirina. She glared at him, but held her tongue.

Chapter 4

For an interminable third day, Keff sat crosslegged on the floor of the Cridi assembly hall. He sat with his chin braced on one palm, elbow on knee, his wrist held to one side so Carialle could see everything that was going on from the miniaturized video pickup on his shirt front.

"Another day of flapping lips and hands in the Main Bog," Keff murmured behind his hand. "I feel like Gulliver in Lilliput."

The humidity was so uncomfortable that in direct countermand of orders from Central Worlds, Keff had stopped wearing uniforms. Instead, he was clad in his least disreputable exercise clothes, fabric made for sweating in. His hair had wound itself into curls, as it always did when it was damp, and he smelled musty. No one else seemed to notice the odor; perhaps his hosts simply couldn't distinguish it in the swamp miasma that hung over everything on this soggy world. Nor did the Cridi pay any attention to the drops running down his face. Like Tall Eyebrow and the others in the ship, some of them made a practice of wearing a film of water to keep their delicate skins from drying out. Others just counted on the ambient humidity, which, Keff thought, was more than sufficient.

The room's decor reflected the possibility of wet delegates. The ceiling rolled back as easily to allow a passing downpour into the chamber as the view of a sunset or a rainbow. Low, comfortable seats shaped for either sitting upright, crouching, or lounging had soft, water-repellent covers; bright white light came from thick, enclosed bubbles hanging overhead; wooden tables were sealed in plastic, or perhaps made of a naturally resinous wood—Keff hadn't had a chance yet to examine one closely. Every time he approached a sitting group, perforce on hands and knees in the low-ceilinged room, stone-faced security frogs came out of the woodwork and herded him back to his spot.

"At least they're allowing you to stay," Carialle said. "It's a foot in the door. You could be stuck out here with me, watching the swamp gurgle, and listening to the security guards babble formulae at each other."

"I'm getting no forrader in advancing the cause of the Central Worlds," Keff said, forlornly watching Tall Eyebrow and the others, separated among three huge groups of Cridi, answering questions. Long Hand was perched in one of the chairs, waving her hands to get the attention of a pair of natives who were squabbling in high-pitched voices. "All during that muddy tour yesterday and the day before, I kept trying to tell them about the Central Worlds, but Big Voice over there kept saying the conclave hadn't yet discussed whether to allow input from an outworlder that would result in any kind of social engineering, when they've never met an outworlder before. Once they've discussed the topic, we have to wait until they've had input from every other city on the planet before proceeding. The final decision rests with the Council of Eight. I'm not allowed to influence anyone, particularly not with the fact of my being an alien. It's a bureaucracy. Our mission, to encounter strange new holdups and fascinating new ways to tie red tape where no frog has gone before."

"Isn't anyone talking to you?"

"Oh, yes, on and off, but more out of curiosity than diplomatic interest. I think," Keff said, smiling and making a seated bow to a passing delegate, "I'm serving a function all the same. The Cridi are learning not to be afraid of us. That's good. If they see me as a clown, I just have to coddle my own ego. The problem is they treat me rather like a talking dog, a non-sentient that is a wonder because it can pronounce recognizable words. I would be most concerned that they wouldn't take the Central Worlds seriously enough. There's no future alliance possible without respect."

"Respect comes with knowledge. They are getting used to you. They've never seen anything like you—or me. As with humans, it sounds like they've run into very few, if any, sentient species beside their own. It *would* be like one of their dogs starting to talk, if they have dogs. So far I've only seen those blobbies and lizardings they keep for pets. In time, they'll get used to the idea that you do think for yourself. Be thankful that they don't think you're a monster. I was a little worried after that first group took off screaming. They could have burned out Frankenstein *and* his castle with Core power."

"So they could." Keff shifted uncomfortably, pulling the folds of his sweatshirt away from his back. "I'd just prefer to be in the midst of things instead of merely observing. It looks like Tall Eyebrow could use my help." He glanced over at the group surrounding the Ozranian Frog Prince.

"Tch, greedy. Look, they're friendly. You're getting an unprecedented privilege to have the first peep at an entirely new world, something anyone in Xeno would kill for."

Keff brightened, sitting up straighter, ignoring the smell and the sog. "That's true. Alien Outreach chose us. It's us, partner, first and foremost, no matter what. I want to see everything. And I need to look sharp. I keep missing details."

"Well, that's what I'm here for," Carialle said complacently. "My drives haven't stopped humming for the last eighty hours. Just ask your friendly neighborhood shellperson for a free, money-back guaranteed review."

Keff grinned. "If only it was that easy. It has to be in *my* head, too. I wish *I* had extended memory banks." There was so much that was different in the way the Cridi lived on their homeworld than on Ozran. Isolated as he was, he felt as if he was only one more fact away from sensory overload.

At first he had wondered if the Cridian amphibioids had abandoned their amulet power system, since no amulets were in evidence. Carialle had been the first to point out the circuits, like fine gold filigree, that were either worn on, or bonded to the ends of the Cridi's long fingers. It was a tremendous advancement in the technology. To access Core power, the user merely positioned his or her hand, as if inserting the fingertips into the niches on a device, the way humans would use a virtual-reality glove, and they were in touch, so to speak, with the Core. Keff knew that Tall Eyebrow and the other Ozranian visitors were uncomfortable using their antique amulets in front of the homeworlders, but he'd assured them that they should be proud to display them, as symbols, if nothing else. The amulets represented hard-won equality after years of deprivation. Besides, their race had a natural predilection for telekinesis, unlike their newfound allies, the humans. That was an advantage that no archaic equipment could devalue. It didn't dispel the Ozranians' discomfort entirely, but it helped. Keff would have given anything to be able to use an amulet, archaic or no, to be dry just for an hour. His boots were beginning to smell moldy. He considered hiking back to the ship through the rain to get a pair of sandals.

Carialle broke into his reverie.

"Oh, look. Company's coming. One of the 'eight great.' "

Keff glanced up. One of the dignitaries from the Cridi delegation made her way through the crowd and stopped before Keff. She wore a red cloak that was secured at her throat and wrists with gold bands instead of the silver bangles she had worn to meet the ship. Keff guessed from his limited knowledge of Cridi biology that she was fairly young, but still considered an adult. He tried to straighten the crumples out of his shirt.

The hands moved swiftly. "Can your mind reach me?"

Keff responded, "I sign your language, gentle-female."

She gestured a little impatiently. "Why you here?"

"To make a bridge between your world and ours. To make friends with another race who has its own science, its own space system. We have met many new peoples, but have always had to help them develop . . . ."

He would have gone on, but he sensed that the female was getting bored. "What's wrong?" he asked.

"Too long," she replied, emphatically. "*Old.* Like three." She swung around to point at the Ozranian delegates in turn, lingering briefly on Tall Eyebrow. She turned again and fixed her beady gaze on him. "Old."

"Old? How would she know how old I . . ." Keff repeated, bewildered, then was enlightened. "Ah! You mean the language we are using is old. Antiquated." The concept was just out of the reach of his Cridi hand-vocabulary, so he had to reach for it. Encouragingly, the female frog watched him struggle with his explanation, nodding when he made sense to her. "We sound like *ancestors* to you?"

She tipped her little face up and stretched her neck slightly three times, like she was bobbing her head against something from underneath.

"Yes."

"Whew! So that's the problem," Keff said, running his hand back through his hair, and remembering just in time that the gesture wasn't going to offend the Cridi, having a neutral meaning like "low ceiling." "Hey, Cari, that's wonderful!"

"Ah," she said, sardonically. "You're not a monster. You're just dull."

"Yes, but think of it. This would be just the same as if I went back to Old Earth and addressed them in Latin. But you see," he continued, dropping back into Cridi for the female, "that is what I learned from Tall Eyebrow, and his society has had none of the global changes of your people. You must help us to learn the new way of speaking. We are willing."

His visitor launched into a flurry of hand signals that Keff could tell had been abbreviated from the ones he knew, plus complicated overtones in the language of science. He was glad he'd learned the long form first, or he'd never have recognized some of the subtleties. He prayed that his translation program was picking up all of her spoken words. Later he'd commune with the Intentional Translator and see what it would make of all the murmurs, squeaks, chirps and trills.

"Ah. See," she signed in her clipped style. The trills translated to a formula for condensing large numbers into small. "I apologize, but it boring watch the long forms. That is why none speaks you."

"That tells me something," Carialle said quietly in his ear. "It means that the Cridi weren't as dependent upon the power controller system when TE's progenitors left for Ozran. Otherwise they'd have had more voice and less hands then, too, the easier to communicate over remote frequencies. I predict that in another thousand years their language will be all verbal. Hand-sign will just be a topic for some doctoral dissertation."

"I'd love to take you up on a bet, Lady Fair," Keff

said, wryly. "You'll just have to remember to check in another millenium for me."

"Ah, Sir Knight, I shall." Carialle's voice was tender.

"Who speak to?" Big Eyes asked.

"To Carialle," he said. "She's my partner. She lives in the ship that brought us here."

"Curious," she said. "Have scanned. Life support absolute?"

"Yes. Very efficient, too."

"Interested in engineering. Degreed."

"Really? What branch?" Keff was starting to get the hang of her abbreviated conversation.

"Aerospace," said her hands, and she added a long vocal trill. IT translated it as a complex navigation formula.

"There's luck," Carialle said in Keff's ear.

"I'll say. You must be the person we've been waiting for. Tell me about Cridi's space program," Keff said eagerly. Big Eyes waved away his request nonchalantly.

"None talk right now," she said.

"Won't she talk about it, or isn't there anything going on?" Carialle asked.

"I don't know," Keff said. "Listen to IT babbling about two potential meanings. Could it be another one of those 'don't tell the alien' subjects?" He broached this suggestion gently to Big Eyes, who openly ignored the question. In fact, she seemed impatient.

"Not now. I worst tell. Father. Much else to see now I know." She pointed at Long Hand, who was giving a dissertation on the farming techniques used on Ozran. "Observe. You asked. I help. Cut middles," she signed to him, lifting an imaginary section out of something with her flattened hands held parallel. Big Eyes repeated key phrases with sign language, and interspersed them with verbal signs that tightened up the long strings of symbolism to the few necessary. Keff had thought the Ozranian version of Cridi sign language was terse and to the point. Big Eyes reduced it still further, to the essence of meaning.

"Very efficient," Keff said, trying to match her gestures. "Cari, I can reprogram IT to give me two choices of expression—dialects, if you will, depending on which planet I'm on, Cridi or Ozran. This is worth at least one paper for *Scientific Galactican* or *Linguistics Today*."

"If Xeno will let you declassify this data so soon. Remember we're the diplomatic advance scout. You'll probably have to teach the combination languages to the reps yet to come."

"All part of the service." He glanced over at Tall Eyebrow again, who was trying to answer questions from three delegates at once, all of whom were clamoring for his sole attention. "He looks as confused as I feel." He turned to Big Eyes. "Excuse me. Talk to my friend."

"Stay," she said, with an urgent gesture and a high-pitched peep that indicated an exponent of urgency. "Elders."

Keff looked around. Two more of the eight, Smooth Hand and Big Voice, were making their way toward him, followed by the usual entourage of aides and flunkeys. Like Big Eyes, they wore modified capes of various colors and lengths attached at throat and wrists.

"You are here already," Smooth Hand said to Big Eyes. "Have you broached discussion with him yet?"

"No," Big Eyes said briefly. "We acquaint."

"Good," Smooth Hand signed. "Here are six of the eight members of the conclave council representatives, so our discussion may be of significance."

"Now's your big chance to impress them," Carialle said.

"Maybe they've made a decision on joining Central Worlds," Keff said, wishing he'd sacrificed comfort for dignity and worn the uniform after all. "How serve, gentle-ones?" he asked, keeping the signs as short as he could. The young female up-nodded encouragingly toward him.

Always a quick study, but unwilling to sacrifice courtesy for speed, Keff tried to incorporate his new friend's lessons in his handspeech. Working from discussions he had had with Tall Eyebrow about traditional protocol, he gave Smooth Hand the respect due the oldest member of the conclave, then greeted the others, ending with Big Eyes. She gave him a quick gesture of approval with joined thumb and long forefinger.

"That was a hash," Keff murmured to Carialle without moving his lips. "The Minute Waltz in eight seconds."

"Looked fine from here," Carialle said. "And they seem happy."

"In return," Smooth Hand said, "we greet you." Keff bowed his head as deeply as he could, and waited.

As usual, Big Voice took the lead in the discussion. The stout amphibioid pushed forward to the center of the group and glared at Keff, who glanced at Smooth Hand for direction. Instead of attempting to overbear the pompous councillor, the old one stood back with an air of indulgence. Keff assumed an air of respectful attention that made Big Eyes' eponymous features twinkle with amusement. Big Voice began his dissertation with exaggerated movements of his elbows designed to clear away anyone standing within half a meter of him. Everyone edged away. Keff carefully pulled in his knees.

"Stranger to this world, we are grateful that you return to us lost descendants of our ancestors," Big Voice gestured hugely. "From the far reaches of the void they come, never thought to have been seen again . . . ." The language of diplomacy appeared to be rooted in both the new and old forms, comprising more sign than was used by Big Eyes—which bored her and the other young members of the council—and more verbiage than Keff's version, which confused the brawn. Keff paused and nodded and smiled in between the flowery statements, waiting for IT to cycle back translations to him utilizing the growing catalog it was picking up of the spoken language. Keff hoped that he would look thoughtful, rather than lost. His brief and polite replies, made when Big Voice stopped for breath, seemed to please his audience.

" . . . And that is how our cousins' journey ended, here on beautiful Cridi."

"We are grateful for your welcome of us."

"You say that you did not know of the Cridi who inhabited Sky Clear?"

"No," Keff said. "We had lost track of some of our own people many hundreds of years ago. They settled on, er, Sky Clear, and thereafter dropped out of communication with us. As it was with your ancestors."

"So, they have been self-governing all this time?" Big Voice asked. "Without the approval of your Central Worlds?"

"Well, not without the approval of the government, but certainly without its knowledge. We lost touch, you see." Keff tried the phrase a couple of ways and hoped they understood.

"So, it is not your Central Worlds who holds the half of Sky Clear?" Big Voice asked.

"Not precisely," Keff said carefully, settling in for a long explanation. "Our people, descendants of *my* ancestors who set out many hundreds of years ago, settled the world alongside yours. To encounter them, we—and they—were as surprised to see one another as you are to meet Tall Eyebrow and his companions."

"But they did not set down upon this world at the same time, nor before the Cridi?"

"He's going somewhere," Carialle said, in between

sound bites from IT in Keff's aural implant. "I don't like what I think he's getting at."

"Neither do I. Not to my knowledge," Keff said out loud, sensing he was treading on tricky ground. "The humans who live on Oz—Sky Clear were not as good recordkeepers as the Cridi." Mentally he crossed his fingers, knowing he was eliding the truth. The early settlers had kept good tape archives of their settlement, and none of it included references to the Cridi except as a curious life-form they thought was indigenous to Ozran.

"Are we to understand that you came to our world only to convey our lost children?" Smooth Hand inquired, interrupting Big Voice by standing in front of him.

Keff was grateful to have a respite from Big Voice's pointed questioning. "That and to ask your people to join the great conclave of planets and beings we call the Central Worlds." Keff had worked out a set of handsigns he found symbolic of those concepts of unity and cooperation. The elder picked it up without a demur, and repeated it to the others. "This organization boasts members from many species besides humanity. We are proud of our diversity. I am instructed to convey the compliments of our government and say that they, and we, would be delighted if you would join."

"Beginning to think no intelligent life existed outside our own," Smooth Hand said, with dry humor. "How many are there?"

"Thousands of inhabited planets, hundreds of intelligent species with uncounted subgroups, millions of non-sentient protected species in various stages of development," Keff said, hoping he was placing the exponents correctly in his voiced phrases.

"Most impressive," Smooth Hand gestured, thoughtfully.

The other councillors chattered formulae at one

another, speculating on the size of Central Worlds' sphere. Keff waved politely for attention.

"I can give you star charts, if you want."

"Yes! Occasional talk of ships passing through our system," Big Eyes said, describing the decline of an arc across the sky. "Believed to be myths. Not know. You?"

"Maybe," Keff said. "Maybe another race. There are countless others out there that we've never met. You might even have neighbors and not know it."

"Maybe the salvage squad," Carialle sputtered in his ear.

"Not in system," Big Voice protested. "That known of old."

"Meteors or myths," the elder said, indulgently. "If not myths, why not land before now? Why were they not curious? All ground control has ever retrieved is rocks. Fly-by saucers are mythical. System has very strange and strong anomalies."

"You can say that again," Carialle said. "That trash heap at the binary end of the heliopause, whew!"

"Shh, Cari," Keff said softly, nodding and smiling at the delegates.

Big Voice hovered above everyone's head and waved for attention. "The presence of so many other worlds containing humans shall then pose no difficulty in moving those off Sky Clear in favor of Cridi."

"Aha!" Carialle said.

"What?" Keff sputtered. "This is a long-established society, sir. It might have been different if you had made such a demand within say, three years of the discovery. Not after a thousand years. That's like saying that dinosaurs have a permanent claim on Burbank, California, on Old Earth just because some of their relatives are buried in the La Brea tar pits."

Big Voice paid no attention to his simile.

"Yes, after a thousand years. If you want the approval

of the conclave to join your Central Worlds, you will
cede Sky Clear to the Cridi. We have prior landing
rights. You have said so yourself." Keff wouldn't have
believed it, but Big Voice's shrill cheeping *did* manage to sound menacing. Two of the six council members present, and a few among the entourage bobbed
up their heads in agreement.

"That's blackmail," Carialle said. "I wonder how much
power he really holds in the conclave. Smooth Hand
looks a little shocked at the tactics."

"We can't afford to find out," Keff said sublingually.
"If, good sir, you would care to examine the records,
you would see that when humans landed on Ozran—
or Sky Clear, if you prefer," he corrected himself, seeing
that Big Voice was swelling fit to pop, "they were
unaware of the presence of the Cridi, owing to the
subterfuge of the Others. See here. Do not ask only
me. Tall Eyebrow himself will explain that the current
generation of Cridi have no objections to sharing the
planet with humans. Small Spot is the archivist. He can
direct you to the correct records."

Another male, wearing a green cape, pushed forward
to get the conclave council's attention. "I withhold
approval because I still do not believe in this story of
a lost colony. These three Cridi must come from
another part of our own world. This is a hoax. A ship
built in secret." A chorus of agreement, plus wild signing came from a portion of the group, obviously this
male's supporters.

"Uh-oh," Carialle said. "Shades of Ozran."

"Snap Fingers, your data is faulty," Smooth Hand said
patiently, shaking his head.

"I would suggest," Keff signed patiently, "that the
internal evidence in the archives, added to the fact that
we humans are here with the Sky Clear delegation, will
prove otherwise."

"Fabricated!"

"But the aliens . . . ?" Smooth Hand began, with a glance at Keff.

"Random chance met!"

"But where?" Big Eyes asked, innocently, "when no whole ship has come in or out of atmosphere for fifty years?"

Big Voice glared fiercely at her.

"Fifty years?" Carialle repeated. "Why hasn't their space program been active for fifty years?"

Keff tried to interrupt the argument to ask, but no one was paying attention to him. The air was full of Cridi. The male in the green cape tapped Smooth Hand's shoulder and flung angry gestures in the old one's face. Big Voice addressed Big Eyes and Snap Fingers alternately, spinning to confront each of them in turn. Creaking broke out all over, making the group sound like a marsh pond in mating season. In spite of the seriousness of the subject, Keff had to try hard not to smile. He hoped fervently that the recording mechanism in IT would be able to distinguish between thirty different Cridi voices when it tried to translate this mess.

Big Voice interrupted with a shrill whistle ordering them to diminish volume. "No decision can be made now! It will take much time for all the archives to be read," he signed.

"Then, please read them," Keff said, sitting up very tall so they had to look up at him. "No decision of any importance should be made in haste."

There was general approval for such a wise suggestion. Big Voice looked upset, as if Keff had stolen his thunder by being reasonable. "We shall read them, you may be assured," he signed, his face grim. "In the meantime, no assurances can be made for or against membership. I shall withhold approval until then myself."

"As you will, gentle-male," Keff said, describing a sitting bow with the flourishes born of long practice.

"Whew!" said Carialle. "At once thrust into the fire and pulled out of it again by the same frog."

"Hot air," signed Big Eyes, merrily. "I am in favor of membership. Many advantages."

"Brash youngster," Smooth Hand said fondly. "Do not decide without all facts."

"Facts dull," Big Eyes said. "Still, should like to see Ozran." She glanced over toward Tall Eyebrow with an approving look. Keff made a mental note to mention the young female's interest to his friend. Then she stood up on her toes and whistled a shrill signal as a tall, thin frog with a mottled skin of a pleasant brownish green entered the big chamber. Keff could tell that he was very old, but he still walked upright. He saw Big Eyes and waved back.

"My father," Big Eyes signed, as the male joined the group. "Narrow Leg I, seventh offspring," Big Eyes offered, presenting the human and the Cridi to one another.

"Seventieth?" Keff asked, singing the number carefully in the highest voice he could muster.

"No," she gestured, and repeated the fluting snatch of song, making sure he saw and heard no decimal multiplier.

"Oops!" Keff exclaimed. "This is an old, thin lad, Big Eyes' dad," he said, playfully to Carialle, noticing the twinkle in the elderly Cridi's eye and deciding at once that he liked him. "No, tad. Tad Pole."

"Oh, Keff," Carialle groaned. Keff snickered. Big Eyes explained Keff to her father with a few gestures, then turned to the human.

"Narrow Leg is head of current space program. Answer questions."

"At last," Keff said, happily. "How do you do, sir?"

"Pleased to meet you," said Narrow Leg. "Wanting to converse on spaceships." He described with a few graceful signs the contours of craft much like Carialle's.

Keff stared. Even for a race that had unusually large and long hands, Tad Pole's were extraordinary. When his hand was closed the tips of the fingers seemed to reach partway down the wrist. The gold filigree amulet circuitry looked like an ancient Chinese aristocrat's fingernail stalls. "May I hope for some increment of your time?"

"At some point, I would love to compare our programs with yours," Keff said. "I expect that we'll be discussing the possibility of Cridi joining the Central Worlds for a while longer."

"Ah!" Narrow Leg squeaked. "A unity of many peoples. Will there be a vote?" he asked the councillors.

"No. Nothing will be settled today," Smooth Hand signed.

"Why not?" Narrow Leg asked.

His daughter made an impatient gesture. "They say reading of archives takes time, then the conclave must discuss everything to death. We and Keff shall be hauled back here again and again. Negotiations held up because there are factions who don't believe Tall Eyebrow and Keff are who they say they are. Non-explanetary."

"Nonsense!" Narrow Leg gestured definitely. "Of course they are! To what purpose, to what end to create an elaborate charade of this nature? Do you think such a creature as this," he indicated Keff, "arose from primordial ooze without us noticing? He is from beyond atmosphere, and, if you will believe your beacons— and you should—from beyond our system. Human," he turned to the brawn. "Will you take me to your spaceship? I would like to see it."

"I should be honored, gentle-male," Keff replied.

"Bring him," Carialle said. "He's one of the few so far who is making sense."

"And my partner will welcome you, also," Keff added. Narrow Leg looked gratified.

"Not settled yet the questioning about sharing Sky Clear," Big Voice interrupted with an alarming shriek meant to regain the floor. "Do you not realize the offense given by involuntary sharing of Sky Clear?"

"Offense?" Keff asked. "Hadn't you better ask Tall Eyebrow about the cooperative colony? Right now humans and Cridi are coexisting rather well. And without much consultation you could abort an experiment that has the possibility of breaking new ground in interspecies cooperation."

Big Voice wasn't interested. "We explored that sector. It is the first of our colonies we have heard from for fifty years. We want it to revert to Cridi, with no interference."

"Fifty years again," Carialle said urgently. "Ask why it's been so long since there's been contact outside the system."

"Yes," said Keff. "Why isn't space program running?"

All the elders except Narrow Leg turned to glare at Big Eyes.

"I have told nothing," she signed indignantly. "He is not stupid. He sees negative indications."

Smooth Hand shook his head, and turned to Keff. "Too many problems, too little funding."

"Too many natural resources are used up," Snap Fingers added. "We have few heavy metals. Send to colonies in centuries past, get no return." He chattered a complex series of descending notes which Keff didn't need IT's help to translate as a losing program. There were outcries of protest, and the brawn kept turning his head to see everyone who wanted his attention.

"Don't think of it in terms of immediate return," Tad Pole complained, pursing his wide lips distastefully. He turned to the crowd. "See here, my friends, you have no respect for the world as it was fifty years ago, when we had a working program. You're ignorant of your own history. So many strides forward were made as a result over hundreds of years of space study! You forget your past!"

"You do not look to the real future! Program failed. Bad use of funds, of the best minds!" signed Snap Fingers. "I and other members of Cridi Inward see no reason to continue burying good food under the swamp. It's a waste of time. Equipment doesn't work properly."

Big Voice took immediate umbrage. "The equipment is properly made and maintained!"

"Well, we keep seeing anomalies on scopes, like other spacecraft," Snap Fingers said, seeing that he had offended the blustering councillor.

"Well, now we know that those could be true," Smooth Hand signed, with a polite nod to Keff.

"That is true. Yet it does not change facts." With less bombastic gestures, Snap Fingers continued. "Our economy could not support any more failures."

"Yes!" Smooth Hand said. "We would like to recoup losses from space program."

"And that is why laying sole claim to Sky Clear is important to Big Voice," Narrow Leg's daughter said, making a distasteful moue. Big Voice emitted his shriek of protest once again, this time with a five-times multiplier attached. Keff winced.

"There is nothing wrong with honest profit!" Big Voice said.

"If profit does not come at the expense of lives," Snap Fingers retorted.

"Gentles, gentles," Keff said, and held up his hands, "please. Facts? I know nothing of your recent history."

Through the confused mixture of Cridi music and gesture, Keff managed to discover that the last *successful* launch of a spacecraft had been fifty years past. Several tries had been made thereafter, but no vehicle had managed to clear the system since then.

"Have received no messages, no artifacts from other colonies," Narrow Leg added, spreading his hands at shoulder level. "Abandoned? Destroyed? Technological setbacks like Sky Clear? We do not know."

"Three launches, three expensive disasters," indicated Snap Fingers. "I blame the equipment."

"As do I," Narrow Leg said.

"No," Big Voice said emphatically. "Not in the last one! It must be because of radiation or ion storms or some unknown natural menace!"

Narrow Leg turned to Keff. "Our space program is crippled. There is something wrong with the drives, or the shielding, that it cannot carry a craft swiftly enough out of the way of space storms, or protect them well. Once out of range of the Core of Cridi, have to rely upon actual machinery, and it has been shoddy."

"How dare you?" Big Voice demanded, embarrassed.

Narrow Leg pointedly turned his back on the other. "The technicians who built can ignore small faults, like badly fitting seals or insufficiently tightened components. Astronauts don't know about them, can't guard using their own devices because range of power is limited to atmosphere of Cridi. Fault—*boom!* Again and again, just out of atmosphere."

"Storms have become more virulent," Snap Fingers said. "Can we trade with the humans for better technology? We have much to offer."

"There is nothing wrong with the technology!" Big Voice said furiously.

"No," Narrow Leg said, coolly, watching the yellow-brown Cridi swell until he looked as if he might pop. "Only with the construction management."

Keff, ever the diplomat, wanted to follow upon Snap Fingers's suggestion. This was much more of what he hoped would happen in council. "Yes, of course we'd be happy to offer machinery or advice, or whatever you need. I know we'd love to exchange goods and ideas with you. We are fascinated with your power control system. We've never seen anything like it. Our, er, brothers and sisters on Ozran have learned to use it, and I know our government has shown an interest in what we've told them."

"And you?" Big Eyes asked.

"Well, at present I can't use it," Keff said, trying to explain his lack of the necessary telekinetic spark.

"Modification?" One frog signed quickly to another. The topic spread around the room, even superseding the discussions in which the three Ozranians were involved.

The room filled with the cheeping of formulae and wild signing of hands.

"There is virtue in the notion of trade, Core technology for superior Central Worlds spacecraft," Smooth Hand said, stroking his jaw with his long fingers.

Big Voice protested once more, but his argument was losing ferocity as he was ignored by everyone around him. "No, not superior! I tell you, it is the ion storms!"

"Sounds unlikely to me," Carialle told Keff, after running her telemetry. "I didn't notice any undue amounts of radiation, or that much floating debris on the outskirts of this system. I'll contact Central Worlds about ion storms in this area. Warn the council I'm about to launch a message probe. Ask them to let it out of atmosphere. I don't want it returned to sender."

Keff conveyed Carialle's information. At once, there was a fresh flurry of argument, which Smooth Hand quickly put down.

"Of course you may communicate with your government," he said genially. "Convey our compliments, and thank them for their assistance."

Tad Pole perked up. "I should still like to witness the launch of your message rocket," he said. "In fact, may I not have a tour of your ship?"

"Tell him he's very welcome," Carialle said. "I'll tidy up. I might even bake a cake."

"I'll tell him," Keff said. "Cari, do you know what

it means that the Cridi have lacked a space program for the last fifty years?"

"Yes," Carialle said with such gusto that Keff winced. "Nothing out of system in all that time. It means the Cridi weren't my salvage squad. I can't tell you how glad that makes me. That only leaves me wondering all the more who they were."

"Don't worry about that now, Cari. We're doing so well with the Cridi. Let's tackle one problem at a time. When this is all shipshape and Bristol fashion, to everyone's satisfaction, I still say we should go out looking for your boojums."

"You bet we will," Carialle said. "But I'm so relieved about the Cridi, I love them all, even that squeaking blowhard, Big Voice."

"I'll tell him so, although I don't think he'll appreciate your description very much."

"Well, think of some diplomatic way to tell him. I'm recording the message to CW now. See you in a few nanos."

Chapter 5

Before he left for the ship with Narrow Leg, Keff collected Tall Eyebrow and the others. Smooth Hand, seeing that all were now on fire to discuss exchanges with the Central Worlds, adjourned the meeting. Tall Eyebrow seemed as if he welcomed the rescue. All four outworlders were grateful to leave, but had to promise to appear in the great hall again in the morning to continue the discussion on citizenship. Narrow Leg led Keff and the Ozranians out of the damp hall and into what was left of the day. It had been raining hard. The air still smelled like a gym locker, but Keff took a deep breath, glad to expand his lungs.

Sunshine glittered on the ornamental paving surrounding the Main Bog building, picking up light from bright specks of mica or quartz. The sculpted, multi-colored granitelike rock felt rough and uneven under his boot soles, but the visual effect was one of undulating ocean waves, most soothing to the eye. Design was important to the Cridi. Keff appreciated their painstaking attention to detail. Plants sprouted out of pillar tops and along the guardrails of ramps. Tall buildings containing hundreds of apartment flats poked up through the thick trees, looking as though they had evolved organically themselves. Since all Cridi had access to Core power and therefore could fly, entrances to the flats were as likely to be up as down: on

93

protruding ledges of smooth stone, in sculpted baskets like giant nests, carved like a child's slide through a miniature waterfall. Mosaics seemed to have been formed by stratification in the rock walls instead of being imposed upon them by artistic hands. Huge golden insects with multiple wings like living jewels hovered over V-shaped blossoms in the many planters, sipping nectar. Keff half-expected one of the Cridi to dart out a long tongue and devour one.

Long Hand looked around her, nodding approvingly. Small Spot just sat down on the sidewalk with his long legs collapsing under him, turning his amulet, a long, thin fingertrap, between his hands. Tall Eyebrow seemed drawn and tired. His skin looked dull amid all the bright stonework.

"How has it been going?" Keff asked him in Standard, once they were out of earshot of the other delegates. Clusters of Cridi hung around the pillared entrance, signing to one another, but more than one cast a curious eye toward the strangers.

"I feel lost," the Frog Prince replied in the human tongue, with a glance at Narrow Leg. The elder Cridi up-nodded politely, after understanding that they were having a private conversation, and turned his head the other way. Keff blessed the old one's tact.

"Why?" Keff asked Tall Eyebrow.

"Technology so far beyond ours," he replied, his small face screwed up, searching for the correct words. "I am at disadvantage to show what my people have done."

"Technology isn't everything," Keff said, soothingly. "You have experience and intelligence. You have overcome incredible obstacles to survive. You've rejuvenated a planet."

"And what is that here?" Tall Eyebrow turned his palms upward. "Nothing."

He paused at the edge of the pavement and looked

up and down the main thoroughfare passing the Main Bog of Greedeek, the Cridi capital city. It had been raining again, and the lanes ran with multiple streams of muddy water. Around him, delegates were taking leave of one another, gliding out or upward toward their homes. Keff could tell that the Frog Prince wished he wasn't groundbound. The taste of power over the last two years on Ozran had spoiled the globe-frog. On the other hand, the mudflow was daunting even to a human. Keff looked down and took a deep breath before raising a foot over the ooze. Tall Eyebrow, too, paused, reaching for his amulet. When he realized it wouldn't work, he glanced up at Keff with a shame-faced expression. Neither of them wanted to test the depth of the viscous goo.

"Here goes anyhow," he said. "I'd better go first."

"Power surge coming up in your direction," Carialle said. At the same time, Keff felt his feet arrested before they sank into the greeny-black mud. His right foot hovered, supported a few centimeters above the surface. He drew his left foot forward. The invisible floor beneath him held.

A shrill whistle of laughter came from behind them. Big Eyes was lifting them and herself, using her power circuitry.

"Technology *is* something," Tall Eyebrow said, gloomily.

"Go on, go on," the female gestured. "Wish to come to ship."

Her father, who had halted when he found that the others had dropped behind, turned to see what was going on.

"How rude of you, daughter," he said. His enormously long fingers folded together.

"I apologize," Narrow Leg signed quickly. "I forgot. I have not met outworlders before. I forgot you," and he indicated Keff, mainly to save Tall Eyebrow embarrassment, "would not have our advantages."

"Quite all right," Keff said, politely. "Your daughter has resc—offered her kind hospitality."

"You mean she has made herself the center of attention," Narrow Leg signed, with a humorous sigh. "Do you think it is easy, after seven children, to find one who stands out so?"

"I think she would stand out," Tall Eyebrow signed, without looking at either of them, "if there were a million children."

The female let out a tinkling laugh, and put her long fingertips on Tall Eyebrow's arm.

"Gallant one," she said, when he raised his head. They looked deeply at one another for a long moment. Grinning fit to pop his jaw, Keff held his breath. Big Eyes tented her fingertips and thumbtips together and dipped her chin toward them. "You're very kind. I am glad you came home to Cridi. Come, let us see the spaceship."

Tall Eyebrow, buoyed on borrowed power and love, strode proudly in the direction of the landing field with Big Eyes beside him.

"This is most impressive," Tad Pole said over and over again, as he stumped about the main cabin of Carialle's ship. "Most impressive."

Possessed of great height for a Cridi, he was able to see over the edges of the consoles from the floor. When he had paced from the food processor to the view tank about a dozen times, he raised himself on a surge of power and floated. Carialle noted the slight surges of power that rose around the old frog's form as he levitated. The homeworld Cridi had such a subtle command of their power system: as different from the Core of Ozran as a scalpel to a sledgehammer. The Cridi generators were, Carialle estimated, as much as five times more powerful. Yet with all the use the locals made of the system, the local environment seemed to show no signs of deterioration or other ill effects. She would have to question Narrow Leg on the technology when he was finished with his tour. She manifested her frog image next to him over the navigation station to describe what he was looking at.

"Thank you for the compliments, gentle-male. This indicates the benchmarking codes for this sector," she said, activating the screen to show Cridi's star in relation to the nearest blue lines. "Sector A is considered galactic center, and the others radiate outward from it."

Tad Pole had accepted the holograph without question, even addressing it directly as if it was a new acquaintance. He pointed at the numerals in the corner of the image.

"So this is where Cridi lies in your reckoning? What does this designation mean?" he asked.

Keff, with the help of IT, tried to render the musical notes for the X, Y, and Z axes. Then he whistled it, and shook his head at himself.

"Oh, fuss and bother," he said. "I can't make an accurate tone when it's important. Well, that's what IT is for." He rummaged around in an instrument locker and came out with the small external speaker that he wore when translation of an alien language was beyond his vocal capabilities. He hooked it into the IT module he wore on his chest next to Carialle's camera eye. "In Sector P, X=248.9, Y=1630.23, Z=876."

"This means nine-tenths?" Narrow Leg asked, pointing to one of the characters, and voiced a very high minor that indicated the negative logarithm.

That led to a quick lesson in Standard decimal notation, and the explanation of Arabic versus Roman numerals, which more closely approximated the Cridi system of written notation. Tad Pole, a quick learner, nodded his head several times appreciatively.

"It is quick and less cumbersome for a screen of

formulae," he said. "Very neat. It may serve as your
first import to our world. Although I do not want my
spacers to become lazy, having an easy way to express
formulae."

"None find it easy to serve Narrow Leg," Big Eyes
said, from the weight bench, where she sat curled up
with her hands around her thin knees, drawing her red
cloak closely against her body. Tall Eyebrow hunched
beside her, eyes wide like a wary animal. "He works
everyone too hard. Himself, too."

"I do nothing unnecessary," the lean, old male admonished his unruly child. "Should like to have documents on numeric system."

"Gladly," Keff signed.

"I will recommend partnership between human
organization and Cridi," Narrow Leg continued.
"Among those who are of sense, I carry weight." He
thumped his chest proudly.

Turning to Tall Eyebrow, he asked, "What do you
call the other?" He circled a forefinger uncertainly. The
Ozranian sat up very straight and put his hand before
his face.

"The One Who Watches From Behind the Walls,"
Tall Eyebrow signed, and spoke her name, "Carialle."

"Carialle," Narrow Leg said. "I thank you for my tour.
Now we are curious about *you*. You do not really look
like one of us, do you, in spite of this flat Cridi which
follows me like a friend?"

"No," Carialle said, signing through the image. "I
resemble Keff, but I am a female of our species." The
white wall beside the visitor displayed images of men
and women from infancy to old age. She erased all the
others and let the adult female image remain, clothing it in the usual garb worn by her Lady Fair holo.
"This is how I usually represent myself, but I am not
mobile on two legs as Keff is." Another series of images
followed, beginning with a human body, surrounding

it in a protective shell, then circuitry and life support tubes, moving outward through every layer until the viewer's eye was outside the titanium pillar beside which Keff was standing. "This ship is my body. I see what is outside with video eyes," she showed some examples of cameras, "and hear with many different kinds of ears." The visitors blinked through a series of images of audio transmitters and receivers, down to the miniaturized implant that Keff wore.

"So different. So very different," Narrow Leg said, awed. "I am glad you have come to our world."

"But you came here for a purpose," Carialle said, resuming her frog image. "I'm sending for data regarding observations on storms and other anomalies in space with special attention to this sector. Keff, I'm piggybacking a message to Simeon to pick up gossip from other ships that have been in this area recently. He'll give us the unofficial scuttle if there's nothing in the records. Watch now."

On the holoview over the main console, Carialle showed the view from the camera over the hatch following the second of her four message rockets. Keff urged Narrow Leg to float as closely as he wanted to the holographic image. The ship's skin peeled back, and the bracket levered the little rocket back, then upright like a child sitting up in bed. An inner hatch closed underneath its tailfins, protecting the other probes from backfire. Carialle sent a command, and the small ring of engines ignited, forming a cushion of fire that elongated into a red tongue as the probe lifted skyward. Carialle changed to another camera view that followed the white-hot dot up through the sky as it gained velocity. It was soon lost from sight.

"It will take a few weeks for the message to get to the outpost of the Central Worlds," Carialle said. "I hope you can put up with us that long."

"It would be our honor, gentle-female. I enjoyed that

very much," Narrow Leg said, nodding thoughtfully. "Very much indeed. And now," he said, recovering his good humor and energy. "You must come to see my ship."

"I felt long ago that we must not lose the heritage of ages," Narrow Leg said as he pointed out feaures of the slender ship on the launch pad. "Space is important. I am old. I remember when the failures began. No one thought anything of it, but when they continued, most gave up all hope. Some saw it as a sign to cease travel into space. Our planet's children, the colonies, had forsaken us, and no project could succeed. Others did not agree. We launched, but the ships exploded just beyond atmosphere, or disappeared before passing the beacons at the edge of our system. I was part of those projects, and I said we should not stop. It has taken me twelve years to achieve funding for this ship, and I will not let anything stop us. The fourth time shall be fortunate."

Keff whistled at the sleek lines of the small ship. As Carialle had said, all the Cridi craft seemed to be about one-sixth to one-third scale to human ships, yet personal quarters were much larger in proportion. Cridi seemed to like a fair bit of headroom. Keff found he was slouching to pass in and out of hatchways, but not actually stooping. Narrow Leg's technology was based upon modular replacements, a notion handed down through the generations to preserve the precious metals and radioactives. Stacks of identical bulkhead panels, numbered in the Cridi way, lay in heaps around the finished craft.

"You have enough here to make another couple of ships," Keff said, kicking one skid.

"One and half," Narrow Leg said. "These plates are designed to fit in over 120 different positions on the craft, both inside and outside. Similar care has been taken with many other components. All circuit boards are the same size, and all plugs, too."

"Are you getting this, Cari?" Keff asked, turning around in a full circle and aiming his transmitter up and down to cover everything.

"Sure am," Carialle said. "It is beautiful. If this is everything it looks like, all hopes Central Worlds has always had for a precisely equal race are achieved. This is as advanced as any CW ship, and it sounds like they've been splitting space for as long as we have, but they've evolved independently. I feel vindicated, and I'm even more glad *we* were the ones to see this. The diplomacy wonks wouldn't give us due credit when they got back from the initial contact mission. When will she be ready to launch?"

Keff relayed the question. Narrow Leg let out a piping laugh.

"When the bureaucrats let me," he said. "They are still arguing about who gets credit for what."

The party reentered the hydroponics section, the first part they had visited upon entering the ship. Small Spot had taken a great fancy to the room, arranged like a jungle garden around a large central bath, and decided he needed to see no more than that. He stood up when Tall Eyebrow appeared.

"How quiet it is in here," Long Hand said, coming in behind. Keff listened. She was right. The incessant peeping and chirping of the technicians could not be heard once the enameled hatch slid shut.

"This is worth recording, senior," Small Spot signed enthusiastically. "Someday, when we are traveling the stars, I should like a room of plants with a pool at its heart."

"Thank you for compliment," Big Eyes signed. "This is my design." Touching Tall Eyebrow's hand, she drew him over to see special details. "It is meant to be quiet during travel. Engine noise absorbed through three layers of paneling. Vibration cut up to 88 percent. Gives mental peace."

"Very impressive," Keff said.

"One has far to go," Narrow Leg added, shaking his old head. "One must be sane when arriving."

"Keff must tell you of the game," Tall Eyebrow said, with enthusiasm. "How humans keep spirit in long transit."

"Uh-oh," Carialle said in Keff's ear. "This is one part I am excising from the record we are bringing back to Xeno. They'll court-martial us, or something, if we spread Myths and Legends to another species. Probably violates a hundred non-interference directives."

Keff, smiling fixedly, bowed to Narrow Leg and his daughter. "I'd be happy to talk about it some time. We have other modifications for comfort that I could offer."

"Gladly received," Narrow Leg said. "I might have forgotten refinements in fifty years."

"Meanwhile, tell me about your propulsion system."

"Gladly," the old one said. He led the way out of the silent chamber with Small Spot reluctantly tagging along behind. The engineering section was the farthest aft, behind cargo storage and more crew quarters.

"I intend this ship to last. It has every fail-safe for survival and ultimate utility. You will see the controls here exactly duplicate those in the command center," he began, but got no farther. A cluster of Cridi security burst into the chamber. Keff froze in place, his muscles held by an invisible suit of armor. Big Voice shouldered his way past the guards and stood with his hands clenched before Narrow Leg.

"The council does not approve of allowing an outworlder on this ship," he signed furiously, interspersing his gestures with angry cheeps of diminishing value equations.

"But it *is* of great worth to have them here," Narrow Leg said, waving a gentle hand. "Until the day we may fly to the Central Worlds in our own ships and show ourselves, this is the only way they can bring back word. Keff is viewing all for Carialle, and she makes a record."

"He's good," Carialle said.

"Yep," Keff murmured. "I'm glad he's on our side."

"Plus," Narrow Leg chirped, having carried on his argument with Big Voice while Keff and Carialle were conferring, "there is undoubtedly little that they do not already know about the theory of space travel. I have requested access to the archives myself. If we preceded them to Sky Clear it was by a few hundred years, that was all. And," he added with fierce stabbings of his remarkably long forefinger in Big Voice's chest, "they have *kept up* their space program, while we have allowed setbacks to keep us confined here. All this is in our own people's writing. You would do well to read the documentation."

"Setbacks?" Big Voice said. "Do you designate the overload of planetary Core 10^3 years ago a setback? Do you call the apocalyptic crash of poorly made colony ship of 85×10 years ago a *setback*?"

"That was first experiment with portable Cores," Big Eyes whispered to Tall Eyebrow and Keff.

"Four x 10^2 years of previously successful space exploration brought to halt by disaster after disaster? Attempts to reconnect with former colonies have only begun in last 10^2 years!" Big Voice stopped, out of breath, to pant angrily.

"We now have open space to meet and interact with a people who were not hampered by constant gaps in space research," Narrow Leg said, without heat.

"This sharing will result in a loss of profit for Cridi industry," Big Voice said, standing his ground. "We will not develop things on our own as we should."

Narrow Leg turned to Keff. "Do all Central Worlds colonies have space travel?"

"Well, no," Keff said. "We require a certain technological and social level to be reached before they can have full membership, but they don't necessarily have to have evolved interstellar travel."

"Don't you see?" Narrow Leg said, turning back to the angry councillor. "This could open up your market to other peoples."

"You'll have to make things larger, though," Keff said, trying out a little exponent humor using IT to describe the proportions between Cridi and humans.

Big Voice was not mollified. "The council will discuss this matter thoroughly and give you their answer." He spun on his flat foot and marched out. The guards, uncertainly, lowered their circuit-covered hands and followed.

"Oh, good," Big Eyes signed behind her fellow councillor's departure. "Then we have *years* to talk about this before he comes back."

Narrow Leg shook his head wearily. "The fellow's a stone—gets set in one place and never moves again."

"What have your people done in space without the Core?" Keff asked.

"Small Core onboard," Narrow Leg said, and his musical whistling described formulae, circuitry, and elemental weights. "It runs on reserve fuel, serves few Cridi intensively for a time until new Core is built on new world. Until then, we walk in mud." His eyes twinkled as a few of the crew-frogs running tests in the engine room caught his signs and shuddered.

"There, you see?" Carialle said, noting their reactions through Keff's body-camera. "Tell Tall Eyebrow he is a hero in spite of his clunky amulet. None of the homeworld Cridi want to go through what his people did."

Keff, careful to make certain Big Eyes saw his signs, relayed Carialle's message to the Frog Prince. The praise made him glow and stand up straighter, especially when the female stared at him with open admiration. Narrow Leg caught Keff's eye behind the two younger Cridi's backs, and up-nodded wisely.

The message rocket streaked out of the system, shedding a burst of glowing electrons as it hurtled through the heliopause. Its passage attracted the attention of a raider ship lying concealed in the asteroid belt just inside the system's invisible barrier.

"Telemetry?" the ship's captain demanded. She was a lean woman with black hair and a thin nose and chin.

"From the reptiles," the navigator confirmed. He stretched out a wing-finger to extrapolate the path of the rocket from its source. He adjusted the computer screen to another view. The second planet had moved along its orbit, but the point of origin based on its current velocity was positive. "Confirmed. It came off the Slime planet."

"Get it," the captain said.

The pilot glanced over his shoulder nervously at her, but he applied thrust while bringing the cranky old drives on-line. The ship decanted from the hollow asteroid and gave chase.

Without looking away from the navigation screen, the captain tilted her head toward the copilot, who acted as communications officer and navigator.

"Send a message to the other ships. Alex is closer, but Autumn's engines are better."

The Thelerie officer nodded. The captain leaned closer, as if willing her ship to greater velocity. They couldn't let the probe get away. The small rocket had a good head start. It would be a miracle if they caught up with it, flying on their rackety old engines. The captain felt the vibration through her feet, sensing each time that connections missed. She was frustrated. There was never time to make the repairs correctly. They never had the right parts. Now, when it was vital for the engines to perform perfectly, they'd lose security in the system because no one had done a tune-up. The ship shuddered and groaned. Suddenly, the cabin went black except for the screens. The captain clutched for something solid to hang on to. The internal stabilizers cut out for a moment, and her wrists were twisted painfully.

"What happened?" she demanded. Her arms hurt, but she didn't let go.

"Cohiro says he's diverting all nonessential power to thrusters," the Thelerie reported.

The captain relaxed, glad her face was hidden by the dark. "Maximum speed, then," she said.

On the screen, the little rocket was a white dot, growing slowly into a dash.

"Can we get near enough to capture it with the tractor?" she asked.

"Not unless we slow it down," her pilot said. Over his shoulder, the captain could see the gauges. They were increasing in speed, but so was the probe.

"Then blast it," the captain said. She braced herself. The whole deck shook as more power was drained away from life support, this time for the weapons.

The white dash ahead of them shuddered slightly, but kept flying. It had slowed down just a bit. The captain urged her ship forward.

"Damaged it slightly," the Thelerie said. "We may catch it now."

The raider homed in on its prey. The captain stared at the streak, feeling her heart pound as it grew larger and larger.

"We're on it," she said. "Prepare to activate tractor."

"Aye, sir," said voices in the dark.

The ship drew up on the probe. The captain watched her screens, seeing the numbers shrink. Closer. Closer.

"Now!" the captain cried. The ship groaned again as power diverted to the tractor ball. "Do you have it?"

"No, sir," the Thelerie said. "I'm trying again."

"Maximum velocity," cried the pilot's voice. "Steady. Steady." The small streak gained detail. The captain could almost count the probe's tail fins.

"Grab it!" the captain ordered.

"I have a lock on it!" the Thelerie announced, just as all the lights went down. Loud grinding echoed through the walls. The captain was thrown to the floor against the backs of the pilot couches. Suddenly, the cabin lights came up again, and a siren wailed under the floors.

"Engines failed," the pilot said apologetically. The crew groaned. The captain pulled herself to her feet.

"Can we catch it?" she said, staring at the screen. The streak had dimmed to a small spot. It gained velocity as it flew, shrinking out of sight.

"No, sir. We've blown half a dozen power connections. Can't go anywhere at all until it's fixed."

"Damn," the captain said, fervently. "Call Alex. Have him come and give us a tow back to the base. Call Autumn to chase . . . never mind. She'd never catch it. We'll have to put out a general message for any crew on its path to intercept it. Can we at least tell Mirina where it's going?"

"It's definitely heading toward Central Worlds, sir," said the pilot, after a glimpse at the navigator's screen. "That's all I can tell you."

The captain sighed heavily. "Give me an open channel. I'd better send right away. Bad news doesn't improve with waiting."

Chapter 6

"See how easy and less cumbersome this is," Tall Eyebrow said, a couple of weeks later, as he and Keff made a quick breakfast in the ship before joining Narrow Legs and Big Eyes at the spaceship facility. Long Hand and Small Spot had left early for meetings with conclave members who wanted clarification of questions they had regarding the archives. Tall Eyebrow had managed to beg off meetings about minutiae, preferring to save himself for constitutional debate and conversations about trade. He was relieved that the council accepted his excuses, allowing him to devote more attention to gaining insights on current Cridi technology and, not incidentally, to spend more time with Big Eyes.

With his knees curled up next to him on the round bench seat, he stretched out his hand and closed his fingers. The food synthesizer turned on, and produced a bowl of greens. As the hatch opened, the bowl flew of its own accord to the table and set itself before Tall Eyebrow with a loud clatter. Some of the contents spattered Keff, who jumped up and brushed at his tunic. The Frog Prince grinned sheepishly.

"Forgive. I am having to refine my heavy touch in order not to crush what I reach for, or send myself flying high up in the air. But, I like it," he said, holding up his hand and turning it so the gold circuitry twinkled in the cabin light. "The council has promised to send sufficient circuitry plus full plans to update the Core of Ozran. It may be possible that all shall have amulets once again, including the mages and magesses."

"Do you think that's a good idea?" Keff asked. "You know most of them will just use it for selfish purposes." He reached for the last of the toast. Carialle was amused by his food choices. Everything he had eaten on the ship for the last several days had contained some stiff fiber. He complained that he'd had enough mush in the Cridi diet, and if he could avoid eating the live insects which were considered a local delicacy, he'd just as soon do so.

"You don't have to give them the new system," Carialle said. "Let the humans keep using the old amulets."

"No!" Tall Eyebrow threw that suggestion away from him with an outthrust hand. "We will all learn responsibility together."

"Attaboy," Keff said, "but long-entrenched privilege is hard to give up."

"True. They have coped well, though further temptation may be hard on them. We will no longer be without oversight from your government, is that not correct?" Tall Eyebrow signed, before picking up his fork. He took one bite, then laid the fork down again to talk. "Nor of mine. I look forward to seeing how well my people can prosper with more Core utility. The transformation of our living quarters will be absolute! More access, more water, better irrigation, less threat from natural pests. We must learn more of the language of science to better communication Ozran-wide. I will give the teachers a current lexicon for teaching the younger generation. We older must pick it up as we go. But we have learned well how to use the amulets. After all these years, our theoretical models proved to be accurate!"

"Good plans, all," Carialle said.

"It's nice to be vindicated, after all your hardship," Keff said. "And now that you're in contact with your homeworld again, the transference of technology will be easier."

"Ah, yes, but what a world we return to! Technology advances beyond our dreams."

"But even we humans have some of these things they're giving you," Keff pointed out.

"It isn't the same," TE said. "These beings look like us. We feel they should be *more* like us, but they are not. It is almost as if we are a different species after so much time. It is confusing that they look like us, but do not think like us. They are more wasteful of resources than we, except in the space program. It is worrying. I do not want our people to become so profligate."

"It'll take more than one generation to do that," Keff assured him.

"The Cridi here do not understand why we have not progressed as they have. I am only able to show that, after a long slide backwards, we are regaining our footing. And that does not impress them."

"It impresses *us*," Carialle said. "You held on to your culture, even your science, with no possibility of relief in sight. That kind of determination is most admirable. Central Worlds certainly was bowled over by our reports."

"But in our own nation we are only *country bumpkins*," TE said, pronouncing the Standard phrase in his high-pitched squeak. Keff blinked his eyes several times. Carialle could see he was controlling his face to keep from bursting out into understandable but inappropriate laughter.

"Don't let them get you down," she said. "After all, how often are you going to see any of them ever again when we take you home?"

"I don't know," TE said. His face was a study in mingled regret and relief. "Big Eyes is . . . " his hands paused briefly, "an interesting person."

"She likes you, too," Keff said.

"But she talks so fast," TE's posture showed despair. "Everyone talks too fast." He settled down dejectedly on the round bench with his legs curled up. "I am a relic."

"You're not a relic," Keff said. "The Cridi have had it easy, and you've virtually lived in a desert war zone. You can't expect most of them to understand what you've been through."

"Besides, you're doing an admirable job," Carialle added. "I've been keeping an ear on the transmissions, and watching the other delegate members whenever I can hook into the mass communication signals. The airwaves are full of interviews with the delegates, portions of the transcripts from the archives, footage from the floor of the Main Bog, color commentators—the full-budget extravaganza. The general consensus is that you are an articulate and strong leader, with an admirable mind. Even the council members who don't agree with you are very impressed with you."

TE studied the floor for a minute while his mobile face went through a series of peculiar grimaces: pride, embarrassment, hope, joy, and shyness. To cover the moment, Keff spoke up eagerly.

"And me?"

"Well, they still think you're a talking dog."

"What?" Keff's face fell.

"I'm joking," Carialle said. "I am joking. You're the flavor of the month. You're the most popular man on Cridi."

"I'm the *only* man on Cridi," Keff pointed out.

"We're lucky there's a free press here. Force of popular opinion will sway the council members who are against us," Carialle said. "You wait and see."

✧   ✧   ✧

As Carialle had predicted, once word had spread around Cridi of their arrival, the public arena had discussed the situation, dissecting it to its very smallest particles of meaning, and had decided that they believed Tall Eyebrow and his party to be truthful about their odyssey from Ozran. Public opinion was split on whether or not to try and reclaim Sky Clear, but all were in favor of trading with the vast human empire which had been their unknown neighbor for centuries.

As the sole representative of the Central Worlds, Keff was their model. Young Cridi he saw in the streets had begun to wear clothes like his, and adopted his posture, even some of his mannerisms. Some even dyed their skin to match his. The hue was disconcerting on hides normally ranging from yellow-green to brown-green.

But the human trait that spread the fastest and most generally was a smile. Strange Cridi smiled at him in imitation of his own crinkly-eyed, dimpled-cheek grin. It was all the rage. Keff sat in the evenings with Carialle, watching the news programs, including video of himself, usually shot from the knees up so that his face was telescoped into an isosceles triangle. The commentators discussed, with terse movements and much cheeping of navigational and trigonometry, the location and profusion of Central Worlds systems. One even pointed out, to Keff's surprise, the system settled by humans that lay quite close to them on the other side of the R-sector benchmark. That was the original trading post that had been the site of Carialle's disaster. Keff watched Carialle's reactions closely, but she was too involved in the ongoing negotiations and recording gigabytes of data for Xeno to be troubled by her memories.

Keff and the Ozranians were invited all over Greedeek and to the other cities on Cridi by homeworlders eager to meet the long-lost travelers and the alien stranger. Every day there were invitations to visit various societies or venues to talk about Sky Clear, or space travel, or the Central Worlds, or humanity in general. Big Eyes assigned herself the task of social secretary for the four, partly as a courtesy service, but partly, too, to be able to spend as much time as possible with Tall Eyebrow. With a humorous eye, she weeded out the frivolous invitations, or those which she said, "would not be useful or fun." The best of the invitations still made for a very full program. Keff and the three Ozranians spoke to three or more groups per day. He doubted that every civic group wanted to see him or the two junior delegates, but Tall Eyebrow had generously insisted on their inclusion. Privately, Keff thought that the Frog Prince wanted Keff and his two companions nearby for confidence. Tall Eyebrow didn't need anyone to lean on. Once he began speaking about the conditions on Ozran, the agriculture, the people that he led and loved, he was transformed from a nervous, sometimes melancholy figure to a dynamic speaker. Or rather, signer. He stopped asking Keff and Carialle to take him back to Ozran, and began to acknowledge that he deserved his place among his ancestors' people.

Keff and Tall Eyebrow also made a point to spend much of their free time with Narrow Leg at the Cridi space facility. The elder enjoyed talking space with Keff and, by extension with Carialle, exchanging ideas and techniques.

"Human technology is good, very good," Narrow Leg asserted. "Refinements we have forgotten, or never known, worth having."

"There's also a few wiggles that I haven't seen," Carialle said. "I've racked my databases, but I've never before seen a system that allows a planet's worth of temporary power supply to be carried in a cargo hold.

If the Cridi government is willing to share that, it'll assuage a lot of hardships for settlers on primitive colony worlds, giving them a pad to work from until they can establish their own systems. The insurmountable trouble is remote control, that's all."

Narrow Leg had the foresight to arrange to have a reporter present at most of the conferences between him and Keff so that all Cridi was party to the discussions.

Over the next weeks, Keff and the others were feted, feasted, and fawned over to exhaustion.

"I'm almost sorry I'm so popular," he confessed to Carialle, as he sat through yet another luncheon where he hunched crosslegged with his meal balanced on his knees. The wooden plate, either a serving platter or a hastily manufactured piece made in proportion to his size, held an unappetizing mess of greens such as Tall Eyebrow and the Ozranians favored, alongside a small clutch of wiggling larvae.

Keff, Tall Eyebrow and his retinue were at the main table in the center of the large room. The Frog Prince, between Smooth Hand and Big Eyes, seemed more relaxed than he had before. Occasionally, Keff felt an invisible hand tap his knee. When he looked up, Tall Eyebrow met his glance, then tilted his head in the direction of this or that conversation. No longer was Sky Clear considered a remote concern. Quite a few local manufacturers and businessfrogs were discussing the possibility of setting up shop on the colony.

Long Hand was fielding such a question from an increasingly insistent Big Voice, who had spread before her holographic photo displays and sheets full of graphs and text.

"But all this, exchanges and imports, must wait, gentle-male," Long Hand protested. "We have no hard currency, and our own exports are few and doubtful

at present. Wait a few years, until we have more concerns going so we can deal with you on a more equal
basis."

Big Voice was undaunted. "I am eager to secure
favorable siting for my manufacturing plants. It means
jobs and opportunity for Cridi there. Such things should
be settled as quickly as possible. Would you approve
of investment from outside, an advance of funds, perhaps, against future interests?"

Long Hand let out a peal of laughter. "We have
nowhere to spend this imaginary money, gentle-male.
All we may do is add your name to the roster of those
interested, and we will be sure to speak to you early
when we have anything to offer. You must wait."

Keff, missing none of the important details of the
conversation because it was all in sign language, smiled
to himself. Big Voice wasn't the only one with an eye
toward future profit, just the most persistent.

A female in gold torc and bracelets rose to her feet
and clicked insistently in her throat for attention.

"Gentle-females and gentle-males," she signed in full
formal language, "we are privileged to welcome the
stranger from the Central Worlds. Please give him your
kind attention."

"Thank you, madam chairfrog," Keff said in Standard, adding the appropriate courtesies in sign language.
"I come to you today to offer your people. . . ."

The Cridi media also clamored for interviews. Keff
did his share, but he urged the commentators who
came to him to take advantage of the returnees
instead.

The most important event of all took place several
weeks after the CK-963 had made landfall. Ten thousand Cridi were packed into a low room like an amphitheater, hundreds of meters long. The rows of seats
were sloped so that the huge audience could see the

stage at the bottom, but the ceiling was quite low. Keff lay on his belly to watch, facing downward in one of the side aisles, sweltering in the high humidity. He had been warned to wear his best tunic, and he had done so. To keep from getting it dirty, he'd snaffled a few huge ear-shaped leaves from a handy plant in the lobby, and used them as a ground sheet. Long, reedlike fronds stuck out every which way from the edges of the leaves. Keff had to push them to one side, and finally tuck them under his body to see.

"Just like it was when we first saw you," Tall Eyebrow said, showing his sharp little fangs in a broad grin, his black eyes glinting, pointing to the waving tendrils. "In the high grass on Ozran."

"I was more comfortable then," Keff said, grinning back. He had to prop himself on his elbows to sign. "The blood's rushing to my head. Try to make this one brief, won't you?"

"If I can, friend Keff, if I can."

Smooth Hand, on his way down with Narrow Leg to take their places at the table on the dais, saw this exchange.

"Do not be in such a hurry to bring this meeting to an end," he said, pausing beside the human and patting him on the shoulder. "You will enjoy it more than any other meeting you have attended."

"What do you mean, sir?" Keff asked. But the old amphibioid would say no more. He put his finger to his lips. Keff shook his head, wryly.

"He's got a secret," Keff said to Narrow Leg. "A human would do exactly the same thing. Interaction between Cridi is so like that of my own people that I'm seeing parallels to our civilization everywhere."

"Some would not like you to say so," Narrow Leg said, with a twinkle in his eye. "But I see it as natural that two such gregarious spacefaring races should ally." As he saw pleased enlightenment dawn in Keff's face, he, too, put a finger to his lips and hurried after Smooth Hand.

"Did you see that, Cari?" Keff said. "What Narrow Leg just said?"

"Unless I read that entirely wrongly, I think we have ourselves an A-class applicant for membership," Carialle said. "Good one, Sir Knight."

"Whew!" Keff breathed out gustily. "For once the brass is going to be pleased with us." He beamed at all of the delegates gathering on the stage, at anyone passing by. His mood was so expansive that he didn't mind moving half a dozen times to accommodate the placement of video pickups and audio cubes. This transmission was going to be beamed worldwide. Keff hoped his view of it was sufficiently good so that his copy could be broadcast throughout the Central Worlds when they got home.

All eight chief councillors, plus the three Ozranians, and Narrow Leg were seated at a long, low table facing the audience. Two small panels of three members of the press sat to either side.

Smooth Hand began in the way that Keff had become used to over many weeks, greeting the visitors and welcoming them to Cridi. He alluded to the sacrifices that all five of them had made to be there, and to the struggles of the Cridi population on Sky Clear. Tactfully, he made no mention of the debate over exclusivity to the colony world. Muttering and surreptitious handsigning in the audience proved that they knew he was leaving it out. Keff knew the question wouldn't be settled quickly. Smooth Hand continued.

"The question was put to the population regarding membership in the Central Worlds. The conclave has been receiving so many favorable votes that the council, even our skeptical members," he up-nodded toward Big Voice and Snap Fingers, "have agreed to hear more about the subject. Will the large stranger Keff come forward and address the full conclave?"

"With pleasure," he signed. He rose to his hands and knees, removed the camera eye he was wearing, and attached it to the wall of the auditorium facing the stage. "Can you see properly, Cari?" he asked.

"Perfectly," she replied. "Recording for posterity. Good luck, my parfait and gentil diplomat."

Keff turned and crawled down the steep slope to the stage amid loud applause mingled with chirps and creaks. Eyes shining, Tall Eyebrow stood up as Keff approached. Big Eyes sprang to her feet. Narrow Leg, moving more slowly, rose next. All the other councillors followed, Big Voice and Snap Fingers reluctantly, until the entire panel, and the audience were slapping out their acclaim. Carefully keeping one hand over his head to avoid bumping into the low ceiling, Keff stood up. He looked out over the audience. Ten thousand Cridi sat before him, but the entire planet was watching or listening. Keff beamed and waved to the ones he knew, feeling like he was standing on the doorstep of destiny. A few young Cridi in the audience, some dressed in human-style tunics, levitated and turned somersaults in midair for joy. Others cheered and cried out Standard phrases they had learned from Keff's media interviews. Smooth Hand signalled for quiet, and signed to Keff to begin his remarks. While the others sat down, Big Eyes remained standing to repeat Keff's speech aloud.

"Thank you for your kind reception," Keff signed, and was amused to hear the phrase reduced to a few notes and trills in the female's high, piping voice. "The Central Worlds is an organization of member states whose purpose is to provide a stable government for the benefit of those planets and stations within its borders. The Central Committee, or CenCom," he enunciated the words and heard Big Eyes repeat it, "is dedicated to reaching out to every people on every planet. To those that have reached a certain level of technological and social advancement, we offer full membership. While my partner, Carialle, and I have found numerous races alien to ourselves in our travels, we always dreamed that one day we would locate that civilization, that people, which had evolved in parallel to ourselves, and were of an equal level in all ways, so that we could be friends and allies, instead of benefactor, patron, or in some cases, a right nuisance."

There was a patter of appreciative laughter. Keff smiled.

"If indeed, you are pleased that the Central Worlds and Cridi have found one another at last, you owe a debt of gratitude to Tall Eyebrow. He, and the leaders who came before him, have preserved Cridi culture on a remote outpost against the most incredible odds, helping it to survive until we discovered it. He is responsible for leading us here so we could be with you today. In the last few weeks I've seen a lot of your planet. I admire your culture. I have seen examples of your art, particularly evident in the architecture and gardens of this beautful city; and strides forward in science. In particular, I want to mention the Core power system, an advance which has never been duplicated in the Central Worlds. You can help us to move into the future. I think we can also help you. And together, we can help support the people of Sky Clear. Thank you very much." He sat down crosslegged next to the dais. Ten thousand pairs of hands pounded together, filling the amphitheater with sound that grew louder and louder until the very walls seemed to shake.

Keff shot a glance at the council. Tall Eyebrow sat proudly erect between Narrow Leg and Big Eyes. Big Voice was conferring energetically with the councillors on either side of him. Smooth Hand let the applause go on, then raised his hands for silence.

"I am sure you have many questions for the tall stranger, now to be called our friend, I hope," he signed, with a slight smile toward Keff. "For now, let your sign be counted. If you approve the approach to Central Worlds, send your vote to your precinct now. Thank you all."

Reporters hurried forward from the side tables and the audience, swamping the panel. Free-floating remote cameras buzzed over their heads and zoomed from face to face, gathering reactions like a species of psychological honey bee. The air was full of flurried gestures and excited Cridi voices. After weeks of intensive training in the spoken language Keff understood more of the verbal exchanges than ever before, and he was delighted with the response.

"Can you hear it, Cari? They want it. They're going to join us."

Carialle sounded amused. "Don't count your chickens in advance, softshell . . . but I think you're right. You should hear some of the scuttlebutt going about on the amulet airwaves. I'm recording the best ones for you to hear later. 'Maximum joy and maximum profit' was the one I heard from Big Voice's media aide."

"And here's the man himself," Keff said, seeing a solemn delegation forcing its way toward them through the crush on the platform. "Good gentle-male."

"Tall stranger," Big Voice signed, *very* politely. "I have exchanged tentative words with Long Hand with regard to the spacecraft concession for Sky Clear. Should this proposition now before us come to pass, I would be concerned that a human delegation might . . . put in a rival bid for choice sites."

"That's the nature of business throughout the universe," Keff signed cheerfully, teasing the pompous amphibioid. Clearly shaken, Big Voice tried again. "Would not Central Committee consider priority for primary sentient species?" His hands fluttered desperately, trying to gauge Keff's response. "Or partnership?" Keff grinned and relented.

"Central Worlds would not take away the rights from one member species in favor of another," he said. "If you can get an exclusive agreement from the Cridi on Sky Clear, the CenCom won't interfere with that at all."

"Thank you," Big Voice signed, gratefully. "Thank you, tall stranger Keff." He moved away, once again in pursuit of Long Hand. Tall Eyebrow, having observed the whole thing from his place on the dais, grinned to show his sharp white teeth. Keff gave him a wink.

More media types swooped in on him, signing or singing questions from all sides. Keff tried to answer them all in turn, knowing he was getting some of the words wrong in his haste, hoping it wouldn't matter. The IT earned its keep that day, translating his spoken replies into Cridi music, so he could carry on two conversations at once.

"Will other humans come to Cridi?" was among the most frequently asked questions. "Will we be able to visit your worlds?"

"You will be most welcome everywhere you go," Keff said. "In fact, we will expect a return visit, just as soon as Narrow Leg's team finishes constructing their first spaceship." He turned to gesture with an open hand toward the old male who stood half a head taller than every other Cridi in the room. He stiffened with pride.

"That is right, and only right," Narrow Leg said, "that we should make our first visit to our new allies in our own spacecraft. And you may take my words straight to heart. We will be ready."

The reporters chirruped excitedly, obviously adding color commentary.

Smooth Hand moved to the center of the dais then, and held up his long, wrinkled hands.

"The tabulation is finished," he signed, and

announced the figures. The numbers were so large that his voice rose almost out of Keff's range of hearing.

"Did I get that right, Cari? Twenty million in favor of membership?"

"Unless your program here split a chip, those in favor of the Central Worlds was 25,697,204. Against: 3,402,110."

Smooth Hand repeated the good news to the crowd, who echoed it as they danced in the aisles. "The measure passes! The measure passes! We join!"

"Sit down, sit down," the elder signed. "There is one thing left to do. *Please.* May we have your attention?"

It took some time until the jubilant Cridi settled back into their seats. The senior councillor turned to Keff.

"This is a great moment for our people. Not only have we rediscovered our lost children, but we make a bond with new friends." He signalled to an aide to come forward.

The silver-torqued frog glided swiftly onto the stage bearing two long rectangles of a high gloss wood. On each was engraved a long screed in an incredibly tiny and intricate script. Beside the Cridi language was the text in Standard. Keff looked up in surprise.

"I helped the engraver with the correct wording," Tall Eyebrow told Keff. "I took it directly from Carialle's file of such documents. You will find it in order, I promise you."

"And I took it from the databanks of your more than unusually helpful IT," Carialle said in his ear.

"You see," Keff said, sublingually. "In no time, you'll look back on the days when you used to laugh at my program."

"I don't see those days receding behind us, Keff," Carialle said, sardonically, "but in this case it came through."

"Is all in order?" Tall Eyebrow asked, concerned.

"I'm absolutely certain it's all right," Keff said,

reassuringly. "I have never seen an official government document look so beautiful."

"You honor us," Smooth Hand said, bowing over his moving hands.

At each side of the document were blank blocks enclosed in festoons of scrollwork, images of vines, flowers, insects and birds. Keff figured out that those were the signature blocks when he managed to decipher his name, picked out delicately in filament-thin characters, running in a border around the right-hand block.

The aide floated over the heads of the crowd and laid the squares of wood neatly beside one another in the center of the table. Smooth Hand followed to stand with one long hand touching each.

Smooth Hand nodded to Keff to join him. The crowd of reporters parted, flowing back into the main audience. Keff fumbled at his tunic pocket and drew out two small devices.

"I'm so excited I nearly forgot these," he said. "These are short-run permanent recorders which I would like to use to immortalize this moment for the CenCom. One is a gift to you, to keep in your admirable archives."

"We thank you for your thoughtfulness," Smooth Hand said. "Your request is granted. Set them where they will catch all of this great moment."

"Well," Keff said, picking up the silver scriber the aide handed him. He tested it against his palm and found it sharp-edged enough to skim off a layer of skin. "This is it, Carialle."

"This is it," she agreed. "A moment for all the Central Worlds, and for us as well. Go for it, Sir Galahad."

"I do it all for you, Lady Fair." He grinned to himself and nodded to the senior councillor.

Smooth Hand looked out across the sea of faces. "All of you bear witness to this moment, in which we find we are not alone in this great galaxy, but among friends." He took his scriber and incised his name in the left-hand block on both blocks of wood. The crowd erupted in cheers and applause. He signalled to Keff, who stepped forward and bowed over the first of the documents.

"Hold it," Carialle's voice said sharply in his ear. "Don't do it."

Keff stopped, arrested with his hand centimeters above the wood. "Why not? What's wrong, Carialle?"

"What is it?" Smooth Hand asked, seeing the human's mouth moving almost silently. "Is something wrong?"

"Cari?"

Her voice in his ear was as crisp and sharp as an artificial-intelligence generated construct. "Don't sign a thing. The entire deal is on hold. I have just received a message back from the CenCom. There's a ship at the perimeter of this system, and they are here to take over negotiations. We are off this mission as of now!"

"What?" Keff demanded. "They can't do that!"

"They can, and have! The CenCom sends its *compliments*, but we are ordered to step back to avoid any 'unforeseen difficulties.' It's the Inspector General's doing. I am so mad that I could just flame out!"

Keff didn't like the edge in her voice. "Try and stay calm, Lady Fair. I'll get out of here and come to you. We'll discuss this." He looked up at the crowd, who were fluttering surreptitious messages at one another, and at Smooth Hand, clearly wondering what was going on. Swallowing his concern for Carialle, he forced a smile to his lips. He hoped his growing command of the Cridi language would sufficiently support him through this delicate moment.

"Gentle-males and gentle-females, I sincerely beg your pardon," he said, setting down the scriber. A few in the audience gasped at his action, and he made a gesture intended to show humility. "I have just been informed that, er, that diplomats senior to Carialle and myself have just arrived in your star system. This is such an important matter that they wish to take part in this ceremony themselves. If you will forgive this terrible breach of manners, may I beg a short delay until they may join us?"

Smooth Hand's face, compressed into a frown of concern, opened up in comprehension. "Ah!" he squeaked. "I see. With the greatest of reluctance, friend Keff, I see no reason why not to allow. We know and trust *you*, but we understand the pressures of state."

There was a general murmur, only partly of agreement, from the rest of the council. Keff heard undertones of distrust and dismay beneath it. Big Voice scowled and crossed his arms as if to say he'd assumed all along the humans would back away at the last minute.

"Thank you, Councillor Smooth Hand, and all the rest of the conclave, gentle-females and gentle-males. I must go and prepare for the arrival of our senior delegates. I . . . we'll be back as soon as we can. If you will excuse me?" He barely waited for the council to signal their assent before he was running up the aisles in a crouch.

"Hold on, Lady Fair," he murmured as he ran out of the hall and into the muddy street. "I'll be with you in just a moment. Don't do anything rash."

"I'm not going to do *anything*," Carialle said, but her voice rose in volume and pitch until he winced. "But Dr. Sennet Maxwell-Corey is going to pay heavily for this. I am *not* crazy!"

Chapter 7

Tall Eyebrow caught up with Keff about twenty meters outside the door, and swept him up on a wave of Core power.

"I will take you swiftly to 'the One Who Watches From Behind the Walls,'" he said.

The two of them flew up over the jungle-fringed city blocks toward the spacefield. Luckily for Keff's atmospheric acrophobia, he had no attention to spare for looking down. He had enough on his hands trying to calm down his partner, who kept up a steady stream of diatribe in his ears.

" . . . Muck-faced, baby-eating, acephalitic *bastard*," Carialle kept saying. "First, he rigged me with a booby trap, illegally, without my knowledge, and set it to go off without waiting to get full data on the situation. Now he sees to our disgrace before the entire Cridi population. What's next?"

"I'm sure we can work out the mistake," Keff said, over and over again. "Just exactly what did they say?"

With admirable control, Tall Eyebrow brought them to a perfect landing on the ramp of the ship. Keff, threw a bare nod over his shoulder for thanks, and ran inside.

"Oh, they were polite," Carialle said. Her voice beat double on his eardrums, coming from the cabin speakers as well as his implant. When he cringed at the sheer

126

power of her vocal volume, she relented and turned it down, deactivating the mastoid bone receiver entirely. "So sorry, but orders are orders."

Keff plumped down in his crash couch. Tall Eyebrow hovered sympathetically near Carialle's titanium pillar.

"Let's see the message," Keff said.

The screen in front of him filled with the hailing graphic used in all Central Worlds Fleet communiques. It vanished, and the image of a man appeared. His long jaws and heavy eyebrows made him look melancholy, but his voice was a pleasantly warm tenor.

"CK-963, this is the DSC-902. Respectful greetings. I am Captain Gavon. I am sending you a tightbeam of messages entrusted to me by the Central Committee. I know the content of these datafiles. I want to assure you in advance that I regret the intrusion as much as you do. Standing by."

The messages followed. As Carialle had dreaded, the first was from the head of Explorations, Dr. Michael Brinker-Levy. His pleasant, dark-skinned face glanced out at them from the screen. He gave them an apologetic smile.

"Carialle and Keff, we have just received communication from the Inspector General for your sectors, Dr. Corey. He had an emergency buoy that you had launched at this point," a star chart overlay his face. "The internal recordings from Telemetry showed you were in no physical peril at the time, but nevertheless show dangerous adrenaline and toxicity levels in your system, Carialle. No updates and no further messages from you were received, except for a routine query for a databank search you sent recently."

"Nonsense," Keff said. "The IG must have heard from SPRIM and MM within microseconds. And what about your complaint for illegal circuit-tapping?"

"*He* oversees all queries about illegalities and

improprieties in this sector," Carialle said bitterly. "And who is watching the watchman?"

Brinker-Levy continued. " . . . I have also had a complaint on your behalf from the oversight agencies, SPRIM and MM, citing personal interference from the Inspector General. Under normal circumstances I would be able to take those into account first. Because you're engaged upon such a delicate negotiation that affects matters at the highest levels, if there is anything wrong, and your judgement is in some way impaired . . . you must understand we cannot take chances, and at this distant remove we have no way of judging for ourselves. Please cooperate in every way with Captain Gavon. He's a good man, and will need your help. Your knowledge of the Cridi culture and language are unsurpassed, and I have always been satisfied with the job you do," here he smiled, "even if you are a little unorthodox. I will take up the subject of your complaints while you are on your way back to Central Worlds, and send you updated information in transit."

"On the way back? What is he talking about?" Keff asked.

"There's more," Carialle said. "This was on the side-band." The visual didn't change from the graphic left after the end of Brinker-Levy's message, but a resonant voice broke over the speakers.

"Hi, gal," Simeon said. "Greetings from SSS-900-C. I received your query. I'm at a loss for natural causes that would have destroyed three starships. No abnormal outbreak of ion storms, comets, or other anomalies observed in your pinpoint area. I'm uploading to you all the data I have for the last fifty years. There's not much. Some of it's your own. That spot between P- and R-sector is rarely explored.

"I'm piggybacking on Exploration's message to you because I heard some scuttlebutt you need to know. Maxwell-Corey's out ringing doorbells again. The first probe caused quite a sensation. Pa-lenty unorthodox. He was going to be in deep spacedust with SPRIM, until the second probe arrived. The data on it was garbled, and your voice sounded woozy. That added fire to his insistence that there's still something wrong with your mind, and you need specialized long-term mental care. I sincerely hope not. He's arguing at the least you're severely overwrought. Keep it together, gal. Greetings to Keff."

The graphic faded, and the unwelcome sight of the Inspector General's mustachioed face flicked into being. Keff found himself unable to resist a sneer. Maxwell-Corey's vendetta against his partner had attained foolish proportions over the years, and he was becoming tired of the pompous bureaucrat and his implausible hobbyhorse. A dozen shrinks had proclaimed Carialle sane, but this control freak could not acknowledge the truth, would not acknowledge it. The tragedy was, he might be able to "prove" it by forcing her into unwitting admissions, recording angry outbursts, and twisting data to suit his purpose.

"CK-963 Carialle, in light of your two communications with the Central Worlds I am ordering you to SSF-863 for a full evaluation. You will brief the replacement team in full and return immediately when you have received this message. Maxwell-Corey out."

The screen blanked. Keff relaxed a little, realizing that his hands were ground into tight fists, and he was standing on the balls of his feet, as if ready to meet an attacker.

Captain Gavon's face reappeared, his long face sympathetic.

"I am sorry," Gavon said, and the catch in his voice showed Keff the diplomat was under a tremendous strain. "We'll be with you in a matter of hours. Gavon out."

"They can't do that to us," Keff said. "We'll fight them, Cari. Cari?"

Carialle didn't answer. She ignored the input from her screens, antennae, and camera eyes. For a moment, just for a moment, at the sound of the Inspector General's mocking voice, her long-buried subconscious had flashed back to a memory she thought had been destroyed with her first ship . . . feeling not so much as hearing a slight vibration from the hull above her, as footsteps stopped—as if someone was laughing at her. Laughing at her helplessness!

No, she said to herself, pulling back into the inmost security of her shell. *I will not let myself be forced. I am not mad. I'm cured!* she cried. *I'm cured, I'm cured, I'm cured.* But the tapping and the sounds of her own screams came back to her. She started counting the seconds again. *One, two, three . . .*

Her power levels all dropped for a dizzying, frightening millisecond. Carialle snapped out of her reverie, and went back on full alert. All scopes were back to normal. She wondered what had happened. Then she became aware that Keff was pounding on her titanium pillar and shouting.

"Carialle! Answer me! Cari!"

"What happened?" she demanded. "I felt a blackout."

The brawn staggered backward, limp with relief. "Tall Eyebrow blinked your power, just once. I'm glad it was enough."

"It was," Carialle said, vastly relieved. "I needed the shock. Thank you, TE." She made her frog image appear. It sketched a graceful half-bow and spread out its hands. The Frog Prince swept a self-deprecatory palm across.

"It was nothing. I was worried."

"I was going to pull the fire bell in a moment," Keff said. "We lost you there, lady."

"I'm sorry," she said. "I . . . I was back *there* again. I was *counting.* Maybe in a way that bastard is right."

"He's not right!" Keff shouted. His normally cheerful face was a furious shade of red. Tall Eyebrow, hovering beside the brawn, shook his head vigorously. "If I could teleport in a blink to where he's laired up, I would find the nearest lavatory and stuff his grinning face down the head. Don't you worry. This is all a mistake. We'll show them the flight path and explain to them what happened. Let's tell Gavon the whole story. I'm sure all he knows is the gossip that's floating around, not the facts."

"I'm not giving up my mission," Carialle said. "We have *earned* this. We've earned the trust of the locals. We shouldn't be removed from the mission. I want to see it through."

"So do I. Let's send a message to Gavon and ask him to reconsider. He can keep us here as aides, and then we can go back to CW." Keff threw himself into his crash couch, and scooted it up to be right in front of the video pickup.

Carialle calculated the location of the DSC-902, and put all she had behind the tightbeam message. All they could do until Gavon replied was wait.

During the time that passed, a few of the Cridi who had been in the amphitheater when Keff had to leave drifted by to visit and make their compliments. A few of the councillors were sympathetic. Unexpectedly, Snap Fingers was one of them.

"I am in business," he signed. "I came up from the merest clerk to my position now as second continental chief. I hate it that bureaucrats would take an assignment away from you. That should not happen. It shows a lack of confidence in you, which I wanted you to know was an error on the part of your superiors. If you were Cridi, I would be proud to have you working for me."

"You are very kind," Carialle's amphibioid image said with its hands.

"I mean what I say," Snap Fingers returned. "We are on opposite sides of the expansion question, but that does not mean we cannot be friends."

"Good people," Tall Eyebrow said, as the councillor departed. "I am proud to know them."

"You are one of them," Keff assured them.

Narrow Leg arrived just as Carialle received Gavon's reply. Tall Eyebrow quickly brought him up to date in sign language while Keff and Carialle listened to the message.

Captain Gavon's thin face looked more haggard, and his long jaw was set. "I have received your transmission. I regret that I have no 'slack' to cut you. Very, very sorry. This is not my idea. I have to follow my orders, too, you know. They are unequivocal and absolutely clear. I sent the messages on in advance so you could prepare."

"Damn," Keff said, watching with chin propped on his fist. He saw the record light pop on, and sat up straight.

"I am sorry, too," Carialle said, sending on a reply. "We did appreciate the extra notice, but it doesn't change the situation here. I don't want to put you on the spot, but you must see how this affects us."

"And what about the psychological effect on the native population of replacing a trusted team with strangers?" Keff put in earnestly. "You must let us stay. We can be of inestimable help to you."

Carialle sent the message, all the while muttering. "Rotoscoped, animated bastard from a bad, grade-D, psycho-horror flick—in 2-D! I don't mean Gavon," Carialle said quickly, in Keff's ear. "I mean the IG."

"*What* is he?" Narrow Leg asked, listening with interest but no comprehension to Carialle's stream of invective. Tall Eyebrow attempted to translate, but gave up almost at once as the spare knowledge he had of

Standard colloquialisms failed him. Carialle realized belatedly that she had left open the communication channels to the frogs' sign-language image, and swiftly blanked the wall.

"The Inspector General has authority over our department, and he has a personal grudge against Carialle," Keff said, explaining more simply. "He is responsible for having us recalled, and the other team taking our place."

"We have no choice," Carialle broke in. "We'll have to lift sooner or later."

"Maybe I can slow down IT so we have to stay through the negotiations," Keff offered.

Carialle's laugh was bitter. "Hah! IT doesn't need to be slowed down. The holes in it leak data like a screen door."

"That's not fair, lady. IT's been doing a wonderful job here."

She was instantly contrite. "I know. That's true. I'm upset."

"You must not leave," Tall Eyebrow said, gesturing frantically, his black eyes wide. "We may never see you again. How will I and my companions return to Ozran?"

"Gavon will take you," Carialle said. "We have no choice. We're off the mission."

"Or I," Narrow Leg said. "My ship is all but ready to launch. I would be proud to escort you home. Besides," he added, with a shrewd and amused glance, "my daughter would not forgive me if I shortened your time together."

Tall Eyebrow looked somewhat mollified and a little abashed.

"But what about trade between my world and yours?" Narrow Leg asked Keff.

"That won't be affected. Even greater authority for decision-making rests with Gavon. We're not really diplomats. Our usual job is exploration of unknown space. Normally we file the preliminary report on a potentially sentient race. We've never been the follow-up team before."

"We prefer you," Narrow Leg said. "We understand one another, you two and I. A diplomat might not be such a seasoned risk-taker. We may not cooperate with this replacement. I can get the council snarled up for years to delay." The high-pitched voice described a geometric progression.

"Don't. Gavon's a good man," Carialle said. She was pleased by the Cridi's offer to side with them, but disliked the idea of fighting her battles unfairly. "Don't blame him for this. Let's see what he says about letting us stay on to help."

Two hours passed. Keff received more visitors from the conclave, and later served a synthesized meal to the Ozranian delegates, Narrow Leg, and Big Eyes, who turned up again in the late evening to sit with Tall Eyebrow. As he ate, Keff kept his eye on the chronometer, impatiently willing a message to come, to beat the next turn of the number.

"Where is it?" he asked. "Gavon's reply should be on a shorter return loop as the ship nears us. The interval ought to have been no more than half an hour by this time. Isn't he speaking to us?"

"Perhaps Simeon's data is incomplete, and there is a dangerous anomaly in-system," Carialle said, her voice remote from the ceiling speakers. "I'm resending."

Nothing came. Keff cleaned up after dinner, and listlessly did his exercises on the Rotoflex with an interested audience of Cridi commenting on the swell and slide of his muscles.

Carialle found the rhythmic *clang! bump!* of the weighted pulleys a soothing, mindless pattern, then all at once it irritated her. She opened input to all her antennae.

She strained her "ears" for transmissions on the CW

ship's frequency, putting the audio of her receivers onto speaker for the others to hear. Keff stopped his deltoid flex and eased the pulleys to a resting position. He looked up hopefully at the sound of static.

"Nothing," Carialle said. "Perhaps Gavon is coming all the way in without speaking to us again."

"Nasty," Keff said. He reached for a towel and wiped his face. "I thought this would be amicable. Maybe I *won't* give him all my files. Let him figure out the subtleties between this and *this*." He made a couple of signs that Carialle, searching the IT database, found to be the symbols for hunger and a mild obscenity regarding mouths and filth. Long Hand looked shocked, Small Spot abashed. Tall Eyebrow and the two Cridi natives grinned widely.

"Wait!" Carialle exclaimed, getting a tickle from her long-distance receiver. "Here's something at last!"

The data-thread was weak and badly garbled. Carialle boosted it, and checked the frequency. It was the same Gavon had been sending on, but the audio portion was mostly static.

" . . . day . . . Intruders . . . May—"

Keff sat up. "Carialle, that sounds bad. Isn't there any more?"

"No."

"Play it again."

Now Carialle strained out a few more of the harmonics and static, and boosted the gain. The message welled up out of the speaker, then faded away again. " . . . ayDAY. INTRUDERS! MAYday . . . ip . . . ." There was no more.

"Something's happened to them," she said. "In the sidebands I'm hearing the ID pulse from their black box, but no ship noise in the low registers, and no more audio messages."

"Intruders!" Keff exclaimed. "They were attacked! How many? Who? Who was it?"

He looked at the Cridi, who shook their heads, signing nervously between one another.

"We've got to help Gavon," Keff said. He shouldered back into his tunic, immediately all business. "Our fellow ship is in trouble. They might need life support assistance." He dared not think of the worst reason the DSC-902 had stopped sending, but concentrated on the possibility of saving the crew.

"I'm starting launch prep now," Carialle snapped out. She activated the control board, and quickly counted green lights. "Tall Eyebrow, Narrow Leg, you'll all have to go. Big Eyes, will you please tell Space Command we request permission to lift. We have an emergency on our hands."

"I will," the young councillor signed, then became still as she squeaked out vocal information through her finger-control transmitters. Carialle heard her voice repeated on first one, then a dozen personal frequencies as the message went out to the command center and members of the conclave via the Core of Cridi.

"I will come with you," Tall Eyebrow said, turning to look from Keff to Carialle's frog image.

Keff shook his head. "Stay here. We could get caught by whatever happened to them, too," he said. "I won't risk you getting hurt. We'll come back as soon as we can."

"I will go now," the Frog Prince insisted. "You may need me." He turned to sign at the local Cridi.

"How long?" Narrow Leg asked Keff. "How long until you go?"

Keff glanced at the board. "Minutes."

"Wait. Give me ten." The old Cridi levitated and flew out of the airlock. He began his high-pitched warbling, too. Big Eyes glanced up, surprised, then followed her father.

They were back within the promised ten minutes, but not alone. Behind them sailed a large crew of Cridi

workers, bearing with them tools and a round device
the size of a medicine ball, and an impressive tangle
of flex, tubes, boxes, and clamps.

Keff peered at it. "It's a ship's Core. But we can't
use it, sir." He waggled his fingers loosely.

"I can," Tall Eyebrow said, holding up his hand, on
which the new finger-stalls gleamed. "Let me help. You
have done so much for me and my people. You may
need more than you have."

"Let him come," Carialle said, interrupting her preparations. "Our tractors may not be equal to what we
might find out there—and we're unarmed."

Keff's face blanked with shock. "Your salvagers? You
think that's who's out there?"

"It's a possibility. There've been several other 'dis-
appearances.' No space anomalies, Simeon said,"
Carialle pointed out. "We're in this sector. I feel there's
a connection to my personal disaster. It's just a guess,
Keff. I have no positive data. I couldn't sell it as a
certainty."

"I trust your guesses more than other people's certainty," Keff said. "I've known you these sixteen years."

The miniature Core was installed by Narrow Leg's
crew with remarkable speed and efficiency. Carialle felt
its power signature, and set up a program so it wouldn't
feed back on her own systems. It responded well to
the technician who tested it, putting in his own frequency number, and to Tall Eyebrow, whose new circuitry was tied in as well.

"Its range is 18,000 kilometers," the shipbuilder said,
with equal references to the X, Y, and Z axes. "Enough
for a planet plus layers of atmosphere plus error fac-
tor."

"That means getting in right on top of the DSC-902,"
Carialle said. "We'd better not miss. I'm calculating
their possible location based on the time signature for

their last transmission. I must work from that assumption."

Keff felt stricken, but he nodded.

Big Eyes waved for attention. "You have permission to lift when you wish." She looked at Tall Eyebrow. "I go, too?"

"No," Keff and Tall Eyebrow signed at once. "You could be in danger."

"We don't know what's out there," Carialle snapped out. "No more arguments. Will you all clear the decks? Keff, TE, secure to station."

"Go in peace and safety," Narrow Leg said. "Return with honor." He turned to Carialle's pillar, as he had seen the others do. "We will assist your launch." The technicians backed away from the blank panel behind which they had secured the Core. They all flew out of the airlock as Carialle shut it on their heels.

"Come back," Big Eyes signed simply to Tall Eyebrow. Then, she was gone.

"Damn M-C," Carialle growled as she lit engines. Flames gathered under her exhaust cones, between the landing fins, wreathing her in light. All her indicators read green and on GO. "This wouldn't have happened at all if he hadn't decided I was about to go rogue. He should have believed me! There's something out there, and it's hostile."

Outside, she observed shadows of Cridi behind the windows of the low buildings at the edge of the field. Farther back, in a great ring around the field, frogs stood, or levitated, or hovered in their saucer-craft, waiting and watching. The infinity of audio broadcast frequencies, both private and public, filled with chatter and speculation, hoping for the first successful launch from their planet in half a Standard century.

"Here goes." She applied thrusters. Carialle felt the invisible hands holding her down to the surface of the planet drop away, and gather at the foot of her ship.

"Ready," Keff said. Tall Eyebrow cheeped an affirmative.

"Brace yourselves," she told the human and the amphibioid as she applied thrust. "Watch your necks."

"Necks?" Keff asked. "Wh—yyyyyyyyy?!"

His question became a strained cry as the g-force pushed his head back. Within a half second of putting on her own engines, Carialle felt the envelope rising under her skirts. It felt like everyone on Cridi was helping to push her into space. The force shoved her hard into the sky like an extra booster rocket, bringing her to breakaway speed in record time. Flames from sheer friction danced down her sides as she cut through the atmosphere and emerged into space, yet her internal temperature remained stable. The Cores, both inside and outside the craft, were protecting her. She felt the exosphere seal behind her, planetary ozone readings returning to normal within milliseconds of her passage. The additional thrust cannoned her forward. She was moving 60% faster than she could have gone unassisted. The shields strained against the additional pressure but were fully capable of holding. She lit her own full engines, corrected course, and opened all her receivers, hoping for word from Gavon's ship. A quick slingshot around Cridi, and she was on her way.

Chapter 8

"This is the end of the ship's ion trail," Keff said, reading the telemetry monitors. The CK-963 zigzagged the empty space between the orbits of the last planet and the asteroid belt that marked the border of the Cridi system. They were within half a million klicks of the planet, a dusty, battered rock rimed with iron oxide red and nickel oxide blue. The sun was a faint flicker of yellow over Keff's right shoulder.

"And this corresponds to the last coordinates from which they transmitted to us," Carialle said. "But where's the ship?" She scanned space around her. There was a little debris, and a very small amount of residual radiation from the right kind of material, but not enough to tell what had happened. The DSC-902 appeared to have crossed the radiopause and disappeared into thin vacuum.

"If the ship was disabled, it couldn't have drifted far," Keff said, staring at the astrogation tank, searching it for artifacts. "If it was towed, where's the engine trail for the other ship?"

"What if Gavon was remotely pulled away?" Tall Eyebrow asked, showing the circuitry on his long fingers.

"The Cores," Carialle said. Keff let out a low whistle. "The pirates who killed them have Cores!"

"That's why somebody has bottled up the Cridi space

140

program," he said. "The Cores have a limited range, but incredible power inside that radius. That technology alone is worth keeping a secret from the rest of the universe."

"I think you're right about the why," Carialle said. "We still don't know who. And at this moment, I am more concerned with *where*."

She was silent for so long Keff wondered if she had suffered another memory flashback. He waited for a long time, then cleared his throat.

"Cari? Are you all right?"

"I'm fine," Carialle said, a little too emphatically. "Apart from being burning mad, I'm just on green. I may not like having another ship come in and usurp my mission, but damn it, I will fight my battles myself. Somebody captured or destroyed one of our vessels, and I am damned well going to know who. Nobody messes with a Central Worlds ship on *my turf*."

"That's the spirit! Evil highway brigands who prey upon the helpless shall not prevail. We will sally forth and beard the miscreants in their den," Keff said, thumping his chest. He kept his voice light, hoping that her train of thought would not lead Carialle back to her memories of isolation. "We shall slay all who do not beg for mercy and swear allegiance to the Cen-Com."

Carialle was amused in spite of her worries. "Thank you, brave Sir Keff. But seriously, who are they? Not Cridi. They wouldn't be shooting at one another, at least not without giving a reason. And it certainly can't be other humans. There's never been any contact with humanity in this system before."

"That is what Narrow Leg and the others assure me," Tall Eyebrow said.

"And word would have gotten back to Central Worlds about the frogs if someone was ambushing their flights and stealing from them. We'd have begun to see artifacts that no one could explain—little spaceships," Carialle said. "Who could resist the Core technology? All three of the last Cridi missions had Cores on board."

"So what does that leave?" Keff asked, feeling the tingle of excitement. "Another race? Another spacegoing alien race?"

"It might be," Carialle said, cautiously. "It's a big universe. But first we must prove that the disappearance of this ship wasn't mere accident, and that it wasn't bad engineering that slew three Cridi vessels."

They explored the outer reaches of the heliopause. Space was pointedly, echoingly empty. Carialle picked up faint traces of engine trails, some ages old by the pattern of their decay. It seemed that most of the Cridi missions, at least as far back as they'd used an ion drive, had exited the system in this direction. It led, not incidentally, directly toward Ozran and away from the bulk of the Central Worlds. Her entry into the solar system was a quarter of the way anticlockwise around the sun, so the new wake she was forming behind her was clear and undisturbed. She used it to check the strength of the trail she was following.

"Aha," she said, as they arced out toward a group of jagged moonlets dancing along in the asteroid belt. "Now I *am* picking up fresh indications from another kind of space drive. Not Cridi."

Keff stared at the astrogation tank. Tall Eyebrow wriggled up next to him to see. Carialle put the view on full light spectrum analysis. The brawn darted a finger toward the lines that sprang into relief, crisscrossing the holographic display like spider web.

"I see it. There are hundreds of them!" he exclaimed. "Someone else is in this system."

"Very strange," Tall Eyebrow signed. "They've been traveling through here for years, but no one has ever made contact with the second planet. They must have been able to tell someone was living there. The noisy airwaves alone would have told them that, even if they couldn't understand the transmissions."

"They wouldn't exactly come visiting if their only motive was robbery," Keff said. "Wait, these are all cold. They're years old."

"Not these," Carialle said, illuminating three traces that converged on an asteroid cluster. "Those are new."

Keff peered closely at the faint image in the tank, then pounded a hand flat on the console. He had spotted movement.

"Cari, reverse course! Quick!"

Almost before the words were out of his mouth, Carialle had looped the ship around. She was heading for cover behind a pocked moonlet before they could sense her. Three strange ships flew out of crevices and holes in one of the asteroids, and were making straight for them. She kept video cameras aimed aft as she looked for a hiding place. Keff studied their pursuers.

The ships' design looked familiar: long, tapered cones bracketed with emplacements for landing gear, communications, and weaponry, but all were old and in poor repair. Flying junkheaps, he thought, with a sniff. His monitors still didn't show a sensor lock from their pursuers. Their sensors showed radiation leak from two of their engines. One was nearing critical point as it poured on power to catch up with them. They were almost ridiculously undermaintained, but Keff felt no urge to laugh.

"Hurry, Cari!"

By comparison, the CK-963 was an angel on the wing. Carialle cornered wide around two halves of a broken rock ten times her size, then hugged in close behind a flattened sphere, searching for a ravine or a cave she could duck into. The sphere's sides were solid. She tried slipping past it unseen, to another huge rock shaped like a flatiron. One of the intruders was waiting just beyond the great wedge's lip. Carialle grimly turned as sharp an angle as she could in the opposite direction.

A red light, infinitesimally small, bloomed on the pursuer's hull.

"Brace!" Carialle cried out as the energy bolt struck her amidships.

The blast tore straight through her shields as though through cellophane. Painful heat ran along her sensors, which then mercifully shut down. Damage control monitors showed her an elongated oval tear in her dorsal hull. Whoops sounded as the alarm went off in the cabin. Emergency systems kicked into operation at once.

Keff kept himself from being thrown across the control console by gripping the crash couch's armrests and hanging on with all his great strength. Tall Eyebrow, hovering, had nothing to grab onto, but pivoted deliberately in the air and somersaulted into the padding of the other couch. The straps rose up and surrounded him like an octopus seizing prey.

"Wish I could do that," Keff said, between gritted teeth. Tall Eyebrow whistled an apology. The pilot's couch engulfed Keff in safety harness. He expelled his breath in a long sigh and let go his grasp on the armrests.

"Thanks. How bad is it?" Keff asked the air.

"Hull breach, minor. Already being fixed," Carialle said shortly.

The automatic repair system quickly pressurized the sector and filled it with self-hardening polymer/metal compound. Nothing vital had been damaged, but Carialle wondered how many of those hits they could take before being destroyed. Her nerve endings still stung. She fed somatotropins to the injured part, and increased her sugar levels slightly.

Keff shook his hands to help the blood flow to the

white and pinched palms, then slammed his fist down on the RECORD button to send a message to CW.

"Mayday. This is the CK-963. We are under attack by three vessels, origin unknown. I am uplinking video of these vessels, plus other data we have gathered regarding the disappearance of a Central Worlds ship in this sector. If we are unable to escape, send fleet ships to the Cridi system at once. We have already taken damage. I repeat, we are under attack—uh-oh!"

The screen caught his attention as the red light on the enemy ship appeared again. "Cari, they're shooting again!"

"I'm moving, I'm moving!" Carialle exclaimed. The ship zigzagged as well as it could to avoid the coming barrage, but she couldn't move far to any side. There was no way to dodge another blast. "Our shields aren't meant to take this."

The Frog Prince once again put his newfound power into operation. His hands whisked back and forth in silent commands. Carialle felt the Core within her walls hum. Suddenly, her hull felt as if it had been dipped in transparent padding. The next bolt of energy, invisible to the naked eye, exploded in a burst of white light against her side. Keff and Tall Eyebrow were jolted around in their couches, but the ship sustained no damage.

"Thanks, TE," Carialle said. "You just earned your keep." The globe-frog signalled a shaky "You're welcome."

The enemy, obviously taken aback that its volley made no impact, sent half a dozen bolts in rapid succession. Carialle attempted to avoid them, but two of them hit her—one in the tail, and one close to the airlock. The white light from their impact momentarily blinded one of her cameras, and the cabin lights faded down for a second. Carialle took the moment of the blast to slide into a narrow alley formed by a winding

DNA-strand of floating rocks. The next blast missed them, exploding a meteorite that peppered the hull noisily with sand. Carialle maneuvered through the belt, hoping to keep the distance between her and her pursuer. It vanished among the rocks.

"How long will your shield hold?" she asked Tall Eyebrow.

"I do not know," he said. "Perhaps long enough, but a sustained volley might overstrain it. Especially if they have a Core, too."

"I'm sending that message to Simeon and the CW right now," Carialle said. "If we lose, no one will ever find us. It'll be weeks, if not months before the message gets home. Someone has to know about these people. They've obviously been using the outskirts of this system as a hideout for years, and no one knew about it."

"You did," Keff said, grimly.

"An unhappy surmise, unluckily turning out to be true. At present, that's no satisfaction," she said briskly.

"Are these the ones?" Keff asked, with a concerned look at her pillar. "Are they your salvage squad?"

"*I don't know*," she said. "I was blind then."

"Do the engines match the configuration?" Keff asked. "Did they make physical contact? Can you recognize the vibration? Frequency emissions?"

"I don't know. After the attack I know my sensors went skewiff, so I might have been filtering all I know through bad information. I'll only know if I can get one of them to walk on me again. And I'm damned if I'll ever let that happen."

She recognized that her voice had grown terse, and made an effort to pull herself together. The moment of indecision and resolution took only microseconds, but she knew Keff had noticed the hesitation.

"I'm fine," she said, making the Lady Fair image appear on the wall. The peach-colored veil from her hennin floated softly around her face, which wore an expression of peace. Keff gave it a skeptical glance, but nodded. Both of them had to concentrate right now on survival.

As they wove through the asteroids, two blips appeared ahead on long range scan. Carialle wondered if her new equipment was more sophisticated than theirs; could she see them before they saw her? It might mean the difference between escape and destruction. Carialle studied her telemetry. Where could she turn to avoid them? Nothing truly safe offered itself. A sharp turn in any direction threw her into the teeth of the celestial meat grinder. Suddenly, a gap opened to starboard. She took it, nipping in just before two bolts lanced through the space she'd been occupying.

"This was probably not a good idea," Carialle said. "One lone, unarmed ship doesn't have a chance against a force of three. We've got to get out of here."

"We still have to find the DSC-902," Keff reminded her. "Even if we can just locate it before we get away, that'll be a help. I'd rather rescue them if we can."

"I'm with you, O brave one, but we need to survive this mission to be of any use to them." She broke off to dodge the first ship, which appeared on the other side of a rock full of holes like Swiss cheese. It fired a few times, through one hole then another. Carialle avoided them all, but felt stone shrapnel ping against her hull. The enemy ship spurred after her. She fled, only to find the lone ship had radioed the other two, who appeared on either side of her at the next wide spot. Carialle calculated the period between spiralling rocks, and ducked upward. The three ships, unable to maneuver with her skill, plummeted forward.

Carialle widened the gap between her and the enemy to half a dozen planet-widths by diving down and through the asteroid belt, and coming out "south"

of the plane of the ecliptic. She made a note of where
the three ships were, and turned back up and into
the stone dance at some distance from them. Her sensors indicated that the enemy had figured out what
she had done and were coming after her, but she was
ahead of them now, scanning for traces of the DSC-
902.

"Do you know, they're fast, but their equipment is
ancient," Carialle said. "I might be able to outlast them
in hide-and-seek, if only we don't get in the way of
sustained fire."

"Your engines are better than any of these brutes,"
Keff said, anxiously watching the aft monitor. One of
the ships, blip number two, was outside the belt now,
pouring on velocity to catch up. "We can outdistance
them. Maybe we can outclass them, too. TE, can we
convince them we've got some heavy armament?"

"How?"

"Grab one of those rocks as we go past, and sling
it backwards toward this fellow."

The globe-frog looked worried. "It will mean relin-
quishing control of the shield," he said.

"We'll have to chance it," Carialle said. "My shields
are 92% intact, and none of those old pots can match
me for maneuverability. Go ahead."

The thick padding around her vanished suddenly,
leaving her feeling chilled as if she was exposed to the
cold of space. Hastily, she rebuilt her defenses. Carialle
felt a momentary drag aft and to port as Tall Eyebrow
hitched his power to a rock about three meters across
and pulled it out of the dance. It sailed along behind
them like a puppy. Carialle turned on all her dorsal
thrusters in a sudden burst, and turned on her belly,
heading back toward the pursuing ship. Tall Eyebrow
made a pushing motion in midair. The rock spiraled
up from Carialle's tail and flew in a tightening pattern
around her body toward the enemy. With the extra

momentum behind it, the missile appeared to elongate in flight.

The enemy ship had only seconds to avoid collision. It veered up and to starboard. Tall Eyebrow reached out to the end of his range to alter the rock's course to match. It got to within a hundred kilometers of the enemy before the lasers exploded it.

"I missed," Tall Eyebrow complained.

"Whew!" Carialle said. "They *have* got fast reflexes."

"More, TE, more!" Keff shouted, as the pirate recovered itself and fired its weapons at them. The Frog Prince threw the shields back into place just in time. Carialle swept deeper into the asteroid belt, and let a cartwheeling rock take the brunt. In the meantime, Tall Eyebrow picked up more chunks of debris to use as weapons. They circled around Carialle's middle like a planetary ring.

"The other two ships are coming," Carialle warned. "If we can disable this one, I can probably outlast the other two."

"We might be able to rely on psychology," Keff said. "If we're wrong, and they don't have the Cores, seeing us throwing rocks around by remote control might make them back up."

"We can only try it," Carialle said. "I'd better show my pretty face, then."

She dove out of the belt, coming out above ship number two. One and three weren't far behind. Burning her thrusters for an extra burst of speed, she got ahead of Ship Two. Tall Eyebrow used the inertia to help launch a series of stone projectiles, one after another, spiraling them down over Carialle's tail and into the path of the other.

The enemy snaked widely, shooting at the speeding rocks. Tall Eyebrow had chosen a good variety for his missiles. Some burst into gravel; some, with heavy metal content, slagged along the edges but kept spinning. One

whirled with sawbladelike inexorability straight into the
path of Ship One, which pulled straight up in an acute
arc. The molten rock narrowly missed its tail fins.

Ship Two, wound too tightly among the asteroids to
flinch, took a pair of fragments amidships. Carialle saw
the leak of atmosphere escape from the side of the
hull. It streamed out in a haze alongside the exhaust.
For the first time she picked up transmissions from
the raiders. She couldn't comprehend the language.

"Keff, listen to this," she said. Keff tilted his head
as she re-ran the recording and raised his eyebrows
at the staccato rhythm of voices. He couldn't understand the deep voices, but he comprehended the
urgency.

"That's an SOS," he said definitely. "TE struck something vital."

"Hit them again, TE," Carialle said. "Aim for the
engines."

The Ozranian continued his bombardment. Because
of the limitations of the Core, he had to depend on
a target maintaining its trajectory from the time he
let go of a rock. With his superior grasp of spatial relations, Carialle only had to make certain he had a constantly updated overview in the astrogation tank. Keff,
a fascinated but helpless bystander, led the cheering
section each time one of Tall Eyebrow's missiles found
its mark.

Battered and leaking, Ship Two eventually dropped
back and out of the race to nurse its damaged hull.
Now that Carialle had proved that her ship wasn't
helpless, the other two ships became cagey. They flew
a wide pattern alongside her, peppering her with laser
fire, trying to herd her into planetoids. Carialle's shields
fell to 68%. Now they were engaged in what Keff
recognized as a true space battle, fought with atlases
instead of micrometers.

Carialle focused her telemetry on what lay ahead.

The going was more difficult here. If they picked up missiles to throw, she would have to remain on her own shields. Ancient comets had passed through this part of the belt again and again, chopping the asteroids into pieces ranging from those meters across to particles almost as small as dust. She worried that she might sustain a breach. On the good side, the cloud of dust seemed to cut off visuals of her to the other ships. On her scopes she saw them veer around uncertainly. Their medium-range sensors were nowhere near as good as hers.

"We can't get them both at once just tossing boulders," Keff said. "Can we set up a kind of chain reaction? What if we spin a big rock, the biggest one TE can handle, into one heading the other way? Could we get it to ricochet back toward the Joy Boys back there? Then we can attack the other more directly."

"I don't see why not," she said. She homed in on a set of nearly spherical fragments ahead, and bracketed them for Tall Eyebrow to see. "How are you at playing pool?"

Carialle let herself be "seen" on the enemies' scopes by surfacing out of the dust clouds. The other ships obligingly took the bait, and spurred to catch up with her. All their strategy for keeping their distance from her was dropped. They meant to kill.

"This had better work," Carialle said. "Otherwise, *we'll* have to run, and hope that the Core holds out until we can make Cridi atmosphere."

With almost a casual deflection of power, the Frog Prince set his chain reaction in motion. The cue ball, a stone sphere twelve meters across, was set spinning into its fellows. Most of the rocks it hit split off in a dozen directions, obvious, easy for the ships following to avoid. The eight ball, a rock dark with magnesium oxide, cannoned forward, gaining velocity toward a quarter-planetoid raddled by the eternal passage of fragments. With delightful precision, Tall Eyebrow had aimed his shot toward an obliquely angled "valley." Carialle saw the eight ball hit one angle of the corner shot and deflect onward, and then she was past it.

The other ships paid no attention to a rock that appeared to have missed. Tall Eyebrow had gathered up another stream of small rocks. He shot them at one ship then the other, in twos and threes, with varying degrees of success. It kept the enemy too busy to fire straight at Carialle, or to pay attention to where they were going. Carialle led them around and back along the trajectory she wanted them to follow. To make sure they could keep up, she dropped velocity slightly, daringly. They passed the alley down which the eight ball hurtled. Ship One was too intent upon Carialle, or perhaps its sensors were too confused by the dust and the flashes from its laser barrage, to pick up the huge rock until it rolled almost straight into its aft section.

The two ventral engines imploded, setting off a chain reaction like the lit fuse on a stick of dynamite that destroyed the rest of the ship.

Carialle heard an outcry on its audio frequency, then silence. Ship Three must have picked up that last, futile message, for it broke off its attack.

"What's it doing?" Keff asked, watching the ship veer deeper into the clouds of debris. Within seconds it was out of visual contact. "Is it coming around to sneak up on us?"

"Not unless it's going all the way around the orbit and coming at us from the front," Carialle said. "It's running away." She slowed down, and made her way cautiously out of the asteroid belt. A further check showed Ship Three really was fleeing. It had put the full width of the belt between itself and Carialle. "It's gone. The field's all ours. Congratulations, TE. It was your marksmanship that saved the day for us."

The Ozranian tipped a hand self-deprecatingly.

"Stop being so modest. You're a genuine hero, and I'm going to tell the world when we get back to Cridi. I'm turning around to see if we can pick up traces of the DSC-902." She swung off sunward from the belt, and turned a huge circle. "Call this your victory roll." The frog image repeated the concept with difficulty. Tall Eyebrow ducked his head.

"Cari, we've done it!" Keff said, dusting his hands together. "That'll neutralize the pirates in this system—killing two and scaring off the third. They'll never shoot at a ship in this place again. If they ever troubled you, you've evened it out now. Probably saved the future of the Cridi space program, too."

"I'm not satisfied," Carialle said, firmly. "I want to be certain that they are the ones. *Were* the ones. I want to see them face-to-face. I have to *know*." She paused, waiting until the adrenaline in her system evened out. "And then I want to haul them back to CenCom and prove to that insufferable bureaucrat and his flunkies that I was not hallucinating. Then, I'll be satisfied."

They returned to the asteroid clump where they first saw the raider ships. Carialle searched for the ion traces, now slightly disturbed by their passage and battle.

Behind the cluster of rocks was a confused knot of trails. Carialle and Keff flew back and forth, trying not to destroy the delicate veins, as they read the order of the events that had gone before they arrived.

"Looks like they were here before," Keff said, thoughtfully, sitting at the console with his chin in his hand. "Then they went away and came back again. Where did they go?"

"I think this is where they waited to ambush the DSC-902," Carialle said. "Look at that mass of exhaust particles. Those three ships accelerated to get there, then sat a long time before kicking out. They did it twice, the second time when they came after us. They did grab the ship with a Core—look at the hard thruster emissions from two ships."

"But what happened to the DSC-902's emissions?" Keff asked, studying the starchart.

Tall Eyebrow let out a little gasp and planted both hands firmly over his mouth and nostrils.

"That's it," Carialle said. "Suffocation. They sealed it up in a forcefield like TE's shield, and carried it away."

"But where did it go?"

Carialle bracketed the traces that led away from the cluster. "If I follow the tangle correctly, they went galactic clockwise."

Not far from the original point of contact, the celestial fragments grew larger, until the belt alongside which they were traveling looked like a gigantic string of brown-red pearls. The spider webbing of ions led from every direction to the largest one. Even from a distance, the artificial structures there were apparent.

"A base!" Keff exclaimed. "Give us a closeup, Cari."

The facility looked like a travesty of the spaceport on Cridi. What must have been a small fuel depot huddled beside a prefabricated dome of extreme age. Both were riddled with pockmarks from meteor strikes. Around them lay debris Carialle recognized with a sinking heart as sections from destroyed or dismembered spaceships. The most recent wreck was frosted white. The residual moisture from the life support system of the DSC-902 had not yet had time to leach away in vacuum. Its hatch and all the cargo bay doors stood open, unspeakably lonely and vulnerable. Lights were on inside.

"Oh, no," Keff whispered. Tall Eyebrow murmured a tiny, sympathetic creak.

"The hull shows half a dozen breaches," Carialle said,

pulling a closeup of the imploded hull plates, showing black holes partially opaqued by the film of ice. "You can see what happened. They held it in place, and they peppered it with laser fire. See how rough the holes are. They were using a mining laser, not weapons grade. I'm getting no trace of radiation from the engines. It looks like our three friends stripped out the drives. No signs of life."

"Bodies?" Keff asked.

Without a word, Carialle magnified a small section of the asteroid's surface. What Keff had taken for a heap of short lengths of tubing in the faint light from the distant sun were half a dozen human bodies. The expression on the staring faces was that of surprise. Keff swallowed hard.

"Those *bastards*."

"There's more," Carialle said. She shifted focus to another one of her cameras. They were above the base now, able to see the ruins on the other side of the structures. Carialle showed them pieces of tiny ships, strewn like discarded toys.

"Even their Cores couldn't protect them," Carialle said.

"Cridi? They did not crash?" TE asked, smashing one of his long hands down on the other.

"They did not crash," Carialle replied grimly. She showed them the parts of the ships. On extreme magnification the pair in the main cabin could see that the pieces showed little damage, except where the laser holes were evident.

"And the crews?" Keff asked, subvocally.

"Dead," Carialle said, without elaborating, but she made a comprehensive recording of the pathetic scatter of small bodies in protective suits near the landing pad. Carialle wished she could not see them. At least she could spare Keff and TE that, and showed them the bodies from a distance. Keff and TE fell silent.

"I hope we blew up the ones carrying the Cores," Carialle said. "This is what the CenCom should see: what happens when that extraordinary power falls into the wrong hands."

"Four ships," Keff said sadly. "All destroyed."

"More," TE signalled suddenly, pulling handfuls of air towards his chest.

"What do you mean?" Carialle asked.

The Ozranian leader tapped the side of his head. "Observation. Please put the pieces in the air for me. Like the puzzle."

"Ah, I get you." Carialle blew up the parts of the ships and placed them in holograph form before him. With lightning speed the Frog Prince reconstructed three small ships from which pieces were missing, but there were parts left over that could not possibly belong to any Cridi ship. Among the leftovers Carialle recognized a nose cone and landing fins of an obsolete model of a human-made ship. She constructed a hologram of the completed ship around the screen image. Keff gawked at Tall Eyebrow.

"How did you *do* that?" he asked.

The Ozran shrugged modestly. "Observation," he repeated.

"That spatial talent of his," Carialle said. "Extraordinary. I'd like to see his people engaged in engineering design work with ours."

"But, see what is left," TE continued. "It is like yours, but not like."

"It's old," Carialle said. "Do you recognize the model, Keff? It dates from fifty or seventy years back. About the time that Cridi got bottled up."

"So a Central Worlds explorer might have found the Cridi before now," Keff said thoughtfully. "These pirates destroyed them before they could get back to report on their findings."

"Maybe they didn't find *Cridi*," Carialle said.

"What do you mean?"

"These thieves don't live on this rock," she said. "They can't. There's no facilities, no supplies, barely any air. They didn't simply intend to destroy the ship, or they would have left the hulk floating where it died. These unknowns are ambushing and robbing starships. This is a chop shop, a staging area. They come from somewhere else. They *go* somewhere else, with the stolen booty. Doesn't it make sense that it's right here, in the system?"

Keff's teeth showed in a feral grin. "It does. We'll find them. We can't let these brutes get away with mass murder." He poked a finger at the shining strands in the holotank. "Shall we see if those ley lines from the engines lead anywhere?"

Chapter 9

"Planet Five," Carialle said, turning all her video
screens to the view of the dark hulk silhouetted by the
distant sun. "The traitors live right here in the Cridi
system."

"Let's take them," Keff said, leaning forward and
slamming his fists together. In the navigation tank,
strands of ion emission joined hundreds more in a skein
around the black sphere, like webs tying up a fly. That
was the center. So close, and yet no one knew it was
here.

"Have you brushed your teeth and said your
prayers?" Carialle asked, interrupting his concentration.
"We can't destroy a base by ourselves, let alone a
planet."

"No," Keff sighed, sitting back. Reason had been
restored. "But we can get data to instruct a CW fleet.
Let's see what's down there."

Keeping in the widest possible orbit, the ship circled
around to sunside. It looked an inhospitable place, but
there were sure signs of habitation, and the three
moons, each the size of Old Earth, could have concealed fleets of pirates. Carialle listened on the frequencies she had observed the three assassins using.
She picked up a familiar drone.

"Landing beacon," she said, putting the sound on
audio for the others. "So far, nothing else. If there are

detection devices out there I'm risking having another force come boiling after me, so I'm keeping thrusters ready to run back toward Cridi if necessary."

"What power emissions are you reading?" Keff asked, studying the astrogation tank.

"Not much. If they have any industrial complexes, they must all be underground. Residual decay in a lot of places on the surface, probably power plants from purloined spaceships. Another refueling depot, in the midst of one enormous junkheap. Radioactive dumping ground, ten degrees north of the equator, far from any of the heat vents. Read this spectroanalysis," she said, putting up a chart on one of her screens. "The atmosphere has a hefty ammonia content."

"Our archives say this burns us," Tall Eyebrow signed, looking at the molecular diagram. "Also smells bad."

"Then I'll need a full breather suit," Keff said, perusing the screen with a critical eye. "Oxygen. Grav assist. Maybe take one or both of the servo drones with me in case the gravity is too much."

"What *are* you talking about?" Carialle asked.

"I want to have a close-up look at the people who were just shooting at us," Keff said, but Carialle recognized the gleam in his eye. He'd looked the same way whenever they were sent on assignment to a planet suspected of sustaining life. He pointed at a spot on the planetary map, a field of craters near the refueling depot. "If you set us down there, I can get in and gather data, and be out before they know it."

"Wait a minute, Sir Knight. Yes, we may have encountered a brand new, sentient species, but that doesn't mean you should fling yourself into their midst."

"Cari, think of it—it's unprecedented. Two intelligent life forms evolving in the same solar system—and never meeting. Think of the furor at Alien Outreach. Think of being the only brainship team ever to bring home a prize like that." Keff began to see glory before his eyes, to hear the congratulations in his ears. Carialle interrupted his reverie.

"It's too dangerous! May I point out you just mentioned that these are the same people who were just shooting at us? Who murdered the crews of at least four starships? And who may have tried to kill me twenty years ago? Surely the ships sent messages with our description and video bits to home control on one of these obscure frequencies I've been trying to monitor. We'd be too easy a target landing near their spaceport, and I don't think they'll buy 'I come in peace' from the ship that just destroyed two or three of their craft. If you get caught, they'll kill you. I won't land."

"I haven't forgotten any of that, Cari, but we can accomplish a great deal if I can infiltrate them successfully. We do need data to support a Central Worlds deployment. I'm good at camouflage. All you have to do is land us very quietly in a nice, deep syncline, and give me sufficient data on the terrain. I'll find a bivouac. It'll take time for the CW ships to reach us . . . ." Keff's eye was distracted from the intractable face of Carialle's Lady Fair image. He turned to stare fully at the navigation tank.

"Cari, jump! There's a ship coming up astern. We can hide behind one of those moons, maybe loop around to the nightside. Hurry! Why aren't your proximity alarms going off? Damn it," he said, hammering a fist down on the console. "I thought we scared that third ship into next Tuesday." He scanned the scopes looking for convenient asteroid belts, planetoids, or ion storms in which they could lose themselves. "There's nothing! We'll have to run. Can you read any armament . . . ?"

"Keff!" Carialle shouted, blinking the displays on and off to get his attention. "It isn't the pirates. It's the Cridi. You'll recognize their configuration by the time it gets into range. Tad Pole persuaded the Cridi to launch their new ship in our defense."

"What?" Keff felt his jaw drop open with shock. "Why didn't you tell me?"

"You've been raving so much I didn't have an edge-wise to fit in a word. Long Hand is transmitting to me from the other ship. IT is translating her sign language to me, but it's slow going, with their rotten screens. Narrow Leg and the others scrambled as soon as we accomplished a successful takeoff. They want to back us up. Small Spot and Long Hand persuaded them to launch in our defense. They came along, and they brought Big Eyes, among others. I'll play you the audio. It's very amusing. I can hear Big Voice chirruping madly in the background behind everyone else."

"Big Eyes comes?" Tall Eyebrow signed, pleased. Keff looked appalled.

"No! Send them home. This is too dangerous."

"They have better defenses than we do, Sir Knight," Carialle said, patiently. "Besides, they want to help us. I think they recognize the risk they're taking."

"We can't let them, Cari," Keff said. Suddenly the small ship came fully into focus. It looked very small and vulnerable. He dashed a hand through his hair and stared desperately at the screen. "The pirates are armed to their masticatory appendages."

"And a moment ago you wanted me to land in their midst," Carialle said sweetly. Keff had a sudden, heart-felt temptation to kick her pillar.

"I'm trained to take risks," he said. "The Cridi are not. Why did they come?"

"Why? Sir Keff, you spent over a month convincing the Cridi to sign on with Central Worlds as a member nation with full privileges. You did a good job. They've taken the concept of alliance seriously, and they mean to back up what they say. How can they prove they're our equals and allies unless we let them?

"But not like this!"

"Then, how?"

"I help," Tall Eyebrow put in, with a quick sign, before Keff could object. "They, too."

"See?" Carialle asked. "I'm proud of them."

Keff wasn't convinced, but suddenly the rust-colored planet off Cari's starboard side looked more menacing. It *would* be useful to have backup. CW Fleet ships were months away. If they scrambled tomorrow, it would still take weeks to close the distance. He glanced at Carialle's pillar.

"Was it unanimous?" he asked.

"By no means," Carialle said. "Snap Fingers and his brood think they should mind their own business. But look at the ones who are risking their lives, who *weren't* sure that ship would even break atmosphere safely. But, there they are."

Keff glanced up slyly through his eyelashes. "Big Voice came, too?"

"Believe it or not, he did."

Keff raised his hands in surrender. "All right. But Alien Outreach isn't going to like this."

"Then, they can lump it," Carialle said firmly. "Would they rather have the pirates running around loose? This is the Cridi's necks on the block, too. It's their system, and for the last fifty years, their menace. These pirates took their freedom, and killed who knows how many Cridi astronauts. The Cridi have a right to be here."

"You're correct, as always, Cari. Let me talk to them. I'm going to eat crow." He sat down in his padded seat before the console. The 1028-square grid appeared on the screen, and coalesced into a rough mosaic of the face of Narrow Leg.

"Captain, Carialle and I welcome you back to space."

"We are successful!" the elderly Cridi squeaked, and IT echoed his tone of triumph. "It flies, it is sound."

"I never doubted it," Keff signed, with a grin. "I've never seen such careful construction. I'm glad you're with us." He cleared his throat, then emitted a short series of chirps. "X equals Y. X plus Y is greater than X. X plus Y is greater than Y. We are equals, and the two of us together are greater than we are alone."

Narrow Leg nodded his head. "That is evident. You honor us. Circling this planet. What must we know about it?"

Carialle spoke up. "We have traced the path of the villains who attacked the diplomatic ship. We have no fleet, no heavy armament, so all we can do is gather information, and send for help from the Central Worlds. We plan to infiltrate the planet's surface."

Narrow Leg's cheeks hollowed, and the faces of the Cridi behind him paled to mint green. They looked terrified, but all of them squeaked up at once.

"Tell us how we may help."

"I didn't want them down here with me," Keff said, sublingually, hunkering himself down further into the crevasse beyond the outskirts of the building they had designated as the spaceport. "I wanted them up there, where they could use their Core to help protect us, and you."

"Nonsense," Carialle said. "There's a delay in response time, even from space. I want them where they can be on the spot if you need them."

Keff didn't protest, but the sound of the plastic globes rolling along the rocky surface of the planet sounded louder than thunder to him. Tall Eyebrow paddled at the head of a party of scouts, heading around toward the other side of the compound. Big Eyes kept up gamely behind him, beside Small Spot and her father, but most of the homeworld Cridi frankly cheated and used their amulet power to levitate their new globes. They bobbed along behind the toiling group, sitting at their ease in the bottom of the transparent spheres.

"Darn it, TE, tell them not to do that," he growled into his helmet's audio pickup. "I know the extra gravity's uncomfortable, but I'd rather take a chance on movement being spotted than extraneous power transmissions." It was bad enough that the Cridi had to use the Core technology to keep the water in the globes from freezing on this cold world. They risked detection of their ship with every deviation from strict survival. "They might at least put down a physical twitch as indigenous wildlife. If there is any. What a bleak place."

A hundred meters away, the lead globe stopped and spun in place. The water inside sloshed upward. Tall Eyebrow made a few signs quickly and with authority toward the other globes. Keff was reminded abruptly that the insecure visitor to the Cridi homeworld was also the leader of the exiled Ozran-born Cridi, who kept his population together, alive, and sane in the most dangerous and deprived of circumstances. He admired the way TE threw in a tactful sign or two that alluded to the difficulty of using a travel globe, but added staccato chops for "absolute necessity." Reluctantly, Big Voice and the others lowered the spheres to the ground. The lead globe rotated 180 degrees, and the party set off again more slowly, but more loudly. Keff flattened himself down so that he could no longer see them. He studied his target.

There appeared to be little activity, but Carialle had detected at least four life-forms in the building. She had a hard time finding body-heat traces. The planet's surface was cold, but it was dotted with hot spots where volcanoes and geothermal vents broke through. Structures placed over these took advantage of the natural heat.

Most of the population had to be below ground, with only a few exits to the open sky. It was impossible to pick out individuals. Ammonia/oxygen flares ignited occasionally, and as swiftly, blew out. Carialle cursed as one trace after another that she was tracking suddenly vanished.

Gravity was approximately one and a half times Standard norm; bearable for short periods. The "spaceport" was a ridge, the edge of a huge crater filled in over eons with dust and debris that had solidified into a flat plain. Architects had bored into, or more likely, *out of* the side of the hill overlooking the plain, and built onto it. Carialle reported that heat traces from inside the building registered at least 35 degrees C. That sounded much nicer than the surrounding landscape, which was bare and dusty where it wasn't covered with discarded junk from hijacked spaceships.

"What do these people eat?" Keff wondered out loud, his voice sounding hollow in his survival suit.

"Look at those domes, built to catch every meager ray, even magnify it," Carialle said. "Perhaps our ammonia-breathers photosynthesize, and live on water."

"Or the cities below ground are full of hydroponics," Keff said. "I don't see enough domes to support a breeding population of mitochondroids." In spite of the peril and the anger he felt at the pirates, he and Carialle had dropped back into the game they loved to play, anticipating the facts about an unknown race. "Is it possible this planet was a lot warmer once? Or do you suppose we've discovered silicophages?"

"It wouldn't be the first discovery of mineral-eaters," Carialle said, after running through her memory banks, "but it would be the first one that attained sentience and space travel."

"In stolen ships," Keff said, flatly. "What do we know about them so far?"

"From the emissions of the ship Tall Eyebrow damaged, body temperatures in range tolerable by humans, between twenty degrees C and forty degrees C. Size, from my readings in the structure ahead of you, they are larger than humans, but smaller than lions. Anything else, I must await data from you and our party of rolling frogs."

"Add to that, intelligent and dangerous," Keff said, nodding, but keeping his eyes pinned on the dome. "Well, I can't wait here forever. TE, I'm moving. Watch the building and stop anything that comes in after me."

"I hear," the small voice said in Standard over the helmet speaker.

Staying flat on his belly, Keff crept over the rise. On the other side was a steeply sloping valley. Long-departed rivers or perhaps the celestial pressures of planetary formation had crazed the plain with shallow canals. Keeping low enough to remain out of sight to occupants of the largest structure, Keff crawled on hands and knees. Fine silt, undisturbed for eons, rose briefly around him, then settled out in the heavy gravity, burying his tracks.

Parked a dozen kilometers away beside the Cridi spaceship in a lonely valley, Carialle watched his progress simultaneously on her charts and through the body-cam he wore on his tunic.

"You're coming to a T-intersection," she said, as Keff paused and reared up on his knees so she could see his precise location. "Take the left branch. No, the left one. The right one leads straight into a deep thermal vent."

Keff made his way along the turnings, wrinkling his nose against the clouds of dust even though he knew they couldn't penetrate his protective suit. His heads-up display told him the half-meter-high bank of fog into which he crawled at a low point in a ditch was heavy with ammonia and traces of other gases reduced to liquid. He gulped. One breach in suit integrity, and he was a green icicle. Never mind; he was committed to his mission. In some small way, he was helping Carialle to lay the ghosts of her past, as well as ridding the Cridi of a menace and avenging the deaths of the Central Worlds diplomatic personnel. A moon in its second quarter rose on the horizon and crept up the sky, throwing a little more light on his path. His canal dipped sharply as he crawled another ten meters, then light from the moon was cut off. In the blackness his suit-lights went on. He paused, waiting for the prickle between his shoulder blades that would tell him he was being watched. Nothing.

"You're almost underneath the building now," Carialle was saying. "If you go around to the right, you'll be in front of that hatchway."

Keff's back began to ache from the heavy gravity. He paused with hands on knees.

"It looks a long way up," he panted, staring at the black shape above him, picked out by distant pinpoint stars. His lungs dragged in oxygen.

"What are you building up all of those muscles if not for an effort like that?" Carialle asked dryly.

When she started making ironic comments, Keff could tell she was the most worried. He just shook his head. In an instant the aches in his lower back and thighs went away. "Just oxygen-starved," he said. "Just a moment." He reached into the gauntlet of his right glove for the control pad, and turned up the nitrox mix slightly. The faint hissing sound was a comfort.

In the gloom the building over his head looked ominous. The slab on which it was built had been slagged out of a lip of the ridge, so the people inside had at least stolen, if not evolved, heavy pyroconstruction equipment.

Keff heaved himself up. The domes began at a meter above the platform, giving him an expanse of blank wall against which he could conceal himself. Ahead of him, the platform widened out away from the domed windows to an apron that bore scorch marks from repeated launches and landings. Limp, metal-bound hoses lay on the ground in skeins. They led from the putative fuel tank, which stood on pylons around a fold of the ridge from the domes. *To protect the glass from explosions,* Keff thought, with an approving nod to the designers. A dusty accordion-pleated hood was bunched up around the entrance to the building. It seemed to be long enough to extend all the way to the edge of the platform. Not at all sophisticated, but it would scarcely ever need major repairs. He took the video pickup off his suit and held it up against the bottom margin of the clear wall.

"Can you see anything, Cari?" he whispered.

"Aqua foliage," Carialle replied. "Spiky, like evergreens—no, more like fan coral. I can't see anything moving, even on infrared. My sensors are still picking up those same four body traces. No one much seems to come up to the surface."

"If they're anything like us, it's too cold for them up here. I'm ten meters from the entrance. Where are you, TE?" Keff asked his suit mike.

"We see you, other side of edge," the globe-frog's voice piped. "Under-by tank-container."

"Back me up. I am going to try and enter. If I am not out in fifteen minutes from the time of my entrance, come in and help me. At that point, revealing we have Core technology will be moot."

"Sir Frog waits," the small voice said. Keff grinned.

He crawled the rest of the way to the rough plascrete arch. The entrance resembled an airlock, devoid of any security devices Keff could recognize. The pirates must have been very confident that no one knew they were here.

"Where are the guards, Cari?" he asked.

"All four are deep inside," she said. "It looks like your best chance."

Keff nodded to himself. "Here goes."

He stood up against the inside edge of the arch, hidden momentarily from sight of anyone in the dome. Carefully, he turned around. Inside a metal frame, two flat bars jutted out from the wall.

"I've only got a fifty-fifty chance of cocking up," he said, and a childhood singsong bubbled up from memory. He waggled his finger playfully between the two bars. "My mother said to pick the very best one, and you are *it*." With that, he stabbed the upper bar. It moved easily under his finger, depressing flat to the wall.

Immediately behind him, something heavy and soft dropped to the ground. Keff spun. He was now curtained into the enclosure by a metal and plastic mesh. Hissing erupted from the wall side. In a few moments, a door, large enough to admit a cargo container, slid upward.

Keff listened before he stepped inside, turning up his external mikes to the maximum. No alarms. No one seemed to have heard the airlock open.

"Looks like I'm all right," he whispered.

"For pity's sake, be careful," Carialle said in his aural implant.

He nodded, knowing she would pick up the physiological signs of the small movement. A blinking light on the other side of the threshold urged him forward into another sealed pocket of air. Keff stepped through just as the heavy door slid downward. It closed silently, which surprised him more than a solid bang would have. He heard more hissing, then the curtain and its fender rose, revealing the interior of the dome. A few spotlights stabbed their beams down at the floor, but mostly the arboretum was lit by the faint, distant sun. Bristly growths sprang out of flat, low dishes made of black ceramic on the shiny floor. The plants themselves—if they were plants—were a riot of neon blue, ultramarine, teal, acid yellow, and interplanetary-distress orange. Keff winced.

"Gack," he said quietly. "Their taste in horticulture is nightmarish."

"I told you so," Carialle said. "The colors suggested

to me that the atmosphere inside was ammonia-heavy, like the outer atmosphere, but it isn't nearly as saturated as I thought. My spectroanalysis shows that it's much more dilute. Less than one-tenth. You could almost breathe it."

"How'm I doing?"

"You're still alone," Carialle said.

"That's strange," Keff said absently, peering around. "Look, could that be furniture?"

He turned so the video pickup on his chest was facing some metal and fabric constructs in a group amid the riot of spiky, sea-colored plants.

"I would say yes." Carialle studied the forms, and ran projections on an ergonomics program in her memory banks. "Something that prefers a sling to a seat—there's no back—so possibly not upright in carriage. It lies supported. A quadruped? Then why wouldn't it simply lie down on pads on the floor?" She drew image after image of arrangements of torsos and limbs, and rejected them all.

"Here are some divan pillows," Keff said. He turned to face fuzzy, covered pads the size of his bunk. "They're huge!"

"Whew!" Carialle whistled in agreement. "Keff, sit on one so I can see how much a body of your weight compresses the material. I need an estimate on what made those dents."

Keff complied, plumping down on one as if exhausted, which indeed he was beginning to be. He sat and gasped for a moment. The heavy gravity was telling on him. He hoped the Cridi were faring all right.

"Let me see," Carialle said. Keff rose and gave her a good view of his impression from different angles. "My estimate stands. I think they weigh about two hundred kilos apiece."

"I am not staying long," Keff said, positively.

Beyond the seating arrangements was an arched

corridor. Like the platform outside, it had been slagged through the mountain with a melter drill of some kind. Down the passageway, Keff spotted the reflected flicker of blue and white lights. It looked familiar. He listened carefully at the entrance for a long time, then tiptoed toward the source of illumination. He passed closed hatchways with the same framed control bars in the wall beside them. At the sudden sound of escaping air, Keff flattened himself into the nearest door frame and held his breath. The noise stopped with a wheeze and a bang.

"Probably a compressor," Carialle commented. "Primitive." Keff nodded, the back of his helmet tapping against the wall. The echo bounded off both ways down the empty hall, sounding like water dripping into a pool.

He waited a moment, then slipped noiselessly into the corridor once again. His heads-up display told him it was three degrees warmer in here than it had been in the atrium. He was undoubtedly already under the lip of the excavated mountain. He looked forward to exploring the labyrinth of caves that underlay this building, but with a suitable escort of CW militia for backup.

"Here's your glow," Carialle said, as he counted the eighth doorway.

"Computer screens," Keff breathed, peering around the frame. On a low table that had once been a galley counter in a Central Worlds ship sat antique CPUs and square monitors. Boxes of jumbled chips and tapes and datasolids sat on the floor beside the table. He edged in so the camera eye on his chest would send the image back to the ship.

"More salvage," Carialle said, severely. "That is a year-old Tambino 90-gig unit. Those are CW special issue screens, and those input peripherals are from half a dozen different systems reaching back a thousand years. And yes, some of that discarded junk is Cridi."

Keff glanced around, wondering how far away the guards were. "Could you crack the data storage system?"

"Sonny, I cut my diodes on tougher stuff than this. Hook me up, and we'll copy everything in the memory. That'll give CenCom plenty to go on."

"What about viruses?"

"Not to worry. I'll isolate the files in a separate section and make them 'read only' outside of that drive base. I have all that spare memory installed for our diplomatic mission. Using it for hacking an enemy system is much more interesting than using it for lists of trade goods and historical texts, wouldn't you say?" There was fierce satisfaction in her voice. "Use the port IT has been attached to. That should be sufficient. You can use the same memory later for language translation."

"Right," Keff said, starting toward the setup. He put one knee on the hanging sling. Suddenly, the computer emitted a loud beep, then a siren wail.

"Oh, no!" he exclaimed, leaping backward. "It's got a proximity alarm. Do they hear me? Are they coming this way?" He stared at the doorway.

"Don't panic," Carialle said, her voice changing to a deep baritone to be heard over the shrill alarms. "I don't hear any high frequencies from motion detectors. It might be a timer."

"It *has* attracted attention. I hear something." Keff's audio pickups detected a faint shuffling sound. "They're coming this way!"

He put one eye around the edge of the door and flung himself backward when he saw a huge shadow looming toward him. "I'm trapped. TE, keep out! I'll get free if I can."

"I hear," the Ozranian's voice said, sounding worried.

"Right you are, Sir Knight," Carialle said, suddenly. "All four bodies are moving toward your location. We've got a visitor coming from space, too."

"What?"

"Looks like Ship Three," she said. "It's alone. I'm tracking . . . updates as available. You hide, now!"

The shuffling sounds grew louder. Keff cast about frantically for a place to hide. He threw himself behind stacks of storage containers just as the feet reached the doorway. Stifling groans of pain from the ribs he bruised in his headlong dive, he flattened himself against the wall and hoped the barrier between him and the aliens was stable.

"They're big ones, all right," Carialle's voice said very quietly in his aural canal. "Two hundred fifty, a hundred seventy, and two hundred ten kilos respectively. The fourth one has gone through to the domes. Probably to watch Ship Three land."

"No way out," Keff said.

"Not yet. Your respiration and blood pressure are up. Take a few deep breaths. Take a drink of water. How is your oxygen supply?"

"Okay," Keff muttered sublingually. He heard a slight sound coming toward him and held his breath. He cursed both CW Exploration and Diplomatic for not allowing their ships to carry even defensive weapons. A stun gun would be useful right now in extricating him from this place. The brutes would kill him with the same lack of pity they showed the crew of the DSC-902. The sound continued past him. The next thing he heard was dragging—one of the aliens hauling in a sling from the atrium. They planned to stay in this room, probably until Ship Three landed. It took a mental effort to restart his breathing. He dragged in a gasp of air, then held his breath again.

"They can't hear you," Carialle reminded him, calmly. "Your helmet muffles sound effectively."

"I know," he whispered, "but because *I* can hear me I think they can. I'll relax."

Keff turned up the gain on his audio pickups. The

aliens were talking. Their voices were surprisingly musical: deep, resonant, like the call of brass horns. He tried to separate the sounds into words and decided he didn't yet have enough data to go on. The hail from the approaching ship came in over the speakers faintly. Apparently Tall Eyebrow's improvised missiles had done some damage to the ship, because the transmission kept cutting in and out. He sensed concern in the voices of the ground crew.

Minutes dragged past. His muscles cramped because of the awkward position in which he lay, but he didn't dare shift to ease them. Sweat began to trickle out of his hairline, over his face and neck, and down between his shoulder blades. It itched infuriatingly. He blinked his eyes to clear drops off his lashes. The chatter of voices, both within the room and on the distant ship, reached a crescendo of agitation. Keff thought he heard the words "Central Worlds," in passing, but decided he was trying to read too much into the meaningless multisyllabic babble. Suddenly there was a hush in the room, and he felt the ground shake. The dome made a grand echo chamber for the *boom!* the ship made when it landed.

"Three point five on the Richter scale at the epicenter," Carialle said. "That ship has no boosters left to soften touchdown. TE did good work. It probably won't be able to to take off again."

"We ought to disable it entirely before we leave here," Keff whispered, "just to make sure."

Hissing and groaning from the airlock compressors heralded the arrival of Ship Three's crew. The ground staff greeted them with unmistakable relief. A couple of them hunched past the gap in the boxes behind which Keff was hiding. He heard the hubbub of vocal greeting, and the shifting of feet as they went through their handshake-equivalent ritual, whatever it was. The brawn maneuvered himself so he could peer through, and got his first glimpse of the aliens. He realized with a shock that their faces were just slightly farther from the floor than his. They did walk on all fours! He willed the new arrivals to stay where they were, and as if they could hear him, they did. At first he saw only partially-opaqued helmets and vast protective suits. One by one, the aliens sat back on invisible haunches, took off the helmets and shed gauntlets. Keff vibrated with impatience until one of them moved in front of the gap again.

"Big flat faces," he told Carialle in staccato bursts of narration, "weird eyes. Sleek head, widens to neck. Sandy pelts, slightly fuzzy, like the garden cushions. Claw hands."

One of them moved too close to the cartons and shut off his view with a slick, oversuited shoulder. Keff withdrew his head very slightly, and waited. The body moved away, and the fabric of the coverall slid downward to reveal the creature's back.

"Cari, they have wings!"

Carialle's voice was a businesslike hum in his ear. "Vestigial wings? That says a lot about the devolution of this planet's bios . . ."

"No," he hissed, excitedly. "Full-sized wings. Like bat's wings, but with longer fur."

"Do you know what that means?" Carialle asked, astonished, adding up the facts in a microsecond. "This planet *isn't* hollow. There's no air mass to support flight. Its surface gravity is huge! That means there are no underground passageways, no millions of separately evolved sentients living cheek by jowl with the Cridi. That's why the difference in the air quality between outside and inside. They're strangers. This is an outpost, too! *Where do they come from?*"

"I don't know!" Keff whispered.

He shifted to get a better view, feeling the boxes with his gloved hands to make sure they wouldn't slip.

He found another gap, closer to the computer setup, and applied his eye to it.

"I keep seeing flashes of claws and talons. I think there's a pair of vestigial fingers on the wings, where, er, where primary feathers would be, beside that pair of hands on the forelimbs that is used for manipulative as well as locomotive purposes. I'm getting a glimpse of heavy haunches."

"That would explain the slings," Carialle's voice said. "Four hands! Fascinating."

Keff heard the ticking of claws on the smooth floor. One of the aliens paused just on the other side of the containers, giving Keff a good look at it. The brawn peered at the set of the narrow head; the placement of the wings on the broad, golden back; the noble, handsome face. "You know, they look rather like griffins."

Carialle immediately accessed the Myths and Legends handbook, found the cross-reference for Griffins, subhead: Gryphons, then cross-referenced it to encyclopediae and classical works from the European subcontinent of Old Earth. "Those griffins had eagles' beaks and lion's tails."

"These have no nose, but those mouths . . . if they are mouths . . ."

The "griffin," answering a query from one of its unseen fellows, spread the halves of its upper lip, and Keff blanched at the sharp white fangs behind it. "That's a mouth, all right," he said. "We need to file a report with the CenCom, but first I have to get out of here."

"How?"

"I don't know, yet," Keff said.

"We will come to help," said a faint voice in his helmet.

"TE, no," he whispered into his audio pickup. "Stay out. Cari, tell them no. Don't let them."

The sound of his own voice dropped like a pin into

the silence of the room. Keff felt the prickles race down his back. He looked up to find a griffin staring down at him, surprise in its vertically-striped eyes. He scrambled crabwise away from it behind the boxes, but there was nowhere to go. The alien followed on all fours, tracking him on the other side of the crates. Panicking, Keff kicked over stacks of containers. They fell heavily, breaking open to scatter components across the feet of the aliens. He dove across the last stack and rolled into an upright position in the corner, hands ready to strike.

"You're right, Sir Knight," Carialle said. "They do look like griffins. Be careful!"

Six of them stood in the room, with the rest crowding the corridor. All of them gawked at him with big, flattish eyes, faces expressionless. None of them moved, but with the advantage of big muscles and wings, they could wait until he was vulnerable. Keeping one hand up in defense, Keff felt his way along the wall, hoping for an escape door, though he'd known this room was a dead end when he had entered. They tracked his progress, calmly, unemotionally, waiting. Their assurance prompted all sorts of horrible scenarios in Keff's imagination. He panted, and his vision swam with blackness around the edges with the difficulty of drawing a deep breath.

One of them moved at last. The lead griffin, the one who had found him, started toward him with wings and spike-like fingers spread. The foreclaws, balancing out the big haunches behind, had fierce talons over ten centimeters long that ticked on the shiny, stone floor. Its big wings obscured the beasts behind so Keff couldn't tell what they were doing. *Mustering for an attack?* Keff flattened himself against the bulkhead, preparing to spring, wondering if his unarmed combat training would help. Where did you pivot to throw something with four legs and an unknown center of gravity? Would tossing it onto its wings disable it long enough for him to escape? The great beast loomed up closer and closer. The top lip split to show the sharp, gleaming fangs and a strip of orange-pink gums above them. The creature was saying something, but Keff could only hear the pounding of blood in his ears.

In the distance, Keff heard the sound of rushing air. The griffins, in a body, turned to look. Keff blessed the distraction. He took his best opportunity, and sprang over their heads.

He had miscalculated the drag of the extra gravity, and fell in the midst of the enemy. Half the aliens were distracted by the noise coming from the domes. The rest turned back to Keff. A couple of them grabbed for his arms with their foreclaws and wing-hands. He rolled away, shaking hard to get loose. The long nails scrabbled on the fabric of his suit. He thought he heard his sleeve rip, and winced. He stood against the wall, panting. More hands reached for him, and his eyes registered a confused blur of wings, claws and eyes. He grabbed a wrist and twisted. One of the griffins cried out. Another added its howl of surprise. Keff, flat on the floor in a jumble of boxes, raised his head as eight globesful of Cridi sailed into the room in midair.

"What takes so long?" Tall Eyebrow's voice said very clearly in Keff's helmet.

"TE, I told you to stay out!" Keff shouted.

To his surprise, the griffins froze in place when they saw the Cridi. Their eyes were wide, not with amazement, Keff thought, but with loathing.

"Slayim!" The word issued with clarion power from one throat, and was echoed by all the others. Every griffin rose to its hind legs and lunged for the Cridi.

Tall Eyebrow stared at the charging griffins for one astonished second, then Big Eyes' globe batted his from behind, sending it careening out of the way just before a griffin landed on it. More of the lithe aliens leaped straight for Big Eyes herself. Narrow Leg's globe shot in front of his daughter's, and the griffins showed their long teeth. The two globes revolved around one another, and bobbed straight upward, with three griffins snapping and clawing for them.

"Hey!" Keff shouted, throwing himself into the fray. "Leave them alone!" He bounded in between two griffins who were on their back toes, giving them almost three meters of reach, clawing for Narrow Leg's pilot, whose globe had retreated to the safety of the ceiling. One of the griffins spread its wings, knocking Keff sprawling and accidentally batting another griffin in the back. The alien who had been struck turned away from Small Spot. The Ozranian was cowering underneath the computer desk. He scooted out from his hiding place and hurried to hover behind a pile of boxes beside Long Hand, under siege from an alien who reached long wing-fingers around from one side of the stack, then the other. Another griffin dove for the two exiles. Keff gathered himself up and launched, ramming the first griffin under the right wing with his shoulder. It turned, a surprised look on its face, its powerful wings battering at him. Keff felt his helmet skew, and the next breath he inhaled hurt. He coughed painfully. He kicked the griffin in the chest, and to his own amazement, sent it sprawling backwards on its tail. The beasts were bottom-heavy! He assessed and docketed this fact, wondering why he was thinking so slowly, and why he heard a roar coming from under his right ear. He felt sick.

"Keff! Seal that," Carialle ordered in stentorian tones. Keff's head was ringing, from nausea and the volume of her voice. "Keff, can you hear me? Your suit has been breached. You're breathing ammoniated air. Are you all right? Keff!"

"Yes," he gasped shortly, and coughed again. He

retched, and caught himself before he threw up. His hands fumbled for the neck of his suit, and he refastened the flapping lip of plastic. Clean, sweet-tasting nitrox flooded his face. Gratefully, he drew in lungfuls. "I'm all right. I. Am. Truly."

Carialle's voice melted with relief. "Thank goodness."

Keff didn't have time to regain his full strength. Two more griffins had joined the pair jumping at Big Voice.

"Aid!" shrieked the plump councillor. "Aid²!"

The other Cridi globes, led by Tall Eyebrow, levitated to assist their compatriot. Swats from claws and wings sent them scattering like a bunch of marbles. Big Eyes' globe hit the wall, and bounced to the floor. The young female lay in her ball of water, her dark eyes staring at nothing. A griffin, spotting her helplessness, tensed its muscular haunches and prepared to spring. A feral grin split its lip.

"Grab them!" Carialle shouted in Keff's ear.

"How?" Keff asked.

"Tell the Cridi! Catch!"

Keff turned and caught Narrow Leg's eye. The human clapped his cupped hands together and pulled the invisible handful toward his body. The elder Cridi nodded sharply.

"Sense!" Narrow Leg's single word echoed through every Cridi amulet. He pointed the fingers of both hands at the griffins, and they froze in place. The springing griffin stiffened in midair, and dropped heavily to the floor on its belly.

The room grew abruptly silent. Ten, ornamental, hexapodal statues in various warlike attitudes glared silent hatred at nothing.

"Nice work," Keff said. He took a deep breath, and sank to the floor. His legs, now aching from lack of oxygen, no longer wished to support him. He felt his sleeve for tears; it was intact. "Good job, everyone. Are you all right?"

"We, yes," Narrow Leg said. "Not used to self-defending. Thank you." Keff only nodded in return. Every other movement hurt.

The Cridi gathered from every corner to assess damage. Tall Eyebrow rolled hastily to his ladyfriend's side. An invisible hand scooped up some of the water in Big Eyes' globe and splashed her cheeks with it. The female blinked. She sat up and turned to smile at him. Tall Eyebrow almost collapsed with relief. Big Eyes clicked her globe gently against his, palm outspread. He opened his hand gently on the inner surface of his sphere, matching hers palm to palm. The two of them floated over to rejoin the others. Keff grinned indulgently.

Big Voice's container was scratched where it had struck the corner of a metal container, but it was not punctured. The stout councillor was voluble in his relief, babbling and waving frantic signs at all of his fellows and Keff. The others, though frightened by the attack, were more curious. Narrow Leg studied the captured aliens closely. He was struck by the hate on each face.

"Their pulses fast," he commented to Keff, near him on the floor. "Anger. Who?"

"I don't know," the human signed. "We've never seen this species before."

"How many?"

"Only ten, what you see here," Keff said.

"Ten?" Big Voice squawked, waving his hands in the confines of his plastic globe. "Thousands! Millions! I thought to be torn alive!"

"Hush!" Big Eyes snapped. She turned to Keff. "Why no more?"

"Because they don't live here," Keff said. "They're invaders. This system is, er, only of Cridi. These come from elsewhere."

"Of course this system is ours," Big Voice said. "Of course." He floated away, muttering about the piles of computer equipment and speculating on their value. "Cridi, alone."

"His mind is clouded," Narrow Leg signed, sympathy on his old face. "Too much to understand at once."

"Most interesting body structure," Carialle said, as Keff looked around at the captives. When the brawn had his breath back again, he hauled himself to his feet. "It feels almost obscene to be able to examine living creatures this way."

"Yes, but it's the only way to study them without getting torn to ribbons," Keff said. "They're strong! Did you see how fast they were moving, even in this gravity? They'd be super-creatures on a Standard planet."

"But they're not natives of this one," Carialle said. "In spite of those magnificent wings they couldn't fly up to get at the Cridi on the ceiling."

"Terrible monsters," Tall Eyebrow signed. He had stayed by Keff as the human took detailed video of the griffins. "More than any in the game we play. Why much hate?"

"I don't know," Keff said. "But I don't think we'd get much of an answer out of them if you released them now."

"What fearsome beings," Long Hand signed, her eyes enormous. Small Spot, color returned to his face, nodded vigorously in agreement.

Narrow Leg rolled in close for a good look, and bumped against Keff's leg for attention. "These are the destroyers of spaceships?"

Keff shook his head. "Ones like them, perhaps. I have no idea if this crew has been around for fifty years."

"We should destroy them," Gap Tooth, one of Tad Pole's crew signed, his small face set. "Killers!"

"We can't do that," Keff said quickly.

"Why not?" Big Eyes demanded. "They killed some of *your* people. Their friends or ancestors killed ours. They die!"

"No!" Keff said. "We don't do things like that. I can't execute anyone. That's against my code of ethics, as well as my instructions."

"Why?" Narrow Leg said, but the question was not for Keff. "Ask them why."

"I can't," Keff said, raising his hands to show helplessness. "I don't speak their language. It would take time to learn theirs. We can't keep these beings like this. I'm frustrated, but any further action is out of my hands. It's up to my superiors to make a decision like this."

"Not our superiors," said Big Voice, catching Keff's sign out of the corner of his eye. "We are superiors."

"But you are under my instructions here," Keff said, signing with strong gestures. "It's always possible that we could be making a mistake. The matter deserves investigation."

All the Cridi broke out in protests. Narrow Leg held up his hands. "Let us be guided by those with experience in such matters. What should we do?"

"We'll disable their spaceship so they can't leave. That will make sure they're here for the CW inspection ships to find. We can search for armaments, and in the meantime, try to discover clues as to where they came from."

"I want to know more about them, too," Carialle said. "This is just an outpost. There is no superior intelligence directing operations from here. I want to hunt them back to their source, find the big fish. I have unanswered questions, too."

Keff repeated Carialle's words to the Cridi. "In the meantime, let's glean what we can from this site."

Chapter 10

"Move in closer to the face, Keff," Carialle instructed, as he walked slowly around the largest griffin. "I want a good look at that upper lip."

Keff did as he was told, with the Cridi in close attendance. They stayed huddled beside him as if in need of his protection. Keff found it ironic since it was their power that was keeping them safe at that moment. More ironically still, Core power was also keeping the griffins alive. The Cridi had made up their minds that the aliens must be condemned to death. Only through a lot of talking and pleading had Keff argued that one couldn't kill them while they were helplessly frozen in place. The mutterings for revenge abated somewhat. Keff was relieved. With luck, an inspection team could be dispatched quickly from a nearby station, to arrive within a few weeks. The matter needed to be investigated before the Cridi decided to take it upon themselves.

"Very interesting," Carialle said, as Keff shifted the camera eye upward. "I think that those apertures in the gumline are nostrils. Yes. On the infrared level I'm seeing warm gas expelled at regular intervals. Admirable dental sets. Whatever their species evolved eating, it fought back."

"It was nearly us," Keff said. "Docket everything and time-stamp it so we can send word home to

Exploration. I don't want anyone else scooping us on the discovery." He walked up behind one being whose long tail was flung up over its back. The tip seemed to twitch, and Keff eyed it suspiciously.

"You are certain that they can't get loose?" he signed to Narrow Leg.

"Held perfectly," the old Cridi said. "Internal pulses may move, but not body."

"Can they see us?" Keff asked.

"Eighty percent probability yes."

"Very interesting," Carialle said, as Keff passed the video pickup around and under the creature's torso. "What beautiful musculature. Look at the evidence of a sophisticated circulatory system. I'm taking internal images to find out whether those organs and orifices around the backside and underside are generative or excretory in function, or a combination. If this was a Terran animal, I'd call it a hermaphrodite. All of this is an educated guess, so far. It's a pity we can't ask them."

"Maybe medical information is in the database," Keff said. "It's time we cracked it."

Tall Eyebrow stayed with Keff. The rest of the Cridi split up to explore the dome structure. Confirming Carialle's guess, they found no access to below-ground excavations, except for heating tunnels that vented to the surface on the ridge high above the domes. The Cridi, recovered from their adventure, were enjoying being the first of their race to explore a new world in fifty years. Keff heard the triumphant chirruping of their high voices echoing in the empty stone corridors. The two councillors, Big Eyes and Big Voice, documented the building and furnishings in their admirably minute shorthand.

Under the baleful auspice of gargoyle wings and fangs, Keff sat down on the sling before the blue-glowing computer screen. He followed Carialle's instructions to disconnect the I/O port for his universal translation device, and hooked it to the computer's small processing unit.

Carialle fidgeted nervously as Keff made the connection. She checked her data security systems over and over again, looking for potential leaks. She had no wish to allow an alien bug to run rampant through her memory banks. Surely the protections in her chips were sophisticated enough to circumvent any intrusions. Just in case, she added a further layer of noise-suppression between her own memory functions and the empty bay she had prepared.

"Ready?" Keff asked.

"Ready," she said.

"You're on-line, Lady Fair." He sat back in the sling, and she saw a flash of gauntlets as he crossed his arms.

Opening the peripheral to the alien computer, Carialle activated the Tambino's hard storage. She allowed first a trickle, then, when nothing bad happened, a flood of memory to upload.

"There's a lot of garbage," Carialle commented, watching bits of data pass or fail to pass through some of her screens. Bad bytes bounced away, disintegrating into sparkle. Now and again she saw a spray of them like a meteor shower when the crystal structure of the disk-matrix was violated. "They've been experimenting with that keyboard, but they didn't know how to purge bad files or compress over bad sectors. I'm dumping them."

"Wait," Keff said. "Keep them. I might get some linguistics clues out of them."

With a sigh, Carialle rescued the data and put it in a separate memory column. "All yours, Sir Knight, and on your own head be it." She began to see graphics and maps appearing in the datastream. "I think I've located the original astrogation program." The Central Worlds Exploration Service logo, as familiar to her as her own engrams, appeared again and again at the head of files. She ran comparisons with her own memory base at half her normal hyperspeed, to make certain she was processing all of the data carefully. Graphics of star systems blinked by rapidly on her optic and neural inputs, in tandem with the screens in her main cabin and in the griffins' control room. The square script that took the place of Standard notation was unreadable, but it was impossible to confuse the starmaps for anything other than what they were.

"Do any of them mean anything to you?" Keff asked. "Is this a record of their own people's exploration? Do they overlap with CW astrogation?"

"Yes, they do overlap," Carialle said, narrating absently as she checked her internal directories. She allowed various diagrams to linger in the tanks in turn long enough for her brawn's slower consciousness to register them. "Too much. That's an actual space station, and that's a colony system, and that's an asteroid belt with a mining center . . . all this stuff is in Central Worlds records. I can't believe in identical exploration patterns, even identical fly-bys of every single system. That would suggest there are thousands of these junk ships flitting all over the galaxy, unnoticed. This information must have been in the database when it was stolen. Hmm. Some of the files have been accessed recently. The griffins must use it to look for targets, where they pick up their 'merchandise.'"

"The mining lasers they used on us," Keff said grimly, nodding. "They must have forced one of the early victims to show them how the computer system works. What about their own star system—where do *they* live? Does anything stand out? Can you pick out the one that doesn't belong?"

"Of a hundred billion systems? *I* don't keep full files from Exploration—naturally not. They wouldn't fit in my database, and if they did, it wouldn't leave me room for anything else. But I do have an index. It'll just take some time."

"Look at this," Carialle said, about an hour later. Keff stood up from where he'd been doing stretching exercises on the black stone floor and clambered back into the sling. The Cridi, having exhausted the curiosities of the dome, crowded around him. They ignored the griffins.

Carialle accessed Keff's monitor and put up three columns of entries. "All of these match exploration files I possess, but they date from around ten years ago. There's nothing newer, except for a couple of files I *don't* have," Carialle said, highlighting the entries. "I want to see the inside of that ship. Let's cross-reference these with the navicomp onboard. I have an itch in my diodes that says one of these is the lucky number."

"Well, let's spin the wheel and find out," Keff said, rising and laying a hand on the monitor in view of her camera eye. "Cari, does this setup control life support in any way?"

Carialle sent the tiniest filament of a feeler out of the protective shell she had made for herself, and threaded it down through Keff's cable, into the alien database. Beyond the wall, the power fed through a comprehensive filter from a horribly dirty source, probably a thermodynamic-based turbine. She shuddered and backed away from it. This computer had once controlled many other units' systems. The residue of Standard language programming still resided in the CPU, showing titles such as Galley, Engineering, Medical, and Electronic Mail: personal, crew. Carialle felt anger which she quickly extinguished. Retribution for the dead humans and Cridi would come in time, but not at her hands. She let the tendril explore the only other open door that existed in the memory unit, a roughly-hewn portal bristling with bad data. It led to an open communications node and the landing beacon. She guessed by the microseconds it took to reach it that the node lay hundreds of kilometers away on the planet's surface.

"No," she said at last. "Not that I can see. It's a database and ground control, but nothing else."

"Good," Keff said. "I won't kill these people, but I don't want them telling anyone we've been here." He turned to the Cridi, and made a twisting gesture with both hands.

The Cridi responded tentatively at first. Narrow Leg used his amulet to rip the cables from the wall, precipitating a shower of sparks. Tall Eyebrow tore apart the umbilicals joining the peripherals to the main unit with a delicate *pop! pop! pop!* The other Cridi watched. Big Voice, still suffering from shock, put out a tentative hand. He raised the screen a couple of meters in the air, and dropped it. The screen flickered slightly. He picked it up again, and dashed it to the ground, almost under the nose of one of the Griffins. The plastic smashed into particles on the stone floor. Big Voice floated above it, looking triumphant.

"There! There is for my near death!" he exclaimed, his shrill voice rising. "That for the ships who disappeared!" His unholy exultation roused the others. They tore apart the computer components with wrenching gestures, scattering pieces all over the room. Keff, Tall Eyebrow and Narrow Leg watched with dismay and astonishment as civilized engineers and statesmen wreaked destruction with wild eyes and flailing hands.

The outburst was over as quickly as it had begun, and the Cridi stood about in their globes amid the ruins of the computer, looking ashamed of themselves.

"Reaction," Narrow Leg said at last, his hands quivering just a little. "It was bound to come. We must leave before the temptation to further revenge becomes too strong."

Keff agreed. He shepherded the Cridi out of the ruined control room, and into the corridor. He heard no sound but the lonely boom of his own footsteps and the wheeze of the air compressors as he followed the Cridi toward the arboretum. In the corridor, the remaining four aliens who had not participated in the brawl were bunched just outside the door, arrested in the act of leaping forward. Keff felt a shudder. He had been frozen by Core power himself, and felt sympathy for the beasts even if they were killers. Although their faces didn't change, he sensed their reproach—and their anger.

"Let's do this quickly," he said, turning away. "I don't like leaving them like that."

In the arboretum, Keff pushed his way through the spiky, blue foliage to the front of the dome, and looked out. The gangway was still attached to the side of the damaged ship, leaving no gap to the outer atmosphere.

"How did you get in here?" he asked Tall Eyebrow.

The globe-frog pantomimed through the side of his traveling sphere the raising and lowering of a curtain, a door, and another curtain. To demonstrate, he rolled across the glossy floor to the edge of the flexible airlock. Without touching the controls, the Cridi raised the heavy bumper and vanished underneath. Keff heard a faint peeping sound inside. The others floated or rolled after him.

"Aren't you going to raise it enough for me?" he asked through his helmet mike.

"Too thick stiff," Tall Eyebrow's voice said in Standard over Keff's helmet radio, with polite regret.

Shrugging, Keff dropped to his knees, and crawled under the lip. As soon as he was through, the bumper thudded down. Surrounded by round obstructions that caromed into his knees, Keff rose to his feet and used his suit light to find the controls. He hit the framed bar. The great door rose. The Cridi scooted through in a party, with the brawn striding along behind. Keff waited, holding his breath, until the second curtain lifted. Before them, the tube extended out toward a distant light. What illumination there was ran in faint parallel lines along the ceiling. Keff listened, heard nothing, then let himself exhale.

"It *feels* like I'm in a suspense drama," he told Carialle.

"Think of it as another M&L game," she said. "I read no live bodies in the ship. Unless they're capable of telekinesis like the Cridi, they can't trigger any traps on you. Go slow, and I'll look for peculiar chemical or heat traces. Aim the video pickup toward anything suspicious."

The Cridi abandoned any attempt to paddle their globes up the flexible walkway, and levitated a meter above the floor. Big Voice jockeyed his way into point position.

"I shall be the first to go in," he signed, with a self-important cheep over his shoulder at Keff.

"All right," Keff said, with Carialle's reassurance in mind. He caught Big Voice's eye, and signed. "You're an observant man, er, frog. You look out for danger."

The pompous councillor's eyes widened, and he shot back to the group.

"Danger is for humans to detect," he said emphatically. Keff bowed, concealing the grin that poked out both sides of his mouth.

The tube swayed with every step Keff took. The jerking movement made him cough, and he remembered how it felt to take that deep breath of alien atmosphere. Nervously, he checked the right side of his helmet seal every so often to make certain it remained closed.

A clear panel protected the same kind of two-bar

control on the spaceship's side. As Keff raised his hand to it, the panel slid away. He punched the top button and waited. Obediently, the hatch slid upward, revealing a plain, square airlock. Keff gasped in recognition.

"This ship is definitely salvage," he said. "I know where the model came from. It's human-made, and half a century old." He felt along the wall with a gloved hand, looking for the small screwplate that should have been just inside the hatchway, but his fingertips found only a couple of small holes where the rivets had been pried out.

"They must have constructed the whole ship part by part," Carialle said, critically. "The controls appear to be retrofitted, but this airlock came off a much larger vessel."

"Appropriate, since they're larger beings," Keff said. Once he and the Cridi were inside, he looked around, turning his body so Carialle could see everything. The airlock closed, pressurized, and released the group into the main cabin of the ship. Keff showed the camera eye the shabby walls, the meager assortment of furniture.

"They haven't redecorated recently," Carialle said.

"No doubt about it, though," Keff said. "They've been shopping at Central Worlds carryout. We're on to something that the CenCom will want to know all about."

The inside of the ship was spartan. Everything was intended for function, with no concession to aesthetics. The slings and benches in the main cabin were worn, and the impact webbing attached to them sported patches in many places. Wall panels, cobbled together from a dozen ships, showed cracks and crazing where the enamel wasn't simply chipped away. Everything Keff saw was old. Even the mismatched floor panels showed worn and dented surfaces. The Cridi emitted small cheeps of interest. Keff let out a low whistle.

"What a lot of junk," he said. "Where's the up-to-date machinery as we saw in the domes?"

"Status?" Carialle guessed. "This ship might be far down the pecking order and gets what's left after the seniors take their pick. Or merely lack of opportunity. Pirates can't maraud through the rich part of space without people noticing, and we'd *know* if anyone reported rapacious griffins."

"Ours is so much nicer," Narrow Leg signed, with pride, gesturing around at the ship. "This lacks continuity. Could not be safe."

"He's right," Carialle said. "I don't know how this thing flies without blowing up. It was leaking high-rad like the proverbial sieve while it was chasing me."

"How quiet it is in here," Keff said, glancing around. The Cridi huddled in a corner, signing to one another. No sound except the burbling and occasional mechanical crunching of machinery broke the silence. "I'd better make sure the griffins didn't leave us any armed surprises."

Two broad doors were set into the walls, one in the wall to Keff's left, leading forward, and the other directly opposite. He signed to the others to wait, and went to the aft door. It opened onto a corridor, narrow only by griffin standards. Tall Eyebrow signed a quick question at him. Keff shook his head.

"I want to take a look before I let anyone else roam around," he said. "It might be dangerous." The Cridi signalled assent, and stayed close together near the airlock.

The rear section was divided into cargo and sleeping quarters. The bunkroom—for it was clearly that—contained more of the divan pillows, plus a few small possessions enclosed in nets on hooks on the walls. Loops of webbing attached to the hull sported frayed fibers.

"Looks like the artificial gravity goes out all the time," Keff commented to Carialle. He fingered one of the bundles, identifying a scarf, some ornamental jewelery, and a soft, fuzzy object that he guessed was a child's toy, almost worn out with love.

"Homey, isn't it?" Carialle said tinnily in his ear. "You'd never guess that these were bloodthirsty pirates, who murder and rob with such efficiency. It took them only hours to strip the DSC-902." Keff shuddered and backed away. Suddenly, the small bundle seemed macabre to him.

The sanitation room bore no resemblance to the one that had been yanked from a CW cargo liner. The facilities were altered to accommodate griffin parts, and the shower had once been two units, welded together. To Keff's surprise, the chamber was spotless. Even the corners had been scrubbed out ruthlessly. He pointed to a residue filling one of the cracks in the enamel.

"Soap," Carialle said, after a moment's analysis. "Or as near as makes never-mind."

"It's all so old," Keff said. "It still strikes me a trifle pathetic."

He went through to the cargo bay. It was full of straps and mounts hanging at all angles from the bulk-heads. Keff recognized the configuration. It was used for securing odd-shaped and delicate cargo. He felt naked shock when he saw that some of the artifacts bound into the shockfoam cradles were of recent CW manufacture. He recognized life support equipment, booster engine parts, even coils upon coils of commu-nication cable. One of the containers lashed into place bore the logo of the DSC-902. Something inside him twisted into a solid knot.

"Pathetic?" Carialle said.

"You're right," Keff said, fighting words past the lump. He was angry, and surprised at the intensity of the emotion. "They're not worth my sympathy. I have work to do."

He searched through the cargo area, yanking open

bulkhead cabinets, then went back to the dormitory, and poked through every bundle, every drawer and niche. At last, he tried turning over the bed pillows. His gloves slipped on the furry surface, but he seized a fold of the cloth, and wrenched upward. They were remarkably heavy, and he found himself sitting on the floor next to the third one, panting.

"Keff!" Carialle shouted in his ear. Her voice sounded alarmed. "What are you doing?" The brawn glanced up, as if suddenly aware of his surroundings.

"I'm . . . looking around," he said, but he knew his voice didn't sound convincing, and Carialle, from nearly sixteen years of experience, wasn't convinced.

"You're looking for something of mine, aren't you?" she asked, her voice soft. "You want to find proof positive that these are my salvagers."

"Well, yes," he admitted, feeling sheepish. He got to his feet and looked down at the sad, lumpy bedding. He kicked it with a toe.

"Sir Knight, you're my best friend and the finest protector a lady could wish for," she said firmly, "but the frogs are waiting, and it would be cruel to leave those aliens playing statue for much longer, even if they are killers. Let's finish up and get out of here."

"But what if there's something here?"

"Someone else will find it, not us," she said firmly. "My gut-level, as much as I feel anything down there, is that we've seen all there is on this ship. Remember that these might not be the same ones."

"I'd hate to think that there were two bunches of pirates roving around out there," Keff said, but he turned and went back to the main cabin.

"Coincidences have occurred before," Carialle said, but now Keff wasn't convinced. "In any case, these are the foot soldiers. I want the top bird."

"What is it *you* want to do?" Keff asked, but he already knew. It was what he wanted as well.

"I want to find their home system," she said. "I have to know what kind of culture fosters a history of mass piracy."

"Right you are, my lady," Keff said, then paused. "You know, Diplomacy and Maxwell-Corey ordered us home. That message they sent with the ship said to relinquish the mission and return."

"Bugger that for a game of soldiers, to quote you," Carialle said at once. "They just want me back under their eye so they can prove me mad. Everything changed when the griffins attacked the DSC-902. Their orders no longer apply. I need to follow this lead up, so I can show them the truth once and for all."

"But if these aren't the ones?" Keff asked.

"Then I'll know. But I'll never find out if we go back. The IG will slap me into protective custody, another highfalutin name for mental confinement. I'll never be satisfied with a remote report. I have to know. I *have* to. In the meantime, we're in pursuit of piratical perpetrators." The P's popped explosively in his ear. "Are you with me?"

"Always and for ever," Keff said. Resolutely, he strode back to the main cabin. With the Cridi in tow, he went into the fore corridor that led to the bridge.

The computer system was substantially like the one in the dome. All parts were of human manufacture. Some showed hard wear, especially the input peripherals. The navicomp, an ancient model of the kind used by vacuum miners, had been augmented by several different and mutually exclusive hard-memory storage units.

"This group knows how to program," Carialle said. "I wonder why a race with the capability to get into space doesn't build its own equipment?"

"Why buy the cow when you can get the milk?" Keff sat down on the sling with Cridi hovering on both sides. "Ready?" he asked Carialle.

"Ready."

He hooked into the information transfer port, and waited anxiously, with one hand on either side of the small screen, staring into its depths, while Carialle sifted the contents of the hard-storage. He could only sense fleeting impressions of individual star system maps as she read the memory and copied it into protected database.

"We have a match." Her voice sounded triumphant. "Three star systems, put in relatively recently."

"What are they?" Keff said, as the graphics appeared in the 2-D display.

"No can tell, Sir Knight. They're in an alien typography. The keyboard must have been altered to create their symbols. There are sixty-eight. Your first clue to their language. Enjoy."

Keff groaned. "Do you mean this is a dead end?"

"Not at all." There was a long pause, and the stars spun by again, accompanied by colored screens full of square letters. "The flight recorder shows that two of them have been visited more than once. And you'll never guess where one of them is!"

"I give up."

"Right next door. The binary mate, PLE-329-JK6—straight across the lowermost boundary of P-sector. I followed the visual log entries, and I could identify half of the visuals from my personal memory."

"That's incredible!" Keff exclaimed, then paused. "No, that's logical. Why else would they go to so much trouble to prevent a lot of traffic in this part of the galaxy?"

"My thinking exactly," Carialle said. "So that's where we go. We try it first, and if it's wrong, we go on to the next one. One of these has to be home base."

"Right. We try them one by one," Keff said.

Tall Eyebrow and Narrow Leg had been watching Keff curiously, hearing half the conversation. Keff looked at them guiltily. He'd forgotten that he was not alone, and his companions were intelligent. And motivated.

"Where to go next? This map?" the Cridi captain asked, pointing at the screen with a long finger.

"You should all go home now," Keff said. "I thank you for your help and support, but I can't ask you to do any more."

"But we would do much more," Narrow Leg signed, his old eyes wise in the wrinkled, green face. "You have done much for us, opening the way. Together, we defeated. You seek a voyage to unknown, to find truth. We wish also. We go with you."

"But your own people need you for defense," Keff said. "It's one thing to have you accompany us in your own system, and quite another to subject you to unknown danger. Your ship is not prepared for a long space voyage. You . . . with respect, you lack training."

"Give us training, then," Narrow Leg said. "We need also to find this truth. Many lives were lost—ships, years, lost also. I want explanations. If you say they are not to be found here, then we go to where they are."

"I will train them," Tall Eyebrow said, tapping himself on the chest. "To survive—I know this."

"Ship is ready interstellar travel," Narrow Leg said, with a throwaway gesture. "All supplies were loaded on board at departure. As for defense, half my crew are assembling two more ships from old ones and new parts. Cridi will be defended in atmosphere and out of atmosphere."

Keff shook his head at the old male's expansive signs.

"Captain, it'll take a long time to reach our destination, and we may not even find what we're looking for at this first stop. It could, no, it *will* be dangerous. I can't let you . . . er, take such important conclave councillors as Big Voice."

Narrow Leg didn't miss the subtlety. He rolled a

beady black eye at Keff. "That fat one will be all right. There is no time to waste. We must not divert back to Cridi. You must be after the villains track to source."

"We come, too," Tall Eyebrow said, sweeping his hands to include his two companions and Big Eyes.

"Yes," Big Eyes agreed, with a brilliant glance at him. "We follow Tall Eyebrow. Experienced twice in space."

"Cari? We have to pursue this to the end, but they don't."

"I'm torn," Carialle said. "We could use the backup. It won't come from CW for ages, even providing they know where we are going, which they do not, and we're not armed. The Cridi want to be our allies. On the other hand, I don't like it that they're entirely without experience. Particularly, I do not like flying interplanetary distances with a possibly explosive emotional problem."

"Big Voice?" Keff asked sublingually, without moving his lips.

"He's the only one who's manifested openly so far. Who knows if any of the others will destabilize during a long trip."

Tall Eyebrow had not missed Keff's eye passing from Cridi to Cridi. "I vouch for each," he said in Standard. "They will not fail."

"I think you'd better ask them," Keff said, both in Standard and sign. Tall Eyebrow looked a question at Narrow Leg, who raised his thin shoulders eloquently and let them drop. Big Eyes made a tentative sign, then glanced at Keff. He heard a faint peep as one of the engineers spoke through the amulet link.

"Privacy," Carialle said.

"Right you are," Keff said. He turned his back on them and studied the navigation tank. After a brief conference, punctuated by shrill exclamations and much rolling about the deck, Keff felt a tap against his leg. He looked down at Tall Eyebrow.

"It is decided. We will come with you." He looked at the other seven Cridi. "We are all willing to go. The crew also." Big Voice, at the front of the group nodded vigorously, and favored Keff with a humanlike smile.

"I wish to come. Otherwise this one," he pointed to Narrow Leg, "blames me for spoiling virgin ship flight."

"You will be acclaimed hero, once home," Big Eyes squeaked, with mischief in her eyes. Big Voice relaxed back in his globe, a happy expression on his face. "All will recognize . . . ."

"No," Tall Eyebrow said, stopping her with a downward stroke of his hand. He turned to Keff. "Not for that reason. He will go because he recognizes his fear and uncertainty, as we all do. No one goes just to prevent us from turning back."

"I am selfish," Big Eyes said, her exuberance dimmed slightly by shame. She covered her eyes with her hands, then peeped coyly between her fingers at Keff. She was so cute he couldn't help but smile.

"I go," Big Voice insisted. "Who else will see you do right? Also, I must meet the leaders of"—here he hooked his long thumbs together and spread his hands in imitation of wings—"griffins." "I wish to know *why* they hate us. I must ask. We will . . . negotiate." He paused before the last sign and glanced at Narrow Leg as if defying him to laugh. "You must teach us what we do not know." Keff smiled down at him. At last he understood why the plump amphibioid was one of the eight most important frogs on Cridi.

"Thank you," he said. "It'll be good to have you along."

"And we will teach you the joys of Myths and Legends," Tall Eyebrow squeaked happily.

As soon as Keff had disconnected from the ship computer's I/O port, the Cridi destroyed the unit with the same thoroughness that they had the one in the dome. Keff examined the rest of the control board and indicated the communication set and guidance system. Tall Eyebrow delicately disassembled those, taking care to leave life support intact. The lights dimmed briefly, but came up again with a steady glow. At a nod from Narrow Leg, the ship's engineer and two of the crew went aft ahead of the rest of the group. Keff heard clashing and breaking sounds. When the three Cridi rejoined the others in the ship's main cabin, they bore between them a Core unit. It was old, and looked to be in bad shape.

"I'd forgotten about that," Keff said. Narrow Leg looked grim.

"We, never," the commander said. "And this ship will not rise again. We have destroyed the engine. Let us leave now."

Free to use Core power, the Cridi swept their globes and Keff high over the dusty landscape, back toward the small valley where the ships lay hidden. Unwilling to look straight down, Keff turned his gaze back over his shoulder toward the dome, watching it until it vanished among the battered ridges. He signed a question to Narrow Leg.

"What about the griffins?"

"We can hold them all as long as need," the old Cridi replied.

"Good. Release them when we leave orbit," Keff said. "I think we're safe, but I want to make sure."

Narrow Leg sketched a quick OK with his long fingers.

"I want you to hear this, Keff," Carialle said. "I'm shipping this off to the CenCom, and it's the last word they're going to hear from us until we find 'Griffin Central.'"

"You sound so serious, Lady Fair," Keff said. He

smiled at the frogs who glanced over when they noticed the movement of his head.

"Never more in my life, but this is plain mutiny. I won't send it unless you give me your all-clear. I want to live to report to the Inspector General. If there's the least chance, I will show him who was crawling over my skin twenty years ago, and that he's been harassing me for nothing, but I refuse to endanger *you*. All I need is a single piece of my first ship for proof or an eyewitness, and if it's anywhere, it's in one of those three systems. Recording:

"'This is the CK-963,'" her voice said, sharp and metallic in intonation in his ear. "'We wish to confirm absolutely that the DSC-902 was the victim of a fatal attack by alien forces. Three ships, carrying stolen Cridi artifacts and CW mining lasers, ambushed the DSC-902 while on its way into this system for a purely peaceful mission. All the crew are dead. Ten of the perpetrators have been marooned on the fifth planet from the Cridi sun. Video accompanying this message will show that this is a life-form with which Central Worlds is unfamiliar. We are following information received, to what we believe to be the aliens' home-world at once. Coordinates for three potential systems are in the visual portion of this message. We will transmit again with further information when we have reached our final destination. Carialle out.' What do you think?"

"Send it, lady," Keff said, firmly. "I'll be aboard in five minutes."

Chapter 11

As if the paralysis had never been, movement returned to the ten Thelerie. Those who had been poised for battle fell over, and those whose eyes had been frozen open blinked. No one spoke for a moment. Everyone exercised their muscles, and simply enjoyed the freedom. Then they took heed of their surroundings. The mess was heartbreaking.

"I do not understand, Autumn," Crescent Moon blurted out, pieces of the precious computer clutched in all four of his hands. "Why did the human destroy our equipment? I've done my best to keep this station exactly as the Manual directs. It was neat, it was clean—and now, look!" The ground control commander sounded as near to trilling as a child. "Was he angry with our performance?"

Autumn still kept her eyes closed, waiting for tear fluid to wash away the dust from her large, flat corneas. "You do not understand, Crescent. There are other humans than the Melange. You have never seen them. You showed aptitude for the computer, so it was the wisdom of the Melange that you went here before spending any time reiving. It is a shame."

"It was the wisdom of the Melange," Crescent said, defiantly. The other station crew all dipped their heads and wings in a worshipful manner. "But this human did behave strangely."

Rivulet shook his head. "He did not even speak properly. His hands moved often, but not his mouth. He wasn't like those from whom we receive goods, nor like those for whom we provide."

"I think he is a captive of the Slime," Dawn piped up in his high, musical voice. "He is under their spell. They've directed the Slime Ball," he pronounced the human phrase most carefully, "to alter his mind. You know the power the Ball has. We do not know all its secrets."

"Yes!" Rivulet agreed, holding out a claw. "See how he cowered from us, when he should know we are his to command."

"We are not slaves of Humans," one protested.

"No, no, but they give us all gifts in exchange for our aid," Captain Autumn said, pausing to consider. She lifted a wing claw. "This human needs rescue. My eyes were turned toward the screens when I froze under the monsters' power. I saw which maps he looked at. He wishes to go to Thelerie. Though he could not speak, his signs grew more frantic when he saw that chart. He can receive aid there, and be freed of the Slime. He was trying to tell us."

"Ah!" The soft voices chorused together for a moment as the Thelerie realized the truth in the leader's words.

"We should warn the others the Slime are heading toward the Center," Rivulet insisted.

"How?" Autumn asked. "The Slime tore our communicator to bits." A wing swept over the shattered console. "I am sure they treated our poor ship the same." She turned to Dawn. "See how things stand. Send a message to the Melange if you can."

The second flicked a claw at the rest of the crew. They dragged on their shipsuits and pattered out into the corridor after him. Autumn began to pick up the broken pieces with all her hands. Crescent and the other three ground crew bent to help. Though distressing, the debris was finite. In a short time, the wreckage was all cleared away.

"I feel better," Crescent said, sitting down on his haunches and blowing a puff of air so his upper lip vibrated. "Now I do not feel as though I broke the trust."

Autumn smiled, showing her fangs. Crescent was a simple soul at heart. Once a problem was out of sight, it was gone. "There is wisdom in hard work."

She donned her shipsuit and went out to her craft. Dawn sat amidst the pieces of the control panel, shaking his great head from side to side. The captain looked down at him.

"How bad, my friend?"

"Perhaps the human stayed the Slime's fury," the lieutenant said. "The communication deck is destroyed, but the filtration systems are intact."

Autumn felt the breath leave her body. "We cannot warn the Center in time. The Slime will be ahead of us."

"Very far, I'm afraid," Dawn said, his large eyes worried. "The engine is ruined, but it was in Stage Four breakdown anyway. The landing finished it off."

"The engine?" For the first time Autumn's expression brightened. "Ah." She wheeled on her haunches and trotted down the corridor toward the cargo compartment.

With pleasure she surveyed the secured racks of parts from the CW ship. She was proud that her crew had responded so quickly with the others when the call came from Phyllis that there was a second invader, after the slim ship had escaped them into the atmosphere of the Slime planet. This large ship moved more slowly than the first, so it was easy for the reivers to get into position at the system's perimeter.

As in the three examples in the Manual, the large

ship did all the things an enemy would. It signalled them, ordered them to halt, and invoked the authority of the Central Worlds. Verje Bisman, and after him his child, Aldon Bisman, had from the earliest days, reminded the Thelerie that Central Worlds was the enemy. The See-Double-Yew comprised a few planets who stockpiled goods taken from decent beings and refused to allow access to them, even in great need. That was anathema to the Melange, who insisted that all people who could pay, in one coin or another, should have entitlement to all goods. That seemed right and proper.

The Melange had taken goods from this aggressor, to distribute or keep as need dictated. The prize under their feet would have fetched a good price, but Autumn needed it herself now.

At her direction, Dawn and the others knelt to take up the floor plates. Their muscles swelled under their hides as they pulled the heavy metal panels aside to uncover the biggest cargo cradle of all.

Nestled in it a piece of machinery—an engine, a prize, a work of mechanical art. Autumn regarded it with affection and awe. The Central Worlds ship must have been nearly new. Inspection seals etched on the finest metal film were still affixed in the correct places on the engine's surface. The whole unit gleamed. With a claw-finger, Autumn traced the inscription on the largest piece of film: Dee-Ess-See-Nine-Oh-Too.

"Install it in place of our old one. It will give us greater speed and stability for our journey back to Thelerie."

Heartbeat, the youngest of them all, tilted her head up toward her captain, eyes full of despair.

"But the navigation system was destroyed by the Slime."

Autumn tapped the youngster with a wing-finger. "Have you no faith in your own soul? Center. Find your way back to the Center. It may take us many days to reach home, but we shall survive. I regret that we cannot warn Mirina in time. We can only hope she hears the messages we sent when the ship first entered the system."

"Damn that ship," Rivulet said. "I wish they will be lost in the Void forever."

"But it was beautiful, wasn't it?" Heartbeat said, looking at the others with rapture shining from her eyes. "So new." Her hands fumbled on the smooth sides of the engine. "So perfect."

Autumn smiled indulgently. "Someday, such ships will be ours, too. In the meantime, we must tend what we have. Work carefully. Remember all your lessons from the Manual." Heartbeat ducked her head shyly.

Dawn began to sing quietly under his breath. Autumn recognized the anthem: "Thelerie, Heart of the Galaxy." She picked up the melody, her strong baritone joining with his. The others added their voices, their lips spreading with smiles of inner joy. Autumn leaned back on her mighty haunches to help lift the engine. The music helped give the six strength. With a deep breath and a hoist, the unit was out of the cradle and onto the deck.

Sacred orders from the humans dictated that the drive mountings should be made adjustable to take any component that offered itself, though lesser manuals Autumn had seen did not allow for such open tolerances. Their Humans were wiser than those who wrote the books. Hoses, connections, control cables—all were snapped or fastened or sealed into place in very little time. Autumn, taking only a moment to stand back and approve her crew's handiwork, directed the crew into the ship. She guided Heartbeat to the navigator's chair. Dawn took his place in the pilot's sling and engaged the engine. Its soft purr surprised them all. It was so mild, yet so powerful, compared to the old one.

"The Wisdom of the Melange," Dawn said, settling his wings on his back with a satisfied twitch.

"They are wise," Autumn agreed, and turned to Heartbeat. "Now, center, child, *center*. Make the wise ones proud of you."

The youngster bent her attention on the tank full of stars before her. Autumn stood back to watch, half proud and half sad.

They would mourn their lost ones on the way home.

"Cold, damned rock," snarled Bisman from behind the pilot's chair, as the ship swung into an orbit around Coltera. "Why in the hope of paradise would anyone spend more than a minute here?"

"Because it's theirs," Zonzalo Don said, with a surprised look at the leader. "That's what this girl I met said."

"Don't knock the place too hard in front of the inhabitants," Mirina said, turning up a palm in appeal. "I don't want them to kick our base off planet."

"Sacred, high lady," Bisman sneered sarcastically, making her wince, "I was born here. I flew with my father around *those moons* when I was a tot. We brought them their first replacement compressors. Don't tell me how to behave with them."

"I apologize," she said, staring him levelly in the eyes. She was stung, but damned if she'd show it. "I know. The nag was automatic. We have few friends in any part of the galaxy. It's important to me that we keep them, especially if they're kin." The raider straightened up, surprised at Mirina's easy surrender.

"Hell, yes, it's important, Miri," Bisman said, slowly, sounding more reasonable than Mirina had heard him in ages. "That's just sense. And you don't insult 'em if you want 'em to buy what you've got. Loyalty goes only so far. But, spacedust, they'd take what's in our hold if we called their mothers mudworms!" He laughed, and slapped Zonzalo on the shoulder. "Get Leader Fontrose on the line, kiddo. Tell him who we are and what we've got. Then call Twilight and tell her we're coming in for refueling."

"Aye, sir," the youth said, with a humorous glance at his sister.

"Fuel pods, radio-ac insulation, enviro-suits—I smell *profit*," Bisman said, rubbing his hands together in pleasurable anticipation.

"So do I," Mirina said. For a moment they forgot the pressures of the past, and hard times, and smiled at one another the way they used to. It didn't last. In an instant, Bisman reverted back to his normal, harsh self. Mirina hugged herself against imagined cold as the older man turned away with brisk efficiency to the board.

She felt eyes on her. When she glanced up, the young Thelerie, Sunset, was turning his head quickly back to his control board. Mirina had seen sympathy on his face. She walked over and patted him on the wing joint.

"You've got a kind heart, youngster," she said quietly. "And you do good work. Keep it up."

He looked up at her, his huge eyes glowing with worship. "Thank you, Mirina."

"Which way's your homeworld?" she asked.

Sunset put up a wing-finger at once, directed aft and to starboard, tracking Thelerie upward as the ship he rode in transited an orbit around the planetoid. His natural gift was a comfort to her, something constant to hold onto in their chancy travels. She wished she could do that: point to her home, no matter how distant it was. She wished she had a home to point to. The ship on which she had been born was scrapped and recycled before she started primary education. Sunset looked at her with a soft, mournful expression, and Mirina realized she'd let her feelings show on her face. She slapped the Thelerie on the shoulder in unconscious imitation of Bisman.

"Thanks, youngster," she said, then nodded to Zonzalo when he signalled her that the communication link was open.

"Greetings, leader!" she said, pulling a bright face for the screentank. "Will you be glad we visited you today!"

Aldon Bisman kicked the ground and spat. Muddy yellow-brown pebbles scattered against the crates of unimaginably precious air-recirculation valves. Mirina was annoyed, but she contained herself.

"What do you mean, seven thousand apiece?" Bisman said to Mirchu Fontrose, a thin, short, sallow-faced man. "What's this character think he's playing at?"

"All we can afford, Aldon, my old friend," Fontrose said, mournfully. "Unless you'd consider extending us further credit. You know we're good for it."

Mirina folded her arms and watched her partner's face. She was tempted to tell the colony leader to fold his offer into a point of singularity and put it in his eye, but this was Bisman's home, and his show.

"Crap," Bisman said, levelly. "They're worth ten. I know that if I sell them to you at seven, you'll be out of orbit the second we're gone. You'll take them to the bazaar on Phait and sell them yourself for that. I could have done that myself, and you'd be stuck paying eleven or worse to the traders. Ten."

Fontrose and the colonists on Coltera were prone to what Mirina's mother called "poor-mouthing." Even though their gem-mining brought in a good credit, they always made believe they were on the edge of starvation. Nothing could have been a greater lie. Opals, especially ones of the clarity and depth of color that they coaxed out of that impossibly dense matrix, were always in demand, however illicit the market. Coltera wasn't an official CW colony. The independent miners who discovered the strike had checked ownership of this small and marginal world. They hid the signs of success and squatted, staking a homesteading claim through the housing office, as if only one family lived here, registered as subsistence wheat farmers. Ridiculous, Mirina thought, since there was no soil. In the meantime, the opals began to appear on the gray market, traded for fabulous profits that were split up among the whole of the colony. The irony of it all was that the family registered with CenCom government received a subsidy for earning below the poverty level.

A lot of independent thinkers had elected to "disappear" and end up here, falling off the CW tax records much as she and the raiders had. When one didn't pay tax, one had money for a lot of things. Like pressure units.

She glanced around the cul-de-sac at the raised mound that surrounded them on each side. Behind every one of those doorways was a domicile, half a mansion in size. Their mining equipment, state of the art for extracting delicate opal, was so new the enamel wasn't scratched. Mirina caught a glimpse of their shabby, red ship standing among the rock loaders, and was sufficiently irritated into speaking.

"The price goes up while you stall," she said, tapping her foot, deliberately sounding unreasonable. "When it goes up to twelve, we leave."

Fontrose cringed away from her. "All right, all right. Don't rush me. Don't rush me. That's a lot of money, you know. I suppose you came by it honestly, eh?" He peered from one face to another. Bisman quirked one side of his mouth.

"Salvage," he said simply, flipping a hand up toward space. "Found it out there, somewhere. You know." Fontrose raised his hands in surrender.

"All right, all right, I won't ask."

"Eleven," Mirina said warningly.

"Wait! Wait!" Fontrose turned to her, alarmed. "Please, dear lady, don't raise things until we've had a chance to talk about your first offer. Now, I thought eight and a half . . . ."

A long-legged figure stumbled down the steps of the raiders' ship and ran toward them headlong. Mirina recognized Zonzalo, and wondered why he was so agitated. She stopped him with a fierce glance when he was still half a dozen meters from the group. He gestured with his hands and eyebrows, trying to signal urgency. He stopped waving at her when Fontrose turned to glance at him, but started his semaphoring again as soon as he looked away. Bisman shot her a look of annoyance.

"Go back, Zon," she said at last. "Check and see how they're coming with those containers."

"Miri!" came a choked squawk from Zonzalo. Fontrose swiveled to stare openly. Bisman looked exasperated. Mirina smiled at Fontrose, dangerously, but politely.

"Excuse me just one moment. A matter of crew discipline."

The colony leader nodded, and Bisman took the distraction as an opportunity to move in to close the sale.

"Now, while she's gone, my old friend, let's get the price to where we both like it."

"What is it?" Mirina hissed. Her younger brother was hopping up and down with nerves. "How dare you interrupt a negotiation?"

"It's dire! Twilight's been holding a message for us from Autumn on Base Eight. They've been attacked by a Central Worlds ship. They need help."

"What are we supposed to do about it?" Mirina asked, annoyed. "We're too bloody far away to do anything now. That message will be weeks old!"

"We ought to go and check out Autumn's report," the boy insisted.

"Check out what? If Autumn got word out, then someone was alive to operate the communications board."

"What the hell is going on?" Bisman asked, coming up between them.

"Base Eight's had a run-in with CW ships," Zonzalo said, wide-eyed.

"So what?"

"So, it's been discovered by the authorities," the boy said. "We have to help them."

"Zon, this is not a vid-show. We're ages away from there. Autumn will just have to abandon the place," Mirina said. "She's a survivor. She'll get the rest of the crews out of there."

"Too bad about Base Eight," Bisman said, scratching his unshaven chin. "It lasted a long time. My dad established that one when I was a boy. I spent time there myself."

"But CW might find the Slime," Zonzalo said. "They'll talk."

"Who cares? They don't know who we are," Bisman said, impatient to get back to the negotiations. "Besides, they stopped kicking a long time ago. One ship is no big deal. They'll come, they'll go. In the meantime, we can go back and mine the skies around Planet Two with impact grenades, to make sure no one gets offworld, no matter how many visitors they get from CenCom." His eyes grew dreamy. "Maybe a blanket bombardment, keep kicking them until the whole planet blow up. Always wanted to see how much that Slime defense system could take."

"Stop it, damn you," Mirina said, inter never knew whether his *enfant terrible* act or not. "We'll just abandon the b don't know where we are or where w word to Phyllis and Autumn and the others to destroy the equipment, and evacuate. There's no need to cause further loss of life."

Bisman turned on her, one finger thrust upward under her chin, eyes flashing dangerously. "Enough of that, brawn. I'm tired of it. You lost one friend, one brain. I've seen hundreds of friends, family, even lovers die over the thirty years I've been out here. You're here where *my people* live. Do you want to know how many holes there are in my family?"

"I know," Mirina said, staring him straight back in the eye. "You've told me again and again."

"And I know. Charles this. Charles that." His scorn pummeled her, and she gaped at him. He shoved his face close to hers, backing her out of the negotiation circle until she was trapped between him and somebody's front door. "I don't care any more! You don't like death, huh? You don't want to see anyone else die. *It blunts your edge*, woman. You should be able to kill to protect yourself. Why should just one death affect you *so much*?"

"Because I thought he could never die," she shouted, feeling her heart constrict and squeeze the words out of her. Bisman backed away, and Mirina caught her breath. Her eyes stung and she knew she was blinking back tears. Sensing a personal matter, Fontrose had turned delicately away, but he couldn't avoid having heard her. Bisman and Zonzalo stared. Mirina glared back defiantly. She had admitted the truth to herself at last, the secret she'd been keeping locked away for eight years. She felt like screaming some more, but she kept control. Her voice stayed level and low. "Because no one ever understood how much I love being in space. How I *have* to be there. He felt the same way."

l, you couldn't sleep with him, couldn't even im. What the hell good was he as a partner?" spat at the ground, and Mirina hated him.

As she looked laser bolts at his back, the co-leader went back to Fontrose, who had moved away. Mirina shook her head, willing her rage to subside. You could *not* explain the brain/brawn relationship to someone who hadn't experienced it. No one else could understand. Bisman never had shown notable signs of sensitivity. She was a fool to expect it.

She turned to Zonzalo. He had stayed alongside them to make sure she was all right, but also a few paces away, well out of the line of verbal fire between his sister and her partner. He fidgeted anxiously, and nodded his head with a slight, hopeful smile. Mirina smiled back, but her eyes were serious.

"We abandon the Slime system, Zon. The Slime don't have a clue who's been out there on Planet Five all those years. We've never left any live captives, so they can't tell Central Worlds authority what we look like. There's not much left on the base. I regret leaving the computer system behind, but it's anonymous. No Standard files anywhere. It's all in Thelerie."

Zonzalo's mouth stretched in a slow smile. "So when CW finds it, they won't be able to read it anyway. Pretty good, Madam Don."

"I didn't do it to please you," she snapped. "I did it so the Thelerie could use it more easily in emergencies. I hope they can get out."

"Soft in the head, dammit," Bisman said, coming back. He looked pleased with himself. He brandished a plastic card in his hand: the agreement struck with Fontrose, thumbprinted and secured. "Ten. What did I tell you? We'll have to do something about that infiltrator, if it's still hanging around Base Eight space when we're back there. We'll strike hard, a fast. One ship shouldn't be so hard to be our advantage, the Slime Ball."

"I'm not convinced that unit will l much longer," Mirina said, uneas' getting steadily weaker over the last couple of years. It needed to be fixed, and none of them had the remotest idea how it worked. Only blind chance had led his engineers to discover what it was all those years ago when they took it off the Slime ship. Only sheerest coincidence had allowed them to install the three Balls in reiver ships and gotten them to work without blowing up. Bisman relied too heavily on it, and that concerned Mirina. Their operation shouldn't turn on a single piece of equipment. She'd said so for years.

"It'll be fine. You worry too much," Bisman said, flicking the card between his fingertips.

Zonzalo tried to add a touch of optimism. "We'll probably hear an update from Autumn as we head back in that direction. Another message is probably on its way now. I'm sure they destroyed that ship. It was only one, and we have three on that base."

"Right," said Bisman, grabbing Mirina's arm and leading the way toward the ship. "In the meantime, we've got a delivery for the Thelerie. Don't you like being thought of as a goddess? Bringing aid from the heavens to bring wings to the winged?"

Mirina lay in a bunk in the guest cave and listened to the echoes far down the hall. Bisman and his old cronies had decided to make a night of it in the settlement, and dragged Zonzalo and Sunset along for fun. No matter how hard she pressed to keep the youngsters on the ship, Bisman countered her every argument. He couldn't see any good reason for sequestering them on his home planet. At least he didn't insist on taking them off on strange ports. Mirina was responsible for Zonzalo, and she felt responsible for Sunset. He was the most gormless, innocent creature she'd ever shipped with, even more so than any other Thelerie. hadn't a guileful cell in his body, and he took every- precious humans said as the mathematical truth. Stars knew what a less moral band of humans might have done with him.

Moral, hah!

It had been eight years since she'd shipped on with Bisman. Eight, long, damned years. When she had paired with Charles on the CM-702, she'd only kept in touch in a sporadic fashion with Zonzalo. She was sorry now. She should have been more of an influence in his upbringing, taking more of the role of their deceased parents, instead of trusting it to boarding school counselors. But brainships were on almost constant duty in Exploration. Mirina couldn't get free just to mediate a grades dispute or a behavior violation for her brother. Sometimes she didn't even hear about problems until months after they had occurred. She'd failed in her parenting, and that still bothered her.

Not long after Charles died she got a message that Zonzalo had left school and fallen in with Bisman. She hadn't liked the sound of the man at all. Anyone with charm and perseverance could gain influence over her poor, silly, gullible brother, who was still looking for a strong role model to fashion himself after. In this case it could get him killed. Zonzalo hinted deliciously of danger and secret raids accomplished in a fast scout ship. Mirina knew she'd have to go and get her brother away from that crowd. He was the only family she had.

With the reputation of jinx riding her, Mirina couldn't get anyone to help her ship out to find him, nor even get a full hearing on the subject. The authorities paid little attention to a troubled woman babbling about a distant brother and malign influences. The counseling they had given her after Charles' death was inadequate, as if her emotional recovery was of secondary importance to the enormous catastrophe of the death of a brainship. It seemed that no one cared at all about her. She resented that her supervisor in Exploration had not intervened more closely in getting her another

any berth—when it would have done wonders for her
sanity, not to mention her patriotism. Mirina felt that
Central Worlds had let her down at every single opportunity. Refusing to untangle the red tape to help her find
Zonzalo was the last crumb that upset the scale. Never
mind that she thought her brother was in the hands of
pirates, and CW might be able to solve robberies in that
sector. The official budget wasn't set up to handle "free-
lance" missions, her boss had said. Then he'd mined her
file with false complaints of insubordination, so when
she went over his head for help, no one would listen
to her. She left, cursing Central Worlds and all bureaucracy. Now and forever more, she was on her own.

It took every last credit she had to charter a scout
craft to Zonzalo's last known location. Lucky thing it
was a base the pirates used all the time. She hadn't
intended to stay once she had rescued her brother, but
face-to-face, the pirates were a truly pathetic lot. Their
equipment was a hundred years outdated, but even bad
equipment will work if maintained. Their diet was so
unbalanced that crew members were going down sick
with fragile-bone disease and scurvy, even the ones who
weighed 160 kilos. Mirina needed so badly to be needed
that when Zonzalo and a younger, much handsomer
Aldon Bisman pressed her to stay, she did. Central
Worlds had rejected her, but these people wanted her.
They'd pay her anything she asked, just to stay. At the
time the offer was hard to resist.

It took two years before she had them whipped into
a kind of military order that preserved resources and
actually allowed them to build their network outward.
She was a good organizer, but for eight years now, it
seemed, she'd operated on autopilot. She found it
harder every day to break away. The activity kept her
from thinking too hard about where she had come
from, about Charles, and the horrifying accident that
him, and what she was doing.

At long last Mirina was thinking again. She needed to take Zonzalo and leave, cease aiding and abetting criminals. She had become one herself. Little niggles and twinges from her conscience told her that she still owed something to Central Worlds. Even after all the wrong CW had done her, she'd never have met Charles and shipped with him if it wasn't for the brainship program. He had been the single most wonderful thing in her life. An old-fashioned but worldly gentleman, Charles himself would have said it was Mirina's duty to turn herself and the others in, and he'd be right. She shouldn't be here. Not that she ought to try and return to the brain/brawn program: she couldn't. She couldn't even go back to the Central Worlds and try to fit into the mainstream. No job would be safe for her. The authorities undoubtedly had a criminal file on her that would cover a small continent, and she would rather die of torture than be locked up ground-side. The Don family would have to ship out on their own, skipping from remote outpost to remote outpost forever. Again the sensation of desperate lack of belonging rose out of her belly and clutched her throat until she gasped, sobbing. Mirina sat up in bed and braced herself, elbows akimbo with hands on her knees, just breathing. She was doing good here, too—she was! The work they had done with the Thelerie was benevolent and worthwhile. Look at the advances the winged ones had made in only a few years! She hated to leave that, but she needed to go away and take Zonzalo with her.

A good organizer knows how to organize. She lay back on her bunk, and began to take stock of her assets.

Chapter 12

The Cridi were green, in every way. They were inexperienced, scared witless, and, well, physically resembled the chorus line for a production of the comedy musical *Frogs in Space*. Keff's natural exuberance and energy were proving to be just shy of what it took to buoy up an entire crew of aliens through their first experience of long-term space travel. Every day brought new anxieties and fears that just proved how quickly a spacegoing race can forget how it once adapted. He fell into bed at night, completely exhausted.

Things were slightly better now that they had passed the halfway point. Their passage around the trapped magnetic Oort debris, pooled at the balance point between the Cridi system and its sister sun, when all of Carialle's sensors had gone briefly insane, had caused hysteria among the Cridi. It had taken all Keff's tact and patience to keep the other ship's crew from mutinying against Narrow Leg and diving through the anomaly—fatally—back toward their homeworld. Carialle's suggestion, voiced at thunderous volume over all speakers, that both systems must be of identical galactic mass and weight to hold this particular configuration, lured some of the scientists out of their emotional shells to study the phenomenon of twin systems. Narrow Leg and Tall Eyebrow rallied everyone into the project. Keff spent plenty of time answering questions and supplying telemetry scans for their use. An intelligent people, they understood that to occupy their minds fully would help defy the dark. Yet, bogeys crept back nightly, leaving Keff to buoy their hearts up again in the morning.

As he staggered out into the main cabin at the beginning of his shift, in the middle of the second week in space, he glimpsed Cridi from the corner of his eye in half a dozen screens, all staring. They relaxed perceptibly when they saw him. Keff deliberately met each pair of eyes in turn, smiling with confidence. They must have been up since the dot of first shift, waiting for him to appear. Tall Eyebrow, Small Spot, Long Hand, and Big Eyes were in the corner of the cabin near the food synthesizer, the only ones who didn't look nervous.

"I'm not used to this much company," Keff growled under his breath to Carialle. "We've had too many years alone, just the two of us."

"It won't last forever," the brain reminded him, speaking through his aural implant, the lone communication signal that they kept as a private channel. All the others had been left on open broadcast to the Cridi ship so the amphibioids could monitor what was going on; Carialle was also tapped into the frequencies of both functioning Cores. She kept her frog image on the wall of the CK-963 and on one screen of the Cridi ship in case they needed to ask questions while Keff was busy or asleep. "We're doing a public service for them, and they're out to help us with our mission."

"But they're still so scared," Keff said, frustrated.

"They'll get over it once there's something to do."

"I hope so," Keff said. He sat down at the control console, and let out a huge yawn. "They're wearing me out." On the screen over it, two of Narrow Leg's crew stared out. He smiled at them.

"Hello, Gap Tooth and Wide Foot."

"Good mor-ning," they chorused in Standard, faltering only a little over the dipthong.

"That's very good," Keff said, nodding encouragingly. "Have you been studying the drama videos I sent so you could practice listening to colloquial speech?"

"Have," the first one said, then fell back on a combination of sign and numeric squeak. "Interesting, times two—times three! Terror, fire, exciting! N is greater than zero tongue trill sounds. Why?"

Keff stared, baffled. "What do you mean? Which tape were you watching?"

The other Cridi, Wide Foot, held up a card and pronounced the title with great care as she followed the words with a finger. "*Gone with the Wind*," she said, and turned puzzled eyes to him.

"Oh!" Keff smiled, enlightened. "It's a dialect. Trill sounds were sometimes replaced with aspirates in some regional speech patterns on Old Earth."

"Sounds soft," she said, and gave him a timid smile in return. "I like to he-ah such speech. I may adopt it."

"Oh, wonderful," Carialle said, much amused. "A frog with an American Southern accent."

"I think it adds character," Keff said. "I encourage you to experiment," he told Wide Foot.

"I shall."

As Tall Eyebrow and his companions had already proved, the Cridi were rapid learners. They absorbed the *Standard as a Second Language* videos that Carialle dredged out of her memory, and were speaking a form of pidgin by the end of the first week. Keff's own grasp of the Cridi spoken language was increasing every day as a result of answering so many questions. Having no residue of the tongue in his memory, Keff was finding it slower going than the three Ozranians did. Tall Eyebrow was now participating fully in discussions with his long-lost cousins.

Keff was also accumulating a considerable amount of data for the paper he was beginning to write on the evolution of the Cridi languages from a thousand years ago up to the present day.

Language instruction was only part of the program that he, Carialle, Narrow Leg, and Tall Eyebrow had worked out to keep the Cridi sane and functioning throughout the voyage. It also included cultural exchange, elementary space travel, survival techniques, and of course, lessons in how to play Myths and Legends. The new Cridi were about evenly split so far on whether or not they liked the concept of the game, but all agreed it helped to pass the time. Cridi video screens weren't sophisticated enough to produce the quality of holographic images Carialle projected, so they didn't see the same charm in it as the travelers aboard the CK-963. All the Cridi loved her three-D puzzles, which did translate reasonably well.

Carialle also shared the extensive onboard collection of entertainment tapes. Because of the language barrier, she gave them mostly music. The Cridi adored symphonies, folk music, stage musicals, operetta, plainchant, and whatever else she could winkle out of the nooks and crannies of her memory. During one communication period they sang an improvised cantata in the human fashion for her. The shrill quality of their voices sent Keff to his knees with his hands over his ears, but Carialle was touched.

"Only a little in return for all your kindness," Big Eyes had said. "With your help, we are learning not to be afraid of the journey—though all of us wonder what we will find at the end."

Since the Cridi ship ran easily using the remote control manipulation of Core amulets, the crew was able to pursue many activities in the long, empty stretches of space. Narrow Leg had set up a process to manufacture more travel globes. He used the ones Tall Eyebrow had lent them to explore the fifth planet as models, and now the native Cridi had a supply of their own, with plenty of backup units. Tall Eyebrow insisted that part of each day be devoted to learning to use the clear shells, and part for an exercise program to build up the muscles needed to manipulate them easily on a variety of terrains. Though he was aboard the brainship, he monitored exercise periods in both groups of Cridi. He was showing the kind of leadership that had impressed Keff back on the griffins' outpost.

There had been a certain amount of bickering before they'd left the fifth planet over who would travel in which ship. Keff invited any of the Cridi to fly with him and Carialle who wished to, and inadvertently started a three-tongued argument. Narrow Leg insisted that there was room in his ship for all the Cridi. Tall Eyebrow claimed pride of place with the Central Worlds pair. Big Eyes wanted to travel with Tall Eyebrow. Narrow Leg demanded that his daughter stay with him. Big Voice couldn't decide which one he wanted to travel on, and demanded a vote of confidence. They appealed to Keff to mediate. While on the surface, all Keff's statements had to pass through Tall Eyebrow's globe-pickup. From there, they were translated into the subtleties of the spoken language over the amulet link to the Cridi, and through sign language to Small Spot and Long Hand. It was a lengthy process, sometimes frustrating, sometimes amusing. In the end, Keff had excused himself and let the Cridi battle it out among themselves.

The brainship wound up with only four guests: the original Ozran contingent, plus Big Eyes, who shared the second spare bunk with Long Hand. Narrow Leg wasn't happy having his daughter miles away across the cold void, but he had plenty of responsibilities to keep him occupied. This morning, Keff could see the Cridi commander over the shoulder of one of the crew who was plastered to a viewscreen. Narrow Leg was having one of his daily arguments with Big Voice, this time over the travel globes. The stout councillor stood, arms folded, in the bottom half of his globe. He was up to his knees in water, but still trying to maintain his dignity.

"Why do we do without our amulets?" Big Voice said, in sign and squeak. "I do not like these bubbles. Why must we learn to use them? Technology is so far beyond this already!" Tall Eyebrow automatically turned to translate for Keff in Standard voice and Ozranian sign. Keff sat down, keeping one eye on the screen and one eye on TE. He understood most of this argument. It was an old one.

"Because the ammonia in the atmosphere could burn your skin, and there's not enough oxygen to sustain you, and you may have other things to think of there than breathing," Narrow Leg said, every gesture filled with impatience. "Because the engines of our host ships have only so much energy, most of which must be saved to launch us back home, not to be used by the Core. I have told you before. And again."

Tall Eyebrow relayed the answer, and added, "He does not like discomfort. I would give him a mild sample touch of the gas, to show him what he will not believe."

"It would sting," Keff said, "but you could be right. Prove one point, and he might begin to take your word on others."

"I will suggest it to Narrow Leg when we can speak alone," Tall Eyebrow said. "But I have another notion. Big Voice," he called, interrupting the argument. The councillor used a flick of power to swivel, and stood facing him.

"What?" The impatient question came through loud and clear over both Core frequency and speaker.

"You do not have to learn to use the globe," Tall Eyebrow said, standing up and stretching to the maximum of his great height.

"I do not?" Big Voice asked, with a shrill squeak that went up almost above human hearing.

"Not at all," the Ozranian leader said. "You shall gather information for us. You shall remain safe in the ship at all times while the rest of us make our exploration. We will report back to you what we find."

Big Voice stared and spluttered. "That is not correct! Think of my position. I am a high official of the conclave! I should be in the first rank."

Tall Eyebrow shrugged his thin shoulders, a gesture borrowed from Keff. "If you cannot use a globe, you cannot proceed us. The atmosphere is undoubtedly too dangerous. We would not put you in peril of your life. You are, as you say, a high official."

The councillor's eyes narrowed.

"I shall practice," Big Voice said. He glanced at Narrow Leg, whose eyes were wide with amusement. "But only so I may take my rightful place."

Casually, not hurrying at all, Big Voice twisted his hand and curled his fingers. The upper half of his globe lifted, inverted, and fitted itself onto the lower half. Big Voice crouched inside it and resolutely placed his hands on the inside wall. Narrow Leg retreated a few steps as the councillor drove his globe directly at him, heading out into the corridor and away from the video screen.

Tall Eyebrow turned away, chuckling, and rejoined the others. "Every step of the way he fights," he said. "He makes me earn my place."

"You do very well," Keff told him. "I think you're quite a leader. I'd be proud to follow you myself."

Carialle's deep, musical laugh filled the room, and Keff glanced over at her image on the wall. "You should hear him. He's cursing to himself that TE might make him miss out on any of the adventure. In between grunts, that is."

"I am afraid," Big Eyes said, and made a gesture of shame. "I was all excited for adventure; now, prudence."

"It is wise to be afraid, but do not let it paralyze you," Tall Eyebrow signed firmly. He put an arm around her. "You have a healthy body and sharp wits, and the strength of the Core is ours. I may not be a military leader, but I can at least show you how to survive. In terrible conditions we manufactured the globes with which your cousins survive on Sky Clear. You have done that, too. You can learn more. Together we can do better. We can prosper." The young female looked hopeful, encouraging the male to smile. "You teach me more verbal language, I tell you of survival. We exchange as we go."

"Bravo, TE," Carialle whispered over the mastoid implant to Keff.

Big Eyes was obviously impressed, by the way she gazed at Tall Eyebrow—and other Cridi were listening. They were nodding wisely to one another; clearly they found encouragement in the Ozranian leader's words.

"I hope you teach me more than that," the female said at last, with a coy look up under her eyelids. Tall Eyebrow looked pleased and a little flustered.

"They don't need us at all," Keff murmured.

In spite of the discomfort of diminished privacy, Keff found the enforced closeness provided him with wonderful opportunities to observe unique sociological interaction. Once the Cridi began to relax, they reverted to their normal personalities.

Tall Eyebrow and the other two Ozranians were also affected by the lack of privacy. TE seemed torn between his desire to spend every waking moment with Big Eyes, and his need to get away by himself for a while.

"It is too crowded," he had said wistfully to Keff in an unguarded moment. Keff sympathized.

Wisely, the young female perceived that not everyone had grown up in a household crowded with dozens

of children and other relatives, and left TE several
times a day to do other things. She made friends with
Long Hand, too. From the occasional eavesdrop, Keff
discovered that Big Eyes was asking about life on
Ozran. The facts were hard for someone brought up
amid plenty and water, but to her credit, the Cridi
councillor didn't blanch. She and the elder female also
had numerous close conversations in the corner of the
large cabin, glancing at the screens showing the Cridi
in the other ship and giggling behind their palms. Big
Eyes seemed to enjoy Long Hand's sardonic sense of
humor.

Some funny moments were universally shared. Big
Voice had appointed himself Communications Officer.
He solicited messages every day from both ships, and
spent about an hour broadcasting back towards Cridi.
The transmissions were more amusing than useful.
Carialle brought in the frequency so she and Keff could
enjoy the pompous administrator practicing self-aggran-
dizement before the video pickup. Tall Eyebrow and
the others watched with interest the first two days.
Thereafter they turned off the sound and made rude
signs among themselves. Big Voice's tenth transmission
made especially good comedy.

"Further advancement has been made. I have observed
constellations as mapped by our ancestors in their star
charts. I am pleased to let the Council and the con-
stituency of Cridi know that those charts are accurate!"

"Oh, no!" Big Eyes signed merrily, waving her hands
at the 3-D image. "Get away."

"I am pleased that he has allowed the poor navigators to trust those maps that have been in place for a
thousand years," Long Hand gestured, with a sly look
in her eyes.

"Important message from our ship commander,
Narrow Leg," Big Voice continued, picking up a minute
square of white. "We have approached and passed

halfway point of journey, and expect to arrive at our destination soon. This is confirmed by our human companions, Keff and Carialle"—he made the sign of the 'Watcher Within the Walls'—"We are grateful for their input, since they confirm what it is that we learn."

"That's not exactly what you said," Keff said to Carialle. "You told Narrow Leg where we are, and he checked it." Her frog image on the wall made much the same throwing-away gesture that Big Eyes had.

"Let him tell their press whatever he wants," she said. "If it will help public relations, I don't care what he says. Do you think any of them kept listening past the first five minutes?"

"I doubt it," Keff said, sitting down with a thump on the bench of his Rotoflex exercise machine at a good remove from Big Voice's screen. "I don't know why Narrow Leg lets him blather on like that."

The commander, whose face was visible on the screen nearest Keff's bench, must have heard his last remark.

"It serves to unite," the old one said, his wrinkled, pistachio-colored face creasing in a friendly grimace. "It does him no harm, because others have too much tact to tell him he is silly."

"Aren't you afraid all that nonsense will begin to pall? You don't want the folks back home to lose interest in what you're doing because he"—Keff tilted his head toward the main screen—"bores them to death."

Narrow Leg shook his head. "He is too shrewd to allow himself to be boring. And he is not. Every day he finds a new way to make himself ridiculous. It does not matter what the media say, so long as they say something with one's name in it. That is what Big Voice thinks. Most importantly, it keeps our minds off what we are doing. If allowed to brood, I think my folk would go mad. That is why I like your games and puzzles and lessons."

"Thank you," Carialle said. "I wish you'd say that to our administration. They think we are already mad for playing games on long flights."

"I shall," the old one said, with a courtly nod, "at the first available opportunity. How is our progress?"

"Very good," Carialle said. "I was right that the gravity well between the twin systems would destroy the ion trail where it passed closest, but now that we're past it, I'm seeing plenty. I'm also getting traces of low-power radio transmissions from the twin system."

The old one cocked his head to one side and looked pleased. "The fourth planet, yes?"

"Yes. With your people's extensive history of space travel I'm surprised you never explored in the system closest to your own, in spite of the gravity well."

"We did," Narrow Leg said, the pixels in his image updating in waves as he swiveled toward his own computer. "We knew of civilization. Our explorers had images of artifacts, buildings—perhaps houses. Large. See here, now." He waved a hand, and the image that was in front of him superimposed itself on the communication screen between him and Keff. In the Cridi format the view was hard to make out, but on the sides of a rocky, steep gorge, the brawn could make out structures that were clearly artificial.

"Well, I'll be damned," he said, his eyebrows creeping upward into his hairline. "Then why didn't your people ever land there?"

"Already inhabited," the Cridi captain said simply, returning to the screen. "We wished planets for colonization, so we did not pay attention to ones with intelligent life. It was remiss of us," he added grimly. "We should have."

Carialle's frog image looked thoughtful. "Why didn't you make contact with them? They're your nearest neighbors."

Narrow Leg shook his head. "Crude. Too primitive.

We knew they were too far behind us to share civilization. Someday, we thought."

Keff snorted. "Well, it looks like they evolved in a hurry."

"If they're our pirates," Carialle said, warningly. "We might just be following the gang from base to base. Narrow Leg, I'd like to copy your data and send it with ours to the CenCom when we transmit next."

"My honor," the captain said, bowing.

"Just a moment!" Big Voice came up behind the commander. While the three of them had been chatting, the councillor had finished his daily tirade. Clearly he had overheard or overseen the last exchange. "I wish to send such a message to your Central Committee. Today!"

"You can't," Keff said, quickly. He glanced at Carialle's frog image, which spread its big mouth in dismay. He knew they shared the same thought. They didn't want to alert the CenCom just yet that they were flying a joint mission with the Cridi. They had already disobeyed a direct order to return. The next time they made contact with CW there'd be a hue and cry out after them, so they'd better have the proof they needed in hand.

Big Voice looked upset. "Why not? You have communication frequencies as we do."

Carialle's frog image suddenly filled the screens. "Honored councillor," she said, waiting while the IT program filtered her Standard speech into Cridi voice-language, "it would confuse matters for our diplomats. Keff and I are the only members of the Central Worlds with a working knowledge of your language. There is no translator in the CenCom who would be able to appreciate your most important words."

"Ah, I see," Big Voice said, leaning back with his long, spidery hands propped proudly on his chest. "Naturally not. I must wait until I may see them face-to-face—which I hope will not be long."

"No," Keff said. "It'll be as soon as we can make it."

Big Voice left, looking very satisfied.

"Well handled," Narrow Leg signed to them, with very small motions obscured from the rest of the room.

Carialle's hand signs were equally discreet. "We have our bores, too."

A soft sound woke Keff in his cabin. He opened his eyes to the darkness.

"Yes? Who's there?"

"Keff?" Carialle's voice came very softly from his aural implant. "Come on forward. I'm getting clearer transmissions from Planet Four. I think you want to hear these."

Keff pulled on a pair of exercise pants and padded out into the cabin. A soft hum, the sound of the frogs breathing, came from behind the closed room across the corridor. Carialle illuminated a faint line of blue along the wall to guide him. He slid into his chair.

"We just came into range where I could pick up those faint radio signals intact. I think it's telephone conversations, words and pictures."

"Really?" Keff asked, interested enough to wake up almost all the way. "And are they the griffins?"

"See for yourself."

"Paydirt!" Keff exclaimed in an excited hiss. He glanced over his shoulder to see if the Cridi had heard him. He turned back for another good look.

In the tank in front of him, a long, narrow image took shape. The being pictured was indeed a griffin. It was younger and slighter than any of the brutes the team had left behind in the Cridi system. It put the tips of its wing-claws together under its chin in a sort of namaste, then let the wings flip around to its back.

"Freihur," it said, the slit upper lip opening and closing breathily. "Solahiaforn. Zsihivonachaella." A burst of static broke up the picture, and it reformed around the speaker saying, ". . . Volpachur."

"You're right," Keff said. "It does sound like half a telephone conversation. I'm surprised you haven't picked up any mass communication channels."

"Maybe they don't have any," Carialle said. "But isn't this better?"

"A thousand times," Keff said, feeling for the keypad to activate IT. The server controlling the translation program beeped softly to tell him it was operating. "I might be able to separate out some appropriate phrases between now and our arrival. Starting with 'hello,' if that's what that first word meant. 'Freihur,'" he said, trying it out with a trill of his tongue. "How close are we?"

"About five days," Carialle said. " . . . Keff, I feel uneasy."

He felt a twinge of anxiety for her, and gazed at her pillar as if it might give him some clue how to help her. "I know how much of a strain this is on you, personally. You know I'm for you, all the way. I simply don't know how much I can help, if we run into—into anybody."

Carialle sighed. "I don't know how *I'll* react. But thank you for your support. This is the best way to lay my personal demons."

"You're right," Keff said, settling himself more comfortably in front of the screen. "And with this I now stand a better chance of cooperation. This is what I was wishing for after the Cridi froze those griffins. How bad is the gain? Can you get me some more?"

"Cued up and waiting for you, Sir Knight," Carialle said, feeling better in the face of Keff's enthusiasm.

At the beginning of day shift, Carialle watched the Cridi on the other ship reacting with surprise to seeing Keff already up before them. Narrow Leg immediately intuited that something important was afoot.

"What is new?" he asked, in Standard, making his way to the screen nearest the console.

"Good morning, captain," Keff said, still staring at the griffin on the screen, a delicate, sable-furred one with a chip on its front left fang. He swiveled toward the screen. "Language lessons."

"The beasts!" Narrow Leg exclaimed, his hands flying.

"We're close enough to pick up their low-power transmissions," Carialle said, forwarding receiver data to the Cridi technical operator. "I think it's a tower-based, amplitude-modulated system."

"Indeed? The monsters have come far," the Cridi captain said. "No electronics were reported many years past."

"How long?" Keff asked. "My own species went from wood stoves to satellite technology in the same generation."

The Cridi opened his large mouth wide, then closed it. "I have forgotten that progress moves tenfold, and tenfold again. It is long since my people discovered non-motor engines."

"Mine, too," Keff said. "It looks like these people made their leap much more recently."

"Have done so without morals," the Cridi said, almost dismissively. "We shall have much to say to them on that subject."

Keff held up his hands. "Slow down a little, Narrow Leg. I've barely learned how to say 'Greetings,' in their language. It is going to take time."

"We shall help you," Narrow Leg said, resolutely. "It is better to work on a project that will advance our understanding than spend time playing puzzles." He shot an impatient glance at his crew, who were now involved in an interactive game with the brainship.

"I'll take care of that," Carialle said cheerfully. She reached into her peripherals for her game function and clicked it off. Screens all over the Cridi ship went blank, and she heard outraged peeps. Disappointed crew members, suddenly noticing that their captain's eye was upon them, immediately tried to look busy.

"I'll tight-beam them all the linguistic data we have so far," she said.

"Think of it as a new kind of game," Keff said, more lightly than he felt. "We're stalking the wild syntax in its lair."

"No. It is rather another weapon in our hand," the Cridi captain said. "This is the confirmation we have sought, after all: that the marauders are here. That is where retribution begins."

"No!" Carialle interrupted him, with a touch of alarm. "Captain, we are investigating this system to gather information, not start an interstellar war. We're not armed."

"No, you are not, but we are."

"With respect, Captain, we must—and will—stand between you and the griffins if you start a conflict."

"Even though yours have also died at their hands." The old male made it a statement instead of a question.

Keff gulped, the memory of the dead on the asteroid clear in his mind. "That only makes what we have to do that much harder, Narrow Leg. That is the unhappy part of diplomacy."

"In the end such an outcome can only be a tragedy," Narrow Leg said, with a sudden expression of sympathy. "I shall not be the one to sacrifice our friendship. We will help you."

The radio transmissions from the griffin homeworld were primitive and infrequent, but as the two ships neared it, Carialle had no trouble capturing and translating the broadcasts into pictures and sound.

The files they'd gotten from the pirate base computer were put to one side. To Keff and IT those had been no help at all. The overlay of narration in musical horn-call on the astrogation file was unreliable as a point of comparison between the two languages. Where Central Worlds had long commentary on a particular system, there might be a single phrase or two of description in griffin. On a star-chart dismissed by the CW astrogators in four sentences as unimportant, Keff listened to a three-minute horn solo that sounded beautiful, but meant nothing to IT. He couldn't separate the language into words. Here and there, a word in the griffin speech sounded like the CW name for a system: "Farkash," for "Barkus," and so on. The difference was due to the griffin facial physiognomy. Keff wondered what had happened to the human computer operator who had told them how to use the system and pronounced some of the names for them.

In the live transmissions from the planet, Keff saw the creatures speaking in colloquial dialect. After several hours of listening to tape after tape, he was delighted to begin to discern patterns. Each of the messages began with the same word or words of greeting: "Freihur." Keff had his "hello."

"This is my Rosetta stone," he told Tall Eyebrow, with a flourish. "This is the way we can begin to understand the language."

The Frog Prince's eyes shone. He and Big Eyes sat with Keff while he was trying to make some sense out of the griffin tapes during that first day. They imitated the phrases they heard, only two or three octaves higher, flutes playing alongside trombones and trumpets. Keff thought they had reasonably good ears, but it was only music to them. They still lacked any concept of meaning. The Cridi were better at concrete, spatial concepts, rather than abstract, but they retained perfectly what he told them. IT began to pick out sentence patterns, even separating word roots where they were repeated in different combinations. Carialle now had thousands of "telephone conversations" from which Keff could work. He was steadily gleaning vocabulary, where the caller occasionally showed an object to his or her callee. None of it was much help; he doubted he'd have occasion to refer to plants, babies, mixing bowls, or necklaces in a diplomatic conversation, but the use of noun and pronoun patterns was useful. Some of the extra memory that the CW had thoughtfully provided Carialle for the diplomatic mission was coming in very handy. They'd have to see what they could do about keeping it when they returned to base.

Keff stayed at the console, still working on the language question when the Cridi went off for baths and bed. He half-listened to the excited chirps of conversation coming from the spare cabin as the frogs discussed the day's discovery. Soon, the noise died away, and he glimpsed the light go out just before the cabin door slid shut.

He was concerned about what he would find when they made orbit, or landed on the griffin homeworld. Would they have to run for their lives? Were they blundering blindly into a trap? And how would the Cridi react? It would be the end of his and Carialle's careers if they deliberately put the elements together for an interstellar conflict.

And he was concerned about Carialle's state of mind. Their duties as hosts and teachers had taken up much of the personal time they usually spent together. For the first time in years he couldn't guess what she was thinking.

Her determination to pursue the hunt had led her to concentrate most of her attention on it. Her theory that the griffin ship was transiting frequently between the Cridi system and the one next door was borne out by the discovery of the wispy threads of many ion trails. They were delicate, hard to see, and remarkably easy to overshoot. Carialle did a lot of backtracking when the thin traces broke and drifted away where they'd been disturbed by anomalies such as ion storms or comets. Picking up the aud/vid broadcasts and confirming that they were heading for the griffin stronghold should have made her relax, but she seemed more concentrated than ever. Multiplexing astrogation, running the ship, playing M&L with the Cridi, maintaining lines of communication and acting as data librarian pulled her attention in a dozen directions at once. Keff worried that in the midst of it all she was thinking too hard about what lay ahead. What if this turned out to be another dry hole in her search for the beings that once threatened her life and sanity? Where would they go next? The team was risking censure and worse by CenCom, and Maxwell-Corey in particular, by ignoring their orders, and yet they couldn't stay off-line forever. Sooner or later they had to communicate, no matter what that brought in return. True, circumstances had changed a routine mission into an emergency, but would the IG see it that way? M-C already doubted the soundness of Carialle's emotions, enough to jeopardize his own position by rigging her with a telltale missile.

Keff felt his face grow hot, and realized he was still just as mad about M-C's impossible gall as he had been when the message probe had launched. He stood up from the console, commanding IT to save his last hour's progress. Then, he plunked himself down on his exercise bench and started pulling on the weight bars until he began to breathe in rhythm. Soon, the resentment was driven out by the simple beat of the weights clapping together. The tension melted away, replaced by the honest warmth of a good workout. Eyes closed, he smiled at the ceiling.

"Penny for them," Carialle's voice said.

He opened his eyes, but continued to haul on the

pulleys. "I was just thinking we haven't talked in a long time. Just the two of us."

"I've been missing that, too," she said, regretfully. "It takes a lot out of a girl, playing hostess nonstop."

"Same here," Keff said, giving one last massive flex of his shoulders that took all the tension out of the part of his back between the scapulae, and let the weights down gently. "Just now I'm tempted to agree with the IG's assessment that we're nuts."

"Still doubt we're doing the right thing?"

"I wonder," Keff said. He stood up and reached for a towel slung over the back of the Rotoflex. "These people trust us enough to accompany them into the great unknown on their very first spaceflight, with their very first working ship after being grounded for fifty years. So many things could go wrong!"

"But they haven't, Sir Keff," Carialle said, manifesting her Lady Fair image on the wall. It was outlined in white. Keff smiled at her, feeling as if he was meeting an old and beloved friend again after a long, lonely separation. It occurred to him, with characteristic wry humor that it had been a long time since he'd seen a flesh-and-blood woman, either. Time enough for that at mission's end. "Don't overanticipate, my dear friend. I'm not, I promise you. Don't worry about specifics. Just keep on your toes."

"Stand and deliver!" a man's baritone voice barked from beside him. Keff jumped to one side, putting the weight bench between himself and the rude looking villain in a tunic standing in a torchlit doorway. The man was leveling a fearsome sword at his throat. Keff grinned ferociously and edged toward his laser epee, slung handily across the back of one of the crash couches. He realized Carialle had created the aural effect by activating only his left ear implant. The villain paced him with his swordpoint, his black brows lowered over narrow eyes.

"Clever, lady," Keff said. With a quick lift and slide, he unsheathed his sword, and assumed the *en garde* position.

"Put 'em up," she said, in the enemy's deep voice. "We both need a good game, just you and me."

"Right," Keff said, tipping the glowing red point of his blade toward the man's face, and circling it slowly. "Shall we duel with, or without conversation?"

"Oh, with," Carialle said, making the man's image grin ferally. "With, of course."

Chapter 13

The audio channels were full of excited chirping as Carialle and the Cridi ship shifted into orbit over the griffin homeworld.

"We are here!" Tall Eyebrow exclaimed with delight from the crash couch where he was strapped in with Big Eyes. "We have succeeded in reaching this place, all together and with no mishap."

Keff watched as on-screen the clouds parted gently beneath them to reveal a vast and mountainous continent, wedge-shaped, strung from north to south like a harp with silver rivers. On the horizon ahead, a small silver moon rose. Carialle hurtled onward until it passed overhead, and set behind them. A second, larger moon followed, and vanished in turn. A blue ocean swam up, flashed green islands at them, and was replaced by another continent, long and narrow, also mountainous. Keff could see lines of smoke from active volcanoes. Another ocean glided by, this one wider than the first, then the harp reappeared, much closer and larger. Cities showed up in the folds of the mountains, very near the peaks. On extreme magnification, Carialle saw small craft flying, then realized she was seeing griffins on the wing. She showed Keff and the Cridi, who cheeped and peeped over the marvel.

Keff, listening as Carialle monitored active broadcast frequencies for a homing signal, caught Big Voice giving a live play-by-play of the new planet for the benefit of listeners on his homeworld.

"Eleven to the sixth power inhabitants, five oceans, two major continents, but many archipelagoes. Signs are humidity equals point-one atmosphere," Big Voice stated, with great emphasis on the statistics. "It will be uncomfortably dry and hot, but the landing party is prepared for eventualities."

Keff grinned and turned to catch the eyes of the Cridi flying with him.

"Always," Big Eyes said, exasperation evident on her small face. She waved her hands in derisive gesture.

Long Hand watched Carialle's telemetry indicators. "So dry," she said. "It is like Ozran. Some in the other ship will never have experienced such conditions."

"Well, you'll be in water globes," Keff said. "That is, after I make contact and establish parley conditions. I don't want you appearing until I'm sure no one is going to attack us."

"Huh," Small Spot grunted, and raised his hand to show the gleaming finger stalls. "I do not fear. We have the Cores."

"Don't manifest anything that looks like a threat," Keff said.

Tall Eyebrow was studying the astrogation tank carefully, measuring the distance between the two stars that they had just crossed.

"So close. It is a great pity," he said. "These people could have been friends of Cridi and Ozran."

"They still could be," Keff reminded him. "Try to keep an open mind. It may be a fringe group of criminals who've been robbing spaceships. If the government promises to punish the pirates, you could still establish friendly relations—form a Mythological Federation of Planets."

"If they themselves are not involved," Tall Eyebrow said, his small face thoughtful.

The ship rounded the planet twice more at high altitude before beginning to drop. The harp separated into successive bands of tan and blue.

"I've pinpointed the largest population centers," Carialle said, illuminating the planetary map, "but in spite of Keff's suggestions I don't want to land right in the thick of things. Some nice suburban location . . . X marks the spot. I think I detected a flat place I can land."

A blue dot began to glow on the chart about fifty kilometers outside one of the large cities. Narrow Leg's navigator glanced up from her console at the screen nearest him, and nodded to Keff. "Defenses are in place. Yours, too."

"Right," Keff said, taking a deep breath. "Down we go."

Narrow Leg's ship had dropped back to ride into the lower atmosphere on Carialle's tail. Watching her waveform monitor, she was pleased by the precision that the pilot showed, not getting too close and endangering them both, but staying just far enough back that the end of the elongated oval envelope just nipped his afterburners. You'd think he'd been doing it all his life. The hull sensors went off, indicating Carialle's skin temperature had risen to normal reentry temperatures. She checked the hull for leaks in either the skin plates or in the cooling pods underneath. All was well. The Cridi pilot signalled that he would stay in long orbit, and wished Carialle well.

"We will wait for word to come," he said in credible Standard.

"See you downstairs," Carialle said, as the Cridi braked, and sailed on above her head.

Her last, long approach was almost entirely over ocean. She descended very quickly, keeping her speed up until the last minute. She hadn't noticed any telemetry beacons, nor radar signals, as if there wasn't a single ear pointed toward space. Strange when you considered that these people were parasites, preying on the isolated Cridi, that they wouldn't be more cautious about invasion of their own airspace. If she'd had functioning saliva glands, she'd have spat.

"All well, Cari?" Keff asked.

"Yes," she said crisply, increasing visual magnification and turning it toward her chosen landing site. "Are you certain we shouldn't land in a covert location? It's possible. Unless that clunky communication system is concealing a much more sophisticated technology underneath, no one can see me."

"No," Keff said. He had prepared his environment suit and kit before strapping in for approach. The light, transparent gloves flapped loose at his wrists as he clutched the ends of his couch arms. "We're not going in to study them. We're entering as envoys of peace, I hope. If nothing else, this will put them on notice that we have observed their people's crimes, and demand cessation of hostilities. What can they do? Attack the entire CW?"

"It looks as if that was just what they have been doing," Carialle said softly. "One ship at a time. Be careful."

"As Big Voice and the other Cridi are always reminding me, lady, we have the Cores. I'll be fine."

Unsatisfied, Carialle returned the greater part of her attention to what lay ahead. Gravity was approximately 1.2 times Standard. That meant those griffin wings had to lift just that much more and stay aloft in very windy skies. They were *strong*. Keff didn't have the advantage he'd had on the base, when they were all fighting that oppressive gravity. He would tire more quickly than they. Carialle maintained respect for the griffins' musculature, having studied the scans all the way from one star to the other. She was trying hard not to admire the fact their bodies, from about the shoulders back, looked like a Terran great cat, a species which she was fond of watching for its grace. And those claws and teeth!

Beneath her, the tiny islands flitted by. Volcanic in nature, they had been augmented in size by the growth of a calcifying organism like coral, but less acid sensitive. Her imagination and pattern recognition aptitude saw in the shapes of the most proximate four islets a dragonfly, a chick, an old-fashioned handbag, and a ketchup bottle. Vegetation on the islands was of the same gaudy colors as in the pirate base conservatory; not as vivid, but healthier. That heavy-ammonia atmosphere must not have been good for griffin-world plant life, either. The trace in this air was much, much lower, below half a percent. Keff could almost get along with just eyedrops and nose filters, but she insisted he wear a full envirosuit. She knew she was being too protective, like a mother running after her child with overshoes. Keff meant so much to her she felt an unhealthy twinge of fear at the thought that the griffins might be able to get past the Cridi's impressive shield and harm him. Quickly, she purged toxins from her internal system, and allowed a dose of serotonin and stimulants to enter her bloodstream. She felt better at once. Keff wasn't a child. He had had plenty of experience in worse situations than this. He always sounded as if he was about to do something rash, but he also possessed a healthy sense of self-preservation.

Carialle passed over the sandy coast, parting the treeoids in her wake. She was low enough now that the fliers had noticed her, and some winged to catch up. With a burst of speed for which she immediately chided herself as arrogant, she lost them over the first mountain range. There she noticed broadcast towers, of a design that hadn't been used by the Central Worlds in a thousand years or more.

"Do you see that, Keff?" she asked. She froze the image, and was ten kilometers past it by the time he responded.

"Antiquities," he said, leaning forward against the straps over his chest. "Are they still using those?"

"My monitors say that's where the broadcasts were coming from."

"Whew!" Keff said.

Trimming slightly to follow the contour of the land, she dipped into a valley and up over the next, higher, mountain range. On the other side she found the first flat terrain. Even in the cultivated fields there were traces of the acid rainbow colors. She looked forward to finding out what those bright red grains were.

"Crops look healthy, but there's very little heavy cover," she said. The Cridi were wide-eyed. She manifested her frog image near Big Eyes.

"Enjoying yourself?" she asked.

"Yes!" the Cridi squeaked, grinning in the human fashion. Clutching Tall Eyebrow with one arm, she signed with the other hand. "A new landscape, the first! Videos of original landings and colonies do not compare to own eyes!"

In the other ship Carialle could see the entire crew glued to the 3-D tanks. She was glad they felt the way she and Keff did about exploration. The Cridi would be a wonderful addition to Central Worlds. When M-C finally allowed the documents to be signed, that was.

"Look, that's a spaceport," Keff said, picking out a distant feature on the horizon after they cleared the next mountain ridge. He peered at the spiky growths poking up from the flat plain on the terrain map. "That is a spaceport, isn't it? Yes! Look, you can fit right in! Just land there."

"I intended to," Carialle said, impatiently, as she was already dumping velocity. She extended visuals to extreme magnification, trying to discern the landing pads, and find herself an empty slot to set down.

"What a collection of derelicts!" she exclaimed in dismay. "I'm never going to pass for one of *those*. I refuse to try. I do have my pride."

Keff leaned up to peer at the screen and signalled for more magnification. Carialle flung up the image she was viewing. The tiny irregular shapes on the cabin screen suddenly took focus.

"Great stars, you're right," Keff exclaimed, looking as if he didn't know whether to laugh or not. "Those look like they've been cobbled together by committees of people who'd once heard a rumor of a story about a spaceship."

"I have no idea how one of those would fly," Carialle said, "but hit me with a hammer if I ever let their ground crew do maintenance on me."

The field reminded them of the scatter of ship remains on the airless asteroid at the edge of the Cridi system. The three craft that stood on the landing pads had been put together with no practical knowledge of the working details. Exhaust vents were ducted to the outside where they would cause the craft to spin in frictionless space. Fuel tanks were exposed, and in one case, the single hatch hung open to show a control room unprotected by anything so pedestrian as an airlock. And yet two of the ships showed clear signs of having launched and returned safely at least once.

"My internal scans show no shielding in half the bulkheads," Carialle said. "The crew must be suffering from fierce radiation poisoning. If they lived."

"These people are suicidal," Keff said flatly. "Or perhaps they're kamikaze pilots, who refuse to be captured alive."

Carialle was silent a long time while she studied the ships. "I think it's buck ignorance," she said at last. "All the pieces necessary are there, but the instructions for assembling them were in a non-native language, so they did the best that they could."

"Like the pedalcycle I had as a boy," Keff said. "No safety backups at all, but it ran."

"Yes, and that's curious, because the ships that were chasing us had full shields."

Someone must have passed the word that Carialle was on her way. By the time she had tipped up and was beginning her descent, the field and the sky above it was full of griffins. Some of them fluttered gracefully to the ground at a respectful distance, but Carialle counted over a hundred in the air alone, with more in sight in the distance. Their followers were catching them up.

"Are they armed, Cari?" Keff asked, surveying the scene with a wary eye.

"Not with anything that carries a heat signature," she said. "Good heavens, but they're big beasts."

"Those teeth!" Tall Eyebrow signed, a-goggle at the screen.

Carialle stepped down magnification to her more immediate location, and settled neatly toward the landing pad between the taller of the two jalopy spaceships. Measuring her thrust to the minim, Carialle brought her tail to the ground just as her engines shut off.

"Swank," Keff said, grinning. "You look like a candle on a minefield, lady love."

"I intend to outclass the competition right from the start," she said. "All psychological advantage we can gain will be to our benefit, if we ever get to a point where we can negotiate."

"I'm ready," Keff said. "Listen: 'Freihur, co nafri da an colaro, yaro.'" The IT unit on his chest recited in Standard, "Greetings, leader you me take go, please."

"That's fine, if that's what those words mean," Carialle said, skeptically. "Trying to guess from context, it still could mean, 'Greetings, your sister sells rugs in a zoo.'"

Keff didn't bother to defend the honor of his translation program.

"We'll find out," he said, pointing at the short-range screen. "Here come the authorities."

On the field, a white-sided gurney like a medieval siege tower, rolled toward Carialle. The half dozen griffins operating it moved in jerking haste, showing their excitement. An enclosed tunnel with soft bumpers extended and clamped against Carialle's side.

"Ah, so that *was* their design on the remote base," Carialle said. "I'm glad to see they don't steal *everything*."

"Easy, Cari. It's showtime," Keff said.

He stood up and sealed his suit, waiting for the faint hiss as each edge met. With the same care, he put on his helmet, then fastened his gloves. A secure seal. He breathed deeply of the slightly plasticky-tasting air, setting the air-recirculators going. There would be no more sudden breaths of ammonia. He felt excitement warring with nerves in his belly, and told both emotions to quiet down. Another world, another life form on which he would be the first human to step! What an opportunity! It was another notch in his belt, although, technically, Carialle had set foot on the planet first. He pretended to grimace, but he couldn't concentrate on being upset. What would happen to him when he stepped outside the airlock? He wasn't afraid to go, but by the stars, he was wary. On the external screen he could see the crowd of griffins gathered on the landing field. As he was checking his heads-up display, he felt something bump into the back of his legs. He jumped half a meter and spun around in midair.

"What are you doing?" he asked. In the few moments he had his back turned, the four Cridi had climbed into their travel globes, and they were clustered around his feet.

"We are coming with you," Tall Eyebrow signed, rolling back a foot or two so he could look up at Keff's face.

"Oh, no, you're not," Keff said, accompanying his words with firm gestures. "This could be dangerous. Please stay in here and cover me with your amulets. I'm counting on you."

"We would share your peril," Tall Eyebrow said earnestly.

"They tried to kill all of us on that base," Keff pointed out, signalling in exasperation. "Me, they just allowed one of their number to stalk. They went blind mad when they saw *you*."

"They know something of Cridi," Long Hand signed, "having killed three ships with Cridi defenses. It cannot have been easy."

"I do not know why they hate us, since we never did them harm," Big Eyes gestured, her wide mouth pressed into a thin line. "Never in our history have we seen these creatures. We should resent them, but we do not. We only wish to ask why. It is the honor of all Cridi." She added mischievously, "Big Voice would have said so."

"Big Voice wouldn't be diving straight out into their midst! Give me a chance to get this on a friendly footing, then we'll ask them," Keff said, pleadingly. The Cridi conferred for a moment, exchanging signals with the screen on the wall on which Narrow Leg's face appeared.

"Very well," Tall Eyebrow said, turning back to Keff. "We wait."

"Thank you," Keff said formally, with a low bow. He strode into the airlock, and heard the door slide shut and felt the slight drag on his shoulders as Carialle pressurized the cabin around him. His suit inflated slightly around his knees, crotch, elbows, and chest. He braced himself, legs well apart.

"Now, how's that go?" he said out loud. "Hello. Please take me to your leader. 'Freihur, co nafri da an colaro, yaro.'"

"Relax, you've done it a dozen times," Carialle reassured him. "Hold on, they're scanning me." Keff frowned up at the ceiling.

"They are? I didn't think they had anything as sophisticated as scanners."

"I didn't *say* they were sophisticated scanners. It feels like elephants are walking on my hull," Carialle grumbled. She paused, and Keff heard a low hiss beyond the airlock hatch. "Just a moment—if the race we're about to face is hostile, why are they pumping a 90/10 nitrox mix into the airlock?"

"They're *what*?" Keff demanded.

"I swear it by my sainted motherboard," Carialle said. "Look for yourself." The monitor beside him lit up with a specroanalysis of comparative atmospheres. "You'll find the air fragrant, too. Plenty of plant esters."

"Perfume?" Keff felt his jaw drop, and yanked it closed again. "I have to speak to them. Open up." He hurried forward, helmet almost bumping the inner hatch. The door slid partway open, then halted.

Carialle's usually crisp voice was almost tentative. "Be careful, Sir Knight. I'd always rather you return with your shield, than on it."

"So would I, Lady Fair," he said, cheerfully, his voice echoing in his helmet. "But in this case I've got better armor than any dragon. Alert the Cridi to rev up their Core power, and let me go."

The airlock slid open onto a wide flexible tube filled with griffins as far as Keff could see. With one hand flat over his pounding heart, he bowed deeply to them. Two of the great beasts bustled forward, stopping about four paces away, and sat down on their haunches. The narrow clawed hands met under their squared chins in the same gesture of respect he'd seen in a thousand beamed conversations, then the great wings spread as far as they could in the confined space. Then, they waited.

Keff stepped forward, and copied their moves as nearly as he could. "'Freihur, co nafri da an colaro, yaro,'" he said.

"In good time, in good time," the lead griffin said, its upper lip splitting to show the gleaming white fangs beneath. "You are most welcome. Are you in need of refueling? Supplies?"

"Uh . . . no," Keff said, gawking at the being. "Welcome?" His hands were seized and shaken by all the griffins who could reach him. Wings, claws, and faces flashed by him in a blur. "Carialle, did they . . . did they . . . ?"

" . . . speak Standard?" Carialle finished his question. "They sure did. With a respectable accent, too. How in the black hole did they learn it? When? Who from?"

"I don't know! How . . . ?"

"We are so glad to see you, great human," the second griffin said, offering another namaste. "This is a great honor. Never before has one of yours landed in our place."

"Where do they usually land?" Keff asked automatically, struggling to make sense of the situation. "Humans! You know other humans! How? Why—when?" His mental drives were overloaded with the new influx of knowledge. "I never saw any communications with humans in your transmissions." But his greeters did not have a chance to answer. A host of smaller griffins pushed past or sailed over the full-sized beasts, and clustered around him.

"Greetings!" they said, in flutelike voices. "Where do you come from?" "What is this for?"

"This doesn't sound like all the humans they've

encountered were captives," Carialle said, pitching her voice low to be heard. "It sounds perhaps as if they were . . . collaborators?"

"Don't jump to any conclusions, Cari."

"I won't, but it sounds pretty suspicious to me," she said.

Keff spoke over the head of the youngsters surrounding him to the adults beyond. "You know humans?"

The leader's lip split again. The expression was clearly the griffin version of a smile.

"Of course, sacred one. You are but testing me. I know of the Melange."

"Sacred ones?" Keff asked.

"The Melange?" Carialle asked, in Keff's ear. He waved a hand in front of the camera eye for silence so he could concentrate on what the lead griffin was saying. "*Who?* I have no entry for any such name in my database."

"What is Melange?" Keff asked. The leader gave him a puzzled glance that narrowed the center stripe in his large eyes.

"The Melange," the second one repeated, as if no explanation was really needed.

"But . . . ?"

"What are you called, human male-man?" one of the children demanded, tugging at his arm. When he looked down, it drew back, giggling at its own boldness.

"My name is Keff," he said, bending down to look into their faces. In spite of their size, and their weight, which must have been around fifty kilos each, they were like any children galaxy-wide: curious, friendly, bold and shy at the same time, and irresistibly cute. They romped around him on all fours.

"And what does 'Keff' describe?" asked another youngster, pushing in close. Its upper lip opened to show the nares, and it sniffed his hands and knees.

"Me," Keff said, tapping his chest. A couple of the children grabbed his hand with their wingclaws to examine his gauntlet. They exclaimed over the transparent material, running delicate talon-tips up and down his palm. "I, uh, Keff comes from Kefyn, an ancient name of my people."

"Poara, vno!" One of the youngsters had discovered the IT on Keff's chest, and pulled it down for a closer look.

"Uh, please don't touch that," Keff said, pulling his hands free and retaking possession of IT from the enthusiastic fledglings.

"Vidoro, eha," another child said, and giggled, creeping around behind Keff to feel his clear plastic suit. Keff prided himself on his physical prowess, but these children were effortlessly stronger than he. They butted into his knees, patted his waist and chest. Their affectionate, curious touches had the power of a body blow.

"Kids, please, enough," he said, holding up his hands as he felt for a wall to brace himself against. The floor bobbed up and down under his feet, and he grabbed for the edge of the airlock. One of the children rose up on hind legs to get a good look at the tubes running from the back of his helmet into his suit, and Keff overbalanced completely. Flailing for a handhold, he toppled toward the adults. The first griffin grabbed his arms in both of its strong claw hands and set him upright.

"Forgive, sir-madam," the creature said. "My child is bad-mannered."

"It's sir," Keff said. "He—she?—didn't mean any harm."

"Are you all right?" Carialle's voice erupted in his ear. "Your heart is running the three-minute mile."

"I'm fine, Cari," Keff assured her in an undertone. The children, restrained from physical contact by their parents, were bombarding him with questions.

"Do you wish food, human sir? Good food, at the canteen. Human coo-orn, human broccocoli, human meeeat. All good!"

"Uh, maybe later," Keff said. "Tell me about these humans."

"But, sir, *you* are a human."

"They are rather charming," Carialle said, "and I don't want to like them. Not yet."

"I know what you mean," Keff said. "If they're involved in piracy, they must be the most cold-blooded . . ."

"What did you say?" One of the youngsters pricked up its fluffy ears. Keff cursed. These beings must have very sharp hearing. "Who are you talking to?"

"To my friend," Keff said, tapping the IT unit. At least they couldn't hear Carialle. "I am asking her questions."

"Who is your friend?" "Can we meet her?" "Your ship is so pretty. Can I go in?" "Ask us questions. We know answers!"

"Excuse me," Keff said, holding up a forefinger to stem the flood, and addressed himself to the first adult. "What is your name, please?"

"I am Cloudy. My friends here are Shower and Moment." The first Griffin indicated the two nearest him. Others began to call out their names, and Keff decided to count on IT remembering them all for him.

"What do you call this beautiful world, Cloudy?" he asked.

"This is Thelerie, at the Center of all things, but you must know that, human sir."

Keff made the namaste, and saw it repeated by every griffin.

"I must assure you I do not know all that. I am pleased to be here. Cloudy, I am here for a most important reason."

The wide smile flashed again. "Ah, so I know. What commodities do you bring to us?"

"Uh, no commodities. I'm just visiting."

Carialle's voice was a siren in his ear canal. "I knew it, piracy! They trade in contraband!"

"Hush, Carialle!" Keff schooled his expression and waited, smiling.

The griffins looked puzzled, and some of the ones further back exchanged glances. "You are not of the Melange?"

"No," Keff said, firmly. "Who are they?"

"You are teasing us," Shower said, shaking its great head.

"How do you know humans?" Keff said, pressing. "How do you all speak Standard so well?"

They looked knowingly at him.

"You *are* teasing us," Cloudy said, his upper lip spreading again. "We did not know of humans to be so merry."

"They are friendly?" asked Tall Eyebrow, rolling out of the open airlock around Keff's feet, with Small Spot and Big Eyes immediately behind. The griffins looked down at the small globes. Tall Eyebrow looked up at them, wearing his best human-type smile. The curious, striped eyes widened.

"Slllaaayiiim!" the aliens shrieked. The large ones grabbed the small ones, and they backpedaled hastily away in the billowing tube. In moments, the long corridor was empty, and bobbing softly. Keff, thrown off his feet by the jouncing, listened to the shrieks outside on the surface as he climbed up again, using the airlock for a handhold, but his gauntlets scrabbled on smooth enamel. As soon as the corridor had broken open to atmosphere, Carialle had slammed the airlock shut.

"Well, that hasn't changed," Carialle said, into the silence. "Your ancestors must have fought hard, TE."

"This isn't the way to start a detente," Keff said severely, looking down at the Ozranian. His back and elbows hurt where he'd slipped against the side of the ship. "I wish you'd waited inside as I asked you. Now they'll probably call out the militia."

"We will protect you," Big Eyes said firmly, showing her fingerstalls.

Keff swallowed his exasperation. "Please wait here. Please." He held up a hand to forbid any of the Cridi to follow him, and threshed clumsily down the tube toward daylight. Two of the globes levitated and started after him, but he held up a warning hand. The plastic balls subsided to the cloth floor. The Cridi inside them sat down crosslegged in the water at the bottom.

"We wait," Tall Eyebrow said, disappointedly.

Lying flat on his belly Keff poked his head out of the end of the corridor. The landing field was deserted. He squinted up into the bright sky, quickly enough to see hundreds of winged shadows fleeing off in all directions.

"Damn," he said.

"At least they aren't calling out the guards," Carialle said in his ear. "No transmissions from this site, and no warm bodies headed in your direction. My, that's a long way down."

Keff glanced at the ground below him. In their haste, the griffins had shoved the gurney away from the ship. The only way down to the pavement was a drop of almost ten meters.

"Do you want me to open my ramp?" Carialle asked.

"No." Keff pulled himself back into the tube and waded back toward the globe-frogs. "I guess you four win, after all. I need an elevator ride to the ground floor."

To his credit, Tall Eyebrow tried not to look triumphant.

"We come with you?"

"Yes, but under conditions," Keff said. "One, you do what I tell you. Two, you stay out of sight until I think it's all right. Three—well, I'll decide on three if I have to. Agreed?"

The Cridi all nodded vigorously.

"This visiting of a new world is fun," Big Eyes said, her dark eyes shining.

"It is," Keff agreed, as they floated out into the sunshine on a wave of Core power. "The worst thing is that we're not the first humans to land here, Cari. After all this, somebody else gets the credit."

"Cheer up, Sir Keff," Carialle said. "We're in this one for another purpose this time."

"I just wish all our witnesses hadn't run away," Keff said. He forced himself to stare straight ahead and not look down as the four Cridi carried him toward the mountain city where most of the natives had fled.

Chapter 14

"Four heat traces inside that one," Carialle said, as Keff obligingly swept his sensors toward the nearest house on the edge of town.

The habitations of the griffins were a peculiar hodge-podge of modern and primitive architecture strewn throughout the ridges of the high mountain reaches. No one seemed to like to live in the valleys. All of the buildings were of stone; unsurprising in a landscape with few trees. Each house had been constructed with considerable physical labor, using handhewn blocks, and yet, on top of this building and the ones visible nearby were delicate metal antennae, the communications transmitters Carialle had detected from space. The houses were roofed and decorated with the local clay, colored blue and green with trace minerals Carialle identified as copper extractives.

"One thing you can say about them, they do land-scape nicely," Carialle commented, focusing on various details in the large yard. "Although the preponderance of rock gardens would get old fairly quickly."

"Pee-yew!" Keff said, as the globe frogs floated him over a pit. It was carefully bermed to prevent its strong stench from wafting toward the small blue house, so the only place for the stink to go was straight up, toward him. He gestured with frantic hands.

"Put me down! Now!" He dipped dangerously

towards the cesspit, and waved for attention. "No, not in here, over there." He rose through the air once more. Following his signals, the Cridi set him down in the long grass several meters away from the humped construction. Once on the ground, he could see that it was fitted with wide stone steps leading to the lip, and surrounded by handsome gardens that no doubt benefited from the natural fertilizer.

"I see you've found 'the necessary,'" Carialle commented drily.

"You can laugh," Keff said crossly, triggering the stud that controlled air recirculation. "You didn't smell it. It was so bad that it passed the filters in my suit." Grateful to be back on his own feet, he patted the nearest Cridi's globe. Small Spot glanced up at him with large, scared eyes.

"These beasts are not secretly making an attack?" he asked.

"I don't think so," Keff replied. "It does not appear as if we have much to fear from them. They're afraid of *you*."

"Us? They are so many, and we are so few, and yet they do not attack?"

"It would seem not," Keff said. He squeezed his eyes halfway closed to trigger magnification of the house. "Those wires are very new," Keff said. "The contacts have yet to oxidize in spite of the chlorinated atmosphere."

"I am finding it very difficult to believe they continue to live in a semi-primitive state like this after having developed space travel," Carialle said.

"Focused application of technology?" Keff wondered out loud. "Perhaps they have a cultural prohibition against wholesale changes in the environment."

"Yes, but Keff, even sustainable technology could take care of that midden heap in a more aesthetic and less odiferous fashion. Side by side with electric light and telecommunications is that complicated system of water-wheels for ventilation."

"Yes," Big Eyes said. "Why do they not use electricity to run water mills *and* to ventilate? Much more efficient."

"Tradition?" Keff asked, but he wasn't convinced either.

"It's as if all this doesn't belong, as if it has been imposed on the landscape," Carialle said. "Looking at it with an artist's eye, it doesn't make sense. Some scientific advances are used for one purpose, but all other uses are ignored."

Big Eyes, accustomed to luxuries available at the flick of a finger, stared around her at the dry landscape with puzzled eyes. "So barren," she said. "Bleak, primitive."

Tall Eyebrow suddenly looked very sad. "Very much like home on Sky Clear," he gestured. Big Eyes caught the expression on his face, and attempted to apologize.

"It is only that I am not used to it," she said hastily, both in voice and sign. "I do not mean such things cannot be considered attractive."

"I'm going to go speak to the beings in the house," Keff signed, distracting them both from a potentially embarrassing exchange. "Stay close, but don't come out until I signal for you."

With the Cridi in their globes staying low in the tall, crisp grass, Keff circled out of the yard and made his way to the front. A wide but low door, elaborately molded bronze to match the shutters of the wide windows, lay in the exact center of the side of the house, facing a lane.

"Not much in the way of roadbuilders," Carialle said. "But would you be, if you could fly everywhere?"

"Not I," Keff said. He raised his hand to knock, then noticed a cluster of bells hanging just under the eaves. "That's right. They haven't much in the way of knuckles, have they?" He jangled the bells with his fingertips.

In a few moments, the door swung wide. A noseless lion face appeared at his chest level.

"Freihur?" the griffin asked. Its strange eyes darkened as its visitor registered on its consciousness, and it sat back on its haunches. "Za, humancaldifaro!"

"Yes, I'm human. My name is Keff. How do you do? Do you speak Standard?" Keff asked, politely, airing the griffin language he'd elicited from Carialle's telephone tap.

"I . . . yes! Welcome," the griffin said in Standard, in seeming befuddlement. It passed wing-hands over its golden fur, grooming it back into place. "Enter, yaro."

Keff followed his host into the low house. The interior was arranged rather like a nest. All the furniture was made for sinking into or settling on. The big, fluffy pillows looked comfortable. The heavy gravity was wearing on his muscles in spite of the assistance of Core power. Keff would have enjoyed flopping down on the cushion with the silky covering that lay under a sunny window amid potted plants. The windows were unglazed, a blessing in the heat, but were all fitted with screens of a microfine weave to keep out the blowing dust.

Keff was about to ask his host to take him to its leader when he noticed a large square device with a screen on top of it, and a sling shoved hastily to one side. On the screen, another griffin face was peering out. He'd probably interrupted an important gossip session, then realized that his host was looking at him with fearful anticipation.

"Vaniah? Vaniah, soheoslayim, commeadyoslayim Thelerieya," the caller on the screen said. Thelerie the host didn't know which way to go. At last, it plunged away from Keff and punched a button on the box below the other's image. The screen went black.

"Word spreads," Carialle said. "Better to take the bullfrog by the horns."

"You're quite right," Keff said, and whispered into his helmet. By the time his host turned around, the four Cridi were clustered around his feet on the stone floor. The Thelerie backpedaled, protecting its face with folded wings. Its claws scrabbled, and it felt for a piece of furniture to sink down into.

"It's true, you see," Keff said, standing in the doorway so the griffin couldn't flee. "These are my friends. They are harmless and friendly, and wish to come with me to meet your government. Can you help us?"

"They are not killers?" the griffin asked. Its pupils were spread out across its eyes. "I have children . . . ." It glanced nervously toward the corridor. Keff guessed the young ones were beyond one of the two closed doors he could see.

"No," he hurried to assure the Thelerie. "They are civilized beings, who only wish to speak."

"Greetings," Tall Eyebrow said, rolling up in his globe. The griffin's ears swiveled forward.

"I did not know they can speak."

"They can and do," Keff said.

"This is like . . . toys," the Thelerie said, tipping a wary wing-hand toward the globes.

"Means of conveyance," Keff said. "Your world is too dry for them. They are accustomed to a very wet climate. They are at a disadvantage here."

"Ah." The griffin paused to consider. Its eyes lost some of the expression of terror.

"You can almost hear the wheels turn in its head," Carialle said. "'The monsters are vulnerable.'"

"You will be assisting in the cause of global peace," Keff said, encouragingly, hoping to make the wheels turn in the right direction. "And think of the gossip you'll be able to pass on to your friends."

The griffin's upper lip split widely, and its pupils narrowed. "I am not forgetting that," it said, with good humor. "What do you want of me?"

"Will you take me to your leader?" Keff asked.

"I thought that griffin would break the sound barrier flying home," Carialle said, as Keff stood on the balcony looking after it.

"And why not?" Keff asked, making sure he had a good grip on the rail while he brushed fine yellow silt from his suit. The broad, stone building about four levels high was the tallest building in the city. This flat parapet appeared to be the landing pad for Thelerie visiting the structure, avoiding the dusty plain below. Keff felt at a disadvantage as the only being on the planet, including the Cridi visitors, who had no means of independent aerial propulsion. "He's got the exclusive story of the century, but he couldn't go and tell it until he got us here. Or was it a she?"

"But where is here?" Tall Eyebrow wanted to know. Keff and the Cridi were clustered out of sight of anyone looking up.

"Central government," Keff said, rapping with his knuckles on the light, metal window frame. "Or so our guide said. We ought to be uninterrupted at least until he gets back to his screen. That should be enough time to make our presence known. Ah," he said as the gauze-screened doors opened onto a broad room. Two large griffins in leather harness met his eyes with open-mouthed astonishment. "Excuse me. I would like to speak to the being in charge." He threw a glance over his shoulder, but the Cridi globes had hovered up out of sight. "Wait for my signal," he said, with his lips close together.

"We waiting," said a soft voice in his helmet receiver.

"So am I," Carialle said.

Keff marched behind his escort down a wide corridor to a chamber, like a huge eyrie. The outward-slanting walls and square pillars were of a mahogany-colored stone, carved sumptuously in relief, and polished to a gleam. Tiny lamps glimmered in sconces around the walls. Keff saw that they were flames, but of intense brightness for their small size. A dozen Thelerie with white tufts in their golden fur conversed respectfully with one whose coat was nearly entirely white. All of them lounged on embroidered pads before individual carved tables. Near the walls, a dozen or more young and muscular-looking Thelerie sat, holding sharpened bronze weapons that resembled a cross between short jai-alai sticks and back-scratchers. In the corner was a griffin playing on a stringed instrument like a huge dulcimer. The music stopped when the musician spotted Keff. The brawn bowed deeply, and addressed himself to the eldest Thelerie.

"Greetings. I am Keff. My partner, Carialle, and I come in friendship, as a representative of the Central Worlds, to extend the compliments of our government, and to voice grievances brought by some of our member worlds."

"Then you must come in," the elder said, rising from his cushion, and extending his wing-hands toward Keff in a companionable gesture. "You are welcome. I am Noonday, Sayas of Thelerie. These are the Ro-sayo, the assembly of the wise."

Murmurs broke out in the chamber as Keff strode between the guards to the center of the room. He bowed to each of the councillors, centering their faces for his chest camera and Carialle.

"Slayim," he heard repeated over and over again. "Slayim."

"Word has already spread here of our arrival," Carialle said. "Slayim, slayim, slayim."

"Slime," Keff said under his breath, suddenly enlightened. "That's what they've been calling the Cridi."

"For their wet skins," Carialle said. "An uncomplimentary but not unreasonable pejorative. But it's a Standard word."

"It won't remain a mystery long, I hope. May I address this assembly?" Keff asked Noonday. The leader, after looking around at the others and meeting their eyes, nodded his great head.

"Not all speak your tongue, but I shall translate for those of us who do not understand."

"Thank you," Keff said, adjusting IT to pick up the leader's voice. "But first, I must introduce you to your nearest neighbors among the stars."

He stepped past Noonday's cushion and up to the great casement behind him. With a flourish, he threw open the windows, and the four Cridi globes sailed up and in on a wave of wind and dust.

"Slime!"

Brandishing their back-scratchers, the guards at once dove for the four small globes, but they rebounded against another unseen wall of force. They fought and tore at obdurate nothingness with hysterical fury on their big, flat faces.

Gawking, the elderly Ro-sayo leaped off their cushions. They tried to break for the door, the other windows, even out past Keff, who flattened himself against a pillar out of the way. The Thelerie all but rebounded off invisible barriers put there by Cridi Core power, and rushed to the next possible route of escape. Noonday held his place, but he looked aghast.

"You dare to bring our enemy here?" he asked Keff.

Keff hurried to the center of the chaos with his hands outstretched above his head.

"Please! They are not your enemy! They mean you no harm. My friends are called the Cridi. They are your closest neighbors in this part of the galaxy. Their planet circles the twin of your star. They wish to speak because they feel a great wrong has been done them."

"They?" one of the councillors said. It was backed into a corner, its eyes were huge with fear. Its wings were spread out, claw hands poised to defend. "*They* feel wronged?"

"They do," Keff said. "All they ask of you is that you listen to them. Please!"

It took some more moments of scrabbling at the air to realize that though the Thelerie could not leave the chamber, nothing else ill was happening to them. After many glances over their shoulders at the little plastic balls in the middle of the room, they soon stopped hammering on the doors and walls and windows. The small, green aliens sat in the water at the bottom of their travel globes, almost hidden by the circle of guards. The first Thelerie to have spoken closed its big wings, and daringly edged back toward its cushion.

"That's good," Keff said, his voice soothing. Noonday's voice sounded forth one of their multisyllabic sentences like the mellowest of brass horns. "Won't everyone else please sit down?"

"They fear us so," Big Eyes signed, her hands shaking. She was almost invisible behind the wings of the guards, but Keff heard her small voice over his helmet speaker. "I guessed nothing of this. For so many years, we pictured the destroyer of spaceships as great unknown."

"And they saw you as unmentionable monsters," Keff said. He moved in and pushed the guards aside. "We must put an end to those misunderstandings now, and discover the truth."

The guards looked to the Sayas for direction. At Noonday's nod, they withdrew to a distance of only three meters and settled onto their haunches. Keff sensed that they were not really relaxed, but ready to pounce again if needed. Slowly, all of the griffins but one resumed their places. The last, a young and slender councillor, found that its pad was closest to the Cridi. It crept close, set a single foot on the cushion, then fled, shrieking, to pound on the door again.

"Jurrelanyaro! Jurrelanyaro, yaro!" it cried. Keff walked between the cushions to the end of the chamber, feeling every head swivel to follow him. He stopped and bowed to put a gentle hand on the Thelerie's back. It jumped a meter in the air, its wings outspread, and landed facing the brawn.

"I am a human," Keff said, softly but clearly. "Your people trust humans. I mean you no harm. I promise you will not be harmed. Will you trust me?"

The beast's striped pupils fluctuated wide to narrow to wide. It may not have understood his words, but it seemed to comprehend his tone. It nodded its head. Keff stepped out a pace or so from the wall, and offered an encouraging hand.

"Come, then, and take your rightful place," he said. It followed him like a tame deer, all the while staring timorously at the Cridi. At Keff's signal, the globe-frogs stayed absolutely still. The young Thelerie settled down on all four legs, but its wings were open half-way, literally ready for flight. Keff turned to find that Noonday was smiling at him.

"You must have young of your own," the Sayas said. "We listen."

"Thank you," Keff said. "I would like to introduce the Cridi. You call them the Slime, but that is not their right name. Cridi." Noonday repeated his words in the musical Thelerie language. Keff smiled to himself as some of the beings around the room tried the foreign word on their tongues. "My companions are Tall Eyebrow, leader of the Cridi of the Sky Clear colony; Big Eyes, one of the eight conclave council members of their homeworld of Cridi; Small Spot and Long Hand, both of Sky Clear. Since, unexpectedly, we share a common tongue, you may hear in their own voices the complaints that they have."

Every eye turned toward the Cridi. Keff sensed how nervous the four were, but they held themselves bravely upright. When one of the globes wavered slightly out of line, Tall Eyebrow brought it back to its place with a sharp gesture from the wrist. Big Eyes rolled closest to him, and matched hands with him on the inside of their globes. Gradually, the assembly was quiet, awaiting.

"But they cannot speak for themselves," a white-headed Thelerie said, breaking the silence. "They are only creatures."

"They are not," Keff said. "In my ship I have video of their homeworld, and I assure you their attainments in art and science are most impressive."

"Impossible. They are dumb animals!"

"We can speak," Tall Eyebrow said, projecting his voice to carry as well as it could from his small plastic bubble. His words caused a sensation. As the hubbub grew louder, his high voice cut through the noise like a cutting torch. "But we choose Sir Keff to speak for us."

"Thank the stars for that," Noonday said, removing the wing-fingers from his ears. "Telling the truth, your voices are painful. We are not aware of any wrong that we have done these . . . people, er, *Sir* Keff, but you may address us as you please." The senior settled himself down, flipping his wings to his back and arranging his haunches like a big cat.

"I will," Keff said, "as soon as the assembly is complete. I await the arrival of the rest of the Cridi delegation. If you will give permission, and the assurance that they will not be harmed, I will ask them to land." He bowed deeply, sweeping an arm around to the rest of the chamber.

"There are more Slime?" one of the Thelerie asked, flinging its wings about it in the protective posture.

An older assembly member scrabbled up. "We are under attack! Guards!"

"Oh, where is the Melange? They should be

protecting us," a slender Thelerie said, wringing both pairs of hands at its breast.

"Silence!" Noonday's voice rose over them like a hunting horn's call, though he did not move. "I give the guarantee. Bring them, Sir Keff."

"Cari?"

"On their way," Carialle said. "There's just about room to land on that balcony, but Narrow Leg shouldn't push his luck. He's going to set down on the roof . . . just . . . about . . . NOW!"

There was a *boom!* and the thunder of rocket engines shook the council chamber. The Thelerie assembly looked frightened, but none of them broke for the exits. Keff found himself full of admiration for their bravery. In a moment, the shadows of travel globes appeared outside the woven window screens, and the casements opened wide. Naturally, the plump councillor had jock-eyed himself into first place, and entered triumphantly.

"I should have been first, before these others," he signed indignantly at Keff.

"It could have been dangerous," Keff gestured back, in as few gestures as possible.

"No matter!" Big Voice said, punctuating his signs with a squeak, now that all peril was past. "I would have faced it for the sake of my people."

Smiling a little, Keff stood forward, like a court herald, and bowed to the Thelerie.

"Allow me to introduce Big Voice, another one of the Eight, Narrow Leg, captain of the Cridi ship, Gap Tooth, Wide Foot . . . ." As he recited their names, the globes touched down on the polished floor and rolled into an arc around Keff's feet.

"I bid you welcome, Cridi," Noonday said, gravely. "And now, speak. What are these grievances?"

Big Voice rolled out just to one side of Keff, where the human could see and hear his every word.

"I have traveled far and endured many hardships to

ask these words," Big Voice said in carefully practiced Standard. His voice quavered when faced with so many griffins, awake and mobile, but he puffed himself up and continued. "Your people have confined us, you have killed us, you have stolen from us. What I must know is *why*? Why do you hate us? Why do you think us monsters?"

The Thelerie stared at him as the assembly resounded with protest. A younger member of the chamber spoke out.

"The Melange told us you were monsters, that you killed innocent beings. You harmed *their* ships, and would kill us, though we only seek to see what is among the stars. We do not harm your kind. It is the other way around."

"We have never seen your people before." Big Voice shrieked, and several of the Thelerie held their ears. "We do not kill others, and we do not destroy or terrorize. Your Melange has lied to you! Keff is the first human we have ever seen, too!"

"Humans don't lie!" a Thelerie howled angrily, a bassoon counterpoint to Big Voice's piccolo. The plump councillor retreated swiftly into the group of his fellows and hunkered down in his globe.

Keff opened his mouth and shut it again. "I can't say anything," he told Carialle. "If I say humans do lie, then I've started one of those conundrums that makes computers break down."

"What have we stolen?" Noonday asked, in a mild tone intended to calm his listeners. "Will you enumerate your losses?"

"Three power sources, known to us as Cores," Big Voice said, counting on his long fingers, "engines and equipment from our ships, the lives of at least three crews, but most of all, our freedom! We have been imprisoned on our world for fifty of our years, because our ships could not pass the barrier you created!"

Keff translated for the Thelerie, who immediately protested.

"We did not set any barrier," Noonday said, earnestly. "Our people have few ships, which have not crossed out of our star's circuit as of yet. The Melange say we are not ready. It must be their barrier you cannot cross. Surely it is for your own good."

Keff shook his head. "Sayas Noonday, the Cridi don't need any protection of that kind. They are accomplished space travelers, with colonies in other systems."

"Are they?" Noonday asked, eyeing the Cridi with new respect. "They seem so helpless, so . . . lacking in a center."

"Once we were not," Narrow Leg said, speaking up. "I am old of my kind. I remember the first time we lost contact with a ship, fifty revolutions ago. The Melange must have destroyed it without warning, for no word ever came back to us. They kill to keep us from leaving our world."

"No!" The Thelerie protested the idea of the Melange killing. Keff held up his hands, pleading for silence.

"The spacecraft we saw when we landed," Keff urged, pointing out of the window in the general direction of the landing pad. "Did you construct these?"

"Yes," said Noonday proudly. "They are made of gifts from the good humans who have visited us in the past."

"But the parts were not given freely to those humans," Keff said. "I recognized some of the components, and my associates recognized others as Cridi technology. Piracy is a great problem in our culture, too."

"It is not piracy. You were *giving* of these objects to us, honored human," one of the younger Ro-sayo said.

Keff shook his head. "I haven't. Many ships were robbed or destroyed to yield those parts."

"It could not be. The Melange is honorable," the first Thelerie protested. The Ro-sayo broke out in hoots and cries of agreement, with the high-pitched whistles of Cridi voices causing many of them to flinch.

"They might have been taking things that didn't belong to them," Keff said.

"Nonsense!" Noonday said. "Some of our most honored citizens have taken ship with the Melange, sworn allegiance, and brought home goods so that we may fly the stars."

"Who is the Melange?" Keff asked, shouting to be heard.

That question provoked the greatest outburst of them all. Noonday gestured for silence, and turned a hard stare on Keff.

"Who *are* you that you do not know of the Melange?"

"We are travelers," Keff said. "We come from the Central Worlds. That means something to you," he added, as some of the Thelerie conferred hastily among themselves. "Central Worlds is a vast confederation of intelligent peoples, governed by common laws to aid life, health, and prosperity. We go from place to place, meeting new people, and sending word of them back to our Central Committee. I promise you, no word of the Thelerie or of the Melange has ever gotten back to the CenCom."

"But how can this be?" Noonday asked, spreading out all four of his hands. "Humans have given us so much, for so many years. They made themselves one with us, gave us helpful innovations. Why, see," he gestured around him with a narrow wing-finger, "these lamps would never be so small or bright without human machines."

"Cari?" Keff said, turning his body full toward the baroque sconce.

He heard a sharp whistle. "It's a dilute form of heavy-water fuel, Keff, very clean and hot-burning, the sort of high-quality stuff I'd use myself if I could get it. If those valves weren't so small, that whole room would go up, blammo!" Keff blanched.

"Where does the fuel come from?" he asked.

"It lies here and there in the deep places," Noonday said, gesturing vaguely with a few of his hands. "The technology to make use of it was brought to us by humans to our mutual benefit, for which we are very grateful. We assumed that all humankind was behind their good intentions."

"Are there more? More innovations?"

"But, of course," Noonday said, with a gentle smile. It was clear he and the others still did not believe Keff's protestations of ignorance. "For everything the Melange takes from Thelerie, they always bring us gifts, more than fair exchange."

"The Thelerie couldn't be using more than a few million barrels a year for light and heat," Keff said, sublingually. "Leaving a source of quality rocket fuel for whoever knows to come and take it."

"I see why now," Carialle said, "but I still don't know who, or if they connect to me."

The youngest Thelerie, Midnight, stood up and placed an indignant wing-hand on its breast. "You have come here with many accusations. You wrong us, and you wrong our friends and benefactors."

"We do not mean to be offensive," Keff said, "but I assure you we tell the truth. You set great store by honesty. I tell you that we left behind in the Cridi system ten of your people, and they were part of a force that lay in ambush for us." Keff continued over the horrified protestations. "That force was responsible for the destruction of a human-run ship from the Central Worlds. The wreckage of that vessel was found near the ruins of at least three Cridi craft, and parts of many others. I swear to you that this account is true. I have video records of this, and of the beings who confronted us on a planetary base. You see why we must find out the truth here and now."

"I would like to see these 'video,' " the young Ro-sayo said.

"You shall," Keff said. "We do not bring these complaints without proof."

"What you are saying is that *Thelerie* have been involved in acts of piracy," Noonday said. His noble face was drawn into lines of pain. Keff felt concern for the leader.

"Cari, is he all right?" he asked under his breath.

"Not a cardiac involvement," Carialle said, after a moment's assessment, "but his pulses are running very fast. He's sustained a shock, which is no surprise, considering how many bombshells you've lobbed in the last few minutes."

"What do you want of us?" the leader asked at last.

"It would seem that most of our questions could be answered by your friends the humans," Keff said. "Can we meet the Melange?"

Chapter 15

"Where is the other human?" Noonday asked, looking around, over, and under the party as they flew out of the capital city toward the northeast. "I would like to meet it."

"Perhaps later. Carialle stays with the ship at all times," Keff said. "She's . . . very attached to it."

Carialle blew a raspberry in his aural pickup, with the volume turned up just a little higher than was strictly necessary. She observed the neural monitor jump as Keff winced.

"I speak to her by means of small transmitter-receivers on my person," Keff said, pointedly ignoring her. "She hears our words, and sends her greetings to you."

"Ah, thank you and her. I know little of human customs. We in the Sayad do not interact with the Melange ourselves," Noonday admitted, flying ahead of his escort with Keff and Tall Eyebrow for a private word. His great wings beat the air a few times, then spread out to glide on a gusty updraft. "They visit Thelerie only irregularly. I myself only met humans once, very long ago. It was a great honor."

Watching from the camera eye on Keff's chest, Carialle admired the easy play of muscles. Noonday's wings were shaped like those of an eagle, but covered with plushy, golden fur like the body of a bat. The Thelerie were certainly a beautiful folk. She had had plenty of time to go over the anatomical studies and scans they had taken of the griffins left behind on the base, but this was her first time to see them in action, in their own habitat, stress-free. She was attracted to the grace of movement, the artistically right integration of six limbs. Their bodies seemed lithe and smooth, their velvet pelts almost caressing her visual receptors. Should time and circumstances permit, Carialle wanted to ask a few of them to sit, or rather, fly for her, so she could paint them. Carialle's brief glimpse of one of the guards suggested that it was carrying young right now. A scan showed a tiny, six-limbed creature in a thick caul like a soft eggshell inside the uterus. Carialle felt protective of the unborn young. In spite of her worries and misgivings, she was finding herself liking the Thelerie. She chided herself for her sympathies, remembering that these charming beings were responsible for countless deaths, and possibly her own long-ago peril.

"Who, then, is the primary interface with the Melange?" Keff's voice asked. Carialle saw that his pulse rate was up. She checked her telemetry, and found the group was flying at approximately twelve hundred feet, far above his comfort level.

"The Sayas of the Space Program meets with them," Noonday said. "We will ask if it is known when their next appearance is to be."

"Then, why do you all speak our language?" Keff asked, gesturing vaguely.

"Oh, that is in anticipation of when we reach out to the stars," Noonday said, and his eyes widened joyfully. "We want to be ready to communicate at once with the blessed humans who are there."

"Not an unbiased party, is he?" Carialle said, wryly. "I notice he doesn't consider it an honor to meet the Cridi, and they're just as alien as we."

"We're not blessed, Sayas, just another species like you," Keff said.

"Not to us," Noonday said, shaking his head. "It is from a legend that comes from the depths of our history, telling the story about the wingless ones who would come one day and take us where our wings cannot. A most beloved story, by children especially. And one day, you came, and made it true."

"Well, not us. This Melange, whoever they are . . . er, we are honored to have your assistance," Keff said, hesitantly, "and, forgive the discourtesy, but why are *you* taking us to meet this Sayas? Wouldn't this task be easily relegated to a junior Ro-sayo, or a guard?"

The elder's wings tilted back for just a moment, then he flapped hastily to catch up. His forehead was creased, ruffling the plush into furrows.

"Thunderstorm is my child," he said, then said defensively, "Where aptitude exists, should not responsibility follow? If there is any wrongdoing, I wish to know at once. We Thelerie are law-abiding folk. Our . . . *moral* life is strong. As you could see, my assembly was much distressed at the notion that Thelerie were involved with crimes against another people, especially a life-form so physically helpless."

"We are not helpless," Big Voice said indignantly, floating his travel globe close to the Sayas. "You have said that before, but see, we are capable."

Noonday reached out a claw hand to tap the globe. Big Voice ducked automatically. "That is true. By coming along on a flight with those believed to be enemies, I am also demonstrating a measure of trust in you for the assembly. *I* prove you can be friends and allies. As you say, we and the . . . *Cridi* are close neighbors. Neighbors should aid one another in time of need. And in spite of all, even if these charges against Thelerie be true, we must continue to trust in humans. So much of our culture over these last many years is involved intimately with this relationship. They gave us electricity, communication, many things."

"Heat exchangers, humidity controls . . . " Carialle chimed in. "The Thelerie should properly be in a pre-industrial age. The baroque decor is reasonably appropriate to the period, as it was on Earth before electricity. Humans brought all this to them, gave them machines, power, and then space travel, all in the space of fifty years. Strictly against the code of the Central Worlds."

"Well, these humans seem to be doing quite a lot against the code of the Central Worlds," Keff said, under his breath. "We'll know more when we've talked to Thunderstorm. How long until we get there, Noonday?"

"Soon," the Sayas said. The group passed over the ridge of the mountain range separating one great, yellow plain from another. Spare clouds riding the sky above them drew long lines that extended down over the mountaintops in both directions. Noonday directed them down into the narrow shadows between ragged, upthrust monoliths. "This way, for another eighth-arc of the sun at least."

"Plenty of time to get to know one another," Keff said cheerfully, stretching out on his side in the air beside the Thelerie. The Cridi continued to fly him along, and his pulses dropped toward normal as he became more involved in the conversation. Carialle flipped her image of the Sayas from horizontal to vertical to compensate for her brawn's change in position. "You say you're Thunderstorm's parent. Are you his mother or his father? And is he a he or a she?"

"Such differences are not known in our biology," Noonday said, beginning in a lecturer's tone. "Unlike you, we are all made the same way, only changing roles as we mate for offspring. I have borne or sired four children in my life. You would say I am Thunderstorm's mother, for I bore that child sixty-seven turns of the sun ago. We live a long time, here."

Carialle made certain the recording on Keff's signal was perfectly clear. She boxed in auxiliary memory to act as backup, to assure data redundancy. She knew her brawn wouldn't want to let a single erg of information get away.

It was a blow to him that the CK-963 team wasn't really the discoverer of the Thelerie, but he intended at least to be the documentarian whose data made the *Encyclopedia Galactica*, if not the Xeno files. Carialle wished she could have such easy short-term goals, but then, she'd never thought like a softshell. Keff had made her realize her humanity, even made her like it, but she knew they weren't very similar in their outlooks. He was ephemeral. One day, when their twenty-five year assignment was over, she'd be suddenly without him, and it would be a long and sad forever thereafter. It was times like this when she understood how very much she valued him. Keff, with his good humor, optimism, and his enthusiasm for diving into any task no matter how difficult or unsavory, was the best thing that had ever happened to her. He was so fragile, so easily injured, and she was so far away. If the Cridi allowed any harm to come to him . . . !

Realizing she was allowing herself to become melancholy, she gave her system a quick eighth-measure of carbohydrates. If her brain was playing such emotion tricks on her, she must be hungry. She had surely been ignoring the gauges that indicated her blood sugar was unusually low.

Carialle knew she'd been working her system hard. Ever since they hove into this part of space, old memories had been surfacing, giving her flashbacks during her rest-times, and intruding into her conscious mind while she was doing easy tasks like calculations. She saw visions of her first brawn, Fanine, relived the explosion and the rescue, even cast a critical mental eye on the early paintings she had done of space-scapes while in therapy. That should all be behind her, she thought. The interference had made her have to concentrate twice as hard.

Her sensors had been gathering information on the Thelerie ever since they had landed. It was time and past time to send another transmission to the Central Worlds, as a follow-up to the one she had sent from the Cridi system, but she was hesitant. Every event changed their perceptions of the situation. If she and Keff were wrong about the pirates, if the whole construct the two of them had made up about the location and origin of the raiders was incorrect, it was the end of her career, at least. Carialle hoped Keff wouldn't be held responsible—they were *her* incorrect perceptions based on *her* mistakes, arising from *her* disaster. She could always plead guilty to constructive kidnapping, if worst came to worst, to spare Keff an official reprimand. Not that it was likely she would face criminal proceedings, but it was best to be pessimistic where the odious M-C was concerned.

And yet, she found it difficult to believe that this charming and seemingly honest race was involved in piracy and illicit salvage. Of course it wouldn't be illicit for *them* to remove parts from a derelict ship; they wouldn't know it was a legal requirement to post a claim to a wreck with the space agencies. The Sayad had no rules dealing with space salvage yet. And yet, griffins—Thelerie—had been aboard the ships chasing them with mining lasers. Who was fooling whom?

She began to build up a dossier of facts to accompany her message. In it, she stressed the pre-electronic environment in which the Thelerie lived. The most intriguing fact about the modern developments that she and Keff had observed was the limitation of their use. It said clearly that the Thelerie did not understand the mechanisms or the physics behind them. Therefore . . . therefore, another agency was at work. Or was it? Couldn't there simply be a group of griffins who had demanded an education in practical science from spacegoing captives? Then, how had they reached into space in the first place? She and Keff needed that final link in the pattern. With luck, they'd have it before her message reached the CenCom.

On her screen, the Sayas stretched out his beautiful wings and dipped down toward a cluster of buildings on the open plain. Their body-harness glinting in the bright sun, the six guards flew into a protective formation around him. What a picture! Keff and the Cridi dropped back a hundred meters, allowing the Thelerie to approach the installation first.

"My, what a nice little fuel storage facility," Carialle said, just before the image of the square stone building with fluid transfer towers disappeared from Keff's camera eye.

"Isn't it, though?" Keff said. "Now our surmise has another leg to stand on."

Thunderstorm's office was very elegantly furnished, though the structure itself was little more than a stone roof on pillars. The walls consisted of corner-to-corner screens that let in the fresh breezes and bright, yellow sunlight. The cool wind felt so good to Keff after the dusty flight that he opened his filters a little more to allow the circulating air to touch his face. The atmosphere contained really very little ammonia, more of a far-off smell than an all-round stink. It might still harm tender Cridi hides, but exposed human skin might be able to last for longish periods. He thought he could almost take off his envirosuit, but then Carialle would probably go spare. Keff wanted to prevent anything from upsetting her during the investigation of this world. She had trials enough with the entire Mental Sciences division clamoring for brain scans, thanks to the Inspector General. Though it might put him in the brig, Keff would love to relieve the itch in his big toe by burying it halfway up the IG's excretory tract.

Keff occupied himself while they waited for Thunderstorm by studying his surroundings. This installation, at least, was accustomed to receiving humans. The doorframe was over two meters high, instead of the meter and a half that would be adequate for Thelerie to enter on four feet. That seemed to be the only structural consideration. The furniture was all made for griffin comfort—not that Keff would have found it onerous to stretch out on floor pillows, and the sling behind the desk was perfectly adequate as a backless chair. As in the government building, Keff saw very little wood, all of it used as ornament rather than in construction. Some of the small outbuildings around the office seemed to be built of adobe, others of fieldstone and concrete. The Thelerie might have had only one main building material, but they used it with imagination.

To his surprise, they also had paper. Keff grinned at himself. He'd been looking for computer terminals in a culture that still had open cesspits. The broadtopped desk was heaped with white, squarecut sheets, covered with the same square script he recognized from the attack ship's files. *Those* computers had been the aberration. This setting seemed more in line with their sociological development.

"Cari, there's hardly any trees here. What's this made of?" he whispered, moving close to the deskful of documents. His forefinger pointed at the paper, in clear view of the camera eye.

"Straw fiber," she replied at once. "A combination of rice and some native fiber; hard to tell which one without a closer molecular scan. The ink's a combination of an organic compound and finely ground mineral powder. Like India ink, it'd last for centuries. Here comes someone."

Keff looked around. Carialle must have detected the approach of a flying body on sensors. Yes, there . . . Keff saw a shadow, steadily growing in size as the body that cast it neared the ground. He heard voices, the Sayad guards calling out greetings, and a single mellow reply, as a Thelerie of middle years rounded the corner of a pillar, and entered.

Thunderstorm looked remarkably like his mother, but with a broader head and wider feet that lent him an endearingly awkward gait. His coat had only begun to show flecks of white. His smile, when he saw Keff, was an echo of Noonday's sweet expression. Thunderstorm looked suddenly wary as he came closer, and realized he did not recognize Keff. But the evidence was clear: this being interacted frequently and closely with humans.

"We've found our connection, Cari," Keff muttered under his breath.

"A . . . stranger?" Thunderstorm asked, in very good Standard, attempting to show surprise. "Forgive, I am rude. Parent, to what do I owe the honor of your presence?" He sat back on his haunches and made the gesture of respect to Noonday. The elder returned it. When he raised his eyes, they were worried.

"My child, I come on the gravest of errands," the Sayas said. "This human has told me many things that in—imm—?" he looked up at Keff apologetically, "favrekina Thelerieya."

"Implicate, parent," Thunderstorm said, smoothly, but Keff saw his tailtip switch. He was nervous. "Implicate Thelerie in what?"

"Crimes against other races of feings," Noonday said, so agitated she was unable to keep the upper halves of her lip together to pronounce the "b" in "beings."

"But I beg an explanation," Thunderstorm said, turning his head, to avoid making eye contact with his mother or Keff. He knelt behind the sling and lifted his upper body across it. With his right claw hand, he picked up a pen and made a few marks on a sheet of paper. "Why come to me?"

"I am told you are the head of the Thelerie space program," Keff said. "Is that true?"

"It is," Thunderstorm said. "It is wrong to lie."

"Then my business is with you. I come on a matter of peace. I am not alone. Perhaps you may have heard?"

The younger Sayas looked uneasy. "I have heard rumors."

"I won't conceal anything from you," Keff said. "Allow me to introduce my friends."

The globes sailed one by one out of the side of the pavilion, where they had been waiting out of the hot sun. Thunderstorm's pupils nearly spread to the edges of his eyes, and he sat up on his haunches at bay, his wings batting.

"I cannot believe you would bring them here," he gabbled out, staring. "Parent, what have they done to you?"

"Nothing at all," Noonday said, refusing to let Thunderstorm distract her. "What do you know about them?" She lifted her eyelids warningly.

"I have encountered them," Thunderstorm said at last, his wings wavering. "When I served my apprenticeship with the Melange. They are evil beings."

"Not evil," Tall Eyebrow protested.

"By the temple, it can speak!"

"You didn't know, did you?" Keff asked, leaning across the stone desk. "You never saw one alive. Did you assist in the ambush and destruction of one of their spacecraft?"

A Thelerie might not lie, but evidently it would fight to keep from telling a harmful truth. Thunderstorm stared silently down at the pen in his hand.

"Child, speak," Noonday commanded, sounding like

the entire brass section of an orchestra. It took some
time before Thunderstorm could bring himself to open
his mouth.

"You recall our first friend, parent? Verje Bisman?"
Thunderstorm asked, in a very low voice. Noonday
nodded, still watching him carefully. The younger
Thelerie turned to Keff. "I was so young, and full of
awe for the strangers. Before a formal arrangement had
been made between our two peoples, I begged to have
him take me in his ship. He apprenticed me and my
friend Autumn. He seemed fascinated with the Center, though he could not find it himself, and called us
great assets because we could. We flew with him for
some years, going from place to place, accomplishing
missions for his ship. We gathered things no one
wanted, or received them from donors who bargained
hard for their goods," Thunderstorm said, looking
ashamed. "So I thought. I was naive. On the cusp of
the nearest star, we caught a ship that my friend, Verje's
child, Aldon, said contained the greatest prize of all,
and the Slime would not yield it. We were young and
on fire, so we stopped the ship and took it. It was a
great battle, for the Slime seemed to have mystic power
to attack us without touching us. We were very frightened, but in the end we prevailed."

"How long ago?" Carialle's voice demanded.

"How long ago?" Keff echoed.

"Forty-three Standard years," Thunderstorm said,
without looking up. "I knew then we committed crimes.
It was the greatest shame of my life."

"Then he wasn't on any ship that touched me,"
Carialle said. Keff felt some of the tightness in his chest
relax, but he grieved for the Cridi, who were only now
discovering the truth about their losses.

"The second of our ships," Narrow Leg said, his wide
lips flat with disapproval. "Fifteen Cridi lost in that
one."

"Why did you never tell?" Noonday asked.

"I had vowed obedience and silence to the Melange," Thunderstorm said, looking up at his parent. "And I knew shame. I begged to be involved in no more assaults, and the humans agreed. After that, I came home to found the space program, finding apprentices for the Melange to train in the art of maintaining and flying craft. They do learn everything they are taught!" he cried, his eyes darting between Keff's and Noonday's. "We are good pupils, and we consider the trust sacred. When we were told these," he gestured at the globes, "were enemies, we believed. We believed, because the humans were the fulfillers of our dearest dream! Those of us who finished with our apprenticeships never speak of it, but some of us *know* we have done wrong. That is why some have left the space program. I stay. I am weak." The Sayas hung his head. "I thought some day when our own ships were spaceworthy, I would go back and see who the Slime were. I was Centered. I knew how to find my way. And now I am too old, and possibly weaker still."

"I am disgraced. What punishment would you demand of this one?" Noonday asked, turning to Tall Eyebrow, who deferred at once to Big Eyes and Narrow Leg. Keff could see the pain in her eyes, but she faced the Cridi without wavering.

"Only weeks ago we might have demanded his life," Narrow Leg said, eyeing his daughter and Big Voice, who rolled forward, bursting to talk. "We want cooperation. Such raiding must stop. We want peace. We want friendship. At what point in our requirements of reparation would such things be impossible?"

"I am the Sayas," Noonday said. "And Sir Keff is of the fourlimbs of the legends. Though Thunderstorm is my child, his life is in my gift. I would prefer to withhold such a gift, if I can. But in the name of peace, we will do anything you ask. We can't keep back one life when you have lost so many."

The two councillors rolled away from the group, followed by Narrow Leg and Tall Eyebrow. Long Hand, glancing over, decided she'd better be part of the discussion, paddled her globe into the circle, leaving Small Spot by himself, staring up at the Thelerie.

"We, too, have recently reconciled with a deadly enemy," the Ozranian said. "I know what I would say about you, but it is not my decision."

Thunderstorm went down on his belly and folded his wing-hands under his chin to the younger Cridi. "I do not deserve the consideration," he said. "I understand my crime, and I have abetted others. Time does not dull my shame."

"What are they doing?" Noonday asked, watching the Cridi sign furiously among themselves. "Is it a ritual? Why do they not talk?"

"They are talking," Keff said, always happy to teach. "They speak both with their mouths and their hands." He spread his arms, palms outward. "This is the first word of theirs I ever learned. It means 'help.'"

"Perhaps we shall learn this tongue, too, child," Noonday said, miming the symbol with his wing-fingers. "It has grace."

"I will do anything I can to make amends," Thunderstorm said earnestly, getting to his feet. "If I am given a chance."

"First, you will stop calling us Slime," Small Spot said, with emphasis.

The conference ended. Big Voice led the group back to the waiting griffins. Narrow Leg confronted Thunderstorm.

"We will not be guilty of spilling more blood," the Cridi captain said, "so we do not want yours. Our council will be made to agree that we are doing the right thing by sparing you. But until you learn what is right, you don't belong among the stars if you cannot respect those you meet there. We will dismember those ships we saw when we landed. They are unsafe anyhow. Your space program is cancelled as of now. One day you will learn right."

Thunderstorm's mouth fell open. "Don't take away my people's dream!" he exclaimed. He again dropped to his belly before the globes. "Take my life, here, now, honored ones, but don't let a foolish few close the door for all the others!"

"And yet, that is what you and your Melange have done to us," Narrow Leg said, severely. "We have colonies we have not visited in revolutions, nor have we been able to explore new systems."

"But the humans gave us this gift," Thunderstorm wailed. "If we had not been intended to fly among the stars, the humans would not have come!"

"Technically speaking," Keff put in unhappily, "the Central Worlds would forbid anyone giving a new species sophisticated systems until their own culture had developed the requisite sciences. Your own development would seem to be rather far below the minimum."

"This is terrible," Noonday said, clenching his hands. "I do not wish to lose the gift of flight, either. What can we do?" Everyone looked at Keff.

"Nothing at all until you've found the humans responsible," Carialle reminded her brawn.

"We need more detail on the Melange," Keff said. "Everything. How to find them, what they do when they're here, what their ships bring in, what they take with them. We need verification, first, for my government's information, whether this is the same group who destroyed the DSC-902 in the Cridi system."

"If it is in the Slime system, it was the Melange, I promise," Thunderstorm assured them, unhappily. "They are jealous of their territory. I am sorry to use the wrong name," he said bowing his head to Small Spot. "But I have known them fifty years, and you only minutes."

"I understand," Small Spot said.

"Do you believe them, Sir Knight?" Carialle asked.

"I think so," Keff said, tapping the desk with his fingers. "We can confirm to CW that those Thelerie that we left behind on the fifth planet were part of a network of pirates. They'll be on the lookout for more ships with the same modus operandi."

"But not all Thelerie are involved," Carialle said, with a sigh of relief. "I'll put that in my message to CW. They'll be very interested to hear about human involvement in this culture."

"Bets on whether the CenCom or Xeno gets back to us first?" Keff asked, playfully.

"Get back to the job," Carialle said, with a wry inflection. "We need data. We still haven't laid hands on the masterminds, and now we only have until the message reaches the CenCom."

"It's incredible that the secret of the Thelerie hasn't leaked to the rest of the Central Worlds in fifty years," Keff said. He settled on one of the spare slings in Thunderstorm's office. The Cridi stayed near him, not yet trusting their new acquaintances, but curious.

"We thought that it had," Noonday said, a little sadly. Thunderstorm could not meet his parent's eyes.

"Would you give up a free source of fuel?" Carialle asked. "This is a remote corner of the sector yet. If it wasn't for the bulk transport difficulties they might have been bootlegging it to exploration ships and miners. And here's an intelligent workforce who do complicated work without asking awkward questions. I think we ought to be amazed they weren't enslaved by this Melange. There's some vestige of morality in there, whatever else is going on."

"That brings me to another question," Keff said, looking from parent to child. "Why did the Melange take you into space in the first place? No offense, but

I'd be afraid beings who had never known space travel might be a . . . liability."

Thunderstorm's upper lip parted in a smile. "I think to test a hypothesis. We are at the Center, and they wanted to understand Centering."

"Centering?" Keff asked.

"So you truly do not know," Thunderstorm said in surprise, settling down on a cushion in the sun with his wings on his back and his foreclaws thrust out before him like the Sphinx. "This is the heart of the universe." A wing claw rose to gesture from ground to sky to his own breast. "Its heart is our heart. Where we go, we can always return to here. It draws us. It is a part of us, and we a part of it."

"Extraordinary!" Keff exclaimed. "You mean that if I blindfolded you—covered your eyes—and took you anywhere on this planet, you could get home unaided?"

The sharp teeth showed in a quick smile. "Any child could. All do, to prove adulthood. We are never lost. Our legends of long ago said the Center would lead us home from anywhere, even the stars. But the wise ones of the past didn't provide us with the means to try the theory."

"An internal homing beacon. Whew!" Keff whistled. "But this Melange provided the means."

"Don't lead the witness," Carialle said in his ear. "If we give the CenCom this tape, we want it to be clear he is volunteering this information."

"Yes," Noonday answered, from another divan cushion. Her large eyes lifted skyward and turned dreamy. "One bright day in my youth, the humans came from the stars, and took some of our people away with them, including my child." A wingtip swept toward Thunderstorm. "The legends proved true. Those of our young people who travel far with the Melange learn to go other places with relation to our Center, but always return." The wing-finger twirled around but came to rest in front of Noonday's breast. "The Melange were fascinated by our natural talent, and said we could aid them. They find us worthy to travel with them, to fulfill our dreams of sailing where there is no air to tuck beneath our wings. It is a sacred destiny. One which, alas, has been defiled."

"And in return, you give them things of value," Keff said. "What besides innate navigators?"

"It is only fair to trade value for value," Noonday said with gentle conviction. "They have brought us electricity, useful machines such as distant talkers, knowledge, and the friendship of another race. We are pleased to know them. They have been benefactors to the Thelerie. Metal, ores, handworks, cut stones, smelly fuel-water, the use of a few years of a young Thelerie's time—all seem of little worth in comparison."

"So for fifty years someone's been cashing in on these people and giving them stolen spacecraft parts in return," Carialle said.

"The Interplanetary Revenue is gonna give us a rewaaard," Keff chanted in a sing-song under his breath.

"Don't count it yet," Carialle said. "Let's catch these brutes, first. We need the Thelerie to help us."

"I know," Keff said, and looked up at the two griffins, who eyed him curiously every time he stopped to talk to himself. He smiled at them, which seemed to make Noonday relax. Thunderstorm looked even more worried, his wingtips clattering together over his back.

"I represent the Central Worlds, an affiliation of thousands of planets, and many different species," Keff said. "We have rules against the introduction of technology to civilizations that have not yet developed it themselves. Still, there are immense benefits to membership, if you were interested in joining."

"Then we would really become one with humans?" Noonday asked.

"Much more so than with the Melange. From our

point of view, they have interfered with your development." Noonday looked puzzled. Keff struggled to explain in Standard, then in pidgin Thelerie, and gave it up as a bad job. "Well, what was it like before the Melange came?"

"Colder at night without house heaters," Noonday said. "Less cohesive among our people."

"The coms," Thunderstorm explained. "Most families have one now."

Keff sighed. "The CW won't actually take something like those away from a people, would they, Cari?"

"Probably not. There's no destructive potential in personal communications or home furnaces. The spaceships, on the other hand, will have to go."

"All these are good things that the Melange shares with us," Noonday said, the beatific smile on her face. "We joined with them, and it has been of benefit to us all. They always assured us that the gifts they brought were traded from outposts, or scavenged from floating space debris."

"I was some of that debris," Carialle screamed.

Keff winced as his aural implant went into overload. "They couldn't know, Cari," he reminded her. It was the first crack in the reserve she'd shown since they had landed.

"How dare the Melange force this lovely people into piracy," Carialle said furiously. "It violates fifty-seven sections of interplanetary law, it's immoral, and it violates the Prime Directive."

"That's fictional," Keff pointed out.

"I don't care. It's still a good idea. I want these people, and I want to be the one who brings them in to Central Worlds. Now there's no excuse for having picked away at my exoskeleton: there isn't a spacer who flies in the Central Worlds who wouldn't recognize a shell capsule."

"We don't know what happened," Keff said, soothingly.

"We'll find out. You must understand, Noonday, that spaceship parts don't just become available. Our evidence shows that at least some of them were the fruit of ambush and murder. Thunderstorm will admit he knows about that."

"To my shame," the Space Sayas said, covering his eyes. "Forgive me, parent." His voice was muffled behind the folds of his wings.

"Will you help us to stop such crimes?" Keff asked, looking intently at Noonday.

"We always wish to follow the laws," Noonday said, but the Thelerie was uneasy. Keff was convinced she never really knew that their gifts were stolen merchandise. He waited. He knew the griffins were fascinated by humans, and admired them, so he smiled his most charming smile. It worked. The rectangular pupil widened. "We will do anything we can."

"Thank you," Keff said.

Noonday's sweet smile was sad now. "We dreamed of space travel, and when it was given to us, that dream was fulfilled. But it is wrong to accept technology in advance of our understanding, as you say."

"But you don't understand," said Thunderstorm, rising to his feet. "Some of our greatest triumphs! Some of our most reknowned heroes . . . "

" . . . were flying in stolen ships," Noonday finished gently. "It is over. Sit down, child."

"Fifty years," Keff said, stroking his chin thoughtfully. He shook his head.

"Certainly long enough to be an established concern by the time I came to grief," Carialle said.

"We will stop taking from the traders, but you must convince your own kind to stop bringing it to us," Noonday said. "For as long as it continues to be available, someone will buy it. We cannot police everyone. But so long as there is no source, then no one can buy."

"Then we need to find this Melange, and stop the

illicit trade," Keff said. "How do you know when they are coming?"

Thunderstorm rose and opened a low cabinet behind his desk. In it was a communications unit.

"I activate this once a day to receive messages, if there are any."

"Cari!" Keff said, hovering over it.

"Of course, Keff. Tell him to turn it on."

Keff conveyed the order, and the Thelerie tweaked an old-fashioned knob with his claw. He winced at the rising growl that came from the set as its tubes—*tubes*—warmed up. It was of ancient design, possibly of ancient manufacture as well. But it would last nearly forever in this environment, if not subjected to harsh treatment.

"I have the frequency. It's specific, and common, if you happen to hail from Central Worlds. It's in the educational transmissions band."

"Very sly," Keff said. "If a mysterious broadcast comes in over this band, most monitors will think it's kids playing pranks."

"Yes," Carialle said. "In the meantime, I can stay open on that frequency and hear the moment anyone in range uses it."

"Do you ever send a message yourself on this unit?" Keff asked.

"No, never," Thunderstorm said. "I speak to Zonzalo when he calls me, but I do not summon them."

"We have a name," Carialle said. "I can send to the nearest space station for criminal files. Zonzalo what?"

"Don," Thunderstorm said. "He speaks for the leaders, Aldon Fisman and Mirina Don. Mirina is senior sibling of Zonzalo."

"Fisman?" Keff asked. "Related to the first Fisman?"

"Child of that one," Thunderstorm explained. "He is my friend. Strong and fierce, with less warmth than the parent. Mirina embraces the apprentices. She is kindhearted."

"Kindhearted pirates," Carialle said ironically.

"Hush, Cari," Keff said, soothingly. "We have names. Get on to CenCom and let's see how far their records go back."

Carialle opened up her receivers on the frequency she had gleaned from Thunderstorm's unit. With so little on-air traffic on this planet, it should be easy to detect another transmitter. Yes, there it was. Carialle couldn't tell precisely where it was, but she could guess approximately how far away in the direction of the strongest signal, where the antenna lay. She triangulated the location on the maps she had made of Thelerie, and made her best guess. If she had to, she could make a flyover of that region to be certain.

"Got one," she said to Keff, interrupting another information dump from Thunderstorm. From being taciturn and cagey, the Sayas of the space program had become almost too eager to help.

"Only one?" Keff asked. She saw his hand go up in front of his chest with one finger raised, a request for the Thelerie to pause.

"Only one base," Thunderstorm said, as his newfound friend fell silent, communing with the internal voice again. "I will show it to you, if you wish."

"Only one, not too high powered, so our friends count on getting very close to this planet before making contact," Carialle said, running through a quick calculation. "It's north-northeast of you, probably a couple hundred klicks. They're very sure no one will sneak up on them."

"Well, they're wrong," Keff said, smacking one hand into another. "This time, we'll be lying in wait."

"And we freeze them in place," Big Voice said, extending his two fists out in front of him." He rose off the floor above everyone's head, and spun in a circle.

"No, no!" Keff exclaimed, diving for the councillor's globe before it crashed into one of the pavilion's supports. "We need information from them. We can only do that if they're free to move and speak."

"Oh," Big Voice said, looking disappointed as Keff put him back on the floor. "It would be simpler. But how can we do this?"

"I have a cunning plan," Keff said, grinning at the little party in the pavilion. "What do the Melange come here for?"

"To gas up, and to pick up a supply of natural navigators," Carialle said at once.

"Well, to trade," Keff said, clarifying for the others. He sat down in his sling again and held out both hands. "We don't want them to cut and run, we want to talk to them. We're unarmed, and besides, policing is not our job. We gather information. So, what if the next time they come, they find someone here in their particular, secret treasure house, ready to undercut any price they ask for better goods?"

Carialle sounded amused. "They wouldn't automatically identify traders as CW personnel."

"Exactly," Keff said, lifting himself into a pike position with his hands braced on the supports of the sling-chair. "They'd land and try to find out who we are and where we come from.

"They might try to destroy you," Thunderstorm pointed out. "There is no mercy in them."

"It doesn't matter," Keff said. "Once they're out of their ships, they're vulnerable." He plopped back onto the thick, black strap and swung back and forth, pleased with himself.

"We can capture them," Tall Eyebrow said, clamping an imaginary prey between his large hands.

"But you have no trade goods to attract attention," Narrow Leg said. "We have brought nothing."

"That's where you're wrong," Keff said, leaning forward with a grin. "We have some very fine trade goods. Now, listen closely."

Chapter 16

"No more word from Base Eight," Zonzalo said, slapping an impatient hand down on the console. "That ship must have gotten them. It's too late."

Mirina bowed her head to say a quiet farewell to the lost crews. Some of them had been good friends of hers ever since the beginning of her association with the Melange. Some of them were apprentices she had brought on board and taught the ropes; innocents, like Sunset, who was wide-pupiled at the news.

"Are they all dead?" the Thelerie asked, searching his beloved humans' faces.

"We don't know that," Bisman said nonchalantly, brushing off the youngster's question. "The radios might have broken down, that's all. All the stuff's old."

"All of them?" Mirina asked in a sarcastic tone, taking care to keep her voice low. "Three ships and the master transmitter *and* all the backups broke down at once?"

"What do you want me to say?" Bisman hissed between his teeth. "You want the kid yammering to be taken home because he's scared?"

"He ought to know the truth, Aldon," Mirina hissed back, planting a palm in the middle of his chest and pushing. Bisman, taken by surprise, backed up into the bulkhead with a thump. His necklace of curios jangled. He brushed Mirina's hand away, and she put it on her hip. "The idea is that we let him make his own decisions, based on honest information, so he can function on his own one day in space, just like we promised them. If we don't tell him anything, he's just blundering along."

"Huh. Like the rest of us." Bisman turned away to go aft toward the mess, dismissing her. Suddenly, Mirina felt weary of the constant fighting, the dishonesty, the deaths. She strode after Bisman, finally having to run up the corridor to catch him. He turned around when he heard the hurrying footsteps behind him. Mirina beckoned him under a ventilation duct so the noise would cover their voices to the crew on the bridge.

"What?" Bisman demanded, deliberately standing over her so she had to crane her head back to look at him. She refused to let his tactics dismay her.

"Aldon, I want to quit."

"Quit what?" Bisman asked, acidly.

"I'm tired," Mirina said, standing back a pace and easing her head down. She massaged the back of her neck, and felt the tension in the muscles there. "I've been thinking a lot about this lately. This wasn't supposed to be a permanent arrangement, me staying on with you and the others."

"What's to think about?" Bisman asked, his thick, dark eyebrows tented in a puzzled peak over his nose. "We've got an arrangement. We work together, and we make money. That's what you wanted."

"Well, that's what I wanted for a while. Now, I want to stop."

Bisman scowled at her. "You're not serious."

Mirina let out an exasperated sigh. "Yes, I'm serious."

"Why do you want to leave?" Bisman asked. "We're good together."

"We haven't really been *together* in a long time, Aldon," Mirina said, patiently, trying to make him understand. She searched his face. "You know that. Everyone needs change after a while. I've been here

eight years. It's time for me to move on. I *need* to."
Then, daringly, "And I'm taking Zon with me."

Bisman was immediately suspicious. "Why?"

Mirina planted her hands on her ample hips.
"Because that's what I meant to do eight years ago
when I came looking for him," she said, without raising her voice. She could see by his expression that he
finally understood her determination, but he still didn't
like it. "I meant to take him and go. Then I stayed.
Now it's time for us to leave. That's all."

"Miri, honey, you can't go! We need you," Bisman
said, bending his knees so he could look directly into
her eyes. He clasped her upper arms and shook her
gently, a tender look on his face. He rubbed his thumbs
back and forth on her shoulders to the indentation
under her collarbone. Mirina groaned inwardly as she
felt the tingle spread through her body. She knew he
was going to try emotional blackmail, and here it came.
He hadn't touched her like that in over two years. The
contact felt so good, reminding her of the days when
they'd been lovers, but she knew it was only a tool he
was using on her. Suddenly, she felt angry that she
could be so thoroughly manipulated.

"You don't need me," Mirina said, fighting for a clear
mind. "You did once, Aldon, but now the operation is
running well. It's profitable, and everyone's taking good
care of themselves."

"There, you see?" Bisman said, with another friendly
shake. "We're in good shape *because* of you. You've
done so much for us. We wouldn't have grown like this.
Couldn't have. We can't do without you. The Melange
needs you."

"You *needed* me," Mirina said, emphatically. "It isn't
the same thing any more. As soon as we finish this run
to Thelerie, Zon and I are leaving." He heard the hard
tone of her voice and let her go, almost pushing her
away. Mirina felt cold like the void of space fill the

gap between them. Shivers replaced the tingle. No, there hadn't been any residual affection there.

"To hell with you, then," he said, his voice flat. "Go. You've got plenty of money from your shares to go anywhere you want."

"I don't want it." Aha, that surprised him. "I've never taken a thing out of the kitty, Aldon. It's all still there. I'll leave you every credit in exchange for a ship, any ship, even a junker. I can make it run."

"You don't know what you're talking about," Bisman said, making a fist. He held it in midair as if he didn't know what to do with it. For a moment Mirina was afraid he would hit her. Then he slammed his hand against the bulkhead over her shoulder. "You're crazy, the both of you. All right, then. When we make planetfall, you can leave in a ship, and go to hell while you're at it." He threw the last words over his shoulder as he stalked away toward the galley. Always the master of the parting line.

"Thank you, Aldon," Mirina called after him, genuinely grateful. He'd given her his word. Bisman wasn't paying any attention. Probably planning the next raid to make up for the loss of a ship.

She had to think of her own next move, too, after Thelerie. They were only a day or two away. It was going to take some fancy planning to begin life anew without a credit to her name. At least she could top off the tank of whatever vessel Bisman let her have. Thunderstorm's wrecks were available, but they wouldn't get her a light-year before blowing up. Damn it, she thought. She would have liked to stick around until the Thelerie became spaceworthy on their own. They were coming along so well. It would have been this generation that finally made the last step, and she would've been there to see it. Maybe some day she'd meet one of them in a remote outpost somewhere. Maybe they'd remember her. Mirina sighed, her heart and shoulders equally heavy. Maybe not. She went to tell Zonzalo of her decision.

Mirina woke in the dark and stared up at the ceiling. Yes, she had heard something, a noise on the edge of sound. A hiss.

In the utter blackness of her cabin she couldn't see anything, but she sensed that the shape of the space had changed. She could feel the air blowing on her skin from another angle. The door was open, but the corridor lights had been killed. Mirina's remaining senses roared up to high awareness. The pulses of the ship grew loud, and she felt the thrum of the engines in her flesh. Her sense of smell became enhanced, too. Mirina scented sweat and another, less tangible odor, sharp and thin. Fear. The shape of the darkness changed again, as a body moved between her and the source of air.

"Who's there?" she said out loud. The light hiss stopped, but no one spoke. Mirina felt a cold ball of terror in her stomach. She drew her legs to one side, bracing her muscles to spring to her feet on the bunk. Her balance was bad because her hip couldn't lie flat, forcing her knee to stay up. Damn, she wished she had kept in better shape! Complacency might now be the death of her.

The unseen person drew closer. She was almost certain the intruder was alone. Who was it? Why was it there? Such elaborate preparations boded no good to her.

In a voice so calm it surprised her, she said, "I have a laser pistol in my hand. I don't give a damn if the beam goes through you or the bulkhead. I'll give you to three before I start slagging everything in this cabin. One. Two . . ." She threw back the covers from her arms.

The small sound alarmed the intruder. The footsteps,

for the sound *was* feet sliding on the floor, scurried out into the passage. The door ground back into place, and the room regained its proper shape. Mirina clapped her hand to the wall for the lights. After two or three attempts, the switches engaged, flooding the room with white light. Mirina blinked blindly. In a moment, her eyes adjusted, and she scanned the cabin. Nothing looked out of the ordinary. Somebody had disconnected the power to her lights and her door to make his or her work easier, and would join the group expressing shock and outrage in the morning when Mirina would be found conveniently dead. She had foiled the attempt, but the sneak remained at large in the ship, having left no clues as to identity.

She ought to go wake up Bisman, and start an inquiry immediately, and check who, right now, had an elevated pulse. Maybe the sneak left fingerprints on the life-support controls, or footprints on her floor. Then Mirina realized that Bisman couldn't care less any more what happened to her. No clue was worth interrupting sleep.

She beat her hands on her thighs in frustration. How naive of her to think she'd just be allowed to walk away from the Melange! Bisman had gone straight to the mess hall and told everyone the Dons wanted to jump ship. Naturally, the first thought through everyone's mind must have been that she and Zonzalo intended to turn them all in and plead state's evidence. How stupid of her not to take that into account. From now until there was a light-year or so between her and the crew, her life was in danger. She'd better start packing that threatened pistol, and take other precautions. Listening for more footsteps in the hall, Mirina rose and hunted out her toolkit. She disconnected the door's mechanism, so there would be no more surprises, from that source at least.

The next two days were miserable. The raiders shunned even eye contact with the traitor. Mirina had felt lonely before, but she couldn't have anticipated real isolation. Zonzalo was no help. He resented being yanked away from his friends, and what he thought of as a career. He would go with his sister when she left, but he was unhappy, and he let everyone know it, loudly. Mirina was alone in her insistence on their upcoming departure. Fortunately, no one made an attempt on her life during day shift. The atmosphere was growing so hostile that Mirina started wearing the laser pistol on her hip and other weapons concealed about her person. Bisman didn't look at her directly at any time, but she caught sidelong glances when he thought she wasn't paying attention. She wondered what he was thinking.

She anticipated another attack, probably just as she and Zonzalo were ready to leave. They couldn't go, she realized. Not with the knowledge she had of all their operations, all their bases—their identity. By opening her mouth, she'd doomed herself and her brother.

Why hadn't she simply taken Zon and gone away, all those years ago? She'd been a fool. Ignored by the bridge crew, Mirina went back to her cabin and locked herself in.

"Mirina?" Sunset's mellow voice, sweet and sad, came from outside her door on the morning of the third, lonely day.

"Yes?" she asked, without opening it. She checked the monitor camera she had hidden in the bulkhead across from her door during the last dark shift. Nothing there but the back and wings of the young Thelerie. "What do you want?"

"May I see you?" he asked.

"That would be a bad idea right now," she said, keeping her voice flat. She was afraid to show the young Thelerie any warmth, lest Bisman and the others take out their anger on him after the Dons were gone. Or dead.

"Then, when? I must speak."

Mirina sighed. "Come in, but quickly." She reconnected the mechanism and slapped the control. Sunset clattered in on four feet, and stood, his noseless face almost in the works as she pulled the switches apart again.

"You are afraid," he said.

"Yes," she said. Her nervous laugh strangled into a squeak, so she chopped it off. She swung an arm toward the chair at her desk, and lifted one hip onto the edge of her bed. Sunset obediently walked over and slung his midsection across the chair seat. "Don't worry. I can handle it. So, what is it, youngster?"

"The others are talking about you," he said, his wide eyes fixed on her. "I do not wish to question. I am obedient, but you are my friend, and I am concerned."

Mirina was touched. So far even Bisman had failed to corrupt this gentle innocent. If there was anything she could do to make certain he was protected after she was gone, she'd do it.

"Thank you. What did they say?"

"They are afraid you will turn them into the See-Double-Yew," he said. "They fear for their lives."

Mirina laughed bitterly. "Do you think I can go to the authorities?" she asked. "You know what we do, young one. Your eyes are open. They'd lock me up, too. I'd rather die, and they should all know that by now." She flung herself off the bed and paced. "If these idiots want to kill me, all right, let them try! After eight years, if they don't trust me, then I know I stayed too long."

"Don't go," Sunset said, reaching out a claw in a simple gesture that broke her heart. "You are my friend."

"Where's your homeworld?" she asked, her voice suddenly husky. He pointed in the direction of the bridge, his eyes glowing.

"We are very close to the Center now," he said. "Soon, we will be home!"

"You're a good child," she said, coming over to pat his wing joint. "You learn your lessons well. I'm proud of you. Remember that."

"I will," he said. He put his claw hands together under his chin. Mirina repeated the salute. For this one being's sake she felt sorry she was going.

Hungry as she was for personal contact, Mirina sent Sunset back to his post. It would not do for him to remain in her company. After the young Thelerie left, she cursed herself for a poor planner. Why hadn't she thought of his well-being when she decided to leave? The Melange might fall into chaos again after she was gone. This ship could be stranded or captured. That child trusted his sacred humans; that trust should not cost him his life.

Mirina needed a moment alone with Thunderstorm. She would beg him to come up with any pretext at all to pull Sunset off the ship, and forbid any other young Thelerie from going out with the Melange. It was time they all faced the truth of what they were doing.

"No news from Base Eight yet," Zonzalo said over his shoulder to Bisman. Mirina stood in her corner, invisible to the rest of the crew. Bisman, making sure she could see it, walked up and patted the young man on the back. "The last message Thaw heard was the same that we did. An attack, and then nothing." Zonzalo swallowed a couple of times. Bisman shook his head.

"Too bad. What about Thelerie?"

"Thaw reports all is okay planetside. Reports in from some of the other crews with profit statements, particulars when you come by in person. Thaw said they filled the tanks at the landing site. Thunderstorm's been up and back a couple of times."

"Does he have any more apprentices for us?"

Zonzalo shook his head. "Didn't say so."

"Too bad," Bisman repeated in the same expression-less voice, with a glance at Sunset. "This one's doing so well, he might teach another Thelerie what he's learned."

Sunset looked up at Bisman with joy. "I would be honored."

"That's good," Bisman said, amused, and returned to Zonzalo. "Get on to Thunder, and tell him to meet us. We've got some good stuff for him."

"Right," the younger Don said. His eyes turned partway toward his sister, then snapped back to his console. Mirina's cheeks burned. He was distancing himself from her, maybe hoping she'd leave him behind with the others. Well, he was wrong. If she had to knock him unconscious, she was getting him away from Bisman.

"What do you mean, you want to compare values?" Bisman shouted at Thunderstorm over the communication line, waving his arms furiously. The Thelerie pulled back from his video pickup, his wings flat to his back, and his pupils narrowed in distress. "I don't believe what I'm hearing! Compare values? With what?"

"With those brought by the new humans," Thunderstorm said, his upper lip twitching. "I have said that. It is only right, isn't it? To see whether the best deal can be made?"

"*We* give you the best deal, you oversized fuzzy-toy!"

"Who are these other humans with goods to sell?" Mirina asked, pushing in front of Bisman. Zonzalo sat crunched down beside her, staying out of the way. "Thunder, how could you let someone cut in on us? After *we* brought you spaceflight, taught you Standard, and all . . . ."

Bisman rounded on her. "Thought you were out of here," he sneered.

Mirina was not going to let him cow her. "I spent a hell of a lot of time bringing these people up to speed, Aldon. I would think," she turned to the screen again, "they would remember that they owe us something!"

"We do, we do!" Thunderstorm protested, looking from one co-leader to the other in panic. "But you have said we are one with *all* humans. Keff is a human!"

Bisman groaned and slapped his hand to his head. Mirina, in spite of her annoyance, was amused. "That's what you get for feeding them altruistic lines all these years," she said.

"Don't gloat, damn you," Bisman said. "Help me." Mirina, giving Aldon a last, humorous glance, turned back to the screen.

"Who are they, Thunder?" she asked.

"I have spoken with a human named Keff, as I say," Thunderstorm said. "He has many interesting goods. I have seen some of them. He has hull-plates of supreme quality. Thruster pods. Engine conduits. Good equipment, almost new. Some things we have not seen before, a garden that travels in a ship!"

"Who is this guy? What does he look like? Who does he represent?" Bisman demanded.

"He is not as tall as you, Fisman, and broad in the chest, like Mirina. His eyes are the sky, and his hair is the color of good soil," and Thunderstorm described curls by circling a claw next to his head. "He says he represents the Circuit."

"The Circuit?" Mirina echoed, puzzled. "Never heard of them."

"This shouldn't change a thing, Thunder," Bisman said, finally. "We've got goods for you. We'll land 'em, have you look 'em over, and we expect a good exchange for them, as usual. We also need another apprentice or two. Shatz, out by Base 23, needs a navigator for one of his ships. Padwe and Hannah are ready to expand, too."

"I . . . am not sure any are ready to accompany you, honored one," Thunderstorm said. Mirina frowned. Thunder was usually deferential, but he seemed downright scared this time. His wings were pressed hard enough to his sides, Mirina could see the tendons bulge under the fur. "All are too young, too unschooled . . . I hope Sunset is well?"

Mirina signalled to the young Thelerie, who was happy to greet his old mentor. He scrambled over, put his hands under his chin and bowed to the screen.

"I am very well, Thunder," he said. "I look forward to seeing you soon."

"And I you, youngster," Thunderstorm said, with visible relief. The tendons in his wings relaxed.

"There is something wrong down there," Mirina said, when Zonzalo had closed the circuit. "We've got to find out what's going on."

"I'll tell you what's wrong," Bisman snarled, slamming a fist down on the back of Zonzalo's chair. "Somebody's trying to take over our territory. They're going to regret it, damn them."

Thunderstorm turned away from the little console. His wingtips and claws trembled as he tottered back to his desk sling. He collapsed into it. The Cridi, who had stayed well out of range of the communication cabinet's video pickup, clustered around him with concern. Keff raised his eyebrows in a question.

"It is done," the Thelerie said, nodding weakly. "They are coming."

"Good," Keff said. "Tell Noonday. Then we start the ball rolling."

"We are ready," Narrow Leg said, nodding to Tall Eyebrow and Long Hand. "I regret this, in many ways. I do not like being defenseless. I do not like having my ship all to pieces all over a field."

"It won't be for long," Keff assured him. "And you

aren't defenseless. You'll all be staying with Carialle in our ship."

"Is not the Watcher nervous, too?" Big Eyes asked.

Carialle answered via helmet speakers, audible to them all. "I certainly am," she said. "But we're on the way to unraveling a lot of mysteries. It'll be worth it, whatever comes."

The crew of the raider ship united instantly against the notion of a stranger's impinging on their domain. Glashton was in favor of killing the intruder on the spot. When the idea began to gather approval from others, Mirina pushed into the midst of them and in spite of the possibility of danger to herself, shouted them down.

"Quiet! What's the matter with you?" she asked, waving a forefinger under all their noses. "There may be a whole *host* of ships behind this one trader. He could be the vanguard for a traveling fleet! Did you think of that? Sooner or later someone was bound to stumble onto Thelerie. Well? Now someone has!"

"I want to know all about this Circuit," Bisman said, forgetting for the moment that Mirina was *persona non grata*. "I've never so much as heard a rumor about them."

"It's a big galaxy," Mirina said, her hands on her hips. "I learned that back in Exploration when we could find whole systems that had been hidden from scans by spatial anomalies. You'd be surprised how easy it is to hide an empire, let alone a rival . . . trading group."

"Send a message to Varvon, Frost, Hannah, and anybody who might have access to a CW news computer station," Bisman ordered. "I want details. Is the scanner working?"

"Intermittently," Glashton said, with a grimace.

"Take a look and see if this character's alone."

"And what are we going to do in the meantime?" It was an automatic question, responsibility kicking in again. Mirina realized it as soon as the phrase left her mouth.

"We?" Bisman glared down at her, also recognizing the incongruity. She saw his face change from annoyance to the old, worn groove of cooperation. It was stupid of her to get involved again when she had so nearly cut the traces, but she owed the Melange some measure of gratitude, too. She nodded. Bisman smiled grimly.

"We're going to pay a visit to this Keff." He glanced up at Zonzalo and Glashton. "He'll be leaving pretty quickly. Prepare to track where he goes. If the scanner's not working, follow him. We've still got the Slime Ball. We can destroy him and his ship if he gets funny."

"What a junker!" Carialle exclaimed. Keff had carefully turned his torso so she could see the huge, red ship land on the field near Thunderstorm's pavilion. It was immediately surrounded by Thelerie of all ages, some flying forward pushing wheeled ramps, others wrestling refueling hoses from the mighty tanks nestled in the crags at the edge of the plain.

"No doubt about it now," Keff said, the consonants blunted because he was speaking sublingually. "The style is all of a piece with the ships we confronted circling Cridi. We have our culprits. The only question is, are these the leaders of the whole shebang, or will we have to go hunting further?"

Carialle conveyed the question to Noonday, who was in her main cabin with two of her bodyguards and the Cridi. The Sayas glanced up from her perch on the weight bench as Carialle zoomed in as the hatch opened.

"This is Aldon Fisman," Noonday said. "I recall him much younger. It is shameful that I and the Ro-sayo did not take closer notice of our involvement with the Melange. But all was so beneficial, and we never questioned their good intentions."

"It is natural to think they would be as morally good as yourself," Long Hand said kindly. In the ammonia-free atmosphere of Carialle's cabin, the Cridi went without their travel globes. The visiting Thelerie were fascinated, and studied their neighbors openly. In particular, they seemed interested in the Cridi's hands, which were nearly the size of their own claws, which in turn were the same size as Keff's hands. It was a sign, Noonday had said, that they all ought to be friends.

"Bisman is their Sayas, in cooperation with the female who now descends," Noonday told Carialle.

On the screen, a woman and a younger man who resembled one another followed Bisman down the ramp. Next out of the ship was a young Thelerie, his eyes and jaws wide, taking in gulping breaths as if he could not get enough of the air. He took the ramp at a bound, spread his wings, gathered his mighty haunches under him and sprang into the air for pure joy. All of Carialle's pulses seemed to halt for that one moment as he took flight.

"Beautiful," she said. She checked her datatapes. Yes, that lovely moment was recorded forever in her memory banks.

"Freihur!" the young Thelerie cried. "Fanasta, theleriyagliapalo!"

Thunderstorm, a row or two down from Keff, looked up, and his eyes widened with relief.

"Farantasioyera, shafur," he said, with the booming cough that was a Thelerie chuckle, as the apprentice came to a scrabbling landing beside him. The two embraced warmly, claw hands and wings wrapped around one another's bodies.

"Did you get any of that, Keff?" Carialle asked. IT laboriously sorted through the syllables, and produced "greetings, (unintelligible) homeworld joy your coming." Thunderstorm had said, "Proud (unintelligible) return, young (unintelligible)." Carialle guessed that the missing words were names or endearments. Even days of intensive cramming wasn't enough to fill in the blanks in IT's lexicon and grammar.

Keff turned away to answer her. Carialle was disappointed when her view was cut off, but one couldn't have everything.

"I did," he said. "I'm going to have to rely on the Thelerie speaking Standard. The Cridi will be at a double disadvantage. Standard is new to them, too."

"They're very adaptable," Carialle reminded him. "They're doing just fine. And besides, they are better at reading body language than you are."

"Are you *sure* they won't jump in too soon this time?" Keff asked, a little more forcefully than he intended. "We need information, not statues. The second these people find out we're affiliated with the Cridi, they'll clam up."

"Absolutely," Carialle said. "Tall Eyebrow swore to me he will not act unless your very life is in danger, and he has one of my second-best monitors in that box with him. The others are here with me, watching the scopes. They are all hooked up temporarily with the Core inside my bulkhead. Myths and Legends has found a useful purpose at last outside pure pleasure, my dear. While you've been setting up your trading post over the last few days, they've been role-playing with holos of human beings until they know the difference between simple physical-psychological aggression and actual assault. They're as ready as they can be."

"Hmm," Keff said. "Keep your records of the training sessions; I'd like Dr. Chaudri in Psych on SSS-900-C to take a look at them."

"Already saved and stored," Carialle assured him blithely. "I think you have a customer."

Chapter 17

The first thing anyone would notice was the poster.
Mirina saw it on short-range screens before they had
quite landed on the plain. Once she could examine it
in detail, she was impressed.

Painted or printed at the top of the huge, white
signboard was a pair of silhouetted beings, species
indeterminate, exchanging shapeless bundles. Beneath
the image of the traders was depicted pictures of
certain commodities in various recognizable forms that
the trader would accept in exchange for his wares. The
first line was an irregular lump of gold, half in and out
of quartz matrix; the gold was shown next pressed into
an ingot, then as the molecular diagram of the element,
and weight at certain gravity, then as various artifacts
into which gold could be shaped, such as cups, wire,
circuit boards, statues, jewelry. He wishes, Mirina
thought. Other lines showed crystals; from simple
quartzite sand up through diamond and radioactive crys-
talline forms; precious metals; radioactives; iron and
steel; marble, alabaster, and other decorative heavy
stone. Handcrafts were welcome, too. A depiction of
weaving and various finished products showed a real
familiarity with textile manufacture. Jewelry, pottery,
furniture, and practically any type of merchandise
approved by the Central Exchange Commission had
been pictured in minute detail, but still leaving room

for the individual to offer variations. So tidy a mind that could design a sign like this appealed to her. This Keff had a completist's attitude: that everything can be set out so no one misunderstands, and everyone goes away happy. If she'd been staying on with Bisman, she might have suggested such a sign for them.

There were three more lines at the bottom of the signboard, showing various kinds of weapons: guns, lasers, bows, whips, garottes, with a big red X through each. This trader didn't want just anything, Mirina noted. Even if an alien didn't understand what the X or the color red meant at once, it would understand that there was something different about the acceptability of certain things. That showed a kind of morality that she had tried without success to impose on the Melange. No matter. That part of her life would soon be behind her. The signboard was worn and battered, as if it had been in and out of a cargo hold a thousand times. She glanced at the trader in the midst of his wares. Perhaps it had. He certainly looked as if he'd seen a few days himself.

Keff, if it was he, was not a youth. He looked to be about her own age, around forty. A man of middle height with very broad shoulders, trim and fit, he was dressed for comfort in a gaudy tunic and a pair of exercise pants going saggy around the ankle underneath a clear environment suit, the only part of his attire that looked new. The top of the helmet had been opaqued against the hot Thelerie sun. The dark halo threw into prominence his brown, curly hair, and fair skin, made pink by the heat. He was at work straightening piles of goods. Two little, boxy servo robots rumbled up and down the rows between the stacks, putting things back in order or holding up goods for the Thelerie to see. When the raider crew spread out, the boxies accepted them as customers, and held up on display any item by which anyone stopped for more than a few seconds. And what merchandise!

"He's got half a spaceship scattered on the ground," Mirina whispered to Bisman as they pushed their way along the dusty aisle toward the stranger. "Look at that: hull plates, exhaust locks, life-support circuitry—I don't know what that is." She pointed at a green, pressed-plastic tub about three meters across and two deep that had several protuberances sticking inward over the lip. A couple of locals were looking it over with the aim of making a planter out of it.

Thunderstorm and some of his staff were counting small circuit boards through the plastic of a storage pouch. They stopped to give the respectful greeting to the humans, but went back to their examination. Bisman's face crimsoned with suppressed fury over the whole situation. Mirina thought he might go into an apoplectic fit. She was annoyed, too, at the nonchalance this character showed.

"There must be thirty Thelerie here," Bisman said furiously, shouldering past them. More natives were winging in at every moment, landing at a remove from the scatter of merchandise and loping forward curiously. "What happened to security?"

"Thunderstorm can't control every centimeter of this planet," Mirina said, reasonably, glancing back over her shoulder at the Space Sayas. He looked very nervous, and she patted the air in a calming gesture toward him. "I can't believe this stranger's here all alone."

"Fool evidently has no fear," Bisman said. "Can you believe it? He landed on a strange world and set up shop, never thinking anybody might take a shot at him!"

"There's probably some sophisticated armaments in his ship," Mirina speculated, glancing around. She spotted it at last, and wondered how she had missed it. It stood tall and pure of shape in a niche formed by the natural rock wall at the edge of the plateau, like a classical statue in an alcove. "What a beauty!"

Bisman glanced up in the direction she pointed, and whistled as he made a mental estimate.

"There's money behind him," he said, at last. "We ought to be able to help ourselves to some of it."

"You're Keff?" Bisman asked.

"Who wants to know?" Keff said, stacking white enameled plates. The servo came over and took them away from him with a touch of impatience that was all Carialle's. He let go of the piece of hull and straightened up to greet his new "customer."

His eyes were a vivid blue in the pink-cheeked face. Mirina realized with a shock how attractive he was, and unconsciously thrust out one hip and put a hand on it. Keff grinned at her. Abashed, she stood up straight, folding her arms across her chest.

"Hot day, isn't it, friends?" Keff asked.

"You don't seem surprised to see other human beings," she said.

Keff laughed. "When I landed, these nice people addressed me in my own language," he said. "It didn't take a rocket scientist to figure out that they've known human people for a long, long time. They didn't get the language from tapes. There were *chairs* in that building over yonder, though none of the locals can sit on them. And your friend here," he pointed to Thunderstorm, "uses colloquialisms."

"Colloq . . . ?" Bisman waved away the unfamiliar word. "So what if he does? If they're in good working order, who cares?" Though Mirina could tell it was costing him something of an effort, he put out a hand to the stranger. "This is Mirina Don. I'm Aldon Bisman."

"Thought it was Fisman," Keff said exasperatingly. "That's what the locals called you. Just call me Keff."

He was so damned cheerful, Mirina thought, she might like to strangle him herself. Then he turned the intense blue gaze on her, and she felt her cheeks flame with red. He was very, *very* attractive. He looked her up and down, with a quick, insouciant flick of those eyes. She should have been offended, but instead, she threw back her hair and raised her chin in defiance. He gave her a grin of approval.

"Damned Thelerie can't say their damned b's," Bisman said. "When are you moving on?"

"When I've finished doing business," Keff said. He straightened up and looked Bisman in the eye. He might have been several inches shorter than the raider, but Mirina, with the eye of long experience, thought he'd be a match for him. The way Keff stood so naturally on the balls of his feet instead of flat on the soles suggested he *lived* unarmed combat. Formidable, attractive . . . and smack in the middle of the Melange's patch. She had to remember that. He was an intruder. He represented the outside world. It spelled the end of the Thelerie's sheltered existence, and she couldn't have that.

"What kind of goods do you have here?" Mirina asked.

"Oh, see for yourself. I sell a lot of things. I do a rather good line on state-of-the-art spaceship parts, right out of the heart of the CW," Keff said. Mirina exchanged a glance with Bisman, and saw the light of greed in his eyes. And small wonder, too, with that array on the ground.

"Looks like you have a whole spaceship spread out here," Bisman said, conversationally.

Keff laughed again, but a little nervously. "When you pick things up here and there, they accumulate," he said.

"Good guess," Carialle said, auditing the conversation from four hundred meters away. "Good thing he

hasn't got the Cridi's skill for abstract puzzle-solving,
or he'd see for sure! I'm glad your new design doesn't
look like the old ships, Narrow Leg, or these folks
would have spotted the resemblance in an instant. Can't
have that."

Narrow Leg sat on the console in front of the biggest screentank. In Carialle's protective atmosphere, he
and the others were able to move around, free of their
travel globes. They watched the screens around the
main cabin that were not obscured by the shipbuilder's
person.

"I do not like having my ship all to pieces on the
ground," he said, wringing his big hands together as
on the screen Mirina kicked some of the components.
"Do not touch that, silly human!" he wailed shrilly.
"That is a delicate power regulator!"

"This stuff is junk," the woman said, turning over
a brand-new engine accelerator valve still covered with
protective lubricant. "I'll give you fifty credits for it,
no more."

"No, thank you," the unseen Keff said, blithely, his
hand taking the component away from her and setting
it delicately on the top of a servo, who spirited it away.
"It's worth a lot more than that."

"Oh, yes? How do you expect me to make a profit
on it if I pay you more?" Mirina asked. The woman
turned to watch the robot whisk the accelerator valve
to the end of a row and set it down on a rickety folding
table.

"Aren't we greedy?" Carialle commented.

"I don't expect you to make a profit on it; I expect
me to make a profit on it," Keff's voice said. "I expect
you to use it. I prefer to serve the end-user. If you
don't want it, someone else will."

She shrugged. "It's junk. Who else would?"

Narrow Leg's black eyes bulged until Carialle thought
they would pop.

"How dare she denigrate the components of my ship! They are perfect! I rejected eight to the power of six of that valve before choosing that one! It was the product of ten to the power of sixteen calculations and designs!" His voice rose into almost inaudible registers.

"It's a bargaining ploy," Big Eyes said, floating over from her perch on the round table to try to calm her father. She put a gentle hand on his shoulder, and he shook it off irately. "You exist in the rarefied waters of science too much. You should come to the bazaar, and dig through the mud with me some time. Then you would hear worse than this."

"Bah." Narrow Leg was not appeased. He turned to Carialle's frog image on the near bulkhead. "What if they take some of our parts away?"

"We have many spares," Gap Tooth called to him.

"They are all out there, mains and spares," Narrow Leg gestured angrily.

Big Voice was clearly amused to see his old adversary discomfitted for once. With a tiny flick of his fingers, he drew just enough power from Carialle's engines to glide up from the weight bench and over where the shipbuilder was sitting.

"Keff will protect your ship parts," he said.

"And if he cannot?" Narrow Leg demanded, glaring upward. "How do you expect to get home?"

Big Voice snapped his fingers, making the gold fingerstalls click. "We do not need *your* ship. Carialle will bring us back to Cridi."

"I will, if necessary," Carialle promised the anguished captain. "But your craft will be restored as soon as possible."

"I am not happy," Narrow Leg said. He hunched up his kness and wrapped his skinny arms around them. The small bundle shot off the console and disappeared into the lap of the crash couch behind him.

"Leave him alone," Big Eyes signed, flitting away

from the chair like a tadpole swimming in a pond. "It is no use communicating with him when he is like this."

"He should be adaptable, like me," Big Voice said aloud.

From inside the huge chair came a disbelieving "Hah!"

"My child looks nervous," Noonday said, speaking up timidly. "He has shown disrespect to humans, and it weighs upon his conscience." The Sayas and two of her Ro-sayo sat in the corner, out of the way of the Cridi. Noonday occupied Keff's weight bench; and the Ro-sayo, a spare mattress pad from the cargo hold. Carialle switched her monitor away from the conversation Keff was having with the raiders, and zoomed in on Thunderstorm. The Space Sayas went about his shopping as he'd been told to do, but he wasn't happy.

"He's doing fine," Carialle assured his parent, enlarging the view on the screen nearest the weight bench for the sake of the Thelerie visitors. "He did exactly what he was supposed to, to make the Melange jealous. We don't want them thinking too clearly. People blurt things out when they are angry."

"Flurt?" Noonday asked, her beautiful eyes puzzled.

"Speak forcefully without thinking," Carialle said, slowly.

"These learn," Small Spot said, proudly. He sat as close to the Thelerie as they would allow him. "I teach them more Standard, which I know."

"You're doing fine, too," Carialle assured him, privately amused.

"I cannot believe the beauty of this ship, Carialle," Noonday said. "I see, but my eyes must lie—such things as this and the Cridi ship, they are as dreams."

Narrow Leg was somewhat soothed by the compliments. His wrinkled, green face appeared over the top of the crash couch.

"Not a dream. State-of-the-art for now," he peeped.

"We move ahead, always ahead." Carialle transposed the voice to a baritone register and amplified it so Noonday and the others could listen without pain.

"We are getting used to them," Noonday said, to the air. Carialle could tell that she still didn't really understand a human who lived in the walls, nor one who could look like a frog at will, but followed the Cridi's example of behaving as if Carialle was there in the room with them. Shellperson existence was a facet of human experience that had never yet come their way.

She wondered what the CenCom would make of Thelerie, and if they would try to withdraw the technology humans had given them to date, on the grounds that they wouldn't have evolved it yet themselves. She hoped not, but bureaucrats could be so rulebound!

Carialle herself had become completely comfortable with Thelerie. Having had Noonday, Thunderstorm, the Ro-Sayo, and a large number of former members of the Melange tour through her ship during the last several days, she was convinced that none of their gaits matched the footsteps she remembered transiting what was left of her hull after her accident, not even accounting for weightlessness and grav-boots. They were absolved. The question remained: who?

"Well, we might have an offer for you ourselves," Bisman said, rocking back on his heels and staring up at the sun. "We'll take the whole line off your hands, on condition that you take it, and don't come back."

"I can't do that," Keff said. "I have obligations to fulfill."

"The Circuit," Bisman said. Keff nodded. "Where's it based?"

"Oh, here and there," Keff said, too casually.

"Well, it won't be here," Bisman said, not at all fooled. "You have two days, then I want to see your tail-rockets up there." He pointed toward the sky.

"No can do," Keff said, looking pathetically at both leaders. Mirina wasn't moved. "The lady who runs the Circuit would make life miserable for me. You'll understand." And he flashed that insouciant grin once again.

Mirina found that they were getting nowhere with the trader. It stood to reason that a traveler who went around in a fancy ship like that with top-shelf goods like these on the edge of nowhere wouldn't be easy to bluff, but was he too cocky? Bisman might get so frustrated that he would attack him right here. She could stop him, but couldn't prevent the rest of the crew piling in on a fight. At least Zonzalo and Sunset would stay out of it. She'd been very firm in her orders. For whatever reason, neither one argued.

Bisman started some low-level threats on Keff, nothing overt or too nasty, and found his sallies thrown back in his face. Mirina stood by, turning over the odd component or two with her toe. He had some of the damnedest things for sale. Oil paintings? She bent to examine them. A small space-scape caught her eye. She thought she recognized the subject as Dimitri DMK-504-R. Piled anyhow underneath it were the study of a planet she couldn't identify, a lake at sunset, a beautifully detailed portrait of a cat stalking a leaf, and a color sketch of a couple in yellow and silver, holding a baby dressed in deep, burgundy red.

"You've wandered into our patch," Bisman was saying over her head.

"Did you paint these?" Mirina asked, suddenly, interrupting them. She nudged the pile with the side of her foot. "They're good!"

She was rewarded with the warm grin. "No. A friend of mine does them."

"He has talent," Mirina said.

"She. Thank you. I'll pass the compliment along. Maybe you'd like to buy something?" Keff asked, with just the right air of hope.

"Maybe not," Mirina said, crossing her arms again. Good God, he was pushy!

"Oh, then on my next stop here," he said, cheerfully, not at all put off. "You folks get around here much?"

"Now, listen, friend," Bisman said, poking Keff in the chest to get his attention. "There won't be another stop here for you."

"Really?" Keff asked. "I won't ask, 'you and what army,' because I've been watching your toughs gather around me for the last ten minutes, and I promise you I'm just not as green as I am cabbage-looking."

"What?" Mirina demanded, having followed his conversation up until then.

"Save the ancient colloquialisms yourself," Carialle growled in his ear. Keff clicked his tongue in acknowledgement. He had his hand on the top of the red box marked "Medical Waste," where Tall Eyebrow was concealed. One rap, and these brutes would be frozen in place. He hated to show his trump card right away. He would never get what he needed if he was too cocky.

"Sorry," he said, smiling at the woman. "I mean, I was not born yesterday. You don't think for a minute that I don't know how defenseless I *look*." She paused. Keff noticed Bisman's hand sweep down in a gesture that looked casual, but all the other spacers stopped moving toward them.

"So you have some kind of defense in that fancy airplane of yours," Bisman said casually.

"Airplane, hah," Carialle said. "Look at the flying refuse heap he came in."

"Shh! . . . sssure," Keff said. "My . . . employer wouldn't let me out without adequate protection."

"The Circuit," Bisman said flatly.

"You've heard of us?"

"No, I haven't. You could be a fly-by-night operation with one ship and an attitude. I've seen your kind before."

"Started that way yourself, did you?" Keff asked, and had the satisfaction of seeing the pirate start violently.

"The Melange comes from an old family tradition," Bisman corrected him with a sharp look.

"Ah! Your *father*," Keff translated.

The present-day Bisman breasted up to Keff and glared down at him. "Listen, character, you gather up all your debris, and you lift off of this world within thirty Standard hours."

"My boss will get tetchy if I don't come back with a deal," Keff said, plaintively, his hands spread in appeal. Bisman crossed his arms. Out of the corner of his eye, Keff could see the crew on the move again. "No, eh?"

"Too bad," Bisman was saying. "You tell him he's accidentally impinged on hazardous territory."

"She," Keff corrected him. "You wouldn't believe how tough the broad is at the center of the Circuit. Your threats would make her laugh out loud."

"Oh, Keff, I love it!" Carialle's chuckle sounded in his ear. "Tell him it's a neural-synaptic network, which means we're never far away from the active arm of our organization."

Keff passed on Carialle's words, and enjoyed the puzzled look on the pirates' faces as the two did mental translations. Bisman, at least, came up empty.

"What's this tough broad's name?" the older man asked.

"Carialle."

"Carialle what?"

"None of your business," Keff said, nonchalantly, raising his eyebrows.

"It is if we're going to do business with you," Bisman said.

"And who says you are?" Keff asked. "You want me off what you call your patch. Who in the frosty void do you think you are?"

"Look," Bisman said, suddenly looking bored with him. "I don't talk to underlings. I want to talk to this Carialle."

"Hmmm . . . Might be arranged," Keff said.

"I want a meeting. You can arrange it."

"Well, I'll see what I can do," Keff said, bending down to accept a bag of circuit boards from one of the loader robots. He glanced up at Thunderstorm and the young apprentice from the pirate ship. The older Thelerie had an anxious look on his face.

"Fine, fine," Keff called, waving to the Sayas. "I'll put the value down on a slate for you. Keep looking! You never know if you'll find something else you like." He smiled at Bisman. "It may take some time to get a message through to Carialle, but I'll send one right away and tell her you want to talk with her."

"Face-to-face," Bisman said, tapping Keff painfully in the middle of the chest once for every syllable.

While Keff stood there thoughtfully rubbing his chest, Bisman hustled Mirina away. He grabbed Thunderstorm by a claw on the way by.

"Your pavilion," he hissed. "Now!"

Thunderstorm loped unhappily behind them over the stony ground. Mirina could feel the storm of fury growing, but Bisman didn't let fly until they were safely under the roof.

"You're avoiding me," Bisman snapped, rounding at once on the Thelerie. Waving a finger under Thunderstorm's nose, he backed the Sayas up until he bumped into his own desk sling. "Don't try to deny it. I've known you too long. I told you we had stuff for you. You should be buying from us, and only us."

"Tell us about this man," Mirina said, more kindly. The Thelerie looked from one human to the other, clattering his claws together nervously. He settled over the sling and continued tapping his fingertips on the desktop until Bisman glared at him to stop.

"This Keff landed here one day. He said he had goods we might like. And so we do!" Thunderstorm said, miserably. "Things that the Melange has been unable to get for many years, are here! You see the temptation is great. And others saw him before I did, so I could not hide him. They like these goods."

"I understand that," Bisman said. "He's got a few things I might take myself. What I'm talking about is no apprentices. You must have some about ready to ship out. Where are they?"

"I . . . I do not have any I am ready to send. There is more to know."

"Haven't they memorized the Manual?" Mirina asked, puzzled.

"Oh, yes," Thunderstorm said, at once. "In that they are proficient."

"Then what's the hangup?" Bisman asked, banging a fist on the desk. "You know what kind of rewards there are in space travel."

"Yes," Thunderstorm replied, more thoughtfully than usual. "I know."

"So why are you being cagey with us?"

"The air is bad in ships," Thunderstorm said suddenly. "The old ones who I see have weakness in the thorax from lack of elemental acids."

"Chlorine?" Mirina asked.

"Yes," Thunderstorm said.

"Hell, then we'll work out a medical system. Miri . . . no, I'll work something out," Bisman said, dismissing Mirina. She glared, then realized she had no right to complain. He'd accepted her resignation, and he was letting her go.

"It will still take time before any are ready," Thunderstorm said, timidly. "The training continues."

Bisman walked to the entrance of the pavilion. "Next

time I won't take no for an answer, Thunder. There are ships out there who need Thelerie apprentices. Just remember who your friends are." With an apologetic glance back at the terrified Thelerie, Mirina followed him out.

Bisman reported the conversation to the others on the ship. The reivers clustered in the galley grumbled about another setback.

"Dammit, this tears the trip out to Sungali," Glashton said. "Hannah had a collection for us. It's not worth burning the fuel if we have to turn around and bring her a navigator on a separate trip."

"At least we can't blame this problem on the trader," Mirina said.

"No, dammit, but he might have said something that set them off," Bisman said, with growing heat. He kicked a battered cabinet door, adding a black bootmark to the damage he'd done it in hundreds of other temper tantrums. Mirina wouldn't miss that part of Aldon Bisman at all.

"Perhaps he's tired of talking to the families of the ones who don't come home again," she said, pointedly.

"Shut up!" Bisman said, rounding on her. "You want out anyhow. This isn't any of your business anymore." He slammed his hand on the countertop. "I've got to find the pressure point, get Thunder back into line, and soon. These Thelerie are a hell of a lot of trouble."

"Well, why are we bothering to go to so much trouble for them, then?" Zonzalo said with disgust.

"Because the soulfrigging flying barnacles can't get lost, that's why," Bisman exploded. "You know that, you young idiot. They always know their way back home, and everywhere in proportion to home. It happened to me once, being lost without a navigator. I never want that to happen again. Wandering lost in eternity may appeal to you, but it scares me juiceless!"

"And there's the fuel," Mirina said thoughtfully. "I didn't see any Thelerie merchandise out on that field. Did Keff spot the refinery and offer to trade for a tankload?"

"Whatever it is doesn't matter," Bisman said. "We find out what there is to know about this Circuit, and what defenses this Keff is packing in that pretty ship of his. He'll get a meeting set up with this Carialle, and I'll strangle him in front of her as a lesson to stay out of our way."

"And then what?" Mirina asked.

"Then we take care of all of the Circuit," Bisman said. "We've got the Slime Ball, remember?"

"Who knows how many there'll be?" Mirina asked. "The Ball could overheat any day, and then we'll have nothing."

"We've got more than sixty ships and enough armament to carpet a planet," Bisman said offhandedly. "I'll start calling 'em in right away. If he wants to make this system the prize in a blood game, we'll oblige him."

"I don't want the Thelerie hurt!" Mirina said, alarmed at the idea.

"Shut up," Bisman said, facing her down. "Either help, or get out of the way. You're just waiting for an offworld ship now, right?"

It stung, but Mirina had asked for it. "Right," she said. She rose and stalked out of the galley. Zonzalo got up to follow her, but his footsteps stopped at the hatchway. Mirina went back to her cabin alone.

"Are they gone?" Keff asked the air.

"Sealed up in their wretched ship," Carialle said. "They might have a passive scan on you, but it's nothing I'm picking up. Their telemetry equipment is as haphazard as their engines."

"Thank heavens," Keff said. One of the servos rumbled up to him, and he put the Medical Waste box onto its flat top. He slapped the robot's side. "Move it out, quickly. Is the tub full?"

"Big Eyes has it ready and waiting, with an electrolyte shake on the side."

Keff trotted along behind the drone. The sun was setting over the planetary-west horizon, and he glimpsed two moons rising golden above the mountain ranges. Very pretty landscape, he thought, but too, too hot.

"Are you okay in there, TE?" he asked, through his helmet mike.

"Okay," came a faint croak.

"Hurry it up, Cari," Keff said, more concerned. He didn't like the way the globe-frog sounded. Had he stayed outside too long? The servo rumbled around the edge of the stone cliff, and out of sight at last from the pirates' ship. Keff grabbed the crate bodily off its platform and ran with it into the ship. The other Cridi flew around him as soon as he was past the airlock. The lid of the box flew one way, and the little globe lifted straight out.

The sides of the globe were completely misted over with condensation, which broke up as the others moved it. The Frog Prince's body lay at the bottom, immersed in a few liters of water. He roused as Big Eyes wrenched off the upper half of the travel-globe, and sat up. His eyes glistened in an unusually pinched face, but he waved away offers of help to stand. Noonday, who had watched all afternoon with growing admiration, added her concern.

"He will live?" she asked.

"I live," he said, hoarsely. "It is sometimes worse on Sky Clear."

"You're a hero," Keff said. "If you hadn't been there, I couldn't have pulled that off." The Cridi shook his head.

"It is nothing," Tall Eyebrow signed. He licked his lips, which were visibly dry.

"Tchah! Nothing!" Big Eyes flicked her fingers, and the door of the spare cabin flew open. Tall Eyebrow was whisked straight out of the main cabin. Keff ran along behind into the corridor. He heard rather than saw the splash.

"I am all right!" Tall Eyebrow protested in Cridi. "Do not . . . blub!" Big Eyes hands had moved, and Keff suspected she swept a wave of the cool water over her loved one's head. He stuck his head in, and saw gallons of water washing across the floor from the small bathroom.

"He is a hero," Big Eyes said, with a look at Keff and the Thelerie, as she sailed in after him. "He does not complain."

"He does what a leader should," Narrow Leg said, nodding.

"Daddy approves, whether he admits it or not," Carialle said, in Keff's aural receiver. "I do love a love story."

"Seeing him in action, you can't help but admire him," Keff agreed.

"It is true," Noonday said, behind them. "The Cridi are most amazing folk." She gathered her wings about her, avoiding the water flying out of the door of the spare cabin. "Now that night falls I must go back. The Ro-sayo and I have much to discuss. You will accompany us?"

"I'd better not," Keff said. "The Melange will be watching me closely now. The Cridi will go, carrying a receiver so you can hear what Carialle and I say."

Noonday looked up, as if she expected to see the pirates and their surveillance. "But how do I go, if you are watched? They will see me."

"Ah," Keff said. "The extreme cleverness of me! Thunderstorm asked a few of your people to wait on the field. They'll come over and give you cover when we lower the hatch again. You'll be one in a crowd of your people making purchases."

✧   ✧   ✧

The Thelerie were right on time. When Carialle activated the ramp again, Thunderstorm and a cluster of his apprentices fluttered over, some carrying boxes, some carrying other small items. Using Core power, to the great astonishment of the locals, Narrow Leg and the others unloaded the contents of the boxes, and rolled their globes inside.

Tall Eyebrow emerged from the bath with glistening skin. His face still looked rather peaked, but Carialle checked his vital signs, and found them strong. He showed no weakness as he sealed himself into his travel globe. Big Eyes looked at him with dismay.

"You should not go with us," the young female said. "You should rest."

"I am going," Tall Eyebrow argued. "These people have made many sacrifices for us. This is not a risk at all. I am healthy. I must hear what is said."

"You will all be well-maintained," Noonday assured Big Eyes solemnly. "I will look after Tall Eyebrow myself." Big Eyes relented, but grudgingly, and allowed herself to be shut into a plumbing fixture.

"We will be back soon," Narrow Leg said to Keff, via radio, from inside his crate. Each of the Thelerie took one of the containers gingerly in its claw arms, and flew away with it. Shaking his head, he stepped back into the airlock, and Carialle sealed the door.

"A meeting with this tough broad," Carialle said, still enjoying the sound of the phrase. Her Lady Fair image appeared on the wall armed with morningstar and shield. "You mean a holographic manifestation?"

"Yes, but not like that one," Keff said, smiling. "Whatever would work to get the most information out of them. We have to be careful. I don't want them to leave again if there's the least chance an armed ship is on the way, but I don't want to endanger this

population. The Thelerie are vulnerable, and they trust
humans implicitly because of these brutes."

"The Melange are a mixed curse," Carialle said,
thoughtfully. "On the one hand, I'm glad they discovered this race. They're fascinating. On the other hand,
if it had been anyone else, the CW could have nurtured the Thelerie's natural development. Look at this
place. Except for the smelly air, it's almost a type-G
world."

"Yes," Keff said. "I notice the pirates don't bother
with air filters."

Carialle caught the hopeful note in his voice. "No,"
she said flatly. "There is a cumulative effect on your
health. The Cridi have been complaining of the residual
ammonia brought into the cabin in the lungs of the
Thelerie visitors. You keep your suit on."

"Yes, mother," Keff sighed.

Keff had a grasshopper's eye view of the proceedings in the Sayad, from the camera eye carried on
GapTooth's globe. She was carried in a sack by one of
Noonday's guards and released into the Sayad chamber to the horror and protest of the Ro-sayo. She rolled
at once into the angle of one of the carved beams as
the Thelerie glared down into the camera lens.

"Why are they here?" Midnight demanded, as behind
him the Cridi freed themselves from the crates and
other containers.

"As witnesses," Narrow Leg said, flying out of a box
marked "Art Supplies." "And as a conduit for our good
friend Keff."

"But they are enemies!"

"They are not," Noonday said, mildly, settling onto
her divan cushion. She coughed, and was surrounded
at once by Ro-sayo exclaiming concern for her health.
Keff felt pleased that the Sayas was held in such
esteem.

"You are unharmed?" Winter asked her.

"All is well," she assured them. "I have spent a day in deficient atmosphere. The effects will pass quickly." With a wing-finger, she signalled for the doors to be secured. "Let no one in or out, and have a patrol hover about the windows on the outside. Our guests must remain hidden from view." The guards sprang out and away, spreading their wings to obey their leader's command. The Ro-sayo settled down on their cushions, casting wary eyes on the cluster of Cridi. Thunderstorm drew their eyes away by stalking into the center of the circle of counselors.

"Before they speak," he said, "I have a speech to make, of apology to our neighbors, for it is true what Keff told you. I will speak in Standard where I can, for the sake of our listeners."

He went on to detail the history of the Melange. Although Keff couldn't understand all of the Space Sayas' words, he could tell that many in the room were shocked at the revelations he had for them.

"Then all of our accomplishments were based on lies!" Midnight said.

Thunderstorm bowed his head. "I deserve that," he said. "But we may rebuild, and beginning now, with the help of legitimate representatives of humanity, we shall."

"And how do we know that Keff and the unseen Carialle are truly from the See-Double-Yew?" another Ro-sayo demanded.

"Does it matter?" Noonday asked. "I saw the Melange show hostility to a stranger human, telling him to leave Thelerie, and never return. That isn't the act of a being who believes we are all one."

Thunderstorm smiled. "I assure you, I know real See-Double-Yew. I spent many years robbing their bases and stations. Also of these, the Cridi. A number of the parts of the ships that stand on our own landing pad come from their ships."

Midnight stood, and solemnly bowed to the Cridi. "We owe you reparation." He held out a claw hand. Narrow Leg and Tall Eyebrow exchanged small, subtle signs that Keff had to squint to see. Together, the Cridi opened their globes and rose to their full, though inconsiderable, heights. Exposing their delicate skins and lungs to the sharp air was a stunning display of trust that moved Keff deeply. The two leaders stepped forward to take the Thelerie's narrow talon, one at a time. The other Ro-sayo grudgingly, fearfully, stepped forward to clasp hands with the shining, water-clad amphibioids.

"We will take aid and assistance instead," Narrow Leg said. "The parts are obsoleted with the new design, the one that is," he added with regret, "lying dismembered on the field."

"What can we do to assist?" the other Ro-sayo asked.

"Be prepared," Keff said, speaking through an audio receiver on GapTooth's globe. "Our intention is to obtain recorded confessions from the Melange as to their activities in this sector for use by our judicial arm. I'm concerned that if the Melange becomes suspicious that we are from the CW, your well-being could be at stake."

"A certain amount of *fallout* is inevitable," Thunderstorm said, with a shrug of his magnificent wings. "We have contributed to the galaxy's ills by consorting with criminals. Although I absorb all guilt, my people may suffer. I owe all many lives."

"We will not claim them," Big Voice said, rolling forward and puffing himself up majestically. "The thing we must do is get the information needed by Keff and Carialle."

"It is possible that our military is nearby," Carialle added, amused by Big Voice's self-importance. "They must have received our message by now about the Thelerie we left behind on the Cridi system's fifth

planet. They could be here soon to take Bisman and
his crew into custody."

"If they leave, what of it?" Noonday said, spreading her upper lip. "My child says that the Melange
come here often. They have a friendly bond with our
people, whatever they have done to others. A capture
will occur, now or in the future. We offer the aid of
our guardians, if you need them. At present, we will
cooperate to get what it is you seek now."

"I hope so," Carialle said. Keff thought he could
detect wistfulness in her tone. He smiled at her pillar.

"With such friends, Lady Fair, how can we fail?"

Chapter 18

A few days passed after the Cridi returned safely from the capital city. Keff continued to pretend doing business on the high plain near Thunderstorm's enclave.

The longer the Cridi's ship parts were on display, the more interested the pirates became in buying them. Keff was now in possession of a handful of credit chits whose legitimacy and provenance he very much doubted. Narrow Leg, on duty as Keff's guardian in the Medical Waste box, was less of a success than Tall Eyebrow, because he kept a closer eye on his inventions than he did on the human whose life he was supposed to be protecting.

"I do not like these disappearing," he protested into his radio over and over again during the long, hot day. "They go into the pirates' hold, and they go away toward the city—but they are not *here*."

"Relax, Tad Pole," Keff said, out of the corner of his mouth. "We'll get everything back just as soon as we're finished here. Thunderstorm promised me that the parts are being well looked after."

"It must be soon," Narrow Leg said. "All this dust, getting into the components! Impair efficiency!"

"Shh! You're exaggerating, I'm sure," Keff hissed, seeing Bisman coming down the ramp of the raider ship. He hoped the Cridi shriek hadn't been audible.

The leader was stalking toward him with purpose. Keff stopped pretending to tidy his wares, and waited.

"What have you heard?" Bisman asked, without other preamble.

"Nothing yet," Keff said. "I sent the request for a meeting, as you asked me to. It'll take time for the message to meet her. I had to assure her you're not a small-timer, that it would be worth her while doing business with you. I told her you had sixty ships under your command, is that right?"

Bisman spat into the dust next to Keff's feet. "At least sixty. And I've got other resources. Connections."

Keff raised his eyebrows, but the older man was far too canny to take the questioning look as an opening. He shook his head, and Keff grinned, pretending to look sheepish. "Can't blame a fellow for trying."

"You just tell me when she gets here," Bisman said, poking him in the chest again. "I'll talk a lot more when I hear her bona fides."

"All right," Keff said, but to Bisman's back. As soon as he'd had his say, he'd swung around and stalked off in the direction of Thunderstorm's pavilion.

"I do feel sorry for that griffin," he said into his sublingual pickup. "He's taking all the brunt for us."

"You play the part of the up-and-coming flunky to perfection," Carialle said acidly.

"I've always said I should start at the top and work downward," Keff said, forcing a note of cheer into his voice. "Is there any word today?"

"Not a thing," Carialle's voice said, sounding a little strained. "There has been plenty of time for my first transmissions to have reached the nearest space station. I could have *flown* up and back in the time it's taken them to respond."

A couple of the raiders on the edge of Keff's "bazaar" reached for the same book-chip library at the same time, and started to bicker over it. Keff turned his back on them.

"There's always the question, if there was an armed ship in the vicinity, and whether they could send it," he said.

"They might already have sent it," Carialle pointed out. "If it's behind the anomaly, the ship won't receive any more transmissions from us until it clears Cridi system. By then, the Melange, or at least Bisman, could be long gone. Noonday's guards won't be worth a darn against energy weapons. I wish you could have gotten even one base location out of Bisman. *Any* starting point so I don't have to unravel ion threads again."

"He doesn't like me," Keff said, thoughtfully. "More fool he. But he's starting to lose patience. How long can we stall him before he finally loses his temper?"

"If that happens, he'll attack, in which case our cover, and the Cridi's, is blown; or he'll leave. We'd have to give chase, and I don't fancy our chances. That third Core may still be out there somewhere."

Keff rocked back on his heels and looked up at the sky. He stared at a bank of clouds gathering in the northwest, then realized the novelty of atmospheric condensation in such a dry climate. Looked like a head of stratocumulus building. Did it ever rain here? He must ask Thunderstorm.

"We're not policemen," Keff said, "but we can't just let these people go."

"Not until I get what I want," Carialle said. "Once the CW forces land here, that possibility is gone, and *we're* stewed, too. I'll be in a home for the perpetually bewildered, and you'll be flying a troop carrier."

"We're not making much progress," Keff admitted. "I haven't managed to elicit a single confidence out of those people, not in six days. Not a single detail of where they've been in the past, a single event. You'd think they'd be bursting to brag about their successes, but no!"

"It's a tight ship," Carialle agreed. "They keep themselves to themselves with a vengeance. There are organized minds in charge. I'd admire the Melange, if we weren't trying to break through their defenses."

The air grew heavier, and the sky darkened. Keff checked his chronometer. "Looks like weather," he said. "How far away is it?"

"I've been charting a pattern coming in from planetary northwest," Carialle said. "I've been charting a tropical front in the far west. It hit a cold front a thousand kilometers from here, and I admit it whipped up faster than I estimated. You'd better start getting things under cover. You have about ninety Standard minutes."

"Looks like it could be a gully-washer," Keff said, starting to pick merchandise up at once. He signalled for the servo to come over and help.

"Keff," Carialle said. Her voice sounded tentative. "I've been trying to stifle my natural anxieties, but something needs to happen soon. I've . . . I find I've been *counting*."

Counting, as she had twenty years ago, adrift in space, to keep herself sane. Keff felt an urge to run inside the ship, to be close to Carialle, anything to help her calm down. "Have you had any memory flashes?" He started to pick up piles of circuit boards with a burst of nervous energy, then stopped to look around for the boxes.

"No."

"Good. Hang on, Cari. Nothing's different than it was just a few days ago."

"No, we're *nearer* an answer, Keff. I know it. I'm beginning to feel antsy in anticipation of it."

Aggravated at how slowly he was progressing, he glanced toward the humans browsing through the lanes.

The men and women from the Melange had also noticed the lowering sky. They shot glances at him and the tons of merchandise, but moved purposefully toward their own ship. Bisman stood next to the ramp of the raider with his arms crossed and a sneering smile on his face, watching Keff.

"Nice people," he growled, with more force than he'd intended.

"Why?" Narrow Leg asked, hearing Keff's comment.

"Because it's going to rain," he said, in frustration. Movement in the direction of the pavilion caught his eye. "Here comes Thunderstorm, probably to tell me the same thing."

"Rain is rare," Thunderstorm said. "And yet, here is! Do you need assistance?"

"Sure do," Keff said shortly, stacking boxes of components on the robot drone's back. His own worries didn't prevent him from remembering to say, "Thanks."

Thunderstorm started to pick up items with all four of his hands, and gestured to his apprentices with a tilt of his head. The young Thelerie fluttered in at once, and began to help. Across the field, the pirate's ramp ostentatiously clapped shut.

"There's nothing I can do now until the rain's over," Keff said sublingually to Carialle. "Can you last? Otherwise, I'll drag them over to you one by one with my bare hands and torture the truth out of them."

He was rewarded by Carialle's dry chuckle. "No, Sir Keff. That would get you thrown out of the Good Knights Club. I'll make it. Only," she hesitated, "stay by me."

"I'm always here for you, lady love," Keff said, with heartfelt sincerity, "even when I'm ankle deep in dust." He grunted as he hoisted a case of plumbing fixtures over his head, and passed them on to a hovering griffin.

"We will help as soon as the light goes," Narrow Leg's voice squeaked from his concealed post. "The outer shell can wait. Gather the life support and navigation components first!"

"Thanks," Keff said, absently, stopping for a moment to triage the most important items left on the field. He was distracted by his concern for Carialle. Had they set themselves an impossible task, with an implausible deadline?

"Where shall I lay these inside?" a Thelerie voice boomed through the rising wind. Keff sprinted across the darkening field to help her.

Mirina watched on the galley screen as the trader and his two robots scurried to put their merchandise away before the rain came. The small drones rumbled across the rocky plane with impossibly high piles of crates on their backs. It was a credit to AI engineering that not one item fell off all the way across the field and up the ramp of the lovely white ship.

"You're being mean, not letting any of us pitch in and help him," she scolded Bisman, who was watching over her shoulder.

"He's a businessman; he knows the risks," Bisman said, with indecent satisfaction. "Weather's a risk." Mirina shot him a glance filled with disgust. The raindrops were already starting to march across the dusty, tan plain. The Thelerie, who hated getting their fur wet, ran before the wind, hurrying to get undercover before the storm broke in earnest.

Mirina watched for a while, wondering how Keff had ever gotten all that hull plate into his little ship in the first place. He must have been sleeping on containers. You couldn't travel for very long in that kind of discomfort. She guessed he'd probably traded upscale from a much bigger craft, and was now paying the price in smaller quarters. She didn't recognize the design, but it was a honey. She missed being around quality like that. The controls must hum under one's fingers, instead of juddering, clacking, and even breaking loose. Mirina thought she'd like to see her fly.

A crack of thunder erupted and lightning burst like a star splitting apart. Mirina jumped back as the rain began to fall heavily, spikes of silver peppering the golden earth. In moments, the dust turned to mud and began to flow toward them. Mirina had a horrible feeling that the whole ground under them would turn into sticky goo, pulling the ship down into it, drowning them. She hated rain.

"It's a young typhoon," Glashton said, idly, with a glance at the screen. He poured himself a cup of coffee. "Nice to be under cover."

"I wish it would stop," she said, turning away.

"Why? It's just started." Bisman looked at her scornfully. "Nice to get a bit of change. This never happens in space."

"Yes, thank heavens," Mirina said. The others in the galley exchanged pitying looks.

"You weren't born in atmosphere, were you?" Glashton asked.

"Nope," Mirina said, reaching past him toward the replicator and programming herself a combination protein/alcohol cocktail. "They say you don't miss what you never had."

"Like what?" Javoya, the chief engineer jeered. She and Mirina had really never hit it off. Now that Mirina was leaving, the woman had been venting all her saved-up spite.

"Like common sense," Mirina said, coldly. "But then, you wouldn't know, would you?" Zonzalo, and all the others, gawked. Part of Mirina said she was stupid for opening her mouth, but the other part admitted she was human, too.

Grabbing a tool out of her belt, the engineer took a threatening step forward. Mirina found she didn't really care if the woman cut her throat right there, but the other crew members moved between them and made the engineer sit down. Ostentatiously, Mirina took another swig of her drink. Javoya glared. Mirina ignored her, thinking about her own problems. There was no other ship available here on Thelerie for her. She'd have to stay on with Bisman and this increasingly hostile group to the next stop, and maybe the next one after that, until they found a team with one that Bisman could bully, to get rid of the troublesome Dons. The one thing she could depend on was that he would keep his word about a transaction.

Eventually, the engineer tired of her aggressive pose, and threw the spanner down on the table. Everyone relaxed a little.

"Aw, what are we doing still *here*?" Javoya asked, appealing to the others. "It's nice enough. I like Thelerie, but even their hospitality gets to be over-whelming after a while."

"Business," Bisman said shortly.

"Well, let's get on with it already," Glashton said, frowning.

Mirina gestured in the vague direction of the other ship. "We're waiting for word from this Keff's employer about a face-to-face meet. Aldon wants to secure this system for uh—for the Melange."

Glashton made a face at Bisman. "What's the matter, is this guy stalling?"

"I don't know," the leader said, in turn scowling at Mirina. She finished her drink, even the awful coffee-tasting dregs which seemed to be at the bottom of every beverage lately. Everything on the ship was breaking down. A burst of thunder shook the ship. She shut her eyes and told her internal stabilizers to ignore the slight rolling under her seat.

"Spacedust, that's a horror."

"Well, we wouldn't still be here listening to it, if your boyfriend over there wasn't black-holing us," Bisman sneered. Mirina, in spite of her promise to herself not to get involved in any more arguments with him, glowered. He returned the fierce stare, with interest. "You don't want to be with us, madam. Maybe you should go ask Blue Eyes in his new ship to give you a boost offworld."

That reminded everybody of Mirina's upcoming departure. Suddenly, between the rain and the unfriendly glares, the fierce planetary weather felt less threatening.

"Maybe I'll go and see if I can't find out what's holding up the transmission," she said. Very casually, so it didn't look as if she was retreating, Mirina tossed her cup overhand into the disposer, and walked down the corridor. As if they were physical touches, she could feel every eye on her back as she left.

"If you're going, see if you can dicker for the whole load of parts," Bisman called.

"Whew!" Keff said, jumping back out of the way as Carialle closed the cargo bay hatch. "As if there wasn't enough in there with our own things, and your Core."

"It is intact," Narrow Leg said, fussing over the mass of machinery like a mother hen inspecting her chicks. "That is what matters. Oh, *days* lying in all that dust!"

"We have it all safely held in place and dry," Tall Eyebrow said. He closed his small black eyes for a moment. "All is stable. It fits together as neatly as if of a single piece." The Cridi flew or glided nimbly out of Keff's way as he slogged back toward the airlock. Carefully, he removed his environment suit, folding the outside in to keep most of the dust from scattering around the ship. Under the plastic hood, his curls were plastered to his skull with sweat.

"It's a good thing those pirates can't see in there," Keff said to Carialle, pointing down through the floor toward the cargo hold. "They'd wonder how I got the

whole shop in here in the first place. Most of the hull
and the engine casings are still outside. I'm exhausted!"

The human staggered back into the main cabin and
flopped into his crash couch with a sigh. All of his
muscles felt as if they were coming unraveled.

"All that weight training has been good for you,"
Carialle said, manifesting her Lady Fair image on the
wall.

Keff was too out of breath to make a suitable
rejoinder. He made a quick, one-handed gesture in
Cridi that he knew had a slightly rude meaning. The
amphibioids tittered.

A faint vibration ran through the body of the ship.
Keff glanced up.

"Thunder, almost directly above us," Carialle said.
"We are now separated from the rest of the world by
a wall of water."

"Rain," Big Eyes signed dreamily, as Carialle directed
her cameras to different views outside. The sun had
dropped most of the way below the rim of the can-
yon walls, throwing black shadows across half the plain.
The remaining crepuscular rays through the heavy
clouds spotlit the distant plain. In the direction of the
capital city was a double rainbow in almost 270 degrees of arc.

"This is not such a bad place," Big Voice said. "I
would prefer to visit during nice seasons like this."

A slow, very brief, and faint rumble clattered on the
hull. Keff glanced idly at the screen, waiting for the
brilliant fork of lightning.

"That's outside," Carialle said, suddenly interrupting.
She switched one of her screens to show a small,
rounded, bipedal figure standing next to the ship's
landing fin, holding up one upper limb. "One of the
pirates. She's knocking with a rock."

Keff peered much closer, and signalled for magnification. "It's Mirina Don. Wonder what she wants?"

"I don't know," Carialle said. "Let her in. Perhaps one at a time you can get some information out of them about where they were twenty years ago."

"Not a bad notion," Keff said.

"Will it be dangerous to allow her access?" Tall Eyebrow asked.

"I doubt it," Keff replied. "But she can't see you. You'll have to hide."

The Cridi gathered up their belongings with a whisk of Core power. The bowls and cups from their meal flew through the air and sank into the cleaner like pool balls into the corner pocket. Narrow Leg supervised the picking up of travel globes. In a few minutes, the room was as tidy as it had been weeks ago when only Keff inhabited it.

"We will watch to ensure safety for you," Big Eyes assured him. She waved her hand, and the door slid shut.

"I'd better hide, too," Carialle said. She darkened the long slice of the room in front of her pillar, then built an elaborate holographic display of a control panel which she projected from several different angles onto the dark space.

The banging came again.

"I'd better let her in," Keff said. He stepped to the inner airlock hatch as Carialle lowered the ramp. The forlorn figure stumped up the ramp and waited inside as the chamber pressurized. Mirina Don emerged into the corridor and turned back her hood, presenting a sodden face to Keff.

"You left me there standing long enough," she said, resentfully.

"Sorry," he said, smiling an apology. "I was doing a crossword puzzle. What can I do for you?"

The woman shifted uncomfortably. "Er, just visiting. May I come in?"

Keff stepped to one side, and made a slight bow.

"Certainly," he said. "It's nice to have company."

✧   ✧   ✧

Mirina shed her rain poncho and put it up on a hook next to a selection of protective suits in a closet just beyond the airlock. The Circuit sure supplied their people well. Keff had one of everything. One full environmental suit, one light enviro, an empty hook where the plastic thing should have gone that he'd been wearing, packs, both light and heavy, rebreathers, a thing like a shriveled green skin with a clear-plas helmet that was probably for deep-water environments. Whatever the Circuit was, it had money. Mirina sighed for pure envy.

"This way," Keff said. He led the way into the main cabin.

It may not have been a large craft, but it was new and beautifully appointed. Mirina glanced at the shadowed section where the control panel lay. A complicated holographic screentank filling almost half of that wall showed a long-range view of a slice of sky over Thelerie, with both small moons on the horizon over the cloud mass. A heap of boxes prevented her from getting too close, so Mirina stood back to admire the view. Both main stations had crash couches of generous proportion before them, so Keff could run either in equal comfort.

With no one to please but himself, Keff clearly lived most of his life in this room. She strolled over and examined the complicated-looking exercise station in one corner. On the other side of the console, a couple of worn grommets in the floor showed where a piece of heavy equipment had been removed from the alcove. The food synth looked clean and well-maintained. The round table beside it had an interrupted-ring bench with a dished top. Everything was neat, comfortable, and expensive-looking. Mirina wished for something like this for herself so much she hardly heard her host speaking to her.

"May I offer you something to drink?" he said.

"Certainly," Mirina said, peering at the synthesizer and wondering if the newfangled-looking controls were as easy to operate as they looked.

"Oh, no, not that," Keff laughed, and bent to a cabinet hidden in the wall behind the exercise machines. Behind the touch-open panel lay dusty bottles in shock webbing. Mirina stared at a small fortune in fermented beverages. "I have a nice beer. Not so good as a cask-aged brew that's served where it was laid down, but not bad."

"Mmm," Mirina said, appreciatively, unwilling to demand anything specific from the treasure house. Keff continued to paw through the collection. Now and again, she heard a faint clink as a couple of the fragile containers touched.

"Or—here, how about a drop of this? Red wine, from Denubia. Sixteen years old. No, wait," he said, after a pause during which he stared at the wall thoughtfully. He withdrew his selection. "This is better. Six-year-old Frusti."

"My God," Mirina said, staring as he produced a glass cylinder with a square paper label. The glass was dark, but the fluid within was darker yet. "I haven't had wine, *real* wine in years."

"It's real," Keff said, thumbing the synthesizer control for a couple of empty glasses. "Please, sit down."

Mirina watched him draw the cork carefully. She scented the faint headiness as the wine began to breathe, and drew it in appreciatively.

"You shouldn't be wasting this on me," she said, although she hoped he wouldn't take her at her word and put it away. She watched his hands. Nice hands. Square palms, square fingers, but favored with grace as well as strength. "In these parts that single bottle's worth a quarter of your other stock."

"A thing's only worth what people are willing to pay

for it," Keff said, with his engaging grin. "I paid about ten credits for it six years ago when it was grape juice." He tilted the bottle gently to one side. "We ought to chamber the wine for a little while. May I offer you a snack in the meantime?"

Chapter 19

"She has very nice manners," Carialle commented, as Keff produced biscuits and cheese from the sythesizer and put them in the middle of the small table. "She looked skeptical when you offered her your goulash, as if she wasn't expecting it to taste good, but she didn't say a word. Pleasantly surprised, to judge by her expression, and her pulse."

"She's not like the others," Keff said, smelling the wine. It was ready at last.

He held up the decanter, offering it to Mirina. The woman held her glass up for him to fill, and gave him a luminous smile. Keff smiled back, feeling his pulse pound harder. She had smooth and clear skin, with about a dozen freckles dusted over her nose. Her irises were the color of cognac but were rimmed with sable-brown like her lashes. He guessed her age to be about the same as his. One, no, two silver hairs glinted in her straight, dark-brown hair, but that was the only sign of age. Her round face was youthful, though the expression in her eyes was a sorrowful millenium old. He watched her curiously and wondered. At a big space station, with a thousand women around me, would he have noticed her? And yet she was very attractive, intelligent, and cultured, in spite of the company she kept.

"Am I overreacting, Cari?" he asked, under his

breath. "It's been a while since I've seen a pretty woman."

There was a momentary pause, but Carialle's voice was perfectly even, without a hint of sarcasm. "I don't think so, Keff. You're a grown-up. But watch your step, eh?"

Keff smiled at Mirina, and stood up. "Why don't we move over here to finish the wine? The crash couches are much more comfortable." He extended a hand to her and settled her in one reclining chair. He sat down in the other and propped his feet on the console.

"This is delicious," Mirina said, sipping her wine. "And that synthesizer must be absolutely top of the line."

"I think so," Keff said, casually. "I'm not sure. I eat anything. Mostly health shakes." At that, Mirina did make a face, and Keff grinned.

"So," he asked, pouring himself some wine. He set the bottle on the console. "Were you born into the business like your partner? The way the two of you act I assume he's your partner."

Mirina corrected him quickly. "Not really *partners*," she said, with a strong emphasis on the word. "We've worked closely together for about eight years." The woman took a hasty sip of wine, then paused to smile over it. Not long enough to have been involved with Carialle, Keff thought, his heart sinking. She'd hardly have heard tales of a single wreck salvage a dozen years before she came.

"You're not much like him," Keff said, encouragingly. "You've had an education."

"The colloquialisms," she said, with a wicked smile. "You caught that. Yes. He was furious!"

"And some formal training? CW?"

"Good guess, Sir Knight," Carialle said. "Her pulse leaped just then. Dig deeper."

But Mirina had recovered herself quickly.

"That, my dear, was a long time ago," she said, lifting her glass. Only a few drops remained by this time, so she held it out for a refill.

"I'm glad you appreciate it," Keff said. He hoisted himself out of the deep padding, feeling his overtaxed muscles protest, and came over with the bottle. "The wine, I mean. Watch out, or you'll get tipsy. You're not from the same place as Bisman?"

"No. You took the paintings away," Mirina said, pointedly changing the subject. "I wanted to see that spacescape again. I've been to Dimitri."

"Oh, is that where it is?" Keff asked. Mirina nodded. "Never been there myself. Well, it was starting to rain."

"I know," the woman said, and showed a trifle of embarrassment. "Sorry we didn't help you."

Keff shrugged. "Competitors."

"I might like to buy that painting," Mirina said, temptingly.

"No," Carialle said, at once, then relented. " . . . Well, perhaps it wouldn't do any harm. I've had my joy from it. Tell her all right."

"Certainly," Keff said, smiling at his guest. "I'll give you a good price."

Mirina looked very pleased, but suddenly her face fell, and she took another sip of wine. "Never mind," she said. "I can't. I . . . I've run through my budget. I bought . . . something expensive."

"Ah," Keff said, wondering what had suddenly troubled her so deeply. She was staring at a spot on the wall. Keff glanced over his shoulder and wondered if she had seen through the holographic display. No, it was still intact. If anything, Carialle had enhanced the details to make it look even more solid. He cleared his throat, determined to lighten the mood. He went back to his own couch and stretched out luxuriously. "Say, aren't you afraid I might take advantage of your lowered resistance, to send a message to your Melange?"

"Send away," Mirina said, watching him with an amused glint in her eyes. "Couldn't be any worse than what's already happened to me."

"Oh? Confession's good for the soul," Keff said, encouragingly.

Her mind snapped back to whatever had been occupying it, and she stared at nothing again.

"Do I still have a soul?" she asked. Keff opened his mouth, then shut it. The wine had affected her more strongly than he'd guessed. Thunder rumbled, and Keff glanced at the external monitor for the flash of lightning. The storm must be directly overhead. The woman shivered. "I hate rain," she said. "I hate weather. I hate being stuck on a planet. I think I'm only happy out in space. If I had to stay planetbound for the rest of my life I'd kill myself."

"I know what you mean," Keff said, sincerely. "There's nothing like it."

"Yes. I don't want to do anything else," she said. "It's nice enough here, but I want to get out there again." Her eyes tilted up toward the ceiling, and the unseen reaches of space.

"She's a born spacer," Carialle said. "Just a little drunk, I think, but a born spacer."

"Don't you ever get lonely, traveling by yourself?" Mirina asked.

"Not at all," Keff said, sweeping a hand around. "I have . . . " he glanced at where Carialle's pillar should have been visible, and wasn't. " . . . I have all this," he finished.

"It's beautiful," she said, never noticing his hesitation. "You make me wish I had a setup like it."

"Aren't you happy where you are?"

"Are you mad?" she asked, with a pitying scowl. "If it wasn't for the Thelerie, well . . ."

"What about the Thelerie?" Keff asked, quickly.

Mirina looked at him hard. "Are you from Central Worlds?" she asked.

"Reformed," Keff said, with a pious expression that made her laugh, but she was still serious.

"They're a kind, innocent people. I don't want them exploited, do you understand me?"

"Isn't that what you're doing?" Keff asked, very gently.

"No!" Then, more honestly, she added, "Not entirely. We trade with them, but they get value from us, too. My program . . ."

Keff leaned up on one elbow, as if to listen better. Mirina stopped in midsentence, realizing that this dashing, handsome man was pumping her. Keff saw he had gone too far.

"This bottle's empty," he said, swinging himself upright with a casual show of strength that made Mirina's eyes light with appreciation. "Let's see what else is in the cellar. Look at that!" Keff dusted down a squarish container with a glass stopper covered with wax. "I didn't think I had any of this left."

"Your nose ought to be a foot long by now," Carialle said. But Mirina didn't seem to mind. The twenty-five-year-old brandy went down as neatly as the wine had, sip by sip. It loosened up whatever tight grip she'd had on herself, and in time, Keff's careful questions began to elicit answers.

"The program to supply the Thelerie with communication equipment was yours?"

"Yes," she said. "The ones who decided to come home again had seen us using commlinks, thought it was a good idea. No mass communication at all on this planet. Once you were out of sight, you were gone. It was cheap, and they were so grateful! You've got some nice comm circuitry among your merchandise. If the price was right, that is."

"Might knock it down for a friend," Keff said. "I don't have to make anything on it for a good cause."

"I don't care, particularly. The profit's not mine any more anyway. It's the Melange's, and Aldon's. What the hell," Mirina said, expansively, "for the Thelerie, too."

His blue eyes twinkled with understanding. Mirina was reminded of what she used to think Charles looked like. *Careful, girl,* she told herself fiercely. *He's the enemy.* But he was very attractive, she thought, looking at him from under her lashes as she took a sip of the fire-smooth brandy. In return, he gave her a top-to-toe sweep of his eyes that made her gasp for its very insouciance. Unconsciously she shifted position, straightening her shoulders and tilting her head to one side. *Great stars, I'm acting like a coquette!* And yet, it was so nice to relax for a change.

"How long have you been . . . involved with the griffins?" Keff asked.

She wrinkled her eyebrows, trying to place the reference, then her face cleared as she grinned. "I never thought of that, but they do look like griffins. Did heraldic beasts ever really live?"

"I don't think so," said Keff.

"Not much of a student of history, is she?" Carialle asked.

"Don't be a snob, Cari," Keff muttered. "How'd you come to ship out with Bisman?"

"I came on board eight years ago, right after Charles died. Zonzalo—my brother—fell in with them. He thought flying with reivers was a great adventure. I found him on one of their lousy bases, half-starved, with leaky air-recirculation equipment, no organization. So pathetic, I stayed," Mirina said, staring into the amber liquid in her glass. "Shouldn't have stayed but," her shoulders slumped, "but I had nowhere to go, nowhere to take him *to.*"

"Didn't you have to go back to your job, or your

school?" Keff asked. "You know your way around ships, I can tell. A valuable employee like you."

"Lost my position," Mirina said, more shortly than she'd intended. "I've been an idiot, but the Thelerie have been wonderful. They're grateful for everything we do. I've had to force Bisman not to lead them into using polluting machinery. They've got plenty of physical strength and simple machines to take care of motive-force needs, plus, dammit! they can fly. No travel problems. The electronics just help with communications."

"She's really thought this out," Carialle said. "*Here's* the organizing mind."

"I'd give anything if she wasn't involved in a pirate ring," Keff murmured under his breath.

Mirina wasn't really paying attention. "What did you say?"

"Very well thought out," Keff said hastily. "You've done good work. You thought of *everything*. You must be some organizer. I, uh, I think there's room in this for both of our groups. I can't say the Circuit won't cut into your parts business, but I'm willing to take it to the Lady over the ethical framework you've built."

She looked grateful and annoyed at the same time. "We'll want a cut, she said. "We've got expenses. Overhead."

"So've we," Keff said, nonchalantly playing the game.

"We'll negotiate it," Mirina said, compromising. "Well, Aldon will. I . . . don't suppose there's room in *your* organization? For a good planner?"

Keff looked surprised. "Thinking of moving on?"

"I have to," she said.

"Being forced out?"

"No. I just can't stand it any longer. The deaths, and all. Now that everything's at about subsistence level Aldon is getting uncontrollable. I never condoned death; I've always tried to prevent it. I hate death. Can't take any more of it in my life."

"How mysterious for someone in her profession," Carialle said.

"Are you going back to what you did before? Were you a pilot?"

"More than that," Mirina said, then thought about it. "Well, and less." The whole accident came back to her, as it did in her nightmares. She had a final, horrible vision of the dock crew trying to spray down the burning ship, the pillar in the control room slagging into molten metal. All the skin on her hands and face were burned, as she tried to fight her way back aboard, to save him if she could. They held her back. They kept her out! Charles!

She let out a cry that brought Keff to his feet in surprise, then fell into heartbroken sobbing. Keff hurried over and sat down next to her on the molded chair's arm. She was beating her fist on her knee. He captured the hand and held it tightly between his own hands.

"I'm sorry," she said, looking up with tears sheeting down her cheeks. "I'm sorry."

"What's the matter?" Keff asked, squeezing her hand. "Why couldn't you have gotten another berth with someone else?"

"Never anyone else like Charles," she sobbed, turning her face into his tunic front. Keff was so nice and sympathetic, but he *wasn't* Charles. Charles remained dead.

"Go on, tell me about it," Keff said. He felt for a handkerchief, and ended up handing her the napkin that was tucked between her hip and the seat cushion.

In between sobs, Mirina managed to tell the story of the accident.

" . . . I guess my supervisor was right—no, I know he was. I was insubordinate, and I should have stayed in therapy, but my brother was in danger! Why couldn't they have understood that?"

Keff's heart melted with sympathy. Over the top of her head, he looked automatically toward Carialle's pillar. He wrapped his arms around the woman and held her tightly.

"Keff, she was a *brawn*!" Carialle said. "What was the brain's name? Charles? Yes, I remember it. You ought to, as well. Charles CM-702. M must have stood for Mirina. It was a freak accident. Combination of a hazardous cargo, an accident on the loading dock, and bad handling by the ground crew. If they hadn't been at a space station, the brawn would have died, too. The last thing that Charles did before his shell melted down was to order one of his servo robots to pull the brawn out of the burning wreckage. There was hardly anything left for the authorities to identify. Now I know why I didn't recognize her name. It's Mirina Velasquez-Donegal. She and her brother must have shortened it when they adopted *noms-de-guerre*."

"I have heard of the accident," Keff said, out loud. "I knew a brainship had died. Never heard what happened to the brawn."

"Hah!" Mirina said bitterly, into his sleeve. "Exactly." Keff glanced toward Carialle's pillar.

"They let her down, too," Carialle said, just as bitterly, in Keff's ear. "For all they say we're a valuable, respected resource, the bureaucrats still treat us like animated furniture, shells and softskins alike, damn them."

"Horrible! We have to help her."

"We can't," Carialle said, flatly.

"She's been the only moral influence these people have had," Keff said. "It could have been far worse if she hadn't been here."

"But why was she here at all? Why didn't she take her brother and go?"

"You heard her," Keff whispered urgently. "She was needy. She'd had a mental breakdown—and she had to get over it by herself. You know what that feels like."

"I certainly do," Carialle said, every memory of her own accident coming back to her. "But what would our word do for her? Shorten her prison sentence? But no, she wouldn't last in a prison. She said she would rather die than be groundbound. I think she means it. We should separate her from these people anyhow."

"We'll have to think of something," Keff said, frustratedly. He realized Mirina had been talking.

" . . . Wanted help, just a little help," Mirina was saying, a little incoherently. "They figured I'd ask for it when I needed it. But how would I know when? I was just trying to survive, feeling it was my fault when I knew it wasn't. Hot white explosives. No time. Charles saved my life."

"Shh, I know," Keff said. He was torn between worrying about Carialle's mental state, and the growing concern for a fellow brawn. Mirina seemed as if she had been waiting for somebody to talk to for a long time. He just stayed beside her, stroking her hair, and occasionally dabbing the tears off her cheeks with the edge of his sleeve. Poor Mirina, carrying a weight like this all by herself for eight years. He kissed the top of her head, rocking her gently like a child.

"I knew Charles slightly," Carialle said, solemnly. "He was a stodgy old 700. He thought I was too radical. I thought he was embalmed. I'd never met his brawn."

Keff opened his mouth to reveal their secret, but Carialle, reading his mind, stopped him short.

"Don't," she said. "She's been part of this piracy operation."

"We have to help her," Keff insisted.

"Why? She has no loyalty to the CW."

"But she was one of *us*. A brain chose her as his brawn. That means she had that special something. She's . . . less than half a person now. She's broken. You know what that means."

"I know, oh, I know," Carialle said, her voice rising

almost to a keen. She sighed. "You win, Sir Knight. I'll try to think of something we can do for her, some way to help."

Thunder crashed, loudly enough to be heard through the noise insulation. Keff felt Mirina tremble in his arms. He stood up and held out a hand to her. She looked up at him, her caramel eyes drowned with tears, and put her hand in his.

"Perhaps you'd better stay the night," Keff said.

Chapter 20

He awoke looking up at the ceiling. The shifting of a soft weight on his shoulder made him look down. In her sleep, Mirina cuddled her head just a little cosier against his chest. He tightened the arm around her, fitting his wrist warmly into her opulently curved torso. One of her hands opened on his chest, the fingertips playing delicately on his skin. He remembered the touch of those small but strong hands along his back, and smiled. Two lonely people had found an oasis of peace together for a moment. He was content, and hoped she felt the same.

"Keff? I know you're awake." Carialle's voice came softly through his aural implant.

"Just barely," he said sublingually. "Whasup?" He glanced down at Mirina.

"I've checked her sleep pattern. She's in deep delta. Good morning. The rain stopped just before dawn. I've got a ship on extreme long-range sensors. I've sent a hail out on standard frequency. The cavalry's on its way!"

"Hurrah," Keff said quietly, wishing he could cheer. "About time."

"The Cridi want to get out and around for a while. They're rather bored with being cooped up, and I can't run the water-refresher if you're supposed to be alone."

"Mmm," he said. "Tell them I'll go take a real shower, and they can bathe as long as they like."

362

He edged himself out of the bunk carefully, lifting Mirina's head from his shoulder onto the pillow. He left the coverlet tucked around her where his arm had been. She let out a small sigh.

"Probably hasn't felt this safe in ages," Keff said quietly to Carialle. He walked silently toward his bathroom. Carialle must condone his sympathy for Mirina. She was perfectly capable of making the humidity or temperature controls in his private quarters go squiffy out of pettiness, but the air was warm on his naked skin, and even the floor had been heated to a comfortable 18 degrees C.

Keff passed up the sonic cleaner for the shower fixture. He fitted the standards into the depressions in the deck, snapped the extendable envelope out into a rectangular booth two meters high and a meter square, and twisted the water spigots on to full. Jets of water shot out of the metal disk at the top, hammering at the booth floor and sides. An answering rush of water across the corridor told him the Cridi had heard his cue. As soon as the water warmed up to a comfortable temperature, he climbed into the booth and sealed it around him. He stood under the shower for a good twenty-five minutes, until his fingers turned into pale prunes.

"Are they finished, Cari?" Keff asked, as loudly as he dared. His voice sounded curiously dead in the heavy plastic tent.

"They are," Carialle chuckled. "Narrow Leg said they wouldn't have had to do this in stages if you hadn't put their swimming pool in the storeroom."

With a thankful sigh, Keff spun the controls off. He shouldered into his toweling robe and walked back into the sleeping room, rubbing his hair dry with a clean cloth. Mirina stirred and opened her eyes at the small sound. Her eyes crinkled as she grinned at him, embarrassed. She sat up, clasping the coverlet to her body.

"Sorry. Have I slept too long?" she asked.

"Not at all," Keff said. "I've just finished. The bath is yours."

She stretched out her arms, throwing her head back with abandon. "Mmm! I haven't had a refreshing sleep like this in ages. Thank you. And, thank you for last evening." The wickedly coy look, through the eyelashes, returned just for a moment. "I was supposed to come and win concessions from you, but I think I gave up as much as I got."

"My pleasure," Keff said, with a twinkle.

"Thank you. I ought to watch my liquor consumption," Mirina said, seriously. "I shouldn't have talked so much."

"Not at all," Keff said. "I understand. Truly, I do." Mirina gave him a skeptical, almost pitying look. He wished again he could tell her the truth, but Carialle was right. He must not blow their cover too soon, even for a fellow brawn in need.

He extended a hand to help Mirina off the bunk, but she smiled a polite refusal, and dropped lightly onto the soles of her feet. She did accept his spare robe, and trailed off into the steamy, tiled bathroom with an easy, spacer's stride. Keff dressed, listening to her hum happily in the shower.

Once they emerged into the main cabin, there were no signs of the Cridi at all, except that the indicator on the food synthesizer was a little lower than it had been the night before. Mirina didn't notice the discrepancy, but then, she'd had the lion's share of brandy and wine. Keff programmed her a nice breakfast, and poured himself a health shake with extra calcium and vitamin E to help chase away the dregs of a headache that loomed behind his eyes. For all her shamed protest, Mirina looked as if she was rather less worse for the wear than he was.

"Mmm, what's that?" Mirina asked, putting down her

coffee cup. She pointed at a light blinking on Carialle's imaginary console.

"Communications," Carialle said in his ear.

"Communications," Keff echoed, springing up. "The Lady!" He went to one of the real control boards, and punched a button. That one normally activated the lights in the cargo bay, but Mirina wouldn't know that. One of the screens blanked, then filled with the image of Carialle's Lady Fair. Keff blinked. She wore an up-to-date coiffure, and tunic set of gauzy blue fabric with flowing sleeves, plus plenty of sparkling jewelry. She looked expensive, impatient, and very efficient.

"Keff? Is that you?" Carialle's voice asked impatiently.

"Yes, ma'am," Keff said, speaking with his mouth close to the audio pickup just for effect.

"My ship is in range of this planet, ETA two hours. I want a full report. What's this meeting supposed to be about?" Her eyes flicked past Keff to Mirina. "Who is that woman?"

"She's, uh, she's a representative of the other group," Keff said. "The Melange. Mirina Don, er, Carialle."

"Madam," Mirina said.

"Greetings." The eyes returned to Keff. "I'll expect a full briefing in an hour. The meeting will commence when I make orbit. Do you understand?"

"I do, ma'am," Keff said, humbly. The screen blanked. He turned to Mirina. She looked pleased.

"I'll go tell Bisman," she said.

Carialle had her suit-clad image smile at Bisman and his cronies as they stalked into the central cabin. The half-dozen human raiders shed oily, yellow-brown mud from their boots everywhere. She cast her eyes upward in disgust, and enjoyed the scowl on the leader's face as he slung himself into one of the crash couches.

"Upscale meets bargain basement," she said to Keff

over the aural link. "You'll have to tidy that after the meeting's over," she added out loud.

"Yes, ma'am," Keff said, standing obsequiously beside the holographic chair in which her image seated itself. Carialle had set almost all her projective cameras over the end of the room where her painting apparatus usually stood. The rack, and all of her personal paintings, were stowed hastily in the small storeroom behind Keff's cabin. It left her image plenty of room to roam.

"I am Carialle," she said, with a nod of her head. "Greetings, gentlemen, and madam." Carialle nodded to Mirina, clad in a similar shipsuit to the one she'd had on the night before. The ex-brawn seated herself beside her brother at the dining table clear across the cabin. The younger Don was a dark-haired, lanky young man who didn't seem to know what to do with his long arms and legs. Bisman wore a knee-length coat over an open-necked shirt and trousers tucked into his muddy boots. The garments were clean but worn, adding to the impression Mirina had given them of an organization too big for its budget. The only non-human was the young Thelerie, Sunset. "You are all welcome."

"Say, wait a minute," Bisman said, turning his head to the right. He'd made himself comfortable, but something caught his eye. He propelled himself forward to wave a hand through Carialle's midsection. "She's a hologram!" he exclaimed, turning on Keff. "I thought we were meeting with the real thing!"

"You're hearing my real voice," Carialle said, with a trace of haughty annoyance. "And seeing my face. I'm not about to make myself vulnerable to strangers. I'm sure you understand."

"Not being vulnerable, yeah," Bisman said, sitting down again, but not so far back in the couch. He held up one hand and showed them a small commlink on his wrist. "I don't like tricks, either. I want you to know

I'm in radio contact with my ship. If something happens, or if my communications are cut off, my people have orders to attack. We are well armed."

Carialle also read the energy trace of a sidearm concealed under the flap of the coat the man wore. She accorded him another gracious nod. "I understand," she said. "We won't shield transmissions. Sounds like they have the third Core," she told Keff privately. "We'll have to get it away from them."

"Yes, ma'am," Keff said, with a respectful bow.

"Why are you here?" Bisman asked Thunderstorm, who sat on his haunches between the airlock and the corridor to the sleeping cabins.

"I represent Thelerie," the Space Sayas said, very nervously. "As I have for many years."

"This was going to be a discussion between our two organizations, wasn't it?" Bisman asked Carialle.

"Of course, but this being makes a valid point," Carialle said, with a polite gesture toward Thunderstorm. "We are occupying his world, after all."

"Okay," Bisman said, crossing his heels on the console. "He can stay."

"Thank you," Carialle said, politely. She made a point of lifting the corner of her lip delicately at his dirty boots, and he grinned. "Shall we begin?"

Keff bowed again. "Shall I serve refreshments?"

"Go ahead. Thank you. Gentles?" Carialle manifested a glass in her image's hand. The visitors declined beverages, and Keff resumed his stand beside his "employer."

"We're here to talk," Bisman said, impatiently. He tilted his head toward Keff. "Your drone here landed on a world we have an exclusive arrangement with."

"Isn't it up to the inhabitants as to whom they do business with?" Carialle asked, with a lift of her eyebrows. "Thunderstorm, what do you say?"

"I . . . " the Thelerie trembled violently and

clattered his clawtips together. "I do not say anything just now."

Bisman's blood pressure rose slightly, as did the temperature in his face. He had a bad temper, but he controlled it. His associates were watching their leader closely. Their muscle tension was high: in Mirina's case, almost dangerously so. The former brawn was under a lot of stress.

"The Melange has made a lot of progress with them," Bisman said, with emphasis. "We don't like someone just walking in and benefiting from all our work."

"But when there's profit in it . . . ?" Carialle asked.

"Yeah, but we intend to keep it just the way it's been," Bisman said. His blood pressure drew down to normal again. He was on his own ground here, Carialle thought.

"The resources on this planet are very attractive, n'est ce pas? For example, fuel of very high quality."

"Ours. Our refinery, our investment," Bisman said, flatly.

Carialle spread her hands prettily. "But can't we make a bargain?" she asked. "We might like to buy some of this fine fuel. And these people, the Thelerie, are good customers."

"Not a chance," Bisman said. "There's not enough production to supply all of us. The Thelerie need it to run their lamps and heating units. I've got more than sixty ships. How many have you got?"

"Enough," Carialle said. "You'll forgive me not giving out too much information until I know who I'm dealing with."

"We've been around a long time," the older man said, narrowing his eyes at her. He jabbed a finger toward Keff. "I have never heard of you people until we landed and found him here. You come out of nowhere, into established territory, and you act like you've had a mandate from the Invisible Hosts."

Carialle smiled austerely. "Perhaps it does seem as if we've been keeping undercover a little too much."

"Nonexistent, is what I call it." Bisman's voice rose threateningly. Carialle picked up signs of distress from Thunderstorm, who watched the man with wide eyes. He was terrified of Bisman, and Carialle couldn't blame him. He was dangerous.

"And yet, here we are," Carialle said. Her sensors picked up the expected ship orbiting and entering atmosphere. The engine vibration matched patrol ships she'd encountered at many space stations. She listened for an official hail, hoping it was the CW military ship at last. It was curious that there hadn't been any advance instructions for her. She strained her external cameras upward and outward, searching for a glimpse of the descending craft. "Now that we've found one another, we should make arrangements for cooperation where our paths cross."

"Keff!" she said, urgently, while her blandfaced hologram continued a meaningless conversation with the pirate leader. "It's *Ship Three*! They're coming in for a landing. Here!"

"What? Impossible!" Keff muttered to himself, although he was badly shaken. "No, it isn't. The Thelerie are natural navigators. They've Centered their way home."

"But with what? We destroyed their propulsion system."

"We never found the DSC-902's," Keff said glumly. He smiled innocently at Mirina, who was staring at him with open curiosity.

Carialle tried to get the others' attention focused back on herself. "Mr. Bisman, the Circuit is prepared to sell you whatever components and parts you might like, at a good price, but we do believe in coexistence."

"Just a minute," Bisman said, holding up a hand as

his pocket unit signalled. He listened to the small speaker. "What?"

Carialle picked up the transmission herself. She listened helplessly to every word the pirate leader heard. She relayed the broadcast so Keff could hear it, too. His eyes widened, and flicked toward her hiding place.

"They saw them on long-range but now they're sure. Autumn says that Keff's ship is the one who attacked them in Slime space," a woman's voice repeated. "Says the human onboard was under Slime control."

"What? Slime? What about the other ship?"

"No one challenged her on the way in. There's nobody in orbit around Thelerie!"

"What? Well, then where's the transmission in here coming from?" Bisman demanded.

"The ship . . ." Carialle could wait to hear no more. She blocked the signal from the pirate.

Bisman jumped for Keff, and backed him up against the nearest bulkhead with a forearm underneath his throat.

"Who is she?" Bisman demanded. "*Where* is she?"

"There's no one else here," Keff said, innocently, pushing the man's arm down enough to gasp in a breath. His windpipe felt half-crushed. "Just me. The Lady's out in space somewhere."

"That's a lie," the pirate leader said, driving home his statement with another bruising push. "One of my ships says there's nobody out there. She's onboard this vessel. Bring her out!"

"You're wrong, friend . . . " Keff began, but he got no more out. The pirate shoved him up against the enameled panel and bore down in earnest. "Hey!" he whispered, battering the man on the back. He saw black spots dance in his vision. Bisman meant to kill him. Dropping all pretense of amiable obsequity, Keff dug both thumbs into pressure points behind the man's ears, and swept a foot back and across Bisman's ankles, sending the older man stumbling. Keff danced out from the wall on the balls of his feet, not turning his back on Bisman. In the close quarters, though, he was at a disadvantage. The pirate, though an older man, had a long reach, and undoubtedly a long, dishonorable history of dirty fighting. He landed a kidney punch before Keff could get by him. Keff staggered, and aimed a slam of his own for the man's gut. Bisman took about half of it, but he slid sideways in the direction of the airlock. Keff closed the distance, and had to dodge back from a dirty kick. He couldn't let Bisman go, not now.

"They'll have backups in a minute," Carialle said. "The rest of the crew is coming. They're armed, and something on that ship is building up energy." Keff nodded but didn't reply. He was concentrating on disabling Bisman without killing him. Mirina and her brother stood beside the table, staring.

"He's CW?" Zonzalo asked, gaping.

"You lied!" Mirina shouted at Keff. She started toward the airlock, but the combatants blocked her way.

"Luring us in here, pretending to be stupid traders," Bisman panted. He evaded a roundhouse kick Keff aimed at him, grabbed Keff's leg, and propelled him backward over the stack of crates toward the image of the third console. Keff fell helplessly among the boxes. The other humans gasped as he disappeared from view into the holographic illusion. Bisman, with a snarl, dove in after him.

"Cari, I can't see!" Keff cried, as a punch came out of nowhere and knocked his head painfully against the deck.

The time for subterfuge was over. Keff's life could be in danger. At once, Carialle dropped the illusion, revealing wall, pillar, and the two men grappling on the floor. The effect on Mirina Don was electric. Her eyes widened, and her mouth fell open.

"Aldon!" she shrieked at the top of her voice. "She's a *brainship!*"

"Central Worlds!" Bisman growled. With a sudden burst of strength, he yanked a hand free, chopped the smaller man in the throat, and scrambled to his feet. He spun and grabbed Thunderstorm, who had been trying to creep unobtrusively toward the airlock.

"You damned traitor," the pirate snarled. "You were in on this." He yanked the Thelerie back on his haunches and drew his sidearm, shoving it under Thunderstorm's throat.

"Help them," Carialle said to Tall Eyebrow and the listening Cridi, activating the door of the spare cabin. "Now!"

Like a barrage of soap-bubbles, the Cridi poured out of the spare room, and surrounded the pirates.

"Slime!" Zonzalo gasped, flattening himself against the wall as Gap Tooth and Small Spot confronted him. Sunset, the young Thelerie clutched Mirina around the waist, and hid behind her, his golden eyes all pupil, while Big Voice, Wide Foot, and Big Eyes edged them backward.

"Stand back," Bisman said, looking up steadily at the floating globes. "I want out of here, now! I want my people out, too. One by one. If we don't, this damned traitor dies. Now!"

"We freeze him!" Small Spot cried, flinging himself forward to save his friend.

"No!" Carialle saw the tiny movement of Bisman's finger closing just as Small Spot's whammy took effect. She sensed the power buildup, an inexorable burst only temporarily halted.

"Small motor control reaction," she said, over all her speakers. The hologram of the Lady vanished, making the human pirates jump. "He's pulled the trigger. If we don't let him go, the gun will fire anyhow in a moment. If we don't try to contain the blast using Core power, it will explode right here in the cabin. If we do, both Bisman and Thunderstorm will die. Sooner or later I will run out of fuel, then the Core won't be able to contain the blast to just the two of them."

"Can he hear us?" Keff asked.

"Yes," said Narrow Leg, hovering in front of the pirate leader's face, watching his pupils.

"Bisman, we'll let you go," Keff said, edging into Bisman's view with his hands out from his sides. "I'm unarmed, and the Cridi will do what I say. Just let Thunderstorm go. You and your people are free." He jerked his head toward the airlock. Carialle slid open both doors, and lowered the ramp. Zonzalo and the other crew dashed out of the door without hesitation. "You're free to go. No one will stop you. TE, ready to pull his hand back?"

"I am ready," the Frog Prince said, his face grim.

"Okay," Keff said to Small Spot. "Let him go!"

The burst of power released five milliseconds after Tall Eyebrow jerked the human's hand back and away from Thunderstorm's neck. Carialle winced as the bolt burned through her ceiling plates and into a fiberoptic conduit. She set a small part of her consciousness to rerouting the functions the severed fibers controlled. She'd have time to repair the ducting later. The Thelerie stood, dazed, the fact that he was alive and unharmed not yet registering in his mind. Like lightning, Bisman ran a few steps, turned, put a bolt straight into Thunderstorm's chest. Sunset fell beside the body of his mentor, crying out shrilly at the black, burned streak in the center of the golden fur. Bisman loosed a few more shots into the cabin, scattering the Cridi, and filling the room with smoke as lights, screens, and upholstery burst and caught fire. Keff dove underneath the crash couch, pulling Mirina down with him.

Carialle dropped her airlock door, intending to trap the pirate inside. Bisman saw the lights activate, and scowled, but he didn't stop running. He raised the energy weapon again, and shot the controls, freezing the doors. She struggled to find another servo that could pull down the door, but the mechanism reacted too slowly. He was able to roll underneath the door. He ran out and down the ramp and out across the field with deliberate, long, heavy steps that ate up the distance. Their rhythm suddenly matched with something Carialle would never, never forget.

"Keff!" she cried. "It's *him*. It's *his* footsteps!"

Keff scrambled out from his hiding place. "Whose?"

"Bisman!" Carialle said, opening all screens to show the pirate leader running across to his own ship. "He was the one, the one who *walked on me*."

"You're sure?" Keff demanded.

"I couldn't forget it as long as I live. Keff, stop him!" Carialle said desperately. "We have to get him back here. He's the one. He can clear my record, Keff. He can't get away."

Keff dashed for the airlock. He waited impatiently until Carialle had raised it high enough for him to scramble underneath, then dashed down the ramp after Bisman. "Do something about Thunderstorm, for pity's sake," he shouted.

Carialle tried to pull herself together. For once in her life she wished she could go about on two feet, or four, or wings! That man must not get away from her. He held the answers she had been seeking for twenty years. It meant the vindication of her sanity.

But her life was not in danger, and Thunderstorm's was. She pulled herself together and located the nearest transmission tower. With a broad-band sweep, she broke into the thousands and thousands of "phone calls" going on across Thelerie.

"Attention," she said, through the shell of the IT program, wishing that it was up to fluent medical Thelerie. "There is an emergency medical situation on the Melange's plain. Will any healer in the area please come at once?" Hubbub erupted on the open lines as thousands of Thelerie broke into speech all at once, wanting to know more. She repeated her message, shut down the transmission and returned her attention to the inside of her cabin.

"And thus is mass communication born," she said, ironically.

"His heart beats," Big Voice said. He sat on the Thelerie's left, his globe in two pieces behind him. "I know not what else to do, but I can keep that going."

"I am making him breathe," Small Spot said, clasping one of the Thelerie's claw hands in his own. "Come, friend. Inhale, exhale, inhale, exhale. Am I doing too fast?"

"I don't think so," Carialle said. "He's in pain. I wish I could tell you what nerves to deaden, or what drugs to use, but I don't dare interfere. We might cause permanent damage."

"Don't touch him," Sunset cried, trying to scatter the amphibioids away from his mentor's body. He ran at them, flailing his wings. The Cridi gently pushed him back, mildly using Core power. The wound was serious, but it didn't go all the way through the Thelerie's body, for which Carialle was grateful.

It didn't take long for her message to have an effect. On her screen, Carialle saw a very large Thelerie with a pouch around its neck sail over the plain. Carialle flashed her running lights to attract the griffin's attention. The creature changed direction on a wingtip and landed on the ramp. It galloped on all fours up into the ship.

"I was called," it said. "I heal! How to help?" It saw Thunderstorm and hurried toward him, with concerned horn calls. It spilled herbs, vials, and tools out of its pouch onto the deck, and went to work.

Another Thelerie, and another, appeared behind the first. "I, too! I, too! I am called. I will help!"

"Help is here," Big Voice said, leaning close to Thunderstorm's face. "I told you we did not want your life."

Thunderstorm fluttered his eyelids and wingtips feebly, acknowledging the irony of his old enemies working to save him from the wounds of his allies.

Keff ran, keeping his knees up with an effort. His feet grew more caked with mud at every step. The previous night's rain had made the field a mire. Tall Eyebrow had sailed ahead in his globe, then realized Keff wasn't keeping up with him. He and Big Eyes swept back and pulled him out of the mud with a mighty *pop!* Keff checked to make sure he hadn't left his boots behind, then turned all his attention forward.

The red ship fired slugs and energy beams at the approaching human and his companions. With a single sweep of his fingers, Narrow Leg created a barrier of Core power between them. The missiles ricocheted all over the landscape. A gout of mud kicked up with a *bang!* almost right in Keff's face. Hot steam hissed where the energy bolts sizzled into the mud. Keff hoped fervently that Big Voice and the others were protecting Carialle from attack.

Ahead of them, Bisman reached the ramp, and hurtled up it in a few long strides. The heavy metal door began to slide downward.

"They close the hatch!" Narrow Leg signed, meters ahead of Keff. "What to do?"

"Hold it open! Hold the ship," Keff shouted in Cridi at the top of his lungs. The ammoniated air made him hoarse. "Don't let them launch. Carialle needs them alive, awake!"

"We understand," Gap Tooth and Wide Foot signed. They stretched out their skinny arms as best they could in the confines of the plastic bubbles. The rising ramp halted in mid-arc, and jerked hard a few times. The airlock hatch, manipulated by Long Hand, reversed direction and began to inch upward.

"Good," Keff said, urging his small force forward. "Cari, we have them!"

"Get him," Carialle said, speaking so rapidly he had to listen closely to understand. "You have to bring him to me. He's my proof for Maxwell-Corey. That bastard must listen. This is the man. He will talk. He must talk. It wasn't *aliens*; it was a human being, one who should have known better. He knew a brain pillar when he saw one! He must have known!"

"Almost there, Cari," Keff said, willing her to hang on. Only a few hundred meters to go to the red ship. He heard the screech of tortured servos fighting against the pull of Core power. The ramp had opened almost all the way. He heard shouting from inside the ship, saw men and women in shipsuits fighting to lower the airlock doors by hand.

Suddenly, he and the Cridi were all swept straight through the air into the side of the pirate ship. Keff slammed face first into the hull and slid, dazed, down to the ground. The travel globes split apart, leaving the Cridi dry, gasping, and shocked in the hot, ammonia-laden air. There was no doubt about it: the pirates had the third Core in their ship, and they knew how to use it.

More Thelerie healers, landing on the plain in answer to Carialle's call, swooped in and helped pick the small aliens out of the mud. Two hovering griffins lifted Keff free of the ship's side, and set him on his feet.

"It burns, it burns!" Gap Tooth shrieked, batting at her skin with her hands. "The air is hot!"

The Thelerie, though they understood the small beings were distressed, couldn't understand the language. They fluttered around uncertainly. The Cridi had to help themselves. Tall Eyebrow, with Big Eyes swept up in his arms, cried out to the others. "Pick up globes, purify air!"

Narrow Leg, recovering his wits in a flash, started clapping travel globes together around his crew with waves of his fingerstalls. In a moment, all the Cridi were rallying.

"Are you all right?" Keff wheezed. His ribs were sore and bruised, and one of his eyes felt as if it was swelling shut.

"We have no water," Narrow Leg signed swiftly, "but it is only for a short time."

"Right," Keff said, turning around. "Let's get them." Just as he spoke, the pirate ship lit engines. The distraction had been long enough. Bisman managed to launch. The ship rose swiftly, diminishing to a fiery dot in the sky. "Oh, no!"

More Thelerie winged their way over the plain. Keff recognized Noonday and her guardians. He waved at them, and pointed at the other ship that had landed.

"More pirates!" Keff had time to shout, as he turned toward Carialle. This time Tall Eyebrow lifted Keff off his feet even before he gave the signal. The wind rushed into his face as they flew back to the ship.

"Ready to lift as soon as you're on board," Carialle said in his aural pickup.

"That one has the last Core," Narrow Leg shouted, his high voice audible even over the sound of Carialle's rockets igniting.

"I know! We'll stop him," Keff said. "Have you got enough fuel for a pursuit, Cari?" he asked.

"Just enough," Carialle said grimly. "If we don't have to use much more Core power ourselves."

The Cridi and Keff swooped in through the door. The Cridi froze their globes to the walls and Keff grabbed the nearest permanent fixture as the airlock slammed shut and Carialle applied full thrust. He was shoved almost all the way to the floor by sheer force, and the roar of the engines threatened to shake his grip.

"Care, care!" Big Voice shrieked. He and half a dozen healers threw their arms across Thunderstorm's body. Their stentorian voices rose in protest, and the patient moaned. Healing impedimenta went flying in every direction, clattering into the bulkheads.

"Sorry," Carialle said over general audio, not taking the time to manifest her frog image on the wall. "It's going to be a rough ride. Cridi, brace everyone and everything that's rolling around loose!"

"We hear!" the shrill voices responded. The external viewscreens swiftly turned from golden to blue to black as Carialle burst out of atmosphere.

As soon as he could move again after the initial push, Keff handed himself toward the crash couch and flung himself into its depths. He started to strap in, when a small human hand reached up and clutched the side of the chair. Keff sat up, and yanked Mirina Don onto his lap. It was a tight fit, but there was just room for both of them. He pulled the straps over her hip and locked them down. She and Keff were pressed almost face to face.

"Oh, please," she said, her soft brown eyes filled with tears. She appealed to Carialle's pillar. "My brother is on that ship. Aldon will kill him. Zon is my only family. Aldon was going to let us leave after we landed here."

"If you can speak to him, do it," Carialle said, concentrating on following the pirate's path precisely. Not one extra centimeter must come between them. "I don't want him dead. I want to talk to him."

"If I help, will you let us go?" Mirina asked. She looked at Carialle's pillar, and back to Keff, who shook his head sadly. "They'll put me in prison. I couldn't stand it."

"I can't," Keff said, helplessly. The desperate look on her face tore at his heart.

"All we can do is try to save lives," Carialle said crisply. "Talk to him. What's the frequency?"

"Reasonable?" Bisman's fierce grimace filled the whole screen. "Reasonable to land and let a CW flunky pick through my brain? They bought you last night, didn't they? You and that sawed-off muscleman."

Mirina had no time for pride. She could see Zonzalo behind Aldon. The boy looked absolutely terrified. She had to do whatever it took to get him to land without harming her brother. He could call her whatever names he wanted to. She clasped her hands.

"Please, Aldon. Carialle swears she means you no harm. You have some information she wants. Maybe she'll trade you a favor for it."

"No promises," Carialle cut in. "All I want is a talk. What happens after that is up to the CenCom."

"This is what I say to your CenCom," Bisman sneered. He nodded his head to one side, and Mirina saw Glashton's hands move toward the controls for the Slime Ball. A tremendous jerk rocked the brainship. Mirina was flung backwards. She would have fallen if Keff and the Cridi hadn't caught her. She grabbed the edge of the console and leaned in closer.

"We can't take many of those," Carialle said, grimly. "The Thelerie might have fuel we can use, but no repair facilities."

"Please, Aldon," Mirina begged. "Listen to me. Let Zon go. He's never done you any harm. I'm the one you want. Bring him back, and you can do whatever you want to me."

"Go to hell, Mirina. You're a traitor." Bisman turned away from the screen, but at least he didn't cut off contact.

"We need the Cridi," Keff said, over the top of Mirina's head.

"I will help," one of the little green frogs said, floating

away from the Thelerie working on Thunderstorm. "That one is in no danger now."

Mirina was itching to know how the Slime had learned to speak Standard, or why they were so friendly to humans, and she'd give ten years of her life to know how it was flying in midair like that. When Keff gave the order to hang on tight, she dropped back into the crash couch and held onto him. The amphibioid hung like a spider in the air beside the screentank. On it, the image of the reiver ship grew larger and larger.

"All right, Big Voice," Carialle's voice said, softly. "Reach out for the pirate. Gently, but so he knows he's been grappled. Now, hold it, but not hard, like an egg or a piece of fruit. *Now* I wish your landing personnel were here. They know exactly how to do it. Go on. Good."

"So. I see," Big Voice said, gesturing slightly with one surprisingly large hand. The long fingers were coated in a kind of twinkling golden metal. It was a kind of activator. There was a Slime Ball here on this ship. There had been the whole time, and she never knew it!

In the tank, the reiver juddered and hesitated. Mirina was nearly kicked out of the chair by another pull from the Slime Ball aboard the red ship. So this is what it felt like when they used the tractor device on other people: terrifying, inexplicable, intangible, and inexorable. She thrust herself in next to Keff among the padding.

"They must turn back and land at once," another one of the amphibioids ordered, from its place on the wall. "Their Core is overheating! It may explode."

"Mirina," Sunset bleated, from his place on the floor. "Stop the ship jostling! My mentor is injured. This hurts him! How could Bisman do this?"

"He's a bad man, youngster," Mirina said, craning her head over the edge of the chair. Her heart sank at the

terrified Thelerie's face. "I should never have let you
or any of your people come aboard with him. Heaven
knows I shouldn't have done so myself."

"Stop him," Sunset begged Keff.

"I am stopping him," Big Voice said. "Less noise!
Must concentrate."

"Bring it back," Narrow Leg interrupted. "That old
Core has reached its end. Can't you hear the frequency?" He followed this with a series of shrill whistles
that Keff and Carialle inexplicably seemed to understand.

"Oh, no," Keff said, his face set.

"The Slime will kill them all," Sunset said, trembling.

"No." Thunderstorm stirred and raised a feeble wing-
finger to the youth's hand. "They are our friends, too,"
he whispered. "It is not true they are evil. The humans
misled you. I am sorry you learned a lie."

"All I know is broken and lost today," Sunset said,
his noble head drooping. Thunderstorm wrapped a wing
around him. Mirina felt heartsick.

"I've always cared what happened to you," she said
to Sunset.

"That is true," Thunderstorm assured the youngster.
Sunset nodded.

"She is my friend. Zonzalo, too."

"Yes," Mirina said, shortly. "He is." Zonzalo must
survive. As if she could will him back to safety, she
stared at the screen. Bisman's face was shining with
sweat. His fingers clutched the navigation controls as
Glashton fought to control the Slime Ball. The look
on his face told her what the Slime had warned about
was happening. Zonzalo had huddled himself into a
knot of arms and legs and shock webbing. She was
relieved to see that the reivers were too busy trying
to manage the ship to think of using him as a nego-
tiating tool. Big Voice tightened his fingers slightly, and
the crew on the other ship jerked heavily backward.

"Bisman, land or you'll explode," Keff said urgently. "The Cridi say that you don't have much time before the device you're carrying goes critical! We don't want anyone to die. Turn back at once. Hurry!"

Glashton, visible over Aldon's shoulder, nodded a white-eyed yes to him. Mirina breathed a silent thanksgiving as he backed the engines down.

Chapter 21

Carialle timed it so her tailfins touched the ground just before the pirate's did. Keff flung himself up and out of his shock webbing as soon as the altimeter hit zero, not waiting for an all-clear. The Cridi followed him in a stream, except for Big Voice and Small Spot, who elected to stay behind with Thunderstorm and the healers. Tall Eyebrow lifted Keff before he stepped off the ramp, and they sailed lightly over the mud toward the pirate ship. Mirina ran out after them.

"Take me with you!" she shouted. "I have to go to my brother!"

Big Eyes doubled back and picked her up. The woman squeaked in surprise as she was surrounded by an envelope of Core power, then rode in goggling silence the rest of the way.

On the plain near the pavilion, Keff spotted Noonday's white pelt, surrounded by a host of golden backs. Long-eyed like all those of her kind, she saw him long before he'd seen her, and was waving a wing-hand for him to join her. He squinted to bring the artificial lens in his eye to full magnification, and signalled that he was heading toward the newly landed ship. He saw her nod, and go back to talking severely to the others. Keff thought he recognized some of the Thelerie from the remote base in the crowd. The ship behind them was unmistakably Ship Three.

"Hurry!" Narrow Leg cried, flying on ahead as fast as Core power could propel him. "The Core goes critical!"

Tall Eyebrow and the others swept after him. The pirate's ramp lowered, and crew began to pour out of it. Keff and the Cridi flew in over their heads, making for the control room. The pilot stood up. Keff grabbed his wrist and signalled to Wide Foot, who drew him into the air and flew aft toward the exit with him. Zonzalo Don stared up at his sister, hovering in the air with no visible means of support. Keff took him by the shoulders and flung him, with Narrow Leg's help, up into Mirina's arms. Three of the Cridi surrounded Bisman, who cowered down into his chair with his hands above his head. The leader was airborne before he even had a chance to unfold.

"Everybody out!" Keff boomed, pitching his voice over the frightened cries of the crew fleeing for the exit. "Condition red!" He could feel hot gusts of air coming from the aft section. The Core must be back there. No time to remove it. The ship was doomed. "Hurry!"

They emerged into the open air. Waves of heat followed them. The pirates flung themselves out into the mud, gasping for breath.

"It ends," Narrow Leg said. He opened his hands to envelop the group. Keff felt something like a light curtain drop onto his back just before a deafening explosion and a kick of invisible force sent him somersaulting away from the pirates' ship. Plastic globes of Cridi and human bodies hurtled sideways past him. Keff landed with a squashy thud in the yellow mud. He picked himself up on hands and knees, spitting, to watch a plume of fire and smoke rise up from the two halves of the ship, now a hundred meters apart.

"Spacedust," Bisman spat, speaking for the first time.

He had landed face first in the mud a dozen meters from Keff. "The hell was that?"

"Something you stole, and never understood," Keff said. "Tad Pole!" he exclaimed, looking up just in time.

"I see," Narrow Leg said. The old Cridi spread his hands again as the debris from the broken ship began to rain down on them. Sections of circuitry, piping, flaming rags, pieces of hull and deck plate, crates of parts, and thousands of little flat pieces of metal pattered down, and bounded off the invisible forcefield ten meters above them like hailstones pinging against a plexiglass dome. The debris splatted down into the mud around them, peppering the landscape. Hundreds of square fragments of metal hammered down on the invisible shield, bouncing off in all directions. Keff realized with a feeling of shock that he recognized what they were. As soon as Narrow Leg signalled the all-clear, Keff crawled out over the mud, picking through them, searching for one in particular. Suddenly, he spotted the one he was looking for. He pounced on it and put it in his pocket. He turned to his allies and their cowering captives.

"*Now*, let's go back and see Carialle."

Thunderstorm had been settled in Keff's chair like an eagle on its nest, and Noonday occupied the other, so Keff had to stand in the midst of the huge crowd that filled the main cabin. A dozen Thelerie guardians, sitting up on their haunches with their bronze pole-arms ready, surrounded all ten pirates from the hidden base and most of the crew of the now-destroyed raider. The rest were outside, with more of the Sayas's guard. Carialle gazed from a dozen camera eyes at Aldon Bisman, whom Keff had made to stand in front of her pillar. She felt as if she was hammering on a prison door, almost out into the sunshine, if only he would talk! The key was in this obstinate man's mind.

He stood with his hands behind him as if on parade rest, staring straight ahead of him, looking at nothing.

"You were in this vicinity twenty years ago, weren't you?" Carialle asked, zooming in on his face with her closest camera eye. Such an ordinary face: human, male, Earth-Indo-European descent, about sixty, confident, choleric. Apart from empirical data, his face gave away no details. "P-sector, not too far from this system."

The man kept his expression blank, though his respiration went up slightly. Keff reached forward and poked him in the shoulder.

"Tell the lady," Keff said, as Bisman turned his head to glare. "She went to a lot of trouble to have you taken alive. The Cridi would cheerfully have split your ship apart in space and left you to die in vacuum. Talk."

"Yeah," Bisman said, at last. His narrow face was coming out in spectacular bruises, whether from the rough landing or Keff's fists, Carialle could not be sure. "I was there. My father's ship. He found this system fifty years ago. It was close to a new CW trading corridor. Easy meat."

"You were stripping wrecks for parts?" Carialle asked. He nodded silently, suspiciously. She almost trembled to ask the next question. "Do you remember one in P-sector that had been destroyed by an explosion in its fuel tanks? It was a Central Worlds Exploration scout. Twenty years ago. Think. You spent about two hours at it. You walked up and back on the hull, four times, two hundred and thirty steps in all." She saw him start, as if she had read his mind.

"I don't have to think," Bisman said, tightlipped. "Yes, I remember one like that. It was hard to tell if anything good was left, it was in such bad shape. Half the tail was missing, all of the control section was slag."

"Would you swear to that?" Carialle asked at once.

"If I had to." His eyes narrowed suspiciously. "Why?"

"Did you know," Carialle asked, feeling her nerves

prickle and ordered them under control, "that you were stripping a brainship? A live brainship? *My* ship?"

Bisman's cheeks paled and hollowed as his mouth dropped open. His eyes went wide. "I'd *never*," he choked on the last word and tried again. He looked up straight into her camera eye. "Madam, I would never hurt one of you. Never! What kind of character do you think I am?"

"Did you know?" Carialle asked.

"You've killed a lot of people," Mirina asked, shocked, staring at the man. "Why stop at that?"

"You dumb brawn," Bisman said, whirling to point a finger at her through the crowd of upright Thelerie. "You *fool*! Think of how many people you've bilked out of their savings, Madam Don! You're going to prison, too! You don't get any points for virtue."

Mirina was pale, too, but she confronted him bravely. "You can say a lot of things, Aldon, but you can never accuse me of murder. Did you do it?"

"No! I didn't know," he said, turning back to Carialle's pillar. "It wasn't intentional, madam. I'd never have left a living being in space like that. You don't. Spacer's law. If I'd had any idea . . . if there'd been a sign of life. We monitored for transmissions. There was a beacon going, but what about it? You must have been nearly dead, ma'am. I didn't bomb you."

"I know," Carialle said. "It was sabotage."

"They did the job thoroughly," Bisman said, fervently. "You . . . it was a fused lump. I can't believe you were alive in *that*."

"Oh, I was. I could hear you. You *laughed*. I've been hating you for twenty years," Carialle said, "wondering why you didn't help me get out of there."

"I didn't know," Bisman said, his cool poise shattered. "I swear, none of us did. We saw the hulk, and spotted some components I knew we could boost. We were just trying to make a few credits. But I know the law of space, and I'd hope it would protect me too," he said earnestly. "If I'd had the *least* iota you were alive inside it, I'd have towed you somewhere."

"Somewhere?" Keff asked, shoving his face into the man's and making him back up a pace. "Like that illegal base at the edge of the Cridi system, for example? So you could finish your salvage?"

Bisman faced Keff down with a snarl. "We heard nothing, brawn. That ship was dead, dead, dead so far as I was concerned. If you'd seen how it looked, ma'am, compacted downlike, you would think so, too. There were damaged capacitors firing off now and again nearly blinding us or burning through our gloves, backup batteries imploding up and down the hulk. I'd have put any residual warmth down to those. We didn't have the best equipment, ma'am. That's why we were salvaging. There could've been a heartbeat deep in there, but I swear we checked."

"Not enough," Keff growled.

"Keff, let him alone," Carialle said. "I believe you." The prison door opened, and she saw sunlight beyond it. She felt immeasurably better. "Thank you for the truth." She sighed. "I only wish I had some solid proof to add to your statement."

"I have some," Keff said, pulling the scrap of metal out of his tunic pocket. "I found it in the field when it was raining ship parts." He held it up to the nearest camera eye. Carialle zoomed in on it, but she didn't need magnification. The small titanium square said "963." It was her original number plate.

"I never noticed that one," Mirina said. "He had a whole collection of those from the ships we gutted among the junk he collected. They were his trophies. I'd have recognized it if I'd seen it. They gave me Charles's." She took a square of metal out of her pocket and showed it to Carialle's camera eye over the food synthesizer. On the fragment was etched "702." "I suppose you heard the whole story."

"Yes," Carialle said. "I'm sorry."

"Now we have physical proof and a confession," Keff said, rubbing his hands together. "We can take this back to the CenCom and shove it up a certain person's nose."

"We have also heard confessions," Noonday said from her nest, looking around for some manifestation of Carialle's to address. Carialle produced the Lady Fair image on the nearest screen over the console, and had it meet the Sayas' golden gaze. "We have those who have shamed us before you now. What will you have us do with them?"

"You'd better ask the Cridi," Carialle said. "I think they have the first claim on reparation."

Big Voice and a few of the others popped up above the crowd. All of the Melange Thelerie protested. The one called Autumn raised her voice.

"Spare us the Slime!" she said desperately, pushing forward to address the image. The guardians crossed their back-scratchers to bar her way. "Only the sacred humans can dictate our fate. I will otherwise kill all my crew."

"Be silent," Noonday said severely.

"We're not sacred," Keff said, shaking his head, "and by the way, I don't think we're your beings of legend. Do you know, Cari, a little idea occurred to me. Noonday, let me suggest something to you. Your legend concerns four-limbed, wingless creatures from the stars who were supposed to help you winged ones to fly in the void. Is that right?"

"It is our most beloved story," Noonday said, nodding her great head.

"How old is it?" Keff asked.

"How old? Told for, mmm, one thousand six hundred of our years."

"Narrow Leg," Keff asked, turning to the Cridi

captain, "when did the Cridi explore this system and reject it as a possibility for settlement?"

Narrow Leg's eyes twinkled, and he bobbed up and down near the ceiling. The rest of the Cridi looked curious, but he made a few quick hand signals, and they laughed merrily.

"It is possible," he said. "One thousand six hundred revolutions times .88768 equals 1,420 revolutions—yes. It could have been Cridi explorers."

"No!" Autumn said, aghast, gaping at the Cridi. "You assume that all these many years we have revered the *wrong* species?"

"I think that's exactly what you have done," Keff said, rocking back on his heels in satisfaction. "The legend doesn't say how big the beings were, does it?"

"No," Noonday said, peering at him. "It does not."

"Then, it could have been, couldn't it?" Carialle asked, projecting an image of a bipedal being on the wall beside the silhouette of a Thelerie. She made the biped in human proportions, than shrank it to half its original height. "It's more likely they landed here than a stray human ship. They're virtually next door."

"I am disgraced," Autumn said, dropping her gaze to the floor.

The rest of the Thelerie turned to stare at Bisman and the human crew.

"It's not our fault nobody measured your visitors," Bisman said, testily. "Look, we've done a lot for you. "Telephone, gas lights, spaceships . . ."

"You have done much ill, too," Noonday said firmly. "If my child had not admitted the wrongs, if more had been open about their experiences, we would have rejected you long ago." She addressed Carialle. "If you are going back to your Central Worlds, we will keep these bad ones in safe custody until you return."

"There's a lot to do yet," Carialle said. "We can't leave

until we . . . I'm receiving an incoming message," she said to Keff. "And this time, it is a CW ship."

"CK-963, this is DSM-344. Remain where you are. Do not lift ship," the uniformed commander said severely from the central screen. "Repeat: do not lift ship. You are under arrest. Any attempts at escape will result in the destruction of your vessel."

"This is the CK-963," Carialle said. "Why are we under arrest?" There was a brief time lag for the distance between the ship and the planet. By the time the screen cleared again, another human had taken the place of the commander in front of the video pickup, a tall, thin man with graying hair and an overwhelming moustache that had been waxed firmly into submission. To Carialle it was the most unwelcome face in the galaxy. Her blood vessels constricted momentarily, but the shock passed quickly.

"This is Dr. Maxwell-Corey, Carialle," he said, in his thin, irritated voice. "You left the Cridi planet strictly against orders."

Keff interposed himself in front of one of her video pickups at once.

"Dr. Maxwell-Corey, how nice to see you," he said. "The circumstances altered the import of your orders. We had to investigate the destruction of the DSC-902, as we transmitted to you, as soon as possible before the perpetrators got too far away. We found them. You did receive our messages?"

"I did," the Inspector General said peevishly. "You conscripted the Cridi for your illegal activity, endangering them on your mad scramble to justify your longstanding mania, Carialle. This will not sit well with Alien Outreach, or Xeno! On my arrival I am insisting that you be placed in protective custody pending a hearing on charges of constructive kidnapping."

"That's ridiculous. We didn't conscript them," Carialle

said, feeling the adrenaline in her system increase twofold. "They insisted on accompanying us—their right as an intelligent species. They have saved our lives several times. I am very pleased to have had them as allies."

"They should not be there at all!" The IG's hollow cheeks went red with fury. "An insane brainship and her dupe convincing them to chase off after illusory pirates to a so-called secret base on the fifth planet of the Cridi system? Preposterous! There was a base, if you could call it that," M-C said, disdainfully. "But there were no mysterious 'griffins.' Er . . . griffins," he said, as Noonday moved into range of the video. She smiled at him, and he goggled at her. Carialle knew what it was like for a human the first time a Thelerie smiled, parting its lip to show the needle-sharp fangs underneath, and she enjoyed the effect it had on the Inspector General.

"Thelerie," Carialle said, sweetly. "We know. May I present Noonday, Sayas of Thelerie? She is the head of planetary government. The pirates escaped and came here, sir. They have only just arrived. The commander of that ship is called Autumn, and if you will check the video I sent you, you can see that that is indeed the ship, out there on the landing field." She inserted a view from her external camera of Ship Three, lying abandoned on the plain. "I strongly suspect that if you check their engine compartment, they flew here using components from the DSC-902."

"It is true," Autumn admitted, as Noonday's guards hustled her forward. She wrapped her wings protectively about herself. "Our ship had no propulsion unit left. Nor communications."

Maxwell-Corey stared out of the screen. "They speak Standard." He glared at Keff. "This is undoubtedly *your* doing. You have no right to involve this species in anything. They are not members of the Central Worlds, or if what you say is true in your transmission, possessed of their own technology."

"Breaking the Prime Directive again," Carialle said pertly. "Not guilty on that count either, sir. They spoke Standard when we arrived. That's part of the rest of the story we have to tell you."

"I am glad to encounter you, sir," the Sayas said warmly, opening sincere, striped eyes at the Inspector General. "We wish to apply for membership in the Central Worlds. We wish to be one with all of the blessed humans."

"I . . . I'm not really the one you should speak to about membership," Maxwell-Corey admitted, staring at the golden-eyed beast. "Er, blessed humans?"

"Then, who? We are most eager. We would like to be full members."

"I'm afraid that's impossible. You lack the necessary technology," the Inspector General said. "If the report the CK-963 sent me is accurate, all that you possess is stolen or derelict."

"We are sorry about that," Noonday said, dipping her head slightly. "What you say has recently come to my attention. We're willing to make reparation as we can, but we still wish to fly in space."

"Er, I don't see how." M-C looked bemused.

"Fait accompli," Carialle said cheerfully. "They have already been in space numerous times. Plus, they have a viable culture and society. They should be at least given ISS status. The rest will follow."

"We will help them gain access to space," Big Voice piped up, floating close enough to Keff to be included on his camera. Carialle opened up the focus so the IG could see all of the Cridi. "As we began to do many revolutions ago, we will continue. It is only right that we fulfill the promise made so long ago, if such a thing is permitted among the Central Worlds." Behind him, Narrow Leg and the others nodded energetic agreement.

Noonday was very touched. She knelt down onto her belly before the plump councillor. "We accept your offer most gratefully, blessed Cridi."

"Yes," Big Voice said, enjoying himself. "We shall be good patrons to you, and you shall be good customers to us."

Mirina stood, feeling dazed, as the conference went on. Autumn and the others were alive! Relief fought in her belly with worry. What would happen to her and her brother now that the Central Worlds authority was coming?

She felt something tap at her knee. She looked down to see one of Keff's—no, Carialle's drone robots beside her. On its platform was the tiny space-scape of Dimitri. She looked up at the wall. An image appeared, the head of the female executive that Carialle had feigned to fool Bisman. It mouthed a single word. "Go."

Mirina dithered for a moment, but only a moment. Everyone's attention was centered on the image of the Inspector General. She grabbed Zonzalo's arm, and began to edge toward the airlock. Sunset glanced up as she sidled behind him. She beckoned hopefully to him, and he nodded, sliding silently backward, away from his spot next to Thunderstorm. The servo made way for them between the guards around the perimeter of the room. At the threshold of the open airlock, the drone offered her the painting with one of its claw hands, and pointed in the direction of Autumn's ship. Mirina needed no further hint. She started running, Zonzalo and Sunset right behind her.

"And in the meantime," Carialle continued, "we've started you off by breaking up a well-established pirate ring with a fifty-year history of theft and murderous raids. That ought to be good for a bonus." M-C turned a fishy eye on Bisman.

"I want to strike a bargain," Bisman said through gritted teeth. "I want legal representation."

"You have nothing we want," Maxwell-Corey said, haughtily.

"Oh, yes?" Bisman asked. "I can give you names, starting with one of your own ex-brawns. How about that, eh?" He scanned the crowd of Thelerie, Cridi, and humans. "She's the real brain behind the operation." He turned around, searching. "Where's Mirina Don?" he demanded.

"Gone," Keff said, pretending to look astonished. "She must have slipped out in all the confusion."

"Her brother's gone, too," Bisman said, angrily. "They can't get far. There's no ship . . ." He turned to look at Autumn.

"Not much fuel, but it flies," Autumn said. "But there is no navigation equipment aboard for humans to use."

"They have Sunset," Thunderstorm said, softly.

The Inspector General rounded on Keff. "You've let a criminal escape!"

"Not me," Keff said, in all innocence. "I've been standing right here the whole time."

Thunderstorm rumbled a phrase in his own language. Carialle whispered the translation into Keff's ear. "My old friend, you have done a good thing." Keff smiled.

Tall Eyebrow stepped forward and addressed the angry human on the screen.

"Think what you do. If you arrest Keff and Carialle, you will jeopardize the fragile alliance between the Cridi and the Central Worlds. If so, we would certainly insist on every human being removed from Sky Clear, which you call Ozran. We could show in a galactic tribunal it was originally a Cridi colony of extreme long standing. I, Tall Eyebrow," he indicated his name in the Ozranian sign language, "speak as the senior representative."

"What?" M-C demanded. Big Voice pushed in close to the camera eye.

"And no access will become possible to our Core technology," the plump councillor insisted. "Such things are to our friends only. We like Keff and Carialle, yet you withdrew . . . what is word, Keff?"

"Portfolio," Keff said, with an angelic expression.

"Portfolio," Big Voice said. "A pity indeed where so much is in common. We would have traded happily for good spacecraft. But no alliance, no ships, no Cores." He shook his head, imitating the human expression of regret, a gesture that was not lost on Maxwell-Corey.

"But—that was part of the agreement sent by the diplomatic service to Cridi," the Inspector General said, looking from brawn to pillar to Cridi with desperation in his eyes.

"Which they were not able to sign," Carialle pointed out. "We delayed having the documents ratified because *you* sent in another team, and they were killed by the Melange."

"My dear Carialle," M-C said, in amazement, "you were withdrawn from the mission because you had a paranoid episode. Your actions were what held diplomacy hostage, not the destruction of the other ship."

"I did *not* have a paranoid episode," Carialle said, coldly. "I had an anxiety attack, brought on by proximity to the location where I once had a near-fatal accident. It is your interpretation of my reaction that caused you to assume paranoia, and to send another ship. You are ultimately responsible for the unnecessary death of the crew of the shuttle."

"Ah, yes," Maxwell-Corey said, maddeningly tenting his fingers together on his narrow belly. "Now we come to it. Your phantom aliens. Your salvage wreckers."

Carialle played the datatape of Bisman's admission on the transmission frequency, and waited. Maxwell-Corey ignored it at first, staring instead straight at his camera eye. Within moments Carialle observed him leaning closer to the screen. A scan sneaked through the sideband of the bandwidth told her he was manifesting anxiety, with increased levels of adrenaline in his system. He spoke at last.

"Yes, well, you could have extorted such a statement from him."

"Bisman!" Keff called. "Is it true?"

The pirate leader looked up. "Yes," he said, through his teeth.

"Do you see?" Carialle said. "And Keff found my old number plate among his effects." Keff displayed it to the video pickup.

"This is very interesting," M-C said, tapping his fingertips together nervously. "Very interesting indeed."

"Indeed," Carialle echoed, icily. "Then you will find it no surprise to hear that I am bringing a second formal complaint against you. Date-coded messages have already gone out to SPRIM and MM as well as my legal counsel regarding the programming you inserted into my message-beacon system. You overstepped reasonable bounds, and I intend to have you taken to task for it!"

"My dear Carialle, it was for your own good!" the IG protested.

"You've had time to absorb the information," Carialle said. "Am I sane? This is official. I am time-coding your reply. Am I?"

"Evidence suggests that the answer might conceivably be . . . yes," the IG said, after a very long pause and a study of the ceiling. "But the evidence only came to light at this juncture, that is to say, now. I was acting on the information of the time. You *could* have imperiled many people, including yourself."

"When your own psychologists said I wasn't a threat," Carialle said. "When we finish this mission, I'll have something to say to the CenCom, *personally*. I assume we are to complete the mission to the Cridi?"

"Yes, yes," M-C said, defeated. His shoulders sagged. "You're reinstated. You are the best team for the job. I've always had the utmost faith in you."

"They have done such a good job," Tall Eyebrow said, floating up to give his words emphasis. "You must tell it to those of CenCom. And teaching us so much about space travel, including such delightful games as Myths and Legends! Such an important cultural gift!"

The Inspector General sputtered, but he managed to hold his tongue. "I will be down presently. We'll talk about the, er, the details of your mission then. I have much to consider before we land. Maxwell-Corey out."

Keff felt a smirk at the corners of his mouth as the screen blanked. "Bravo, Cari!" he said, applauding her. "And bravo, TE. Thank you for rubbing salt in the wound."

"It is not salt," Tall Eyebrow said, puzzled. "It is truth."

At a gesture from the Sayas' wing-finger, the Sayas' guardians assembled the prisoners, both human and Thelerie, and marched out, leaving only the Cridi, Thunderstorm and Noonday.

"The healing really begins now," Carialle said to Keff, who stood close beside her pillar. "He won't dare to persecute me again."

"Which way did she go, Cari?" Keff asked softly.

"I don't know," Carialle said. "I've blanked it out of my memory. But if I were her I'd run for the balance point. Once she's behind the anomaly she can change direction without being detected." Keff looked at Noonday and Thunderstorm.

"If she comes back, will you treat her kindly?"

"As she has always treated us," Thunderstorm said.

"I feel she is already punished somewhat," Noonday said. "And she has killed no one. She will be allowed."

"Thank you," Keff said, sincerely. He turned to the

Cridi. "Well, TE, I suppose we'll be taking you home to Ozran soon?"

"Much left to do here, for a while," the Frog Prince said. "Must retrieve all parts of the ship, and hope none are damaged. But once it is reassembled, Narrow Leg wants to take us home himself. He would see where Big Eyes will be living. She is staying with me. It will be difficult . . . "

"It will be fine," Big Eyes interrupted him.

"Congratulations!" Keff said. The young female flirted her eyelids shyly at him as she took Tall Eyebrow's hand and interlaced his long fingers in hers.

"Yes," Big Voice said, waddling forward. "Instead, you shall have the honor of taking *me* home to Cridi, where I shall tell story of great heroism of mine. I captured the evil ship. And see the burns on my back where alien gas touched me, yet I continued with rescue of injured Thelerie!"

Carialle sighed deeply, but it was for pure happiness. "Games are good," she said, "but you can't beat real life. We've never had a game where everyone lived happily ever after."

Keff, thinking of Mirina, hurtling away from the planet in a rickety ship, but free, said, "Or as close as it's possible to be."

Carialle's Lady Fair image appeared on the wall and winked solemnly at him. She knew exactly what he was thinking.

The white and blue ship sank gracefully out of the sky like a diva taking a curtain call. It landed softly but heavily on the plain between Carialle's ship and the smoking hulk of the red pirate, and sank a good three meters in the viscous yellow mud. Keff, hovering among the Cridi centimeters over the surface of the plain, was on hand as the gangplank dropped with a splat. Thelerie, including Noonday and most of the

Ro-sayo, swirled in to flit about the ship as soon as the engines shut off. Three security officers in full environment kit and gleaming armored suits trotted out onto the ramp, careful not to step off into the shining goo. They looked up at the gathering crowd, and stared. It only took a moment for them to realize they were looking at three different species of beings. The youngest among them, a thin-faced rating with freckles, stared openmouthed at Cridi and Thelerie until his CO elbowed him. The young man came on guard, his long-barreled gun leveled over his forearm. The CO let out a sharp all-clear whistle, and two more space-suited humans emerged. One, in black armor, must have been the commander of the ship. The other, in official blue and red, was the Inspector General.

"Cari, I'm a little worried," Keff said into his sublingual link as he made a little salute to the ship's crew. The gangplank, under the additional weight of the IG, sank an additional quarter meter into the mud. "Will you be able to handle seeing Maxwell-Corey face-to-face?"

"Oh, don't worry, Keff," Carialle said, confidently. "This time I'm ready for him. Bring him along! And, Keff?"

"Yes?" Keff asked.

"Let him walk!"

DAVID WEBER

Honor Harrington *(cont.)*:

Field of Dishonor

Honor goes home to Manticore—and fights for her life on a battlefield she never trained for, in a private war that offers just two choices: death—or a "victory" that can end only in dishonor and the loss of all she loves....

Other novels by DAVID WEBER:

Mutineers' Moon

"...a good story...reminds me of 1950s Heinlein..."
—*BMP Bulletin*

The Armageddon Inheritance

Sequel to *Mutineers' Moon*.

Path of the Fury

"Excellent...a thinking person's Terminator."
—*Kliatt*

Oath of Swords

An epic fantasy.

with STEVE WHITE:

Insurrection
Crusade

Novels set in the world of the Starfire ™ game system.

And don't miss Steve White's solo novels,
***The Disinherited** and **Legacy**!*

continued ☞

To Read About Great Characters Having Incredible Adventures You Should Try 🚀 🚀 🚀

IF YOU LIKE . . .	YOU SHOULD TRY . . .

Arthurian Legend... *The Winter Prince*
by Elizabeth E. Wein

Computers... Rick Cook's *Wizard's Bane* series

Cats... Larry Niven's *Man-Kzin Wars* series

Cats in Space ed. by Bill Fawcett

Horses... *Hunting Party* and *Sporting Chance*
by Elizabeth Moon

Dun Lady's Jess by Doranna Durgin

**Fantasy Role Playing
  Games...** *The Bard's Tale* ™ Novels
by Mercedes Lackey et al.

The Rose Sea by S.M. Stirling & Holly Lisle

Harry Turtledove's *Werenight* and *Prince of the North*

Computer Games... *The Bard's Tale* ™ Novels
by Mercedes Lackey et al.

The Wing Commander ™ Novels
by Mercedes Lackey, William R. Forstchen, et al.

New . . . St. Joseph

SUNDAY MISSAL

PRAYERBOOK AND HYMNAL

For 2015-2016

THE COMPLETE MASSES FOR SUNDAYS, HOLYDAYS, and the SACRED PASCHAL TRIDUUM

With the People's Parts of Holy Mass
Printed in Boldface Type
and Arranged for Parish Participation

**IN ACCORD WITH THE THIRD TYPICAL EDITION
OF THE ROMAN MISSAL**

**WITH THE "NEW AMERICAN BIBLE" TEXT
FROM THE REVISED SUNDAY LECTIONARY,
SHORT HELPFUL NOTES AND EXPLANATIONS,
AND A TREASURY OF POPULAR PRAYERS**

Dedicated to St. Joseph
Patron of the Universal Church

CATHOLIC BOOK PUBLISHING CORP.
New Jersey

NIHIL OBSTAT: Sr. M. Kathleen Flanagan, S.C., Ph.D.
   Censor Librorum

IMPRIMATUR: ✠ Arthur J. Serratelli, S.S.L., S.T.D., D.D.
   Bishop of Paterson

Published with the approval of the
Committee on Divine Worship,
United States Conference of Catholic Bishops

The St. Joseph Missals have been diligently prepared with the invaluable assistance of a special Board of Editors, including specialists in Liturgy and Sacred Scripture, Catechetics, Sacred Music and Art.

In this new Sunday Missal Edition the musical notations for responsorial antiphons are by Rev. John Selner, S.S.

(T-2016)

ISBN 978-1-941243-41-1

© 2015 by *Catholic Book Publishing Corp.*, N.J.
www.catholicbookpublishing.com
Printed in the U.S.A.

PREFACE

IN the words of the Second Vatican Council in the *Constitution on the Liturgy*, the *Mass* "is an action of Christ the priest and of his body which is the Church; it is a sacred action surpassing all others; no other action of the Church can equal its efficacy by the same title and to the same degree" (art. 7). Hence the Mass is a sacred sign, something visible which brings the invisible reality of Christ to us in the worship of the Father.

The Mass was first instituted as a meal at the Last Supper and became a living memorial of Christ's sacrifice on the cross:

"At the Last Supper, on the night when he was betrayed, our Savior instituted the Eucharistic sacrifice of his body and blood. He did this in order to perpetuate the sacrifice of the Cross throughout the centuries until he should come again, and so to entrust to his beloved spouse, the Church, a memorial of his death and resurrection: a sacrament of love, a sign of unity, a bond of charity, a Paschal banquet in which Christ is eaten, the mind is filled with grace, and a pledge of future glory is given to us.

"The Church, therefore, earnestly desires that Christ's faithful, when present at this mystery of faith, should not be there as strangers or silent spectators; on the contrary, through a good understanding of the rites and prayers they should take part in the sacred action conscious of what they are doing, with devotion and full collaboration. They should be instructed by God's word

7

and be nourished at the table of the Lord's body; they should give thanks to God; by offering the immaculate Victim, not only through the hands of the priests but also with him, they should learn also to offer themselves; through Christ the Mediator, they should be drawn day by day into ever more perfect union with God and with each other, so that . . . God may be all in all" (art. 47-48).

Accordingly, this new Sunday Missal has been edited, in conformity with the latest findings of modern liturgists, especially to enable the people to attain the most active participation.

To insure that "each . . . lay person who has an office to perform [will] do all of, but only, those parts which pertain to his office" (art. 28), a simple method of instant identification of the various parts of the Mass, has been designed, using different typefaces:

(1) **boldface type**—clearly identifies all people's parts for each Mass.

(2) lightface type—indicates the Priest's, Deacon's, or lector's parts.

In order to enable the faithful to prepare for each Mass AT HOME and so participate more actively AT MASS, the editors have added short helpful explanations of the new scripture readings, geared to the spiritual needs of daily life. A large selection of hymns for congregational singing has been included as well as a treasury of private prayers.

We trust that all these special features will help Catholics who use this new St. Joseph Missal to be led—in keeping with the desire of the Church—"to that full, conscious, and active participation in liturgical celebrations which is demanded by the very nature of the liturgy. Such participation by the Christian people as a chosen race, a royal priesthood, a holy nation, a redeemed people (1 Pt 2:9; cf. 2:4-5), is their right and duty by reason of their baptism" (art. 14).

THE ORDER OF MASS TITLES

THE INTRODUCTORY RITES

1. Entrance Chant
2. Greeting
3. Rite for the Blessing and Sprinkling of Water
4. Penitential Act
5. Kyrie
6. Gloria
7. Collect (Proper)

THE LITURGY OF THE WORD

8. First Reading (Proper)
9. Responsorial Psalm (Proper)
10. Second Reading (Proper)
11. Gospel Acclamation (Proper)
12. Gospel Dialogue
13. Gospel Reading (Proper)
14. Homily
15. Profession of Faith (Creed)
16. Universal Prayer

THE LITURGY OF THE EUCHARIST

17. Presentation and Preparation of the Gifts
18. Invitation to Prayer
19. Prayer over the Offerings (Proper)
20. Eucharistic Prayer

21. Preface Dialogue
22. Preface
23. Preface Acclamation
    Eucharistic Prayer
    1, 2, 3, 4
    Reconciliation 1, 2
    Various Needs 1, 2, 3, 4

THE COMMUNION RITE

24. The Lord's Prayer
25. Sign of Peace
26. Lamb of God
27. Invitation to Communion
28. Communion
29. Prayer after Communion (Proper)

THE CONCLUDING RITES

30. Solemn Blessing
31. Final Blessing
32. Dismissal

THE ORDER OF MASS

Options are indicated by A, B, C, D in the margin.

THE INTRODUCTORY RITES

Acts of prayer and penitence prepare us to meet Christ as he comes in Word and Sacrament. We gather as a worshiping community to celebrate our unity with him and with one another in faith.

1 ENTRANCE CHANT `STAND`

If it is not sung, it is recited by all or some of the people.

Joined together as Christ's people, we open the celebration by raising our voices in praise of God who is present among us. This song should deepen our unity as it introduces the Mass we celebrate today.

→ `Turn to Today's Mass`

2 GREETING (3 forms)

When the Priest comes to the altar, he makes the customary reverence with the ministers and kisses the altar. Then, with the ministers, he goes to his chair. After the Entrance Chant, all make the Sign of the Cross:

Priest: In the name of the Father, and of the Son, and of the Holy Spirit.

PEOPLE: **Amen.**

10

The Priest welcomes us in the name of the Lord. We show our union with God, our neighbor, and the Priest by a united response to his greeting.

A ————————————————————

Priest: The grace of our Lord Jesus Christ,
and the love of God,
and the communion of the Holy Spirit
be with you all.

PEOPLE: And with your spirit.

B ———————— OR ————————

Priest: Grace to you and peace from God our Father
and the Lord Jesus Christ.

PEOPLE: And with your spirit.

C ———————— OR ————————

Priest: The Lord be with you.

PEOPLE: And with your spirit.

[Bishop: Peace be with you.

PEOPLE: And with your spirit.]

3 RITE FOR the BLESSING and SPRINKLING OF WATER

From time to time on Sundays, especially in Easter Time, instead of the customary Penitential Act, the Blessing and Sprinkling of Water may take place (see pp. 78-81) as a reminder of Baptism.

4 PENITENTIAL ACT (3 forms)

(Omitted when the Rite for the Blessing and Sprinkling of Water [see pp. 78-81] has taken place or some part of the liturgy of the hours has preceded.)

Before we hear God's word, we acknowledge our sins humbly, ask for mercy, and accept his pardon.

Invitation to repent:

After the introduction to the day's Mass, the Priest invites the people to recall their sins and to repent of them in silence:

Priest: Brethren (brothers and sisters), let us acknowledge our sins,
and so prepare ourselves to celebrate the sacred mysteries.

Then, after a brief silence, one of the following forms is used.

A

Priest and **PEOPLE:**

**I confess to almighty God
and to you, my brothers and sisters,
that I have greatly sinned,
in my thoughts and in my words,
in what I have done and in what I have failed to do,**

They strike their breast:

**through my fault, through my fault,
through my most grievous fault;**

Then they continue:

**therefore I ask blessed Mary ever-Virgin,
all the Angels and Saints,
and you, my brothers and sisters,
to pray for me to the Lord our God.**

B ───────────── OR ─────────────

Priest: Have mercy on us, O Lord.

PEOPLE: For we have sinned against you.

Priest: Show us, O Lord, your mercy.

PEOPLE: And grant us your salvation.

C ───────────── OR─────────────

Priest, or a Deacon or another minister:

> You were sent to heal the contrite of heart:
> Lord, have mercy.

PEOPLE: Lord, have mercy.

Priest or other minister:

> You came to call sinners:
> Christ, have mercy.

PEOPLE: Christ, have mercy.

Priest or other minister:

> You are seated at the right hand of the Father to intercede for us:
>
> Lord, have mercy.

PEOPLE: Lord, have mercy.

───────────

Absolution:

At the end of any of the forms of the Penitential Act:

Priest: May almighty God have mercy on us,
forgive us our sins,
and bring us to everlasting life.

PEOPLE: Amen.

5　KYRIE

Unless included in the Penitential Act, the Kyrie is sung or said by all, with alternating parts for the choir or cantor and for the people:

℣.　Lord, have mercy.

℟.　**Lord, have mercy.**

℣.　Christ, have mercy.

℟.　**Christ, have mercy.**

℣.　Lord, have mercy.

℟.　**Lord, have mercy.**

6　GLORIA

As the Church assembled in the Spirit we praise and pray to the Father and the Lamb.

When the Gloria is sung or said, the Priest or the cantors or everyone together may begin it:

**Glory to God in the highest,
and on earth peace to people of good will.**

**We praise you,
we bless you,
we adore you,
we glorify you,
we give you thanks for your great glory,
Lord God, heavenly King,
O God, almighty Father.**

**Lord Jesus Christ, Only Begotten Son,
Lord God, Lamb of God, Son of the Father,
you take away the sins of the world,
　　have mercy on us;**

you take away the sins of the world,
   receive our prayer;
you are seated at the right hand of the Father,
   have mercy on us.

For you alone are the Holy One,
you alone are the Lord,
you alone are the Most High,
Jesus Christ,
with the Holy Spirit,
in the glory of God the Father.
Amen.

7 COLLECT

The Priest invites us to pray silently for a moment and then, in our name, expresses the theme of the day's celebration and petitions God the Father through the mediation of Christ in the Holy Spirit.

Priest: Let us pray.

→ Turn to Today's Mass

Priest and people pray silently for a while. Then the Priest says the Collect prayer, at the end of which the people acclaim:

PEOPLE: Amen.

THE LITURGY OF THE WORD

The proclamation of God's Word is always centered on Christ, present through his Word. Old Testament writings prepare for him; New Testament books speak of him directly. All of scripture calls us to believe once more and to follow. After the reading we reflect on God's words and respond to them.

As in Today's Mass   `SIT`

8 FIRST READING

At the end of the reading: Reader: **The word of the Lord.**

PEOPLE: Thanks be to God.

9 RESPONSORIAL PSALM

The people repeat the response sung by the cantor the first time and then after each verse.

10 SECOND READING

At the end of the reading: Reader: **The word of the Lord.**

PEOPLE: Thanks be to God.

11 GOSPEL ACCLAMATION   `STAND`

Jesus will speak to us in the Gospel. We rise now out of respect and prepare for his message with the Alleluia.

The people repeat the Alleluia after the cantor's Alleluia and then after the verse. During Lent one of the following invocations is used as a response instead of the Alleluia:

(a) **Glory and praise to you, Lord Jesus Christ!**
(b) **Glory to you, Lord Jesus Christ, Wisdom of God the Father!**
(c) **Glory to you, Word of God, Lord Jesus Christ!**
(d) **Glory to you, Lord Jesus Christ, Son of the Living God!**

(e) **Praise and honor to you, Lord Jesus Christ!**

(f) **Praise to you, Lord Jesus Christ, King of endless glory!**

(g) **Marvelous and great are your works, O Lord!**

(h) **Salvation, glory, and power to the Lord Jesus Christ!**

12 GOSPEL DIALOGUE

Before proclaiming the Gospel, the Deacon asks the Priest: Your blessing, Father. *The Priest says:*

May the Lord be in your heart and on your lips,
that you may proclaim his Gospel worthily and well,
in the name of the Father, and of the Son, ✠ and of
the Holy Spirit. *The Deacon answers:* Amen.

If there is no Deacon, the Priest says inaudibly:

Cleanse my heart and my lips, almighty God,
that I may worthily proclaim your holy Gospel.

13 GOSPEL READING

Deacon (or Priest):
        The Lord be with you.

PEOPLE: And with your spirit.

Deacon (or Priest):

✠ A reading from the holy Gospel according to N.

PEOPLE: Glory to you, O Lord.

At the end:

Deacon (or Priest):
        The Gospel of the Lord.

PEOPLE: Praise to you, Lord Jesus Christ.

Then the Deacon (or Priest) kisses the book, saying inaudibly: Through the words of the Gospel may our sins
be wiped away.

14 HOMILY · SIT

God's word is spoken again in the Homily. The Holy Spirit speaking through the lips of the preacher explains and applies today's biblical readings to the needs of this particular congregation. He calls us to respond to Christ through the life we lead.

15 PROFESSION OF FAITH (CREED) STAND

As a people we express our acceptance of God's message in the Scriptures and Homily. We summarize our faith by proclaiming a creed handed down from the early Church.

All say the Profession of Faith on Sundays.

THE NICENE CREED

I believe in one God,
the Father almighty,
maker of heaven and earth,
of all things visible and invisible.

I believe in one Lord Jesus Christ,
the Only Begotten Son of God,
born of the Father before all ages.
God from God, Light from Light,
true God from true God,
begotten, not made, consubstantial with the Father;
through him all things were made.
For us men and for our salvation
he came down from heaven,
and by the Holy Spirit was incarnate of the Virgin
   Mary,   } *bow*
and became man.

For our sake he was crucified under Pontius Pilate,
he suffered death and was buried,
and rose again on the third day
in accordance with the Scriptures.
He ascended into heaven
and is seated at the right hand of the Father.
He will come again in glory
to judge the living and the dead
and his kingdom will have no end.

I believe in the Holy Spirit, the Lord, the giver of life,
who proceeds from the Father and the Son,
who with the Father and the Son is adored and
   glorified,
who has spoken through the prophets.

I believe in one, holy, catholic and apostolic Church.
I confess one Baptism for the forgiveness of sins
and I look forward to the resurrection of the dead
and the life of the world to come. Amen.

OR ─────── **APOSTLES' CREED** ───────

*Especially during Lent and Easter Time, the Apostles'
Creed may be said after the Homily.*

I believe in God,
the Father almighty,
Creator of heaven and earth,
and in Jesus Christ, his only Son, our Lord,
who was conceived by the Holy Spirit, ⎫ *bow*
born of the Virgin Mary,   ⎭
suffered under Pontius Pilate,
was crucified, died and was buried;
he descended into hell;
on the third day he rose again from the dead;
he ascended into heaven,
and is seated at the right hand of God the Father
    almighty;
from there he will come to judge the living and the dead.

I believe in the Holy Spirit,
the holy catholic Church,
the communion of saints,
the forgiveness of sins,
the resurrection of the body,
and life everlasting. Amen.

16 UNIVERSAL PRAYER   (Prayer of the Faithful)

As a priestly people we unite with one another to pray for today's
needs in the Church and the world.

*After the Priest gives the introduction the Deacon or other
minister sings or says the invocations.*

PEOPLE: Lord, hear our prayer.

(or other response, according to local custom)
At the end the Priest says the concluding prayer:

PEOPLE: Amen.

THE LITURGY OF THE EUCHARIST

17 PRESENTATION AND PREPARATION `SIT`
OF THE GIFTS

While the people's gifts are brought forward to the Priest and are placed on the altar, the Offertory Chant is sung.

Before placing the bread on the altar, the Priest says inaudibly:

Blessed are you, Lord God of all creation,
for through your goodness we have received
the bread we offer you:
fruit of the earth and work of human hands,
it will become for us the bread of life.

If there is no singing, the Priest may say this prayer aloud, and the people may respond:

PEOPLE: Blessed be God for ever.

When he pours wine and a little water into the chalice, the Deacon (or the Priest) says inaudibly:

By the mystery of this water and wine
may we come to share in the divinity of Christ
who humbled himself to share in our humanity.

Before placing the chalice on the altar, he says:

Blessed are you, Lord God of all creation,
for through your goodness we have received
the wine we offer you:
fruit of the vine and work of human hands,
it will become our spiritual drink.

If there is no singing, the Priest may say this prayer aloud, and the people may respond:

PEOPLE: **Blessed be God for ever.**

The Priest says inaudibly:

With humble spirit and contrite heart
may we be accepted by you, O Lord,
and may our sacrifice in your sight this day
be pleasing to you, Lord God.

Then he washes his hands, saying:

Wash me, O Lord, from my iniquity
and cleanse me from my sin.

18 INVITATION TO PRAYER

Priest: Pray, brethren (brothers and sisters),
that my sacrifice and yours
may be acceptable to God,
the almighty Father.

STAND

PEOPLE:

**May the Lord accept the sacrifice at your hands
for the praise and glory of his name,
for our good
and the good of all his holy Church.**

19 PRAYER OVER THE OFFERINGS

*The Priest, speaking in our name, asks the Father to bless
and accept these gifts.*

→ Turn to Today's Mass

At the end, PEOPLE: **Amen.**

20 EUCHARISTIC PRAYER

We begin the eucharistic service of praise and thanksgiving, the center of the entire celebration, the central prayer of worship. We lift our hearts to God, and offer praise and thanks as the Priest addresses this prayer to the Father through Jesus Christ. Together we join Christ in his sacrifice, celebrating his memorial in the holy meal and acknowledging with him the wonderful works of God in our lives.

21 PREFACE DIALOGUE

Priest: The Lord be with you.
PEOPLE: **And with your spirit.**

Priest: Lift up your hearts.
PEOPLE: **We lift them up to the Lord.**

Priest: Let us give thanks to the Lord our God.
PEOPLE: **It is right and just.**

22 PREFACE

As indicated in the individual Masses of this Missal, the Priest may say one of the following Prefaces (listed in numerical order).

23 PREFACE ACCLAMATION

Priest and **PEOPLE:**

Holy, Holy, Holy Lord God of hosts.
Heaven and earth are full of your glory.
Hosanna in the highest.
Blessed is he who comes in the name of the Lord.
Hosanna in the highest. `KNEEL`

Then the Priest continues with one of the following Eucharistic Prayers.

EUCHARISTIC PRAYER .... Choice of ten

1	To you, therefore, most merciful Father ..	p. 24
2	You are indeed Holy, O Lord, the fount ...	p. 31
3	You are indeed Holy, O Lord, and all	p. 34
4	We give you praise, Father most holy	p. 39
R1	You are indeed Holy, O Lord, and from ...	p. 44
R2	You, therefore, almighty Father	p. 49
V1	You are indeed Holy and to be glorified ..	p. 53
V2	You are indeed Holy and to be glorified ..	p. 58
V3	You are indeed Holy and to be glorified ..	p. 63
V4	You are indeed Holy and to be glorified ..	p. 68

The Roman Canon

(This Eucharistic Prayer is especially suitable for Sundays and Masses with proper Communicantes and Hanc igitur.)

[The words within parentheses may be omitted.]

To you, therefore, most merciful Father,
we make humble prayer and petition
through Jesus Christ, your Son, our Lord:
that you accept
and bless ✠ these gifts, these offerings,
these holy and unblemished sacrifices,
which we offer you firstly
for your holy catholic Church.
Be pleased to grant her peace,
to guard, unite and govern her
throughout the whole world,
together with your servant N. our Pope,
and N. our Bishop,
and all those who, holding to the truth,
hand on the catholic and apostolic faith.

Remember, Lord, your servants N. and N.
and all gathered here,
whose faith and devotion are known to you.
For them, we offer you this sacrifice of praise
or they offer it for themselves
and all who are dear to them:
for the redemption of their souls,
in hope of health and well-being,
and paying their homage to you,
the eternal God, living and true.

In communion with those whose memory we
    venerate,
especially the glorious ever-Virgin Mary,
Mother of our God and Lord, Jesus Christ,
† and blessed Joseph, her Spouse,
your blessed Apostles and Martyrs
Peter and Paul, Andrew,
(James, John,
Thomas, James, Philip,
Bartholomew, Matthew,
Simon and Jude;
Linus, Cletus, Clement, Sixtus,
Cornelius, Cyprian,
Lawrence, Chrysogonus,
John and Paul,
Cosmas and Damian)
and all your Saints;
we ask that through their merits and prayers,
in all things we may be defended
by your protecting help.
(Through Christ our Lord. Amen.)

Therefore, Lord, we pray:*
graciously accept this oblation of our service,
that of your whole family;
order our days in your peace,
and command that we be delivered from eternal
    damnation
and counted among the flock of those you have
    chosen.
(Through Christ our Lord. Amen.)

Be pleased, O God, we pray,
to bless, acknowledge,
and approve this offering in every respect;

† * *See p. 95 for proper* Communicantes *and* Hanc igitur.

1 make it spiritual and acceptable,
so that it may become for us
the Body and Blood of your most beloved Son,
our Lord Jesus Christ.

On the day before he was to suffer,
he took bread in his holy and venerable hands,
and with eyes raised to heaven
to you, O God, his almighty Father,
giving you thanks, he said the blessing,
broke the bread
and gave it to his disciples, saying:

Take this, all of you, and eat of it,
for this is my Body,
which will be given up for you.

In a similar way when supper was ended,
he took this precious chalice
in his holy and venerable hands,
and once more giving you thanks, he said the
    blessing
and gave the chalice to his disciples, saying:

Take this, all of you, and drink from it,
for this is the chalice of my Blood,
the Blood of the new and eternal covenant,
which will be poured out for you and for many
for the forgiveness of sins.

Do this in memory of me.

Priest: **The mystery of faith.** *(Memorial Acclamation)*
PEOPLE:

A **We proclaim your Death, O Lord,**
and profess your Resurrection
until you come again.

B When we eat this Bread and drink this Cup,
   we proclaim your Death, O Lord,
   until you come again.

C Save us, Savior of the world,
   for by your Cross and Resurrection
   you have set us free.

Therefore, O Lord,
as we celebrate the memorial of the blessed Passion,
the Resurrection from the dead,
and the glorious Ascension into heaven
of Christ, your Son, our Lord,
we, your servants and your holy people,
offer to your glorious majesty
from the gifts that you have given us,
this pure victim,
this holy victim,
this spotless victim,
the holy Bread of eternal life
and the Chalice of everlasting salvation.

Be pleased to look upon these offerings
with a serene and kindly countenance,
and to accept them,
as once you were pleased to accept
the gifts of your servant Abel the just,
the sacrifice of Abraham, our father in faith,
and the offering of your high priest Melchizedek,
a holy sacrifice, a spotless victim.

In humble prayer we ask you, almighty God:
command that these gifts be borne
by the hands of your holy Angel
to your altar on high

1 in the sight of your divine majesty,
so that all of us, who through this participation at
   the altar
receive the most holy Body and Blood of your Son,
may be filled with every grace and heavenly
   blessing.
(Through Christ our Lord. Amen.)

Remember also, Lord, your servants N. and N.,
who have gone before us with the sign of faith
and rest in the sleep of peace.
Grant them, O Lord, we pray,
and all who sleep in Christ,
a place of refreshment, light and peace.
(Through Christ our Lord. Amen.)

To us, also, your servants, who, though sinners,
hope in your abundant mercies,
graciously grant some share
and fellowship with your holy Apostles and
   Martyrs:
with John the Baptist, Stephen,
Matthias, Barnabas,
(Ignatius, Alexander,
Marcellinus, Peter,
Felicity, Perpetua,
Agatha, Lucy,
Agnes, Cecilia, Anastasia)
and all your Saints;
admit us, we beseech you,
into their company,
not weighing our merits,
but granting us your pardon,
through Christ our Lord.

1

Through whom
you continue to make all these good things,
  O Lord;
you sanctify them, fill them with life,
bless them, and bestow them upon us.

(Concluding Doxology)

Through him, and with him, and in him,
O God, almighty Father,
in the unity of the Holy Spirit,
all glory and honor is yours,
for ever and ever.

All reply: **Amen.**

Continue with the Mass, as on p. 72.

2   EUCHARISTIC PRAYER No. 2

(This Eucharistic Prayer is particularly suitable on Weekdays or for special circumstances.)

STAND

℣. The Lord be with you.
℟. **And with your spirit.**

℣. Lift up your hearts.
℟. **We lift them up to the Lord.**

℣. Let us give thanks to the Lord our God.
℟. **It is right and just.**

It is truly right and just, our duty and our salvation,
always and everywhere to give you thanks, Father
   most holy,
through your beloved Son, Jesus Christ,
your Word through whom you made all things,
whom you sent as our Savior and Redeemer,
incarnate by the Holy Spirit and born of the Virgin.

Fulfilling your will
   and gaining for you a holy people,
he stretched out his hands
   as he endured his Passion,
so as to break the bonds of death
   and manifest the resurrection.

And so, with the Angels and all the Saints
we declare your glory,
as with one voice we acclaim:

2

Holy, Holy, Holy Lord God of hosts.
Heaven and earth are full of your glory.
Hosanna in the highest.
Blessed is he who comes in the name of the Lord.
Hosanna in the highest.

KNEEL

You are indeed Holy, O Lord,
the fount of all holiness.

Make holy, therefore, these gifts, we pray,
by sending down your Spirit upon them like the
    dewfall,
so that they may become for us
the Body and ✚ Blood of our Lord Jesus Christ.

At the time he was betrayed
and entered willingly into his Passion,
he took bread and, giving thanks, broke it,
and gave it to his disciples, saying:

Take this, all of you, and eat of it,
for this is my Body,
which will be given up for you.

In a similar way, when supper was ended,
he took the chalice
and, once more giving thanks,
he gave it to his disciples, saying:

Take this, all of you, and drink from it,
for this is the chalice of my Blood,
the Blood of the new and eternal covenant,
which will be poured out for you and for many
for the forgiveness of sins.

Do this in memory of me.

2 Priest: The mystery of faith. *(Memorial Acclamation)*

PEOPLE:

A We proclaim your Death, O Lord,
and profess your Resurrection
until you come again.

B When we eat this Bread and drink this Cup,
we proclaim your Death, O Lord,
until you come again.

C Save us, Savior of the world,
for by your Cross and Resurrection
you have set us free.

Therefore, as we celebrate
the memorial of his Death and Resurrection,
we offer you, Lord,
the Bread of life and the Chalice of salvation,
giving thanks that you have held us worthy
to be in your presence and minister to you.

Humbly we pray
that, partaking of the Body and Blood of Christ,
we may be gathered into one by the Holy Spirit.

Remember, Lord, your Church,
spread throughout the world,
and bring her to the fullness of charity,
together with *N.* our Pope and *N.* our Bishop
and all the clergy.

In Masses for the Dead, the following may be added:

Remember your servant *N.*,
whom you have called (today)
from this world to yourself.

2

Grant that he (she) who was united with your Son in a
    death like his,
may also be one with him in his Resurrection.

Remember also our brothers and sisters
who have fallen asleep in the hope of the
    resurrection,
and all who have died in your mercy:
welcome them into the light of your face.
Have mercy on us all, we pray,
that with the Blessed Virgin Mary, Mother of
    God,
with blessed Joseph, her Spouse,
with the blessed Apostles,
and all the Saints who have pleased you
    throughout the ages,
we may merit to be coheirs to eternal life,
and may praise and glorify you
through your Son, Jesus Christ.

(Concluding Doxology)

Through him, and with him, and in him,
O God, almighty Father,
in the unity of the Holy Spirit,
all glory and honor is yours,
for ever and ever.
All reply: **Amen.**

Continue with the Mass, as on p. 72.

EUCHARISTIC PRAYER No. 3

(This Eucharistic Prayer may be used with any Preface and preferably on Sundays and feast days.)

You are indeed Holy, O Lord,
and all you have created
rightly gives you praise,
for through your Son our Lord Jesus Christ,
by the power and working of the Holy Spirit,
you give life to all things and make them holy,
and you never cease to gather a people to yourself,
so that from the rising of the sun to its setting
a pure sacrifice may be offered to your name.

Therefore, O Lord, we humbly implore you:
by the same Spirit graciously make holy
these gifts we have brought to you for
    consecration,
that they may become the Body and ✠ Blood
of your Son our Lord Jesus Christ,
at whose command we celebrate these mysteries.

For on the night he was betrayed
he himself took bread,
and, giving you thanks, he said the blessing,
broke the bread and gave it to his disciples,
    saying:

Take this, all of you, and eat of it,
for this is my Body,
which will be given up for you.

In a similar way, when supper was ended,
he took the chalice,

and, giving you thanks, he said the blessing,
and gave the chalice to his disciples, saying:

Take this, all of you, and drink from it,
for this is the chalice of my Blood,
the Blood of the new and eternal covenant,
which will be poured out for you and for many
for the forgiveness of sins.

Do this in memory of me.

Priest: The mystery of faith. *(Memorial Acclamation)*

PEOPLE:

A   We proclaim your Death, O Lord,
and profess your Resurrection
until you come again.

B   When we eat this Bread and drink this Cup,
we proclaim your Death, O Lord,
until you come again.

C   Save us, Savior of the world,
for by your Cross and Resurrection
you have set us free.

Therefore, O Lord, as we celebrate the memorial
of the saving Passion of your Son,
his wondrous Resurrection
and Ascension into heaven,
and as we look forward to his second coming,
we offer you in thanksgiving
this holy and living sacrifice.

Look, we pray, upon the oblation of your Church
and, recognizing the sacrificial Victim by whose
death
you willed to reconcile us to yourself,

3 grant that we, who are nourished
by the Body and Blood of your Son
and filled with his Holy Spirit,
may become one body, one spirit in Christ.

May he make of us
an eternal offering to you,
so that we may obtain an inheritance with your elect,
especially with the most Blessed Virgin Mary,
    Mother of God,
with blessed Joseph, her Spouse,
with your blessed Apostles and glorious Martyrs
(with Saint N.: the Saint of the day or Patron Saint)
and with all the Saints,
on whose constant intercession in your presence
we rely for unfailing help.

May this Sacrifice of our reconciliation,
we pray, O Lord,
advance the peace and salvation of all the world.
Be pleased to confirm in faith and charity
your pilgrim Church on earth,
with your servant N. our Pope and N. our Bishop,
the Order of Bishops, all the clergy,
and the entire people you have gained for your
    own.

Listen graciously to the prayers of this family,
whom you have summoned before you:
in your compassion, O merciful Father,
gather to yourself all your children
scattered throughout the world.

† To our departed brothers and sisters
and to all who were pleasing to you
at their passing from this life,
give kind admittance to your kingdom.

3

There we hope to enjoy for ever the fullness of
    your glory
through Christ our Lord,
through whom you bestow on the world all that
    is good. †

(Concluding Doxology)

Through him, and with him, and in him,
O God, almighty Father,
in the unity of the Holy Spirit,
all glory and honor is yours,
for ever and ever.

All reply: **Amen.**

Continue with the Mass, as on p. 72.

---

† *In Masses for the Dead the following may be said:*

†Remember your servant *N.*
whom you have called (today)
from this world to yourself.
Grant that he (she) who was united with your Son in a
    death like his,
may also be one with him in his Resurrection,
when from the earth
he will raise up in the flesh those who have died,
and transform our lowly body
after the pattern of his own glorious body.
To our departed brothers and sisters, too,
and to all who were pleasing to you
at their passing from this life,
give kind admittance to your kingdom.
There we hope to enjoy for ever the fullness of your glory,
when you will wipe away every tear from our eyes.
For seeing you, our God, as you are,
we shall be like you for all the ages
and praise you without end,
through Christ our Lord,
through whom you bestow on the world all that is good. †

℣. The Lord be with you.
℟. **And with your spirit.**

℣. Lift up your hearts.
℟. **We lift them up to the Lord.**

℣. Let us give thanks to the Lord our God.
℟. **It is right and just.**

It is truly right to give you thanks,
truly just to give you glory, Father most holy,
for you are the one God living and true,
existing before all ages and abiding for all eternity,
dwelling in unapproachable light;
yet you, who alone are good, the source of life,
have made all that is,
so that you might fill your creatures with blessings
and bring joy to many of them by the glory of your
    light.

And so, in your presence are countless hosts of
    Angels,
who serve you day and night
and, gazing upon the glory of your face,
glorify you without ceasing.

With them we, too, confess your name in exultation,
giving voice to every creature under heaven,
as we acclaim:

Holy, Holy, Holy Lord God of hosts.
Heaven and earth are full of your glory.
Hosanna in the highest.

**Blessed is he who comes in the name of the Lord.
Hosanna in the highest.**

4

KNEEL

We give you praise, Father most holy,
for you are great
and you have fashioned all your works
in wisdom and in love.
You formed man in your own image
and entrusted the whole world to his care,
so that in serving you alone, the Creator,
he might have dominion over all creatures.
And when through disobedience he had lost your
    friendship,
you did not abandon him to the domain of death.
For you came in mercy to the aid of all,
so that those who seek might find you.
Time and again you offered them covenants
and through the prophets
taught them to look forward to salvation.

And you so loved the world, Father most holy,
that in the fullness of time
you sent your Only Begotten Son to be our Savior.
Made incarnate by the Holy Spirit
and born of the Virgin Mary,
he shared our human nature
in all things but sin.
To the poor he proclaimed the good news of
    salvation,
to prisoners, freedom,
and to the sorrowful of heart, joy.
To accomplish your plan,
he gave himself up to death,
and, rising from the dead,
he destroyed death and restored life.

4 And that we might live no longer for ourselves
but for him who died and rose again for us,
he sent the Holy Spirit from you, Father,
as the first fruits for those who believe,
so that, bringing to perfection his work in the world,
he might sanctify creation to the full.

Therefore, O Lord, we pray:
may this same Holy Spirit
graciously sanctify these offerings,
that they may become
the Body and ✠ Blood of our Lord Jesus Christ
for the celebration of this great mystery,
which he himself left us
as an eternal covenant.

For when the hour had come
for him to be glorified by you, Father most holy,
having loved his own who were in the world,
he loved them to the end:
and while they were at supper,
he took bread, blessed and broke it,
and gave it to his disciples, saying:

Take this, all of you, and eat of it,
for this is my Body,
which will be given up for you.

In a similar way,
taking the chalice filled with the fruit of the vine,
he gave thanks,
and gave the chalice to his disciples, saying:

Take this, all of you, and drink from it,
for this is the chalice of my Blood,
the Blood of the new and eternal covenant,

4

which will be poured out for you and for many for the forgiveness of sins.

Do this in memory of me.

Priest: The mystery of faith. *(Memorial Acclamation)*

PEOPLE:

A We proclaim your Death, O Lord,
  and profess your Resurrection
  until you come again.

B When we eat this Bread and drink this Cup,
  we proclaim your Death, O Lord,
  until you come again.

C Save us, Savior of the world,
  for by your Cross and Resurrection
  you have set us free.

Therefore, O Lord,
as we now celebrate the memorial of our
  redemption,
we remember Christ's Death
and his descent to the realm of the dead,
we proclaim his Resurrection
and his Ascension to your right hand,
and, as we await his coming in glory,
we offer you his Body and Blood,
the sacrifice acceptable to you
which brings salvation to the whole world.

Look, O Lord, upon the Sacrifice
which you yourself have provided for your Church,
and grant in your loving kindness
to all who partake of this one Bread and one
  Chalice
that, gathered into one body by the Holy Spirit,

4 they may truly become a living sacrifice in Christ
to the praise of your glory.

Therefore, Lord, remember now
all for whom we offer this sacrifice:
especially your servant N. our Pope,
N. our Bishop, and the whole Order of Bishops,
all the clergy,
those who take part in this offering,
those gathered here before you,
your entire people,
and all who seek you with a sincere heart.

Remember also
those who have died in the peace of your Christ
and all the dead,
whose faith you alone have known.

To all of us, your children,
grant, O merciful Father,
that we may enter into a heavenly inheritance
with the Blessed Virgin Mary, Mother of God,
with blessed Joseph, her Spouse,
and with your Apostles and Saints in your kingdom.
There, with the whole of creation,
freed from the corruption of sin and death,
may we glorify you through Christ our Lord,
through whom you bestow on the world all that
  is good.

(Concluding Doxology)

Through him, and with him, and in him,
O God, almighty Father,
in the unity of the Holy Spirit,
all glory and honor is yours,
for ever and ever.

All reply: **Amen.**

Continue with the Mass, as on p. 72.

EUCHARISTIC PRAYER FOR RECONCILIATION I

STAND

℣. The Lord be with you.
℟. **And with your spirit.**

℣. Lift up your hearts.
℟. **We lift them up to the Lord.**

℣. Let us give thanks to the Lord our God.
℟. **It is right and just.**

It is truly right and just
that we should always give you thanks,
Lord, holy Father, almighty and eternal God.

For you do not cease to spur us on
to possess a more abundant life
and, being rich in mercy,
you constantly offer pardon
and call on sinners
to trust in your forgiveness alone.

Never did you turn away from us,
and, though time and again we have broken your
    covenant,
you have bound the human family to yourself
through Jesus your Son, our Redeemer,
with a new bond of love so tight
that it can never be undone.

Even now you set before your people
a time of grace and reconciliation,
and, as they turn back to you in spirit,
you grant them hope in Christ Jesus
and a desire to be of service to all,

43

**R
1**

while they entrust themselves
more fully to the Holy Spirit.

And so, filled with wonder,
we extol the power of your love,
and, proclaiming our joy
at the salvation that comes from you,
we join in the heavenly hymn of countless hosts,
as without end we acclaim:

**Holy, Holy, Holy Lord God of hosts.
Heaven and earth are full of your glory.
Hosanna in the highest.
Blessed is he who comes in the name of the Lord.
Hosanna in the highest.**

KNEEL

You are indeed Holy, O Lord,
and from the world's beginning
are ceaselessly at work,
so that the human race may become holy,
just as you yourself are holy.

Look, we pray, upon your people's offerings
and pour out on them the power of your Spirit,
that they may become the Body and ✠ Blood
of your beloved Son, Jesus Christ,
in whom we, too, are your sons and daughters.

Indeed, though we once were lost
and could not approach you,
you loved us with the greatest love:
for your Son, who alone is just,
handed himself over to death,

R 1

and did not disdain to be nailed for our sake
to the wood of the Cross.

But before his arms were outstretched between
  heaven and earth,
to become the lasting sign of your covenant,
he desired to celebrate the Passover with his
  disciples.

As he ate with them,
he took bread
and, giving you thanks, he said the blessing,
broke the bread and gave it to them, saying:

Take this, all of you, and eat of it,
for this is my Body,
which will be given up for you.

In a similar way, when supper was ended,
knowing that he was about to reconcile all things
  in himself
through his Blood to be shed on the Cross,
he took the chalice, filled with the fruit of the
  vine,
and once more giving you thanks,
handed the chalice to his disciples, saying:

Take this, all of you, and drink from it,
for this is the chalice of my Blood,
the Blood of the new and eternal covenant,
which will be poured out for you and for many
for the forgiveness of sins.
Do this in memory of me.

R
1

PEOPLE:

A We proclaim your Death, O Lord,
and profess your Resurrection
until you come again.

B When we eat this Bread and drink this Cup,
we proclaim your Death, O Lord,
until you come again.

C Save us, Savior of the world,
for by your Cross and Resurrection
you have set us free.

Therefore, as we celebrate
the memorial of your Son Jesus Christ,
who is our Passover and our surest peace,
we celebrate his Death and Resurrection from the
    dead,
and looking forward to his blessed Coming,
we offer you, who are our faithful and merciful
    God,
this sacrificial Victim
who reconciles to you the human race.

Look kindly, most compassionate Father,
on those you unite to yourself
by the Sacrifice of your Son,
and grant that, by the power of the Holy Spirit,
as they partake of this one Bread and one
    Chalice,
they may be gathered into one Body in Christ,
who heals every division.

R 1

Be pleased to keep us always
in communion of mind and heart,
together with N. our Pope and N. our Bishop.
Help us to work together
for the coming of your Kingdom,
until the hour when we stand before you,
Saints among the Saints in the halls of heaven,
with the Blessed Virgin Mary, Mother of God,
the blessed Apostles and all the Saints,
and with our deceased brothers and sisters,
whom we humbly commend to your mercy.

Then, freed at last from the wound of corruption
and made fully into a new creation,
we shall sing to you with gladness
the thanksgiving of Christ,
who lives for all eternity.

(Concluding Doxology)

Through him, and with him, and in him,
O God, almighty Father,
in the unity of the Holy Spirit,
all glory and honor is yours,
for ever and ever.

The people respond: **Amen.**

Continue with the Mass, as on p. 72.

EUCHARISTIC PRAYER FOR
RECONCILIATION II

℣.   The Lord be with you.

℟.   **And with your spirit.**

℣.   Lift up your hearts.

℟.   **We lift them up to the Lord.**

℣.   Let us give thanks to the Lord our God.

℟.   **It is right and just.**

It is truly right and just
that we should give you thanks and praise,
O God, almighty Father,
for all you do in this world,
through our Lord Jesus Christ.

For though the human race
is divided by dissension and discord,
yet we know that by testing us
you change our hearts
to prepare them for reconciliation.

Even more, by your Spirit you move human hearts
that enemies may speak to each other again,
adversaries join hands,
and peoples seek to meet together.

By the working of your power
it comes about, O Lord,
that hatred is overcome by love,
revenge gives way to forgiveness,
and discord is changed to mutual respect.

Therefore, as we give you ceaseless thanks
with the choirs of heaven,

we cry out to your majesty on earth,
and without end we acclaim:

Holy, Holy, Holy Lord God of hosts.
Heaven and earth are full of your glory.
Hosanna in the highest.
Blessed is he who comes in the name of the Lord.
Hosanna in the highest.

You, therefore, almighty Father,   `KNEEL`
we bless through Jesus Christ your Son,
who comes in your name.
He himself is the Word that brings salvation,
the hand you extend to sinners,
the way by which your peace is offered to us.
When we ourselves had turned away from you
on account of our sins,
you brought us back to be reconciled, O Lord,
so that, converted at last to you,
we might love one another
through your Son,
whom for our sake you handed over to death.

And now, celebrating the reconciliation
Christ has brought us,
we entreat you:
sanctify these gifts by the outpouring of your Spirit,
that they may become the Body and ✠ Blood of
    your Son,
whose command we fulfill
when we celebrate these mysteries.

For when about to give his life to set us free,
as he reclined at supper,
he himself took bread into his hands,

R 2

and, giving you thanks, he said the blessing,
broke the bread and gave it to his disciples, saying:

Take this, all of you, and eat of it,
for this is my Body,
which will be given up for you.

In a similar way, on that same evening,
he took the chalice of blessing in his hands,
confessing your mercy,
and gave the chalice to his disciples, saying:

Take this, all of you, and drink from it,
for this is the chalice of my Blood,
the Blood of the new and eternal covenant,
which will be poured out for you and for many
for the forgiveness of sins.

Do this in memory of me.

Priest: The mystery of faith. *(Memorial Acclamation)*

PEOPLE:

A We proclaim your Death, O Lord,
and profess your Resurrection
until you come again.

B When we eat this Bread and drink this Cup,
we proclaim your Death, O Lord,
until you come again.

C Save us, Savior of the world,
for by your Cross and Resurrection
you have set us free.

Celebrating, therefore, the memorial
of the Death and Resurrection of your Son,
who left us this pledge of his love,
we offer you what you have bestowed on us,
the Sacrifice of perfect reconciliation.

R 2

Holy Father, we humbly beseech you
to accept us also, together with your Son,
and in this saving banquet
graciously to endow us with his very Spirit,
who takes away everything
that estranges us from one another.

May he make your Church a sign of unity
and an instrument of your peace among all people
and may he keep us in communion
with N. our Pope and N. our Bishop
and all the Bishops
and your entire people.

Just as you have gathered us now at the table of
    your Son,
so also bring us together,
with the glorious Virgin Mary, Mother of God,
with your blessed Apostles and all the Saints,
with our brothers and sisters
and those of every race and tongue
who have died in your friendship.
Bring us to share with them the unending banquet
    of unity
in a new heaven and a new earth,
where the fullness of your peace will shine forth
in Christ Jesus our Lord.

(Concluding Doxology)

Through him, and with him, and in him,
O God, almighty Father,
in the unity of the Holy Spirit,
all glory and honor is yours,
for ever and ever.

The people respond: **Amen.**

Continue with the Mass, as on p. 72.

EUCHARISTIC PRAYER FOR USE IN MASSES FOR VARIOUS NEEDS I

STAND

℣. The Lord be with you.

℟. **And with your spirit.**

℣. Lift up your hearts.

℟. **We lift them up to the Lord.**

℣. Let us give thanks to the Lord our God.

℟. **It is right and just.**

It is truly right and just to give you thanks
and raise to you a hymn of glory and praise,
O Lord, Father of infinite goodness.

For by the word of your Son's Gospel
you have brought together one Church
from every people, tongue, and nation,
and, having filled her with life by the power of
    your Spirit,
you never cease through her
to gather the whole human race into one.

Manifesting the covenant of your love,
she dispenses without ceasing
the blessed hope of your Kingdom
and shines bright as the sign of your faithfulness,
which in Christ Jesus our Lord
you promised would last for eternity.

And so, with all the Powers of heaven,
we worship you constantly on earth,
while, with all the Church,
as one voice we acclaim:

Holy, Holy, Holy Lord God of hosts.
Heaven and earth are full of your glory.
Hosanna in the highest.
Blessed is he who comes in the name of the Lord.
Hosanna in the highest.

KNEEL

You are indeed Holy and to be glorified, O God,
who love the human race
and who always walk with us on the journey of life.
Blessed indeed is your Son,
present in our midst
when we are gathered by his love
and when, as once for the disciples, so now for us,
he opens the Scriptures and breaks the bread.

Therefore, Father most merciful,
we ask that you send forth your Holy Spirit
to sanctify these gifts of bread and wine,
that they may become for us
the Body and ✠ Blood
of our Lord Jesus Christ.

On the day before he was to suffer,
on the night of the Last Supper,
he took bread and said the blessing,
broke the bread and gave it to his disciples, saying:

Take this, all of you, and eat of it,
for this is my Body,
which will be given up for you.

In a similar way, when supper was ended,
he took the chalice, gave you thanks
and gave the chalice to his disciples, saying:

V 1

Take this, all of you, and drink from it,
for this is the chalice of my Blood,
the Blood of the new and eternal covenant,
which will be poured out for you and for many
for the forgiveness of sins.

Do this in memory of me.

Priest: **The mystery of faith.** *(Memorial Acclamation)*

PEOPLE:

A We proclaim your Death, O Lord,
and profess your Resurrection
until you come again.

B When we eat this Bread and drink this Cup,
we proclaim your Death, O Lord,
until you come again.

C Save us, Savior of the world,
for by your Cross and Resurrection
you have set us free.

Therefore, holy Father,
as we celebrate the memorial of Christ your Son,
   our Savior,
whom you led through his Passion and Death on
   the Cross
to the glory of the Resurrection,
and whom you have seated at your right hand,
we proclaim the work of your love until he comes
   again
and we offer you the Bread of life
and the Chalice of blessing.

Look with favor on the oblation of your Church,
in which we show forth

the paschal Sacrifice of Christ that has been
    handed on to us,
and grant that, by the power of the Spirit of your
    love,
we may be counted now and until the day of
    eternity
among the members of your Son,
in whose Body and Blood we have communion.

Lord, renew your Church (which is in N.)
by the light of the Gospel.
Strengthen the bond of unity
between the faithful and the pastors of your people,
together with N. our Pope, N. our Bishop,
and the whole Order of Bishops,
that in a world torn by strife
your people may shine forth
as a prophetic sign of unity and concord.

Remember our brothers and sisters (N. and N.),
who have fallen asleep in the peace of your Christ,
and all the dead, whose faith you alone have
    known.
Admit them to rejoice in the light of your face,
and in the resurrection give them the fullness of
    life.

Grant also to us,
when our earthly pilgrimage is done,
that we may come to an eternal dwelling place
and live with you for ever;
there, in communion with the Blessed Virgin Mary,
    Mother of God,
with the Apostles and Martyrs,

V1

(with Saint *N*.: the Saint of the day or Patron)
and with all the Saints,
we shall praise and exalt you
through Jesus Christ, your Son.

(Concluding Doxology)

Through him, and with him, and in him,
O God, almighty Father,
in the unity of the Holy Spirit,
all glory and honor is yours,
for ever and ever.

The people respond: **Amen.**

Continue with the Mass, as on p. 72.

EUCHARISTIC PRAYER FOR USE IN MASSES FOR VARIOUS NEEDS II

STAND

℣. The Lord be with you.
℟. **And with your spirit.**

℣. Lift up your hearts.
℟. **We lift them up to the Lord.**

℣. Let us give thanks to the Lord our God.
℟. **It is right and just.**

It is truly right and just, our duty and our salvation,
always and everywhere to give you thanks,
Lord, holy Father,
creator of the world and source of all life.

For you never forsake the works of your wisdom,
but by your providence are even now at work in our midst.
With mighty hand and outstretched arm
you led your people Israel through the desert.
Now, as your Church makes her pilgrim journey in the world,
you always accompany her
by the power of the Holy Spirit
and lead her along the paths of time
to the eternal joy of your Kingdom,
through Christ our Lord.

And so, with the Angels and Saints,
we, too, sing the hymn of your glory,
as without end we acclaim:

57

V 2

Holy, Holy, Holy Lord God of hosts.
Heaven and earth are full of your glory.
Hosanna in the highest.
Blessed is he who comes in the name of the Lord.
Hosanna in the highest.

KNEEL

You are indeed Holy and to be glorified, O God,
who love the human race
and who always walk with us on the journey of life.
Blessed indeed is your Son,
present in our midst
when we are gathered by his love,
and when, as once for the disciples, so now for us,
he opens the Scriptures and breaks the bread.

Therefore, Father most merciful,
we ask that you send forth your Holy Spirit
to sanctify these gifts of bread and wine,
that they may become for us
the Body and ✠ Blood
of our Lord Jesus Christ.

On the day before he was to suffer,
on the night of the Last Supper,
he took bread and said the blessing,
broke the bread and gave it to his disciples, saying:

Take this, all of you, and eat of it,
for this is my Body,
which will be given up for you.

In a similar way, when supper was ended,
he took the chalice, gave you thanks
and gave the chalice to his disciples, saying:

Take this, all of you, and drink from it,
for this is the chalice of my Blood,
the Blood of the new and eternal covenant,
which will be poured out for you and for many
for the forgiveness of sins.

Do this in memory of me.

Priest: **The mystery of faith.** *(Memorial Acclamation)*

PEOPLE:

A **We proclaim your Death, O Lord,**
   and profess your Resurrection
   until you come again.

B **When we eat this Bread and drink this Cup,**
   we proclaim your Death, O Lord,
   until you come again.

C **Save us, Savior of the world,**
   for by your Cross and Resurrection
   you have set us free.

Therefore, holy Father,
as we celebrate the memorial of Christ your Son,
   our Savior,
whom you led through his Passion and Death on
   the Cross
to the glory of the Resurrection,
and whom you have seated at your right hand,
we proclaim the work of your love until he comes
   again
and we offer you the Bread of life
and the Chalice of blessing.

Look with favor on the oblation of your Church,
in which we show forth

V 2 the paschal Sacrifice of Christ that has been
handed on to us,
and grant that, by the power of the Spirit of your
love,
we may be counted now and until the day of
eternity
among the members of your Son,
in whose Body and Blood we have communion.

And so, having called us to your table, Lord,
confirm us in unity,
so that, together with N. our Pope and N. our
Bishop,
with all Bishops, Priests and Deacons,
and your entire people,
as we walk your ways with faith and hope,
we may strive to bring joy and trust into the world.

Remember our brothers and sisters (N. and N.),
who have fallen asleep in the peace of your Christ,
and all the dead, whose faith you alone have
known.
Admit them to rejoice in the light of your face,
and in the resurrection give them the fullness of
life.

Grant also to us,
when our earthly pilgrimage is done,
that we may come to an eternal dwelling place
and live with you for ever;
there, in communion with the Blessed Virgin Mary,
Mother of God,
with the Apostles and Martyrs,
(with Saint N.: the Saint of the day or Patron)

and with all the Saints,
we shall praise and exalt you
through Jesus Christ, your Son.

(Concluding Doxology)

Through him, and with him, and in him,
O God, almighty Father,
in the unity of the Holy Spirit,
all glory and honor is yours,
for ever and ever.

The people respond: **Amen.**

Continue with the Mass, as on p. 72.

STAND

℣. The Lord be with you.
℟. **And with your spirit.**

℣. Lift up your hearts.
℟. **We lift them up to the Lord.**

℣. Let us give thanks to the Lord our God.
℟. **It is right and just.**

It is truly right and just, our duty and our salvation,
always and everywhere to give you thanks,
holy Father, Lord of heaven and earth,
through Christ our Lord.

For by your Word you created the world
and you govern all things in harmony.
You gave us the same Word made flesh as Mediator,
and he has spoken your words to us
and called us to follow him.
He is the way that leads us to you,
the truth that sets us free,
the life that fills us with gladness.

Through your Son
you gather men and women,
whom you made for the glory of your name,
into one family,
redeemed by the Blood of his Cross
and signed with the seal of the Spirit.

Therefore, now and for ages unending,
with all the Angels,

V 3

we proclaim your glory,
as in joyful celebration we acclaim:

Holy, Holy, Holy Lord God of hosts.
Heaven and earth are full of your glory.
Hosanna in the highest.
Blessed is he who comes in the name of the Lord.
Hosanna in the highest.

KNEEL

You are indeed Holy and to be glorified, O God,
who love the human race
and who always walk with us on the journey of life.
Blessed indeed is your Son,
present in our midst
when we are gathered by his love
and when, as once for the disciples, so now for us,
he opens the Scriptures and breaks the bread.

Therefore, Father most merciful,
we ask that you send forth your Holy Spirit
to sanctify these gifts of bread and wine,
that they may become for us
the Body and ✠ Blood
of our Lord Jesus Christ.

On the day before he was to suffer,
on the night of the Last Supper,
he took bread and said the blessing,
broke the bread and gave it to his disciples, saying:

Take this, all of you, and eat of it,
for this is my Body,
which will be given up for you.

V 3 In a similar way, when supper was ended,
he took the chalice, gave you thanks
and gave the chalice to his disciples, saying:

Take this, all of you, and drink from it,
for this is the chalice of my Blood,
the Blood of the new and eternal covenant,
which will be poured out for you and for many
for the forgiveness of sins.

Do this in memory of me.

Priest: **The mystery of faith.** *(Memorial Acclamation)*

PEOPLE:

A **We proclaim your Death, O Lord,**
and profess your Resurrection
until you come again.

B **When we eat this Bread and drink this Cup,**
we proclaim your Death, O Lord,
until you come again.

C **Save us, Savior of the world,**
for by your Cross and Resurrection
you have set us free.

Therefore, holy Father,
as we celebrate the memorial of Christ your Son,
    our Savior,
whom you led through his Passion and Death on
    the Cross
to the glory of the Resurrection,
and whom you have seated at your right hand,
we proclaim the work of your love until he comes
    again
and we offer you the Bread of life
and the Chalice of blessing.

V 3

Look with favor on the oblation of your Church,
in which we show forth
the paschal Sacrifice of Christ that has been
    handed on to us,
and grant that, by the power of the Spirit of your
    love,
we may be counted now and until the day of
    eternity
among the members of your Son,
in whose Body and Blood we have communion.

By our partaking of this mystery, almighty Father,
give us life through your Spirit,
grant that we may be conformed to the image of
    your Son,
and confirm us in the bond of communion,
together with N. our Pope and N. our Bishop,
with all other Bishops,
with Priests and Deacons,
and with your entire people.

Grant that all the faithful of the Church,
looking into the signs of the times by the light of
    faith,
may constantly devote themselves
to the service of the Gospel.

Keep us attentive to the needs of all
that, sharing their grief and pain,
their joy and hope,
we may faithfully bring them the good news of
    salvation
and go forward with them
along the way of your Kingdom.

**V
3**
Remember our brothers and sisters (*N.* and *N.*),
who have fallen asleep in the peace of your Christ,
and all the dead, whose faith you alone have known.
Admit them to rejoice in the light of your face,
and in the resurrection give them the fullness of life.

Grant also to us,
when our earthly pilgrimage is done,
that we may come to an eternal dwelling place
and live with you for ever;
there, in communion with the Blessed Virgin Mary,
    Mother of God,
with the Apostles and Martyrs,
(with Saint *N.*: the Saint of the day or Patron)
and with all the Saints,
we shall praise and exalt you
through Jesus Christ, your Son.

(Concluding Doxology)

Through him, and with him, and in him,
O God, almighty Father,
in the unity of the Holy Spirit,
all glory and honor is yours,
for ever and ever.

The people respond: **Amen.**

Continue with the Mass, as on p. 72.

EUCHARISTIC PRAYER FOR USE IN MASSES FOR VARIOUS NEEDS IV

V 4

STAND

℣. The Lord be with you.
℟. **And with your spirit.**

℣. Lift up your hearts.
℟. **We lift them up to the Lord.**

℣. Let us give thanks to the Lord our God.
℟. **It is right and just.**

It is truly right and just, our duty and our salvation,
always and everywhere to give you thanks,
Father of mercies and faithful God.

For you have given us Jesus Christ, your Son,
as our Lord and Redeemer.

He always showed compassion
for children and for the poor,
for the sick and for sinners,
and he became a neighbor
to the oppressed and the afflicted.

By word and deed he announced to the world
that you are our Father
and that you care for all your sons and daughters.

And so, with all the Angels and Saints,
we exalt and bless your name
and sing the hymn of your glory,
as without end we acclaim:

V
4

Holy, Holy, Holy Lord God of hosts.
Heaven and earth are full of your glory.
Hosanna in the highest.
Blessed is he who comes in the name of the Lord.
Hosanna in the highest.

`KNEEL`

You are indeed Holy and to be glorified, O God,
who love the human race
and who always walk with us on the journey of life.
Blessed indeed is your Son,
present in our midst
when we are gathered by his love
and when, as once for the disciples, so now for us,
he opens the Scriptures and breaks the bread.

Therefore, Father most merciful,
we ask that you send forth your Holy Spirit
to sanctify these gifts of bread and wine,
that they may become for us
the Body and ✝ Blood
of our Lord Jesus Christ.

On the day before he was to suffer,
on the night of the Last Supper,
he took bread and said the blessing,
broke the bread and gave it to his disciples, saying:

Take this, all of you, and eat of it,
for this is my Body,
which will be given up for you.

In a similar way, when supper was ended,
he took the chalice, gave you thanks
and gave the chalice to his disciples, saying:

**V
4**

Take this, all of you, and drink from it,
for this is the chalice of my Blood,
the Blood of the new and eternal covenant,
which will be poured out for you and for many
for the forgiveness of sins.

Do this in memory of me.

Priest: **The mystery of faith.** *(Memorial Acclamation)*

PEOPLE:

A We proclaim your Death, O Lord,
  and profess your Resurrection
  until you come again.

B When we eat this Bread and drink this Cup,
  we proclaim your Death, O Lord,
  until you come again.

C Save us, Savior of the world,
  for by your Cross and Resurrection
  you have set us free.

Therefore, holy Father,
as we celebrate the memorial of Christ your Son,
  our Savior,
whom you led through his Passion and Death on
  the Cross
to the glory of the Resurrection,
and whom you have seated at your right hand,
we proclaim the work of your love until he comes
  again
and we offer you the Bread of life
and the Chalice of blessing.

Look with favor on the oblation of your Church,
in which we show forth

V 4 the paschal Sacrifice of Christ that has been handed on to us,
and grant that, by the power of the Spirit of your love,
we may be counted now and until the day of eternity
among the members of your Son,
in whose Body and Blood we have communion.

Bring your Church, O Lord,
to perfect faith and charity,
together with N. our Pope and N. our Bishop,
with all Bishops, Priests and Deacons,
and the entire people you have made your own.

Open our eyes
to the needs of our brothers and sisters;
inspire in us words and actions
to comfort those who labor and are burdened.
Make us serve them truly,
after the example of Christ and at his command.
And may your Church stand as a living witness
to truth and freedom,
to peace and justice,
that all people may be raised up to a new hope.

Remember our brothers and sisters (N. and N.),
who have fallen asleep in the peace of your Christ,
and all the dead, whose faith you alone have known.
Admit them to rejoice in the light of your face,
and in the resurrection give them the fullness of life.

Grant also to us,
when our earthly pilgrimage is done,
that we may come to an eternal dwelling place
and live with you for ever;
there, in communion with the Blessed Virgin Mary,
   Mother of God,
with the Apostles and Martyrs,
(with Saint *N.*: the Saint of the day or Patron)
and with all the Saints,
we shall praise and exalt you
through Jesus Christ, your Son.

(Concluding Doxology)

Through him, and with him, and in him,
O God, almighty Father,
in the unity of the Holy Spirit,
all glory and honor is yours,
for ever and ever.

The people respond: **Amen.**

Continue with the Mass, as on p. 72.

THE COMMUNION RITE

To prepare for the paschal meal, to welcome the Lord, we pray for forgiveness and exchange a sign of peace. Before eating Christ's Body and drinking his Blood, we must be one with him and with all our brothers and sisters in the Church.

24 THE LORD'S PRAYER　　　STAND

Priest:　At the Savior's command
　　　　and formed by divine teaching,
　　　　we dare to say:

Priest and **PEOPLE**:

**Our Father, who art in heaven,
hallowed be thy name;
thy kingdom come,
thy will be done
on earth as it is in heaven.
Give us this day our daily bread,
and forgive us our trespasses,
as we forgive those who trespass against us;
and lead us not into temptation,
but deliver us from evil.**

Priest:　Deliver us, Lord, we pray, from every evil,
　　　　graciously grant us peace in our days,
　　　　that, by the help of your mercy,
　　　　we may be always free from sin
　　　　and safe from all distress,
　　　　as we await the blessed hope
　　　　and the coming of our Savior, Jesus Christ.

PEOPLE: **For the kingdom,
the power and the glory are yours
now and for ever.**

25 SIGN OF PEACE

The Church is a community of Christians joined by the Spirit in love. It needs to express, deepen, and restore its peaceful unity before eating the one Body of the Lord and drinking from the one cup of salvation. We do this by a sign of peace.

The Priest says the prayer for peace:

Lord Jesus Christ,
who said to your Apostles:
Peace I leave you, my peace I give you,
look not on our sins,
but on the faith of your Church,
and graciously grant her peace and unity
in accordance with your will.
Who live and reign for ever and ever.

PEOPLE: **Amen.**

Priest: The peace of the Lord be with you always.

PEOPLE: **And with your spirit.**

Deacon (or Priest):
Let us offer each other the sign of peace.

The people exchange a sign of peace, communion and charity, according to local customs.

26 LAMB OF GOD

Christians are gathered for the "breaking of the bread," another name for the Mass. In Communion, though many we are made one body in the one bread, which is Christ.

The Priest breaks the host over the paten and places a small piece in the chalice, saying quietly:

May this mingling of the Body and Blood
of our Lord Jesus Christ
bring eternal life to us who receive it.

Meanwhile the following is sung or said:

PEOPLE:

> **Lamb of God, you take away the sins of the
>   world,
>   have mercy on us.
> Lamb of God, you take away the sins of the
>   world,
>   have mercy on us.
> Lamb of God, you take away the sins of the
>   world,
>   grant us peace.**

The invocation may even be repeated several times if the breaking of the bread is prolonged. Only the final time, however, is grant us peace said.

KNEEL

We pray in silence and then voice words of humility and hope as our final preparation before meeting Christ in the Eucharist.

Before Communion, the Priest says quietly one of the following prayers:

Lord Jesus Christ, Son of the living God,
who, by the will of the Father
and the work of the Holy Spirit,
through your Death gave life to the world,
free me by this, your most holy Body and Blood,
from all my sins and from every evil;
keep me always faithful to your commandments,
and never let me be parted from you.

—————————— OR ——————————

May the receiving of your Body and Blood,
Lord Jesus Christ,
not bring me to judgment and condemnation,
but through your loving mercy
be for me protection in mind and body
and a healing remedy.

27 INVITATION TO COMMUNION*

*The Priest genuflects, takes the host and, holding it
slightly raised above the paten or above the chalice, while
facing the people, says aloud:*

Priest: Behold the Lamb of God,
behold him who takes away the sins of the
world.
Blessed are those called to the supper of
the Lamb.

Priest and **PEOPLE** (once only):

Lord, I am not worthy
that you should enter under my roof,
but only say the word
and my soul shall be healed.

*Before reverently consuming the Body of Christ, the Priest
says quietly:*

May the Body of Christ
keep me safe for eternal life.

*Then, before reverently consuming the Blood of Christ,
he takes the chalice and says quietly:*

May the Blood of Christ
keep me safe for eternal life.

* See Guidelines on pp. 664-665.

28 COMMUNION

He then gives Communion to the people.

Priest: **The Body of Christ.** Communicant: **Amen.**
Priest: **The Blood of Christ.** Communicant: **Amen.**

The Communion Psalm or other appropriate chant is sung while Communion is given to the faithful. If there is no singing, the Communion Antiphon is said.

→ **Turn to Today's Mass**

The vessels are purified by the Priest or Deacon or acolyte. Meanwhile he says quietly:

What has passed our lips as food, O Lord,
may we possess in purity of heart,
that what has been given to us in time
may be our healing for eternity.

After Communion there may be a period of sacred silence, or a canticle of praise or a hymn may be sung.

29 PRAYER AFTER COMMUNION   STAND

The Priest prays in our name that we may live the life of faith since we have been strengthened by Christ himself. Our *Amen* makes his prayer our own.

Priest: **Let us pray.**

Priest and people may pray silently for a while unless silence has just been observed. Then the Priest says the Prayer after Communion.

→ **Turn to Today's Mass**

At the end, **PEOPLE: Amen.**

THE CONCLUDING RITES

We have heard God's Word and eaten the Body of Christ. Now it is time for us to leave, to do good works, to praise and bless the Lord in our daily lives.

30 SOLEMN BLESSING STAND

After any brief announcements, the Blessing and Dismissal follow:

Priest: The Lord be with you.

PEOPLE: And with your spirit.

31 FINAL BLESSING

Priest: **May almighty God bless you, the Father, and the Son, ✣ and the Holy Spirit.**

PEOPLE: Amen.

On certain days or occasions, this formula of blessing is preceded, in accordance with the rubrics, by another more solemn formula of blessing (pp. 97-105) or by a prayer over the people (pp. 105-110).

32 DISMISSAL

Deacon (or Priest):

A Go forth, the Mass is ended.

B Go and announce the Gospel of the Lord.

C Go in peace, glorifying the Lord by your life.

D Go in peace.

PEOPLE: Thanks be to God.

If any liturgical service follows immediately, the rites of dismissal are omitted.

RITE FOR THE BLESSING
AND SPRINKLING OF WATER

If this rite is celebrated during Mass, it takes the place of the usual Penitential Act at the beginning of Mass.

After the greeting, the Priest stands at his chair and faces the people. With a vessel containing the water to be blessed before him, he calls upon the people to pray in these or similar words:

Dear brethren (brothers and sisters),
let us humbly beseech the Lord our God
to bless this water he has created,
which will be sprinkled on us
as a memorial of our Baptism.
May he help us by his grace
to remain faithful to the Spirit we have received.

And after a brief pause for silence, he continues with hands joined:

Almighty ever-living God,
who willed that through water,
the fountain of life and the source of purification,
even souls should be cleansed
and receive the gift of eternal life;
be pleased, we pray, to ✚ bless this water,
by which we seek protection on this your day, O Lord.
Renew the living spring of your grace within us
and grant that by this water we may be defended
from all ills of spirit and body,
and so approach you with hearts made clean
and worthily receive your salvation.
Through Christ our Lord. ℟. **Amen.**

Or:

Almighty Lord and God,
who are the source and origin of all life,

whether of body or soul,
we ask you to ✤ bless this water,
which we use in confidence
to implore forgiveness for our sins
and to obtain the protection of your grace
against all illness and every snare of the enemy.
Grant, O Lord, in your mercy,
that living waters may always spring up for our
    salvation,
and so may we approach you with a pure heart
and avoid all danger to body and soul.
Through Christ our Lord. ℟. **Amen.**

Or (during Easter Time):

Lord our God,
in your mercy be present to your people's prayers,
and, for us who recall the wondrous work of our creation
and the still greater work of our redemption,
graciously ✤ bless this water.
For you created water to make the fields fruitful
and to refresh and cleanse our bodies.
You also made water the instrument of your mercy:
for through water you freed your people from slavery
and quenched their thirst in the desert;
through water the Prophets proclaimed the new
    covenant
you were to enter upon with the human race;
and last of all,
through water, which Christ made holy in the Jordan,
you have renewed our corrupted nature
in the bath of regeneration.
Therefore, may this water be for us
a memorial of the Baptism we have received,
and grant that we may share
in the gladness of our brothers and sisters
who at Easter have received their Baptism.
Through Christ our Lord. ℟. **Amen.**

Where the circumstances of the place or the custom of the people suggest that the mixing of salt be preserved in the blessing of water, the Priest may bless salt, saying:

We humbly ask you, almighty God:
be pleased in your faithful love to bless ✚ this salt
you have created,
for it was you who commanded the prophet Elisha
to cast salt into water,
that impure water might be purified.
Grant, O Lord, we pray,
that, wherever this mixture of salt and water is sprinkled,
every attack of the enemy may be repulsed
and your Holy Spirit may be present
to keep us safe at all times.
Through Christ our Lord. ℟. **Amen.**

Then he pours the salt into the water, without saying anything.

Afterward, taking the aspergillum, the Priest sprinkles himself and the ministers, then the clergy and people, moving through the church, if appropriate.

Meanwhile, one of the following chants, or another appropriate chant is sung.

Outside Easter Time

ANTIPHON 1 Ps 51 (50):9

Sprinkle me with hyssop, O Lord, and I shall be cleansed; wash me and I shall be whiter than snow.

ANTIPHON 2 Ez 36:25-26

I will pour clean water upon you, and you will be made clean of all your impurities, and I shall give you a new spirit, says the Lord.

HYMN Cf. 1 Pt 1:3-5

Blessed be the God and Father of our Lord Jesus Christ, who in his great mercy has given us new birth into a living hope through the Resurrection of Jesus Christ from

the dead, into an inheritance that will not perish, preserved for us in heaven for the salvation to be revealed in the last time!

During Easter Time

ANTIPHON 1 Cf. Ez 47:1-2, 9

I saw water flowing from the Temple, from its right-hand side, alleluia: and all to whom this water came were saved and shall say: Alleluia, alleluia.

ANTIPHON 2 Cf. Zeph 3:8; Ez 36:25

On the day of my resurrection, says the Lord, alleluia, I will gather the nations and assemble the kingdoms and I will pour clean water upon you, alleluia.

ANTIPHON 3 Cf. Dn 3:77, 79

You springs and all that moves in the waters, sing a hymn to God, alleluia.

ANTIPHON 4 1 Pt 2:9

O chosen race, royal priesthood, holy nation, proclaim the mighty works of him who called you out of darkness into his wonderful light, alleluia.

ANTIPHON 5

From your side, O Christ, bursts forth a spring of water, by which the squalor of the world is washed away and life is made new again, alleluia.

When he returns to his chair and the singing is over, the Priest stands facing the people and, with hands joined, says:

May almighty God cleanse us of our sins,
and through the celebration of this Eucharist
make us worthy to share at the table of his Kingdom.
℟. **Amen**.

Then, when it is prescribed, the hymn Gloria in excelsis (Glory to God in the highest) *is sung or said.*

PREFACES

PREFACE I OF ADVENT (P 1)

The two comings of Christ

(From the First Sunday of Advent to December 16)

It is truly right and just, our duty and our salvation,
always and everywhere to give you thanks,
Lord, holy Father, almighty and eternal God,
through Christ our Lord.

For he assumed at his first coming
the lowliness of human flesh,
and so fulfilled the design you formed long ago,
and opened for us the way to eternal salvation,
that, when he comes again in glory and majesty
and all is at last made manifest,
we who watch for that day
may inherit the great promise
in which now we dare to hope.

And so, with Angels and Archangels,
with Thrones and Dominions,
and with all the hosts and Powers of heaven,
we sing the hymn of your glory,
as without end we acclaim: ➜ No. 23, p. 23

PREFACE II OF ADVENT (P 2)

The twofold expectation of Christ

(From December 17 to December 24)

It is truly right and just, our duty and our salvation,
always and everywhere to give you thanks,
Lord, holy Father, almighty and eternal God,
through Christ our Lord.

For all the oracles of the prophets foretold him,
the Virgin Mother longed for him
with love beyond all telling,

82

John the Baptist sang of his coming
and proclaimed his presence when he came.

It is by his gift that already we rejoice
at the mystery of his Nativity,
so that he may find us watchful in prayer
and exultant in his praise.

And so, with Angels and Archangels,
with Thrones and Dominions,
and with all the hosts and Powers of heaven,
we sing the hymn of your glory,
as without end we acclaim: → No. 23, p. 23

PREFACE I OF THE NATIVITY OF THE LORD (P 3)

Christel the Light

(For the Nativity of the Lord, its Octave Day and within the Octave)

It is truly right and just, our duty and our salvation,
always and everywhere to give you thanks,
Lord, holy Father, almighty and eternal God.

For in the mystery of the Word made flesh
a new light of your glory has shone upon the eyes of our
    mind,
so that, as we recognize in him God made visible,
we may be caught up through him in love of things invisible.

And so, with Angels and Archangels,
with Thrones and Dominions,
and with all the hosts and Powers of heaven,
we sing the hymn of your glory,
as without end we acclaim: → No. 23, p. 23

PREFACE II OF THE NATIVITY OF THE LORD (P 4)

The restoration of all things in the Incarnation

(For the Nativity of the Lord, its Octave Day and within the Octave)

It is truly right and just, our duty and our salvation,
always and everywhere to give you thanks,
Lord, holy Father, almighty and eternal God,
through Christ our Lord.

For on the feast of this awe-filled mystery,
though invisible in his own divine nature,

he has appeared visibly in ours;
and begotten before all ages,
he has begun to exist in time;
so that, raising up in himself all that was cast down,
he might restore unity to all creation
and call straying humanity back to the heavenly Kingdom.

And so, with all the Angels, we praise you,
as in joyful celebration we acclaim: → No. 23, p. 23

PREFACE III OF THE NATIVITY OF THE LORD (P 5)

The exchange in the Incarnation of the Word

(For the Nativity of the Lord, its Octave Day and within the Octave)

It is truly right and just, our duty and our salvation,
always and everywhere to give you thanks,
Lord, holy Father, almighty and eternal God,
through Christ our Lord.

For through him the holy exchange that restores our life
has shone forth today in splendor:
when our frailty is assumed by your Word
not only does human mortality receive unending honor
but by this wondrous union we, too, are made eternal.

And so, in company with the choirs of Angels,
we praise you, and with joy we proclaim: → No. 23, p. 23

PREFACE I OF LENT (P 8)

The spiritual meaning of Lent

It is truly right and just, our duty and our salvation,
always and everywhere to give you thanks,
Lord, holy Father, almighty and eternal God,
through Christ our Lord.

For by your gracious gift each year
your faithful await the sacred paschal feasts
with the joy of minds made pure,
so that, more eagerly intent on prayer
and on the works of charity,
and participating in the mysteries
by which they have been reborn,

they may be led to the fullness of grace
that you bestow on your sons and daughters.

And so, with Angels and Archangels,
with Thrones and Dominions,
and with all the hosts and Powers of heaven,
we sing the hymn of your glory,
as without end we acclaim: → No. 23, p. 23

PREFACE II OF LENT (P 9)
Spiritual penance

It is truly right and just, our duty and our salvation,
always and everywhere to give you thanks,
Lord, holy Father, almighty and eternal God.

For you have given your children a sacred time
for the renewing and purifying of their hearts,
that, freed from disordered affections,
they may so deal with the things of this passing world
as to hold rather to the things that eternally endure.

And so, with all the Angels and Saints,
we praise you, as without end we acclaim: → No. 23, p. 23

PREFACE I OF EASTER I (P 21)
The Paschal Mystery

(At the Easter Vigil, is said "on this night"; on Easter Sunday and throughout the Octave
of Easter, is said "on this day"; on other days of Easter Time, is said "in this time.")

It is truly right and just, our duty and our salvation,
at all times to acclaim you, O Lord,
but (on this night / on this day / in this time) above all
to laud you yet more gloriously,
when Christ our Passover has been sacrificed.

For he is the true Lamb
who has taken away the sins of the world;
by dying he has destroyed our death,
and by rising, restored our life.

Therefore, overcome with paschal joy,
every land, every people exults in your praise
and even the heavenly Powers, with the angelic hosts,
sing together the unending hymn of your glory,
as they acclaim: → No. 23, p. 23

PREFACE II OF EASTER (P 22)
New life in Christ

It is truly right and just, our duty and our salvation,
at all times to acclaim you, O Lord,
but in this time above all to laud you yet more gloriously,
when Christ our Passover has been sacrificed.

Through him the children of light rise to eternal life
and the halls of the heavenly Kingdom
are thrown open to the faithful;
for his Death is our ransom from death,
and in his rising the life of all has risen.

Therefore, overcome with paschal joy,
every land, every people exults in your praise
and even the heavenly Powers, with the angelic hosts,
sing together the unending hymn of your glory,
as they acclaim:					➙ No. 23, p. 23

PREFACE III OF EASTER (P 23)
Christ living and always interceding for us

It is truly right and just, our duty and our salvation,
at all times to acclaim you, O Lord,
but in this time above all to laud you yet more gloriously,
when Christ our Passover has been sacrificed.

He never ceases to offer himself for us
but defends us and ever pleads our cause before you:
he is the sacrificial Victim who dies no more,
the Lamb, once slain, who lives for ever.

Therefore, overcome with paschal joy,
every land, every people exults in your praise
and even the heavenly Powers, with the angelic hosts,
sing together the unending hymn of your glory,
as they acclaim:					➙ No. 23, p. 23

PREFACE IV OF EASTER (P 24)
*The restoration of the universe through the
Paschal Mystery*

It is truly right and just, our duty and our salvation,
at all times to acclaim you, O Lord,

but in this time above all to laud you yet more gloriously,
when Christ our Passover has been sacrificed.

For, with the old order destroyed,
a universe cast down is renewed,
and integrity of life is restored to us in Christ.

Therefore, overcome with paschal joy,
every land, every people exults in your praise
and even the heavenly Powers, with the angelic hosts,
sing together the unending hymn of your glory,
as they acclaim: ➔ No. 23, p. 23

PREFACE V OF EASTER (P 25)

Christ, Priest and Victim

It is truly right and just, our duty and our salvation,
at all times to acclaim you, O Lord,
but in this time above all to laud you yet more gloriously,
when Christ our Passover has been sacrificed.

By the oblation of his Body,
he brought the sacrifices of old to fulfillment
in the reality of the Cross
and, by commending himself to you for our salvation,
showed himself the Priest, the Altar, and the Lamb of
   sacrifice.

Therefore, overcome with paschal joy,
every land, every people exults in your praise
and even the heavenly Powers, with the angelic hosts,
sing together the unending hymn of your glory,
as they acclaim: ➔ No. 23, p. 23

PREFACE I OF THE ASCENSION OF THE LORD (P 26)

The mystery of the Ascension
(Ascension to the Saturday before Pentecost inclusive)

It is truly right and just, our duty and our salvation,
always and everywhere to give you thanks,
Lord, holy Father, almighty and eternal God.

For the Lord Jesus, the King of glory,
conqueror of sin and death,

ascended (today) to the highest heavens,
as the Angels gazed in wonder.

Mediator between God and man,
judge of the world and Lord of hosts,
he ascended, not to distance himself from our lowly state
but that we, his members, might be confident of following
where he, our Head and Founder, has gone before.

Therefore, overcome with paschal joy,
every land, every people exults in your praise
and even the heavenly Powers, with the angelic hosts,
sing together the unending hymn of your glory,
as they acclaim: ➜ No. 23, p. 23

PREFACE II OF THE ASCENSION OF THE LORD (P 27)

The mystery of the Ascension
(Ascension to the Saturday before Pentecost inclusive)

It is truly right and just, our duty and our salvation,
always and everywhere to give you thanks,
Lord, holy Father, almighty and eternal God,
through Christ our Lord.

For after his Resurrection
he plainly appeared to all his disciples
and was taken up to heaven in their sight,
that he might make us sharers in his divinity.

Therefore, overcome with paschal joy,
every land, every people exults in your praise
and even the heavenly Powers, with the angelic hosts,
sing together the unending hymn of your glory,
as they acclaim: ➜ No. 23, p. 23

PREFACE I OF THE SUNDAYS IN ORDINARY TIME (P 29)

The Paschal Mystery and the People of God

It is truly right and just, our duty and our salvation,
always and everywhere to give you thanks,
Lord, holy Father, almighty and eternal God,
through Christ our Lord.

For through his Paschal Mystery,
he accomplished the marvelous deed,

by which he has freed us from the yoke of sin and death,
summoning us to the glory of being now called
a chosen race, a royal priesthood,
a holy nation, a people for your own possession,
to proclaim everywhere your mighty works,
for you have called us out of darkness
into your own wonderful light.

And so, with Angels and Archangels,
with Thrones and Dominions,
and with all the hosts and Powers of heaven,
we sing the hymn of your glory,
as without end we acclaim: → No. 23, p. 23

PREFACE II OF THE SUNDAYS IN ORDINARY TIME (P 30)

The mystery of salvation

It is truly right and just, our duty and our salvation,
always and everywhere to give you thanks,
Lord, holy Father, almighty and eternal God,
through Christ our Lord.

For out of compassion for the waywardness that is ours,
he humbled himself and was born of the Virgin;
by the passion of the Cross he freed us from unending death,
and by rising from the dead he gave us life eternal.

And so, with Angels and Archangels,
with Thrones and Dominions,
and with all the hosts and Powers of heaven,
we sing the hymn of your glory,
as without end we acclaim: → No. 23, p. 23

PREFACE III OF THE SUNDAYS IN ORDINARY TIME (P 31)

The salvation of man by a man

It is truly right and just, our duty and our salvation,
always and everywhere to give you thanks,
Lord, holy Father, almighty and eternal God.

For we know it belongs to your boundless glory,
that you came to the aid of mortal beings with your divinity
and even fashioned for us a remedy out of mortality itself,
that the cause of our downfall

might become the means of our salvation,
through Christ our Lord.

Through him the host of Angels adores your majesty
and rejoices in your presence for ever.
May our voices, we pray, join with theirs
in one chorus of exultant praise, as we acclaim:
→ No. 23, p. 23

PREFACE IV OF THE SUNDAYS IN ORDINARY TIME (P 32)

The history of salvation

It is truly right and just, our duty and our salvation,
always and everywhere to give you thanks,
Lord, holy Father, almighty and eternal God,
through Christ our Lord.

For by his birth he brought renewal
to humanity's fallen state,
and by his suffering, canceled out our sins;
by his rising from the dead
he has opened the way to eternal life,
and by ascending to you, O Father,
he has unlocked the gates of heaven.

And so, with the company of Angels and Saints,
we sing the hymn of your praise,
as without end we acclaim:
→ No. 23, p. 23

PREFACE V OF THE SUNDAYS IN ORDINARY TIME (P 33)

Creation

It is truly right and just, our duty and our salvation,
always and everywhere to give you thanks,
Lord, holy Father, almighty and eternal God.

For you laid the foundations of the world
and have arranged the changing of times and seasons;
you formed man in your own image
and set humanity over the whole world in all its wonder,
to rule in your name over all you have made
and for ever praise you in your mighty works,
through Christ our Lord.

And so, with all the Angels, we praise you,
as in joyful celebration we acclaim: → No. 23, p. 23

PREFACE VI OF THE SUNDAYS IN ORDINARY TIME (P 34)

The pledge of the eternal Passover

It is truly right and just, our duty and our salvation,
always and everywhere to give you thanks,
Lord, holy Father, almighty and eternal God.

For in you we live and move and have our being,
and while in this body
we not only experience the daily effects of your care,
but even now possess the pledge of life eternal.

For, having received the first fruits of the Spirit,
through whom you raised up Jesus from the dead,
we hope for an everlasting share in the Paschal Mystery.

And so, with all the Angels, we praise you,
as in joyful celebration we acclaim: → No. 23, p. 23

PREFACE VII OF THE SUNDAYS IN ORDINARY TIME (P 35)

Salvation through the obedience of Christ

It is truly right and just, our duty and our salvation,
always and everywhere to give you thanks,
Lord, holy Father, almighty and eternal God.

For you so loved the world
that in your mercy you sent us the Redeemer,
to live like us in all things but sin,
so that you might love in us what you loved in your Son,
by whose obedience we have been restored to those gifts
   of yours
that, by sinning, we had lost in disobedience.

And so, Lord, with all the Angels and Saints,
we, too, give you thanks, as in exultation we acclaim:
→ No. 23, p. 23

PREFACE VIII OF THE SUNDAYS IN ORDINARY TIME (P 36)

The Church united by the unity of the Trinity

It is truly right and just, our duty and our salvation,
always and everywhere to give you thanks,
Lord, holy Father, almighty and eternal God.

For, when your children were scattered afar by sin,
through the Blood of your Son and the power of the Spirit,
you gathered them again to yourself,
that a people, formed as one by the unity of the Trinity,
made the body of Christ and the temple of the Holy Spirit,
might, to the praise of your manifold wisdom,
be manifest as the Church.

And so, in company with the choirs of Angels,
we praise you, and with joy we proclaim: ➙ No. 23, p. 23

PREFACE I OF THE MOST HOLY EUCHARIST (P 47)
The Sacrifice and the Sacrament of Christ

It is truly right and just, our duty and our salvation,
always and everywhere to give you thanks,
Lord, holy Father, almighty and eternal God,
through Christ our Lord.

For he is the true and eternal Priest,
who instituted the pattern of an everlasting sacrifice
and was the first to offer himself as the saving Victim,
commanding us to make this offering as his memorial.
As we eat his flesh that was sacrificed for us,
we are made strong,
and, as we drink his Blood that was poured out for us,
we are washed clean.

And so, with Angels and Archangels,
with Thrones and Dominions,
and with all the hosts and Powers of heaven,
we sing the hymn of your glory,
as without end we acclaim: ➙ No. 23, p. 23

PREFACE II OF THE MOST HOLY EUCHARIST (P 48)
The fruits of the Most Holy Eucharist

It is truly right and just, our duty and our salvation,
always and everywhere to give you thanks,
Lord, holy Father, almighty and eternal God,
through Christ our Lord.

For at the Last Supper with his Apostles,
establishing for the ages to come the saving memorial of
the Cross,
he offered himself to you as the unblemished Lamb,
the acceptable gift of perfect praise.

Nourishing your faithful by this sacred mystery,
you make them holy, so that the human race,
bounded by one world,
may be enlightened by one faith
and united by one bond of charity.

And so, we approach the table of this wondrous Sacrament,
so that, bathed in the sweetness of your grace,
we may pass over to the heavenly realities here foreshadowed.

Therefore, all creatures of heaven and earth
sing a new song in adoration,
and we, with all the host of Angels,
cry out, and without end we acclaim: ➡ No. 23, p. 23

PREFACE I FOR THE DEAD (P 77)
The hope of resurrection in Christ

It is truly right and just, our duty and our salvation,
always and everywhere to give you thanks,
Lord, holy Father, almighty and eternal God,
through Christ our Lord.

In him the hope of blessed resurrection has dawned,
that those saddened by the certainty of dying
might be consoled by the promise of immortality to come.
Indeed for your faithful, Lord,
life is changed not ended,
and, when this earthly dwelling turns to dust,
an eternal dwelling is made ready for them in heaven.

And so, with Angels and Archangels,
with Thrones and Dominions,
and with all the hosts and Powers of heaven,
we sing the hymn of your glory,
as without end we acclaim: ➡ No. 23, p. 23

PREFACE II FOR THE DEAD (P 78)
Christ died so that we might live

It is truly right and just, our duty and our salvation,
always and everywhere to give you thanks,
Lord, holy Father, almighty and eternal God,
through Christ our Lord.

For as one alone he accepted death,
so that we might all escape from dying;
as one man he chose to die,
so that in your sight we all might live for ever.

And so, in company with the choirs of Angels,
we praise you, and with joy we proclaim: ➥ No. 23, p. 23

PREFACE III FOR THE DEAD (P 79)
Christ, the salvation and the life

It is truly right and just, our duty and our salvation,
always and everywhere to give you thanks,
Lord, holy Father, almighty and eternal God,
through Christ our Lord.

For he is the salvation of the world,
the life of the human race,
the resurrection of the dead.

Through him the host of Angels adores your majesty
and rejoices in your presence for ever.
May our voices, we pray, join with theirs
in one chorus of exultant praise, as we acclaim:
➥ No. 23, p. 23

PREFACE IV FOR THE DEAD (P 80)
From earthly life to heavenly glory

It is truly right and just, our duty and our salvation,
always and everywhere to give you thanks,
Lord, holy Father, almighty and eternal God.

For it is at your summons that we come to birth,
by your will that we are governed,
and at your command that we return,
on account of sin,
to that earth from which we came.

And when you give the sign,
we who have been redeemed by the Death of your Son,
shall be raised up to the glory of his Resurrection.

And so, with the company of Angels and Saints,
we sing the hymn of your praise,
as without end we acclaim: → No. 23, p. 23

PREFACE V FOR THE DEAD (P 81)
Our resurrection through the victory of Christ

It is truly right and just, our duty and our salvation,
always and everywhere to give you thanks,
Lord, holy Father, almighty and eternal God.

For even though by our own fault we perish,
yet by your compassion and your grace,
when seized by death according to our sins,
we are redeemed through Christ's great victory,
and with him called back into life.

And so, with the Powers of heaven,
we worship you constantly on earth,
and before your majesty
without end we acclaim: → No. 23, p. 23

PROPER COMMUNICANTES
AND HANC IGITUR

FOR EUCHARISTIC PRAYER I (THE ROMAN CANON)

Communicantes for the Nativity of the Lord
and throughout the Octave

Celebrating the most sacred night (day)
on which blessed Mary the immaculate Virgin
brought forth the Savior for this world,
and in communion with those whose memory we venerate,
especially the glorious ever-Virgin Mary,
Mother of our God and Lord, Jesus Christ,† etc., p. 25.

Communicantes for the Epiphany of the Lord

Celebrating the most sacred day
on which your Only Begotten Son,
eternal with you in your glory,
appeared in a human body, truly sharing our flesh,

and in communion with those whose memory we venerate,
especially the glorious ever-Virgin Mary,
Mother of our God and Lord, Jesus Christ,† etc., p. 25.

Communicantes for Easter

Celebrating the most sacred night (day)
of the Resurrection of our Lord Jesus Christ in the flesh,
and in communion with those whose memory we venerate,
especially the glorious ever-Virgin Mary,
Mother of our God and Lord, Jesus Christ,† etc., p. 25.

Hanc Igitur for the Easter Vigil
until the Second Sunday of Easter

Therefore, Lord, we pray:
graciously accept this oblation of our service,
that of your whole family,
which we make to you
also for those to whom you have been pleased to give
the new birth of water and the Holy Spirit,
granting them forgiveness of all their sins;
order our days in your peace,
and command that we be delivered from eternal damnation
and counted among the flock of those you have chosen.
(Through Christ our Lord. Amen.)   → *Canon*, p. 25.

Communicantes for the Ascension of the Lord

Celebrating the most sacred day
on which your Only Begotten Son, our Lord,
placed at the right hand of your glory
our weak human nature,
which he had united to himself,
and in communion with those whose memory we venerate,
especially the glorious ever-Virgin Mary,
Mother of our God and Lord, Jesus Christ,† etc., p. 25.

Communicantes for Pentecost Sunday

Celebrating the most sacred day of Pentecost,
on which the Holy Spirit
appeared to the Apostles in tongues of fire,
and in communion with those whose memory we venerate,
especially the glorious ever-Virgin Mary,
Mother of our God and Lord, Jesus Christ,† etc., p. 25.

BLESSINGS AT THE END OF MASS AND PRAYERS OVER THE PEOPLE

SOLEMN BLESSINGS

The following blessings may be used, at the discretion of the Priest, at the end of the celebration of Mass, or of a Liturgy of the Word, or of the Office, or of the Sacraments.

The Deacon or, in his absence, the Priest himself, says the invitation: Bow down for the blessing. *Then the Priest, with hands extended over the people, says the blessing, with all responding:* **Amen**.

I. For Celebrations in the Different Liturgical Times

1. ADVENT

May the almighty and merciful God,
by whose grace you have placed your faith
in the First Coming of his Only Begotten Son
and yearn for his coming again,
sanctify you by the radiance of Christ's Advent
and enrich you with his blessing. ℞. **Amen.**

As you run the race of this present life,
may he make you firm in faith,
joyful in hope and active in charity. ℞. **Amen.**

So that, rejoicing now with devotion
at the Redeemer's coming in the flesh,
you may be endowed with the rich reward of eternal life
when he comes again in majesty. ℞. **Amen.**

And may the blessing of almighty God,
the Father, and the Son, ✠ and the Holy Spirit,
come down on you and remain with you for ever. ℞. **Amen.**

2. THE NATIVITY OF THE LORD

May the God of infinite goodness,
who by the Incarnation of his Son has driven darkness from the world
and by that glorious Birth has illumined this most holy night (day),
drive far from you the darkness of vice
and illumine your hearts with the light of virtue. ℞. **Amen.**

97

May God, who willed that the great joy
of his Son's saving Birth
be announced to shepherds by the Angel,
fill your minds with the gladness he gives
and make you heralds of his Gospel. ℟. **Amen.**

And may God, who by the Incarnation
brought together the earthly and heavenly realm,
fill you with the gift of his peace and favor
and make you sharers with the Church in heaven. ℟. **Amen.**

And may the blessing of almighty God,
the Father, and the Son, ✖ and the Holy Spirit,
come down on you and remain with you for ever. ℟. **Amen.**

3. THE BEGINNING OF THE YEAR

May God, the source and origin of all blessing,
grant you grace,
pour out his blessing in abundance,
and keep you safe from harm throughout the year. ℟. **Amen.**

May he give you integrity in the faith,
endurance in hope,
and perseverance in charity
with holy patience to the end. ℟. **Amen.**

May he order your days and your deeds in his peace,
grant your prayers in this and in every place,
and lead you happily to eternal life. ℟. **Amen.**

And may the blessing of almighty God,
the Father, and the Son, ✖ and the Holy Spirit,
come down on you and remain with you for ever. ℟. **Amen.**

4. THE EPIPHANY OF THE LORD

May God, who has called you
out of darkness into his wonderful light,
pour out in kindness his blessing upon you
and make your hearts firm
in faith, hope and charity. ℟. **Amen.**

And since in all confidence you follow Christ,
who today appeared in the world
as a light shining in darkness,

may God make you, too,
a light for your brothers and sisters. ℟. **Amen.**

And so when your pilgrimage is ended,
may you come to him
whom the Magi sought as they followed the star
and whom they found with great joy, the Light from Light,
who is Christ the Lord. ℟. **Amen.**

And may the blessing of almighty God,
the Father, and the Son, ✠ and the Holy Spirit,
come down on you and remain with you for ever. ℟. **Amen.**

5. THE PASSION OF THE LORD

May God, the Father of mercies,
who has given you an example of love
in the Passion of his Only Begotten Son,
grant that, by serving God and your neighbor,
you may lay hold of the wondrous gift of his blessing.
℟. **Amen.**

So that you may receive the reward of everlasting life from
him,
through whose earthly Death
you believe that you escape eternal death. ℟. **Amen.**

And by following the example of his self-abasement,
may you possess a share in his Resurrection. ℟. **Amen.**

And may the blessing of almighty God,
the Father, and the Son, ✠ and the Holy Spirit,
come down on you and remain with you for ever. ℟. **Amen.**

6. EASTER TIME

May God, who by the Resurrection of his Only Begotten Son
was pleased to confer on you
the gift of redemption and of adoption,
give you gladness by his blessing. ℟. **Amen.**

May he, by whose redeeming work
you have received the gift of everlasting freedom,
make you heirs to an eternal inheritance. ℟. **Amen.**

And may you, who have already risen with Christ
in Baptism through faith,

by living in a right manner on this earth,
be united with him in the homeland of heaven. ℟. **Amen.**

And may the blessing of almighty God,
the Father, and the Son, ✠ and the Holy Spirit,
come down on you and remain with you for ever. ℟. **Amen.**

7. THE ASCENSION OF THE LORD

May almighty God bless you,
for on this very day his Only Begotten Son
pierced the heights of heaven
and unlocked for you the way
to ascend to where he is. ℟. **Amen.**

May he grant that,
as Christ after his Resurrection
was seen plainly by his disciples,
so when he comes as Judge
he may show himself merciful to you for all eternity.
℟. **Amen.**

And may you, who believe he is seated
with the Father in his majesty,
know with joy the fulfillment of his promise
to stay with you until the end of time. ℟. **Amen.**

And may the blessing of almighty God,
the Father, and the Son, ✠ and the Holy Spirit,
come down on you and remain with you for ever. ℟. **Amen.**

8. THE HOLY SPIRIT

May God, the Father of lights,
who was pleased to enlighten the disciples' minds
by the outpouring of the Spirit, the Paraclete,
grant you gladness by his blessing
and make you always abound with the gifts of the same
   Spirit. ℟. **Amen.**

May the wondrous flame that appeared above the disciples,
powerfully cleanse your hearts from every evil
and pervade them with its purifying light. ℟. **Amen.**

And may God, who has been pleased to unite many
   tongues

in the profession of one faith,
give you perseverance in that same faith
and, by believing, may you journey from hope to clear
    vision. ℟. **Amen.**

And may the blessing of almighty God,
the Father, and the Son, ✠ and the Holy Spirit,
come down on you and remain with you for ever. ℟. **Amen.**

9. ORDINARY TIME I

May the Lord bless you and keep you. ℟. **Amen.**

May he let his face shine upon you
and show you his mercy. ℟. **Amen.**

May he turn his countenance towards you
and give you his peace. ℟. **Amen.**

And may the blessing of almighty God,
the Father, and the Son, ✠ and the Holy Spirit,
come down on you and remain with you for ever. ℟. **Amen.**

10. ORDINARY TIME II

May the peace of God,
which surpasses all understanding,
keep your hearts and minds
in the knowledge and love of God,
and of his Son, our Lord Jesus Christ. ℟. **Amen.**

And may the blessing of almighty God,
the Father, and the Son, ✠ and the Holy Spirit,
come down on you and remain with you for ever. ℟. **Amen.**

11. ORDINARY TIME III

May almighty God bless you in his kindness
and pour out saving wisdom upon you. ℟. **Amen.**

May he nourish you always with the teachings of the faith
and make you persevere in holy deeds. ℟. **Amen.**

May he turn your steps towards himself
and show you the path of charity and peace. ℟. **Amen.**

And may the blessing of almighty God,
the Father, and the Son, ✠ and the Holy Spirit,
come down on you and remain with you for ever. ℟. **Amen.**

12. ORDINARY TIME IV

May the God of all consolation order your days in his peace
and grant you the gifts of his blessing. ℟. **Amen.**

May he free you always from every distress
and confirm your hearts in his love. ℟. **Amen.**

So that on this life's journey
you may be effective in good works,
rich in the gifts of hope, faith and charity,
and may come happily to eternal life. ℟. **Amen.**

And may the blessing of almighty God,
the Father, and the Son, ✠ and the Holy Spirit,
come down on you and remain with you for ever. ℟. **Amen.**

13. ORDINARY TIME V

May almighty God always keep every adversity far from you
and in his kindness pour out upon you the gifts of his
    blessing. ℟. **Amen.**

May God keep your hearts attentive to his words,
that they may be filled with everlasting gladness. ℟. **Amen.**

And so, may you always understand what is good and right,
and be found ever hastening along
in the path of God's commands,
made coheirs with the citizens of heaven. ℟. **Amen.**

And may the blessing of almighty God,
the Father, and the Son, ✠ and the Holy Spirit,
come down on you and remain with you for ever. ℟. **Amen.**

14. ORDINARY TIME VI

May God bless you with every heavenly blessing,
make you always holy and pure in his sight,
pour out in abundance upon you the riches of his glory,
and teach you with the words of truth;
may he instruct you in the Gospel of salvation,
and ever endow you with fraternal charity.
Through Christ our Lord. ℟. **Amen.**

And may the blessing of almighty God,
the Father, and the Son, ✠ and the Holy Spirit,
come down on you and remain with you for ever. ℟. **Amen.**

II. For Celebrations of the Saints

15. THE BLESSED VIRGIN MARY

May God, who through the childbearing of the Blessed
    Virgin Mary
willed in his great kindness to redeem the human race,
be pleased to enrich you with his blessing. ℟. **Amen.**

May you know always and everywhere the protection of
    her,
through whom you have been found worthy to receive the
    author of life. ℟. **Amen.**

May you, who have devoutly gathered on this day,
carry away with you the gifts of spiritual joys and heavenly
    rewards. ℟. **Amen.**

And may the blessing of almighty God,
the Father, and the Son, ✠ and the Holy Spirit,
come down on you and remain with you for ever. ℟. **Amen.**

16. SAINTS PETER AND PAUL, APOSTLES

May almighty God bless you,
for he has made you steadfast in Saint Peter's saving
    confession
and through it has set you on the solid rock of the Church's
    faith. ℟. **Amen.**

And having instructed you
by the tireless preaching of Saint Paul,
may God teach you constantly by his example
to win brothers and sisters for Christ. ℟. **Amen.**

So that by the keys of St. Peter and the words of St. Paul,
and by the support of their intercession,
God may bring us happily to that homeland
that Peter attained on a cross
and Paul by the blade of a sword. ℟. **Amen.**

And may the blessing of almighty God,
the Father, and the Son, ✚ and the Holy Spirit,
come down on you and remain with you for ever. ℟. **Amen.**

17. THE APOSTLES

May God, who has granted you
to stand firm on apostolic foundations,
graciously bless you through the glorious merits
of the holy Apostles *N.* and *N.* (the holy Apostle *N.*). ℟.
    Amen.

And may he, who endowed you
with the teaching and example of the Apostles,
make you, under their protection,
witnesses to the truth before all. ℟. **Amen.**

So that through the intercession of the Apostles,
you may inherit the eternal homeland,
for by their teaching you possess firmness of faith. ℟. **Amen.**

And may the blessing of almighty God,
the Father, and the Son, ✚ and the Holy Spirit,
come down on you and remain with you for ever. ℟. **Amen.**

18. ALL SAINTS

May God, the glory and joy of the Saints,
who has caused you to be strengthened
by means of their outstanding prayers,
bless you with unending blessings. ℟. **Amen.**

Freed through their intercession from present ills
and formed by the example of their holy way of life,
may you be ever devoted
to serving God and your neighbor. ℟. **Amen.**

So that, together with all,
you may possess the joys of the homeland,
where Holy Church rejoices
that her children are admitted in perpetual peace
to the company of the citizens of heaven. ℟. **Amen.**

And may the blessing of almighty God,
the Father, and the Son, ✚ and the Holy Spirit,
come down on you and remain with you for ever. ℟. **Amen.**

III. Other Blessings

19. FOR THE DEDICATION OF A CHURCH

May God, the Lord of heaven and earth,
who has gathered you today for the dedication of this
    church,
make you abound in heavenly blessings. ℟. **Amen.**

And may he, who has willed that all his scattered children
should be gathered together in his Son,
grant that you may become his temple
and the dwelling place of the Holy Spirit. ℟. **Amen.**

And so, when you are thoroughly cleansed,
may God dwell within you
and grant you to possess with all the Saints
the inheritance of eternal happiness. ℟. **Amen.**

And may the blessing of almighty God,
the Father, ✝ and the Son, ✝ and the Holy ✝ Spirit,
come down on you and remain with you for ever. ℟. **Amen.**

20. IN CELEBRATIONS FOR THE DEAD

May the God of all consolation bless you,
for in his unfathomable goodness he created the human
    race,
and in the Resurrection of his Only Begotten Son
he has given believers the hope of rising again. ℟. **Amen.**

To us who are alive, may God grant pardon for our sins,
and to all the dead, a place of light and peace. ℟. **Amen.**

So may we all live happily for ever with Christ,
whom we believe truly rose from the dead. ℟. **Amen.**

And may the blessing of almighty God,
the Father, and the Son, ✝ and the Holy Spirit,
come down on you and remain with you for ever. ℟. **Amen.**

PRAYERS OVER THE PEOPLE

*The following prayers may be used, at the discretion
of the Priest, at the end of the celebration of Mass,
or of a Liturgy of the Word, or of the Office, or of the
Sacraments.*

The Deacon or, in his absence, the Priest himself, says the invitation: Bow down for the blessing. *Then the Priest, with hands outstretched over the people, says the prayer, with all responding:* **Amen**.

After the prayer, the Priest always adds: And may the blessing of almighty God, the Father, and the Son, ✚ and the Holy Spirit, come down on you and remain with you for ever. ℟. **Amen**.

1. Be gracious to your people, O Lord,
   and do not withhold consolation on earth
   from those you call to strive for heaven.
   Through Christ our Lord.

2. Grant, O Lord, we pray,
   that the Christian people
   may understand the truths they profess
   and love the heavenly liturgy
   in which they participate.
   Through Christ our Lord.

3. May your people receive your holy blessing,
   O Lord, we pray,
   and, by that gift,
   spurn all that would harm them
   and obtain what they desire.
   Through Christ our Lord.

4. Turn your people to you with all their heart,
   O Lord, we pray,
   for you protect even those who go astray,
   but when they serve you with undivided heart,
   you sustain them with still greater care.
   Through Christ our Lord.

5. Graciously enlighten your family, O Lord, we pray,
   that by holding fast to what is pleasing to you,
   they may be worthy to accomplish all that is good.
   Through Christ our Lord.

6. Bestow pardon and peace, O Lord, we pray,
   upon your faithful,
   that they may be cleansed from every offense

and serve you with untroubled hearts.
Through Christ our Lord.

7. May your heavenly favor, O Lord, we pray,
   increase in number the people subject to you
   and make them always obedient to your commands.
   Through Christ our Lord.

8. Be propitious to your people, O God,
   that, freed from every evil,
   they may serve you with all their heart
   and ever stand firm under your protection.
   Through Christ our Lord.

9. May your family always rejoice together, O God,
   over the mysteries of redemption they have celebrated,
   and grant its members the perseverance
   to attain the effects that flow from them.
   Through Christ our Lord.

10. Lord God, from the abundance of your mercies
    provide for your servants and ensure their safety,
    so that, strengthened by your blessings,
    they may at all times abound in thanksgiving
    and bless you with unending exultation.
    Through Christ our Lord.

11. Keep your family, we pray, O Lord,
    in your constant care,
    so that, under your protection,
    they may be free from all troubles
    and by good works show dedication to your name.
    Through Christ our Lord.

12. Purify your faithful, both in body and in mind,
    O Lord, we pray,
    so that, feeling the compunction you inspire,
    they may be able to avoid harmful pleasures
    and ever feed upon your delights.
    Through Christ our Lord.

13. May the effects of your sacred blessing, O Lord,
    make themselves felt among your faithful,

to prepare with spiritual sustenance the minds of all,
that they may be strengthened by the power of your
   love
to carry out works of charity.
Through Christ our Lord.

14. The hearts of your faithful submitted to your name,
entreat your help, O Lord,
and since without you they can do nothing that is just,
grant by your abundant mercy
that they may both know what is right
and receive all that they need for their good.
Through Christ our Lord.

15. Hasten to the aid of your faithful people
who call upon you, O Lord, we pray,
and graciously give strength in their human weakness,
so that, being dedicated to you in complete sincerity,
they may find gladness in your remedies
both now and in the life to come.
Through Christ our Lord.

16. Look with favor on your family, O Lord,
and bestow your endless mercy on those who seek it:
and just as without your mercy,
they can do nothing truly worthy of you,
so through it,
may they merit to obey your saving commands.
Through Christ our Lord.

17. Bestow increase of heavenly grace
on your faithful, O Lord;
may they praise you with their lips,
with their souls, with their lives;
and since it is by your gift that we exist,
may our whole lives be yours.
Through Christ our Lord.

18. Direct your people, O Lord, we pray,
with heavenly instruction,
that by avoiding every evil
and pursuing all that is good,
they may earn not your anger

but your unending mercy.
Through Christ our Lord.

19. Be near to those who call on you, O Lord,
    and graciously grant your protection
    to all who place their hope in your mercy,
    that they may remain faithful in holiness of life
    and, having enough for their needs in this world,
    they may be made full heirs of your promise for eternity.
    Through Christ our Lord.

20. Bestow the grace of your kindness
    upon your supplicant people, O Lord,
    that, formed by you, their creator,
    and restored by you, their sustainer,
    through your constant action they may be saved.
    Through Christ our Lord.

21. May your faithful people, O Lord, we pray,
    always respond to the promptings of your love
    and, moved by wholesome compunction,
    may they do gladly what you command,
    so as to receive the things you promise.
    Through Christ our Lord.

22. May the weakness of your devoted people
    stir your compassion, O Lord, we pray,
    and let their faithful pleading win your mercy,
    that what they do not presume upon by their merits
    they may receive by your generous pardon.
    Through Christ our Lord.

23. In defense of your children, O Lord, we pray,
    stretch forth the right hand of your majesty,
    so that, obeying your fatherly will,
    they may have the unfailing protection
    of your fatherly care.
    Through Christ our Lord.

24. Look, O Lord, on the prayers of your family,
    and grant them the assistance they humbly implore,
    so that, strengthened by the help they need,
    they may persevere in confessing your name.
    Through Christ our Lord.

25. Keep your family safe, O Lord, we pray,
    and grant them the abundance of your mercies,
    that they may find growth
    through the teachings and the gifts of heaven.
    Through Christ our Lord.

26. May your faithful people rejoice, we pray, O Lord,
    to be upheld by your right hand,
    and, progressing in the Christian life,
    may they delight in good things
    both now and in the time to come.
    Through Christ our Lord.

ON FEASTS OF SAINTS

27. May the Christian people exult, O Lord,
    at the glorification of the illustrious members of your
        Son's Body,
    and may they gain a share in the eternal lot
    of the Saints on whose feast day
    they reaffirm their devotion to you,
    rejoicing with them for ever in your glory.
    Through Christ our Lord.

28. Turn the hearts of your people
    always to you, O Lord, we pray,
    and, as you give them the help of such great patrons as
        these,
    grant also the unfailing help of your protection.
    Through Christ our Lord.

"Pray that you have the strength to escape . . . and to stand before the Son of Man."

NOVEMBER 29, 2015

1st SUNDAY OF ADVENT

ENTRANCE ANT. Cf. Ps 25 (24):1-3   [Hope]
To you, I lift up my soul, O my God. In you, I have trusted; let me not be put to shame. Nor let my enemies exult over me; and let none who hope in you be put to shame.   → No. 2, p. 10 (Omit Gloria)

COLLECT   [Meeting Christ]
Grant your faithful, we pray, almighty God,
the resolve to run forth to meet your Christ
with righteous deeds at his coming,
so that, gathered at his right hand,
they may be worthy to possess the heavenly Kingdom.
Through our Lord Jesus Christ, your Son,
who lives and reigns with you in the unity of the Holy
    Spirit,
one God, for ever and ever. ℟. **Amen.** ↓

FIRST READING Jer 33:14-16   [The Lord's Messiah]

Jeremiah reveals the promise of the Lord made to the House of Israel. A shoot from David shall do what is right and just. Judah and Jerusalem shall be safe.

A reading from the Book of the Prophet Jeremiah

THE days are coming, says the LORD, when I will fulfill the promise I made to the house of Israel and Judah. In those days, in that time, I will raise up for David a just shoot; he shall do what is right and just in the land. In those days Judah shall be safe and Jerusalem shall dwell secure; this is what they shall call her: "The LORD our justice."—The word of the Lord. ℟. **Thanks be to God.** ↓

RESPONSORIAL PSALM Ps 25   [Eye on God]

℟. To   you, O   Lord,   I   lift   my   soul.

Your ways, O LORD, make known to me;
   teach me your paths,
guide me in your truth and teach me,
   for you are God my savior,
   and for you I wait all the day.

℟. **To you, O Lord, I lift my soul.**

Good and upright is the LORD;
   thus he shows sinners the way.
He guides the humble to justice,
   and teaches the humble his way.

℟. **To you, O Lord, I lift my soul.**

All the paths of the LORD are kindness and constancy
   toward those who keep his covenant and his decrees.
The friendship of the LORD is with those who fear him,
   and his covenant, for their instruction.

℟. **To you, O Lord, I lift my soul.** ↓

SECOND READING 1 Thes 3:12—4:2   [Lives Pleasing to God]

Paul prays that the Lord will increase his love among the
Thessalonians. In turn they must live a life pleasing to God
so that they may progress in the way of perfection.

A reading from the first Letter of Saint Paul to
the Thessalonians

BROTHERS and sisters: May the Lord make you
increase and abound in love for one another and
for all, just as we have for you, so as to strengthen your
hearts, to be blameless in holiness before our God and
Father at the coming of our Lord Jesus with all his holy
ones. Amen.

Finally, brothers and sisters, we earnestly ask and
exhort you in the Lord Jesus that, as you received from
us how you should conduct yourselves to please God—
and as you are conducting yourselves—you do so even
more. For you know what instructions we gave you
through the Lord Jesus.—The word of the Lord.
℟. **Thanks be to God.** ↓

ALLELUIA Ps 85:8   [God's Salvation]
℟. **Alleluia, alleluia.**
Show us, Lord, your love;
and grant us your salvation.
℟. **Alleluia, alleluia.** ↓

GOSPEL Lk 21:25-28, 34-36   [Prayerful Vigilance]

Jesus tells his disciples that there will be signs for his second coming. The sun, moon, stars, anguish among people,
fright—these will warn of his coming. They should watch,
pray and stand secure before the Son of Man.

℣. The Lord be with you. ℟. **And with your spirit.**
✝ A reading from the holy Gospel according to Luke.
℟. **Glory to you, O Lord.**

JESUS said to his disciples: "There will be signs in the sun, the moon, and the stars, and on earth nations will be in dismay, perplexed by the roaring of the sea and the waves. People will die of fright in anticipation of what is coming upon the world, for the powers of the heavens will be shaken. And then they will see the Son of Man coming in a cloud with power and great glory. But when these signs begin to happen, stand erect and raise your heads because your redemption is at hand.

"Beware that your hearts do not become drowsy from carousing and drunkenness and the anxieties of daily life, and that day catch you by surprise like a trap. For that day will assault everyone who lives on the face of the earth. Be vigilant at all times and pray that you have the strength to escape the tribulations that are imminent and to stand before the Son of Man."—The Gospel of the Lord. ℟. **Praise to you, Lord Jesus Christ.**   → No. 15, p. 18

PRAYER OVER THE OFFERINGS   [Eternal Redemption]

Accept, we pray, O Lord, these offerings we make,
gathered from among your gifts to us,
and may what you grant us to celebrate devoutly here
   below
gain for us the prize of eternal redemption.
Through Christ our Lord.
℟. **Amen.**   → No. 21, p. 22 (Pref. P 1)

COMMUNION ANT. Ps 85 (84):13   [God's Bounty]
The Lord will bestow his bounty, and our earth shall yield its increase. ↓

PRAYER AFTER COMMUNION   [Love for Heaven]

May these mysteries, O Lord,
in which we have participated,

profit us, we pray,
for even now, as we walk amid passing things,
you teach us by them
to love the things of heaven
and hold fast to what endures.
Through Christ our Lord.
℟. **Amen.**   → No. 30, p. 77

Optional Solemn Blessings, p. 97, and Prayers over the People, p. 105

"John went throughout the whole region of the Jordan, proclaiming a baptism of repentance."

DECEMBER 6

2nd SUNDAY OF ADVENT

ENTRANCE ANT. Cf. Is 30:19, 30   [Lord of Salvation]

O people of Sion, behold, the Lord will come to save the nations, and the Lord will make the glory of his voice heard in the joy of your heart.

→ No. 2, p. 10 (Omit Gloria)

COLLECT   [Heavenly Wisdom]

Almighty and merciful God,
may no earthly undertaking hinder those
who set out in haste to meet your Son,
but may our learning of heavenly wisdom
gain us admittance to his company.
Who lives and reigns with you in the unity of the Holy Spirit,
one God, for ever and ever. ℟. **Amen.** ↓

FIRST READING Bar 5:1-9   [God's Favor on Jerusalem]

Baruch tells Jerusalem of God's favor. God will gather the people together that Israel may grow secure in the glory of God. He leads in joy, mercy, and justice.

116

A reading from the Book of the Prophet Baruch

JERUSALEM, take off your robe of mourning and
    misery;
    put on the splendor of glory from God forever:
wrapped in the cloak of justice from God,
    bear on your head the mitre
    that displays the glory of the eternal name.
For God will show all the earth your splendor:
    you will be named by God forever
    the peace of justice, the glory of God's worship.

Up, Jerusalem! stand upon the heights;
    look to the east and see your children
gathered from the east and the west
    at the word of the Holy One,
    rejoicing that they are remembered by God.
Led away on foot by their enemies they left you:
    but God will bring them back to you
    borne aloft in glory as on royal thrones.
For God has commanded
    that every lofty mountain be made low,
and that the age-old depths and gorges
    be filled to level ground,
    that Israel may advance secure in the glory of God.
The forests and every fragrant kind of tree
    have overshadowed Israel at God's command;
for God is leading Israel in joy
    by the light of his glory,
    with his mercy and justice for company.
The word of the Lord. ℟. **Thanks be to God.** ↓

RESPONSORIAL PSALM Ps 126   [The Lord's Wonders]

℟. **The Lord has done great things for us; we are filled with joy.**

When the LORD brought back the captives of Zion,
   we were like men dreaming.
Then our mouth was filled with laughter,
   and our tongue with rejoicing.

℟. **The Lord has done great things for us; we are filled
   with joy.**

Then they said among the nations,
   "The LORD has done great things for them."
The LORD has done great things for us;
   we are glad indeed.

℟. **The Lord has done great things for us; we are filled
   with joy.**

Restore our fortunes, O LORD,
   like the torrents in the southern desert.
Those who sow in tears
   shall reap rejoicing.

℟. **The Lord has done great things for us; we are filled
   with joy.**

Although they go forth weeping,
   carrying the seed to be sown,
they shall come back rejoicing,
   carrying their sheaves.

℟. **The Lord has done great things for us; we are filled
   with joy.** ↓

SECOND READING Phil 1:4-6, 8-11 [Cooperating with Joy]

Paul rejoices in the progress of faith among the
Philippians. He is sure that God who began this good work
will help it grow. Paul prays that their love may even more
abound that they may be rich in harvest.

A reading from the Letter of Saint Paul
to the Philippians

BROTHERS and sisters: I pray always with joy in
my every prayer for all of you, because of your

partnership for the gospel from the first day until now.
I am confident of this, that the one who began a good
work in you will continue to complete it until the day
of Christ Jesus. God is my witness, how I long for all of
you with the affection of Christ Jesus. And this is my
prayer: that your love may increase ever more and
more in knowledge and every kind of perception, to
discern what is of value, so that you may be pure and
blameless for the day of Christ, filled with the fruit of
righteousness that comes through Jesus Christ for the
glory and praise of God.—The word of the Lord.
℟. **Thanks be to God.** ↓

ALLELUIA Lk 3:4, 6   [Prepare the Way]
℟. **Alleluia, alleluia.**
Prepare the way of the Lord, make straight his paths:
all flesh shall see the salvation of God.
℟. **Alleluia, alleluia.** ↓

GOSPEL Lk 3:1-6   [Prepare for the Lord]
    Luke outlines some historical facts at the time of John the
    Baptist's preaching. It is the fulfillment of the prophecy of
    Isaiah. John prepares the way for the Lord.

℣. The Lord be with you. ℟. **And with your spirit.**
✤ A reading from the holy Gospel according to Luke.
℟. **Glory to you, O Lord.**

IN the fifteenth year of the reign of Tiberius Caesar,
when Pontius Pilate was governor of Judea, and
Herod was tetrarch of Galilee, and his brother Philip
tetrarch of the region of Ituraea and Trachonitis, and
Lysanias was tetrarch of Abilene, during the high
priesthood of Annas and Caiaphas, the word of God
came to John the son of Zechariah in the desert. John
went throughout the whole region of the Jordan, proclaiming a baptism of repentance for the forgiveness

of sins, as it is written in the book of the words of the
prophet Isaiah:

A voice of one crying out in the desert:
"Prepare the way of the Lord,
    make straight his paths.
Every valley shall be filled
    and every mountain and hill shall be made low.
The winding roads shall be made straight,
    and the rough ways made smooth,
and all flesh shall see the salvation of God."

The Gospel of the Lord. ℟. **Praise to you, Lord Jesus
Christ.**   ➔ No. 15, p. 18

PRAYER OVER THE OFFERINGS   [Our Offering]

Be pleased, O Lord, with our humble prayers and
    offerings,
and, since we have no merits to plead our cause,
come, we pray, to our rescue
with the protection of your mercy.
Through Christ our Lord.
℟. **Amen.**   ➔ No. 21, p. 22 (Pref. P 1)

COMMUNION ANT. Bar 5:5; 4:36   [Coming Joy]

**Jerusalem, arise and stand upon the heights, and
behold the joy which comes to you from God.** ↓

PRAYER AFTER COMMUNION   [Wise Judgment]

Replenished by the food of spiritual nourishment,
we humbly beseech you, O Lord,
that, through our partaking in this mystery,
you may teach us to judge wisely the things of earth
and hold firm to the things of heaven.
Through Christ our Lord.
℟. **Amen.**   ➔ No. 30, p. 77

Optional Solemn Blessings, p. 97, Prayers over the People, p. 105

"Hail, full of grace! The Lord is with you."

DECEMBER 8

THE IMMACULATE CONCEPTION
OF THE BLESSED VIRGIN MARY

Patronal Feastday
of the United States of America

Solemnity

ENTRANCE ANT. Is 61:10   [Mary Rejoices in the Lord]

I rejoice heartily in the Lord, in my God is the joy of
my soul; for he has clothed me with a robe of salvation, and wrapped me in a mantle of justice, like a
bride adorned with her jewels.   → No. 2, p. 10

COLLECT   [Admitted to God's Presence]

O God, who by the Immaculate Conception of the
   Blessed Virgin
prepared a worthy dwelling for your Son,
grant, we pray,
that, as you preserved her from every stain
by virtue of the Death of your Son, which you foresaw,
so, through her intercession,
we, too, may be cleansed and admitted to your presence.

Through our Lord Jesus Christ, your Son,
who lives and reigns with you in the unity of the Holy
   Spirit,
one God, for ever and ever. ℟. **Amen.** ↓

FIRST READING Gn 3:9-15, 20   [Promise of the Redeemer]
   In the Garden, humankind enjoys an intimacy with God. It
   is disrupted by sin, and the free and happy relationship
   between humankind and God is broken.

A reading from the Book of Genesis

AFTER the man, Adam, had eaten of the tree the
Lord God called to the man and asked him, "Where
are you?" He answered, "I heard you in the garden; but I
was afraid, because I was naked, so I hid myself." Then
he asked, "Who told you that you were naked? You have
eaten, then, from the tree of which I had forbidden you
to eat!" The man replied, "The woman whom you put
here with me—she gave me fruit from the tree, and so I
ate it." The Lord God then asked the woman, "Why did
you do such a thing?" The woman answered, "The serpent tricked me into it, so I ate it."
   Then the Lord God said to the serpent:
   "Because you have done this, you shall be banned
      from all the animals
      and from all the wild creatures;
   on your belly shall you crawl,
      and dirt shall you eat
      all the days of your life.
   I will put enmity between you and the woman,
      and between your offspring and hers;
   he will strike at your head
      while you strike at his heel."
   The man called his wife Eve, because she became
the mother of all the living.—The word of the Lord. ℟.
Thanks be to God. ↓

RESPONSORIAL PSALM Ps 98   [God's Salvation]

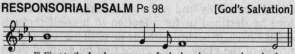

℟. Sing to the Lord a new song, for he has done marvelous deeds.

Sing to the LORD a new song,
  for he has done wondrous deeds;
his right hand has won victory for him,
  his holy arm.

℟. **Sing to the Lord a new song, for he has done marvelous deeds.**

The LORD has made his salvation known:
  in the sight of the nations he has revealed his justice.
He has remembered his kindness and his faithfulness
  toward the house of Israel.

℟. **Sing to the Lord a new song, for he has done marvelous deeds.**

All the ends of the earth have seen
  the salvation by our God.
Sing joyfully to the LORD, all you lands;
  break into song; sing praise.

℟. **Sing to the Lord a new song, for he has done marvelous deeds.** ↓

SECOND READING Eph 1:3-6, 11-12   [God's Saving Plan]

God is praised for revealing his plan of salvation. Whatever God wills he works effectively and surely to accomplish. Let us make his will our will.

A reading from the letter of Saint Paul to the Ephesians

BROTHERS and sisters: Blessed be the God and Father of our Lord Jesus Christ, who has blessed us in Christ with every spiritual blessing in the heavens, as he chose us in him, before the foundation of the world, to be holy and without blemish before him. In love he destined us for adoption to himself through Jesus Christ, in accord with the favor of his will, for the praise of the glory of his grace that he granted us in the beloved.

In him we were also chosen, destined in accord with the purpose of the One who accomplishes all things according to the intention of his will, so that we might exist for the praise of his glory, we who first hoped in Christ.—The word of the Lord. ℟. **Thanks be to God.** ↓

ALLELUIA Cf. Lk 1:28   [Blessed among Women]

℟. **Alleluia, alleluia.**
Hail, Mary, full of grace, the Lord is with you;
blessed are you among women.
℟. **Alleluia, alleluia.** ↓

GOSPEL Lk 1:26-38   [Mary's Great Holiness]

Mary has received a promise of supreme grace and blessing and accepts it in faith, assenting to God's Word with her "Amen."

℣. The Lord be with you. ℟. **And with your spirit.**
✛ A reading from the holy Gospel according to Luke.
℟. **Glory to you, O Lord.**

THE angel Gabriel was sent from God to a town of Galilee called Nazareth, to a virgin betrothed to a man named Joseph, of the house of David, and the virgin's name was Mary. And coming to her, he said, "Hail, full of grace! The Lord is with you." But she was greatly troubled at what was said and pondered what sort of greeting this might be. Then the angel said to her, "Do not be afraid, Mary, for you have found favor with God. Behold, you will conceive in your womb and bear a son, and you shall name him Jesus. He will be great and will be called Son of the Most High, and the Lord God will give him the throne of David his father, and he will rule over the house of Jacob forever, and of his Kingdom there will be no end." But Mary said to the angel, "How can this be, since I have no relations with a man?" And the angel said to her in reply, "The Holy Spirit will come upon you, and the power of the Most High will overshadow you. Therefore the child to be born will be called holy, the Son of God. And behold, Elizabeth, your relative, has also conceived a son in her old age, and this is the sixth month for her who was called barren; for nothing will be impossible for God." Mary said, "Behold, I am the handmaid of the Lord. May it be done to me according to your word." Then the angel departed from her.—The Gospel of the Lord. ℟. **Praise to you, Lord Jesus Christ.**

→ No. 15, p. 18

PRAYER OVER THE OFFERINGS
[Helped by Mary's Intercession]
Graciously accept the saving sacrifice
which we offer you, O Lord,
on the Solemnity of the Immaculate Conception
of the Blessed Virgin Mary,
and grant that, as we profess her,
on account of your prevenient grace,
to be untouched by any stain of sin,
so, through her intercession,
we may be delivered from all our faults.
Through Christ our Lord.
℟. **Amen.** ↓

PREFACE (P 58)   [Mary Our Advocate]
℣. The Lord be with you. ℟. **And with your spirit.**
℣. Lift up your hearts. ℟. **We lift them up to the Lord.**
℣. Let us give thanks to the Lord our God. ℟. **It is right and just.**

It is truly right and just, our duty and our salvation,
always and everywhere to give you thanks,
Lord, holy Father, almighty and eternal God.

For you preserved the most Blessed Virgin Mary
from all stain of original sin,
so that in her, endowed with the rich fullness of your
   grace,
you might prepare a worthy Mother for your Son
and signify the beginning of the Church,
his beautiful Bride without spot or wrinkle.

She, the most pure Virgin, was to bring forth a Son,
the innocent Lamb who would wipe away our offenses;
you placed her above all others
to be for your people an advocate of grace
and a model of holiness.

And so, in company with the choirs of Angels,
we praise you, and with joy we proclaim:

→ No. 23, p. 23

COMMUNION ANT.   [Glorious Things Spoken of Mary]
**Glorious things are spoken of you, O Mary, for from
you arose the sun of justice, Christ our God.** ↓

PRAYER AFTER COMMUNION   [Heal Our Wounds]
May the Sacrament we have received,
O Lord our God,
heal in us the wounds of that fault
from which in a singular way
you preserved Blessed Mary in her Immaculate
   Conception.
Through Christ our Lord.
℟. **Amen.**   → No. 30, p. 77

Optional Solemn Blessings, p. 97, and Prayers over the People, p. 105

"[John] preached good news to the people."

DECEMBER 13

3rd SUNDAY OF ADVENT

ENTRANCE ANT. Phil 4:4-5   [Mounting Joy]

Rejoice in the Lord always; again I say, rejoice. Indeed, the Lord is near. ➜ No. 2, p. 10 (Omit Gloria)

COLLECT   [Joy of Salvation]

O God, who see how your people
faithfully await the feast of the Lord's Nativity,
enable us, we pray,
to attain the joys of so great a salvation
and to celebrate them always
with solemn worship and glad rejoicing.
Through our Lord Jesus Christ, your Son,
who lives and reigns with you in the unity of the Holy
    Spirit,
one God, for ever and ever. ℟. **Amen.** ↓

FIRST READING Zep 3:14-18a [Joy Over the Mighty Savior]

Zephaniah writes that Israel should shout for joy. Her King, the Lord, is in her midst. The Lord is a mighty savior. Israel should not be discouraged.

127

A reading from the Book of the Prophet Zephaniah

SHOUT for joy, O daughter Zion!
　Sing joyfully, O Israel!
Be glad and exult with all your heart,
　　O daughter Jerusalem!
The LORD has removed the judgment against you,
　he has turned away your enemies;
the King of Israel, the LORD, is in your midst,
　　you have no further misfortune to fear.
On that day, it shall be said to Jerusalem:
　　Fear not, O Zion, be not discouraged!
The LORD, your God, is in your midst,
　　a mighty savior;
he will rejoice over you with gladness,
　　and renew you in his love,
he will sing joyfully because of you,
　　as one sings at festivals.
The word of the Lord. ℟. **Thanks be to God.** ↓

RESPONSORIAL PSALM Is 12　　[Joy Over the Holy One]

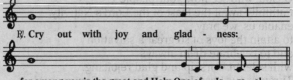

℟. Cry out with joy and glad - ness:

for among you is the great and Holy One of　Is - ra - el.

God indeed is my savior;
　I am confident and unafraid.
My strength and my courage is the LORD,
　and he has been my savior.
With joy you will draw water
　at the fountain of salvation.

℟. **Cry out with joy and gladness: for among you is the
　great and Holy One of Israel.**

Give thanks to the LORD, acclaim his name;
   among the nations make known his deeds,
   proclaim how exalted is his name.

℞. **Cry out with joy and gladness: for among you is the great and Holy One of Israel.**

Sing praise to the LORD for his glorious achievement;
   let this be known throughout all the earth.
Shout with exultation, O city of Zion,
   for great in your midst
   is the Holy One of Israel!

℞. **Cry out with joy and gladness: for among you is the great and Holy One of Israel.** ↓

SECOND READING Phil 4:4-7   [Rejoice in the Lord]

Christians should rejoice in the Lord. They should take their prayers and petitions to him. God will watch over his children.

A reading from the Letter of Saint Paul
to the Philippians

B ROTHERS and sisters: Rejoice in the Lord always.
I shall say it again: rejoice! Your kindness should be known to all. The Lord is near. Have no anxiety at all, but in everything, by prayer and petition, with thanksgiving, make your requests known to God. Then the peace of God that surpasses all understanding will guard your hearts and minds in Christ Jesus.—The word of the Lord. ℞. **Thanks be to God.** ↓

ALLELUIA Is 61:1 (cited in Lk 4:18)   [Glad Tidings]

℞. **Alleluia, alleluia.**
The Spirit of the Lord is upon me,
because he has anointed me
to bring glad tidings to the poor.
℞. **Alleluia, alleluia.** ↓

GOSPEL Lk 3:10-18   [Majesty of the Messiah]

John preached a law of sharing. He baptized and admonished all to be just and loving and to pray. John tells the people about the majesty of the Messiah.

℣. The Lord be with you. ℟. **And with your spirit.**

✠ A reading from the holy Gospel according to Luke.
℟. **Glory to you, O Lord.**

THE crowds asked John the Baptist, "What should we do?" He said to them in reply, "Whoever has two cloaks should share with the person who has none. And whoever has food should do likewise." Even tax collectors came to be baptized and they said to him, "Teacher, what should we do?" He answered them, "Stop collecting more than what is prescribed." Soldiers also asked him, "And what is it that we should do?" He told them, "Do not practice extortion, do not falsely accuse anyone, and be satisfied with your wages."

Now the people were filled with expectation, and all were asking in their hearts whether John might be the Christ. John answered them all, saying, "I am baptizing you with water, but one mightier than I is coming. I am not worthy to loosen the thongs of his sandals. He will baptize you with the Holy Spirit and fire. His winnowing fan is in his hand to clear his threshing floor and to gather the wheat into his barn, but the chaff he will burn with unquenchable fire." Exhorting them in many other ways, he preached good news to the people.— The Gospel of the Lord. ℟. **Praise to you, Lord Jesus Christ.**   ➜ No. 15, p. 18

PRAYER OVER THE OFFERINGS   [Unceasing Sacrifice]

May the sacrifice of our worship, Lord, we pray,
be offered to you unceasingly,
to complete what was begun in sacred mystery
and powerfully accomplish for us your saving work.

Through Christ our Lord.
℟. **Amen.**   ➜ No. 21, p. 22 (Pref. P 1 or 2)

COMMUNION ANT. Cf. Is 35:4   [Trust in God]
**Say to the faint of heart: Be strong and do not fear.
Behold, our God will come, and he will save us.** ↓

PRAYER AFTER COMMUNION   [Preparation for Christ]
We implore your mercy, Lord,
that this divine sustenance may cleanse us of our faults
and prepare us for the coming feasts.
Through Christ our Lord.
℟. **Amen.**   ➜ No. 30, p. 77

Optional Solemn Blessings, p. 97, and Prayers over the People, p. 105

*"Blessed are you among women, and blessed is the fruit
of your womb."*

DECEMBER 20

4th SUNDAY OF ADVENT

ENTRANCE ANT. Cf. Is 45:8   [The Advent Plea]
**Drop down dew from above, you heavens, and let the
clouds rain down the Just One; let the earth be opened
and bring forth a Savior.** ➜ No. 2, p. 10 (Omit Gloria)

COLLECT   [From Suffering to Glory]

Pour forth, we beseech you, O Lord,
your grace into our hearts,
that we, to whom the Incarnation of Christ your Son
was made known by the message of an Angel,
may by his Passion and Cross
be brought to the glory of his Resurrection.
Who lives and reigns with you in the unity of the Holy
  Spirit,
one God, for ever and ever. R̶. **Amen.** ↓

FIRST READING Mi 5:1-4a   [The Messiah from Bethlehem]

Micah speaks of the glory of Bethlehem, a lone town
among the people of Judah. From Bethlehem shall come
forth the promised one who shall stand firm and strong in
the Lord.

A reading from the Book of the Prophet Micah

THUS says the LORD:
  You, Bethlehem-Ephrathah,
    too small to be among the clans of Judah,
from you shall come forth for me
    one who is to be ruler in Israel;
whose origin is from of old,
    from ancient times.
Therefore the LORD will give them up, until the time
    when she who is to give birth has borne,
and the rest of his kindred shall return
    to the children of Israel.
He shall stand firm and shepherd his flock
    by the strength of the LORD,
    in the majestic name of the LORD, his God;
and they shall remain, for now his greatness
    shall reach to the ends of the earth;
    he shall be peace.
The word of the Lord. R̶. **Thanks be to God.** ↓

RESPONSORIAL PSALM Ps 80   [Turn to the Lord]

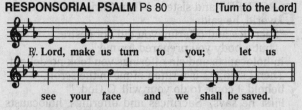

R̶. Lord, make us turn to you; let us see your face and we shall be saved.

O shepherd of Israel, hearken,
   from your throne upon the cherubim, shine forth.
Rouse your power,
   and come to save us.

R̶. **Lord, make us turn to you; let us see your face and we shall be saved.**

Once again, O LORD of hosts,
   look down from heaven, and see;
take care of this vine,
   and protect what your right hand has planted,
   the son of man whom you yourself made strong.

R̶. **Lord, make us turn to you; let us see your face and we shall be saved.**

May your help be with the man of your right hand,
   with the son of man whom you yourself made
      strong.
Then we will no more withdraw from you;
   give us new life, and we will call upon your name.

R̶. **Lord, make us turn to you; let us see your face and we shall be saved.** ↓

SECOND READING Heb 10:5-10   [Doing God's Will]
   Jesus said the sacrifices, sin offerings and holocausts did not delight the Lord. But he has come to do the will of God—to establish a second covenant.

   A reading from the Letter to the Hebrews

B ROTHERS and sisters: When Christ came into the
world, he said:
"Sacrifice and offering you did not desire,
   but a body you prepared for me;
in holocausts and sin offerings you took no delight.
Then I said, 'As is written of me in the scroll,
behold, I come to do your will, O God.' "
First he says, "Sacrifices and offerings, holocausts
and sin offerings, you neither desired nor delighted
in." These are offered according to the law. Then he
says, "Behold, I come to do your will." He takes away
the first to establish the second. By this "will," we have
been consecrated through the offering of the body of
Jesus Christ once for all.—The word of the Lord.
℟. **Thanks be to God.** ↓

ALLELUIA Lk 1:38   **[The Lord's Handmaid]**
℟. **Alleluia, alleluia.**
Behold, I am the handmaid of the Lord.
May it be done to me according to your word.
℟. **Alleluia, alleluia.** ↓

GOSPEL Lk 1:39-45   **[The Visitation]**
**Mary went to visit Elizabeth who was also blessed by the
Holy Spirit. Elizabeth greeted Mary: "Blessed are you
among women and blessed is the fruit of your womb."**

℣. The Lord be with you. ℟. **And with your spirit.**
✚ A reading from the holy Gospel according to Luke.
℟. **Glory to you, O Lord.**

M ARY set out and traveled to the hill country in
haste to a town of Judah, where she entered the
house of Zechariah and greeted Elizabeth. When
Elizabeth heard Mary's greeting, the infant leaped in
her womb, and Elizabeth, filled with the Holy Spirit,
cried out in a loud voice and said, "Blessed are you
among women, and blessed is the fruit of your womb.

And how does this happen to me, that the mother of my Lord should come to me? For at the moment the sound of your greeting reached my ears, the infant in my womb leaped for joy. Blessed are you who believed that what was spoken to you by the Lord would be fulfilled."—The Gospel of the Lord. ℟. **Praise to you, Lord Jesus Christ.**   → No. 15, p. 18

PRAYER OVER THE OFFERINGS   [Power of the Spirit]

May the Holy Spirit, O Lord,
sanctify these gifts laid upon your altar,
just as he filled with his power the womb of the Blessed
    Virgin Mary.
Through Christ our Lord.
℟. **Amen.**   → No. 21, p. 22 (Pref. P 2)

COMMUNION ANT. Is 7:14   [The Virgin Mother]

Behold, a Virgin shall conceive and bear a son; and his name will be called Emmanuel. ↓

PRAYER AFTER COMMUNION   [Worthy Celebration]

Having received this pledge of eternal redemption,
we pray, almighty God,
that, as the feast day of our salvation draws ever nearer,
so we may press forward all the more eagerly
to the worthy celebration of the mystery of your Son's
    Nativity.
Who lives and reigns for ever and ever.
℟. **Amen.**   → No. 30, p. 77

Optional Solemn Blessings, p. 97, and Prayers over the People, p. 105

The Word is made flesh.

DECEMBER 25

THE NATIVITY OF THE LORD [CHRISTMAS]

Solemnity

AT THE MASS DURING THE NIGHT

ENTRANCE ANT. Ps 2:7   [Son of God]
The Lord said to me: You are my Son. It is I who have begotten you this day.   → No. 2, p. 10

OR   [True Peace]
Let us all rejoice in the Lord, for our Savior has been born in the world. Today true peace has come down to us from heaven.   → No. 2, p. 10

COLLECT   [Eternal Gladness]
O God, who have made this most sacred night
radiant with the splendor of the true light,
grant, we pray, that we, who have known the mysteries
   of his light on earth,
may also delight in his gladness in heaven.
Who lives and reigns with you in the unity of the Holy
   Spirit,
one God, for ever and ever. ℟. **Amen.** ↓

FIRST READING Is 9:1-6   [The Messiah's Kingdom]

> The spell of darkness, the shame of sin is broken—the Prince of light is born to us.

A reading from the Book of the Prophet Isaiah

THE people who walked in darkness
  have seen a great light;
upon those who dwelt in the land of gloom
  a light has shone.
You have brought them abundant joy
  and great rejoicing,
as they rejoice before you as at the harvest,
  as people make merry when dividing spoils.
For the yoke that burdened them,
  the pole on their shoulder,
and the rod of their taskmaster
  you have smashed, as on the day of Midian.
For every boot that tramped in battle,
  every cloak rolled in blood,
  will be burned as fuel for flames.
For a child is born to us, a son is given us;
  upon his shoulder dominion rests.
They name him Wonder-Counselor, God-Hero,
  Father-Forever, Prince of Peace.
His dominion is vast
  and forever peaceful,
from David's throne, and over his kingdom,
  which he confirms and sustains
by judgment and justice,
  both now and forever.
The zeal of the LORD of hosts will do this!
The word of the Lord. ℟. **Thanks be to God.** ↓

RESPONSORIAL PSALM Ps 96   [Bless the Lord]

℟. Today is born our Sav - ior, Christ the Lord.

Sing to the LORD a new song;
  sing to the LORD, all you lands.
Sing to the LORD; bless his name.

℟. **Today is born our Savior, Christ the Lord.**

Announce his salvation, day after day.
  Tell his glory among the nations;
    among all peoples, his wondrous deeds.

℟. **Today is born our Savior, Christ the Lord.**

Let the heavens be glad and the earth rejoice;
  let the sea and what fills it resound;
    let the plains be joyful and all that is in them!
Then shall all the trees of the forest exult.

℟. **Today is born our Savior, Christ the Lord.**

They shall exult before the LORD, for he comes;
  for he comes to rule the earth.
He shall rule the world with justice
  and the peoples with his constancy.

℟. **Today is born our Savior, Christ the Lord.** ↓

SECOND READING Ti 2:11-14   [Salvation for All]
  We look to the second coming of Christ in glory. Through
  his cross we are freed from the darkness of sin.

  A reading from the Letter of Saint Paul to Titus

B ELOVED: The grace of God has appeared, saving
  all and training us to reject godless ways and
worldly desires and to live temperately, justly, and
devoutly in this age, as we await the blessed hope, the
appearance of the glory of our great God and savior
Jesus Christ, who gave himself for us to deliver us
from all lawlessness and to cleanse for himself a people as his own, eager to do what is good.—The word of
the Lord. ℟. **Thanks be to God.** ↓

ALLELUIA Lk 2:10-11   [Great Joy]

℟. **Alleluia, alleluia.**
I proclaim to you good news of great joy:
today a Savior is born for us,
Christ the Lord.
℟. **Alleluia, alleluia.** ↓

GOSPEL Lk 2:1-14   [Birth of Christ]

Rejoice in the good news—our Savior is born, and he is
revealed to us by the witness of shepherds.

℣. The Lord be with you. ℟. **And with your spirit.**
✠ A reading from the holy Gospel according to Luke.
℟. **Glory to you, O Lord.**

IN those days a decree went out from Caesar
Augustus that the whole world should be enrolled.
This was the first enrollment, when Quirinius was governor of Syria. So all went to be enrolled, each to his
own town. And Joseph too went up from Galilee from
the town of Nazareth to Judea, to the city of David that
is called Bethlehem, because he was of the house and
family of David, to be enrolled with Mary, his
betrothed, who was with child. While they were there,
the time came for her to have her child, and she gave
birth to her firstborn son. She wrapped him in swaddling clothes and laid him in a manger, because there
was no room for them in the inn.

Now there were shepherds in that region living in
the fields and keeping the night watch over their flock.
The angel of the Lord appeared to them and the glory
of the Lord shone around them, and they were struck
with great fear. The angel said to them, "Do not be
afraid; for behold, I proclaim to you good news of
great joy that will be for all the people. For today in the
city of David a savior has been born for you who is
Christ and Lord. And this will be a sign for you: you

will find an infant wrapped in swaddling clothes and lying in a manger." And suddenly there was a multitude of the heavenly host with the angel, praising God and saying:

"Glory to God in the highest
  and on earth peace to those on whom his favor rests."

The Gospel of the Lord. ℟. **Praise to you, Lord Jesus Christ.**   → No. 15, p. 18

The Creed is said. All kneel at the words and by the Holy Spirit was incarnate.

PRAYER OVER THE OFFERINGS   [Become Like Christ]

May the oblation of this day's feast
be pleasing to you, O Lord, we pray,
that through this most holy exchange
we may be found in the likeness of Christ,
in whom our nature is united to you.
Who lives and reigns for ever and ever.
℟. **Amen.**   → No. 21, p. 22 (Pref. P 3-5)

When the Roman Canon is used, the proper form of the Communicantes *(In communion with those) is said.*

COMMUNION ANT. Jn 1:14   [Glory of Christ]
The Word became flesh, and we have seen his glory. ↓

PRAYER AFTER COMMUNION   [Union with Christ]

Grant us, we pray, O Lord our God,
that we, who are gladdened by participation
in the feast of our Redeemer's Nativity,
may through an honorable way of life become worthy of union with him.
Who lives and reigns for ever and ever.
℟. **Amen.**   → No. 30, p. 77

Optional Solemn Blessings, p. 97, and Prayers over the People, p. 105

AT THE MASS AT DAWN

ENTRANCE ANT. Cf. Is 9:1, 5; Lk 1:33   [Prince of Peace]

Today a light will shine upon us, for the Lord is born for us; and he will be called Wondrous God, Prince of peace, Father of future ages: and his reign will be without end.   → No. 2, p. 10

COLLECT   [Light of Faith]

Grant, we pray, almighty God,
that, as we are bathed in the new radiance of your
    incarnate Word,
the light of faith, which illumines our minds,
may also shine through in our deeds.
Through our Lord Jesus Christ, your Son,
who lives and reigns with you in the unity of the Holy
    Spirit,
one God, for ever and ever.
℟. **Amen.** ↓

FIRST READING Is 62:11-12   [The Savior's Birth]

Our Savior comes. He makes us a holy people and redeems
us.

A reading from the Book of the Prophet Isaiah

SEE, the LORD proclaims
    to the ends of the earth:
say to daughter Zion,
    your savior comes!
Here is his reward with him,
    his recompense before him.
They shall be called the holy people,
    the redeemed of the LORD,
and you shall be called "Frequented,"
    a city that is not forsaken.
The word of the Lord. ℟. **Thanks be to God.** ↓

RESPONSORIAL PSALM Ps 97   [Be Glad in the Lord]

℟.   A light will shine on us this day: the Lord is born for us.

The LORD is king; let the earth rejoice;
   let the many isles be glad.
The heavens proclaim his justice,
   and all peoples see his glory.

℟. **A light will shine on us this day: the Lord is born for us.**

Light dawns for the just;
   and gladness, for the upright of heart.
Be glad in the LORD, you just,
   and give thanks to his holy name.

℟. **A light will shine on us this day: the Lord is born for us.** ↓

SECOND READING Ti 3:4-7   [Saved by God's Mercy]

By God's mercy we are saved from sin. Jesus became man that we might through him receive the Spirit.

A reading from the Letter of Saint Paul to Titus

BELOVED:
  When the kindness and generous love
    of God our savior appeared,
  not because of any righteous deeds we had done
    but because of his mercy,
  he saved us through the bath of rebirth
    and renewal by the Holy Spirit,
  whom he richly poured out on us
    through Jesus Christ our savior,
  so that we might be justified by his grace
    and become heirs in hope of eternal life.
The word of the Lord. ℟. **Thanks be to God.** ↓

ALLELUIA Lk 2:14   [Glory to God]

℟. **Alleluia, alleluia.**

Glory to God in the highest,
and on earth peace to those
on whom his favor rests.

℟. **Alleluia, alleluia.** ↓

GOSPEL Lk 2:15-20   [Jesus, the God-Man]

**The wonder of salvation is revealed to the shepherds and
to us. The love of God is manifest because he is with us.**

℣. The Lord be with you. ℟. **And with your spirit.**

✜ A reading from the holy Gospel according to Luke.

℟. **Glory to you, O Lord.**

WHEN the angels went away from them to heaven,
the shepherds said to one another,"Let us go, then,
to Bethlehem to see this thing that has taken place, which
the Lord has made known to us." So they went in haste
and found Mary and Joseph, and the infant lying in the
manger. When they saw this, they made known the message that had been told them about this child. All who
heard it were amazed by what had been told them by the
shepherds. And Mary kept all these things, reflecting on
them in her heart. Then the shepherds returned, glorifying and praising God for all they had heard and seen, just
as it had been told to them.—The Gospel of the Lord.

℟. **Praise to you, Lord Jesus Christ.**   → No. 15, p. 18

The Creed is said. All kneel at the words and by the Holy
Spirit was incarnate.

PRAYER OVER THE OFFERINGS   [Gift of Divine Life]

May our offerings be worthy, we pray, O Lord,
of the mysteries of the Nativity this day,
that, just as Christ was born a man and also shone forth
    as God,
so these earthly gifts may confer on us what is divine.
Through Christ our Lord.

℟. **Amen.**   → No. 21, p. 22 (Pref. P 3-5)

When the Roman Canon is used, the proper form of the Communicantes *(In communion with those) is said.*

COMMUNION ANT. Cf. Zec 9:9   [The Holy One]

Rejoice, O Daughter Sion; lift up praise, Daughter Jerusalem: Behold, your King will come, the Holy One and Savior of the world. ↓

PRAYER AFTER COMMUNION   [Fullness of Faith]

Grant us, Lord, as we honor with joyful devotion
the Nativity of your Son,
that we may come to know with fullness of faith
the hidden depths of this mystery
and to love them ever more and more.
Through Christ our Lord.
℟. **Amen.**   → No. 30, p. 77

Optional Solemn Blessings, p. 97, and Prayers over the People, p. 105

AT THE MASS DURING THE DAY

ENTRANCE ANT. Cf. Is 9:5   [The Gift of God's Son]

A child is born for us, and a son is given to us; his scepter of power rests upon his shoulder, and his name will be called Messenger of great counsel.
→ No. 2, p. 10

COLLECT   [Share in Christ's Divinity]

O God, who wonderfully created the dignity of human
 nature
and still more wonderfully restored it,
grant, we pray,
that we may share in the divinity of Christ,
who humbled himself to share in our humanity.
Who lives and reigns with you in the unity of the Holy
 Spirit,
one God, for ever and ever. ℟. **Amen.** ↓

FIRST READING Is 52:7-10   [Your God Is King]

The good news, the Gospel—the Lord comforts his people by announcing our salvation.

A reading from the Book of the Prophet Isaiah

HOW beautiful upon the mountains
are the feet of him who brings glad tidings,
announcing peace, bearing good news,
    announcing salvation, and saying to Zion,
    "Your God is King!"

Hark! Your sentinels raise a cry,
    together they shout for joy,
for they see directly, before their eyes,
    the LORD restoring Zion.
Break out together in song,
    O ruins of Jerusalem!
For the LORD comforts his people,
    he redeems Jerusalem.
The LORD has bared his holy arm
    in the sight of all the nations;
all the ends of the earth will behold
    the salvation of our God.
The word of the Lord. ℟. **Thanks be to God.** ↓

RESPONSORIAL PSALM Ps 98   [Sing a New Song]

℟. All the ends of the earth have seen the saving power of God.

Sing to the LORD a new song,
    for he has done wondrous deeds;
his right hand has won victory for him,
    his holy arm.

℟. **All the ends of the earth have seen the saving power of God.**

The LORD has made his salvation known:
  in the sight of the nations he has revealed his jus-
      tice.
He has remembered his kindness and his faithful-
    ness
  toward the house of Israel.

℟. **All the ends of the earth have seen the saving
  power of God.**

All the ends of the earth have seen
  the salvation by our God.
Sing joyfully to the LORD, all you lands;
  break into song; sing praise.

℟. **All the ends of the earth have seen the saving
  power of God.**

Sing praise to the LORD with the harp,
  with the harp and melodious song.
With trumpets and the sound of the horn
  sing joyfully before the King, the LORD.

℟. **All the ends of the earth have seen the saving
  power of God.** ↓

SECOND READING Heb 1:1-6 [God Speaks through Jesus]
  Now God speaks to us more clearly than ever before. His
  Son is with us—God is with us; we are his people.

    A reading from the Letter to the Hebrews

B ROTHERS and sisters: In times past, God spoke in
  partial and various ways to our ancestors through
the prophets; in these last days, he has spoken to us
through the Son, whom he made heir of all things and
through whom he created the universe,
    who is the refulgence of his glory, the very imprint
      of his being,
    and who sustains all things by his mighty word.
    When he had accomplished purification from sins,

he took his seat at the right hand of the Majesty on
    high,
as far superior to the angels
as the name he has inherited is more excellent than
    theirs.
For to which of the angels did God ever say:
You are my son; this day I have begotten you?
Or again:
I will be a father to him, and he shall be a son to me?
And again, when he leads the firstborn into the
world, he says:
Let all the angels of God worship him.
The word of the Lord. ℟. **Thanks be to God.** ↓

ALLELUIA   [Adore the Lord]
℟. **Alleluia, alleluia.**
A holy day has dawned upon us.
Come, you nations, and adore the Lord.
For today a great light has come upon the earth.
℟. **Alleluia, alleluia.** ↓

GOSPEL Jn 1:1-18 or 1:1-5, 9-14   [The True Light]
    **The Word of God is the living Word. The Word became
    flesh and lives in our midst.**

*[If the "Shorter Form" is used, the indented text in brackets is
omitted.]*

℣. The Lord be with you. ℟. **And with your spirit.**
✠ A reading from the holy Gospel according to John.
℟. **Glory to you, O Lord.**

IN the beginning was the Word,
    and the Word was with God,
    and the Word was God.
He was in the beginning with God.
All things came to be through him,
    and without him nothing came to be.
What came to be through him was life,
    and this life was the light of the human race;

the light shines in the darkness,
   and the darkness has not overcome it.
      [A man named John was sent from God. He
      came for testimony, to testify to the light, so
      that all might believe through him. He was not
      the light, but came to testify to the light.]
The true light, which enlightens everyone, was coming
into the world.
   He was in the world,
      and the world came to be through him,
      but the world did not know him.
   He came to what was his own,
      but his own people did not accept him.

But to those who did accept him he gave power to
become children of God, to those who believe in his
name, who were born not by natural generation nor by
human choice nor by a man's decision but of God.
   And the Word became flesh
      and made his dwelling among us,
      and we saw his glory,
      the glory as of the Father's only Son,
      full of grace and truth.
         [John testified to him and cried out, saying,
         "This was he of whom I said, 'The one who is
         coming after me ranks ahead of me because
         he existed before me.' " From his fullness we
         have all received, grace in place of grace,
         because while the law was given through
         Moses, grace and truth came through Jesus
         Christ. No one has ever seen God. The only
         Son, God, who is at the Father's side, has
         revealed him.]
The Gospel of the Lord. ℟. **Praise to you, Lord Jesus
Christ.**   → No. 15, p. 18

The Creed is said. All kneel at the words and by the Holy Spirit was incarnate.

PRAYER OVER THE OFFERINGS   [Reconciliation]

Make acceptable, O Lord, our oblation on this solemn day,
when you manifested the reconciliation
that makes us wholly pleasing in your sight
and inaugurated for us the fullness of divine worship.
Through Christ our Lord.
℟. **Amen.**   → No. 21, p. 22 (Pref. P 3-5)

When the Roman Canon is used, the proper form of the Communicantes *(In communion with those) is said.*

COMMUNION ANT. Cf. Ps 98 (97):3   [God's Power]

All the ends of the earth have seen the salvation of our God. ↓

PRAYER AFTER COMMUNION   [Giver of Immortality]

Grant, O merciful God,
that, just as the Savior of the world, born this day,
is the author of divine generation for us,
so he may be the giver even of immortality.
Who lives and reigns for ever and ever.
℟. **Amen.**   → No. 30, p. 77

Optional Solemn Blessings, p. 97, and Prayers over the People, p. 105

*"He went down with them and came to Nazareth,
and was obedient to them."*

DECEMBER 27

THE HOLY FAMILY OF
JESUS, MARY, AND JOSEPH

Feast

ENTRANCE ANT. Lk 2:16   [Jesus, Mary, and Joseph]
**The shepherds went in haste, and found Mary and
Joseph and the Infant lying in a manger.** ➔ No. 2, p. 10

COLLECT   [Shining Example]

O God, who were pleased to give us
the shining example of the Holy Family,
graciously grant that we may imitate them
in practicing the virtues of family life and in the bonds
   of charity,
and so, in the joy of your house,
delight one day in eternal rewards.
Through our Lord Jesus Christ, your Son,
who lives and reigns with you in the unity of the Holy
   Spirit,
one God, for ever and ever. ℟. **Amen.** ↓

*The following readings (except the Gospel) are optional. In
their place, the readings for Year A, pp. 155-157 may be used.*

FIRST READING 1 Sm 1:20-22, 24-28   [God's Creative Love]

This reading teaches us that motherhood and life are a gift of God. The presence of children in a family signals the continuation of life and manifests the newness of God's love, which gives origin to ever new creatures.

A reading from the first Book of Samuel

IN those days Hannah conceived, and at the end of her term bore a son whom she called Samuel, since she had asked the LORD for him. The next time her husband Elkanah was going up with the rest of his household to offer the customary sacrifice to the LORD and to fulfill his vows, Hannah did not go, explaining to her husband, "Once the child is weaned, I will take him to appear before the LORD and to remain there forever; I will offer him as a perpetual nazirite."

Once Samuel was weaned, Hannah brought him up with her, along with a three-year-old bull, an ephah of flour, and a skin of wine, and presented him at the temple of the LORD in Shiloh. After the boy's father had sacrificed the young bull, Hannah, his mother, approached Eli and said: "Pardon, my lord! As you live, my lord, I am the woman who stood near you here, praying to the LORD. I prayed for this child, and the LORD granted my request. Now I, in turn, give him to the LORD; as long as he lives, he shall be dedicated to the LORD." Hannah left Samuel there.—The word of the Lord. ℟. **Thanks be to God.** ↓

RESPONSORIAL PSALM Ps 84   [Love for God's House]

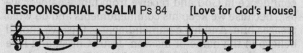

℟. Blessed   are they who dwell in your house, O Lord.

How lovely is your dwelling place, O LORD of hosts!
  My soul yearns and pines for the courts of the LORD.
My heart and my flesh cry out for the living God.

℟. **Blessed are they who dwell in your house, O Lord.**

Happy they who dwell in your house!
    Continually they praise you.
Happy the men whose strength you are!
    Their hearts are set upon the pilgrimage.

℟. **Blessed are they who dwell in your house, O Lord.**

O LORD of hosts, hear our prayer;
    hearken, O God of Jacob!
O God, behold our shield,
    and look upon the face of your anointed.

℟. **Blessed are they who dwell in your house, O Lord.** ↓

SECOND READING 1 Jn 3:1-2, 21-24   [Children of God]

Every family must be a mirror of the divine love because the root of every love is God. Therefore, members of a family should deal lovingly with one another.

A reading from the first Letter of Saint John

BELOVED: See what love the Father has bestowed on us that we may be called the children of God. And so we are. The reason the world does not know us is that it did not know him. Beloved, we are God's children now; what we shall be has not yet been revealed. We do know that when it is revealed we shall be like him, for we shall see him as he is.

Beloved, if our hearts do not condemn us, we have confidence in God and receive from him whatever we ask, because we keep his commandments and do what pleases him. And his commandment is this: we should believe in the name of his Son, Jesus Christ, and love one another just as he commanded us. Those who keep his commandments remain in him, and he in them, and the way we know that he remains in us is from the Spirit he gave us.—The word of the Lord. ℟. **Thanks be to God.** ↓

ALLELUIA Cf. Acts 16:14b   [Open Hearts]

℟. **Alleluia, alleluia.**

Open our hearts, O Lord,

to listen to the words of your Son.

℟. **Alleluia, alleluia.** ↓

GOSPEL Lk 2:41-52   [Jesus Was Obedient to Them]

> Jesus and his parents go to Jerusalem for the Passover.
> Upon returning, Jesus is separated from them. Mary and
> Joseph find him in the temple teaching. When Mary asked
> why, Jesus replied that he must be doing his Father's work.
> Jesus returned with Mary and Joseph to Nazareth.

℣. The Lord be with you. ℟. **And with your spirit.**

✤ A reading from the holy Gospel according to Luke.

℟. **Glory to you, O Lord.**

EACH year Jesus' parents went to Jerusalem for the
feast of Passover, and when he was twelve years old,
they went up according to festival custom. After they
had completed its days, as they were returning, the boy
Jesus remained behind in Jerusalem, but his parents did
not know it. Thinking that he was in the caravan, they
journeyed for a day and looked for him among their relatives and acquaintances, but not finding him, they
returned to Jerusalem to look for him. After three days
they found him in the temple, sitting in the midst of the
teachers, listening to them and asking them questions,
and all who heard him were astounded at his understanding and his answers. When his parents saw him,
they were astonished, and his mother said to him, "Son,
why have you done this to us? Your father and I have
been looking for you with great anxiety." And he said to
them, "Why were you looking for me? Did you not know
that I must be in my Father's house?" But they did not
understand what he said to them. He went down with
them and came to Nazareth, and was obedient to them;
and his mother kept all these things in her heart. And

Jesus advanced in wisdom and age and favor before God
and man.—The Gospel of the Lord. ℟. **Praise to you,
Lord Jesus Christ.** → No. 15, p. 18

PRAYER OVER THE OFFERINGS [Grace and Peace]

We offer you, Lord, the sacrifice of conciliation,
humbly asking that,
through the intercession of the Virgin Mother of God
    and Saint Joseph,
you may establish our families firmly in your grace
    and your peace.
Through Christ our Lord.
℟. **Amen.** → No. 21, p. 22 (Pref. P 3-5)

When the Roman Canon is used, the proper form of the
Communicantes (In communion with those) *is said.*

COMMUNION ANT. Bar 3:38 [God with Us]
**Our God has appeared on the earth, and lived among
us.** ↓

PRAYER AFTER COMMUNION [Imitate Their Example]

Bring those you refresh with this heavenly Sacrament,
most merciful Father,
to imitate constantly the example of the Holy Family,
so that, after the trials of this world,
we may share their company for ever.
Through Christ our Lord.
℟. **Amen.** → No. 30, p. 77

Optional Solemn Blessings, p. 97, and Prayers over the People, p. 105

The following readings from Year A may be used in place of the optional ones given on pp. 151-153.

FIRST READING Sir 3:2-6, 12-14   [Duties toward Parents]

Fidelity to Yahweh implies many particular virtues, and among them Sirach gives precedence to duties toward parents. He promises atonement for sin to those who honor their parents.

A reading from the Book of Sirach

GOD sets a father in honor over his children;
a mother's authority he confirms over her sons.
Whoever honors his father atones for sins,
   and preserves himself from them.
When he prays, he is heard;
   he stores up riches who reveres his mother.
Whoever honors his father is gladdened by children,
   and when he prays, is heard.
Whoever reveres his father will live a long life;
   he obeys his father who brings comfort to his
      mother.

My son, take care of your father when he is old;
   grieve him not as long as he lives.
Even if his mind fail, be considerate of him;
   revile him not all the days of his life;
kindness to a father will not be forgotten,
   firmly planted against the debt of your sins
      —a house raised in justice to you.
The word of the Lord. ℟. **Thanks be to God.** ↓

RESPONSORIAL PSALM Ps 128   [Happiness in Families]

℟. **Bles - sed are those who fear   the Lord and walk in   his ways.**

Blessed is everyone who fears the LORD,
   who walks in his ways!

For you shall eat the fruit of your handiwork;
    blessed shall you be, and favored.

℟. **Blessed are those who fear the Lord and walk in
    his ways.**

Your wife shall be like a fruitful vine
    in the recesses of your home;
your children like olive plants
    around your table.

℟. **Blessed are those who fear the Lord and walk in
    his ways.**

Behold, thus is the man blessed
    who fears the LORD.
The LORD bless you from Zion:
    may you see the prosperity of Jerusalem
    all the days of your life.

℟. **Blessed are those who fear the Lord and walk in
    his ways.** ↓

SECOND READING Col 3:12-21 or 3:12-17

[Plan for Family Life]

    Paul describes the life a Christian embraces through
    Baptism.

*[If the "Shorter Form" is used, the indented text in brackets is
omitted.]*

A reading from the Letter of Saint Paul to the Colossians

BROTHERS and sisters: Put on, as God's chosen
ones, holy and beloved, heartfelt compassion,
kindness, humility, gentleness, and patience, bearing
with one another and forgiving one another, if one has
a grievance against another; as the Lord has forgiven
you, so must you also do. And over all these put on
love, that is, the bond of perfection. And let the peace
of Christ control your hearts, the peace into which you
were also called in one body. And be thankful. Let the

word of Christ dwell in you richly, as in all wisdom you teach and admonish one another, singing psalms, hymns, and spiritual songs with gratitude in your hearts to God. And whatever you do, in word or in deed, do everything in the name of the Lord Jesus, giving thanks to God the Father through him.

> [Wives, be subordinate to your husbands, as is proper in the Lord. Husbands, love your wives, and avoid any bitterness toward them. Children, obey your parents in everything, for this is pleasing to the Lord. Fathers, do not provoke your children, so they may not become discouraged.]

The word of the Lord. ℟. **Thanks be to God.** ↓

ALLELUIA Col 3:15a, 16a   [Peace of Christ]

℟. **Alleluia, alleluia.**
Let the peace of Christ control your hearts;
let the word of Christ dwell in you richly.
℟. **Alleluia, alleluia.**

"He was named Jesus, . . ."

JANUARY 1, 2016

SOLEMNITY OF MARY, THE HOLY MOTHER OF GOD

ENTRANCE ANT.   [Hail, Holy Mother]

Hail, Holy Mother, who gave birth to the King who rules heaven and earth for ever.   ➥ No. 2, p. 10

OR Cf. Is 9:1, 5; Lk 1:33   [Wondrous God]

Today a light will shine upon us, for the Lord is born for us; and he will be called Wondrous God, Prince of peace, Father of future ages: and his reign will be without end.   ➥ No. 2, p. 10

COLLECT   [Mary's Intercession]

O God, who through the fruitful virginity of Blessed
    Mary
bestowed on the human race
the grace of eternal salvation,
grant, we pray,
that we may experience the intercession of her,
through whom we were found worthy
to receive the author of life,
our Lord Jesus Christ, your Son.

158

Who lives and reigns with you in the unity of the Holy
  Spirit,
one God, for ever and ever.
℞. **Amen.** ↓

FIRST READING Nm 6:22-27   [The Aaronic Blessing]

> **God speaks to Moses instructing him to have Aaron and
> the Israelites pray that he may answer their prayers with
> blessings.**

A reading from the Book of Numbers

THE LORD said to Moses: "Speak to Aaron and his
  sons and tell them: This is how you shall bless the
Israelites. Say to them:

The LORD bless you and keep you!
The LORD let his face shine upon you, and be gra-
  cious to you!
The LORD look upon you kindly and give you peace!

So shall they invoke my name upon the Israelites and
I will bless them."—The word of the Lord. ℞. **Thanks
be to God.** ↓

RESPONSORIAL PSALM Ps 67   [God Bless Us]

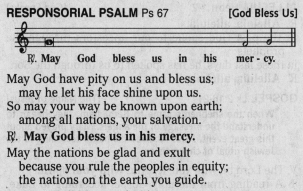

℞. **May   God   bless   us   in   his   mer - cy.**

May God have pity on us and bless us;
  may he let his face shine upon us.
So may your way be known upon earth;
  among all nations, your salvation.

℞. **May God bless us in his mercy.**

May the nations be glad and exult
  because you rule the peoples in equity;
  the nations on the earth you guide.

℞. **May God bless us in his mercy.**

May the peoples praise you, O God;
 may all the peoples praise you!
May God bless us,
 and may all the ends of the earth fear him!

℟. **May God bless us in his mercy.** ↓

SECOND READING Gal 4:4-7   [Heirs by God's Design]
 **God sent Jesus, his Son, born of Mary, to deliver all from
 the bondage of sin and slavery to the law. By God's choice
 we are heirs of heaven.**

A reading from the Letter of Saint Paul to the Galatians

BROTHERS and sisters: When the fullness of time
 had come, God sent his Son, born of a woman,
born under the law, to ransom those under the law, so
that we might receive adoption as sons. As proof that
you are sons, God sent the Spirit of his Son into our
hearts, crying out, "Abba, Father!" So you are no longer
a slave but a son, and if a son then also an heir,
through God.—The word of the Lord. ℟. **Thanks be to
God.** ↓

ALLELUIA Heb 1:1-2   [God Speaks]
℟. **Alleluia, alleluia.**
In the past God spoke to our ancestors through the
 prophets;
in these last days, he has spoken to us through the Son.
℟. **Alleluia, alleluia.** ↓

GOSPEL Lk 2:16-21   [The Name of Jesus]
 **When the shepherds came to Bethlehem, they began to
 understand the message of the angels. Mary prayed about
 this great event. Jesus received his name according to the
 Jewish ritual of circumcision.**

℣. The Lord be with you. ℟. **And with your spirit.**
✛ A reading from the holy Gospel according to Luke.
℟. **Glory to you, O Lord.**

THE shepherds went in haste to Bethlehem and found Mary and Joseph, and the infant lying in the manger. When they saw this, they made known the message that had been told them about this child. All who heard it were amazed by what had been told them by the shepherds. And Mary kept all these things, reflecting on them in her heart. Then the shepherds returned, glorifying and praising God for all they had heard and seen, just as it had been told to them.

When eight days were completed for his circumcision, he was named Jesus, the name given him by the angel before he was conceived in the womb.—The Gospel of the Lord. ℟. **Praise to you, Lord Jesus Christ.**

→ No. 15, p. 18

PRAYER OVER THE OFFERINGS   [Rejoice in Grace]

O God, who in your kindness begin all good things
and bring them to fulfillment,
grant to us, who find joy in the Solemnity of the holy
    Mother of God,
that, just as we glory in the beginnings of your grace,
so one day we may rejoice in its completion.
Through Christ our Lord. ℟. **Amen.** ↓

PREFACE (P 56)   [Mary, Virgin and Mother]

℣. The Lord be with you. ℟. **And with your spirit.**
℣. Lift up your hearts. ℟. **We lift them up to the Lord.**
℣. Let us give thanks to the Lord our God. ℟. **It is right and just.**

It is truly right and just, our duty and our salvation,
always and everywhere to give you thanks,
Lord, holy Father, almighty and eternal God,
and to praise, bless, and glorify your name
on the Solemnity of the Motherhood
of the Blessed ever-Virgin Mary.

For by the overshadowing of the Holy Spirit
she conceived your Only Begotten Son,
and without losing the glory of virginity,
brought forth into the world the eternal Light,
Jesus Christ our Lord.

Through him the Angels praise your majesty,
Dominions adore and Powers tremble before you.
Heaven and the Virtues of heaven and the blessed
　　Seraphim
worship together with exultation.
May our voices, we pray, join with theirs
in humble praise, as we acclaim:　　➡ No. 23, p. 23

When the Roman Canon is used, the proper form of the
Communicantes (In communion with those) *is said.*

COMMUNION ANT. Heb 13:8　　　　　**[Jesus Forever]**

Jesus Christ is the same yesterday, today, and for ever. ↓

PRAYER AFTER COMMUNION　　　**[Mother of the Church]**

We have received this heavenly Sacrament with joy,
　　O Lord:
grant, we pray,
that it may lead us to eternal life,
for we rejoice to proclaim the blessed ever-Virgin Mary
Mother of your Son and Mother of the Church.
Through Christ our Lord.
℟. **Amen.**　　　　　　　　　　➡ No. 30, p. 77

Optional Solemn Blessings, p. 97, and Prayers over the People, p. 105

"They prostrated themselves and did him homage."

JANUARY 3

THE EPIPHANY OF THE LORD

Solemnity

AT THE VIGIL MASS (January 2)

ENTRANCE ANT. Cf. Bar 5:5   **[Arise, Jerusalem]**

Arise, Jerusalem, and look to the East and see your children gathered from the rising to the setting of the sun.   → No. 2, p. 10

COLLECT   **[Splendor of God's Majesty]**

May the splendor of your majesty, O Lord, we pray,
shed its light upon our hearts,
that we may pass through the shadows of this world
and reach the brightness of our eternal home.
Through our Lord Jesus Christ, your Son,
who lives and reigns with you in the unity of the Holy
  Spirit,
one God, for ever and ever.
℟. **Amen.** ↓

FIRST READING Is 60:1-6   [Glory of God's Church]

> Jerusalem is favored by the Lord. Kings and peoples will come before you. The riches of the earth will be placed at the gates of Jerusalem.

A reading from the Book of the Prophet Isaiah

RISE up in splendor, Jerusalem! Your light has come,
   the glory of the Lord shines upon you.
See, darkness covers the earth,
   and thick clouds cover the peoples;
but upon you the LORD shines,
   and over you appears his glory.
Nations shall walk by your light,
   and kings by your shining radiance.
Raise your eyes and look about;
   they all gather and come to you:
your sons come from afar,
   and your daughters in the arms of their nurses.

Then you shall be radiant at what you see,
   your heart shall throb and overflow,
for the riches of the sea shall be emptied out before
     you,
   the wealth of nations shall be brought to you.
Caravans of camels shall fill you,
   dromedaries from Midian and Ephah;
all from Sheba shall come
   bearing gold and frankincense,
   and proclaiming the praises of the LORD.
The word of the Lord. ℟. **Thanks be to God.** ↓

RESPONSORIAL PSALM Ps 72   [The Messiah-King]

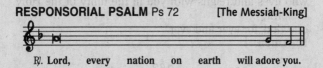

℟. **Lord,   every   nation   on   earth   will adore you.**

O God, with your judgment endow the king,
   and with your justice, the king's son;
he shall govern your people with justice
   and your afflicted ones with judgment.

℟. **Lord, every nation on earth will adore you.**

Justice shall flower in his days,
   and profound peace, till the moon be no more.
May he rule from sea to sea,
   and from the River to the ends of the earth.

℟. **Lord, every nation on earth will adore you.**

The kings of Tarshish and the Isles shall offer gifts;
   the kings of Arabia and Seba shall bring tribute.
All kings shall pay him homage,
   all nations shall serve him.

℟. **Lord, every nation on earth will adore you.**

For he shall rescue the poor man when he cries out,
   and the afflicted when he has no one to help him.
He shall have pity for the lowly and the poor;
   the lives of the poor he shall save.

℟. **Lord, every nation on earth will adore you.** ↓

SECOND READING Eph 3:2-3a, 5-6   [Good News for All]

   Paul admits that God has revealed the divine plan of salvation to him. Not only the Jews, but also the whole Gentile world, will share in the Good News.

A reading from the Letter of Saint Paul to the Ephesians

BROTHERS and sisters: You have heard of the stewardship of God's grace that was given to me for your benefit, namely, that the mystery was made known to me by revelation. It was not made known to people in other generations as it has now been revealed to his holy apostles and prophets by the Spirit: that the Gentiles are coheirs, members of the same body, and copartners in the promise in Christ

Jesus through the gospel.—The word of the Lord.
℟. **Thanks be to God.** ↓

ALLELUIA Mt 2:2   [Leading Star]

℟. **Alleluia, alleluia.**
We saw his star at its rising
and have come to do him homage.
℟. **Alleluia, alleluia.** ↓

GOSPEL Mt 2:1-12   [Magi with Gifts]

King Herod, being jealous of his earthly crown, was threatened by the coming of another king. The magi from the east followed the star to Bethlehem from which a ruler was to come.

℣. The Lord be with you. ℟. **And with your spirit.**
✠ A reading from the holy Gospel according to Matthew. ℟. **Glory to you, O Lord.**

WHEN Jesus was born in Bethlehem of Judea, in the days of King Herod, behold, magi from the east arrived in Jerusalem, saying, "Where is the newborn king of the Jews? We saw his star at its rising and have come to do him homage." When King Herod heard this, he was greatly troubled, and all Jerusalem with him. Assembling all the chief priests and the scribes of the people, he inquired of them where the Christ was to be born. They said to him, "In Bethlehem of Judea, for thus it has been written through the prophet:

And you, Bethlehem, land of Judah,
    are by no means least among the rulers of Judah;
since from you shall come a ruler,
    who is to shepherd my people Israel."

Then Herod called the magi secretly and ascertained from them the time of the star's appearance. He sent them to Bethlehem and said, "Go and search diligently for the child. When you have found him, bring me word, that I too may go and do him homage." After their audience with the king they set out. And behold, the star that they had seen at its rising preceded them, until it came and stopped over the place where the child was. They were overjoyed at seeing the star, and on entering the house they saw the child with Mary his mother. They prostrated themselves and did him homage. Then they opened their treasures and offered him gifts of gold, frankincense, and myrrh. And having been warned in a dream not to return to Herod, they departed for their country by another way.—The Gospel of the Lord. ℟. **Praise to you, Lord Jesus Christ.**   → No. 15, p. 18

PRAYER OVER THE OFFERINGS   [Render Praise]

Accept we pray, O Lord, our offerings,
in honor of the appearing of your Only Begotten Son
and the first fruits of the nations,
that to you praise may be rendered
and eternal salvation be ours.
Through Christ our Lord. ℟. **Amen.** ↓

PREFACE (P 6)   [Jesus Revealed to All]

℣. The Lord be with you. ℟. **And with your spirit.**
℣. Lift up your hearts. ℟. **We lift them up to the Lord.**
℣. Let us give thanks to the Lord our God. ℟. **It is right and just.**

It is truly right and just, our duty and our salvation,
always and everywhere to give you thanks,
Lord, holy Father, almighty and eternal God.

For today you have revealed the mystery
of our salvation in Christ
as a light for the nations,
and, when he appeared in our mortal nature,
you made us new by the glory of his immortal nature.

And so, with Angels and Archangels,
with Thrones and Dominions,
and with all the hosts and Powers of heaven,
we sing the hymn of your glory,
as without end we acclaim: ➙ No. 23, p. 23

COMMUNION ANT. Cf. Rev 21:23   [Walking by God's Light]
**The brightness of God illumined the holy city Jeru-
salem, and the nations will walk by its light.** ↓

PRAYER AFTER COMMUNION   [True Treasure]

Renewed by sacred nourishment,
we implore your mercy, O Lord,
that the star of your justice
may shine always bright in our minds
and that our true treasure may ever consist in our
    confession of you.
Through Christ our Lord.
℞. **Amen.**   ➙ No. 30, p. 77

Optional Solemn Blessings, p. 97, and Prayers over the People, p. 105

AT THE MASS DURING THE DAY

ENTRANCE ANT. Cf. Mal 3:1; 1 Chr 29:12 [Lord and Ruler]

Behold, the Lord, the Mighty One, has come; and kingship is in his grasp, and power and dominion.

→ No. 2, p. 10

COLLECT [Behold Glory]

O God, who on this day
revealed your Only Begotten Son to the nations
by the guidance of a star,
grant in your mercy
that we, who know you already by faith,
may be brought to behold the beauty of your sublime
    glory.
Through our Lord Jesus Christ, your Son,
who lives and reigns with you in the unity of the Holy
    Spirit,
one God, for ever and ever.
R̷. **Amen.** ↓

The readings for this Mass can be found beginning on p. 164.

PRAYER OVER THE OFFERINGS [Offering of Jesus]

Look with favor, Lord, we pray,
on these gifts of your Church,
in which are offered now not gold or frankincense or
    myrrh,
but he who by them is proclaimed,
sacrificed and received, Jesus Christ.
Who lives and reigns for ever and ever.
R̷. **Amen.** → Pref. P 6, p. 167

When the Roman Canon is used, the proper form of the
Communicantes (In communion with those) *is said.*

COMMUNION ANT. Cf. Mt 2:2   [Adore the Lord]

We have seen his star in the East, and have come with gifts to adore the Lord. ↓

PRAYER AFTER COMMUNION   [Heavenly Light]

Go before us with heavenly light, O Lord,
always and everywhere,
that we may perceive with clear sight
and revere with true affection
the mystery in which you have willed us to participate.
Through Christ our Lord.
℟. **Amen.** → No. 30, p. 77

Optional Solemn Blessings, p. 97, and Prayers over the People, p. 105

"You are my beloved Son; with you I am well pleased."

JANUARY 10

THE BAPTISM OF THE LORD

Feast

ENTRANCE ANT. Cf. Mt 3:16-17   [Beloved Son]

After the Lord was baptized, the heavens were opened,
and the Spirit descended upon him like a dove, and the
voice of the Father thundered: This is my beloved Son,
with whom I am well pleased.   → No. 2, p. 10

COLLECT   [Children by Adoption]

Almighty ever-living God,
who, when Christ had been baptized in the River Jordan
and as the Holy Spirit descended upon him,
solemnly declared him your beloved Son,
grant that your children by adoption,
reborn of water and the Holy Spirit,
may always be well pleasing to you.
Through our Lord Jesus Christ, your Son,
who lives and reigns with you in the unity of the Holy
    Spirit,
one God, for ever and ever. ℟. **Amen.** ↓

171

OR   [God Became Man]

O God, whose Only Begotten Son
has appeared in our very flesh,
grant, we pray, that we may be inwardly transformed
through him whom we recognize as outwardly like
   ourselves.
Who lives and reigns with you in the unity of the Holy
   Spirit,
one God, for ever and ever. ℟. **Amen.** ↓

*The following readings (except the Gospel) are optional. In
their place, the readings for Year A, pp. 177-178, may be used.*

FIRST READING Is 40:1-5, 9-11   [Promise of Salvation]

   Isaiah's central message is an announcement of salvation
   for the people of God. He reveals God as a Shepherd-King,
   attracting and ever caring for his people.

A reading from the Book of the Prophet Isaiah

COMFORT, give comfort to my people,
   says your God.
Speak tenderly to Jerusalem, and proclaim to her
   that her service is at an end,
   her guilt is expiated;
indeed, she has received from the hand of the Lord
   double for all her sins.
     A voice cries out:
In the desert prepare the way of the Lord!
   Make straight in the wasteland a highway for our
     God!
Every valley shall be filled in,
   every mountain and hill shall be made low;
the rugged land shall be made a plain,
   the rough country, a broad valley.
Then the glory of the Lord shall be revealed,
   and all people shall see it together;
   for the mouth of the Lord has spoken.

Go up onto a high mountain,
  Zion, herald of glad tidings;
cry out at the top of your voice,
  Jerusalem, herald of good news!
Fear not to cry out
  and say to the cities of Judah:
  Here is your God!
Here comes with power
  the Lord GOD,
  who rules by a strong arm;
here is his reward with him,
  his recompense before him.
Like a shepherd he feeds his flock;
  in his arms he gathers the lambs,
carrying them in his bosom,
  and leading the ewes with care.

The word of the Lord. ℟. **Thanks be to God.** ↓

RESPONSORIAL PSALM Ps 104   **[Creator and Redeemer]**

  ℟. O   bless   the   Lord,   my   soul.

O LORD, my God, you are great indeed!
  you are clothed with majesty and glory,
robed in light as with a cloak.
  You have spread out the heavens like a tent-cloth.

℟. **O bless the Lord, my soul.**

You have constructed your palace upon the waters.
  You make the clouds your chariot;
you travel on the wings of the wind.
  You make the winds your messengers,
and flaming fire your ministers.

℟. **O bless the Lord, my soul.**

How manifold are your works, O LORD!
  In wisdom you have wrought them all—

the earth is full of your creatures;
    the sea also, great and wide,
in which are schools without number
    of living things both small and great.

℟. **O bless the Lord, my soul.**

They look to you to give them food in due time.
    When you give it to them, they gather it;
when you open your hand, they are filled with good
        things.

℟. **O bless the Lord, my soul.**

If you take away their breath, they perish and return to
        the dust.
    When you send forth your spirit, they are created,
and you renew the face of the earth.

℟. **O bless the Lord, my soul.** ↓

SECOND READING Ti 2:11-14; 3:4-7 [Called through Baptism]

**God anointed Jesus the Savior with the Holy Spirit and
power. Jesus is the Lord of all, and he brought healing to
all who were in the grip of the devil.**

A reading from the Letter of Paul to Titus

BELOVED: The grace of God has appeared, saving
all and training us to reject godless ways and
worldly desires and to live temperately, justly, and
devoutly in this age, as we await the blessed hope, the
appearance of the glory of our great God and savior
Jesus Christ, who gave himself for us to deliver us
from all lawlessness and to cleanse for himself a people as his own, eager to do what is good.

    When the kindness and generous love
        of God our savior appeared,
    not because of any righteous deeds we had done
        but because of his mercy,
    he saved us through the bath of rebirth
        and renewal by the Holy Spirit,

whom he richly poured out on us
    through Jesus Christ our savior,
so that we might be justified by his grace
    and become heirs in hope of eternal life.
The word of the Lord. ℟. **Thanks be to God.** ↓

ALLELUIA Cf. Lk 3:16   [Baptism with the Spirit]
℟. **Alleluia, alleluia.**
John said: One mightier than I is coming;
he will baptize you with the Holy Spirit and with fire.
℟. **Alleluia, alleluia.** ↓

GOSPEL Lk 3:15-16, 21-22   [Beloved Son]
    **The Spirit of God is seen coming upon Christ. The words
    of Isaiah are beginning to be fulfilled.**

℣. The Lord be with you. ℟. **And with your spirit.**
✠ A reading from the holy gospel according to Luke.
℟. **Glory to you, O Lord.**

THE people were filled with expectation, and all were
asking in their hearts whether John might be the
Christ. John answered them all, saying, "I am baptizing
you with water, but one mightier than I is coming. I am
not worthy to loosen the thongs of his sandals. He will
baptize you with the Holy Spirit and fire."

    After all the people had been baptized and Jesus
also had been baptized and was praying, heaven was
opened and the Holy Spirit descended upon him in
bodily form like a dove. And a voice came from heaven, "You are my beloved Son; with you I am well
pleased."—The Gospel of the Lord. ℟. **Praise to you,
Lord Jesus Christ.**   → No. 15, p. 18

PRAYER OVER THE OFFERINGS   [Christ's Revelation]
Accept, O Lord, the offerings
we have brought to honor the revealing of your
    beloved Son,
so that the oblation of your faithful
may be transformed into the sacrifice of him

who willed in his compassion
to wash away the sins of the world.
Who lives and reigns for ever and ever. ℟. **Amen.** ↓

PREFACE (P 7)   [New Gift of Baptism]

℣. The Lord be with you. ℟. **And with your spirit.**
℣. Lift up your hearts. ℟. **We lift them up to the Lord.**
℣. Let us give thanks to the Lord our God. ℟. **It is right and just.**

It is truly right and just, our duty and our salvation,
always and everywhere to give you thanks,
Lord, holy Father, almighty and eternal God.

For in the waters of the Jordan
you revealed with signs and wonders a new Baptism,
so that through the voice that came down from heaven
we might come to believe in your Word dwelling
    among us,
and by the Spirit's descending in the likeness of a dove
we might know that Christ your Servant
has been anointed with the oil of gladness
and sent to bring the good news to the poor.

And so, with the Powers of heaven,
we worship you constantly on earth,
and before your majesty
without end we acclaim: → No. 23, p. 23

COMMUNION ANT. Jn 1:32, 34   [Witness to God's Son]

**Behold the One of whom John said: I have seen and
testified that this is the Son of God.** ↓

PRAYER AFTER COMMUNION   [Children in Truth]

Nourished with these sacred gifts,
we humbly entreat your mercy, O Lord,
that, faithfully listening to your Only Begotten Son,
we may be your children in name and in truth.
Through Christ our Lord.
℟. **Amen.**   → No. 30, p. 77

Optional Solemn Blessings, p. 97, and Prayers over the People, p. 105

The following readings from Year A may be used in place of the optional ones given on pp. 172-175, excluding Gospel.

FIRST READING Is 42:1-4, 6-7   [Works of the Messiah]
The prophet Isaiah sees the spirit upon the Lord's servant who will proclaim the "good news" to the poor, freedom to prisoners and joy to those in sorrow.

A reading from the Book of the Prophet Isaiah

THUS says the Lord:
Here is my servant whom I uphold,
    my chosen one with whom I am pleased,
upon whom I have put my spirit;
    he shall bring forth justice to the nations,
not crying out, not shouting,
    not making his voice heard in the street.
A bruised reed he shall not break,
    and a smoldering wick he shall not quench,
until he establishes justice on the earth;
    the coastlands will wait for his teaching.

I, the LORD, have called you for the victory of justice,
    I have grasped you, by the hand;
I formed you, and set you
    as a covenant of the people,
    a light for the nations,
to open the eyes of the blind,
    to bring out prisoners from confinement,
    and from the dungeon, those who live in darkness.
The word of the Lord. ℟. **Thanks be to God.** ↓

RESPONSORIAL PSALM Ps 29   [Peace for God's People]

℟. The Lord will bless his peo-ple with peace.

Give to the LORD, you sons of God,
    give to the LORD glory and praise,
give to the LORD the glory due his name;
    adore the LORD in holy attire.

℟. **The Lord will bless his people with peace.**

The voice of the LORD is over the waters,
   the LORD, over vast waters.
The voice of the LORD is mighty;
   the voice of the LORD is majestic.

℟. **The Lord will bless his people with peace.**

The God of glory thunders,
   and in his temple all say, "Glory!"
The LORD is enthroned above the flood;
   the LORD is enthroned as king forever.

℟. **The Lord will bless his people with peace.** ↓

SECOND READING Acts 10:34-38   [Anointed to Do Good]

   God anointed Jesus the Savior with the Holy Spirit and
   power. Jesus is the Lord of all, and he brought healing to
   all who were in the grip of the devil.

A reading from the Acts of the Apostles

PETER proceeded to speak to those gathered in the
house of Cornelius, saying: "In truth, I see that God
shows no partiality. Rather, in every nation whoever
fears him and acts uprightly is acceptable to him. You
know the word that he sent to the Israelites as he proclaimed peace through Jesus Christ, who is Lord of all,
what has happened all over Judea, beginning in
Galilee after the baptism that John preached, how God
anointed Jesus of Nazareth with the Holy Spirit and
power. He went about doing good and healing all those
oppressed by the devil, for God was with him."—The
word of the Lord. ℟. **Thanks be to God.** ↓

ALLELUIA Cf. Mk 9:7   [Hear Him]
℟. **Alleluia, alleluia.**
The heavens were opened and the voice of the Father
   thundered:
This is my beloved Son, listen to him.
℟. **Alleluia, alleluia.**

———————

"Jesus told them, 'Fill the jars with water.'"

JANUARY 17

2nd SUNDAY IN ORDINARY TIME

ENTRANCE ANT. Ps 66 (65):4   **[Proclaim His Glory]**

All the earth shall bow down before you, O God, and shall sing to you, shall sing to your name, O Most High!   ➔ No. 2, p. 10

COLLECT   **[Peace on Our Times]**

Almighty ever-living God,
who govern all things,
both in heaven and on earth,
mercifully hear the pleading of your people
and bestow your peace on our times.
Through our Lord Jesus Christ, your Son,
who lives and reigns with you in the unity of the Holy
    Spirit,
one God, for ever and ever.
℟. **Amen.** ↓

FIRST READING Is 62:1-5   [God's Love for His People]

"Zion," "Jerusalem," is the people of God and God describes his love and concern for us in terms of the joy of a bridegroom.

A reading from the Book of the Prophet Isaiah

FOR Zion's sake I will not be silent,
   for Jerusalem's sake I will not be quiet,
until her vindication shines forth like the dawn
   and her victory like a burning torch.

Nations shall behold your vindication,
   and all the kings your glory;
you shall be called by a new name
   pronounced by the mouth of the LORD.
You shall be a glorious crown in the hand of the LORD,
   a royal diadem held by your God.
No more shall people call you "Forsaken,"
   or your land "Desolate,"
but you shall be called "My Delight,"
   and your land "Espoused."
For the LORD delights in you
   and makes your land his spouse.
As a young man marries a virgin,
   your Builder shall marry you;
and as a bridegroom rejoices in his bride
   so shall your God rejoice in you.
The word of the Lord. ℟. **Thanks be to God.** ↓

RESPONSORIAL PSALM Ps 96   [Proclaim God's Deeds]

℟. **Proclaim his marvelous deeds to all   the   na - tions.**

Sing to the LORD a new song;
   sing to the LORD, all you lands.
Sing to the LORD; bless his name.

℞. **Proclaim his marvelous deeds to all the nations.**

Announce his salvation, day after day.
Tell his glory among the nations;
  among all peoples, his wondrous deeds.

℞. **Proclaim his marvelous deeds to all the nations.**

Give to the LORD, you families of nations,
  give to the LORD glory and praise;
  give to the LORD the glory due his name!

℞. **Proclaim his marvelous deeds to all the nations.**

Worship the LORD in holy attire.
  Tremble before him, all the earth;
say among the nations: The LORD is king.
  He governs the peoples with equity.

℞. **Proclaim his marvelous deeds to all the nations.** ↓

SECOND READING 1 Cor 12:4-11 [Gifts of the Holy Spirit]
  **The gifts of God come from the same Spirit. The gifts are
  diverse but the Spirit is one; and the gifts are given to unite
  not separate us.**

A reading from the first Letter of Saint Paul
to the Corinthians

BROTHERS and sisters: There are different kinds of
spiritual gifts but the same Spirit; there are different forms of service but the same Lord; there are different workings but the same God who produces all of them in everyone. To each individual the manifestation of the Spirit is given for some benefit. To one is given through the Spirit the expression of wisdom; to another, the expression of knowledge according to the same Spirit; to another, faith by the same Spirit; to another, gifts of healing by the one Spirit; to another, mighty deeds; to another, prophecy; to another, discernment of spirits; to another, varieties of tongues; to another, interpretation of tongues. But one and the same Spirit

produces all of these, distributing them individually to each person as he wishes.—The word of the Lord. ℟. **Thanks be to God.** ↓

ALLELUIA Cf. 2 Thes 2:14   [We Are Called]
℟. **Alleluia, alleluia.**
God has called us through the Gospel
to possess the glory of our Lord Jesus Christ.
℟. **Alleluia, alleluia.** ↓

In place of the Alleluia which is given for each Sunday in Ordinary Time, another may be selected.

GOSPEL Jn 2:1-11   [Jesus Reveals His Glory]
Christ the Lord reveals his glory, and the kingdom of God is at hand.

℣. The Lord be with you. ℟. **And with your spirit.**
✠ A reading from the holy Gospel according to John.
℟. **Glory to you, O Lord.**

THERE was a wedding at Cana in Galilee, and the mother of Jesus was there. Jesus and his disciples were also invited to the wedding. When the wine ran short, the mother of Jesus said to him, "They have no wine." And Jesus said to her, "Woman, how does your concern affect me? My hour has not yet come." His mother said to the servers, "Do whatever he tells you." Now there were six stone water jars there for Jewish ceremonial washings, each holding twenty to thirty gallons. Jesus told them, "Fill the jars with water." So they filled them to the brim. Then he told them, "Draw some out now and take it to the headwaiter." So they took it. And when the headwaiter tasted the water that had become wine, without knowing where it came from—although the servers who had drawn the water knew—, the headwaiter called the bridegroom and said to him, "Everyone serves good wine first, and then when people have drunk freely, an inferior one; but you have kept the good wine until now." Jesus did this as the beginning of his signs at Cana in Galilee and so revealed his glory, and his disciples began to believe in him.—The Gospel of the Lord. ℟. **Praise to you, Lord Jesus Christ.**   ➙ No. 15, p. 18

PRAYER OVER THE OFFERINGS   [Work of Redemption]

Grant us, O Lord, we pray,
that we may participate worthily in these mysteries,
for whenever the memorial of this sacrifice is celebrated
the work of our redemption is accomplished.
Through Christ our Lord.
℟. **Amen.**   ➙ No. 21, p. 22 (Pref. P 29-36)

COMMUNION ANT. Ps 23 (22):5   [Thirst Quenched]

You have prepared a table before me, and how precious is the chalice that quenches my thirst. ↓

OR 1 Jn 4:16   [God's Love]

We have come to know and to believe in the love that God has for us. ↓

PRAYER AFTER COMMUNION   [One in Heart]

Pour on us, O Lord, the Spirit of your love,
and in your kindness
make those you have nourished
by this one heavenly Bread
one in mind and heart.
Through Christ our Lord.
℟. **Amen.**   ➙ No. 30, p. 77

Optional Solemn Blessings, p. 97, and Prayers over the People, p. 105

"The eyes of all in the synagogue looked intently at him."

JANUARY 24

3rd SUNDAY IN ORDINARY TIME

ENTRANCE ANT. Cf. Ps 96 (95):1, 6   [Sing to the Lord]

O sing a new song to the Lord; sing to the Lord, all the earth. In his presence are majesty and splendor, strength and honor in his holy place.   → No. 2, p. 10

COLLECT   [Abound in Good Works]

Almighty ever-living God,
direct our actions according to your good pleasure,
that in the name of your beloved Son
we may abound in good works.
Through our Lord Jesus Christ, your Son,
who lives and reigns with you in the unity of the Holy
  Spirit,
one God, for ever and ever.
℞. **Amen.** ↓

FIRST READING Neh 8:2-4a, 5-6, 8-10   [God's Law]

The people of God return to their homeland, rebuild the
temple, and now listen to the proclamation of the law of
God.

A reading from the Book of the Prophet Nehemiah

EZRA the priest brought the law before the assembly, which consisted of men, women, and those children old enough to understand. Standing at one end of the open place that was before the Water Gate, he read out of the book from daybreak till midday, in the presence of the men, the women, and those children old enough to understand; and all the people listened attentively to the book of the law. Ezra the scribe stood on a wooden platform that had been made for the occasion. He opened the scroll so that all the people might see it—for he was standing higher up than any of the people—; and, as he opened it, all the people rose. Ezra blessed the LORD, the great God, and all the people, their hands raised high, answered, "Amen, amen!" Then they bowed down and prostrated themselves before the LORD, their faces to the ground. Ezra read plainly from the book of the law of God, interpreting it so that all could understand what was read. Then Nehemiah, that is, His Excellency, and Ezra the priest-scribe and the Levites who were instructing the people said to all the people: "Today is holy to the LORD your God. Do not be sad, and do not weep"—for all the people were weeping as they heard the words of the law. He said further: "Go, eat rich foods and drink sweet drinks, and allot portions to those who had nothing prepared; for today is holy to our LORD. Do not be saddened this day, for rejoicing in the LORD must be your strength!"—The word of the Lord. ℟. **Thanks be to God.** ↓

RESPONSORIAL PSALM Ps 19   [Spirit and Life]

℟. Your   words,   Lord,   are   Spir-it and life.

The law of the LORD is perfect,
    refreshing the soul;

the decree of the LORD is trustworthy,
  giving wisdom to the simple.

℞. **Your words, Lord, are Spirit and life.**

The precepts of the LORD are right,
  rejoicing the heart;
the command of the LORD is clear,
  enlightening the eye.

℞. **Your words, Lord, are Spirit and life.**

The fear of the LORD is pure,
  enduring forever;
the ordinances of the LORD are true,
  all of them just.

℞. **Your words, Lord, are Spirit and life.**

Let the words of my mouth and the thought of my
    heart
  find favor before you,
O LORD, my rock and my redeemer.

℞. **Your words, Lord, are Spirit and life. ↓**

SECOND READING 1 Cor 12:12-30 or 12:12-14, 27 **[One Body]**
> **By baptism we begin to become Christians, Christ takes
> possession of us, and we must grow with him.**

*[If the "Shorter Form" is used, the indented text in brackets is
omitted.]*

A reading from the first Letter of Saint Paul
to the Corinthians

BROTHERS and sisters: As a body is one though it
has many parts, and all the parts of the body,
though many, are one body, so also Christ. For in one
Spirit we were all baptized into one body, whether
Jews or Greeks, slaves or free persons, and we were all
given to drink of one Spirit.

  Now the body is not a single part, but many.

[If a foot should say, "Because I am not a hand I do not belong to the body," it does not for this reason belong any less to the body. Or if an ear should say, "Because I am not an eye I do not belong to the body," it does not for this reason belong any less to the body. If the whole body were an eye, where would the hearing be? If the whole body were hearing, where would the sense of smell be? But as it is, God placed the parts, each one of them, in the body as he intended. If they were all one part, where would the body be? But as it is, there are many parts, yet one body. The eye cannot say to the hand, "I do not need you," nor again the head to the feet, "I do not need you." Indeed, the parts of the body that seem to be weaker are all the more necessary, and those parts of the body that we consider less honorable we surround with greater honor, and our less presentable parts are treated with greater propriety, whereas our more presentable parts do not need this. But God has so constructed the body as to give greater honor to a part that is without it, so that there may be no division in the body, but that the parts may have the same concern for one another. If one part suffers, all the parts suffer with it; if one part is honored, all the parts share its joy.]

Now you are Christ's body, and individually parts of it.

[Some people God has designated in the church to be, first, apostles; second, prophets; third, teachers; then, mighty deeds; then gifts of healing, assistance, administration, and varieties of tongues. Are all apostles? Are all prophets? Are all teachers? Do all work mighty deeds? Do all have gifts of healing? Do all speak in tongues? Do all interpret?]

The word of the Lord. ℟. **Thanks be to God.** ↓

ALLELUIA Cf. Lk 4:18   [Glad Tidings]

R̷. **Alleluia, alleluia.**

The Lord sent me to bring glad tidings to the poor,
and to proclaim liberty to captives.

R̷. **Alleluia, alleluia.** ↓

GOSPEL Lk 1:1-4; 4:14-21   [Proclaiming the Good News]

Jesus proclaims the "good news" to the poor, and
announces the fulfillment of the prophetic vision of Isaiah.

V̷. The Lord be with you. R̷. **And with your spirit.**

✝ A reading from the holy Gospel according to Luke.

R̷. **Glory to you, O Lord.**

SINCE many have undertaken to compile a narrative of the events that have been fulfilled among us,
just as those who were eyewitnesses from the beginning and ministers of the word have handed them
down to us, I too have decided, after investigating
everything accurately anew, to write it down in an
orderly sequence for you, most excellent Theophilus,
so that you may realize the certainty of the teachings
you have received.

Jesus returned to Galilee in the power of the Spirit,
and news of him spread throughout the whole region.
He taught in their synagogues and was praised by all.

He came to Nazareth, where he had grown up, and
went according to his custom into the synagogue on
the sabbath day. He stood up to read and was handed
a scroll of the prophet Isaiah. He unrolled the scroll
and found the passage where it was written:

The Spirit of the Lord is upon me,
*   because he has anointed me*
*   to bring glad tidings to the poor.*
He has sent me to proclaim liberty to captives
*   and recovery of sight to the blind,*
*   to let the oppressed go free,*
*   and to proclaim a year acceptable to the Lord.*

Rolling up the scroll, he handed it back to the attendant and sat down, and the eyes of all in the synagogue looked intently at him. He said to them, "Today this Scripture passage is fulfilled in your hearing."— The Gospel of the Lord. ℟. **Praise to you, Lord Jesus Christ.**   ➔ No. 15, p. 18

PRAYER OVER THE OFFERINGS   [Offerings for Salvation]

Accept our offerings, O Lord, we pray,
and in sanctifying them
grant that they may profit us for salvation.
Through Christ our Lord.
℟. **Amen.**   ➔ No. 21, p. 22 (Pref. P 29-36)

COMMUNION ANT. Cf. Ps 34 (33):6   [Radiance]

Look toward the Lord and be radiant; let your faces not be abashed. ↓

OR Jn 8:12   [Light of Life]

I am the light of the world, says the Lord; whoever follows me will not walk in darkness, but will have the light of life. ↓

PRAYER AFTER COMMUNION   [New Life]

Grant, we pray, almighty God,
that, receiving the grace
by which you bring us to new life,
we may always glory in your gift.
Through Christ our Lord.
℟. **Amen.**   ➔ No. 30, p. 77

Optional Solemn Blessings, p. 97, and Prayers over the People, p. 105

"But Jesus passed through the midst of them and went away."

JANUARY 31

4th SUNDAY IN ORDINARY TIME

ENTRANCE ANT. Ps 106 (105):47   **[Save Us]**

Save us, O Lord our God! And gather us from the nations, to give thanks to your holy name, and make it our glory to praise you.   → No. 2, p. 10

COLLECT   **[Christian Love]**

Grant us, Lord our God,
that we may honor you with all our mind,
and love everyone in truth of heart.
Through our Lord Jesus Christ, your Son,
who lives and reigns with you in the unity of the Holy
  Spirit,
one God, for ever and ever.
℟. **Amen.** ↓

FIRST READING Jer 1:4-5, 17-19   **[Call of Jeremiah]**

  Jeremiah is called by the Father to be his spokesman. He will be rejected but receives the promise of God that he will support him against his adversaries.

A reading from the Book of the Prophet Jeremiah

THE word of the LORD came to me, saying:
  Before I formed you in the womb I knew you,
  before you were born I dedicated you,
  a prophet to the nations I appointed you.

But do you gird your loins;
  stand up and tell them
  all that I command you.
Be not crushed on their account,
  as though I would leave you crushed before them;
for it is I this day
  who have made you a fortified city,
a pillar of iron, a wall of brass,
  against the whole land:
against Judah's kings and princes,
  against its priests and people.
They will fight against you but not prevail over you,
  for I am with you to deliver you, says the LORD.
The word of the Lord. ℟. **Thanks be to God.** ↓

RESPONSORIAL PSALM Ps 71   [Proclaim the Lord's Salvation]

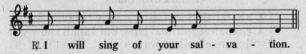

℟. I   will   sing   of   your   sal - va - tion.

In you, O LORD, I take refuge;
  let me never be put to shame.
In your justice rescue me, and deliver me;
  incline your ear to me, and save me.

℟. **I will sing of your salvation.**

Be my rock of refuge,
  a stronghold to give me safety,
  for you are my rock and my fortress.
O my God, rescue me from the hand of the wicked.

℟. **I will sing of your salvation.**

For you are my hope, O Lord;
    my trust, O God, from my youth.
On you I depend from birth;
    from my mother's womb you are my strength.

℟. **I will sing of your salvation.**

My mouth shall declare your justice,
    day by day your salvation.
O God, you have taught me from my youth,
    and till the present I proclaim your wondrous deeds.

℟. **I will sing of your salvation.** ↓

SECOND READING 1 Cor 12:31—13:13 or 13:4-13

[The Power of Love]

Love, the virtue of charity, surpasses all. It rises above everything. All gifts will pass away, but the supernatural virtue of love will never fail.

[If the "Shorter Form" is used, the indented text in brackets is omitted.]

A reading from the first Letter of Saint Paul
to the Corinthians

[B ROTHERS and sisters: Strive eagerly for the greatest spiritual gifts. But I shall show you a still more excellent way.

If I speak in human and angelic tongues, but do not have love, I am a resounding gong or a clashing cymbal. And if I have the gift of prophecy, and comprehend all mysteries and all knowledge; if I have all faith so as to move mountains, but do not have love, I am nothing. If I give away everything I own, and if I hand my body over so that I may boast, but do not have love, I gain nothing.]

Love is patient, love is kind. It is not jealous, it is not pompous, it is not inflated, it is not rude, it does not seek its own interests, it is not quick–tempered, it does not brood over injury, it does not rejoice over wrongdoing but rejoices with the truth. It bears all things, believes all things, hopes all things, endures all things.

Love never fails. If there are prophecies, they will be brought to nothing; if tongues, they will cease; if knowledge, it will be brought to nothing. For we know partially and we prophesy partially, but when the perfect comes, the partial will pass away. When I was a child, I used to talk as a child, think as a child, reason as a child; when I became a man, I put aside childish things. At present we see indistinctly, as in a mirror, but then face to face. At present I know partially; then I shall know fully, as I am fully known. So faith, hope, love remain, these three; but the greatest of these is love.—The word of the Lord. ℟. **Thanks be to God.** ↓

ALLELUIA Lk 4:18   [Glad Tidings]

℟. **Alleluia, alleluia.**
The Lord sent me to bring glad tidings to the poor,
to proclaim liberty to captives.
℟. **Alleluia, alleluia.** ↓

GOSPEL Lk 4:21-30   [Preaching Salvation]
Jesus is rejected by his own neighbors. They resented his strong reminder of the past rejections of the prophets. In baptism and the sacraments we are united to Jesus. Like him we must bear our crosses.

℣. The Lord be with you. ℟. **And with your spirit.**
✝ A reading from the holy Gospel according to Luke.
℟. **Glory to you, O Lord.**

JESUS began speaking in the synagogue, saying: "Today this Scripture passage is fulfilled in your hearing." And all spoke highly of him and were amazed at the gracious words that came from his mouth. They also asked, "Isn't this the son of Joseph?" He said to them, "Surely you will quote me this proverb, 'Physician, cure yourself,' and say, 'Do here in your native place the things that we heard were done in Capernaum.'" And he said, "Amen, I say to you, no prophet is accepted in his own native place. Indeed, I tell you, there were many widows in Israel in the days of Elijah when the sky was closed for three and a half years and a severe famine spread over the entire land. It was to none of these that Elijah was sent, but only to a widow in Zarephath in the land of Sidon. Again, there were many lepers in Israel during the time of Elisha the prophet; yet not one of them was cleansed, but only Naaman the Syrian." When the people in the synagogue heard this, they were all filled with fury. They rose up, drove him out of the town, and led him to the brow of the hill on which their town had been built, to hurl him down headlong. But Jesus passed through the midst of them and went away.—The Gospel of the Lord. ℟. **Praise to you, Lord Jesus Christ.**

→ No. 15, p. 18

PRAYER OVER THE OFFERINGS [Sacrament of Redemption]

O Lord, we bring to your altar
these offerings of our service:
be pleased to receive them, we pray,
and transform them
into the Sacrament of our redemption.
Through Christ our Lord.
℟. **Amen.**

→ No. 21, p. 22 (Pref. P 29-36)

COMMUNION ANT. Cf. Ps 31 (30):17-18   [Save Me]

Let your face shine on your servant. Save me in your merciful love. O Lord, let me never be put to shame, for I call on you. ↓

OR Mt 5:3-4   [Poor in Spirit]

Blessed are the poor in spirit, for theirs is the Kingdom of Heaven. Blessed are the meek, for they shall possess the land. ↓

PRAYER AFTER COMMUNION   [True Faith]

Nourished by these redeeming gifts,
we pray, O Lord,
that through this help to eternal salvation
true faith may ever increase.
Through Christ our Lord.
℟. **Amen.**   → No. 30, p. 77

Optional Solemn Blessings, p. 97, and Prayers over the People, p. 105

"They caught a great number of fish . . ."

FEBRUARY 7

5th SUNDAY IN ORDINARY TIME

ENTRANCE ANT. Ps 95 (94):6-7   [Adoration]

O come, let us worship God and bow low before the God who made us, for he is the Lord our God.

→ No. 2, p. 10

COLLECT   [God's Protection]

Keep your family safe, O Lord, with unfailing care,
that, relying solely on the hope of heavenly grace,
they may be defended always by your protection.
Through our Lord Jesus Christ, your Son,
who lives and reigns with you in the unity of the Holy
  Spirit,
one God, for ever and ever.
℟. **Amen.** ↓

FIRST READING Is 6:1-2a, 3-8   [Call of Isaiah]

**The prophet, aware of his own unworthiness, is fearful.
Purged of sin he accepts the call of the Father.**

A reading from the Book of the Prophet Isaiah

IN the year King Uzziah died, I saw the Lord seated
on a high and lofty throne, with the train of his garment filling the temple. Seraphim were stationed
above.

They cried one to the other, "Holy, holy, holy is the
LORD of hosts! All the earth is filled with his glory!" At
the sound of that cry, the frame of the door shook and
the house was filled with smoke.

Then I said, "Woe is me, I am doomed! For I am a
man of unclean lips, living among a people of unclean
lips; yet my eyes have seen the King, the LORD of
hosts!" Then one of the seraphim flew to me, holding
an ember that he had taken with tongs from the altar.

He touched my mouth with it, and said, "See, now
that this has touched your lips, your wickedness is
removed, your sin purged."

Then I heard the voice of the Lord saying, "Whom
shall I send? Who will go for us?" "Here I am," I said;
"send me!"—The word of the Lord. ℟. **Thanks be to
God.** ↓

RESPONSORIAL PSALM Ps 138   [Gratitude to God]

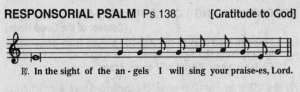

℟. In the sight of the an‑gels I will sing your praise‑es, Lord.

I will give thanks to you, O LORD, with all my heart,
   for you have heard the words of my mouth;
    in the presence of the angels I will sing your praise;
I will worship at your holy temple
   and give thanks to your name.

℟. **In the sight of the angels I will sing your praises,
Lord.**

Because of your kindness and your truth;
   for you have made great above all things
   your name and your promise.
When I called, you answered me;
   you built up strength within me.

℟. **In the sight of the angels I will sing your praises,
Lord.**

All the kings of the earth shall give thanks to you,
   O LORD,
   when they hear the words of your mouth;
and they shall sing of the ways of the LORD:
   "Great is the glory of the LORD."

℟. **In the sight of the angels I will sing your praises,
Lord.**

Your right hand saves me.
   The LORD will complete what he has done for me;
your kindness, O LORD, endures forever;
   forsake not the work of your hands.

℟. **In the sight of the angels I will sing your praises,
Lord.** ↓

SECOND READING 1 Cor 15:1-11 or 15:3-8, 11

[Content of the Good News]

Through God's favor, the Apostle turned from persecution to preaching the "good news" like Isaiah. Christ has died, Christ is risen, Christ will come again.

[If the "Shorter Form" is used, the indented text in brackets is omitted.]

A reading from the first Letter of Saint Paul
to the Corinthians

[I AM reminding you, brothers and sisters, of the gospel I preached to you, which you indeed received and in which you also stand. Through it you are also being saved, if you hold fast to the word I preached to you, unless you believed in vain.]

For* I handed on to you as of first importance what I also received: that Christ died for our sins in accordance with the Scriptures; that he was buried; that he was raised on the third day in accordance with the Scriptures; that he appeared to Cephas, then to the Twelve. After that, he appeared to more than five hundred brothers at once, most of whom are still living, though some have fallen asleep. After that he appeared to James, then to all the apostles. Last of all, as to one born abnormally, he appeared to me.

[For I am the least of the apostles, not fit to be called an apostle, because I persecuted the church of God. But by the grace of God I am what I am, and his grace to me has not been ineffective. Indeed, I have toiled harder than all of them; not I, however, but the grace of God that is with me.]

Therefore, whether it be I or they, so we preach and so you believed.—The word of the Lord. ℟. **Thanks be to God.** ↓

***

* *The Shorter Form begins "Brothers and sisters:"*

ALLELUIA Mt 4:19   [Fishers of Men]

℟. **Alleluia, alleluia.**
Come after me
and I will make you fishers of men.
℟. **Alleluia, alleluia.**

GOSPEL Lk 5:1-11   [Call of Peter]

Peter confesses: "I am a sinful man," and is reassured by
Christ. Then together with James and John he leaves
everything to become his follower.

℣. The Lord be with you. ℟. **And with your spirit.**
✣ A reading from the holy Gospel according to Luke.
℟. **Glory to you, O Lord.**

WHILE the crowd was pressing in on Jesus and listening to the word of God, he was standing by
the Lake of Gennesaret. He saw two boats there alongside the lake; the fishermen had disembarked and
were washing their nets. Getting into one of the boats,
the one belonging to Simon, he asked him to put out a
short distance from the shore. Then he sat down and
taught the crowds from the boat. After he had finished
speaking, he said to Simon, "Put out into deep water
and lower your nets for a catch." Simon said in reply,
"Master, we have worked hard all night and have
caught nothing, but at your command I will lower the
nets." When they had done this, they caught a great
number of fish and their nets were tearing. They sig-
naled to their partners in the other boat to come to
help them. They came and filled both boats so that the
boats were in danger of sinking. When Simon Peter
saw this, he fell at the knees of Jesus and said, "Depart
from me, Lord, for I am a sinful man." For astonishment at the catch of fish they had made seized him and
all those with him, and likewise James and John, the
sons of Zebedee, who were partners of Simon. Jesus

said to Simon, "Do not be afraid; from now on you will be catching men." When they brought their boats to the shore, they left everything and followed him.—The Gospel of the Lord. ℟. **Praise to you, Lord Jesus Christ.**   ➔ No. 15, p. 18

PRAYER OVER THE OFFERINGS   [Eternal Life]

O Lord our God,
who once established these created things
to sustain us in our frailty,
grant, we pray,
that they may become for us now
the Sacrament of eternal life.
Through Christ our Lord.
℟. **Amen.**   ➔ No. 21, p. 22 (Pref. P 29-36)

COMMUNION ANT. Cf. Ps 107 (106):8-9   [The Lord's Mercy]

Let them thank the Lord for his mercy, his wonders for the children of men, for he satisfies the thirsty soul, and the hungry he fills with good things. ↓

OR Mt 5:5-6   [Those Who Mourn]

Blessed are those who mourn, for they shall be consoled. Blessed are those who hunger and thirst for righteousness, for they shall have their fill. ↓

PRAYER AFTER COMMUNION   [Salvation and Joy]

O God, who have willed that we be partakers
in the one Bread and the one Chalice,
grant us, we pray, so to live
that, made one in Christ,
we may joyfully bear fruit
for the salvation of the world.
Through Christ our Lord.
℟. **Amen.**   ➔ No. 30, p. 77

Optional Solemn Blessings, p. 97, and Prayers over the People, p. 105

"Jesus said . . . 'You shall not put the Lord, your God, to the test.'"

FEBRUARY 14

1st SUNDAY OF LENT

ENTRANCE ANT. Cf. Ps 91 (90):15-16   [Length of Days]

When he calls on me, I will answer him; I will deliver him and give him glory, I will grant him length of days.

       → No. 2, p. 10 (Omit Gloria)

COLLECT   [Grow in Understanding]

Grant, almighty God,
through the yearly observances of holy Lent,
that we may grow in understanding
of the riches hidden in Christ
and by worthy conduct pursue their effects.
Through our Lord Jesus Christ, your Son,
who lives and reigns with you in the unity of the Holy
   Spirit,
one God, for ever and ever.
℟. **Amen.** ↓

FIRST READING Dt 26:4-10   [Confession of Faith]

The fruits of our labor are gifts from God. Before we use and enjoy them we should first acknowledge his bounty with dedication and thanks.

A reading from the Book of Deuteronomy

MOSES spoke to the people, saying: "The priest shall receive the basket from you and shall set it in front of the altar of the LORD, your God. Then you shall declare before the LORD, your God, 'My father was a wandering Aramean who went down to Egypt with a small household and lived there as an alien. But there he became a nation great, strong, and numerous. When the Egyptians maltreated and oppressed us, imposing hard labor upon us, we cried to the LORD, the God of our fathers, and he heard our cry and saw our affliction, our toil, and our oppression. He brought us out of Egypt with his strong hand and outstretched arm, with terrifying power, with signs and wonders; and bringing us into this country, he gave us this land flowing with milk and honey. Therefore, I have now brought you the firstfruits of the products of the soil which you, O LORD, have given me.' And having set them before the LORD, your God, you shall bow down in his presence."—The word of the Lord. ℟. **Thanks be to God.** ↓

RESPONSORIAL PSALM Ps 91   [Call for God's Help]

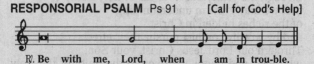

℟. Be with me, Lord, when I am in trou-ble.

You who dwell in the shelter of the Most High,
  who abide in the shadow of the Almighty,
say to the LORD, "My refuge and fortress,
  my God in whom I trust."
℟. **Be with me, Lord, when I am in trouble.**

No evil shall befall you,
　　nor shall affliction come near your tent,
for to his angels he has given command about you,
　　that they guard you in all your ways.

℟. **Be with me, Lord, when I am in trouble.**

Upon their hands they shall bear you up,
　　lest you dash your foot against a stone.
You shall tread upon the asp and the viper;
　　you shall trample down the lion and the dragon.

℟. **Be with me, Lord, when I am in trouble.**

Because he clings to me, I will deliver him;
　　I will set him on high because he acknowledges my
　　　　name.
He shall call upon me, and I will answer him;
　　I will be with him in distress;
I will deliver him and glorify him.

℟. **Be with me, Lord, when I am in trouble.** ↓

SECOND READING Rom 10:8-13   [Creed of Christians]
　　**Holiness (justification) is rooted in faith. Believe in your
　　heart that Jesus is raised from the dead.**

A reading from the Letter of Saint Paul to the Romans

BROTHERS and sisters: What does Scripture say? *The
word is near you, in your mouth and in your heart*—
that is, the word of faith that we preach—, for, if you confess with your mouth that Jesus is Lord and believe in
your heart that God raised him from the dead, you will
be saved. For one believes with the heart and so is justified, and one confesses with the mouth and so is saved.
For the Scripture says, *No one who believes in him will
be put to shame.* For there is no distinction between Jew
and Greek; the same Lord is Lord of all, enriching all
who call upon him. For "everyone who calls on the name
of the Lord will be saved."—The word of the Lord. ℟.
Thanks be to God. ↓

VERSE BEFORE THE GOSPEL Mt 4:4b [Source of Life]

℟. **Praise to you, Lord Jesus Christ, king of endless glory!***

One does not live on bread alone,
but on every word that comes forth from the mouth of God.

℟. **Praise to you, Lord Jesus Christ, king of endless glory!** ↓

GOSPEL Lk 4:1-13 [Practicing Our Creed]

Jesus is fully human and overcomes the temptation of Satan. As Messiah he will not resort to expediency.

℣. The Lord be with you. ℟. **And with your spirit.**

✠ A reading from the holy Gospel according to Luke.

℟. **Glory to you, O Lord.**

FILLED with the Holy Spirit, Jesus returned from the Jordan and was led by the Spirit into the desert for forty days, to be tempted by the devil. He ate nothing during those days, and when they were over he was hungry. The devil said to him, "If you are the Son of God, command this stone to become bread." Jesus answered him, "It is written, *One does not live on bread alone.*" Then he took him up and showed him all the kingdoms of the world in a single instant. The devil said to him, "I shall give to you all this power and glory; for it has been handed over to me, and I may give it to whomever I wish. All this will be yours, if you worship me." Jesus said to him in reply, "It is written:

You shall worship the Lord, your God,
and him alone shall you serve."

Then he led him to Jerusalem, made him stand on the parapet of the temple, and said to him, "If you are the Son of God, throw yourself down from here, for it is written:

He will command his angels concerning you,
to guard you,

* See p. 16 for other Gospel Acclamations.

and:

> *With their hands they will support you,*
> *lest you dash your foot against a stone."*

Jesus said to him in reply, "It also says, *You shall not put the Lord, your God, to the test."* When the devil had finished every temptation, he departed from him for a time.—The Gospel of the Lord. ℟. **Praise to you, Lord Jesus Christ.**   ➜ No. 15, p. 18

PRAYER OVER THE OFFERINGS   [Sacred Time]

Give us the right dispositions, O Lord, we pray,
to make these offerings,
for with them we celebrate the beginning
of this venerable and sacred time.
Through Christ our Lord. ℟. **Amen.** ↓

PREFACE (P 12)   [Christ's Abstinence]

℣. The Lord be with you. ℟. **And with your spirit.**
℣. Lift up your hearts. ℟. **We lift them up to the Lord.**
℣. Let us give thanks to the Lord our God. ℟. **It is right and just.**

It is truly right and just, our duty and our salvation,
always and everywhere to give you thanks,
Lord, holy Father, almighty and eternal God,
through Christ our Lord.

By abstaining forty long days from earthly food,
he consecrated through his fast
the pattern of our Lenten observance
and, by overturning all the snares of the ancient serpent,
taught us to cast out the leaven of malice,
so that, celebrating worthily the Paschal Mystery,
we might pass over at last to the eternal paschal feast.

And so, with the company of Angels and Saints,
we sing the hymn of your praise,
as without end we acclaim: ➜ No. 23, p. 23

COMMUNION ANT. Mt 4:4 [Life-Giving Word]

One does not live by bread alone, but by every word that comes forth from the mouth of God. ↓

OR Cf. Ps 91 (90):4 [Refuge in God]

The Lord will conceal you with his pinions, and under his wings you will trust. ↓

PRAYER AFTER COMMUNION [Heavenly Bread]

Renewed now with heavenly bread,
by which faith is nourished, hope increased,
and charity strengthened,
we pray, O Lord,
that we may learn to hunger for Christ,
the true and living Bread,
and strive to live by every word
which proceeds from your mouth.
Through Christ our Lord.
℞. **Amen.** ↓

The Deacon or, in his absence, the Priest himself, says the invitation: Bow down for the blessing.

PRAYER OVER THE PEOPLE [Bountiful Blessing]

May bountiful blessing, O Lord, we pray,
come down upon your people,
that hope may grow in tribulation,
virtue be strengthened in temptation,
and eternal redemption be assured.
Through Christ our Lord.
℞. **Amen.**

→ No. 32, p. 77

"And behold, two men were conversing with him, Moses and Elijah."

FEBRUARY 21

2nd SUNDAY OF LENT

ENTRANCE ANT. Cf. Ps 27 (26):8-9 [God's Face]

Of you my heart has spoken: Seek his face. It is your face, O Lord, that I seek; hide not your face from me.
→ No. 2, p. 10 (Omit Gloria)

OR Cf. Ps 25 (24):6, 2, 22 [God's Merciful Love]

Remember your compassion, O Lord, and your merciful love, for they are from of old. Let not our enemies exult over us. Redeem us, O God of Israel, from all our distress.
→ No. 2, p. 10 (Omit Gloria)

COLLECT [Nourish Us]

O God, who have commanded us
to listen to your beloved Son,
be pleased, we pray,
to nourish us inwardly by your word,
that, with spiritual sight made pure,

we may rejoice to behold your glory.
Through our Lord Jesus Christ, your Son,
who lives and reigns with you in the unity of the Holy
    Spirit,
one God, for ever and ever. ℟. **Amen.** ↓

FIRST READING Gn 15:5-12, 17-18 [Covenant with Abram]

> By faith Abram finds favor with the Lord. The Lord makes
> a covenant, that is, establishes a special relationship, with
> Abram and his descendants.

A reading from the Book of Genesis

THE Lord God took Abram outside and said: "Look
up at the sky and count the stars, if you can. Just
so," he added, "shall your descendants be." Abram put
his faith in the LORD, who credited it to him as an act
of righteousness.

He then said to him, "I am the LORD who brought you
from Ur of the Chaldeans to give you this land as a
possession." "O Lord GOD," he asked, "how am I to
know that I shall possess it?" He answered him, "Bring
me a three-year-old heifer, a three-year-old she-goat, a
three-year-old ram, a turtledove, and a young pigeon."
Abram brought him all these, split them in two, and
placed each half opposite the other; but the birds he
did not cut up. Birds of prey swooped down on the car-
casses, but Abram stayed with them. As the sun was
about to set, a trance fell upon Abram, and a deep, terrifying darkness enveloped him.

When the sun had set and it was dark, there
appeared a smoking fire pot and a flaming torch,
which passed between those pieces. It was on that
occasion that the LORD made a covenant with Abram,
saying: "To your descendants I give this land, from the
Wadi of Egypt to the Great River, the Euphrates."—The
word of the Lord. ℟. **Thanks be to God.** ↓

RESPONSORIAL PSALM Ps 27   [Union with God]

℟. The Lord is my light and my sal - va - tion.

The LORD is my light and my salvation;
   whom should I fear?
The LORD is my life's refuge;
   of whom should I be afraid?

℟. **The Lord is my light and my salvation.**

Hear, O LORD, the sound of my call;
   have pity on me, and answer me.
Of you my heart speaks; you my glance seeks.

℟. **The Lord is my light and my salvation.**

Your presence, O LORD, I seek.
   Hide not your face from me;
do not in anger repel your servant.
   You are my helper: cast me not off.

℟. **The Lord is my light and my salvation.**

I believe that I shall see the bounty of the LORD
   in the land of the living.
Wait for the LORD with courage;
   be stouthearted, and wait for the LORD.

℟. **The Lord is my light and my salvation.** ↓

SECOND READING Phil 3:17—4:1 or 3:20—4:1
                              [Citizenship in Heaven]

Paul exhorts us to turn away from worldly pleasures and to reject sin. He reminds us that we are not of this world.

[If the "Shorter Form" is used, the indented text in brackets is omitted.]

A reading from the Letter of Saint Paul to the Philippians

   *[JOIN with others in being imitators of me,
      brothers and sisters, and observe those who

---
* *The Shorter Form adds "Brothers and sisters."*

thus conduct themselves according to the model you have in us. For many, as I have often told you and now tell you even in tears, conduct themselves as enemies of the cross of Christ. Their end is destruction. Their God is their stomach; their glory is in their "shame." Their minds are occupied with earthly things.

But] our citizenship is in heaven, and from it we also await a savior, the Lord Jesus Christ. He will change our lowly body to conform with his glorified body by the power that enables him also to bring all things into subjection to himself.

Therefore, my brothers and sisters, whom I love and long for, my joy and crown, in this way stand firm in the Lord.*—The word of the Lord. ℟. **Thanks be to God.** ↓

VERSE BEFORE THE GOSPEL Cf. Mt 17:5   [Hear Him]

℟. **Praise and honor to you, Lord Jesus Christ!****
From the shining cloud the Father's voice is heard:
This is my beloved Son, hear him.
℟. **Praise and honor to you, Lord Jesus Christ!** ↓

GOSPEL Lk 9:28b-36   [Listen to Jesus]

The glory of Christ is revealed, and God manifests the special mission of Christ.

℣. The Lord be with you. ℟. **And with your spirit.**
✚ A reading from the holy Gospel according to Luke.
℟. **Glory to you, O Lord.**

JESUS took Peter, John, and James and went up the mountain to pray. While he was praying his face changed in appearance and his clothing became dazzling white. And behold, two men were conversing with him, Moses and Elijah, who appeared in glory and spoke of his exodus that he was going to accom-

---

* The Shorter Form adds "beloved."
** See p. 16 for other Gospel Acclamations.

plish in Jerusalem. Peter and his companions had been overcome by sleep, but becoming fully awake, they saw his glory and the two men standing with him. As they were about to part from him, Peter said to Jesus, "Master, it is good that we are here; let us make three tents, one for you, one for Moses, and one for Elijah." But he did not know what he was saying. While he was still speaking, a cloud came and cast a shadow over them, and they became frightened when they entered the cloud. Then from the cloud came a voice that said, "This is my chosen Son; listen to him." After the voice had spoken, Jesus was found alone. They fell silent and did not at that time tell anyone what they had seen.— The Gospel of the Lord. ℟. **Praise to you, Lord Jesus Christ.**

→ No. 15, p. 18

PRAYER OVER THE OFFERINGS   [Cleanse Our Faults]

May this sacrifice, O Lord, we pray,
cleanse us of our faults
and sanctify your faithful in body and mind
for the celebration of the paschal festivities.
Through Christ our Lord.
℟. **Amen.** ↓

PREFACE (P 13)   [Jesus in Glory]

℣. The Lord be with you. ℟. **And with your spirit.**
℣. Lift up your hearts. ℟. **We lift them up to the Lord.**
℣. Let us give thanks to the Lord our God. ℟. **It is right and just.**

It is truly right and just, our duty and our salvation,
always and everywhere to give you thanks,
Lord, holy Father, almighty and eternal God,
through Christ our Lord.

For after he had told the disciples of his coming Death,
on the holy mountain he manifested to them his glory,

to show, even by the testimony of the law and the
　prophets,
that the Passion leads to the glory of the Resurrection.

And so, with the Powers of heaven,
we worship you constantly on earth,
and before your majesty
without end we acclaim:　　　　　→ No. 23, p. 23

COMMUNION ANT. Mt 17:5　　　　　[Son of God]
**This is my beloved Son, with whom I am well pleased;
listen to him.** ↓

PRAYER AFTER COMMUNION　　　[Things of Heaven]
As we receive these glorious mysteries,
we make thanksgiving to you, O Lord,
for allowing us while still on earth
to be partakers even now of the things of heaven.
Through Christ our Lord.
℟. **Amen.** ↓

*The Deacon or, in his absence, the Priest himself, says the
invitation:* Bow down for the blessing.

PRAYER OVER THE PEOPLE　　　[Faithful to the Gospel]
Bless your faithful, we pray, O Lord,
with a blessing that endures for ever,
and keep them faithful
to the Gospel of your Only Begotten Son,
so that they may always desire and at last attain
that glory whose beauty he showed in his own Body,
to the amazement of his Apostles.
Through Christ our Lord.
℟. **Amen.**　　　　　　　　　　　→ No. 32, p. 77

"It may bear fruit in the future."

FEBRUARY 28

3rd SUNDAY OF LENT

On this Sunday is celebrated the First Scrutiny in preparation for the Baptism of the catechumens who are to be admitted to the Sacraments of Christian Initiation at the Easter Vigil. The Ritual Mass for the First Scrutiny is found on p. 219.

ENTRANCE ANT. Cf. Ps 25 (24):15-16   [Eyes on God]

My eyes are always on the Lord, for he rescues my feet from the snare. Turn to me and have mercy on me, for I am alone and poor. → No. 2, p. 10 (Omit Gloria)

OR Ez 36:23-26   [A New Spirit]

When I prove my holiness among you, I will gather you from all the foreign lands; and I will pour clean water upon you and cleanse you from all your impurities, and I will give you a new spirit, says the Lord.
→ No. 2, p. 10 (Omit Gloria)

COLLECT   [Fasting, Prayer, Almsgiving]

O God, author of every mercy and of all goodness,
who in fasting, prayer and almsgiving

213

have shown us a remedy for sin,
look graciously on this confession of our lowliness,
that we, who are bowed down by our conscience,
may always be lifted up by your mercy.
Through our Lord Jesus Christ, your Son,
who lives and reigns with you in the unity of the Holy
      Spirit,
one God, for ever and ever. ℟. **Amen.** ↓

FIRST READING Ex 3:1-8a, 13-15   [The Name of God]

The Lord God calls Moses to lead his people and reveals
his name to Moses.

A reading from the Book of Exodus

MOSES was tending the flock of his father-in-law
Jethro, the priest of Midian. Leading the flock
across the desert, he came to Horeb, the mountain of
God. There an angel of the LORD appeared to Moses in
fire flaming out of a bush. As he looked on, he was surprised to see that the bush, though on fire, was not consumed. So Moses decided, "I must go over to look at this
remarkable sight, and see why the bush is not burned."
   When the LORD saw him coming over to look at it
more closely, God called out to him from the bush,
"Moses! Moses!" He answered, "Here I am." God said,
"Come no nearer! Remove the sandals from your feet,
for the place where you stand is holy ground. I am the
God of your fathers," he continued, "the God of
Abraham, the God of Isaac, the God of Jacob." Moses
hid his face, for he was afraid to look at God. But the
LORD said, "I have witnessed the affliction of my people
in Egypt and have heard their cry of complaint against
their slave drivers, so I know well what they are suffering. Therefore I have come down to rescue them from
the hands of the Egyptians and lead them out of that
land into a good and spacious land, a land flowing
with milk and honey."

Moses said to God, "But when I go to the Israelites and say to them, 'The God of your fathers has sent me to you,' if they ask me, 'What is his name?' what am I to tell them?" God replied, "I am who am." Then he added, "This is what you shall tell the Israelites: I AM sent me to you."

God spoke further to Moses, "Thus shall you say to the Israelites: The LORD, the God of your fathers, the God of Abraham, the God of Isaac, the God of Jacob, has sent me to you.

"This is my name forever;
thus am I to be remembered through all generations."

The word of the Lord. ℟. **Thanks be to God.** ↓

RESPONSORIAL PSALM Ps 103   [The Lord's Kindness]

℟. The Lord is   kind and mer - ci - ful.

Bless the LORD, O my soul;
and all my being, bless his holy name.
Bless the LORD, O my soul,
and forget not all his benefits.

℟. **The Lord is kind and merciful.**

He pardons all your iniquities,
he heals all your ills.
He redeems your life from destruction,
he crowns you with kindness and compassion.

℟. **The Lord is kind and merciful.**

The LORD secures justice
and the rights of all the oppressed.
He has made known his ways to Moses,
and his deeds to the children of Israel.

℟. **The Lord is kind and merciful.**

Merciful and gracious is the LORD,
  slow to anger and abounding in kindness.
For as the heavens are high above the earth,
  so surpassing is his kindness toward those who fear
  him.

℟. **The Lord is kind and merciful.** ↓

SECOND READING 1 Cor 10:1-6, 10-12

[Avoid Overconfidence]

We must remain steadfast in our faith. We cannot become overconfident even though we are the recipients of God's favor and grace.

A reading from the first Letter of Saint Paul
to the Corinthians

I DO not want you to be unaware, brothers and sisters, that our ancestors were all under the cloud and all passed through the sea, and all of them were baptized into Moses in the cloud and in the sea. All ate the same spiritual food, and all drank the same spiritual drink, for they drank from a spiritual rock that followed them, and the rock was the Christ. Yet God was not pleased with most of them, for they were struck down in the desert.

These things happened as examples for us, so that we might not desire evil things, as they did. Do not grumble as some of them did, and suffered death by the destroyer. These things happened to them as an example, and they have been written down as a warning to us, upon whom the end of the ages has come. Therefore, whoever thinks he is standing secure should take care not to fall.—The word of the Lord. ℟. **Thanks be to God.** ↓

VERSE BEFORE THE GOSPEL Mt 4:17   [Repent]

℟. **Glory and praise to you, Lord Jesus Christ!***
Repent, says the Lord;

---

* See p. 16 for other Gospel Acclamations.

the kingdom of heaven is at hand.
℟. **Glory and praise to you, Lord Jesus Christ!** ↓

GOSPEL Lk 13:1-9   [Time To Reform]

Jesus tells us to reform and repent. Time will run out, and
no one can ever count on another year. Now is the time!

℣. The Lord be with you. ℟. **And with your spirit.**
✦ A reading from the holy Gospel according to Luke.
℟. **Glory to you, O Lord.**

SOME people told Jesus about the Galileans whose
blood Pilate had mingled with the blood of their
sacrifices. Jesus said to them in reply, "Do you think
that because these Galileans suffered in this way they
were greater sinners than all other Galileans? By no
means! But I tell you, if you do not repent, you will all
perish as they did! Or those eighteen people who were
killed when the tower at Siloam fell on them—do you
think they were more guilty than everyone else who
lived in Jerusalem? By no means! But I tell you, if you
do not repent, you will all perish as they did!"

And he told them this parable: "There once was a
person who had a fig tree planted in his orchard, and
when he came in search of fruit on it but found none,
he said to the gardener, 'For three years now I have
come in search of fruit on this fig tree but have found
none. So cut it down. Why should it exhaust the soil?'
He said to him in reply, 'Sir, leave it for this year also,
and I shall cultivate the ground around it and fertilize
it; it may bear fruit in the future. If not you can cut it
down.' "—The Gospel of the Lord. ℟. **Praise to you,
Lord Jesus Christ.**   → No. 15, p. 18

PRAYER OVER THE OFFERINGS   [Pardon]

Be pleased, O Lord, with these sacrificial offerings,
and grant that we who beseech pardon for our own sins,
may take care to forgive our neighbor.
Through Christ our Lord.
℟. **Amen.**   → No. 21, p. 22 (Pref. P 8-9)

When the Gospel of the Samaritan Woman is read, see p. 224 for Preface (P 14).

COMMUNION ANT. Ps 84 (83):4-5   [God's House]

The sparrow finds a home, and the swallow a nest for her young: by your altars, O Lord of hosts, my King and my God. Blessed are they who dwell in your house, for ever singing your praise. ↓

When the Gospel of the Samaritan Woman is read:

COMMUNION ANT. Jn 4:13-14   [Water of Eternal Life]

For anyone who drinks it, says the Lord, the water I shall give will become in him a spring welling up to eternal life. ↓

PRAYER AFTER COMMUNION   [Nourishment from Heaven]

As we receive the pledge
of things yet hidden in heaven
and are nourished while still on earth
with the Bread that comes from on high,
we humbly entreat you, O Lord,
that what is being brought about in us in mystery
may come to true completion.
Through Christ our Lord. ℟. **Amen.** ↓

The Deacon or, in his absence, the Priest himself, says the invitation: Bow down for the blessing.

PRAYER OVER THE PEOPLE   [Love of God and Neighbor]

Direct, O Lord, we pray, the hearts of your faithful,
and in your kindness grant your servants this grace:
that, abiding in the love of you and their neighbor,
they may fulfill the whole of your commands.
Through Christ our Lord.
℟. **Amen.**   → No. 32, p. 77

MASS FOR THE FIRST SCRUTINY

This Mass is celebrated when the First Scrutiny takes place during the Rite of Christian Initiation of Adults, usually on the 3rd Sunday of Lent. The readings may be used in any case.

ENTRANCE ANT. Ez 36:23-26   [A New Spirit]

When I prove my holiness among you, I will gather you from all the foreign lands and I will pour clean water upon you and cleanse you from all your impurities, and I will give you a new spirit, says the Lord.

→ No. 2, p. 10 (Omit Gloria)

OR Cf. Is 55:1   [Drink Joyfully]

Come to the waters, you who are thirsty, says the Lord; you who have no money, come and drink joyfully.

→ No. 2, p. 10 (Omit Gloria)

COLLECT   [Fashioned Anew]

Grant, we pray, O Lord,
that these chosen ones may come worthily and wisely
to the confession of your praise,
so that in accordance with that first dignity
which they lost by original sin
they may be fashioned anew through your glory.
Through our Lord Jesus Christ, your Son,
who lives and reigns with you in the unity of the Holy Spirit,
one God, for ever and ever. ℟. **Amen.** ↓

FIRST READING Ex 17:3-7   [Water from Rock]

The Israelites murmured against God in their thirst. God directs Moses to strike a rock with his staff, and water issues forth.

A reading from the Book of Exodus

IN those days, in their thirst for water, the people grumbled against Moses, saying, "Why did you ever make us leave Egypt? Was it just to have us die here of thirst with our children and our livestock?" So Moses cried out to the LORD, "What shall I do with this people? A little more and they will stone me!" The LORD answered Moses, "Go over there in front of the people, along with some of the elders of Israel, holding in your hand, as you go, the staff with which you struck the river. I will be standing there in front of you on the rock in Horeb. Strike the rock, and the water will flow from it for the people to drink." This Moses did, in the presence of the elders of Israel. The place was called Massah and Meribah, because the Israelites quarreled there and tested the LORD, saying, "Is the LORD in our midst or not?"— The word of the Lord. ℟. **Thanks be to God.** ↓

RESPONSORIAL PSALM Ps 95   [The Lord Our Rock]

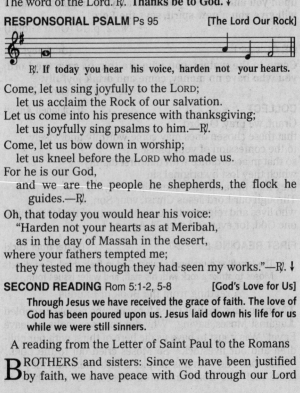

℟. If today you hear his voice, harden not your hearts.

Come, let us sing joyfully to the LORD;
  let us acclaim the Rock of our salvation.
Let us come into his presence with thanksgiving;
  let us joyfully sing psalms to him.—℟.

Come, let us bow down in worship;
  let us kneel before the LORD who made us.
For he is our God,
  and we are the people he shepherds, the flock he guides.—℟.

Oh, that today you would hear his voice:
  "Harden not your hearts as at Meribah,
  as in the day of Massah in the desert,
where your fathers tempted me;
  they tested me though they had seen my works."—℟. ↓

SECOND READING Rom 5:1-2, 5-8   [God's Love for Us]
Through Jesus we have received the grace of faith. The love of God has been poured upon us. Jesus laid down his life for us while we were still sinners.

A reading from the Letter of Saint Paul to the Romans

BROTHERS and sisters: Since we have been justified by faith, we have peace with God through our Lord

Jesus Christ, through whom we have gained access by faith to this grace in which we stand, and we boast in hope of the glory of God.

And hope does not disappoint, because the love of God has been poured out into our hearts through the Holy Spirit who has been given to us. For Christ, while we were still helpless, died at the appointed time for the ungodly. Indeed, only with difficulty does one die for a just person, though perhaps for a good person one might even find courage to die. But God proves his love for us in that while we were still sinners Christ died for us.—The word of the Lord. ℟. **Thanks be to God.** ↓

VERSE BEFORE THE GOSPEL Cf. Jn 4:42, 15   [Living Water]

℟. **Glory and praise to you, Lord Jesus Christ!***
Lord, you are truly the Savior of the world;
give me living water, that I may never thirst again.
℟. **Glory and praise to you, Lord Jesus Christ!** ↓

GOSPEL Jn 4:5-42 or 4:5-15, 19b-26, 39, 40-42   [Samaritan Woman]

> Jesus speaks to the Samaritan woman at the well. He searches her soul, and she recognizes him as a prophet. Jesus speaks of the water of eternal life. He also notes the fields are ready for harvest.

[If the "Shorter Form" is used, the indented text in brackets is omitted.]

℣. The Lord be with you. ℟. **And with your spirit.**
✤ A reading from the holy Gospel according to John.
℟. **Glory to you, O Lord.**

JESUS came to a town of Samaria called Sychar, near the plot of land that Jacob had given to his son Joseph. Jacob's well was there. Jesus, tired from his journey, sat down there at the well. It was about noon.

A woman of Samaria came to draw water. Jesus said to her, "Give me a drink." His disciples had gone into the

---

* *See p. 16 for other Gospel Acclamations.*

town to buy food. The Samaritan woman said to him, "How can you, a Jew, ask me, a Samaritan woman, for a drink?"—For Jews use nothing in common with Samaritans.—Jesus answered and said to her, "If you knew the gift of God and who is saying to you, 'Give me a drink,' you would have asked him and he would have given you living water." The woman said to him, "Sir, you do not even have a bucket and the cistern is deep; where then can you get this living water? Are you greater than our father Jacob, who gave us this cistern and drank from it himself with his children and his flocks?" Jesus answered and said to her, "Everyone who drinks this water will be thirsty again; but whoever drinks the water I shall give will never thirst; the water I shall give will become in him a spring of water welling up to eternal life." The woman said to him, "Sir, give me this water, so that I may not be thirsty or have to keep coming here to draw water."

[Jesus said to her, "Go call your husband and come back." The woman answered and said to him, "I do not have a husband." Jesus answered her, "You are right in saying, 'I do not have a husband.' For you have had five husbands, and the one you have now is not your husband. What you have said is true."]

[The woman said to him, "Sir,] I can see that you are a prophet. Our ancestors worshiped on this mountain; but you people say that the place to worship is in Jerusalem." Jesus said to her, "Believe me, woman, the hour is coming when you will worship the Father neither on this mountain nor in Jerusalem. You people worship what you do not understand; we worship what we understand, because salvation is from the Jews. But the hour is coming, and is now here, when true worshippers will worship the Father in Spirit and truth; and indeed the Father seeks such people to worship him. God is Spirit, and those who worship him must worship in Spirit and truth." The woman said to him, "I know that the Messiah is coming, the one called the

Christ; when he comes, he will tell us everything." Jesus said to her, "I am he, the one speaking with you."

[At that moment his disciples returned, and were amazed that he was talking with a woman, but still no one said, "What are you looking for?" or "Why are you talking with her?" The woman left her water jar and went into the town and said to the people, "Come see a man who told me everything I have done. Could he possibly be the Christ?" They went out of the town and came to him. Meanwhile, the disciples urged him, "Rabbi, eat." But he said to them, "I have food to eat of which you do not know." So the disciples said to one another, "Could someone have brought him something to eat?" Jesus said to them, "My food is to do the will of the one who sent me and to finish his work. Do you not say, 'In four months the harvest will be here'? I tell you, look up and see the fields ripe for the harvest. The reaper is already receiving payment and gathering crops for eternal life, so that the sower and reaper can rejoice together. For here the saying is verified that 'One sows and another reaps.' I sent you to reap what you have not worked for; others have done the work, and you are sharing the fruits of their work."]

Many of the Samaritans of that town began to believe in him [because of the word of the woman who testified, "He told me everything I have done."]* When the Samaritans came to him, they invited him to stay with them; and he stayed there two days. Many more began to believe in him because of his word, and they said to the woman, "We no longer believe because of your word; for we have heard for ourselves, and we know that this is truly the savior of the world."—The Gospel of the Lord. ℞.
Praise to you, Lord Jesus Christ.   ➔ No. 15, p. 18

----

* *Appears only in Longer Form.*

PRAYER OVER THE OFFERINGS   [Merciful Grace]

May your merciful grace prepare your servants, O Lord,
for the worthy celebration of these mysteries
and lead them to it by a devout way of life.
Through Christ our Lord.
℟. **Amen.** ↓

PREFACE (P 14)   [Gift of Faith]

℣. The Lord be with you. ℟. **And with your spirit.**
℣. Lift up your hearts. ℟. **We lift them up to the Lord.**
℣. Let us give thanks to the Lord our God. ℟. **It is right and just.**

It is truly right and just, our duty and our salvation,
always and everywhere to give you thanks,
Lord, holy Father, almighty and eternal God,
through Christ our Lord.

For when he asked the Samaritan woman for water to
    drink,
he had already created the gift of faith within her
and so ardently did he thirst for her faith,
that he kindled in her the fire of divine love.

And so we, too, give you thanks
and with the Angels
praise your mighty deeds, as we acclaim: → No. 23, p. 23

When the Roman Canon is used, in the section Memento,
Domine (Remember, Lord, your servants) *there is a com-
memoration of the godparents, and the proper form of the*
Hanc igitur *(Therefore, Lord, we pray), is said.*

Remember, Lord, your servants
who are to present your chosen ones
for the holy grace of your Baptism,

(Here the names of the godparents are read out.)

and all gathered here,
whose faith and devotion are known to you . . . (p. 24)

Therefore, Lord, we pray:
graciously accept this oblation
which we make to you for your servants,
whom you have been pleased
to enroll, choose and call for eternal life
and for the blessed gift of your grace.
(Through Christ our Lord. Amen.)

The rest follows the Roman Canon, pp. 25-29.

When Eucharistic Prayer II is used, after the words and all
the clergy, *the following is added:*

Remember also, Lord, your servants
who are to present these chosen ones
at the font of rebirth.

When Eucharistic Prayer III is used, after the words the
entire people you have gained for your own, *the following
is added:*

Assist your servants with your grace,
O Lord, we pray,
that they may lead these chosen ones by word and example
to new life in Christ, our Lord.

COMMUNION ANT. Cf. Jn 4:14   [Water of Eternal Life]
**For anyone who drinks it, says the Lord, the water I shall
give will become in him a spring welling up to eternal
life.** ↓

PRAYER AFTER COMMUNION   [God's Protection]
Give help, O Lord, we pray,
by the grace of your redemption
and be pleased to protect and prepare
those you are to initiate
through the Sacraments of eternal life.
Through Christ our Lord.
℟. **Amen.**   → No. 30, p. 77

Optional Solemn Blessings, p. 97, and Prayers over the People, p. 105

"Father, I have sinned against heaven and against you."

MARCH 6

4th SUNDAY OF LENT

On this Sunday is celebrated the Second Scrutiny in preparation for the Baptism of the catechumens who are to be admitted to the Sacraments of Christian Initiation at the Easter Vigil. The Ritual Mass for the Second Scrutiny is found on p. 232.

ENTRANCE ANT. Cf. Is 66:10-11   **[Rejoice]**

Rejoice, Jerusalem, and all who love her. Be joyful, all who were in mourning; exult and be satisfied at her consoling breast.   → No. 2, p. 10 (Omit Gloria)

COLLECT   **[Devotion and Faith]**

O God, who through your Word
reconcile the human race to yourself in a wonderful way,
grant, we pray,
that with prompt devotion and eager faith
the Christian people may hasten
toward the solemn celebrations to come.
Through our Lord Jesus Christ, your Son,

who lives and reigns with you in the unity of the Holy
   Spirit,
one God, for ever and ever. ℟. **Amen.** ↓

FIRST READING Jos 5:9a, 10-12   [Food for the Israelites]

The people of God celebrate the Passover in the promised
land, and as a sign that they are "home," the manna from
heaven is no longer provided.

A reading from the Book of Joshua

T HE LORD said to Joshua: "Today I have removed the
   reproach of Egypt from you."
   While the Israelites were encamped at Gilgal on the
plains of Jericho, they celebrated the Passover on the
evening of the fourteenth of the month. On the day
after the Passover, they ate of the produce of the land
in the form of unleavened cakes and parched grain. On
that same day after the Passover, on which they ate of
the produce of the land, the manna ceased. No longer
was there manna for the Israelites, who that year ate
of the yield of the land of Canaan.—The word of the
Lord. ℟. **Thanks be to God.** ↓

RESPONSORIAL PSALM Ps 34   [The Lord's Goodness]

℟. Taste and see   the   goodness   of   the Lord.

I will bless the LORD at all times;
   his praise shall be ever in my mouth.
Let my soul glory in the LORD;
   the lowly will hear me and be glad.

℟. **Taste and see the goodness of the Lord.**

Glorify the LORD with me,
   let us together extol his name.
I sought the LORD, and he answered me
   and delivered me from all my fears.

℟. **Taste and see the goodness of the Lord.**

Look at him that you may be radiant with joy,
   and your faces may not blush with shame.
When the poor one called out, the LORD heard,
   and from all his distress he saved him.

℟. **Taste and see the goodness of the Lord.** ↓

SECOND READING 2 Cor 5:17-21   [Reconciliation]

Christ, the ambassador, reconciles all to God. Our transgressions find forgiveness in him so that we might become the very holiness of God.

A reading from the second Letter of Saint Paul
to the Corinthians

BROTHERS and sisters: Whoever is in Christ is a new creation: the old things have passed away; behold, new things have come. And all this is from God, who has reconciled us to himself through Christ and given us the ministry of reconciliation, namely, God was reconciling the world to himself in Christ, not counting their trespasses against them and entrusting to us the message of reconciliation. So we are ambassadors for Christ, as if God were appealing through us. We implore you on behalf of Christ, be reconciled to God. For our sake he made him to be sin who did not know sin, so that we might become the righteousness of God in him.—The word of the Lord. ℟. **Thanks be to God.** ↓

VERSE BEFORE THE GOSPEL Lk 15:18   [Return Home]

℟. **Glory to you, Word of God, Lord Jesus Christ!***
I will get up and go to my Father and shall say to him:
Father, I have sinned against heaven and against you.
℟. **Glory to you, Word of God, Lord Jesus Christ!** ↓

----

* See p. 16 for other Gospel Acclamations.

GOSPEL Lk 15:1-3, 11-32   [The Prodigal Son]

Our loving Father is always ready to forgive the truly repentant.

℣. The Lord be with you. ℟. **And with your spirit.**
✢ A reading from the holy Gospel according to Luke.
℟. **Glory to you, O Lord.**

TAX collectors and sinners were all drawing near to listen to Jesus, but the Pharisees and scribes began to complain, saying, "This man welcomes sinners and eats with them." So to them Jesus addressed this parable: "A man had two sons, and the younger son said to his father, 'Father, give me the share of your estate that should come to me.' So the father divided the property between them. After a few days, the younger son collected all his belongings and set off to a distant country where he squandered his inheritance on a life of dissipation. When he had freely spent everything, a severe famine struck that country, and he found himself in dire need. So he hired himself out to one of the local citizens who sent him to his farm to tend the swine. And he longed to eat his fill of the pods on which the swine fed, but nobody gave him any. Coming to his senses he thought, 'How many of my father's hired workers have more than enough food to eat, but here am I, dying from hunger. I shall get up and go to my father and I shall say to him, "Father, I have sinned against heaven and against you. I no longer deserve to be called your son; treat me as you would treat one of your hired workers."' So he got up and went back to his father. While he was still a long way off, his father caught sight of him, and was filled with compassion. He ran to his son, embraced him and kissed him. His son said to him, 'Father, I have sinned against heaven and against you; I no longer deserve to be called your son.' But his father ordered his servants,

'Quickly bring the finest robe and put it on him; put a ring on his finger and sandals on his feet. Take the fattened calf and slaughter it. Then let us celebrate with a feast, because this son of mine was dead, and has come to life again; he was lost, and has been found.' Then the celebration began. Now the older son had been out in the field and, on his way back, as he neared the house, he heard the sound of music and dancing. He called one of the servants and asked what this might mean. The servant said to him, 'Your brother has returned and your father has slaughtered the fattened calf because he has him back safe and sound.' He became angry, and when he refused to enter the house, his father came out and pleaded with him. He said to his father in reply, 'Look, all these years I served you and not once did I disobey your orders; yet you never gave me even a young goat to feast on with my friends. But when your son returns who swallowed up your property with prostitutes, for him you slaughter the fattened calf.' He said to him, 'My son, you are here with me always; everything I have is yours. But now we must celebrate and rejoice, because your brother was dead and has come to life again; he was lost and has been found.' "—The Gospel of the Lord. ℟. **Praise to you, Lord Jesus Christ.**   ➜ No. 15, p. 18

PRAYER OVER THE OFFERINGS   [Eternal Remedy]

We place before you with joy these offerings,
which bring eternal remedy, O Lord,
praying that we may both faithfully revere them
and present them to you, as is fitting,
for the salvation of all the world.
Through Christ our Lord.
℟. **Amen.**   ➜ No. 21, p. 22 (Pref. P 8-9)

When the Gospel of the Man Born Blind is read, see p. 237 for Preface (P 15).

COMMUNION ANT. Lk 15:32   [Rejoice]
You must rejoice, my son, for your brother was dead and has come to life; he was lost and is found. ↓

When the Gospel of the Man Born Blind is read:

COMMUNION ANT. Cf. Jn 9:11, 38   [Spiritual Sight]
The Lord anointed my eyes: I went, I washed, I saw and I believed in God. ↓

PRAYER AFTER COMMUNION   [Illuminate Our Hearts]

O God, who enlighten everyone who comes into this
   world,
illuminate our hearts, we pray,
with the splendor of your grace,
that we may always ponder
what is worthy and pleasing to your majesty
and love you in all sincerity.
Through Christ our Lord.
℟. **Amen.** ↓

The Deacon or, in his absence, the Priest himself, says the invitation: Bow down for the blessing.

PRAYER OVER THE PEOPLE   [Life-Giving Light]

Look upon those who call to you, O Lord,
and sustain the weak;
give life by your unfailing light
to those who walk in the shadow of death,
and bring those rescued by your mercy from every evil
to reach the highest good.
Through Christ our Lord.
℟. **Amen.**   → No. 32, p. 77

MASS FOR THE SECOND SCRUTINY

This Mass is celebrated when the Second Scrutiny takes place during the Rite of Christian Initiation of Adults, usually on the 4th Sunday of Lent. The readings may be used in any case.

ENTRANCE ANT. Cf. Ps 25 (24):15-16   [Have Mercy]

My eyes are always on the Lord, for he rescues my feet from the snare. Turn to me and have mercy on me, for I am alone and poor.   → No. 2, p. 10 (Omit Gloria)

COLLECT   [Spiritual Joy]

Almighty ever-living God,
give to your Church an increase in spiritual joy,
so that those once born of earth
may be reborn as citizens of heaven.
Through our Lord Jesus Christ, your Son,
who lives and reigns with you in the unity of the Holy Spirit,
one God, for ever and ever. ℟. **Amen.** ↓

FIRST READING 1 Sm 16:1b, 6-7, 10-13a   [The Lord's Anointed]

> God directs Samuel to anoint David king. God looks into the heart of each person.

A reading from the first Book of Samuel

THE LORD said to Samuel: "Fill your horn with oil, and be on your way. I am sending you to Jesse of Bethlehem, for I have chosen my king from among his sons."

As Jesse and his sons came to the sacrifice, Samuel looked at Eliab and thought, "Surely the LORD's anointed is here before him." But the LORD said to Samuel: "Do not judge from his appearance or from his lofty stature, because I have rejected him. Not as man sees does God see, because man sees the appearance but the LORD looks into the heart." In the same way Jesse presented seven sons before Samuel, but Samuel said to Jesse, "The LORD has not chosen any one of these." Then Samuel asked Jesse, "Are these all the sons you have?" Jesse replied, "There is still the youngest, who is tending the sheep." Samuel said to Jesse, "Send for him; we will

not begin the sacrificial banquet until he arrives here." Jesse
sent and had the young man brought to them. He was ruddy,
a youth handsome to behold and making a splendid appearance. The LORD said, "There—anoint him, for this is the one!"
Then Samuel, with the horn of oil in hand, anointed him in
the presence of his brothers; and from that day on, the spirit of the LORD rushed upon David.—The word of the Lord.
℟. **Thanks be to God.** ↓

RESPONSORIAL PSALM Ps 23   [The Lord's Protection]

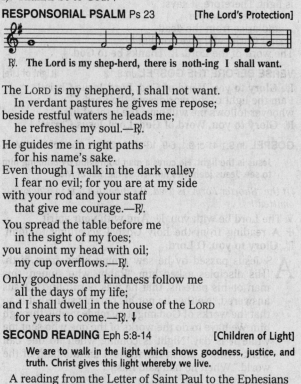

℟.   **The Lord is my shep-herd, there is noth-ing I shall want.**

The LORD is my shepherd, I shall not want.
   In verdant pastures he gives me repose;
beside restful waters he leads me;
   he refreshes my soul.—℟.

He guides me in right paths
   for his name's sake.
Even though I walk in the dark valley
   I fear no evil; for you are at my side
with your rod and your staff
   that give me courage.—℟.

You spread the table before me
   in the sight of my foes;
you anoint my head with oil;
   my cup overflows.—℟.

Only goodness and kindness follow me
   all the days of my life;
and I shall dwell in the house of the LORD
   for years to come.—℟. ↓

SECOND READING Eph 5:8-14   [Children of Light]

   We are to walk in the light which shows goodness, justice, and
   truth. Christ gives this light whereby we live.

A reading from the Letter of Saint Paul to the Ephesians

B ROTHERS and sisters: You were once darkness, but now you are light in the Lord. Live as children of light, for light produces every kind of goodness and righteousness and truth. Try to learn what is pleasing to the Lord. Take no part in the fruitless works of darkness; rather expose them, for it is shameful even to mention the things done by them in secret; but everything exposed by the light becomes visible, for everything that becomes visible is light. Therefore, it says:

"Awake, O sleeper,
    and arise from the dead,
    and Christ will give you light."
The word of the Lord. ℟. **Thanks be to God.** ↓

VERSE BEFORE THE GOSPEL Jn 8:12   [Light of Life]

℟. **Glory to you, Word of God, Lord Jesus Christ!***
I am the light of the world, says the Lord;
whoever follows me will have the light of life.
℟. **Glory to you, Word of God, Lord Jesus Christ!** ↓

GOSPEL Jn 9:1-41 or 9:1, 6-9, 13-17, 34-38   [Cure of Blind Man]

Jesus is the light. He cures a man born blind by bringing him to see. Jesus identifies himself as the Son of Man.

[If the "Shorter Form" is used, the indented text in brackets is omitted.]

℣. The Lord be with you. ℟. **And with your spirit.**
✚ A reading from the holy Gospel according to John.
℟. **Glory to you, O Lord.**

A S Jesus passed by he saw a man blind from birth. [His disciples asked him, "Rabbi, who sinned, this man or his parents, that he was born blind?" Jesus answered, "Neither he nor his parents sinned; it is so that the works of God might be made visible through him. We have to do the works of the one who sent me while it is day. Night is coming when no one can work. While I am in the world, I am the light of the world." When he had said this,]

———
* See p. 16 for other Gospel Acclamations.

he spat on the ground and made clay with the saliva, and smeared the clay on his eyes, and said to him, "Go wash in the Pool of Siloam"—which means Sent—. So he went and washed, and came back able to see.

His neighbors and those who had seen him earlier as a beggar said, "Isn't this the one who used to sit and beg?" Some said, "It is," but others said, "No, he just looks like him." He said, "I am."

[So they said to him, "How were your eyes opened?" He replied, "The man called Jesus made clay and anointed my eyes and told me, 'Go to Siloam and wash.' So I went there and washed and was able to see." And they said to him, "Where is he?" He said, "I don't know."]

They brought the one who was once blind to the Pharisees. Now Jesus had made clay and opened his eyes on a sabbath. So then the Pharisees also asked him how he was able to see. He said to them, "He put clay on my eyes, and I washed, and now I can see." So some of the Pharisees said, "This man is not from God, because he does not keep the sabbath." But others said, "How can a sinful man do such signs?" And there was a division among them. So they said to the blind man again, "What do you have to say about him, since he opened your eyes?" He said, "He is a prophet."

[Now the Jews did not believe that he had been blind and gained his sight until they summoned the parents of the one who had gained his sight. They asked them, "Is this your son, who you say was born blind? How does he now see?" His parents answered and said, "We know that this is our son and that he was born blind. We do not know how he sees now, nor do we know who opened his eyes. Ask him, he is of age; he can speak for himself." His parents said this because they were afraid of the Jews, for the Jews had already agreed that if anyone acknowl-

edged him as the Christ, he would be expelled from
the synagogue. For this reason his parents said, "He
is of age; question him."

So a second time they called the man who had
been blind and said to him, "Give God the praise! We
know that this man is a sinner." He replied, "If he is a
sinner, I do not know. One thing I do know is that I was
blind and now I see." So they said to him, "What did he
do to you? How did he open your eyes?" He answered
them, "I told you already and you did not listen. Why do
you want to hear it again? Do you want to become his
disciples, too?" They ridiculed him and said, "You are
that man's disciple; we are disciples of Moses! We
know that God spoke to Moses, but we do not know
where this one is from." The man answered and said to
them, "This is what is so amazing, that you do not know
where he is from, yet he opened my eyes. We know that
God does not listen to sinners, but if one is devout and
does his will, he listens to him. It is unheard of that
anyone ever opened the eyes of a person born blind. If
this man were not from God, he would not be able to
do anything."]

They answered and said to him, "You were born totally in
sin, and are you trying to teach us?" Then they threw him
out.

When Jesus heard that they had thrown him out, he
found him and said, "Do you believe in the Son of Man?"
He answered and said, "Who is he, sir, that I may believe
in him?" Jesus said to him, "You have seen him, and the
one speaking with you is he." He said, "I do believe, Lord,"
and he worshiped him.

[Then Jesus said, "I came into this world for judgment, so that those who do not see might see, and
those who do see might become blind."

Some of the Pharisees who were with him
heard this and said to him, "Surely we are not also

blind, are we?" Jesus said to them, "If you were blind,
you would have no sin; but now you are saying, 'We
see,' so your sin remains."]

The Gospel of the Lord. ℟. **Praise to you, Lord Jesus
Christ.**   → No. 15, p. 18

PRAYER OVER THE OFFERINGS   [Eternal Remedy]

We place before you with joy these offerings,
which bring eternal remedy, O Lord,
praying that we may both faithfully revere them
and present them to you, as is fitting,
for those who seek salvation.
Through Christ our Lord. ℟. **Amen.** ↓

PREFACE (P 15)   [From Darkness to Radiance]

℣. The Lord be with you. ℟. **And with your spirit.**
℣. Lift up your hearts. ℟. **We lift them up to the Lord.**
℣. Let us give thanks to the Lord our God. ℟. **It is right
and just.**

It is truly right and just, our duty and our salvation,
always and everywhere to give you thanks,
Lord, holy Father, almighty and eternal God,
through Christ our Lord.

By the mystery of the Incarnation,
he has led the human race that walked in darkness
into the radiance of the faith
and has brought those born in slavery to ancient sin
through the waters of regeneration
to make them your adopted children.

Therefore, all creatures of heaven and earth
sing a new song in adoration,
and we, with all the host of Angels,
cry out, and without end acclaim: → No. 23, p. 23

*The commemoration of the godparents in the Eucharistic
Prayers takes place as above (pp. 224, 225) and, if the Roman
Canon is used, the proper form of the* Hanc igitur *(Therefore,*

Lord, we pray) *is said, as in the First Scrutiny (p. 225). The rest follows the Roman Canon, pp. 25–29.*

COMMUNION ANT. Cf. Jn 9:11, 38   [Spiritual Sight]

The Lord anointed my eyes: I went, I washed, I saw and I believed in God. ↓

PRAYER AFTER COMMUNION   [God's Kindness]

Sustain your family always in your kindness,
O Lord, we pray,
correct them, set them in order,
graciously protect them under your rule,
and in your unfailing goodness
direct them along the way of salvation.
Through Christ our Lord.
℟. **Amen.**   → No. 30, p. 77

Optional Solemn Blessings, p. 97, and Prayers over the People, p. 105

"Go, and from now on do not sin any more."

MARCH 13

5th SUNDAY OF LENT

On this Sunday is celebrated the Third Scrutiny in preparation for the Baptism of the catechumens who are to be admitted to the Sacraments of Christian Initiation at the Easter Vigil. The Ritual Mass for the Third Scrutiny is found on p. 245.

ENTRANCE ANT. Cf. Ps 43 (42):1-2   **[Rescue Me]**
Give me justice, O God, and plead my cause against a nation that is faithless. From the deceitful and cunning rescue me, for you, O God, are my strength.

→ No. 2, p. 10 (Omit Gloria)

COLLECT   **[Walk in Charity]**

By your help, we beseech you, Lord our God,
may we walk eagerly in that same charity
with which, out of love for the world,
your Son handed himself over to death.
Through our Lord Jesus Christ, your Son,
who lives and reigns with you in the unity of the Holy
    Spirit,

239

one God, for ever and ever.
℟. **Amen.** ↓

FIRST READING Is 43:16-21   [Hope for the Future]

A call to look with hope to the future. God is not dead. Look around you and see his wonderful works.

A reading from the Book of the Prophet Isaiah

T HUS says the LORD,
who opens a way in the sea
   and a path in the mighty waters,
who leads out chariots and horsemen,
   a powerful army,
till they lie prostrate together, never to rise,
   snuffed out and quenched like a wick.
Remember not the events of the past,
   the things of long ago consider not;
see, I am doing something new!
   Now it springs forth, do you not perceive it?
In the desert I make a way,
   in the wasteland, rivers.
Wild beasts honor me,
   jackals and ostriches,
for I put water in the desert
   and rivers in the wasteland
   for my chosen people to drink,
the people whom I formed for myself,
   that they might announce my praise.
The word of the Lord. ℟. **Thanks be to God.** ↓

RESPONSORIAL PSALM Ps 126   [Joy of the Redeemed]

℟. **The Lord has done great things for us;   we are filled with joy.**

When the LORD brought back the captives of Zion,
   we were like men dreaming.

Then our mouth was filled with laughter,
  and our tongue with rejoicing.

℟. **The Lord has done great things for us; we are filled
    with joy.**

Then they said among the nations,
  "The LORD has done great things for them."
The LORD has done great things for us;
  we are glad indeed.

℟. **The Lord has done great things for us; we are filled
    with joy.**

Restore our fortunes, O LORD,
  like the torrents in the southern desert.
Those that sow in tears
  shall reap rejoicing.

℟. **The Lord has done great things for us; we are filled
    with joy.**

Although they go forth weeping,
  carrying the seed to be sown,
they shall come back rejoicing,
  carrying their sheaves.

℟. **The Lord has done great things for us; we are filled
    with joy.** ↓

SECOND READING Phil 3:8-14   [Life in Christ]

**Faith in Christ is our salvation, but we cannot relax. We
must continue, while in this life, to strive for the good
things of life in Christ—heaven.**

A reading from the Letter of Saint Paul to
the Philippians

BROTHERS and sisters: I consider everything as a
loss because of the supreme good of knowing
Christ Jesus my Lord. For his sake I have accepted the
loss of all things and I consider them so much rubbish,
that I may gain Christ and be found in him, not having

any righteousness of my own based on the law but that
which comes through faith in Christ, the righteousness
from God, depending on faith to know him and the
power of his resurrection and the sharing of his sufferings by being conformed to his death, if somehow I
may attain the resurrection from the dead.

It is not that I have already taken hold of it or have
already attained perfect maturity, but I continue my
pursuit in hope that I may possess it, since I have
indeed been taken possession of by Christ Jesus.
Brothers and sisters, I for my part do not consider
myself to have taken possession. Just one thing: forgetting what lies behind but straining forward to what
lies ahead, I continue my pursuit toward the goal, the
prize of God's upward calling, in Christ Jesus.—The
word of the Lord. ℟. **Thanks be to God.** ↓

VERSE BEFORE THE GOSPEL Jl 2:12-13 [Return to God]
℟. **Praise and honor to you, Lord Jesus Christ!***
Even now, says the Lord,
return to me with your whole heart;
for I am gracious and merciful.
℟. **Praise and honor to you, Lord Jesus Christ!** ↓

GOSPEL Jn 8:1-11   [Christ's Forgiveness]
By his example and works the Lord teaches us that God
extends his mercy to sinners to free them from slavery to sin.

℣. The Lord be with you. ℟. **And with your spirit.**
✠ A reading from the holy Gospel according to John.
℟. **Glory to you, O Lord.**

JESUS went to the Mount of Olives. But early in the
morning he arrived again in the temple area, and all
the people started coming to him, and he sat down and
taught them. Then the scribes and the Pharisees

---

* See p. 16 for other Gospel Acclamations.

brought a woman who had been caught in adultery and made her stand in the middle. They said to him, "Teacher, this woman was caught in the very act of committing adultery. Now in the law, Moses command-ed us to stone such women. So what do you say?" They said this to test him, so that they could have some charge to bring against him. Jesus bent down and began to write on the ground with his finger. But when they continued asking him, he straightened up and said to them, "Let the one among you who is without sin be the first to throw a stone at her." Again he bent down and wrote on the ground. And in response, they went away one by one, beginning with the elders. So he was left alone with the woman before him. Then Jesus straightened up and said to her, "Woman, where are they? Has no one condemned you?" She replied, "No one, sir." Then Jesus said, "Neither do I condemn you. Go, and from now on do not sin any more."—The Gospel of the Lord. ℟. **Praise to you, Lord Jesus Christ.**   ➙ No. 15, p. 18

PRAYER OVER THE OFFERINGS   [Hear Us]

Hear us, almighty God,
and, having instilled in your servants
the teachings of the Christian faith,
graciously purify them
by the working of this sacrifice.
Through Christ our Lord.
℟. **Amen.**   ➙ No. 21, p. 22 (Pref. P 8-9)

When the Gospel of Lazarus is read, see p. 249 for Preface (P 16).

COMMUNION ANT. Jn 8:10-11   [Sin No More]

Has no one condemned you, woman? No one, Lord. Neither shall I condemn you. From now on, sin no more. ↓

When the Gospel of Lazarus is read:

COMMUNION ANT. Cf. Jn 11:26 [Eternal Life]
Everyone who lives and believes in me will not die for ever, says the Lord. ↓

PRAYER AFTER COMMUNION [Union with Jesus]
We pray, almighty God,
that we may always be counted among the members of
   Christ,
in whose Body and Blood we have communion.
Who lives and reigns for ever and ever.
℞. **Amen.** ↓

*The Deacon or, in his absence, the Priest himself, says the
invitation:* Bow down for the blessing.

PRAYER OVER THE PEOPLE [Gift of Mercy]
Bless, O Lord, your people,
who long for the gift of your mercy,
and grant that what, at your prompting, they desire
they may receive by your generous gift.
Through Christ our Lord.
℞. **Amen.** → No. 32, p. 77

MASS FOR THE THIRD SCRUTINY

This Mass is celebrated when the Third Scrutiny takes place during the Rite of Christian Initiation of Adults, usually on the 5th Sunday of Lent. The readings may be used in any case.

ENTRANCE ANT. Cf. Ps 18 (17):5-7   [The Lord Hears Me]

The waves of death rose about me; the pains of the nether-world surrounded me. In my anguish I called to the Lord; and from his holy temple he heard my voice.

→ No. 2, p. 10 (Omit Gloria)

COLLECT   [Chosen Ones]

Grant, O Lord, to these chosen ones
that, instructed in the holy mysteries,
they may receive new life at the font of Baptism
and be numbered among the members of your Church.
Through our Lord Jesus Christ, your Son,
who lives and reigns with you in the unity of the Holy Spirit,
one God, for ever and ever. ℟. **Amen.** ↓

FIRST READING Ez 37:12-14   [The Lord's Promise]

The Lord promises to bring his people back to their home-land. He will be with them and they will know him.

A reading from the Book of the Prophet Ezekiel

THUS says the LORD God: O my people, I will open your graves and have you rise from them, and bring you back to the land of Israel. Then you shall know that I am the LORD, when I open your graves and have you rise from them, O my people! I will put my spirit in you that you may live, and I will settle you upon your land; thus you shall know that I am the LORD. I have promised, and I will do it, says the LORD.—The word of the Lord. ℟. **Thanks be to God.** ↓

RESPONSORIAL PSALM Ps 130   [Mercy and Redemption]

℟. With the Lord there is mer-cy   and fullness of redemption.

Out of the depths I cry to you, O LORD;
  LORD, hear my voice!
Let your ears be attentive
  to my voice in supplication.

℟. **With the Lord there is mercy and fullness of redemption.**

If you, O LORD, mark iniquities,
  LORD, who can stand?
But with you is forgiveness,
  that you may be revered.—℟.

I trust in the LORD;
  my soul trusts in his word.
More than sentinels wait for the dawn,
  let Israel wait for the LORD.—℟.

For with the LORD is kindness
  and with him is plenteous redemption;
and he will redeem Israel
  from all their iniquities.—℟. ↓

SECOND READING Rom 8:8-11   [Indwelling of Christ's Spirit]

  **The followers of Jesus live in the Spirit of God. The same
  Spirit who brought Jesus back to life will bring mortal bodies to life since God's Spirit dwells in them.**

  A reading from the Letter of Saint Paul to the Romans

B ROTHERS and sisters: Those who are in the flesh cannot please God. But you are not in the flesh; on the
contrary, you are in the spirit, if only the Spirit of God
dwells in you. Whoever does not have the Spirit of Christ
does not belong to him. But if Christ is in you, although
the body is dead because of sin, the spirit is alive because
of righteousness. If the Spirit of the one who raised Jesus
from the dead dwells in you, the one who raised Christ
from the dead will give life to your mortal bodies also,
through his Spirit dwelling in you.—The word of the Lord.
℟. **Thanks be to God.** ↓

VERSE BEFORE THE GOSPEL Jn 11:25a, 26   [Resurrection]

℟. **Praise and honor to you, Lord Jesus Christ!***
I am the resurrection and the life, says the Lord;
whoever believes in me, even if he dies, will never die.
℟. **Praise and honor to you, Lord Jesus Christ!** ↓

GOSPEL Jn 11:1-45 or 11:3-7, 17, 20-27, 33b-45   [Lazarus]

**Lazarus, the brother of Martha and Mary, died and was
buried. When Jesus came, he assured them that he was the
resurrection and the life. Jesus gave life back to Lazarus.**

*[If the "Shorter Form" is used, the indented text in brackets is
omitted.]*

℣. The Lord be with you. ℟. **And with your spirit.**
✚ A reading from the holy Gospel according to John.
℟. **Glory to you, O Lord.**

[N OW a man was ill, Lazarus from Bethany, the
village of Mary and her sister Martha. Mary
was the one who had anointed the Lord with perfumed oil and dried his feet with her hair; it was her
brother Lazarus who was ill.]
[So] the sisters** sent word to Jesus saying, "Master, the
one you love is ill." When Jesus heard this he said, "This
illness is not to end in death, but is for the glory of God,
that the Son of God may be glorified through it." Now Jesus
loved Martha and her sister and Lazarus. So when he heard
that he was ill, he remained for two days in the place where
he was. Then after this he said to his disciples, "Let us go
back to Judea."

[The disciples said to him, "Rabbi, the Jews were just
trying to stone you, and you want to go back there?"
Jesus answered, "Are there not twelve hours in a day?
If one walks during the day, he does not stumble,
because he sees the light of this world. But if one walks
at night, he stumbles, because the light is not in him."

---

* *See p. 16 for other Gospel Acclamations.*
** *The Shorter Form adds "of Lazarus."*

He said this, and then told them, "Our friend Lazarus is asleep, but I am going to awaken him." So the disciples said to him, "Master, if he is asleep, he will be saved." But Jesus was talking about his death, while they thought that he meant ordinary sleep. So then Jesus said to them clearly, "Lazarus has died. And I am glad for you that I was not there, that you may believe. Let us go to him." So Thomas, called Didymus, said to his fellow disciples, "Let us also go to die with him."]

When Jesus arrived, he found that Lazarus had already been in the tomb for four days.

[Now Bethany was near Jerusalem, only about two miles away. And many of the Jews had come to Martha and Mary to comfort them about their brother.]

When Martha heard that Jesus was coming, she went to meet him; but Mary sat at home. Martha said to Jesus, "Lord, if you had been here, my brother would not have died. But even now I know that whatever you ask of God, God will give you." Jesus said to her, "Your brother will rise." Martha said to him, "I know he will rise, in the resurrection on the last day." Jesus told her, "I am the resurrection and the life; whoever believes in me, even if he dies, will live, and everyone who lives and believes in me will never die. Do you believe this?" She said to him, "Yes, Lord. I have come to believe that you are the Christ, the Son of God, the one who is coming into the world."

[When she had said this, she went and called her sister Mary secretly, saying, "The teacher is here and is asking for you." As soon as she heard this, she rose quickly and went to him. For Jesus had not yet come into the village, but was still where Martha had met him. So when the Jews who were with her in the house comforting her saw Mary get up quickly and go out, they followed her, presuming that she was going to the tomb to weep there. When Mary came to where Jesus was and saw him, she fell at his feet and said to him, "Lord, if you had been here, my brother would not

have died." When Jesus saw her weeping and the
    Jews who had come with her weeping,]
he became perturbed and deeply troubled, and said,
"Where have you laid him?" They said to him, "Sir, come
and see." And Jesus wept. So the Jews said, "See how he
loved him." But some of them said, "Could not the one who
opened the eyes of the blind man have done something so
that this man would not have died?"

So Jesus, perturbed again, came to the tomb. It was a
cave, and a stone lay across it. Jesus said, "Take away the
stone." Martha, the dead man's sister, said to him, "Lord,
by now there will be a stench; he has been dead for four
days." Jesus said to her, "Did I not tell you that if you
believe you will see the glory of God?" So they took away
the stone. And Jesus raised his eyes and said, "Father, I
thank you for hearing me. I know that you always hear
me; but because of the crowd here I have said this, that
they may believe that you sent me." And when he had said
this, he cried out in a loud voice, "Lazarus, come out!" The
dead man came out, tied hand and foot with burial bands,
and his face was wrapped in a cloth. So Jesus said to
them, "Untie him and let him go."

Now many of the Jews who had come to Mary and seen
what he had done began to believe in him.—The Gospel
of the Lord. ℟. **Praise to you, Lord Jesus Christ.**

→ No. 15, p. 18

PREFACE (P 16)   [God Raised Lazarus]

PRAYER OVER THE OFFERINGS   [Hear Us]

Hear us, almighty God,
and, having instilled in your servants
the first fruits of the Christian faith,
graciously purify them by the working of this sacrifice.
Through Christ our Lord. ℟. **Amen.** ↓

PREFACE (P 16)   [God Raised Lazarus]

℣. The Lord be with you. ℟. **And with your spirit.**
℣. Lift up your hearts. ℟. **We lift them up to the Lord.**

℣. Let us give thanks to the Lord our God. ℟. **It is right and just.**

It is truly right and just, our duty and our salvation,
always and everywhere to give you thanks,
Lord, holy Father, almighty and eternal God,
through Christ our Lord.

For as true man he wept for Lazarus his friend
and as eternal God raised him from the tomb,
just as, taking pity on the human race,
he leads us by sacred mysteries to new life.

Through him the host of Angels adores your majesty
and rejoices in your presence for ever.
May our voices, we pray, join with theirs
in one chorus of exultant praise, as we acclaim:

→ No. 23, p. 23

*The commemoration of the godparents in the Eucharistic
Prayers takes place as above (pp. 224, 225) and, if the Roman
Canon is used, the proper form of the* Hanc igitur *(Therefore,
Lord, we pray) is said, as in the First Scrutiny (p. 225). The rest
follows the Roman Canon, pp. 25-29.*

COMMUNION ANT. Cf. Jn 11:26   [Obtain Grace]
**Everyone who lives and believes in me will not die for
ever, says the Lord.** ↓

PRAYER AFTER COMMUNION   [Joy at Salvation]
May your people be at one, O Lord, we pray,
and in wholehearted submission to you
may they obtain this grace:
that, safe from all distress,
they may readily live out their joy at being saved
and remember in loving prayer those to be reborn.
Through Christ our Lord.
℟. **Amen.**   → No. 30, p. 77

Optional Solemn Blessings, p. 97, and Prayers over the People, p. 105

*"Blessed are you, who have come
in your abundant mercy!"*

MARCH 20

PALM SUNDAY OF THE PASSION
OF THE LORD

*On this day the Church recalls the entrance of Christ the
Lord into Jerusalem to accomplish his Paschal Mystery.
Accordingly, the memorial of this entrance of the Lord takes
place at all Masses, by means of the Procession or the Solemn
Entrance before the principal Mass or the Simple Entrance
before other Masses. The Solemn Entrance, but not the
Procession, may be repeated before other Masses that are
usually celebrated with a large gathering of people.*

*It is desirable that, where neither the Procession nor the
Solemn Entrance can take place, there be a sacred celebration
of the Word of God on the messianic entrance and on the
Passion of the Lord, either on Saturday evening or on Sunday
at a convenient time.*

The Commemoration of the Lord's Entrance
into Jerusalem

FIRST FORM: THE PROCESSION

*At an appropriate hour, a gathering takes place at a smaller
church or other suitable place other than inside the church*

to which the procession will go. The faithful hold branches in their hands.

Meanwhile, the following antiphon or another appropriate chant is sung.

ANTIPHON Mt 21:9   [Hosanna]

Hosanna to the Son of David;
blessed is he who comes
in the name of the Lord,
the King of Israel.
Hosanna in the highest.

After this, the Priest and people sign themselves, while the Priest says: In the name of the Father, and of the Son, and of the Holy Spirit. *Then he greets the people in the usual way. A brief address is given, in which the faithful are invited to participate actively and consciously in the celebration of this day, in these or similar words:*

Dear brethren (brothers and sisters),
since the beginning of Lent until now
we have prepared our hearts by penance and charitable
     works.
Today we gather together to herald with the whole
     Church
the beginning of the celebration
of our Lord's Paschal Mystery,
that is to say, of his Passion and Resurrection.
For it was to accomplish this mystery
that he entered his own city of Jerusalem.
Therefore, with all faith and devotion,
let us commemorate
the Lord's entry into the city for our salvation,
following in his footsteps,
so that, being made by his grace partakers of the Cross,
we may have a share also in his Resurrection and in his
     life.

After the address, the Priest says one of the following prayers with hands extended.

PRAYER   [Following Christ]

Let us pray.
Almighty ever-living God,
sanctify ✛ these branches with your blessing,
that we, who follow Christ the King in exultation,
may reach the eternal Jerusalem through him.
Who lives and reigns for ever and ever. ℟. **Amen.** ↓

OR   [Christ in Triumph]

Increase the faith of those who place their hope in you,
    O God,
and graciously hear the prayers of those who call on you,
that we, who today hold high these branches
to hail Christ in his triumph,
may bear fruit for you by good works accomplished in
    him.
Who lives and reigns for ever and ever.
℟. **Amen.** ↓

*The Priest sprinkles the branches with holy water without
saying anything.*

*Then a Deacon or, if there is no Deacon, a Priest, proclaims
in the usual way the Gospel concerning the Lord's entrance
according to one of the four Gospels.*

GOSPEL Lk 19:28-40   [Jesus' Triumphal Entry]

**In triumphant glory Jesus comes into Jerusalem. The peo-
ple spread their cloaks on the ground for him, wave olive
branches, and sing in his honor.**

℣. The Lord be with you. ℟. **And with your spirit.**
✛ A reading from the holy Gospel according to Luke.
℟. **Glory to you, O Lord.**

JESUS proceeded on his journey up to Jerusalem. As
he drew near to Bethphage and Bethany at the place
called the Mount of Olives, he sent two of his disciples.
He said, "Go into the village opposite you, and as you
enter it you will find a colt tethered on which no one has

ever sat. Untie it and bring it here. And if anyone should ask you, 'Why are you untying it?' you will answer, 'The Master has need of it.'" So those who had been sent went off and found everything just as he had told them. And as they were untying the colt, its owners said to them, "Why are you untying this colt?" They answered, "The Master has need of it." So they brought it to Jesus, threw their cloaks over the colt, and helped Jesus to mount. As he rode along, the people were spreading their cloaks on the road; and now as he was approaching the slope of the Mount of Olives, the whole multitude of his disciples began to praise God aloud with joy for all the mighty deeds they had seen. They proclaimed:

"Blessed is the king who comes
   in the name of the Lord.
Peace in heaven
   and glory in the highest."

Some of the Pharisees in the crowd said to him, "Teacher, rebuke your disciples." He said in reply, "I tell you, if they keep silent, the stones will cry out!"—The Gospel of the Lord. ℟. **Praise to you, Lord Jesus Christ**.

After the Gospel, a brief homily may be given. Then, to begin the Procession, an invitation may be given by a Priest or a Deacon or a lay minister, in these or similar words:

Dear brethren (brothers and sisters),
like the crowds who acclaimed Jesus in Jerusalem,
let us go forth in peace.

OR

Let us go forth in peace.
℟. **In the name of Christ. Amen**.

The Procession to the church where Mass will be celebrated then sets off in the usual way. If incense is used, the thurifer goes first, carrying a thurible with burning incense, then an acolyte or another minister, carrying a cross decorated with palm branches according to local custom, between two ministers with lighted candles. Then follow the Deacon carrying the Book of the Gospels, the Priest with the ministers, and, after them, all the faithful carrying branches.

As the Procession moves forward, the following or other suitable chants in honor of Christ the King are sung by the choir and people.

ANTIPHON 1   [Hosanna]

The children of the Hebrews, carrying olive branches, went to meet the Lord, crying out and saying: Hosanna in the highest.

If appropriate, this antiphon is repeated between the strophes (verses) of the following Psalm.

PSALM 24 (23)   [The King of Glory]

The LORD's is the earth and its fullness, the world, and those who dwell in it. It is he who set it on the seas; on the rivers he made it firm. *(The antiphon is repeated.)*

Who shall climb the mountain of the LORD? The clean of hands and pure of heart, whose soul is not set on vain things, who has not sworn deceitful words.
(The antiphon is repeated.)

Blessings from the LORD shall he receive, and right reward from the God who saves him. Such are the people who seek him, who seek the face of the God of Jacob.
(The antiphon is repeated.)

O gates, lift high your heads; grow higher, ancient doors. Let him enter, the king of glory! Who is this king of glory? The LORD, the mighty, the valiant; the LORD, the valiant in war. *(The antiphon is repeated.)*

O gates, lift high your heads; grow higher, ancient doors.

Let him enter, the king of glory!
Who is this king of glory?
He, the LORD of hosts,
he is the king of glory.   *(The antiphon is repeated.)*

ANTIPHON 2   [Hosanna]

The children of the Hebrews spread their garments on
   the road,
crying out and saying: Hosanna to the Son of David;
blessed is he who comes in the name of the Lord.

*If appropriate, this antiphon is repeated between the strophes
(verses) of the following Psalm.*

PSALM 47 (46)   [The Great King]

All peoples, clap your hands.
Cry to God with shouts of joy!
For the LORD, the Most high, is awesome,
the great king over all the earth. *(The antiphon is repeated.)*

He humbles peoples under us
and nations under our feet.
Our heritage he chose for us,
the pride of Jacob whom he loves.
God goes up with shouts of joy.
The LORD goes up with trumpet blast.
                    (The antiphon is repeated.)
Sing praise for God; sing praise!
Sing praise to our king; sing praise!
God is king of all earth.
Sing praise with all your skill. *(The antiphon is repeated.)*

God reigns over the nations.
God sits upon his holy throne.
The princes of the peoples are assembled
with the people of the God of Abraham.
The rulers of the earth belong to God,
who is greatly exalted.   *(The antiphon is repeated.)*

Hymn to Christ the King

Chorus:

Glory and honor and praise be to you, Christ, King and Redeemer,

to whom young children cried out loving Hosannas with joy.

All repeat: **Glory and honor . . .**

Chorus:

Israel's King are you, King David's magnificent offspring;

you are the ruler who come blest in the name of the Lord.

All repeat: **Glory and honor . . .**

Chorus:

Heavenly hosts on high unite in singing your praises;

men and women on earth and all creation join in.

All repeat: **Glory and honor . . .**

Chorus:

Bearing branches of palm, Hebrews came crowding to greet you;

see how with prayers and hymns we come to pay you our vows.

All repeat: **Glory and honor . . .**

Chorus:

They offered gifts of praise to you, so near to your Passion;

see how we sing this song now to you reigning on high.

All repeat: **Glory and honor . . .**

Chorus:

Those you were pleased to accept; now accept our gifts of devotion,

good and merciful King, lover of all that is good.

All repeat: **Glory and honor . . .**

As the procession enters the church, there is sung the following responsory or another chant, which should speak of the Lord's entrance.

RESPONSORY

℟. **As the Lord entered the holy city, the children of the Hebrews proclaimed the resurrection of life. Waving their branches of palm, they cried: Hosanna in the Highest.**

℣. **When the people heard that Jesus was coming to Jerusalem, they went out to meet him. Waving their branches of palm, they cried: Hosanna in the Highest.**

When the Priest arrives at the altar, he venerates it and, if appropriate, incenses it. Then he goes to the chair, where he puts aside the cope, if he has worn one, and puts on the chasuble. Omitting the other Introductory Rites of the Mass and, if appropriate, the Kyrie (Lord, have mercy), *he says the Collect of the Mass, and then continues the Mass in the usual way.*

SECOND FORM: THE SOLEMN ENTRANCE

When a procession outside the church cannot take place, the entrance of the Lord is celebrated inside the church by means of a Solemn Entrance before the principal Mass.

Holding branches in their hands, the faithful gather either outside, in front of the church door, or inside the church itself. The Priest and ministers and a representative group of the faithful go to a suitable place in the church outside the sanctuary, where at least the greater part of the faithful can see the rite.

While the Priest approaches the appointed place, the antiphon Hosanna *or another appropriate chant is sung. Then the blessing of branches and the proclamation of the Gospel of the Lord's entrance into Jerusalem take place as above (pp. 253-254). After the Gospel, the Priest processes solemnly with the ministers and the representative group of the faithful through the church to the sanctuary, while the responsory* As the Lord entered *(above) or another appropriate chant is sung.*

*Arriving at the altar, the Priest venerates it. He then goes to the
chair and, omitting the Introductory Rites of the Mass and, if
appropriate, the* Kyrie (Lord, have mercy), *he says the
Collect of the Mass, and then continues the Mass in the usual
way.*

THIRD FORM: THE SIMPLE ENTRANCE

*At all other Masses of this Sunday at which the Solemn
Entrance is not held, the memorial of the Lord's entrance
into Jerusalem takes place by means of a Simple Entrance.*

*While the Priest proceeds to the altar, the Entrance Antiphon
with its Psalm (below) or another chant on the same theme is
sung. Arriving at the altar, the Priest venerates it and goes to
the chair. After the Sign of the Cross, he greets the people and
continues the Mass in the usual way.*

*At other Masses, in which singing at the entrance cannot
take place, the Priest, as soon as he has arrived at the altar
and venerated it, greets the people, reads the Entrance
Antiphon, and continues the Mass in the usual way.*

ENTRANCE ANT. Cf. Jn 12:1, 12-13; Ps 24 (23): 9-10
[Hosanna in the Highest]

**Six days before the Passover, when the Lord came
into the city of Jerusalem, the children ran to meet
him; in their hands they carried palm branches and
with a loud voice cried out: Hosanna in the highest!
Blessed are you, who have come in your abundant
mercy!**

**O gates, lift high your heads; grow higher, ancient
doors. Let him enter, the king of glory! Who is this
king of glory? He, the Lord of hosts, he is the king of
glory. Hosanna in the highest! Blessed are you, who
have come in your abundant mercy!**

AT THE MASS

*After the Procession or Solemn Entrance the Priest begins the
Mass with the Collect.*

COLLECT   [Patient Suffering]

Almighty ever-living God,
who as an example of humility for the human race to
   follow
caused our Savior to take flesh and submit to the Cross,
graciously grant that we may heed his lesson of patient
   suffering
and so merit a share in his Resurrection.
Who lives and reigns with you in the unity of the Holy
   Spirit,
one God, for ever and ever.
℟. **Amen.** ↓

FIRST READING Is 50:4-7   [Christ's Suffering]
   **The sufferings of God's servant will not deter him from
   faith in God.**

   A reading from the Book of the Prophet Isaiah

T HE Lord GOD has given me
    a well-trained tongue,
that I might know how to speak to the weary
    a word that will rouse them.
Morning after morning
    he opens my ear that I may hear;
and I have not rebelled,
    have not turned back.
I gave my back to those who beat me,
    my cheeks to those who plucked my beard;
my face I did not shield
    from buffets and spitting.

The Lord GOD is my help,
    therefore I am not disgraced;
I have set my face like flint,
    knowing that I shall not be put to shame.
The word of the Lord. ℟. **Thanks be to God.** ↓

RESPONSORIAL PSALM Ps 22   [Christ's Abandonment]

℟. My God, my God, why have you a-ban - doned me?

All who see me scoff at me;
  they mock me with parted lips, they wag their
    heads:
"He relied on the Lord; let him deliver him,
  let him rescue him, if he loves him."

℟. **My God, my God, why have you abandoned me?**

Indeed, many dogs surround me,
  a pack of evildoers closes in upon me;
they have pierced my hands and my feet;
  I can count all my bones.

℟. **My God, my God, why have you abandoned me?**

They divide my garments among them,
  and for my vesture they cast lots.
But you, O Lord, be not far from me;
  O my help, hasten to aid me.

℟. **My God, my God, why have you abandoned me?**

I will proclaim your name to my brethren;
  in the midst of the assembly I will praise you:
"You who fear the Lord, praise him;
  all you descendants of Jacob, give glory to him;
  revere him, all you descendants of Israel!"

℟. **My God, my God, why have you abandoned me?** ↓

SECOND READING Phil 2:6-11   [Humility]
Jesus Christ is Lord!
A reading from the Letter of Saint Paul
to the Philippians

CHRIST Jesus, though he was in the form of God,
did not regard equality with God
something to be grasped.

Rather, he emptied himself,
  taking the form of a slave,
  coming in human likeness;
  and found human in appearance,
  he humbled himself,
  becoming obedient to the point of death,
  even death on a cross.
Because of this, God greatly exalted him
  and bestowed on him the name
  which is above every name,
  that at the name of Jesus
  every knee should bend,
  of those in heaven and on earth and under the earth,
  and every tongue confess that
  Jesus Christ is Lord,
  to the glory of God the Father.
The word of the Lord. ℟. **Thanks be to God.** ↓

VERSE BEFORE THE GOSPEL Phil 2:8-9 [Obedient to Death]

℟. **Praise to you, Lord Jesus Christ, King of endless
  glory!***

Christ became obedient to the point of death,
even death on the cross.
Because of this, God greatly exalted him
and bestowed on him the name which is above every
  name.

℟. **Praise to you, Lord Jesus Christ, King of endless
  glory!** ↓

GOSPEL Lk 22:14—23:56 or 23:1-49   [The Passion]
  **Attend to the account of Christ's last days, and consider
  how he suffered that we might have faith. By his Holy
  Cross he has saved the world.**

When the Shorter Form is read, see pp. 267-270.

* See p. 16 for other Gospel Acclamations.

The fourteen subheadings introduced into the reading enable those who so desire to meditate on this text while making the Stations of the Cross.

The Passion may be read by lay readers, with the part of Christ, if possible, read by a Priest. The Narrator is noted by N, the words of Jesus by a ✝ and the words of others by V (Voice) and C (Crowd). The parts of the Crowd (C) printed in boldface type may be recited by the people.

We participate in the Passion narrative in several ways: by reading it and reflecting on it during the week ahead; by listening with faith as it is proclaimed; by respectful posture during the narrative; by reverent silence after the passage about Christ's Death. We do not hold the palms during the reading on Palm Sunday.

The message of the liturgy in proclaiming the Passion narratives in full is to enable the assembly to see vividly the love of Christ for each person, despite their sins, a love that even death could not vanquish. The crimes during the Passion of Christ cannot be attributed indiscriminately to all Jews of that time, nor to Jews today. The Jewish people should not be referred to as though rejected or cursed, as if this view followed from Scripture. The Church ever keeps in mind that Jesus, his mother Mary, and the Apostles were Jewish. As the Church has always held, Christ freely suffered his Passion and Death because of the sins of all, that all might be saved.

This week we are challenged by the Passion narrative to reflect on the way we are living up to our baptismal promises of dying with Christ to sin and living with him for God.

N. THE Passion of our Lord Jesus Christ according to Luke.

1. THE HOLY EUCHARIST

N. WHEN the hour came, Jesus took his place at table with the apostles. He said to them, ✝ "I have eagerly desired to eat this Passover with you before I suffer, for, I tell you, I shall not eat it again until there is fulfillment in the kingdom of God."

N. Then he took a cup, gave thanks, and said, ✟ "Take this and share it among yourselves; for I tell you that from this time on I shall not drink of the fruit of the vine until the kingdom of God comes." **N.** Then he took the bread, said the blessing, broke it, and gave it to them, saying, ✟ "This is my body, which will be given for you; do this in memory of me." **N.** And likewise the cup after they had eaten, saying, ✟ "This cup is the new covenant in my blood, which will be shed for you.

2. THE BETRAYER

✟ "**A**ND yet behold, the hand of the one who is to betray me is with me on the table; for the Son of Man indeed goes as it has been determined; but woe to that man by whom he is betrayed." **N.** And they began to debate among themselves who among them would do such a deed.

3. WHO IS GREATEST?

N. **T**HEN an argument broke out among them about which of them should be regarded as the greatest. He said to them, ✟ "The kings of the Gentiles lord it over them and those in authority over them are addressed as 'Benefactors'; but among you it shall not be so. Rather, let the greatest among you be as the youngest, and the leader as the servant. For who is greater: the one seated at table or the one who serves? Is it not the one seated at table? I am among you as the one who serves. It is you who have stood by me in my trials; and I confer a kingdom on you, just as my Father has conferred one on me, that you may eat and drink at my table in my kingdom; and you will sit on thrones judging the twelve tribes of Israel.

4. PETER'S DENIALS FORETOLD

✟ "**S**IMON, Simon, behold Satan has demanded to sift all of you like wheat, but I have prayed that your own faith may not fail; and once you have turned back, you must strengthen your brothers." **N.** He said to him, **V.** "Lord, I am prepared to go to prison and to die with you." **N.** But he replied, ✠ "I tell you, Peter, before the cock crows this day, you will deny three times that you know me."

N. He said to them, ✠ "When I sent you forth without a money bag or a sack or sandals, were you in need of anything?" **C.** "No, nothing," **N.** they replied. He said to them, ✠ "But now one who has a money bag should take it, and likewise a sack, and one who does not have a sword should sell his cloak and buy one. For I tell you that this Scripture must be fulfilled in me, namely, *He was counted among the wicked;* and indeed what is written about me is coming to fulfillment." **N.** Then they said, **C.** "Lord, look, there are two swords here." **N.** But he replied, ✠ "It is enough!"

5. THE AGONY IN THE GARDEN

N. THEN going out, he went, as was his custom, to the Mount of Olives, and the disciples followed him. When he arrived at the place he said to them, ✠ "Pray that you may not undergo the test." **N.** After withdrawing about a stone's throw from them and kneeling, he prayed, saying, ✠ "Father, if you are willing, take this cup away from me; still, not my will but yours be done." **N.** And to strengthen him an angel from heaven appeared to him. He was in such agony and he prayed so fervently that his sweat became like drops of blood falling on the ground. When he rose from prayer and returned to his disciples, he found them sleeping from grief. He said to them, ✠ "Why are you sleeping? Get up and pray that you may not undergo the test."

6. JESUS ARRESTED

N. WHILE he was still speaking, a crowd approached and in front was one of the Twelve, a man named Judas. He went up to Jesus to kiss him. Jesus said to him, ✙ "Judas, are you betraying the Son of Man with a kiss?" **N.** His disciples realized what was about to happen, and they asked, **C. "Lord, shall we strike with a sword?" N.** And one of them struck the high priest's servant and cut off his right ear. But Jesus said in reply, ✙ "Stop, no more of this!" **N.** Then he touched the servant's ear and healed him. And Jesus said to the chief priests and temple guards and elders who had come for him, ✙ "Have you come out as against a robber, with swords and clubs? Day after day I was with you in the temple area, and you did not seize me; but this is your hour, the time for the power of darkness."

7. PETER'S DENIAL

N. AFTER arresting him they led him away and took him into the house of the high priest; Peter was following at a distance. They lit a fire in the middle of the courtyard and sat around it, and Peter sat down with them. When a maid saw him seated in the light, she looked intently at him and said, **C. "This man too was with him." N.** But he denied it saying, **V.** "Woman, I do not know him." **N.** A short while later someone else saw him and said, **C. "You too are one of them"; N.** but Peter answered, **V.** "My friend, I am not." **N.** About an hour later, still another insisted, **C. "Assuredly, this man too was with him, for he also is a Galilean." N.** But Peter said, **V.** "My friend, I do not know what you are talking about." **N.** Just as he was saying this, the cock crowed, and the Lord turned and looked at Peter; and Peter remembered the word of the Lord, how he had said to him, "Before the cock crows today, you will deny me three times." He went out and began to weep bitterly.

[8. JESUS BEFORE THE SANHEDRIN]

N. The men who held Jesus in custody were ridiculing and beating him. They blindfolded him and questioned him, saying, **C. "Prophesy! Who is it that struck you?"**

N. And they reviled him in saying many other things against him.

When day came the council of elders of the people met, both chief priests and scribes, and they brought him before their Sanhedrin. They said, **C. "If you are the Christ, tell us,"** N. but he replied to them, ✣ "If I tell you, you will not believe, and if I question, you will not respond. But from this time on the Son of Man will be seated at the right hand of the power of God." **N.** They all asked, **C. "Are you then the Son of God?" N.** He replied to them, ✣ "You say that I am." **N.** Then they said, **C. "What further need have we for testimony? We have heard it from his own mouth."**

[Beginning of Shorter Form]

9. JESUS BEFORE PILATE

N.*THE elders of the people, chief priests and scribes arose and brought him before Pilate. They brought charges against him, saying, **C. "We found this man misleading our people; he opposes the payment of taxes to Caesar and maintains that he is the Christ, a king." N.** Pilate asked him, **V.** "Are you the king of the Jews?" **N.** He said to him in reply, ✣ "You say so." **N.** Pilate then addressed the chief priests and the crowds, **V.** "I find this man not guilty." **N.** But they were adamant and said, **C. "He is inciting the people with his teaching throughout all Judea, from Galilee where he began even to here."**

N. On hearing this Pilate asked if the man was a Galilean; and upon learning that he was under Herod's jurisdiction, he sent him to Herod who was in Jerusalem at that time. Herod was very glad to see Jesus; he had been wanting to see him for a long time, for he had heard about him and had been hoping to see him perform some sign. He questioned him at length, but he gave him no

---

* *The Longer Form reads: "Then the whole assembly of them. . . ."*

answer. The chief priests and scribes, meanwhile, stood by accusing him harshly. Herod and his soldiers treated him contemptuously and mocked him, and after clothing him in resplendent garb, he sent him back to Pilate. Herod and Pilate became friends that very day, even though they had been enemies formerly.

[*10. JESUS AGAIN BEFORE PILATE*]

N. Pilate then summoned the chief priests, the rulers, and the people and said to them, **V.** "You brought this man to me and accused him of inciting the people to revolt. I have conducted my investigation in your presence and have not found this man guilty of the charges you have brought against him, nor did Herod, for he sent him back to us. So no capital crime has been committed by him. Therefore I shall have him flogged and then release him."

N. BUT all together they shouted out, **C. "Away with this man! Release Barabbas to us."** **N.**—Now Barabbas had been imprisoned for a rebellion that had taken place in the city and for murder.—Again Pilate addressed them, still wishing to release Jesus, but they continued their shouting, **C. "Crucify him! Crucify him!"** **N.** Pilate addressed them a third time, **V.** "What evil has this man done? I found him guilty of no capital crime. Therefore I shall have him flogged and then release him." **N.** With loud shouts, however, they persisted in calling for his crucifixion, and their voices prevailed. The verdict of Pilate was that their demand should be granted. So he released the man who had been imprisoned for rebellion and murder, for whom they asked, and he handed Jesus over to them to deal with as they wished.

11. THE WAY OF THE CROSS

N. AS they led him away they took hold of a certain Simon, a Cyrenian, who was coming in from the country; and after laying the cross on him, they made him carry it behind Jesus. A large crowd of people followed Jesus, including many women who mourned and lamented him. Jesus turned to them and said, ✠ "Daughters of Jerusalem, do not weep for me; weep instead for yourselves and for your children, for indeed, the days are coming when people will say, 'Blessed are the barren, the wombs that never bore and the breasts that never nursed.' At that time people will say to the mountains, 'Fall upon us!' and to the hills, 'Cover us!' for if these things are done when the wood is green what will happen when it is dry?"

[12. THE CRUCIFIXION]

N. Now two others, both criminals, were led away with him to be executed.

W HEN they came to the place called the Skull, they crucified him and the criminals there, one on his right, the other on his left. Then Jesus said, ✠ "Father, forgive them, they know not what they do." **N.** They divided his garments by casting lots. The people stood by and watched; the rulers, meanwhile, sneered at him and said, **C.** "He saved others, let him save himself if he is the chosen one, the Christ of God." **N.** Even the soldiers jeered at him. As they approached to offer him wine they called out, **C.** "If you are King of the Jews, save yourself." **N.** Above him there was an inscription that read, "THIS IS THE KING OF THE JEWS."

Now one of the criminals hanging there reviled Jesus, saying, **V.** "Are you not the Christ? Save yourself and us." **N.** The other, however, rebuking him, said in reply, **V.** "Have you no fear of God, for you are subject to the same condemnation? And indeed, we have been condemned justly, for the sentence we received corresponds to our crimes, but this man has done nothing criminal." **N.** Then he said, **V.** "Jesus, remember me when you come into your kingdom." **N.** He replied to him, ✠ "Amen, I say to you, today you will be with me in Paradise."

13. JESUS DIES ON THE CROSS

N. IT was now about noon and darkness came over the whole land until three in the afternoon because of an eclipse of the sun. Then the veil of the temple was torn down the middle. Jesus cried out in a loud voice, ✠ "Father, into your hands I commend my spirit"; **N.** and when he had said this he breathed his last.

Here all kneel and pause for a short time.

The centurion who witnessed what had happened glorified God and said, **V.** "This man was innocent beyond doubt." **N.** When all the people who had gathered for this spectacle saw what had happened, they returned home beating their breasts; but all his acquaintances stood at a distance, including the women who had followed him from Galilee and saw these events.

[End of Shorter Form]

14. THE BURIAL

N. NOW there was a virtuous and righteous man named Joseph who, though he was a member of the council, had not consented to their plan of action. He came from the Jewish town of Arimathea and was awaiting the kingdom of God. He went to Pilate and asked for the body of Jesus. After he had taken the body down, he wrapped it in a linen cloth and laid him in a rock-hewn tomb in which no one had yet been buried. It was the day of preparation, and the sabbath was about to begin. The women who had come from Galilee with him followed behind, and when they had seen the tomb and the way in which his body was laid in it, they returned and prepared spices and perfumed oils. Then they rested on the sabbath according to the commandment.—The Gospel of the Lord. ℟. **Praise to you Lord Jesus Christ.**   ➜ No. 15, p. 18

After the narrative of the Passion, a brief homily should take place, if appropriate. A period of silence may also be observed.

PRAYER OVER THE OFFERINGS   [Reconciled with God]

Through the Passion of your Only Begotten Son, O Lord,
may our reconciliation with you be near at hand,
so that, though we do not merit it by our own deeds,
yet by this sacrifice made once for all,
we may feel already the effects of your mercy.
Through Christ our Lord. ℟. **Amen.** ↓

PREFACE (P 19)   [Purchased Our Justification]

℣. The Lord be with you. ℟. **And with your spirit.**
℣. Lift up your hearts. ℟. **We lift them up to the Lord.**
℣. Let us give thanks to the Lord our God. ℟. **It is right and just.**

It is truly right and just, our duty and our salvation,
always and everywhere to give you thanks,
Lord, holy Father, almighty and eternal God,
through Christ our Lord.

For, though innocent, he suffered willingly for sinners
and accepted unjust condemnation to save the guilty.
His Death has washed away our sins,
and his Resurrection has purchased our justification.

And so, with all the Angels,
we praise you, as in joyful celebration we acclaim:

➜ No. 23, p. 23

COMMUNION ANT. Mt 26:42   [God's Will]

Father, if this chalice cannot pass without my drinking it, your will be done. ↓

PRAYER AFTER COMMUNION   [Nourishing Gifts]

Nourished with these sacred gifts,
we humbly beseech you, O Lord,

that, just as through the death of your Son
you have brought us to hope for what we believe,
so by his Resurrection
you may lead us to where you call.
Through Christ our Lord.
℟. **Amen.** ↓

*The Deacon or, in his absence, the Priest himself, says the
invitation:* Bow down for the blessing.

PRAYER OVER THE PEOPLE   [God's Family]

Look, we pray, O Lord, on this your family,
for whom our Lord Jesus Christ
did not hesitate to be delivered into the hands of the
    wicked
and submit to the agony of the Cross.
Who lives and reigns for ever and ever.
℟. **Amen.**   ➜ No. 32, p. 77

"The Spirit of the Lord is upon me."

MARCH 24

THURSDAY OF HOLY WEEK
[HOLY THURSDAY]

THE CHRISM MASS

This Mass, which the Bishop concelebrates with his presbyterate, should be, as it were, a manifestation of the Priests' communion with their Bishop. Accordingly it is desirable that all the Priests participate in it, insofar as is possible, and during it receive Communion even under both kinds. To signify the unity of the presbyterate of the diocese, the Priests who concelebrate with the Bishop should be from different regions of the diocese.

In accord with traditional practice, the blessing of the Oil of the Sick takes place before the end of the Eucharistic Prayer, but the blessing of the Oil of Catechumens and the consecration of the Chrism take place after Communion. Nevertheless, for pastoral reasons, it is permitted for the entire rite of blessing to take place after the Liturgy of the Word.

ENTRANCE ANT. Rev 1:6   [Kingdom of Priests]
Jesus Christ has made us into a kingdom, priests for his God and Father. To him be glory and power for ever and ever. Amen.   → No. 2, p. 10

The Gloria *is said.*

COLLECT   [Faithful Witnesses]

O God, who anointed your Only Begotten Son with the
  Holy Spirit
and made him Christ and Lord,
graciously grant
that, being made sharers in his consecration,
we may bear witness to your Redemption in the world.
Through our Lord Jesus Christ, your Son,
who lives and reigns with you in the unity of the Holy
  Spirit,
one God, for ever and ever. ℟. **Amen.** ↓

FIRST READING Is 61:1-3ab, 6a, 8b-9   [The Lord's Anointed]

**The prophet, anointed by God to bring the Good News to
the poor, proclaims a message filled with hope. It is one
that replaces mourning with gladness.**

A reading from the Book of the Prophet Isaiah

THE Spirit of the Lord GOD is upon me,
  because the LORD has anointed me;
He has sent me to bring glad tidings to the poor,
  to heal the brokenhearted,
To proclaim liberty to the captives
  and release to the prisoners,
To announce a year of favor from the LORD
  and a day of vindication by our God,
  to comfort all who mourn;
To place on those who mourn in Zion
  a diadem instead of ashes,
To give them oil of gladness in place of mourning,
  a glorious mantle instead of a listless spirit.
You yourselves shall be named priests of the LORD,
  ministers of our God you shall be called.

I will give them their recompense faithfully,
  a lasting covenant I will make with them.

Their descendants shall be renowned among the
  nations,
    and their offspring among the peoples;
  All who see them shall acknowledge them
    as a race the LORD has blessed.
The word of the Lord. ℟. **Thanks be to God.** ↓

RESPONSORIAL PSALM Ps 89   [God the Savior]

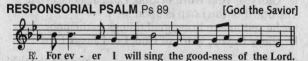

  ℟. For ev - er I will sing the good-ness of the Lord.

"I have found David, my servant;
  with my holy oil I have anointed him,
that my hand may be always with him,
  and that my arm may make him strong."—℟.

"My faithfulness and my kindness shall be with him,
  and through my name shall his horn be exalted.
He shall say of me, 'You are my father,
  my God, the Rock my savior.' "—℟. ↓

SECOND READING Rv 1:5-8   [The Alpha and the Omega]
God says, "I am the Alpha and the Omega, the one who is
and who was and who is to come, the almighty!" All shall
see God as he comes amid the clouds.

A reading from the Book of Revelation

[GRACE to you and peace] from Jesus Christ, who is
the faithful witness, the firstborn of the dead and
ruler of the kings of earth. To him who loves us and has
freed us from our sins by his Blood, who has made us
into a Kingdom, priests for his God and Father, to him
be glory and power forever and ever! Amen.
  Behold, he is coming amid the clouds,
    and every eye will see him,
      even of those who pierced him.
  All the peoples of the earth will lament him.
    Yes. Amen.

"I am the Alpha and the Omega," says the Lord God, "the one who is and who was and who is to come, the almighty!"—The word of the Lord. ℟. **Thanks be to God.** ↓

VERSE BEFORE THE GOSPEL Is 61:1 (cited in Lk 4:18)

[Glad Tidings]

℟. **Glory to you, Word of God, Lord Jesus Christ!*
The Spirit of the LORD is upon me
for he sent me to bring glad tidings to the poor.
℟. **Glory to you, Word of God, Lord Jesus Christ!** ↓

GOSPEL Lk 4:16-21   [Christ the Messiah]
Jesus reads in the synagogue at Nazareth the words of Isaiah quoted in the first reading. Jesus is the Anointed One. He tells the people that today Isaiah's prophecy is fulfilled.

℣. The Lord be with you. ℟. **And with your spirit.**
✝ A reading from the holy Gospel according to Luke.
℟. **Glory to you, O Lord.**

J ESUS came to Nazareth, where he had grown up, and went according to his custom into the synagogue on the sabbath day. He stood up to read and was handed a scroll of the prophet Isaiah. He unrolled the scroll and found the passage where it was written:
The Spirit of the Lord is upon me,
because he has anointed me
to bring glad tidings to the poor.
He has sent me to proclaim liberty to captives
and recovery of sight to the blind,
to let the oppressed go free,
and to proclaim a year acceptable to the Lord.
Rolling up the scroll, he handed it back to the attendant and sat down, and the eyes of all in the synagogue looked intently at him. He said to them, "Today this Scripture passage is fulfilled in your hearing."—

* See p. 16 for other Gospel Acclamations.

The Gospel of the Lord. ℟. **Praise to you, Lord Jesus Christ.** ↓

After the reading of the Gospel, the Bishop preaches the Homily in which, taking his starting point from the text of the readings proclaimed in the Liturgy of the Word, he speaks to the people and to his Priests about priestly anointing, urging the Priests to be faithful in their office and calling on them to renew publicly their priestly promises.

Renewal of Priestly Promises

After the Homily, the Bishop speaks with the Priests in these or similar words.

Beloved sons,
on the anniversary of that day
when Christ our Lord conferred his priesthood
on his Apostles and on us,
are you resolved to renew,
in the presence of your Bishop and God's holy people,
the promises you once made?
Priests: I am.

Bishop:
Are you resolved to be more united with the Lord Jesus
and more closely conformed to him,
denying yourselves and confirming those promises
about sacred duties towards Christ's Church
which, prompted by love of him,
you willingly and joyfully pledged
on the day of your priestly ordination?
Priests: I am.

Bishop:
Are you resolved to be faithful stewards of the mysteries
    of God
in the Holy Eucharist and the other liturgical rites
and to discharge faithfully the sacred office of teaching,
following Christ the Head and Shepherd,
not seeking any gain,

but moved only by zeal for souls?
Priests: I am.

Then, turned towards the people, the Bishop continues:

As for you, dearest sons and daughters,
pray for your Priests,
that the Lord may pour out his gifts abundantly upon
    them,
and keep them faithful as ministers of Christ, the High
    Priest,
so that they may lead you to him,
who is the source of salvation.
People: Christ, hear us. Christ, graciously hear us.

Bishop:
And pray also for me,
that I may be faithful to the apostolic office
entrusted to me in my lowliness
and that in your midst I may be made day by day
a living and more perfect image of Christ,
the Priest, the Good Shepherd,
the Teacher and the Servant of all.
People: Christ, hear us. Christ, graciously hear us.

Bishop:
May the Lord keep us all in his charity
and lead all of us,
shepherds and flock,
to eternal life.
All: Amen.

The Creed is not said.   → No. 17, p. 20

PRAYER OVER THE OFFERINGS   [New Life]

May the power of this sacrifice, O Lord, we pray,
mercifully wipe away what is old in us
and increase in us grace of salvation and newness of life.
Through Christ our Lord.
℟. **Amen.** ↓

PREFACE (P 20)   [Continuation of Christ's Priesthood]

℣. The Lord be with you. ℟. **And with your spirit.**
℣. Lift up your hearts. ℟. **We lift them up to the
Lord.** ℣. Let us give thanks to the Lord our God. ℟. **It
is right and just.**

It is truly right and just, our duty and our salvation,
always and everywhere to give you thanks,
Lord, holy Father, almighty and eternal God.

For by the anointing of the Holy Spirit
you made your Only Begotten Son
High Priest of the new and eternal covenant,
and by your wondrous design were pleased to decree
that his one Priesthood should continue in the Church.

For Christ not only adorns with a royal priesthood
the people he has made his own,
but with a brother's kindness he also chooses men
to become sharers in his sacred ministry
through the laying on of hands.

They are to renew in his name
the sacrifice of human redemption,
to set before your children the paschal banquet,
to lead your holy people in charity,
to nourish them with the word
and strengthen them with the Sacraments.

As they give up their lives for you
and for the salvation of their brothers and sisters,
they strive to be conformed to the image of Christ
    himself
and offer you a constant witness of faith and love.

And so, Lord, with all the Angels and Saints,
we, too, give you thanks, as in exultation we acclaim:

→ No. 23, p. 23

COMMUNION ANT. Ps 89 (88):2   [The Lord's Fidelity]

I will sing for ever of your mercies, O Lord; through all ages my mouth will proclaim your fidelity. ↓

PRAYER AFTER COMMUNION   [Renewed in Christ]

We beseech you, almighty God,
that those you renew by your Sacraments
may merit to become the pleasing fragrance of Christ.
Who lives and reigns for ever and ever.
℞. **Amen.**   → No. 30, p. 77

Optional Solemn Blessings, p. 97, and Prayers over the People, p. 105

"Do this in remembrance of me."

MARCH 24

THE SACRED PASCHAL TRIDUUM
THURSDAY OF THE LORD'S SUPPER
[HOLY THURSDAY]

AT THE EVENING MASS

The Evening Mass of the Lord's Supper commemorates the institution of the Holy Eucharist and the sacrament of Holy Orders. It was at this Mass that Jesus changed bread and wine into his Body and

Blood. He then directed his disciples to carry out this same ritual:
"Do this in remembrance of me."

ENTRANCE ANT. Cf. Gal 6:14   [Glory in the Cross]

**We should glory in the Cross of our Lord Jesus Christ,
in whom is our salvation, life and resurrection,
through whom we are saved and delivered.**

→ No. 2, p. 10

The Gloria in excelsis *(Glory to God in the highest) is
said. While the hymn is being sung, bells are rung, and when
it is finished, they remain silent until the* Gloria in excelsis
*of the Easter Vigil, unless, if appropriate, the Diocesan
Bishop has decided otherwise. Likewise, during this same
period, the organ and other musical instruments may be used
only so as to support the singing.*

COLLECT   [Fullness of Charity]

O God, who have called us to participate
in this most sacred Supper,
in which your Only Begotten Son,
when about to hand himself over to death,
entrusted to the Church a sacrifice new for all eternity,
the banquet of his love,
grant, we pray,
that we may draw from so great a mystery,
the fullness of charity and of life.
Through our Lord Jesus Christ, your Son,
who lives and reigns with you in the unity of the Holy
   Spirit,
one God, for ever and ever. ℟. **Amen.** ↓

FIRST READING Ex 12:1-8, 11-14   [The First Passover]

For the protection of the Jewish people, strict religious and
dietary instructions are given to Moses by God. The law of
the Passover meal requires that the doorposts and lintels
of each house be marked with the blood of the sacrificial
animal so that the LORD can "go through Egypt striking
down every firstborn of the land, both man and beast."

A reading from the Book of Exodus

THE LORD said to Moses and Aaron in the land of Egypt, "This month shall stand at the head of your calendar; you shall reckon it the first month of the year. Tell the whole community of Israel: On the tenth of this month every one of your families must procure for itself a lamb, one apiece for each household. If a family is too small for a whole lamb, it shall join the nearest household in procuring one and shall share in the lamb in proportion to the number of persons who partake of it. The lamb must be a year-old male and without blemish. You may take it from either the sheep or the goats. You shall keep it until the fourteenth day of this month, and then, with the whole assembly of Israel present, it shall be slaughtered during the evening twilight. They shall take some of its blood and apply it to the two doorposts and the lintel of every house in which they partake of the lamb. That same night they shall eat its roasted flesh with unleavened bread and bitter herbs.

"This is how you are to eat it: with your loins girt, sandals on your feet and your staff in hand, you shall eat like those who are in flight. It is the Passover of the LORD. For on this same night I will go through Egypt, striking down every firstborn of the land, both man and beast, and executing judgment on all the gods of Egypt—I, the LORD! But the blood will mark the houses where you are. Seeing the blood, I will pass over you; thus, when I strike the land of Egypt, no destructive blow will come upon you.

"This day shall be a memorial feast for you, which all your generations shall celebrate with pilgrimage to the LORD, as a perpetual institution."—The word of the Lord. ℞. **Thanks be to God.** ↓

RESPONSORIAL PSALM Ps 116   [Thanksgiving]

℟. Our bless - ing - cup is a com -
mun - ion with the Blood of Christ.

How shall I make a return to the LORD
    for all the good he has done for me?
The cup of salvation I will take up,
    and I will call upon the name of the LORD.—℟.

Precious in the eyes of the LORD
    is the death of his faithful ones.
I am your servant, the son of your handmaid;
    you have loosed my bonds.—℟.

To you will I offer sacrifice of thanksgiving,
    and I will call upon the name of the LORD.
My vows to the LORD I will pay
    in the presence of all his people.—℟. ↓

SECOND READING 1 Cor 11:23-26   [The Lord's Supper]

Paul recounts the events of the Last Supper which were
handed down to him. The changing of bread and wine into
the Body and Blood of the Lord proclaimed again his
death. It was to be a sacrificial meal.

A reading from the first Letter of Saint Paul
to the Corinthians

BROTHERS and sisters: I received from the Lord
what I also handed on to you, that the Lord Jesus,
on the night he was handed over, took bread, and, after
he had given thanks, broke it and said, "This is my
body that is for you. Do this in remembrance of me." In
the same way also the cup, after supper, saying, "This
cup is the new covenant in my blood. Do this, as often

as you drink it, in remembrance of me." For as often as you eat this bread and drink the cup, you proclaim the death of the Lord until he comes.—The word of the Lord. ℟. **Thanks be to God.** ↓

VERSE BEFORE THE GOSPEL Jn 13:34 [Love One Another]

℟. **Praise to you, Lord Jesus Christ, King of endless glory!***

I give you a new commandment, says the Lord:
love one another as I have loved you.

℟. **Praise to you, Lord Jesus Christ, King of endless glory!** ↓

GOSPEL Jn 13:1-15   [Love and Service]

Jesus washes the feet of his disciples to prove to them his sincere love and great humility which they should imitate. He teaches them that, although free from sin and not unworthy to receive his most holy body and blood, they should be purified of all evil inclinations.

℣. The Lord be with you. ℟. **And with your spirit.**

✚ A reading from the holy Gospel according to John.
℟. **Glory to you, O Lord.**

BEFORE the feast of Passover, Jesus knew that his hour had come to pass from this world to the Father. He loved his own in the world and he loved them to the end. The devil had already induced Judas, son of Simon the Iscariot, to hand him over. So, during supper, fully aware that the Father had put everything into his power and that he had come from God and was returning to God, he rose from supper and took off his outer garments. He took a towel and tied it around his waist. Then he poured water into a basin and began to wash the disciples' feet and dry them with the towel around his waist. He came to Simon Peter, who said to him, "Master, are you going to wash

* See p. 16 for other Gospel Acclamations.

my feet?" Jesus answered and said to him, "What I am doing, you do not understand now, but you will understand later." Peter said to him, "You will never wash my feet." Jesus answered him, "Unless I wash you, you will have no inheritance with me." Simon Peter said to him, "Master, then not only my feet, but my hands and head as well." Jesus said to him, "Whoever has bathed has no need except to have his feet washed, for he is clean all over; so you are clean, but not all." For he knew who would betray him; for this reason, he said, "Not all of you are clean."

So when he had washed their feet and put his garments back on and reclined at table again, he said to them, "Do you realize what I have done for you? You call me 'teacher' and 'master,' and rightly so, for indeed I am. If I, therefore, the master and teacher, have washed your feet, you ought to wash one another's feet. I have given you a model to follow, so that as I have done for you, you should also do."—The Gospel of the Lord. ℟. **Praise to you, Lord Jesus Christ.**

After the proclamation of the Gospel, the Priest gives a homily in which light is shed on the principal mysteries that are commemorated in this Mass, namely, the institution of the Holy Eucharist and of the priestly Order, and the commandment of the Lord concerning fraternal charity.

The Washing of Feet

After the Homily, where a pastoral reason suggests it, the Washing of Feet follows.

The men who have been chosen are led by the ministers to seats prepared in a suitable place. Then the Priest (removing his chasuble if necessary) goes to each one, and, with the help of the ministers, pours water over each one's feet and then dries them.

Meanwhile some of the following antiphons or other appropriate chants are sung.

ANTIPHON 1 Cf. Jn 13:4, 5, 15   [Jesus' Example]

After the Lord had risen from supper,
he poured water into a basin
and began to wash the feet of his disciples:
he left them this example.

ANTIPHON 2 Cf. Jn 13:12, 13, 15   [Do Likewise]

The Lord Jesus, after eating supper with his disciples,
washed their feet and said to them:
Do you know what I, your Lord and Master, have done
    for you?
I have given you an example, that you should do like-
    wise.

ANTIPHON 3 Jn 13:6, 7, 8   [Peter's Understanding]

Lord, are you to wash my feet? Jesus said to him in
    answer:
If I do not wash your feet, you will have no share with
    me.

℣. So he came to Simon Peter and Peter said to him:
—Lord.

℣. What I am doing, you do not know for now,
but later you will come to know.
—Lord.

ANTIPHON 4 Cf. Jn 13:14   [Service]

If I, your Lord and Master, have washed your feet,
how much more should you wash each other's feet?

ANTIPHON 5 Jn 13:35   [Identified by Love]

This is how all will know that you are my disciples:
if you have love for one another.

℣. **Jesus said to his disciples:**
—**This is how.**

ANTIPHON 6 Jn 13:34   [New Commandment]

I give you a new commandment,
that you love one another
as I have loved you, says the Lord.

ANTIPHON 7 1 Cor 13:13   [Greatest Is Charity]

Let faith, hope and charity, these three, remain among
   you,
but the greatest of these is charity.

℣. **Now faith, hope and charity, these three, remain;**
but the greatest of these is charity.
—**Let.**

*After the Washing of Feet, the Priest washes and dries his
hands, puts the chasuble back on, and returns to the chair,
and from there he directs the Universal Prayer.*

The Creed is not said.

The Liturgy of the Eucharist

*At the beginning of the Liturgy of the Eucharist, there may
be a procession of the faithful in which gifts for the poor may
be presented with the bread and wine.*

*Meanwhile the following, or another appropriate chant, is
sung.*

[Christ's Love]

Ant. **Where true charity is dwelling, God is present there.**

℣. **By the love of Christ we have been brought to-**
   gether:
℣. **let us find in him our gladness and our pleasure;**
℣. **may we love him and revere him, God the living,**
℣. **and in love respect each other with sincere hearts.**

Ant. **Where true charity is dwelling, God is present there.**

℣. So when we as one are gathered all together,
℣. let us strive to keep our minds free of division;
℣. may there be an end to malice, strife and quarrels,
℣. and let Christ our God be dwelling here among us.

Ant. Where true charity is dwelling, God is present there.

℣. May your face thus be our vision, bright in glory,
℣. Christ our God, with all the blessed Saints in
　　heaven:
℣. such delight is pure and faultless, joy unbounded,
℣. which endures through countless ages world with-
　　out end. Amen.　　　　　　　　→ No. 17, p. 20

PRAYER OVER THE OFFERINGS　　[Work of Redemption]

Grant us, O Lord, we pray,
that we may participate worthily in these mysteries,
for whenever the memorial of this sacrifice is celebrated
the work of our redemption is accomplished.
Through Christ our Lord.
℟. Amen.　　　　　　　→ No. 21, p. 22 (Pref. P 47)

*When the Roman Canon is used, this special form of it is said,
with proper formulas for the* Communicantes *(In communion with those),* Hanc igitur *(Therefore, Lord, we pray),
and* Qui pridie *(On the day before he was to suffer).*

To you, therefore, most merciful Father,
we make humble prayer and petition
through Jesus Christ, your Son, our Lord:
that you accept
and bless ✠ these gifts, these offerings,
these holy and unblemished sacrifices,
which we offer you firstly
for your holy catholic Church.
Be pleased to grant her peace,
to guard, unite and govern her

throughout the whole world,
together with your servant N. our Pope
and N. our Bishop,
and all those who, holding to the truth,
hand on the catholic and apostolic faith.

Remember, Lord, your servants N. and N.
and all gathered here,
whose faith and devotion are known to you.
For them we offer you this sacrifice of praise
or they offer it for themselves
and all who are dear to them:
for the redemption of their souls,
in hope of health and well-being,
and paying their homage to you,
the eternal God, living and true.

Celebrating the most sacred day
on which our Lord Jesus Christ
was handed over for our sake,
and in communion with those whose memory we
    venerate,
especially the glorious ever-Virgin Mary,
Mother of our God and Lord, Jesus Christ,
and † blessed Joseph, her Spouse,
your blessed Apostles and Martyrs
Peter and Paul, Andrew,
(James, John,
Thomas, James, Philip,
Bartholomew, Matthew, Simon and Jude;
Linus, Cletus, Clement, Sixtus,
Cornelius, Cyprian,
Lawrence, Chrysogonus,
John and Paul,
Cosmas and Damian)
and all your Saints;
we ask that through their merits and prayers,
in all things we may be defended

by your protecting help.
(Through Christ our Lord. Amen.)

Therefore, Lord, we pray:
graciously accept this oblation of our service,
that of your whole family,
which we make to you
as we observe the day
on which our Lord Jesus Christ
handed on the mysteries of his Body and Blood
for his disciples to celebrate;
order our days in your peace,
and command that we be delivered from eternal
   damnation
and counted among the flock of those you have chosen.
(Through Christ our Lord. Amen.)

Be pleased, O God, we pray,
to bless, acknowledge,
and approve this offering in every respect;
make it spiritual and acceptable,
so that it may become for us
the Body and Blood of your most beloved Son,
our Lord Jesus Christ.

On the day before he was to suffer
for our salvation and the salvation of all,
that is today,
he took bread in his holy and venerable hands,
and with eyes raised to heaven
to you, O God, his almighty Father,
giving you thanks, he said the blessing,
broke the bread
and gave it to his disciples, saying:

Take this, all of you, and eat of it,
for this is my Body,
which will be given up for you.

In a similar way, when supper was ended,
he took this precious chalice
in his holy and venerable hands,
and once more giving you thanks, he said the blessing
and gave the chalice to his disciples, saying:

Take this, all of you, and drink from it,
for this is the chalice of my Blood,
the Blood of the new and eternal covenant,
which will be poured out for you and for many
for the forgiveness of sins.

Do this in memory of me.

The rest follows the Roman Canon, pp. 26-29.

COMMUNION ANT. 1 Cor 11:24-25   [In Memory of Christ]

**This is the Body that will be given up for you; this is
the Chalice of the new covenant in my Blood, says the
Lord; do this, whenever you receive it, in memory of
me.** ↓

*After the distribution of Communion, a ciborium with hosts for
Communion on the following day is left on the altar. The Priest,
standing at the chair, says the Prayer after Communion.*

PRAYER AFTER COMMUNION   [Renewed]

Grant, almighty God,
that, just as we are renewed
by the Supper of your Son in this present age,
so we may enjoy his banquet for all eternity.
Who lives and reigns for ever and ever. ℟. **Amen.**

The Transfer of the Most Blessed Sacrament

*After the Prayer after Communion, the Priest puts incense in
the thurible while standing, blesses it and then, kneeling,
incenses the Blessed Sacrament three times. Then, having
put on a white humeral veil, he rises, takes the ciborium, and
covers it with the ends of the veil.*

A procession is formed in which the Blessed Sacrament, accompanied by torches and incense, is carried through the church to a place of repose prepared in a part of the church or in a chapel suitably decorated. A lay minister with a cross, standing between two other ministers with lighted candles leads off. Others carrying lighted candles follow. Before the Priest carrying the Blessed Sacrament comes the thurifer with a smoking thurible. Meanwhile, the hymn Pange, lingua *(exclusive of the last two stanzas) or another eucharistic chant is sung.*

PANGE LINGUA   [Adoring the Lord]

Sing my tongue, the Savior's glory,
Of his flesh the mystery sing;
Of his blood all price exceeding,
Shed by our immortal king,
Destined for the world's redemption,
From a noble womb to spring.

Of a pure and spotless Virgin
Born for us on earth below,
He, as man with man conversing,
Stayed the seeds of truth to sow;
Then he closed in solemn order
Wondrously his life of woe.

On the night of that Last Supper,
Seated with his chosen band,
He, the paschal victim eating,
First fulfills the law's command;
Then as food to all his brethren
Gives himself with his own hand.

Word made Flesh, the bread of nature,
By his word to flesh he turns;
Wine into his blood he changes:
What though sense no change discerns,
Only be the heart in earnest,
Faith her lesson quickly learns.

When the procession reaches the place of repose, the Priest, with the help of the Deacon if necessary, places the ciborium in the tabernacle, the door of which remains open. Then he puts incense in the thurible and, kneeling, incenses the Blessed Sacrament, while Tantum ergo Sacramentum *or another eucharistic chant is sung. Then the Deacon or the Priest himself places the Sacrament in the tabernacle and closes the door.*

Down in adoration falling,
Lo! the sacred host we hail,
Lo! o'er ancient forms departing
Newer rites of grace prevail;
Faith for all defects supplying,
Where the feeble senses fail.

To the everlasting Father,
And the Son who reigns on high
With the Holy Spirit proceeding
Forth from each eternally,
Be salvation, honor, blessing,
Might and endless majesty.
Amen.

After a period of adoration in silence, the Priest and ministers genuflect and return to the sacristy.

At an appropriate time, the altar is stripped and, if possible, the crosses are removed from the church. It is expedient that any crosses which remain in the church be veiled.

The faithful are invited to continue adoration before the Blessed Sacrament for a suitable length of time during the night, according to local circumstances, but after midnight the adoration should take place without solemnity.

"And bowing his head, [Jesus] handed over the spirit."

MARCH 25

FRIDAY OF THE PASSION OF THE LORD
[GOOD FRIDAY]

CELEBRATION OF THE PASSION OF THE LORD

The liturgy of Good Friday recalls graphically the Passion and Death of Jesus. The reading of the Passion describes the suffering and Death of Jesus. Today we show great reverence for the crucifix, the sign of our redemption.

On this and the following day, by a most ancient tradition, the Church does not celebrate the Sacraments at all, except for Penance and the Anointing of the Sick. On the afternoon of this day, about three o'clock (unless a later hour is chosen for a pastoral reason), there takes place the celebration of the Lord's Passion.

The Priest and the Deacon, if a Deacon is present, wearing red vestments as for Mass, go to the altar in silence and, after making a reverence to the altar, prostrate themselves or, if appropriate, kneel and pray in silence for a while. All others kneel. Then the Priest, with the ministers, goes to the chair where, facing the people, who are standing, he says, with hands extended, one of the following prayers, omitting the invitation Let us pray.

PRAYER   [Sanctify Your Servants]
Remember your mercies, O Lord,
and with your eternal protection sanctify your servants,
for whom Christ your Son,
by the shedding of his Blood,
established the Paschal Mystery.
Who lives and reigns for ever and ever. ℟. **Amen.** ↓

OR   [Image of Christ]
O God, who by the Passion of Christ your Son, our Lord,
abolished the death inherited from ancient sin
by every succeeding generation,
grant that just as, being conformed to him,
we have borne by the law of nature
the image of the man of earth,
so by the sanctification of grace
we may bear the image of the Man of heaven.
Through Christ our Lord. ℟. **Amen.** ↓

FIRST PART: THE LITURGY OF THE WORD

FIRST READING Is 52:13—53:12   [Suffering and Glory]
**The suffering Servant shall be raised up and exalted. The
Servant remains one with all people in sorrow and yet dis-
tinct from each of them in innocence of life and total service to God. The doctrine of expiatory suffering finds
supreme expression in these words.**

A reading from the Book of the Prophet Isaiah

SEE, my servant shall prosper,
he shall be raised high and greatly exalted.
Even as many were amazed at him—
    so marred was his look beyond human semblance
    and his appearance beyond that of the sons of
        man—
so shall he startle many nations,
    because of him kings shall stand speechless;
for those who have not been told shall see,
    those who have not heard shall ponder it.

Who would believe what we have heard?
    To whom has the arm of the LORD been revealed?
He grew up like a sapling before him,
    like a shoot from the parched earth;
there was in him no stately bearing to make us look
      at him,
    nor appearance that would attract us to him.
He was spurned and avoided by people,
    a man of suffering, accustomed to infirmity,
one of those from whom people hide their faces,
    spurned, and we held him in no esteem.

Yet it was our infirmities that he bore,
    our sufferings that he endured,
while we thought of him as stricken,
    as one smitten by God and afflicted.
But he was pierced for our offenses,
    crushed for our sins;
upon him was the chastisement that makes us whole,
    by his stripes we were healed.
We had all gone astray like sheep,
    each following his own way;
but the LORD laid upon him
    the guilt of us all.

Though he was harshly treated, he submitted
    and opened not his mouth;
like a lamb led to the slaughter
    or a sheep before the shearers,
    he was silent and opened not his mouth.
Oppressed and condemned, he was taken away,
    and who would have thought any more of his
      destiny?
When he was cut off from the land of the living,
    and smitten for the sin of his people,
a grave was assigned him among the wicked
    and a burial place with evildoers,
though he had done no wrong
    nor spoken any falsehood.

But the Lord was pleased
  to crush him in infirmity.

If he gives his life as an offering for sin,
  he shall see his descendants in a long life,
    and the will of the LORD shall be accomplished
      through him.

Because of his affliction
  he shall see the light in fullness of days;
through his suffering, my servant shall justify many,
  and their guilt he shall bear.

Therefore I will give him his portion among the great,
  and he shall divide the spoils with the mighty,
because he surrendered himself to death
  and was counted among the wicked;
and he shall take away the sins of many,
  and win pardon for their offenses.

The word of the Lord. ℟. **Thanks be to God.** ↓

RESPONSORIAL PSALM Ps 31   [Trust in God]

℟. Fa - ther, in - to your hands I com - mend my spir - it.

In you, O LORD, I take refuge;
  let me never be put to shame.
  In your justice rescue me.
Into your hands I commend my spirit;
  you will redeem me, O LORD, O faithful God.

℟. **Father, into your hands I commend my spirit.**

For all my foes I am an object of reproach,
  a laughingstock to my neighbors, and a dread to my
    friends;
  they who see me abroad flee from me.
I am forgotten like the unremembered dead;
  I am like a dish that is broken.

℟. **Father, into your hands I commend my spirit.**

But my trust is in you, O LORD;
  I say, "You are my God."
In your hands is my destiny; rescue me
  from the clutches of my enemies and my persecutors.

℟. **Father, into your hands I commend my spirit.**

Let your face shine upon your servant;
  save me in your kindness.
Take courage and be stouthearted,
  all you who hope in the LORD.

℟. **Father, into your hands I commend my spirit.** ↓

SECOND READING Heb 4:14-16; 5:7-9   [Access to Christ]

The theme of the compassionate high priest appears again
in this passage. In him the Christian can approach God
confidently and without fear. Christ learned obedience
from his sufferings whereby he became the source of eternal life for all.

A reading from the Letter to the Hebrews

B ROTHERS and sisters: Since we have a great high
priest who has passed through the heavens, Jesus,
the Son of God, let us hold fast to our confession. For
we do not have a high priest who is unable to sympa-
thize with our weaknesses, but one who has similarly
been tested in every way, yet without sin. So let us confidently approach the throne of grace to receive mercy
and to find grace for timely help.

In the days when Christ was in the flesh, he offered
prayers and supplications with loud cries and tears to
the one who was able to save him from death, and he
was heard because of his reverence. Son though he
was, he learned obedience from what he suffered; and
when he was made perfect, he became the source of
eternal salvation for all who obey him.—The word of
the Lord. ℟. **Thanks be to God.** ↓

VERSE BEFORE THE GOSPEL Phil 2:8-9 [Obedient for Us]

℟. **Praise and honor to you, Lord Jesus Christ!*****
Christ became obedient to the point of death,
even death on a cross.
Because of this, God greatly exalted him
and bestowed on him the name which is above every
    other name.
℟. **Praise and honor to you, Lord Jesus Christ!**

GOSPEL Jn 18:1—19:42   [Christ's Passion]

Finally the Passion is read in the same way as on the preceding Sunday. The narrator is noted by N, the words of Jesus by a ✝ and the words of others by V (Voice) and C (Crowd). The parts of the Crowd (C) printed in boldface type may be recited by the people.

It is important for us to understand the meaning of Christ's sufferings today. See the note on p. 263.

> **The beginning scene is Christ's agony in the garden. Our Lord knows what is to happen. The Scriptures recount the betrayal, the trial, the condemnation, and the crucifixion of Jesus.**

N. ❡HE Passion of our Lord Jesus Christ according
    to John

1. JESUS IS ARRESTED

N. JESUS went out with his disciples across the
    Kidron valley to where there was a garden, into
which he and his disciples entered. Judas his betrayer
also knew the place, because Jesus had often met
there with his disciples. So Judas got a band of soldiers and guards from the chief priests and the
Pharisees and went there with lanterns, torches, and
weapons. Jesus, knowing everything that was going to
happen to him, went out and said to them, ✝ "Whom
are you looking for?" **N.** They answered him, **C. "Jesus
the Nazorean." N.** He said to them, ✝ "I AM." **N.** Judas
his betrayer was also with them. When he said

* *See p. 16 for other Gospel Acclamations.*

to them, "I AM," they turned away and fell to the ground. So he again asked them, ✠ "Whom are you looking for?" **N.** They said, **C.** **"Jesus the Nazorean."** **N.** Jesus answered, ✠ "I told you that I AM. So if you are looking for me, let these men go." **N.** This was to fulfill what he had said, "I have not lost any of those you gave me." Then Simon Peter, who had a sword, drew it, struck the high priest's slave, and cut off his right ear. The slave's name was Malchus. Jesus said to Peter, ✠ "Put your sword into its scabbard. Shall I not drink the cup that the Father gave me?"

N. So the band of soldiers, the tribune, and the Jewish guards seized Jesus, bound him, and brought him to Annas first. He was the father-in-law of Caiaphas, who was high priest that year. It was Caiaphas who had counseled the Jews that it was better that one man should die rather than the people.

2. PETER'S FIRST DENIAL

N. **S**IMON Peter and another disciple followed Jesus. Now the other disciple was known to the high priest, and he entered the courtyard of the high priest with Jesus. But Peter stood at the gate outside. So the other disciple, the acquaintance of the high priest, went out and spoke to the gatekeeper and brought Peter in. Then the maid who was the gatekeeper said to Peter, **C.** **"You are not one of this man's disciples, are you?"** **N.** He said, **V.** "I am not." **N.** Now the slaves and the guards were standing around a charcoal fire that they had made, because it was cold, and were warming themselves. Peter was also standing there keeping warm.

3. THE INQUIRY BEFORE ANNAS

N. **T**HE high priest questioned Jesus about his disciples and about his doctrine. Jesus answered him, ✠ "I have spoken publicly to the world. I have always taught in a synagogue or in the temple area where all the Jews gather, and in secret I have said nothing. Why ask me? Ask those who heard me what I said to them. They know what I said." **N.** When he had said this, one of the temple guards standing there struck Jesus and said, **V.** "Is this the way you answer the high priest?" **N.** Jesus answered him, ✠ "If I have spoken wrongly, testify to the wrong; but if I have spoken rightly, why do you strike me?" **N.** Then Annas sent him bound to Caiaphas the high priest.

4. THE FURTHER DENIALS

N. **N**OW Simon Peter was standing there keeping warm. And they said to him, **C.** **"You are not one of his disciples, are you?"** **N.** He denied it and said, **V.** "I am not." **N.** One of the slaves of the high priest, a relative of the one whose ear Peter had cut off, said, **C. "Didn't I see you in the garden with him?"** **N.** Again Peter denied it. And immediately the cock crowed.

5. JESUS BROUGHT BEFORE PILATE

N. **T**HEN they brought Jesus from Caiaphas to the praetorium. It was morning. And they themselves did not enter the praetorium, in order not to be defiled so that they could eat the Passover. So Pilate came out to them and said, **V.** "What charge do you bring against this man?" **N.** They answered and said to him, **C. "If he were not a criminal, we would not have handed him over to you."** **N.** At this, Pilate said to them, **V.** "Take him yourselves, and judge him according to your law." **N.** The Jews answered him, **C. "We do not have the right to execute anyone,"** **N.** in order that the word of Jesus might be fulfilled that he said indicating the kind of death he would die.

[6. JESUS QUESTIONED BY PILATE]

So Pilate went back into the praetorium and summoned Jesus and said to him, **V.** "Are you the King of the Jews?" **N.** Jesus answered, ✠ "Do you say this on your own or have others told you about me?" **N.** Pilate answered, **V.** "I am not a Jew, am I? Your own nation and the chief priests handed you over to me. What have you done?" **N.** Jesus answered, ✠ "My kingdom does not belong to this world. If my kingdom did belong to this world, my attendants would be fighting to keep me from being handed over to the Jews. But as it is, my kingdom is not here." **N.** So Pilate said to him, **V.** "Then you are a king?" **N.** Jesus answered, ✠ "You say I am a king. For this I was born and for this I came into the world, to testify to the truth. Everyone who belongs to the truth listens to my voice." **N.** Pilate said to him, **V.** "What is truth?"

7. BARABBAS CHOSEN OVER JESUS

N. WHEN he had said this, he again went out to the Jews and said to them, **V.** "I find no guilt in him. But you have a custom that I release one prisoner to you at Passover. Do you want me to release to you the King of the Jews?" **N.** They cried out again, **C.** **"Not this one but Barabbas!"** **N.** Now Barabbas was a revolutionary.

8. JESUS IS SCOURGED

N. THEN Pilate took Jesus and had him scourged. And the soldiers wove a crown out of thorns and placed it on his head, and clothed him in a purple cloak, and they came to him and said, **C.** **"Hail, King of the Jews!"** **N.** And they struck him repeatedly.

[9. JESUS IS PRESENTED TO THE CROWD]

Once more Pilate went out and said to them, **V.** "Look, I am bringing him out to you, so that you may know that I find no guilt in him." **N.** So Jesus came out, wearing the crown of thorns and the purple cloak. And Pilate said to them, **V.** "Behold, the man!" **N.** When the chief priests and the guards saw him they cried out, **C. "Crucify him, crucify him!"** N. Pilate said to them, V. "Take him yourselves and crucify him. I find no guilt in him." N. The Jews answered, **C. "We have a law, and according to that law he ought to die, because he made himself the Son of God."**

[*10. JESUS AGAIN QUESTIONED BY PILATE*]

N. Now when Pilate heard this statement, he became even more afraid, and went back into the praetorium and said to Jesus, V. "Where are you from?" N. Jesus did not answer him. So Pilate said to him, V. "Do you not speak to me? Do you not know that I have power to release you and I have power to crucify you?" [N. Jesus answered him,] ✠ "You would have no power over me if it had not been given to you from above. For this reason the one who handed me over to you has the greater sin."

[*11. JESUS SENTENCED TO BE CRUCIFIED*]

N. Consequently, Pilate tried to release him; but the Jews cried out, **C. "If you release him, you are not a Friend of Caesar. Everyone who makes himself a king opposes Caesar."**

N. When Pilate heard these words he brought Jesus out and seated him on the judge's bench in the place called Stone Pavement, in Hebrew, Gabbatha. It was preparation day for Passover, and it was about noon. And he said to the Jews, V. "Behold, your king!" N. They cried out, **C. "Take him away, take him away! Crucify him!"** N. Pilate said to them, V. "Shall I crucify your king?" N. The chief priests answered, **C. "We have no king but Caesar."** N. Then he handed him over to them to be crucified.

12. CRUCIFIXION AND DEATH

N. SO they took Jesus, and, carrying the cross himself, he went out to what is called the Place of the Skull, in Hebrew, Golgotha. There they crucified him, and with him two others, one on either side, with Jesus in the middle. Pilate also had an inscription written and put on the cross. It read, "Jesus the Nazorean, the King of the Jews." Now many of the Jews read this inscription, because the place where Jesus was crucified was near the city; and it was written in Hebrew, Latin, and Greek. So the chief priests of the Jews said to Pilate, **C. "Do not write 'The King of the Jews,' but that he said, 'I am the King of the Jews.' "** N. Pilate answered, V. "What I have written, I have written."

N. When the soldiers had crucified Jesus, they took his clothes and divided them into four shares, a share for each soldier. They also took his tunic, but the tunic was seamless, woven in one piece from the top down. So they said to one another, **C. "Let's not tear it, but cast lots for it to see whose it will be,"** N. in order that the passage of Scripture might be fulfilled that says:

They divided my garments among them,
    and for my vesture they cast lots.

This is what the soldiers did. Standing by the cross of Jesus were his mother and his mother's sister, Mary the wife of Clopas, and Mary of Magdala. When Jesus saw his mother and the disciple there whom he loved he said to his mother, ✠ "Woman, behold, your son." N. Then he said to the disciple, ✠ "Behold, your mother." N. And from that hour the disciple took her into his home.

After this, aware that everything was now finished, in order that the Scripture might be fulfilled, Jesus said, ✠ "I thirst." N. There was a vessel filled with common wine. So they put a sponge soaked in wine on a sprig of hyssop and put it up to his mouth. When Jesus had taken the wine, he said, ✠ "It is finished." And bowing his head, he handed over the spirit.

Here all kneel and pause for a short time.

13. THE BLOOD AND WATER

N. **N**OW since it was preparation day, in order that the bodies might not remain on the cross on the sabbath, for the sabbath day of that week was a solemn one, the Jews asked Pilate that their legs be broken and that they be taken down. So the soldiers came and broke the legs of the first and then of the other one who was crucified with Jesus. But when they came to Jesus and saw that he was already dead, they did not break his legs, but one soldier thrust his lance into his side, and immediately blood and water flowed out. An eyewitness has testified, and his testimony is true; he knows that he is speaking the truth, so that you also may come to believe. For this happened so that the Scripture passage might be fulfilled:

Not a bone of it will be broken.

And again another passage says:

They will look upon him whom they have pierced.

14. BURIAL OF JESUS

N. **A**FTER this, Joseph of Arimathea, secretly a disciple of Jesus for fear of the Jews, asked Pilate if he could remove the body of Jesus. And Pilate permitted it. So he came and took his body. Nicodemus, the one who had first come to him at night, also came bringing a mixture of myrrh and aloes weighing about one hundred pounds. They took the body of Jesus and bound it with burial cloths along with the spices, according to the Jewish burial custom. Now in the place where he had been crucified there was a garden, and in the garden a new tomb, in which no one had yet been buried. So they laid Jesus there because of the Jewish preparation day; for the tomb was close by.— The Gospel of the Lord. ℟. **Praise to you, Lord Jesus Christ.**

THE SOLEMN INTERCESSIONS

The Liturgy of the Word concludes with the Solemn Intercessions, which take place in this way: the Deacon, if a Deacon is present, or if he is not, a lay minister, stands at the ambo, and sings or says the invitation in which the intention is expressed. Then all pray in silence for a while, and afterwards the Priest, standing at the chair or, if appropriate, at the altar, with hands extended, sings or says the prayer. The faithful may remain either kneeling or standing throughout the entire period of the prayers. Before the Priest's prayer, in accord with tradition, it is permissible to use the Deacon's invitations Let us kneel—Let us stand, *with all kneeling for silent prayer.*

I. For Holy Church

Let us pray, dearly beloved, for the holy Church of God,
that our God and Lord be pleased to give her peace,
to guard her and to unite her throughout the whole
  world
and grant that, leading our life in tranquility and quiet,
we may glorify God the Father almighty.

Prayer in silence. Then the Priest says:

Almighty ever-living God,
who in Christ revealed your glory to all the nations,
watch over the works of your mercy,
that your Church, spread throughout all the world,
may persevere with steadfast faith in confessing your
  name.
Through Christ our Lord. ℟. **Amen.** ↓

II. For the Pope

Let us pray also for our most Holy Father Pope N.,
that our God and Lord,
who chose him for the Order of Bishops,
may keep him safe and unharmed for the Lord's holy
  Church,
to govern the holy People of God.

Prayer in silence. Then the Priest says:

Almighty ever-living God,
by whose decree all things are founded,
look with favor on our prayers
and in your kindness protect the Pope chosen for us,
that, under him, the Christian people,
governed by you their maker,
may grow in merit by reason of their faith.
Through Christ our Lord. ℟. **Amen.** ↓

III. For all orders and degrees of the faithful

Let us pray also for our Bishop *N.*,
for all Bishops, Priests, and Deacons of the Church
and for the whole of the faithful people.

Prayer in silence. Then the Priest says:

Almighty ever-living God,
by whose Spirit the whole body of the Church
is sanctified and governed,
hear our humble prayer for your ministers,
that, by the gift of your grace,
all may serve you faithfully.
Through Christ our Lord. ℟. **Amen.** ↓

IV. For catechumens

Let us pray also for (our) catechumens,
that our God and Lord
may open wide the ears of their inmost hearts
and unlock the gates of his mercy,
that, having received forgiveness of all their sins
through the waters of rebirth,
they, too, may be one with Christ Jesus our Lord.

Prayer in silence. Then the Priest says:

Almighty ever-living God,
who make your Church ever fruitful with new offspring,
increase the faith and understanding of (our)
    catechumens,
that, reborn in the font of Baptism,

they may be added to the number of your adopted
children.
Through Christ our Lord. ℟. **Amen.** ↓

V. For the unity of Christians

Let us pray also for all our brothers and sisters who
believe in Christ,
that our God and Lord may be pleased,
as they live the truth,
to gather them together and keep them in his one
Church.

Prayer in silence. Then the Priest says:

Almighty ever-living God,
who gather what is scattered
and keep together what you have gathered,
look kindly on the flock of your Son,
that those whom one Baptism has consecrated
may be joined together by integrity of faith
and united in the bond of charity.
Through Christ our Lord. ℟. **Amen.** ↓

VI. For the Jewish people

Let us pray also for the Jewish people,
to whom the Lord our God spoke first,
that he may grant them to advance in love of his name
and in faithfulness to his covenant.

Prayer in silence. Then the Priest says:

Almighty ever-living God,
who bestowed your promises on Abraham and his
descendants,
graciously hear the prayers of your Church,
that the people you first made your own
may attain the fullness of redemption.
Through Christ our Lord. ℟. **Amen.** ↓

VII. For those who do not believe in Christ

Let us pray also for those who do not believe in Christ,
that, enlightened by the Holy Spirit,
they, too, may enter on the way of salvation.

Prayer in silence. Then the Priest says:

Almighty ever-living God,
grant to those who do not confess Christ
that, by walking before you with a sincere heart,
they may find the truth
and that we ourselves, being constant in mutual love
and striving to understand more fully the mystery of
    your life,
may be made more perfect witnesses to your love in the
    world.
Through Christ our Lord.
℟. **Amen.** ↓

VIII. For those who do not believe in God

Let us pray also for those who do not acknowledge God,
that, following what is right in sincerity of heart,
they may find the way to God himself.

Prayer in silence. Then the Priest says:

Almighty ever-living God,
who created all people
to seek you always by desiring you
and, by finding you, come to rest,
grant, we pray,
that, despite every harmful obstacle,
all may recognize the signs of your fatherly love
and the witness of the good works
done by those who believe in you,
and so in gladness confess you,
the one true God and Father of our human race.
Through Christ our Lord. ℟. **Amen.** ↓

IX. For all in public office

Let us pray also for those in public office,
that our God and Lord
may direct their minds and hearts according to his will
for the true peace and freedom of all.

Prayer in silence. Then the Priest says:

Almighty ever-living God,
in whose hand lies every human heart
and the rights of peoples,
look with favor, we pray,
on those who govern with authority over us,
that throughout the whole world,
the prosperity of peoples,
the assurance of peace,
and freedom of religion
may through your gift be made secure.
Through Christ our Lord. ℟. **Amen.** ↓

X. For those in tribulation

Let us pray, dearly beloved,
to God the Father almighty,
that he may cleanse the world of all errors,
banish disease, drive out hunger,
unlock prisons, loosen fetters,
granting to travelers safety, to pilgrims return,
health to the sick, and salvation to the dying.

Prayer in silence. Then the Priest says:

Almighty ever-living God,
comfort of mourners, strength of all who toil,
may the prayers of those who cry out in any tribulation
come before you,
that all may rejoice,
because in their hour of need
your mercy was at hand.
Through Christ our Lord. ℟. **Amen.** ↓

SECOND PART: THE ADORATION OF THE HOLY CROSS

After the Solemn Intercessions, the solemn Adoration of the Holy Cross takes place. Of the two forms of the showing of the Cross presented here, the more appropriate one, according to pastoral needs, should be chosen.

The Showing of the Holy Cross: First Form

The Deacon accompanied by ministers, or another suitable minister, goes to the sacristy, from which, in procession, accompanied by two ministers with lighted candles, he carries the Cross, covered with a violet veil, through the church to the middle of the sanctuary.

The Priest, standing before the altar and facing the people, receives the Cross, uncovers a little of its upper part and elevates it while beginning the Ecce lignum Crucis (Behold the wood of the Cross). *He is assisted in singing by the Deacon or, if need be, by the choir. All respond,* Come, let us adore. *At the end of the singing, all kneel and for a brief moment adore in silence, while the Priest stands and holds the Cross raised.*

Behold the wood of the Cross,
on which hung the salvation of the world.

℟. **Come, let us adore.**

Then the Priest uncovers the right arm of the Cross and again, raising up the Cross, begins, Behold the wood of the Cross *and everything takes place as above.*

Finally, he uncovers the Cross entirely and, raising it up, he begins the invitation Behold the wood of the Cross *a third time and everything takes place like the first time.*

The Showing of the Holy Cross: Second Form

The Priest or the Deacon accompanied by ministers, or another suitable minister, goes to the door of the church, where he receives the unveiled Cross, and the ministers take lighted candles; then the procession sets off through the church to the sanctuary. Near the door, in the middle of the church and before the entrance of the sanctuary, the one who carries the Cross elevates it, singing, Behold the wood of the Cross, *to which all respond,* Come, let us adore. *After each response all kneel and for a brief moment adore in silence, as above.*

The Adoration of the Holy Cross

Then, accompanied by two ministers with lighted candles, the Priest or the Deacon carries the Cross to the entrance of the sanctuary or to another suitable place and there puts it down or hands it over to the ministers to hold. Candles are placed on the right and left sides of the Cross.

For the Adoration of the Cross, first the Priest Celebrant alone approaches, with the chasuble and his shoes removed, if appropriate. Then the clergy, the lay ministers, and the faithful approach, moving as if in procession, and showing reverence to the Cross by a simple genuflection or by some other sign appropriate to the usage of the region, for example, by kissing the Cross.

Only one Cross should be offered for adoration. If, because of the large number of people, it is not possible for all to approach individually, the Priest, after some of the clergy and faithful have adored, takes the Cross and, standing in the middle before the altar, invites the people in a few words to adore the Holy Cross and afterwards holds the Cross elevated higher for a brief time, for the faithful to adore it in silence.

While the adoration of the Holy Cross is taking place, the antiphon Crucem tuam adoramus (We adore your Cross, O Lord), *the Reproaches, the hymn* Crux fidelis (Faithful Cross) *or other suitable chants are sung, during which all who have already adored the Cross remain seated.*

Chants to Be Sung during the Adoration of the Holy Cross

ANTIPHON   [Holy Cross]

Ant. **We adore your Cross, O Lord,
we praise and glorify your holy Resurrection,
for behold, because of the wood of a tree
joy has come to the whole world.**

**May God have mercy on us and bless us;
may he let his face shed its light upon us
and have mercy on us.** Cf. Ps 67 (66):2

And the antiphon is repeated: **We adore . . .**

THE REPROACHES

Parts assigned to one of the two choirs separately are indicated by the numbers 1 (first choir) and 2 (second choir); parts sung by both choirs together are marked: 1 and 2. Some of the verses may also be sung by two cantors.

I

1 and 2: **My people, what have I done to you?
Or how have I grieved you? Answer me!**

1: **Because I led you out of the land of Egypt,
you have prepared a Cross for your Savior.**

1: **Hagios o Theos,**

2: **Holy is God,**

1: **Hagios Ischyros,**

2: **Holy and Mighty,**

1: **Hagios Athanatos, eleison himas.**

2: **Holy and Immortal One, have mercy on us.**

1 and 2: **Because I led you out through the desert forty
    years
and fed you with manna and brought you into
    a land of plenty,
you have prepared a Cross for your Savior.**

1: **Hagios o Theos,**

2: **Holy is God,**

1: **Hagios Ischyros,**

2: **Holy and Mighty,**

1: **Hagios Athanatos, eleison himas.**

2: **Holy and Immortal One, have mercy on us.**

1 and 2: **What more should I have done for you and have not done?**

> **Indeed, I planted you as my most beautiful chosen vine**
> **and you have turned very bitter for me,**
> **for in my thirst you gave me vinegar to drink**
> **and with a lance you pierced your Savior's side.**

1: **Hagios o Theos,**

2: **Holy is God,**

1: **Hagios Ischyros,**

2: **Holy and Mighty,**

1: **Hagios Athanatos, eleison himas.**

2: **Holy and Immortal One, have mercy on us.**

II

Cantors:

I scourged Egypt for your sake with its firstborn sons, and you scourged me and handed me over.

1 and 2 repeat:

My people, what have I done to you?
Or how have I grieved you? Answer me!

Cantors:

I led you out from Egypt as Pharaoh lay sunk in the Red Sea,
and you handed me over to the chief priests.

1 and 2 repeat:

My people . . .

Cantors:

I opened up the sea before you,
and you opened my side with a lance.

1 and 2 repeat:

My people . . .

Cantors:

**I went before you in a pillar of cloud,
and you led me into Pilate's palace.**

1 and 2 repeat:

My people . . .

Cantors:

**I fed you with manna in the desert,
and on me you rained blows and lashes.**

1 and 2 repeat:

My people . . .

Cantors:

**I gave you saving water from the rock to drink,
and for drink you gave me gall and vinegar.**

1 and 2 repeat:

My people . . .

Cantors:

**I struck down for you the kings of the Canaanites,
and you struck my head with a reed.**

1 and 2 repeat:

My people . . .

Cantors:

**I put in your hand a royal scepter,
and you put on my head a crown of thorns.**

1 and 2 repeat:

My people . . .

Cantors:

**I exalted you with great power,
and you hung me on the scaffold of the Cross.**

1 and 2 repeat:

My people . . .

HYMN [Faithful Cross]

All:

Faithful Cross the Saints rely on,
Noble tree beyond compare!
Never was there such a scion,
Never leaf or flower so rare.
Sweet the timber, sweet the iron,
Sweet the burden that they bear!

Cantors:

Sing, my tongue, in exultation
Of our banner and device!
Make a solemn proclamation
Of a triumph and its price:
How the Savior of creation
Conquered by his sacrifice!

All:

Faithful Cross the Saints rely on,
Noble tree beyond compare!
Never was there such a scion,
Never leaf or flower so rare.

Cantors:

For, when Adam first offended,
Eating that forbidden fruit,
Not all hopes of glory ended
With the serpent at the root:
Broken nature would be mended
By a second tree and shoot.

All:

Sweet the timber, sweet the iron,
Sweet the burden that they bear!

Cantors:

Thus the tempter was outwitted
By a wisdom deeper still:
Remedy and ailment fitted,
Means to cure and means to kill;

That the world might be
    acquitted,
Christ would do his Father's will.

All:

Faithful Cross the Saints rely on,
Noble tree beyond compare!
Never was there such a scion,
Never leaf or flower so rare.

Cantors:

So the Father, out of pity
For our self-inflicted doom,
Sent him from the heavenly city
When the holy time had come:
He, the Son and the Almighty,
Took our flesh in Mary's womb.

All:

Sweet the timber, sweet the iron,
Sweet the burden that they bear!

Cantors:

Hear a tiny baby crying,
Founder of the seas and strands;
See his virgin Mother tying
Cloth around his feet and hands;
Find him in a manger lying
Tightly wrapped in swaddling-
    bands!

All:

Faithful Cross the Saints rely on,
Noble tree beyond compare!
Never was there such a scion,
Never leaf or flower so rare.

Cantors:

So he came, the long-expected,
Not in glory, not to reign;
Only born to be rejected,

Choosing hunger, toil and pain,
Till the scaffold was erected
And the Paschal Lamb was slain.

All:

Sweet the timber, sweet the iron,
Sweet the burden that they bear!

Cantors:

No disgrace was too abhorrent:
Nailed and mocked and parched
   he died;
Blood and water, double war-
   rant,
Issue from his wounded side,
Washing in a mighty torrent
Earth and stars and oceantide.

All:

Faithful Cross the Saints rely on,
Noble tree beyond compare!
Never was there such a scion,
Never leaf or flower so rare.

Cantors:

Lofty timber, smooth your
   roughness,
Flex your boughs for blossom-
   ing;
Let your fibers lose their tough-
   ness,
Gently let your tendrils cling;

Lay aside your native gruffness,
Clasp the body of your King!

All:

Sweet the timber, sweet the iron,
Sweet the burden that they bear!

Cantors:

Noblest tree of all created,
Richly jeweled and embossed:
Post by Lamb's blood conse-
   crated;
Spar that saves the tempest-
   tossed;
Scaffold-beam which, elevated,
Carries what the world has cost!

All:

Faithful Cross the Saints rely on,
Noble tree beyond compare!
Never was there such a scion,
Never leaf or flower so rare.

*The following conclusion is
never to be omitted:*

All:

Wisdom, power, and adoration
To the blessed Trinity
For redemption and salvation
Through the Paschal Mystery,
Now, in every generation,
And for all eternity. Amen.

*In accordance with local circumstances or popular traditions
and if it is pastorally appropriate, the* Stabat Mater *may be
sung, as found in the Graduale Romanum, or another suitable
chant in memory of the compassion of the Blessed Virgin Mary.*

*When the adoration has been concluded, the Cross is carried
by the Deacon or a minister to its place at the altar. Lighted
candles are placed around or on the altar or near the Cross.*

THIRD PART: HOLY COMMUNION

A cloth is spread on the altar, and a corporal and the Missal put in place. Meanwhile the Deacon or, if there is no Deacon, the Priest himself, putting on a humeral veil, brings the Blessed Sacrament back from the place of repose to the altar by a shorter route, while all stand in silence. Two ministers with lighted candles accompany the Blessed Sacrament and place their candlesticks around or upon the altar.

When the Deacon, if a Deacon is present, has placed the Blessed Sacrament upon the altar and uncovered the ciborium, the Priest goes to the altar and genuflects.

Then the Priest, with hands joined, says aloud:

At the Savior's command
and formed by divine teaching,
we dare to say:

The Priest, with hands extended says, and all present continue:

Our Father . . .

With hands extended, the Priest continues alone:

Deliver us, Lord, we pray, from every evil,
graciously grant peace in our days,
that, by the help of your mercy,
we may be always free from sin
and safe from all distress,
as we await the blessed hope
and the coming of our Savior, Jesus Christ.

The people conclude the prayer, acclaiming:

For the kingdom, the power and the glory are yours now and for ever.

Then the Priest, with hands joined, says quietly:

May the receiving of your Body and Blood,
Lord Jesus Christ,
not bring me to judgment and condemnation,
but through your loving mercy

be for me protection in mind and body
and a healing remedy.

*The Priest then genuflects, takes a particle, and, holding it
slightly raised over the ciborium, while facing the people,
says aloud:*

Behold the Lamb of God,
behold him who takes away the sins of the world.
Blessed are those called to the supper of the Lamb.

And together with the people he adds once:

**Lord, I am not worthy
that you should enter under my roof,
but only say the word
and my soul shall be healed.**

*And facing the altar, he reverently consumes the Body of
Christ, saying quietly: May the Body of Christ keep me
safe for eternal life.*

*He then proceeds to distribute Communion to the faithful.
During Communion, Psalm 22 (21) or another appropriate
chant may be sung.*

*When the distribution of Communion has been completed,
the ciborium is taken by the Deacon or another suitable
minister to a place prepared outside the church or, if circumstances so require, it is placed in the tabernacle.*

Then the Priest says: Let us pray, *and, after a period of
sacred silence, if circumstances so suggest, has been
observed, he says the Prayer after Communion.*

[Devoted to God]

Almighty ever-living God,
who have restored us to life
by the blessed Death and Resurrection of your Christ,
preserve in us the work of your mercy,
that, by partaking of this mystery,
we may have a life unceasingly devoted to you.
Through Christ our Lord.
℟. **Amen.** ↓

For the Dismissal the Deacon or, if there is no Deacon, the Priest himself, may say the invitation Bow down for the blessing.

Then the Priest, standing facing the people and extending his hands over them, says this:

PRAYER OVER THE PEOPLE   [Redemption Secured]

May abundant blessing, O Lord, we pray,
descend upon your people,
who have honored the Death of your Son
in the hope of their resurrection:
may pardon come,
comfort be given,
holy faith increase,
and everlasting redemption be made secure.
Through Christ our Lord.

℟. **Amen.** ↓

And all, after genuflecting to the Cross, depart in silence.

After the celebration, the altar is stripped, but the Cross remains on the altar with two or four candlesticks.

MARCH 26

HOLY SATURDAY

On Holy Saturday the Church waits at the Lord's tomb in prayer and fasting, meditating on his Passion and Death and on his Descent into Hell, and awaiting his Resurrection.

The Church abstains from the Sacrifice of the Mass, with the sacred table left bare, until after the solemn Vigil, that is, the anticipation by night of the Resurrection, when the time comes for paschal joys, the abundance of which overflows to occupy fifty days.

"He is not here, but he has been raised."

MARCH 26

THE EASTER VIGIL
IN THE HOLY NIGHT

By most ancient tradition, this is the night of keeping vigil for the Lord (Ex 12:42), in which, following the Gospel admonition (Lk 12:35-37), the faithful, carrying lighted lamps in their hands, should be like those looking for the Lord when he returns, so that at his coming he may find them awake and have them sit at his table.

Of this night's Vigil, which is the greatest and most noble of all solemnities, there is to be only one celebration in each church. It is arranged, moreover, in such a way that after the Lucernarium and Easter Proclamation (which constitutes the first part of this Vigil), Holy Church meditates on the wonders the Lord God has done for his people from the beginning, trusting in his word and promise (the second part, that is, the Liturgy of the Word) until, as day approaches, with new members reborn in Baptism (the third part), the Church is called to the table the Lord has prepared for his people, the memorial of his Death and Resurrection until he comes again (the fourth part).

Candles should be prepared for all who participate in the Vigil. The lights of the church are extinguished.

FIRST PART:
THE SOLEMN BEGINNING OF THE VIGIL
OR LUCERNARIUM

The Blessing of the Fire and Preparation of the Candle

A blazing fire is prepared in a suitable place outside the church. When the people are gathered there, the Priest approaches with the ministers, one of whom carries the paschal candle. The processional cross and candles are not carried.

Where, however, a fire cannot be lit outside the church, the rite is carried out as below, p. 324.

The Priest and faithful sign themselves while the Priest says:
In the name of the Father, and of the Son, and of the Holy Spirit, *and then he greets the assembled people in the usual way and briefly instructs them about the night vigil in these or similar words:*

[Keeping the Lord's Paschal Solemnity]
Dear brethren (brothers and sisters),
on this most sacred night,
in which our Lord Jesus Christ
passed over from death to life,
the Church calls upon her sons and daughters,
scattered throughout the world,
to come together to watch and pray.
If we keep the memorial
of the Lord's paschal solemnity in this way,
listening to his word and celebrating his mysteries,
then we shall have the sure hope
of sharing his triumph over death
and living with him in God.

Then the Priest blesses the fire, saying with hands extended:

Let us pray.   **[Fire of God's Glory]**

O God, who through your Son
bestowed upon the faithful the fire of your glory,
sanctify ✚ this new fire, we pray,

and grant that,
by these paschal celebrations,
we may be so inflamed with heavenly desires,
that with minds made pure
we may attain festivities of unending splendor.
Through Christ our Lord. ℟. **Amen.** ↓

After the blessing of the new fire, one of the ministers brings the paschal candle to the Priest, who cuts a cross into the candle with a stylus. Then he makes the Greek letter Alpha above the cross, the letter Omega below, and the four numerals of the current year between the arms of the cross, saying meanwhile:

1. Christ yesterday and today *(he cuts a vertical line);*
2. the Beginning and the End *(he cuts a horizontal line);*
3. the Alpha *(he cuts the letter Alpha above the vertical line);*
4. and the Omega *(he cuts the letter Omega below the vertical line).*
5. All time belongs to him *(he cuts the first numeral of the current year in the upper left corner of the cross);*
6. and all the ages *(he cuts the second numeral of the current year in the upper right corner of the cross).*
7. To him be glory and power *(he cuts the third numeral of the current year in the lower left corner of the cross);*
8. through every age and for ever. Amen *(he cuts the fourth numeral of the current year in the lower right corner of the cross).*

```
      A
   2  |  0
   ───┼───
   1  |  6
      Ω
```

When the cutting of the cross and of the other signs has been completed, the Priest may insert five grains of incense into the candle in the form of a cross, meanwhile saying:

1. By his holy   1
2. and glorious wounds,   4 2 5
3. may Christ the Lord   3
4. guard us
5. and protect us. Amen.

Where, because of difficulties that may occur, a fire is not lit, the blessing of fire is adapted to the circumstances. When the people are gathered in the church as on other occasions, the Priest comes to the door of the church, along with the ministers carrying the paschal candle. The people, insofar as is possible, turn to face the Priest.

The greeting and address take place as above, p. 322; then the fire is blessed and the candle is prepared, as above, pp. 322-323.

The Priest lights the paschal candle from the new fire, saying:

May the light of Christ rising in glory
dispel the darkness of our hearts and minds.

Procession

When the candle has been lit, one of the ministers takes burning coals from the fire and places them in the thurible, and the Priest puts incense into it in the usual way. The Deacon or, if there is no Deacon, another suitable minister, takes the paschal candle and a procession forms. The thurifer with the smoking thurible precedes the Deacon or other minister who carries the paschal candle. After them follows the Priest with the ministers and the people, all holding in their hands unlit candles.

At the door of the church the Deacon, standing and raising up the candle, sings:

The Light of Christ.

And all reply:

Thanks be to God.

The Priest lights his candle from the flame of the paschal candle.

Then the Deacon moves forward to the middle of the church and, standing and raising up the candle, sings a second time:

The Light of Christ.

And all reply:

Thanks be to God.

All light their candles from the flame of the paschal candle and continue in procession.

When the Deacon arrives before the altar, he stands facing the people, raises up the candle and sings a third time:

The Light of Christ.

And all reply:

Thanks be to God.

Then the Deacon places the paschal candle on a large candlestand prepared next to the ambo or in the middle of the sanctuary.

And lights are lit throughout the church, except for the altar candles.

The Easter Proclamation (Exsultet)

Arriving at the altar, the Priest goes to his chair, gives his candle to a minister, puts incense into the thurible and blesses the incense as at the Gospel at Mass. The Deacon goes to the Priest and saying, Your blessing, Father, *asks for and receives a blessing from the Priest, who says in a low voice:*

May the Lord be in your heart and on your lips,
that you may proclaim his paschal praise worthily and well,
in the name of the Father and of the Son, ✠ and of the Holy Spirit.

The Deacon replies: Amen. ↓

This blessing is omitted if the Proclamation is made by someone who is not a Deacon.

The Deacon, after incensing the book and the candle, proclaims the Easter Proclamation (Exsultet) at the ambo or at a lectern, with all standing and holding lighted candles in their hands.

The Easter Proclamation may be made, in the absence of a Deacon, by the Priest himself or by another concelebrating Priest. If, however, because of necessity, a lay cantor sings the Proclamation, the words Therefore, dearest friends *up to the end of the invitation are omitted, along with the greeting* The Lord be with you.

[*When the Shorter Form is used, omit the italicized parts.*]

Exult, let them exult, the hosts of heaven,
exult, let Angel ministers of God exult,
let the trumpet of salvation
sound aloud our mighty King's triumph!
Be glad, let earth be glad, as glory floods her,
ablaze with light from her eternal King,
let all corners of the earth be glad,
knowing an end to gloom and darkness.
Rejoice, let Mother Church also rejoice,
arrayed with the lightning of his glory,
let this holy building shake with joy,
filled with the mighty voices of the peoples.
(Therefore, dearest friends,
standing in the awesome glory of this holy light,
invoke with me, I ask you,
the mercy of God almighty,
that he, who has been pleased to number me,
though unworthy, among the Levites,
may pour into me his light unshadowed,
that I may sing this candle's perfect praises).

(℣. The Lord be with you. ℟. **And with your spirit.**)
℣. Lift up your hearts. ℟. **We lift them up to the Lord.**
℣. Let us give thanks to the Lord our God. ℟. **It is right and just.**

It is truly right and just,
with ardent love of mind and heart
and with devoted service of our voice,
to acclaim our God invisible, the almighty Father,
and Jesus Christ, our Lord, his Son, his Only Begotten.

Who for our sake paid Adam's debt to the eternal Father,
and, pouring out his own dear Blood,
wiped clean the record of our ancient sinfulness.

These then are the feasts of Passover,
in which is slain the Lamb, the one true Lamb,
whose Blood anoints the doorposts of believers.

This is the night,
when once you led our forebears, Israel's children,
from slavery in Egypt
and made them pass dry-shod through the Red Sea.

This is the night
that with a pillar of fire
banished the darkness of sin.

This is the night
that even now, throughout the world,
sets Christian believers apart from worldly vices
and from the gloom of sin,
leading them to grace
and joining them to his holy ones.

This is the night,
when Christ broke the prison-bars of death
and rose victorious from the underworld.

Our birth would have been no gain,
had we not been redeemed.
O wonder of your humble care for us!
O love, O charity beyond all telling,
to ransom a slave you gave away your Son!

O truly necessary sin of Adam,
destroyed completely by the Death of Christ!

O happy fault
that earned so great, so glorious a Redeemer!

O truly blessed night,
worthy alone to know the time and hour
when Christ rose from the underworld!

This is the night
of which it is written:
The night shall be as bright as day,
dazzling is the night for me,
and full of gladness.

The sanctifying power of this night
dispels wickedness, washes faults away,
restores innocence to the fallen, and joy to mourners,
drives out hatred, fosters concord, and brings down the
    mighty.

On this, your night of grace, O holy Father,
accept this candle, a solemn offering,
the work of bees and of your servants' hands,
an evening sacrifice of praise,
this gift from your most holy Church.

But now we know the praises of this pillar,
which glowing fire ignites for God's honor,
a fire into many flames divided,
yet never dimmed by sharing of its light,
for it is fed by melting wax,
drawn out by mother bees
to build a torch so precious.

O truly blessed night,
when things of heaven are wed to those of earth,
and divine to the human.

Shorter Form only:
On this, your night of grace, O holy Father,
accept this candle, a solemn offering,
the work of bees and of your servants' hands,
an evening sacrifice of praise,
this gift from your most holy Church.

Therefore, O Lord,
we pray you that this candle,

hallowed to the honor of your name,
may persevere undimmed,
to overcome the darkness of this night.
Receive it as a pleasing fragrance,
and let it mingle with the lights of heaven.
May this flame be found still burning
by the Morning Star:
the one Morning Star who never sets,
Christ your Son,
who, coming back from death's domain,
has shed his peaceful light on humanity,
and lives and reigns for ever and ever.
℟. **Amen.** ↓

SECOND PART:
THE LITURGY OF THE WORD

*In this Vigil, the mother of all Vigils, nine readings are provid-
ed, namely seven from the Old Testament and two from the
New (the Epistle and Gospel), all of which should be read
whenever this can be done, so that the character of the Vigil,
which demands an extended period of time, may be preserved.*

*Nevertheless, where more serious pastoral circumstances
demand it, the number of readings from the Old Testament
may be reduced, always bearing in mind that the reading of
the Word of God is a fundamental part of this Easter Vigil. At
least three readings should be read from the Old Testament,
both from the Law and from the Prophets, and their respec-
tive Responsorial Psalms should be sung. Never, moreover,
should the reading of chapter 14 of Exodus with its canticle
be omitted.*

*After setting aside their candles, all sit. Before the readings
begin, the Priest instructs the people in these or similar words:*

[Listen with Quiet Hearts]

Dear brethren (brothers and sisters),
now that we have begun our solemn Vigil,
let us listen with quiet hearts to the Word of God.

Let us meditate on how God in times past saved his
   people
and in these, the last days, has sent us his Son as our
   Redeemer.
Let us pray that our God may complete this paschal
   work of salvation
by the fullness of redemption.

*Then the readings follow. A reader goes to the ambo and pro-
claims the reading. Afterwards a psalmist or a cantor sings or
says the Psalm with the people making the response. Then all
rise, the Priest says,* Let us pray *and, after all have prayed
for a while in silence, he says the prayer corresponding to the
reading. In place of the Responsorial Psalm a period of
sacred silence may be observed, in which case the pause after*
Let us pray *is omitted.*

FIRST READING Gn 1:1—2:2 or 1:1, 26-31a **[God Our Creator]**

> **God created the world and all that is in it. He saw that it
> was good. This reading from the first book of the Bible
> shows that God loved all that he made.**

*[If the "Shorter Form" is used, the indented text in brackets is
omitted.]*

A reading from the Book of Genesis

IN the beginning, when God created the heavens and
the earth,
   [the earth was a formless wasteland, and darkness
   covered the abyss, while a mighty wind swept over
   the waters.

      Then God said, "Let there be light," and there
   was light. God saw how good the light was. God
   then separated the light from the darkness. God
   called the light "day," and the darkness he called
   "night." Thus evening came, and morning followed—the first day.

      Then God said, "Let there be a dome in the
   middle of the waters, to separate one body of
   water from the other." And so it happened: God

made the dome, and it separated the water above the dome from the water below it. God called the dome "the sky." Evening came, and morning followed—the second day.

Then God said, "Let the water under the sky be gathered into a single basin, so that the dry land may appear." And so it happened: the water under the sky was gathered into its basin, and the dry land appeared. God called the dry land "the earth," and the basin of the water he called "the sea." God saw how good it was. Then God said, "Let the earth bring forth vegetation: every kind of plant that bears seed and every kind of fruit tree on earth that bears fruit with its seed in it." And so it happened: the earth brought forth every kind of plant that bears seed and every kind of fruit tree on earth that bears fruit with its seed in it. God saw how good it was. Evening came, and morning followed—the third day.

Then God said: "Let there be lights in the dome of the sky, to separate day from night. Let them mark the fixed times, the days and the years, and serve as luminaries in the dome of the sky, to shed light upon the earth." And so it happened: God made the two great lights, the greater one to govern the day, and the lesser one to govern the night; and he made the stars. God set them in the dome of the sky, to shed light upon the earth, to govern the day and the night, and to separate the light from the darkness. God saw how good it was. Evening came, and morning followed—the fourth day.

Then God said, "Let the water teem with an abundance of living creatures, and on the earth let birds fly beneath the dome of the sky." And so it happened: God created the great sea monsters and all kinds of swimming creatures with which the water teems, and all kinds of winged birds. God saw how good it was, and God blessed them, saying, "Be fertile, multiply, and fill the water of the seas; and let the birds multiply on the earth." Evening came, and morning followed—the fifth day.

Then God said, "Let the earth bring forth all kinds of living creatures: cattle, creeping things, and wild animals of all kinds." And so it happened: God made all kinds of wild animals, all kinds of cattle, and all kinds of creeping things of the earth. God saw how good it was. Then]

God said: "Let us make man in our image, after our likeness. Let them have dominion over the fish of the sea, the birds of the air, and the cattle, and over all the wild animals and all the creatures that crawl on the ground."

God created man in his image;
in the divine image he created him;
male and female he created them.

God blessed them, saying: "Be fertile and multiply; fill the earth and subdue it. Have dominion over the fish of the sea, the birds of the air, and all the living things that move on the earth." God also said: "See, I give you every seed-bearing plant all over the earth and every tree that has seed-bearing fruit on it to be your food; and to all the animals of the land, all the birds of the air, and all the living creatures that crawl on the ground, I give all the green plants for food." And so it happened. God looked at everything he had made, and he found it very good.

[Evening came, and morning followed—the sixth day.

Thus the heavens and the earth and all their array were completed. Since on the seventh day God was finished with the work he had been doing, he rested on the seventh day from all the work he had undertaken.]

The word of the Lord. ℟. **Thanks be to God.** ↓

RESPONSORIAL PSALM Ps 104   **[Come, Holy Spirit]**

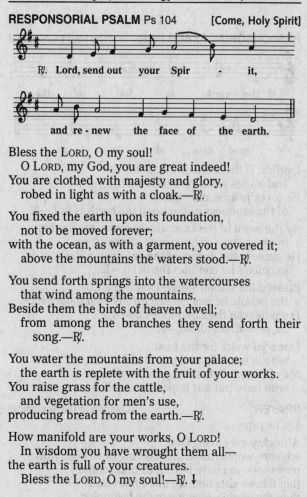

℟. Lord, send out your Spir - it,
and re - new the face of the earth.

Bless the LORD, O my soul!
   O LORD, my God, you are great indeed!
You are clothed with majesty and glory,
   robed in light as with a cloak.—℟.

You fixed the earth upon its foundation,
   not to be moved forever;
with the ocean, as with a garment, you covered it;
   above the mountains the waters stood.—℟.

You send forth springs into the watercourses
   that wind among the mountains.
Beside them the birds of heaven dwell;
   from among the branches they send forth their
      song.—℟.

You water the mountains from your palace;
   the earth is replete with the fruit of your works.
You raise grass for the cattle,
   and vegetation for men's use,
producing bread from the earth.—℟.

How manifold are your works, O LORD!
   In wisdom you have wrought them all—
the earth is full of your creatures.
   Bless the LORD, O my soul!—℟. ↓

OR

RESPONSORIAL PSALM Ps 33   [The Lord's Goodness]

R̸. The earth is full of the good - ness of the Lord.

Upright is the word of the LORD,
 and all his works are trustworthy.
He loves justice and right;
 of the kindness of the LORD the earth is full.—R̸.

By the word of the LORD the heavens were made;
 by the breath of his mouth all their host.
He gathers the waters of the sea as in a flask;
 in cellars he confines the deep.—R̸.

Blessed the nation whose God is the LORD,
 the people he has chosen for his own inheritance.
From heaven the LORD looks down;
 he sees all mankind.—R̸.

Our soul waits for the LORD,
 who is our help and our shield.
May your kindness, O LORD, be upon us
 who have put our hope in you.—R̸. ↓

PRAYER   [Creation in the Beginning]
Let us pray.

Almighty ever-living God,
who are wonderful in the ordering of all your works,
may those you have redeemed understand
that there exists nothing more marvelous
than the world's creation in the beginning

except that, at the end of the ages,
Christ our Passover has been sacrificed.
Who lives and reigns for ever and ever. ℟. **Amen.** ↓

OR

PRAYER (On the creation of man) [Eternal Joys]

O God, who wonderfully created human nature
and still more wonderfully redeemed it,
grant us, we pray,
to set our minds against the enticements of sin,
that we may merit to attain eternal joys.
Through Christ our Lord. ℟. **Amen.** ↓

SECOND READING Gn 22:1-18 or 22:1-2, 9a, 10-13, 15-18

[Obedience to God]

**Abraham is obedient to the will of God. Because God asks
him, without hesitation he prepares to sacrifice his son
Isaac. In the new order, God sends his Son to redeem man
by his death on the cross.**

*[If the "Shorter Form" is used, the indented text in brackets is
omitted.]*

A reading from the Book of Genesis

GOD put Abraham to the test. He called to him,
"Abraham!" "Here I am," he replied. Then God
said: "Take your son Isaac, your only one, whom you
love, and go to the land of Moriah. There you shall
offer him up as a holocaust on a height that I will point
out to you."

[Early the next morning Abraham saddled
his donkey, took with him his son Isaac, and two
of his servants as well, and with the wood that he
had cut for the holocaust, set out for the place of
which God had told him.

On the third day Abraham got sight of the
place from afar. Then he said to his servants: "Both
of you stay here with the donkey, while the boy

and I go on over yonder. We will worship and then come back to you." Thereupon Abraham took the wood for the holocaust and laid it on his son Isaac's shoulders, while he himself carried the fire and the knife. As the two walked on together, Isaac spoke to his father Abraham. "Father!" Isaac said. "Yes, son," he replied. Isaac continued, "Here are the fire and the wood, but where is the sheep for the holocaust?" "Son," Abraham answered, "God himself will provide the sheep for the holocaust." Then the two continued going forward.]

When they came to the place of which God had told him, Abraham built an altar there and arranged the wood on it.

[Next he tied up his son Isaac, and put him on top of the wood on the altar.]

Then he reached out and took the knife to slaughter his son. But the LORD's messenger called to him from heaven, "Abraham, Abraham!" "Here I am," he answered. "Do not lay your hand on the boy," said the messenger. "Do not do the least thing to him. I know now how devoted you are to God, since you did not withhold from me your own beloved son." As Abraham looked about, he spied a ram caught by its horns in the thicket. So he went and took the ram and offered it up as a holocaust in place of his son.

[Abraham named the site Yahweh-yireh; hence people now say, "On the mountain the LORD will see."]

Again the LORD's messenger called to Abraham from heaven and said: "I swear by myself, declares the LORD, that because you acted as you did in not withholding from me your beloved son, I will bless you abundantly and make your descendants as countless as the stars of the sky and the sands of the seashore; your descendants shall take possession of the gates of their enemies, and in your descendants all the nations of the earth shall find blessing—all this because you obeyed my command."—The word of the Lord. ℟. **Thanks be to God.** ↓

RESPONSORIAL PSALM Ps 16   [God Our Hope]

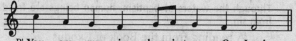

℟. You   are   my   in - her - i - tance, O   Lord.

O Lord, my allotted portion and my cup,
    you it is who hold fast my lot.
I set the Lord ever before me;
    with him at my right I shall not be disturbed.—℟.

Therefore my heart is glad and my soul rejoices,
    my body, too, abides in confidence;
because you will not abandon my soul to the nether-
    world,
    nor will you suffer your faithful one to undergo cor-
    ruption.—℟.

You will show me the path to life,
    fullness of joys in your presence,
    the delights at your right hand forever.—℟. ↓

PRAYER   [Entering into Grace]

Let us pray.

O God, supreme Father of the faithful,
who increase the children of your promise
by pouring out the grace of adoption
throughout the whole world
and who through the Paschal Mystery
make your servant Abraham father of nations,
as once you swore,
grant, we pray,
that your peoples may enter worthily
into the grace to which you call them.

Through Christ our Lord.

R/. **Amen.** ↓

THIRD READING Ex 14:15—15:1   [Exodus]

Moses leads the Israelites out of Egypt. He opens a path of escape through the Red Sea. God protects his people. Through the waters of baptism, human beings are freed from sin.

A reading from the Book of Exodus

THE LORD said to Moses, "Why are you crying out to me? Tell the Israelites to go forward. And you, lift up your staff and, with hand outstretched over the sea, split the sea in two, that the Israelites may pass through it on dry land. But I will make the Egyptians so obstinate that they will go in after them. Then I will receive glory through Pharaoh and all his army, his chariots and charioteers. The Egyptians shall know that I am the LORD, when I receive glory through Pharaoh and his chariots and charioteers."

The angel of God, who had been leading Israel's camp, now moved and went around behind them. The column of cloud also, leaving the front, took up its place behind them, so that it came between the camp of the Egyptians and that of Israel. But the cloud now became dark, and thus the night passed without the rival camps coming any closer together all night long. Then Moses stretched out his hand over the sea, and the LORD swept the sea with a strong east wind throughout the night and so turned it into dry land. When the water was thus divided, the Israelites marched into the midst of the sea on dry land, with the water like a wall to their right and to their left.

The Egyptians followed in pursuit; all Pharaoh's horses and chariots and charioteers went after them right into the midst of the sea. In the night watch just before dawn the LORD cast through the column of the fiery cloud upon the Egyptian force a glance that threw it into a panic; and he so clogged their chariot wheels that they could hardly drive. With that the Egyptians sounded the retreat before Israel, because the Lord was fighting for them against the Egyptians.

Then the Lord told Moses, "Stretch out your hand over the sea, that the water may flow back upon the Egyptians, upon their chariots and their charioteers." So Moses stretched out his hand over the sea, and at dawn the sea flowed back to its normal depth. The Egyptians were fleeing head on toward the sea, when the Lord hurled them into its midst. As the water flowed back, it covered the chariots and the charioteers of Pharaoh's whole army which had followed the Israelites into the sea. Not a single one of them escaped. But the Israelites had marched on dry land through the midst of the sea, with the water like a wall to their right and to their left. Thus the Lord saved Israel on that day from the power of the Egyptians. When Israel saw the Egyptians lying dead on the seashore and beheld the great power that the Lord had shown against the Egyptians, they feared the Lord and believed in him and in his servant Moses.

Then Moses and the Israelites sang this song to the Lord:

I will sing to the Lord, for he is gloriously triumphant;
horse and chariot he has cast into the sea.
The word of the Lord. ℟. **Thanks be to God.** ↓

RESPONSORIAL PSALM Ex 15   [God the Savior]

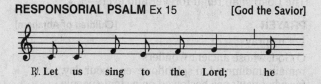

℟. Let   us   sing   to   the   Lord;   he

has cov-ered him-self　　in glo - ry.

I will sing to the LORD, for he is gloriously triumphant;
　horse and chariot he has cast into the sea.
My strength and my courage is the LORD,
　and he has been my savior.
He is my God, I praise him;
　the God of my father, I extol him.

℟. **Let us sing to the Lord; he has covered himself in
　glory.**

The LORD is a warrior,
　LORD is his name!
Pharaoh's chariots and army he hurled into the sea;
　the elite of his officers were submerged into the Red
　　Sea.—℟.

The flood waters covered them,
　they sank into the depths like a stone.
Your right hand, O LORD, magnificent in power,
　your right hand, O LORD, has shattered the enemy.
　　—℟.

You brought in the people you redeemed
　and planted them on the mountain of your inheri-
　　tance—
the place where you made your seat, O LORD,
　the sanctuary, O LORD, which your hands estab-
　　lished.
The LORD shall reign forever and ever.—℟. ↓

PRAYER　　　　　　　　　　　　　　[Children of Abraham]
Let us pray.

O God, whose ancient wonders
remain undimmed in splendor even in our day,
for what you once bestowed on a single people,

freeing them from Pharaoh's persecution
by the power of your right hand,
now you bring about as the salvation of the nations
through the waters of rebirth,
grant, we pray, that the whole world
may become children of Abraham
and inherit the dignity of Israel's birthright.
Through Christ our Lord. ℟. **Amen.** ↓

OR

PRAYER [Reborn]

O God, who by the light of the New Testament
have unlocked the meaning
of wonders worked in former times,
so that the Red Sea prefigures the sacred font
and the nation delivered from slavery
foreshadows the Christian people,
grant, we pray, that all nations,
obtaining the privilege of Israel by merit of faith,
may be reborn by partaking of your Spirit.
Through Christ our Lord. ℟. **Amen.** ↓

FOURTH READING Is 54:5-14 [God's Love]

For a time, God hid from his people, but his love for them is everlasting. He takes pity on them and promises them prosperity.

A reading from the Book of the Prophet Isaiah

T HE One who has become your husband is your
  Maker;
    his name is the LORD of hosts;
your redeemer is the Holy One of Israel,
    called God of all the earth.
The LORD calls you back,
    like a wife forsaken and grieved in spirit,
    a wife married in youth and then cast off,
    says your God.
For a brief moment I abandoned you,
    but with great tenderness I will take you back.

In an outburst of wrath, for a moment
    I hid my face from you;
but with enduring love I take pity on you,
    says the LORD, your redeemer.
This is for me like the days of Noah,
    when I swore that the waters of Noah
    should never again deluge the earth;
so I have sworn not to be angry with you,
    or to rebuke you.
Though the mountains leave their place
    and the hills be shaken,
my love shall never leave you
    nor my covenant of peace be shaken,
    says the LORD, who has mercy on you.
O afflicted one, storm-battered and unconsoled,
    I lay your pavements in carnelians,
    and your foundations in sapphires;
I will make your battlements of rubies,
    your gates of carbuncles,
    and all your walls of precious stones.
All your sons shall be taught by the LORD,
    and great shall be the peace of your children.
In justice shall you be established,
    far from the fear of oppression,
    where destruction cannot come near you.
The word of the Lord. ℟. **Thanks be to God.** ↓

RESPONSORIAL PSALM Ps 30   **[God Our Help]**

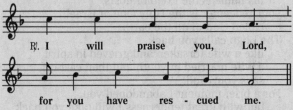

℟. I will praise you, Lord,
for you have res-cued me.

I will extol you, O LORD, for you drew me clear
　　and did not let my enemies rejoice over me.
O LORD, you brought me up from the netherworld;
　　you preserved me from among those going down
　　　into the pit.—R̶/.

Sing praise to the LORD, you his faithful ones,
　　and give thanks to his holy name.
For his anger lasts but a moment;
　　a lifetime, his good will.
At nightfall, weeping enters in,
　　but with the dawn, rejoicing.—R̶/.

Hear, O LORD, and have pity on me;
　　O LORD, be my helper.
You changed my mourning into dancing;
　　O LORD, my God, forever will I give you thanks.—R̶/. ↓

PRAYER　　　　　　　　　　[Fulfillment of God's Promise]

Let us pray.

Almighty ever-living God,
surpass, for the honor of your name,
what you pledged to the Patriarchs by reason of their
　　faith,
and through sacred adoption increase the children of
　　your promise,
so that what the Saints of old never doubted would come
　　to pass
your Church may now see in great part fulfilled.
Through Christ our Lord. R̶/. **Amen.** ↓

*Alternatively, other prayers may be used from among those
which follow the readings that have been omitted.*

FIFTH READING Is 55:1-11　　　　[God of Forgiveness]
　　God is a loving Father and he calls his people back. He
　　promises an everlasting covenant with them. God is mer-
　　ciful, generous, and forgiving.

A reading from the Book of the Prophet Isaiah

THUS says the LORD:
 All you who are thirsty,
   come to the water!
You who have no money,
   come, receive grain and eat;
come, without paying and without cost,
   drink wine and milk!
Why spend your money for what is not bread;
   your wages for what fails to satisfy?
Heed me, and you shall eat well,
   you shall delight in rich fare.
Come to me heedfully,
   listen, that you may have life.
I will renew with you the everlasting covenant,
   the benefits assured to David.
As I made him a witness to the peoples,
   a leader and commander of nations,
so shall you summon a nation you knew not,
   and nations that knew you not shall run to you,
because of the LORD, your God,
   the Holy One of Israel, who has glorified you.

Seek the LORD while he may be found,
   call him while he is near.
Let the scoundrel forsake his way,
   and the wicked man his thoughts;
let him turn to the LORD for mercy;
   to our God, who is generous in forgiving.
For my thoughts are not your thoughts,
   nor are your ways my ways, says the LORD.
As high as the heavens are above the earth,
   so high are my ways above your ways,
   and my thoughts above your thoughts.

For just as from the heavens
   the rain and snow come down

and do not return there
till they have watered the earth,
making it fertile and fruitful,
giving seed to the one who sows
and bread to the one who eats,
so shall my word be
that goes forth from my mouth;
my word shall not return to me void,
but shall do my will,
achieving the end for which I sent it.

The word of the Lord. ℟. **Thanks be to God.** ↓

RESPONSORIAL PSALM Is 12   [Make Known God's Deeds]

℟. You will draw water joyfully from the springs of salvation.

God indeed is my savior;
I am confident and unafraid.
My strength and my courage is the LORD,
and he has been my savior.
With joy you will draw water
at the fountain of salvation.—℟.

Give thanks to the LORD, acclaim his name;
among the nations make known his deeds,
proclaim how exalted is his name.—℟.

Sing praise to the LORD for his glorious achievement;
let this be known throughout all the earth.
Shout with exultation, O city of Zion,
for great in your midst
is the Holy One of Israel!—℟. ↓

PRAYER [Progress in Virtue]

Let us pray.

Almighty ever-living God,
sole hope of the world,
who by the preaching of your Prophets
unveiled the mysteries of this present age,
graciously increase the longing of your people,
for only at the prompting of your grace
do the faithful progress in any kind of virtue.
Through Christ our Lord. ℟. **Amen.** ↓

SIXTH READING Bar 3:9-15, 32—4:4 [Walk in God's Ways]

> Baruch tells the people of Israel to walk in the ways of
> God. They have to learn prudence, wisdom, understand-
> ing. Then they will have peace forever.

A reading from the Book of the Prophet Baruch

HEAR, O Israel, the commandments of life:
listen, and know prudence!
How is it, Israel,
    that you are in the land of your foes,
    grown old in a foreign land,
defiled with the dead,
    accounted with those destined for the netherworld?
You have forsaken the fountain of wisdom!
    Had you walked in the way of God,
    you would have dwelt in enduring peace.
Learn where prudence is,
    where strength, where understanding;
that you may know also
    where are length of days, and life,
    where light of the eyes, and peace.
Who has found the place of wisdom,
    who has entered into her treasuries?

The One who knows all things knows her;
    he has probed her by his knowledge—

the One who established the earth for all time,
    and filled it with four-footed beasts;
he who dismisses the light, and it departs,
    calls it, and it obeys him trembling;
before whom the stars at their posts
    shine and rejoice;
when he calls them, they answer, "Here we are!"
    shining with joy for their Maker.
Such is our God;
    no other is to be compared to him:
he has traced out all the way of understanding,
    and has given her to Jacob, his servant,
    to Israel, his beloved son.

Since then she has appeared on earth,
    and moved among people.
She is the book of the precepts of God,
    the law that endures forever;
all who cling to her will live,
    but those will die who forsake her.
Turn, O Jacob, and receive her:
    walk by her light toward splendor.
Give not your glory to another,
    your privileges to an alien race.
Blessed are we, O Israel;
    for what pleases God is known to us!
The word of the Lord. ℟. **Thanks be to God.** ↓

RESPONSORIAL PSALM Ps 19   [Words of Eternal Life]

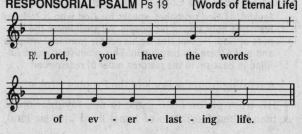

℟. Lord, you have the words of ev - er - last - ing life.

The law of the LORD is perfect,
  refreshing the soul;
the decree of the LORD is trustworthy,
  giving wisdom to the simple.

℞. **Lord, you have the words of everlasting life.**

The precepts of the LORD are right,
  rejoicing the heart;
the command of the LORD is clear,
  enlightening the eye.—℞.

The fear of the LORD is pure,
  enduring forever;
the ordinances of the LORD are true,
  all of them just.—℞.

They are more precious than gold,
  than a heap of purest gold;
sweeter also than syrup
  or honey from the comb.—℞. ↓

PRAYER   [Unfailing Protection]

Let us pray.

O God, who constantly increase your Church
by your call to the nations,
graciously grant
to those you wash clean in the waters of Baptism
the assurance of your unfailing protection.
Through Christ our Lord. ℞. **Amen.** ↓

SEVENTH READING Ez 36:16-17a, 18-28 [God's People]

Ezekiel, as God's prophet, speaks for God who is to keep
his name holy among his people. All shall know the holiness of God. He will cleanse his people from idol worship
and make them his own again. This promise is again fulfilled in baptism in the restored order of redemption.

A reading from the Book of the Prophet Ezekiel

THE word of the LORD came to me, saying: Son of
man, when the house of Israel lived in their land,

they defiled it by their conduct and deeds. Therefore I poured out my fury upon them because of the blood that they poured out on the ground, and because they defiled it with idols. I scattered them among the nations, dispersing them over foreign lands; according to their conduct and deeds I judged them. But when they came among the nations wherever they came, they served to profane my holy name, because it was said of them: "These are the people of the Lord, yet they had to leave their land." So I have relented because of my holy name which the house of Israel profaned among the nations where they came. Therefore say to the house of Israel: Thus says the Lord God: Not for your sakes do I act, house of Israel, but for the sake of my holy name, which you profaned among the nations to which you came. I will prove the holiness of my great name, profaned among the nations, in whose midst you have profaned it. Thus the nations shall know that I am the Lord, says the Lord God, when in their sight I prove my holiness through you. For I will take you away from among the nations, gather you from all the foreign lands, and bring you back to your own land. I will sprinkle clean water upon you to cleanse you from all your impurities, and from all your idols I will cleanse you. I will give you a new heart and place a new spirit within you, taking from your bodies your stony hearts and giving you natural hearts. I will put my spirit within you and make you live by my statutes, careful to observe my decrees. You shall live in the land I gave your fathers; you shall be my people, and I will be your God.—The word of the Lord. ℞. **Thanks be to God.** ↓

When Baptism is celebrated, Responsorial Psalm 42 is used; when Baptism is not celebrated, Is 12 or Ps 51 is used.

RESPONSORIAL PSALM Ps 42   [Longing for God]

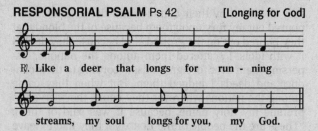

℟. Like a deer that longs for run - ning streams, my soul longs for you, my God.

Athirst is my soul for God, the living God.
  When shall I go and behold the face of God?—℟.

I went with the throng
  and led them in procession to the house of God,
amid loud cries of joy and thanksgiving,
  with the multitude keeping festival.—℟.

Send forth your light and your fidelity;
  they shall lead me on
and bring me to your holy mountain,
  to your dwelling-place.—℟.

Then will I go into the altar of God,
  the God of my gladness and joy;
then will I give you thanks upon the harp,
  O God, my God!—℟. ↓

OR

*When Baptism is not celebrated, the Responsorial Psalm
after the Fifth Reading (Is 12:2-3, 4bcd, 5-6) as above, p. 345,
may be used; or the following:*

RESPONSORIAL PSALM Ps 51   [A Clean Heart]

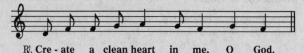

℟. Cre - ate a clean heart in me, O God.

A clean heart create for me, O God,
  and a steadfast spirit renew within me.
Cast me not out from your presence,
  and your Holy Spirit take not from me.—℟.

Give me back the joy of your salvation,
  and a willing spirit sustain in me.
I will teach transgressors your ways,
  and sinners shall return to you.—℟.

For you are not pleased with sacrifices;
  should I offer a holocaust, you would not accept it.
My sacrifice, O God, is a contrite spirit;
  a heart contrite and humbled, O God, you will not
    spurn.—℟. ↓

PRAYER   [Human Salvation]
Let us pray.

O God of unchanging power and eternal light,
look with favor on the wondrous mystery of the whole
  Church
and serenely accomplish the work of human salvation,
which you planned from all eternity;
may the whole world know and see
that what was cast down is raised up,
what had become old is made new,
and all things are restored to integrity through Christ,
just as by him they came into being.
Who lives and reigns for ever and ever. ℟. **Amen.** ↓

OR

PRAYER   [Confirm Our Hope]
O God, who by the pages of both Testaments
instruct and prepare us to celebrate the Paschal Mystery,
grant that we may comprehend your mercy,
so that the gifts we receive from you this night

may confirm our hope of the gifts to come.
Through Christ our Lord. ℟. **Amen.** ↓

*After the last reading from the Old Testament with its
Responsorial Psalm and its prayer, the altar candles are lit,
and the Priest intones the hymn* Gloria in excelsis Deo
(Glory to God in the highest), *which is taken up by all,
while bells are rung, according to local custom.*

COLLECT   [Renewed in Body and Mind]

O God, who make this most sacred night radiant
with the glory of the Lord's Resurrection,
stir up in your Church a spirit of adoption,
so that, renewed in body and mind,
we may render you undivided service.
Through our Lord Jesus Christ, your Son,
who lives and reigns with you in the unity of the Holy
    Spirit,
one God, for ever and ever. ℟. **Amen.** ↓

Then the reader proclaims the reading from the Apostle.

EPISTLE Rom 6:3-11   [Alive in Christ]

**By Baptism the Christian is not merely identified with the
dying Christ, who has won a victory over sin, but is introduced into the very act by which Christ died to sin.**

A reading from the Letter of Saint Paul to the Romans

BROTHERS and sisters: Are you unaware that we
who were baptized into Christ Jesus were baptized
into his death? We were indeed buried with him
through baptism into death, so that, just as Christ was
raised from the dead by the glory of the Father, we too
might live in newness of life.

For if we have grown into union with him through a
death like his, we shall also be united with him in the
resurrection. We know that our old self was crucified
with him, so that our sinful body might be done away
with, that we might no longer be in slavery to sin. For

a dead person has been absolved from sin. If, then, we have died with Christ, we believe that we shall also live with him. We know that Christ, raised from the dead, dies no more; death no longer has power over him. As to his death, he died to sin once and for all; as to his life, he lives for God. Consequently, you too must think of yourselves as being dead to sin and living for God in Christ Jesus.—The word of the Lord. ℟. **Thanks be to God.** ↓

After the Epistle has been read, all rise, then the Priest solemnly intones the Alleluia *three times, raising his voice by a step each time, with all repeating it. If necessary, the psalmist intones the* Alleluia.

RESPONSORIAL PSALM Ps 118   [God's Mercy]

℟. Al - le - lu - ia.   Al - le - lu - ia.   Al - le - lu - ia.

Give thanks to the LORD, for he is good,
   for his mercy endures forever.
Let the house of Israel say,
   "His mercy endures forever."—℟.

The right hand of the LORD has struck with power;
   the right hand of the LORD is exalted.
I shall not die, but live,
   and declare the works of the LORD.—℟.

The stone which the builders rejected
   has become the cornerstone.
By the LORD has this been done;
   it is wonderful in our eyes.—℟. ↓

The Priest, in the usual way, puts incense in the thurible and blesses the Deacon. At the Gospel lights are not carried, but only incense.

GOSPEL Lk 24:1-12   [The Resurrection]

> Christ has died, Christ has risen, Christ will come again!
> God's mercy brings us forgiveness and salvation.

℣. The Lord be with you. ℟. **And with your spirit.**
✠ A reading from the holy Gospel according to Luke.
℟. **Glory to you, O Lord.**

A T daybreak on the first day of the week the women
who had come from Galilee with Jesus took the
spices they had prepared and went to the tomb. They
found the stone rolled away from the tomb; but when
they entered, they did not find the body of the Lord
Jesus. While they were puzzling over this, behold, two
men in dazzling garments appeared to them. They were
terrified and bowed their faces to the ground. They said
to them, "Why do you seek the living one among the
dead? He is not here, but he has been raised. Remember
what he said to you while he was still in Galilee, that the
Son of Man must be handed over to sinners and be crucified, and rise on the third day." And they remembered
his words. Then they returned from the tomb and
announced all these things to the eleven and to all the
others. The women were Mary Magdalene, Joanna, and
Mary the mother of James; the others who accompanied
them also told this to the apostles, but their story seemed
like some nonsense and they did not believe them. But
Peter got up and ran to the tomb, bent down, and saw the
burial cloths alone; then he went home amazed at what
had happened.—The Gospel of the Lord. ℟. **Praise to
you, Lord Jesus Christ.**

After the Gospel, the Homily, even if brief, is not to be omitted.

THIRD PART:
CELEBRATION OF THE SACRAMENTS OF INITIATION

The following is adapted from the Rite of Christian Initiation of Adults.

Celebration of Baptism

PRESENTATION OF THE CANDIDATES

An assisting Deacon or other minister calls the candidates for Baptism forward and their godparents present them. The Invitation to Prayer and the Litany of the Saints follow.

INVITATION TO PRAYER   [Supportive Prayer]

The Priest addresses the following or a similar invitation for the assembly to join in prayer for the candidates for Baptism.

Dearly beloved,
with one heart and one soul, let us by our prayers
come to the aid of these our brothers and sisters in their
    blessed hope,
so that, as they approach the font of rebirth,
the almighty Father may bestow on them
all his merciful help.

LITANY OF THE SAINTS   [Petitioning the Saints]

The singing of the Litany of the Saints is led by cantors and may include, at the proper place, names of other saints (for example, the titular of the church, the patron saints of the place or of those to be baptized) or petitions suitable to the occasion.

Lord, have mercy.
Lord, have mercy.

Christ, have mercy.
Christ, have mercy.

Lord, have mercy.
Lord, have mercy.

Holy Mary, Mother of God,
    pray for us.

Saint Michael, **pray for us.**

Holy Angels of God, **pray for us.**

Saint John the Baptist, **pray for us.**

Saint Joseph, **pray for us.**

Saint Peter and Saint Paul, **pray for us.**

Saint Andrew, **pray for us.**

Saint John, **pray for us.**

Saint Mary Magdalene, **pray for us.**

Saint Stephen, **pray for us.**

Saint Ignatius of Antioch, **pray for us.**

Saint Lawrence, **pray for us.**

Saint Perpetua and Saint Felicity, **pray for us.**

Saint Agnes, **pray for us.**

Saint Gregory, **pray for us.**

Saint Augustine, **pray for us.**

Saint Athanasius, **pray for us.**

Saint Basil, **pray for us.**

Saint Martin, **pray for us.**

Saint Benedict, **pray for us.**

Saint Francis and Saint Dominic, **pray for us.**

Saint Francis Xavier, **pray for us.**

Saint John Vianney, **pray for us.**

Saint Catherine of Siena, **pray for us.**

Saint Teresa of Jesus, **pray for us.**

All holy men and women, Saints of God, **pray for us.**

Lord, be merciful, **Lord, deliver us, we pray.**

From all evil, **Lord, deliver us, we pray.**

From every sin, **Lord, deliver us, we pray.**

From everlasting death, **Lord, deliver us, we pray.**

By your Incarnation, **Lord, deliver us, we pray.**

By your Death and Resurrection, **Lord, deliver us, we pray.**

By the outpouring of the Holy Spirit, **Lord, deliver us, we pray.**

Be merciful to us sinners, **Lord, we ask you, hear our prayer.**

Bring these chosen ones to new birth through the grace of Baptism, **Lord, we ask you, hear our prayer.**

Jesus, Son of the living God, **Lord, we ask you, hear our prayer.**

Christ, hear us. **Christ, hear us.**

Christ, graciously hear us. **Christ, graciously hear us.**

BLESSING OF BAPTISMAL WATER   [Grace-Filled Water]

The Priest then blesses the baptismal water, saying the following prayer with hands extended:

O God, who by invisible power
accomplish a wondrous effect
through sacramental signs
and who in many ways have prepared water, your creation,
to show forth the grace of Baptism;

O God, whose Spirit
in the first moments of the world's creation
hovered over the waters,
so that the very substance of water
would even then take to itself the power to sanctify;

O God, who by the outpouring of the flood
foreshadowed regeneration,
so that from the mystery of one and the same element of water
would come an end to vice and a beginning of virtue;

O God, who caused the children of Abraham
to pass dry-shod through the Red Sea,
so that the chosen people,
set free from slavery to Pharaoh,
would prefigure the people of the baptized;

O God, whose Son,
baptized by John in the waters of the Jordan,
was anointed with the Holy Spirit,
and, as he hung upon the Cross,
gave forth water from his side along with blood,
and after his Resurrection, commanded his disciples:
"Go forth, teach all nations, baptizing them
in the name of the Father and of the Son and of the Holy Spirit,"
look now, we pray, upon the face of your Church
and graciously unseal for her the fountain of Baptism.

May this water receive by the Holy Spirit
the grace of your Only Begotten Son,
so that human nature, created in your image
and washed clean through the Sacrament of Baptism
from all the squalor of the life of old,
may be found worthy to rise to the life of newborn
  children
through water and the Holy Spirit.

*And, if appropriate, lowering the paschal candle into the
water either once or three times, he continues:*

May the power of the Holy Spirit,
O Lord, we pray,
come down through your Son
into the fullness of this font,

and, holding the candle in the water, he continues:

so that all who have been buried with Christ
by Baptism into death
may rise again to life with him.
Who lives and reigns with you in the unity of the Holy
  Spirit,
one God, for ever and ever. ℟. **Amen.**

*Then the candle is lifted out of the water, as the people
acclaim:*

**Springs of water, bless the Lord;
praise and exalt him above all for ever.**

THE BLESSING OF WATER   [Memorial of Baptism]

*If no one present is to be baptized and the font is not to be
blessed, the Priest introduces the faithful to the blessing of
water, saying:*

Dear brothers and sisters,
let us humbly beseech the Lord our God
to bless this water he has created,
which will be sprinkled upon us
as a memorial of our Baptism.

May he graciously renew us,
that we may remain faithful to the Spirit
whom we have received.

*And after a brief pause in silence, he proclaims the following
prayer, with hands extended:*

Lord our God,
in your mercy be present to your people
who keep vigil on this most sacred night,
and, for us who recall the wondrous work of our creation
and the still greater work of our redemption,
graciously bless this water.
For you created water to make the fields fruitful
and to refresh and cleanse our bodies.
You also made water the instrument of your mercy:
for through water you freed your people from slavery
and quenched their thirst in the desert;
through water the Prophets proclaimed the new
    covenant
you were to enter upon with the human race;
and last of all,
through water, which Christ made holy in the Jordan,
you have renewed our corrupted nature
in the bath of regeneration.

Therefore, may this water be for us
a memorial of the Baptism we have received,
and grant that we may share
in the gladness of our brothers and sisters,
who at Easter have received their Baptism.
Through Christ our Lord.
℟. **Amen.**

RENUNCIATION OF SIN AND PROFESSION OF FAITH
[Witnessing to Our Faith]

*If there are baptismal candidates, the Priest, in a series of
questions to which the candidates reply, **I do**, asks the candidates to renounce sin and profess their faith.*

BAPTISM [Children of God]

The Priest baptizes each candidate either by immersion or by the pouring of water.

N., I baptize you in the name of the Father, and of the Son, and of the Holy Spirit.

EXPLANATORY RITES

The celebration of Baptism continues with the explanatory rites, after which the celebration of Confirmation normally follows.

ANOINTING AFTER BAPTISM [Chrism of Salvation]

If the Confirmation of those baptized is separated from their Baptism, the Priest anoints them with chrism immediately after Baptism.

The God of power and Father of our Lord Jesus Christ has freed you from sin
and brought you to new life
through water and the Holy Spirit.

He now anoints you with the chrism of salvation,
so that, united with his people,
you may remain for ever a member of Christ
who is Priest, Prophet, and King.

Newly baptized: **Amen.**

In silence each of the newly baptized is anointed with chrism on the crown of the head.

CLOTHING WITH A BAPTISMAL GARMENT
[Clothed in Christ]

The garment used in this Rite may be white or of a color that conforms to local custom. If circumstances suggest, this Rite may be omitted.

N. and N., you have become a new creation
and have clothed yourselves in Christ.

Receive this baptismal garment
and bring it unstained to the judgment seat of our Lord
    Jesus Christ,
so that you may have everlasting life.

Newly baptized: **Amen.**

PRESENTATION OF A LIGHTED CANDLE [Light of Christ]

*The Priest takes the Easter candle in his hands or touches it,
saying:*

Godparents, please come forward to give to the newly
baptized the light of Christ.

*A godparent of each of the newly baptized goes to the Priest,
lights a candle from the Easter candle, then presents it to the
newly baptized.*

You have been enlightened by Christ.
Walk always as children of the light
and keep the flame of faith alive in your hearts.
When the Lord comes, may you go out to meet him
with all the saints in the heavenly kingdom.

Newly baptized: **Amen.**

The Renewal of Baptismal Promises

INVITATION   [Call to Renewal]

*After the celebration of Baptism, the Priest addresses the com-
munity, in order to invite those present to the renewal of their
baptismal promises; the candidates for reception into full communion join the rest of the community in this renunciation of
sin and profession of faith. All stand and hold lighted candles.*

The Priest may use the following or similar words.

Dear brethren (brothers and sisters), through the
    Paschal Mystery
we have been buried with Christ in Baptism,
so that we may walk with him in newness of life.
And so, now that our Lenten observance is concluded,
let us renew the promises of Holy Baptism,

by which we once renounced Satan and his works
and promised to serve God in the holy Catholic Church.
And so I ask you:

A   [Reject Evil]

Priest: Do you renounce Satan?
All: **I do.**

Priest: And all his works?
All: **I do.**

Priest: And all his empty show?
All: **I do.**

B

Priest: Do you renounce sin,
  so as to live in the freedom of the children of God?
All: **I do.**

Priest: Do you renounce the lure of evil,
  so that sin may have no mastery over you?
All: **I do.**

Priest: Do you renounce Satan,
  the author and prince of sin?
All: **I do.**

PROFESSION OF FAITH   [I Believe]

Then the Priest continues:

Priest: Do you believe in God,
      the Father almighty,
        Creator of heaven and earth?
All: **I do.**

Priest: Do you believe in Jesus Christ, his only Son, our
        Lord,
      who was born of the Virgin Mary,
      suffered death and was buried,
      rose again from the dead
      and is seated at the right hand of the Father?
All: **I do.**

Priest: Do you believe in the Holy Spirit,
the holy catholic Church,
the communion of saints,
the forgiveness of sins,
the resurrection of the body,
and life everlasting?

All: **I do.**

And the Priest concludes:

And may almighty God, the Father of our Lord Jesus
  Christ,
who has given us new birth by water and the Holy Spirit
and bestowed on us forgiveness of our sins,
keep us by his grace,
in Christ Jesus our Lord,
for eternal life.

All: **Amen.**

SPRINKLING WITH BAPTISMAL WATER   [Water of Life]

*The Priest sprinkles all the people with the blessed baptismal
water, while all sing the following song or any other that is
baptismal in character.*

Antiphon

**I saw water flowing from the Temple,
from its right-hand side, alleluia;
and all to whom this water came were saved
and shall say: Alleluia, alleluia.**

Celebration of Reception

INVITATION   [Call To Come Forward]

*If Baptism has been celebrated at the font, the Priest, the
assisting ministers, and the newly baptized with their godparents proceed to the sanctuary. As they do so the assembly
may sing a suitable song.*

*Then in the following or similar words the Priest invites the
candidates for reception, along with their sponsors, to come
into the sanctuary and before the community to make a profession of faith.*

N. and N., of your own free will you have asked to be received into the full communion of the Catholic Church. You have made your decision after careful thought under the guidance of the Holy Spirit. I now invite you to come forward with your sponsors and in the presence of this community to profess the Catholic faith. In this faith you will be one with us for the first time at the eucharistic table of the Lord Jesus, the sign of the Church's unity.

PROFESSION BY THE CANDIDATES   [Belief in Church]

When the candidates for reception and their sponsors have taken their places in the sanctuary, the Priest asks the candidates to make the following profession of faith. The candidates say:

I believe and profess all that the holy Catholic Church believes, teaches, and proclaims to be revealed by God.

ACT OF RECEPTION   [Full Communion]

Then the candidates with their sponsors go individually to the Priest, who says to each candidate (laying his right hand on the head of any candidate who is not to receive Confirmation):

N., the Lord receives you into the Catholic Church.
His loving kindness has led you here,
so that in the unity of the Holy Spirit
you may have full communion with us
in the faith that you have professed in the presence of
   his family.

Celebration of Confirmation

INVITATION   [Strength in the Spirit]

The newly baptized with their godparents and, if they have not received the Sacrament of Confirmation, the newly received with their sponsors, stand before the Priest. He first speaks briefly to the newly baptized and the newly received in these or similar words.

My dear candidates for Confirmation, by your Baptism you have been born again in Christ and you have become members of Christ and of his priestly people. Now you are to share in the outpouring of the Holy Spirit among us, the Spirit sent by the Lord upon his apostles at Pentecost and given by them and their successors to the baptized.

The promised strength of the Holy Spirit, which you are to receive, will make you more like Christ and help you to be witnesses to his suffering, death, and resurrection. It will strengthen you to be active members of the Church and to build up the Body of Christ in faith and love.

My dear friends, let us pray to God our Father, that he will pour out the Holy Spirit on these candidates for Confirmation to strengthen them with his gifts and anoint them to be more like Christ, the Son of God.

All pray briefly in silence.

LAYING ON OF HANDS   [Gifts of the Spirit]

The Priest holds his hands outstretched over the entire group of those to be confirmed and says the following prayer.

Almighty God, Father of our Lord Jesus Christ,
who brought these your servants to new birth
by water and the Holy Spirit,
freeing them from sin:
send upon them, O Lord, the Holy Spirit, the Paraclete;
give them the spirit of wisdom and understanding,
the spirit of counsel and fortitude,
the spirit of knowledge and piety;

fill them with the spirit of the fear of the Lord.
Through Christ our Lord.
℟. **Amen.**

ANOINTING WITH CHRISM   [Sealed in the Spirit]

*Either or both godparents and sponsors place the right hand
on the shoulder of the candidate; and a godparent or a spon-
sor of the candidate gives the candidate's name to the minister of the sacrament. During the conferral of the sacrament
an appropriate song may be sung.*

*The minister of the sacrament dips his right thumb in the
chrism and makes the Sign of the Cross on the forehead of the
one to be confirmed as he says:*

N., be sealed with the Gift of the Holy Spirit.
Newly confirmed: **Amen.**
Minister: Peace be with you.
Newly confirmed: **And with your spirit.**

*After all have received the sacrament, the newly confirmed as
well as the godparents and sponsors are led to their places in
the assembly.*

*[Since the Profession of Faith is not said, the Universal
Prayer (no. 16, p. 19) begins immediately and for the first time
the neophytes take part in them.]*

FOURTH PART:

THE LITURGY OF THE EUCHARIST

*The Priest goes to the altar and begins the Liturgy of the
Eucharist in the usual way.*

*It is desirable that the bread and wine be brought forward by
the newly baptized or, if they are children, by their parents
or godparents.*

PRAYER OVER THE OFFERINGS   [God's Saving Work]

Accept, we ask, O Lord,
the prayers of your people

with the sacrificial offerings,
that what has begun in the paschal mysteries
may, by the working of your power,
bring us to the healing of eternity.
Through Christ our Lord.
℟. **Amen.**

➜ No. 21, p. 22 (Pref P 21: on this night above all)

*In the Eucharistic Prayer, a commemoration is made of the
baptized and their godparents in accord with the formulas
which are found in the Roman Missal and Roman Ritual for
each of the Eucharistic Prayers.*

COMMUNION ANT. 1 Cor 5:7-8   [Purity and Truth]

**Christ our Passover has been sacrificed; therefore let
us keep the feast with the unleavened bread of purity
and truth, alleluia.** ↓

Psalm 118 (117) may appropriately be sung.

PRAYER AFTER COMMUNION   [One in Mind and Heart]

Pour out on us, O Lord, the Spirit of your love,
and in your kindness make those you have nourished
by this paschal Sacrament
one in mind and heart.
Through Christ our Lord. ℟. **Amen.**

SOLEMN BLESSING   [God's Blessings]

May almighty God bless you
through today's Easter Solemnity
and, in his compassion,
defend you from every assault of sin. ℟. **Amen.**

And may he, who restores you to eternal life
in the Resurrection of his Only Begotten,
endow you with the prize of immortality. ℟. **Amen.**

Now that the days of the Lord's Passion have drawn to a
   close,
may you who celebrate the gladness of the Paschal Feast
come with Christ's help, and exulting in spirit,
to those feasts that are celebrated in eternal joy.
℟. **Amen.**

And may the blessing of almighty God,
the Father, and the Son, ✠ and the Holy Spirit,
come down on you and remain with you for ever.
℟. **Amen.** ↓

*The final blessing formula from the Rite of Baptism of Adults
or of Children may also be used, according to circumstances.*

*To dismiss the people the Deacon or, if there is no Deacon, the
Priest himself sings or says:*

Go forth, the Mass is ended, alleluia, alleluia.

Or:

Go in peace, alleluia, alleluia.

℟. **Thanks be to God, alleluia, alleluia.**

This practice is observed throughout the Octave of Easter.

"I have risen, and I am with you still."

MARCH 27

EASTER SUNDAY

ENTRANCE ANT. Cf. Ps 139 (138):18, 5-6

[Christ's Resurrection]

I have risen, and I am with you still, alleluia. You have laid your hand upon me, alleluia. Too wonderful for me, this knowledge, alleluia, alleluia. → No. 2, p. 10

OR Lk 24:34; cf. Rv 1:6 [Glory and Power]

The Lord is truly risen, alleluia. To him be glory and power for all the ages of eternity, alleluia, alleluia.
→ No. 2, p. 10

COLLECT [Renewal]

O God, who on this day,
through your Only Begotten Son,
have conquered death
and unlocked for us the path to eternity,
grant, we pray, that we who keep
the solemnity of the Lord's Resurrection
may, through the renewal brought by your Spirit,
rise up in the light of life.
Through our Lord Jesus Christ, your Son,

who lives and reigns with you in the unity of the Holy
 Spirit,
one God, for ever and ever. ℟. **Amen.** ↓

FIRST READING Acts 10:34a, 37-43 [Salvation in Christ]

**In his sermon Peter sums up the "good news," the Gospel.
Salvation comes through Christ, the beloved Son of the
Father, the anointed of the Holy Spirit.**

A reading from the Acts of the Apostles

PETER proceeded to speak and said: "You know
what has happened all over Judea, beginning in
Galilee after the baptism that John preached, how God
anointed Jesus of Nazareth with the Holy Spirit and
power. He went about doing good and healing all those
oppressed by the devil, for God was with him. We are
witnesses of all that he did both in the country of the
Jews and in Jerusalem. They put him to death by hanging him on a tree. This man God raised on the third day
and granted that he be visible, not to all the people, but
to us, the witnesses chosen by God in advance, who ate
and drank with him after he rose from the dead. He
commissioned us to preach to the people and testify
that he is the one appointed by God as judge of the living and the dead. To him all the prophets bear witness,
that everyone who believes in him will receive forgiveness of sins through his name."—The word of the Lord.
℟. **Thanks be to God.** ↓

RESPONSORIAL PSALM Ps 118 [The Day of the Lord]

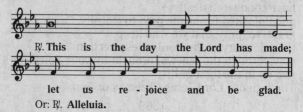

℟. This is the day the Lord has made;
let us re - joice and be glad.
Or: ℟. **Alleluia.**

Give thanks to the LORD, for he is good,
  for his mercy endures forever.
Let the house of Israel say,
  "His mercy endures forever."

℟. **This is the day the Lord has made; let us rejoice
  and be glad.**

Or: ℟. **Alleluia.**

"The right hand of the LORD has struck with power;
  the right hand of the LORD is exalted.
I shall not die, but live,
  and declare the works of the LORD."

℟. **This is the day the Lord has made; let us rejoice
  and be glad.**

Or: ℟. **Alleluia.**

The stone which the builders rejected
  has become the cornerstone.
By the LORD has this been done;
  it is wonderful in our eyes.

℟. **This is the day the Lord has made; let us rejoice
  and be glad.**

Or: ℟. **Alleluia.** ↓

*One of the following texts may be chosen as the Second
Reading.*

SECOND READING Col 3:1-4   [Seek Heavenly Things]

> **Look to the glory of Christ in which we share because our
> lives are hidden in him (through baptism) and we are des-
> tined to share in the glory.**

A reading from the Letter of Saint Paul to the Colossians

B ROTHERS and sisters: If then you were raised with
  Christ, seek what is above, where Christ is seated
at the right hand of God. Think of what is above, not of
what is on earth. For you have died, and your life is
hidden with Christ in God. When Christ your life
appears, then you too will appear with him in glory.—
The word of the Lord. ℟. **Thanks be to God.** ↓

OR

SECOND READING 1 Cor 5:6b-8   [Change of Heart]

Turn away from your old ways, from sin. Have a change of heart; be virtuous.

A reading from the first Letter of Saint Paul
to the Corinthians

BROTHERS and sisters: Do you not know that a little yeast leavens all the dough? Clear out the old yeast, so that you may become a fresh batch of dough, inasmuch as you are unleavened. For our paschal lamb, Christ, has been sacrificed. Therefore, let us celebrate the feast, not with the old yeast, the yeast of malice and wickedness, but with the unleavened bread of sincerity and truth.—The word of the Lord. ℟. **Thanks be to God.** ↓

SEQUENCE *(Victimae paschali laudes)*   [Hymn to the Victor]

Christians, to the Paschal Victim
    Offer your thankful praises!
A Lamb the sheep redeems;
    Christ, Who only is sinless,
    Reconciles sinners to the Father.
Death and life have contended in that combat stu-
        pendous:
    The Prince of life, who died, reigns immortal.
Speak, Mary, declaring
    What you saw, wayfaring.
"The tomb of Christ, who is living,
    The glory of Jesus' resurrection;
Bright angels attesting,
    The shroud and napkin resting.
Yes, Christ my hope is arisen;
    To Galilee he goes before you."
Christ indeed from death is risen, our new life ob-
        taining.
    Have mercy, victor King, ever reigning!
    Amen. Alleluia. ↓

ALLELUIA Cf. 1 Cor 5:7b-8a   [Joy in the Lord]

℟. **Alleluia, alleluia.**
Christ, our paschal lamb, has been sacrificed;
let us then feast with joy in the Lord.
℟. **Alleluia, alleluia.** ↓

(For Morning Mass)

GOSPEL Jn 20:1-9   [Renewed Faith]

Let us discover the empty tomb and ponder this mystery, and like Christ's first followers be strengthened in our faith.

℣. The Lord be with you. ℟. **And with your spirit.**
✣ A reading from the holy Gospel according to John.
℟. **Glory to you, O Lord.**

ON the first day of the week, Mary of Magdala came to the tomb early in the morning, while it was still dark, and saw the stone removed from the tomb. So she ran and went to Simon Peter and to the other disciple whom Jesus loved, and told them, "They have taken the Lord from the tomb, and we don't know where they put him." So Peter and the other disciple went out and came to the tomb. They both ran, but the other disciple ran faster than Peter and arrived at the tomb first; he bent down and saw the burial cloths there, but did not go in. When Simon Peter arrived after him, he went into the tomb and saw the burial cloths there, and the cloth that had covered his head, not with the burial cloths but rolled up in a separate place. Then the other disciple also went in, the one who had arrived at the tomb first, and he saw and believed. For they did not yet understand the Scripture that he had to rise from the dead.—The Gospel of the Lord. ℟. **Praise to you, Lord Jesus Christ.**

➜ No. 15, p. 18

In Easter Sunday Masses which are celebrated with a congregation, the rite of the renewal of baptismal promises may take place after the Homily, according to the text used at the Easter Vigil (p. 361). In that case the Creed is omitted.

OR

GOSPEL Lk 24:1-12   [The Resurrection]
See p. 354.

(For an Afternoon or Evening Mass)

GOSPEL Lk 24:13-35   [The Messiah's Need To Suffer]
   Let us accept the testimony of these two witnesses that
   our hearts may burn with the fire of faith.

℣. The Lord be with you. ℟. **And with your spirit.**
✛ A reading from the holy Gospel according to Luke.
℟. **Glory to you, O Lord.**

T HAT very day, the first day of the week, two of
   Jesus' disciples were going to a village seven miles
from Jerusalem called Emmaus, and they were conversing about all the things that had occurred. And it
happened that while they were conversing and debat-
ing, Jesus himself drew near and walked with them,
but their eyes were prevented from recognizing him.
He asked them, "What are you discussing as you walk
along?" They stopped, looking downcast. One of them,
named Cleopas, said to him in reply, "Are you the only
visitor to Jerusalem who does not know of the things
that have taken place there in these days?" And he
replied to them, "What sort of things?" They said to
him, "The things that happened to Jesus the Nazarene,
who was a prophet mighty in deed and word before
God and all the people, how our chief priests and
rulers both handed him over to a sentence of death
and crucified him. But we were hoping that he would
be the one to redeem Israel; and besides all this, it is
now the third day since this took place. Some women
from our group, however, have astounded us: they
were at the tomb early in the morning and did not find
his body; they came back and reported that they had

indeed seen a vision of angels who announced that he was alive. Then some of those with us went to the tomb and found things just as the women had described, but him they did not see." And he said to them, "Oh, how foolish you are! How slow of heart to believe all that the prophets spoke! Was is not necessary that the Christ should suffer these things and enter into his glory?" Then beginning with Moses and all the prophets, he interpreted to them what referred to him in all the Scriptures. As they approached the village to which they were going, he gave the impression that he was going on farther. But they urged him, "Stay with us, for it is nearly evening and the day is almost over." So he went in to stay with them. And it happened that, while he was with them at table, he took bread, said the blessing, broke it, and gave it to them. With that their eyes were opened and they recognized him, but he vanished from their sight. They said to each other, "Were not our hearts burning within us while he spoke to us on the way and opened the Scriptures to us?" So they set out at once and returned to Jerusalem where they found gathered together the eleven and those with them who were saying, "The Lord has truly been raised and has appeared to Simon!" Then the two recounted what had taken place on the way and how he was made known to them in the breaking of bread.—The Gospel of the Lord. ℟. **Praise to you, Lord Jesus Christ.**   → No. 15, p. 18

However, in Easter Sunday Masses which are celebrated with a congregation, the rite of the renewal of baptismal promises may take place after the Homily, according to the text used at the Easter Vigil (p. 361). In that case the Creed is omitted.

PRAYER OVER THE OFFERINGS [Reborn and Nourished]

Exultant with paschal gladness, O Lord,
we offer the sacrifice

by which your Church
is wondrously reborn and nourished.
Through Christ our Lord. ℟. **Amen.**

➙ No. 21, p. 22 (Pref. P 21: on this day above all)

When the Roman Canon is used, the proper forms of the
Communicantes *(In communion with those)* and Hanc
igitur *(Therefore, Lord, we pray) are said.*

COMMUNION ANT. 1 Cor 5:7-8   [Purity and Truth]
**Christ our Passover has been sacrificed, alleluia;
therefore let us keep the feast with the unleavened
bread of purity and truth, alleluia, alleluia.** ↓

PRAYER AFTER COMMUNION   [Glory of Resurrection]
Look upon your Church, O God,
with unfailing love and favor,
so that, renewed by the paschal mysteries,
she may come to the glory of the resurrection.
Through Christ our Lord.
℟. **Amen.**

➙ No. 30, p. 77

*To impart the blessing at the end of Mass, the Priest may
appropriately use the formula of Solemm Blessing for the
Mass of the Easter Vigil, p. 367.*

For the dismissal of the people, there is sung or said:

Go forth, the Mass is ended, alleluia, alleluia.

OR

Go in peace, alleluia, alleluia.

℟. **Thanks be to God, alleluia, alleluia.**

"Thomas answered . . . , 'My Lord and my God!' "

APRIL 3

2nd SUNDAY OF EASTER
(or of Divine Mercy)

ENTRANCE ANT. 1 Pt 2:2   **[Long for Spiritual Milk]**

Like newborn infants, you must long for the pure,
spiritual milk, that in him you may grow to salvation,
alleluia.   → No. 2, p. 10

OR 4 Esdr 2:36-37   **[Give Thanks]**

Receive the joy of your glory, giving thanks to God,
who has called you into the heavenly Kingdom, alleluia.   → No. 2, p. 10

COLLECT   **[Kindle Faith]**

God of everlasting mercy,
who in the very recurrence of the paschal feast
kindle the faith of the people you have made your own,
increase, we pray, the grace you have bestowed,
that all may grasp and rightly understand
in what font they have been washed,
by whose Spirit they have been reborn,

377

by whose Blood they have been redeemed.
Through our Lord Jesus Christ, your Son,
who lives and reigns with you in the unity of the Holy
   Spirit,
one God, for ever and ever. ℟. **Amen.** ↓

FIRST READING Acts 5:12-16   [Signs and Wonders]
**Through signs and wonders—miracles—the Lord supports
the work of the Apostles and leads people to the Faith.**

A reading from the Acts of the Apostles

MANY signs and wonders were done among the
people at the hands of the apostles. They were all
together in Solomon's portico. None of the others
dared to join them, but the people esteemed them. Yet
more than ever, believers in the Lord, great numbers of
men and women, were added to them. Thus they even
carried the sick out into the streets and laid them on
cots and mats so that when Peter came by, at least his
shadow might fall on one or another of them. A large
number of people from the towns in the vicinity of
Jerusalem also gathered, bringing the sick and those
disturbed by unclean spirits, and they were all
cured.—The word of the Lord. ℟. **Thanks be to God.** ↓

RESPONSORIAL PSALM Ps 118 [The Lord's Goodness]

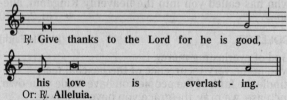

℟. **Give thanks to the Lord for he is good,
his love is everlast - ing.**
Or: ℟. **Alleluia.**

Let the house of Israel say,
   "His mercy endures forever."
Let the house of Aaron say,
   "His mercy endures forever."

Let those who fear the Lḭṟṟ say,
    "His mercy endures forever."

℟. **Give thanks to the Lord for he is good, his love is everlasting.**

Or: ℟. **Alleluia.**

I was hard pressed and was falling,
    but the Lḭṟṟ helped me.
My strength and my courage is the Lḭṟṟ,
    and he has been my savior.
The joyful shout of victory
    in the tents of the just:

℟. **Give thanks to the Lord for he is good, his love is everlasting.**

Or: ℟. **Alleluia.**

The stone which the builders rejected
    has become the cornerstone.
By the Lḭṟṟ has this been done;
    it is wonderful in our eyes.
This is the day the Lḭṟṟ has made;
    let us be glad and rejoice in it.

℟. **Give thanks to the Lord for he is good, his love is everlasting.** ↓

Or: ℟. **Alleluia.** ↓

SECOND READING Rv 1:9-11a, 12-13, 17-19
                    [The First and the Last]

In symbol and allegory the glory of the Lord is depicted.

A reading from the Book of Revelation

I, JOHN, your brother, who share with you the distress, the kingdom, and the endurance we have
in Jesus, found myself on the island called Patmos
because I proclaimed God's word and gave testimony
to Jesus. I was caught up in spirit on the Lord's day
and heard behind me a voice as loud as a trumpet,

which said, "Write on a scroll what you see." Then I turned to see whose voice it was that spoke to me, and when I turned, I saw seven gold lampstands and in the midst of the lampstands one like a son of man, wearing an ankle-length robe, with a gold sash around his chest.

When I caught sight of him, I fell down at his feet as though dead. He touched me with his right hand and said, "Do not be afraid. I am the first and the last, the one who lives. Once I was dead, but now I am alive forever and ever. I hold the keys to death and the netherworld. Write down, therefore, what you have seen, and what is happening, and what will happen afterwards."—The word of the Lord. ℟. **Thanks be to God.** ↓

ALLELUIA Jn 20:29   [Blind Faith]

℟. **Alleluia, alleluia.**
You believe in me, Thomas, because you have seen me,
    says the Lord;
blessed are they who have not seen me, but still believe!
℟. **Alleluia, alleluia.** ↓

GOSPEL Jn 20:19-31   [Living Faith]
   Jesus is risen; he comes and stands before his disciples. He
   encourages them and strengthens their faith.

℣. The Lord be with you. ℟. **And with your spirit.**
✠ A reading from the holy Gospel according to John.
℟. **Glory to you, O Lord.**

ON the evening of that first day of the week, when the doors were locked, where the disciples were, for fear of the Jews, Jesus came and stood in their midst and said to them, "Peace be with you." When he had said this, he showed them his hands and his side. The disciples rejoiced when they saw the Lord. Jesus said to them again, "Peace be with you. As the Father has sent me, so

I send you." And when he had said this, he breathed on them and said to them, "Receive the Holy Spirit. Whose sins you forgive are forgiven them, and whose sins you retain are retained."

Thomas, called Didymus, one of the Twelve, was not with them when Jesus came. So the other disciples said to him, "We have seen the Lord." But he said to them, "Unless I see the mark of the nails in his hands and put my finger into the nailmarks and put my hand into his side, I will not believe."

Now a week later his disciples were again inside and Thomas was with them. Jesus came, although the doors were locked, and stood in their midst and said, "Peace be with you." Then he said to Thomas, "Put your finger here and see my hands, and bring your hand and put it into my side, and do not be unbelieving, but believe." Thomas answered and said to him, "My Lord and my God!" Jesus said to him, "Have you come to believe because you have seen me? Blessed are those who have not seen and have believed."

Now Jesus did many other signs in the presence of his disciples that are not written in this book. But these are written that you may come to believe that Jesus is the Christ, the Son of God, and that through this belief you may have life in his name.—The Gospel of the Lord. ℟. **Praise to you, Lord Jesus Christ.**   ➔ No. 15, p. 18

PRAYER OVER THE OFFERINGS   [Unending Happiness]

Accept, O Lord, we pray,
the oblations of your people
(and of those you have brought to new birth),
that, renewed by confession of your name and by
    Baptism,
they may attain unending happiness.
Through Christ our Lord. ℟. **Amen.**

          ➔ No. 21, p. 22 (Pref. P 21: on this day above all)

When the Roman Canon is used, the proper forms of the Communicantes (In communion with those) *and* Hanc igitur (Therefore, Lord, we pray) *are said.*

COMMUNION ANT. Cf. Jn 20:27　　　　　　[Believe]

Bring your hand and feel the place of the nails, and do not be unbelieving but believing, alleluia. ↓

PRAYER AFTER COMMUNION　　　[Devout Reception]

Grant, we pray, almighty God,
that our reception of this paschal Sacrament
may have a continuing effect
in our minds and hearts.
Through Christ our Lord.
℟. **Amen.**　　　　　　　　　　　　→ No. 30, p. 77

Optional Solemn Blessings, p. 97, and Prayers over the People, p. 105

For the dismissal of the people, there is sung or said: Go forth, the Mass is ended alleluia, alleluia. *Or:* Go in peace, alleluia, alleluia. *The people respond:* **Thanks be to God, alleluia, alleluia.**

"He said to them, 'Cast the net over the right side of the boat.'"

3rd SUNDAY OF EASTER

ENTRANCE ANT. Cf. Ps 66 (65):1-2   [Praise the Lord]

Cry out with joy to God, all the earth; O sing to the glory of his name. O render him glorious praise, alleluia.   ➙ No. 2, p. 10

COLLECT   [Hope of Resurrection]

May your people exult for ever, O God,
in renewed youthfulness of spirit,
so that, rejoicing now in the restored glory of our
    adoption,
we may look forward in confident hope
to the rejoicing of the day of resurrection.
Through our Lord Jesus Christ, your Son,
who lives and reigns with you in the unity of the Holy
    Spirit,
one God, for ever and ever. ℟. **Amen.** ↓

FIRST READING Acts 5:27-32, 40b-41 **[Preaching the Name]**

With a strong faith the Apostles persevere in the mission that Christ gave them.

A reading from the Acts of the Apostles

WHEN the captain and the court officers had brought the apostles in and made them stand before the Sanhedrin, the high priest questioned them, "We gave you strict orders, did we not, to stop teaching in that name? Yet you have filled Jerusalem with your teaching and want to bring this man's blood upon us." But Peter and the apostles said in reply, "We must obey God rather than men. The God of our ancestors raised Jesus, though you had him killed by hanging him on a tree. God exalted him at his right hand as leader and savior to grant Israel repentance and forgiveness of sins. We are witnesses of these things, as is the Holy Spirit whom God has given to those who obey him."

The Sanhedrin ordered the apostles to stop speaking in the name of Jesus, and dismissed them. So they left the presence of the Sanhedrin, rejoicing that they had been found worthy to suffer dishonor for the sake of the name.—The word of the Lord. ℟. **Thanks be to God.** ↓

RESPONSORIAL PSALM Ps 30   **[Divine Security]**

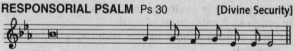

    ℟. **I will praise you, Lord, for you have res-cued me.**

    Or: ℟. **Alleluia.**

I will extol you, O LORD, for you drew me clear
    and did not let my enemies rejoice over me.
O LORD, you brought me up from the netherworld;
    you preserved me from among those going down
      into the pit.

℟. **I will praise you, Lord, for you have rescued me.**
Or: ℟. **Alleluia.**

Sing praise to the LORD, you his faithful ones,
  and give thanks to his holy name.
For his anger lasts but a moment;
  a lifetime, his good will.
At nightfall, weeping enters in,
  but with the dawn, rejoicing.

℟. **I will praise you, Lord, for you have rescued me.**

Or: ℟. **Alleluia.**

Hear, O LORD, and have pity on me;
  O LORD, be my helper.
You changed my mourning into dancing;
  O LORD, my God, forever will I give you thanks.

℟. **I will praise you, Lord, for you have rescued me.** ↓

Or: ℟. **Alleluia.** ↓

SECOND READING Rv 5:11-14   [The Throne of God]
  **The power and the glory of God are acclaimed by his cre-
  ation.**

A reading from the Book of Revelation

I, JOHN, looked and heard the voices of many angels
who surrounded the throne and the living creatures and the elders. They were countless in number,
and they cried out in a loud voice:
  "Worthy is the Lamb that was slain
    to receive power and riches, wisdom and strength,
    honor and glory and blessing."
Then I heard every creature in heaven and on earth
and under the earth and in the sea, everything in the
universe, cry out:
  "To the one who sits on the throne and to the Lamb
    be blessing and honor, glory and might,
    forever and ever."
The four living creatures answered, "Amen," and the
elders fell down and worshiped.—The word of the
Lord. ℟. **Thanks be to God.** ↓

ALLELUIA   [Creator of All]

℟. **Alleluia, alleluia.**
Christ is risen, creator of all;
he has shown pity on all people.
℟. **Alleluia, alleluia.** ↓

GOSPEL Jn 21:1-19 or 21:1-14   [Christ Is Lord]

**Again the risen Savior appears to his disciples in a very
human way. Peter in three affirmations rejects his triple
denial and again hears the call "Follow me."**

*[If the "Shorter Form" is used, the indented text in brackets is
omitted.]*

℣. The Lord be with you. ℟. **And with your spirit.**
✠ A reading from the holy Gospel according to John.
℟. **Glory to you, O Lord.**

A T that time, Jesus revealed himself again to his
disciples at the Sea of Tiberias. He revealed himself in this way. Together were Simon Peter, Thomas
called Didymus, Nathanael from Cana in Galilee,
Zebedee's sons, and two others of his disciples. Simon
Peter said to them, "I am going fishing." They said to
him, "We also will come with you." So they went out
and got into the boat, but that night they caught nothing. When it was already dawn, Jesus was standing on
the shore; but the disciples did not realize that it was
Jesus. Jesus said to them, "Children, have you caught
anything to eat?" They answered him, "No." So he said
to them, "Cast the net over the right side of the boat
and you will find something." So they cast it, and were
not able to pull it in because of the number of fish. So
the disciple whom Jesus loved said to Peter, "It is the
Lord." When Simon Peter heard that it was the Lord,
he tucked in his garment, for he was lightly clad, and
jumped into the sea. The other disciples came in the
boat, for they were not far from shore, only about a
hundred yards, dragging the net with the fish. When

they climbed out on shore, they saw a charcoal fire
with fish on it and bread. Jesus said to them, "Bring
some of the fish you just caught." So Simon Peter went
over and dragged the net ashore full of one hundred
fifty-three large fish. Even though there were so many,
the net was not torn. Jesus said to them, "Come, have
breakfast." And none of the disciples dared to ask him,
"Who are you?" because they realized it was the Lord.
Jesus came over and took the bread and gave it to
them, and in like manner the fish. This was now the
third time Jesus was revealed to his disciples after
being raised from the dead.

[When they had finished breakfast, Jesus said
to Simon Peter, "Simon, son of John, do you love
me more than these?" Simon Peter answered him,
"Yes, Lord, you know that I love you." Jesus said to
him, "Feed my lambs." He then said to Simon Peter
a second time, "Simon, son of John, do you love
me?" Simon Peter answered him, "Yes, Lord, you
know that I love you." Jesus said to him, "Tend my
sheep." Jesus said to him the third time, "Simon,
son of John, do you love me?" Peter was distressed
that Jesus had said to him a third time, "Do you
love me?" and he said to him, "Lord, you know
everything; you know that I love you." Jesus said
to him, "Feed my sheep. Amen, amen, I say to you,
when you were younger, you used to dress yourself and go where you wanted; but when you grow
old, you will stretch out your hands, and someone
else will dress you and lead you where you do not
want to go." He said this signifying by what kind
of death he would glorify God. And when he had
said this, he said to him, "Follow me."]

The Gospel of the Lord. ℟. **Praise to you, Lord Jesus
Christ.**   → No. 15, p. 18

PRAYER OVER THE OFFERINGS   [Exultant Church]

Receive, O Lord, we pray,
these offerings of your exultant Church,
and, as you have given her cause for such great
   gladness,
grant also that the gifts we bring
may bear fruit in perpetual happiness.
Through Christ our Lord.
℟. **Amen.**   → No. 21, p. 22 (Pref. P 21-25)

COMMUNION ANT. Cf. Lk 24:35   [Christ's Presence]

The disciples recognized the Lord Jesus in the breaking of the bread, alleluia. ↓

OR Cf. Jn 21:12-13   [Come and Eat]

Jesus said to his disciples: Come and eat. And he took bread and gave it to them, alleluia. ↓

PRAYER AFTER COMMUNION   [The Lord's Kindness]

Look with kindness upon your people, O Lord,
and grant, we pray,
that those you were pleased to renew by eternal
   mysteries
may attain in their flesh
the incorruptible glory of the resurrection.
Through Christ our Lord.
℟. **Amen.**   → No. 30, p. 77

Optional Solemn Blessings, p. 97, and Prayers over the People, p. 105

"My sheep hear my voice."

APRIL 17

4th SUNDAY OF EASTER

ENTRANCE ANT. Cf. Ps 33 (32):5-6   [God the Creator]
The merciful love of the Lord fills the earth; by the word of the Lord the heavens were made, alleluia.

→ No. 2, p. 10

COLLECT   [Joys of Heaven]
Almighty ever-living God,
lead us to a share in the joys of heaven,
so that the humble flock may reach
where the brave Shepherd has gone before.
Who lives and reigns with you in the unity of the Holy
   Spirit,
one God, for ever and ever.
℟. **Amen.** ↓

FIRST READING Acts 13:14, 43-52   [Salvation in Jesus]
   As missionaries, Paul and Barnabas meet with some success and encounter strong opposition. Steadfastness in
   faith is a source of joy.

389

A reading from the Acts of the Apostles

PAUL and Barnabas continued on from Perga and reached Antioch in Pisidia. On the sabbath they entered the synagogue and took their seats. Many Jews and worshipers who were converts to Judaism followed Paul and Barnabas, who spoke to them and urged them to remain faithful to the grace of God.

On the following sabbath almost the whole city gathered to hear the word of the Lord. When the Jews saw the crowds, they were filled with jealousy and with violent abuse contradicted what Paul said. Both Paul and Barnabas spoke out boldly and said, "It was necessary that the word of God be spoken to you first, but since you reject it and condemn yourselves as unworthy of eternal life, we now turn to the Gentiles. For so the Lord has commanded us, *I have made you a light to the Gentiles, that you may be an instrument of salvation to the ends of the earth.*"

The Gentiles were delighted when they heard this and glorified the word of the Lord. All who were destined for eternal life came to believe, and the word of the Lord continued to spread through the whole region. The Jews, however, incited the women of prominence who were worshipers and the leading men of the city, stirred up a persecution against Paul and Barnabas, and expelled them from their territory.

So they shook the dust from their feet in protest against them, and went to Iconium. The disciples were filled with joy and the Holy Spirit.—The word of the Lord. ℟. **Thanks be to God.** ↓

RESPONSORIAL PSALM Ps 100   [The Lord Is God]

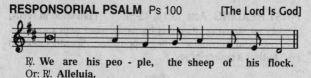

℟. **We are his peo - ple, the sheep of his flock.**
Or: ℟. **Alleluia.**

Sing joyfully to the LORD, all you lands;
    serve the LORD with gladness;
    come before him with joyful song.

℟. **We are his people, the sheep of his flock.**

Or: ℟. **Alleluia.**

Know that the LORD is God;
    he made us, his we are;
    his people, the flock he tends.

℟. **We are his people, the sheep of his flock.**

Or: ℟. **Alleluia.**

The LORD is good:
    his kindness endures forever,
    and his faithfulness, to all generations.

℟. **We are his people, the sheep of his flock.** ↓

Or: ℟. **Alleluia.** ↓

SECOND READING Rv 7:9, 14b-17 [The Blood of the Lamb]
    Those who remain faithful despite severe persecution will
    find their reward is to be with God and restored to peace.

A reading from the Book of Revelation

I, JOHN, had a vision of a great multitude, which no
    one could count, from every nation, race, people,
and tongue. They stood before the throne and before
the Lamb, wearing white robes and holding palm
branches in their hands.

Then one of the elders said to me, "These are the
ones who have survived the time of great distress; they
have washed their robes and made them white in the
blood of the Lamb.

"For this reason they stand before God's throne
    and worship him day and night in his temple.
The one who sits on the throne will shelter them.
They will not hunger or thirst anymore,
    nor will the sun or any heat strike them.

For the Lamb who is in the center of the throne
    will shepherd them
    and lead them to springs of life-giving water,
    and God will wipe away every tear from their eyes."
The word of the Lord. ℟. **Thanks be to God.** ↓

ALLELUIA Jn 10:14   [God's Sheep]
℟. **Alleluia, alleluia.**
I am the good shepherd, says the Lord;
I know my sheep, and mine know me.
℟. **Alleluia, alleluia.**

GOSPEL Jn 10:27-30   [The Good Shepherd]
    **Jesus proclaims his oneness with the Father. His love for
    us is so great that he brings us eternal life.**

℣. The Lord be with you. ℟. **And with your spirit.**
✤ A reading from the holy Gospel according to John.
℟. **Glory to you, O Lord.**

JESUS said: "My sheep hear my voice. I know them,
and they follow me. I give them eternal life, and
they shall never perish. No one can take them out of
my hand. My Father, who has given them to me, is
greater than all, and no one can take them out of the
Father's hand. The Father and I are one."—The Gospel
of the Lord. ℟. **Praise to you, Lord Jesus Christ.**
➜ No. 15, p. 18

PRAYER OVER THE OFFERINGS   [Unending Joy]
Grant, we pray, O Lord,
that we may always find delight in these paschal
    mysteries,
so that the renewal constantly at work within us
may be the cause of our unending joy.
Through Christ our Lord.
℟. **Amen.**   ➜ No. 21, p. 22 (Pref. P 21-25)

COMMUNION ANT.   [The Risen Shepherd]

The Good Shepherd has risen, who laid down his life for his sheep and willingly died for his flock, alleluia. ↓

PRAYER AFTER COMMUNION   [Kind Shepherd]

Look upon your flock, kind Shepherd,
and be pleased to settle in eternal pastures
the sheep you have redeemed
by the Precious Blood of your Son.
Who lives and reigns for ever and ever.
℟. **Amen.**   → No. 30, p. 77

Optional Solemn Blessings, p. 97, and Prayers over the People, p. 105

"I give you a new commandment: love one another."

APRIL 24

5th SUNDAY OF EASTER

ENTRANCE ANT. Cf. Ps 98 (97):1-2   [Wonders of the Lord]

O sing a new song to the Lord, for he has worked wonders; in the sight of the nations he has shown his deliverance, alleluia.   → No. 2, p. 10

COLLECT   [Much Fruit]

Almighty ever-living God,
constantly accomplish the Paschal Mystery within us,
that those you were pleased to make new in Holy
    Baptism
may, under your protective care, bear much fruit
and come to the joys of life eternal.
Through our Lord Jesus Christ, your Son,
who lives and reigns with you in the unity of the Holy
    Spirit,
one God, for ever and ever.
℟. **Amen.** ↓

FIRST READING Acts 14:21-27   [Conversion of the Gentiles]

The life we have through Faith is not easy. We must struggle against many difficulties, even temptations, on our journey to eternal life.

A reading from the Acts of the Apostles

A FTER Paul and Barnabas had proclaimed the good news to that city and made a considerable number of disciples, they returned to Lystra and to Iconium and to Antioch. They strengthened the spirits of the disciples and exhorted them to persevere in the faith, saying, "It is necessary for us to undergo many hardships to enter the kingdom of God." They appointed elders for them in each church and, with prayer and fasting, commended them to the Lord in whom they had put their faith. Then they traveled through Pisidia and reached Pamphylia. After proclaiming the word at Perga they went down to Attalia. From there they sailed to Antioch, where they had been commended to the grace of God for the work they had now accomplished. And when they arrived, they called the church together and reported what God had done with them and how he had opened the door of faith to the Gentiles.—The word of the Lord.
℟. **Thanks be to God.** ↓

RESPONSORIAL PSALM Ps 145   [The Kingdom of God]

℟. **I will praise your name for ev - er, my king and my God.**
Or: ℟. **Alleluia.**

The LORD is gracious and merciful,
    slow to anger and of great kindness.
The LORD is good to all
    and compassionate toward all his works.

℟. **I will praise your name for ever, my king and my God.**
Or: ℟. **Alleluia.**

Let all your works give you thanks, O Lᴏʀᴅ,
  and let your faithful ones bless you.
Let them discourse of the glory of your kingdom
  and speak of your might.

℟. **I will praise your name for ever, my king and my God.**

Or: ℟. **Alleluia.**

Let them make known your might to the children
    of Adam,
  and the glorious splendor of your kingdom.
Your kingdom is a kingdom for all ages,
  and your dominion endures through all generations.

℟. **I will praise your name for ever, my king and my
  God.** ↓

Or: ℟. **Alleluia.** ↓

SECOND READING Rv 21:1-5a   [God's Dwelling]

In the Kingdom of God all things are made new.

A reading from the Book of Revelation

THEN I, John, saw a new heaven and a new earth.
The former heaven and the former earth had
passed away, and the sea was no more. I also saw the
holy city, a new Jerusalem, coming down out of heav-
en from God, prepared as a bride adorned for her husband. I heard a loud voice from the throne saying,
"Behold, God's dwelling is with the human race. He
will dwell with them and they will be his people and
God himself will always be with them as their God. He
will wipe every tear from their eyes, and there shall be
no more death or mourning, wailing or pain, for the
old order has passed away."

The One who sat on the throne said, "Behold, I make
all things new."—The word of the Lord. ℟. **Thanks be
to God.** ↓

ALLELUIA Jn 13:34   [Love One Another]

℟. **Alleluia, alleluia.**

I give you a new commandment, says the Lord:
love one another as I have loved you.

℟. **Alleluia, alleluia.** ↓

GOSPEL Jn 13:31-33a, 34-35   [The New Commandment]

> Jesus is about to be betrayed yet he teaches us the way to
> glory—the way he will go. It is the way of love.

℣. The Lord be with you. ℟. **And with your spirit.**

✤ A reading from the holy Gospel according to John.

℟. **Glory to you, O Lord.**

WHEN Judas had left them, Jesus said, "Now is the
Son of Man glorified, and God is glorified
in him. If God is glorified in him, God will also glorify
him in himself, and God will glorify him at once. My children, I will be with you only a little while longer. I give
you a new commandment: love one another. As I have
loved you, so you also should love one another. This is
how all will know that you are my disciples, if you have
love for one another."—The Gospel of the Lord. ℟. **Praise
to you, Lord Jesus Christ.**   → No. 15, p. 18

PRAYER OVER THE OFFERINGS   [Guided by God's Truth]

O God, who by the wonderful exchange effected in this
    sacrifice
have made us partakers of the one supreme Godhead,
grant, we pray,
that, as we have come to know your truth,
we may make it ours by a worthy way of life.
Through Christ our Lord.

℟. **Amen.**   → No. 21, p. 22 (Pref. P 21-25)

COMMUNION ANT. Cf. Jn 15:1, 5   [Union with Christ]

**I am the true vine and you are the branches, says the
Lord. Whoever remains in me, and I in him, bears fruit
in plenty, alleluia.** ↓

PRAYER AFTER COMMUNION　　[New Life]

Graciously be present to your people, we pray, O Lord, and lead those you have imbued with heavenly mysteries
to pass from former ways to newness of life.
Through Christ our Lord.
℟. **Amen.**　　→ No. 30, p. 77

Optional Solemn Blessings, p. 97, and Prayers over the People, p. 105

"The Father will send [the Holy Spirit] in my name."

MAY 1

6th SUNDAY OF EASTER

ENTRANCE ANT. Cf. Is 48:20　　[Spiritual Freedom]
Proclaim a joyful sound and let it be heard; proclaim to the ends of the earth: The Lord has freed his people, alleluia.　　→ No. 2, p. 10

COLLECT　　[Heartfelt Devotion]
Grant, almighty God,
that we may celebrate with heartfelt devotion these days of joy,

which we keep in honor of the risen Lord,
and that what we relive in remembrance
we may always hold to in what we do.
Through our Lord Jesus Christ, your Son,
who lives and reigns with you in the unity of the Holy
    Spirit,
one God, for ever and ever. ℟. **Amen.** ↓

FIRST READING   Acts 15:1-2, 22-29   [Settling a Dispute]
The Church faces its first test caused by inner dissensions and she shows how, guided by the Spirit, charity will prevail.

A reading from the Acts of the Apostles

SOME who had come down from Judea were instructing the brothers, "Unless you are circumcised according to the Mosaic practice, you cannot be saved." Because there arose no little dissension and debate by Paul and Barnabas with them, it was decided that Paul, Barnabas, and some of the others should go up to Jerusalem to the apostles and elders about this question.

The apostles and elders, in agreement with the whole church, decided to choose representatives and to send them to Antioch with Paul and Barnabas. The ones chosen were Judas, who was called Barsabbas, and Silas, leaders among the brothers. This is the letter delivered by them:

"The apostles and the elders, your brothers, to the brothers in Antioch, Syria, and Cilicia of Gentile origin: greetings. Since we have heard that some of our number who went out without any mandate from us have upset you with their teachings and disturbed your peace of mind, we have with one accord decided to choose representatives and to send them to you along with our beloved Barnabas and Paul, who have dedicated their lives to the name of our Lord Jesus Christ. So we are sending Judas and Silas who will also convey this same message by word of mouth: 'It is the decision of the Holy Spirit and of us not to place on you any burden beyond these necessities, namely, to abstain from meat sacrificed to idols, from blood, from meats of strangled animals, and from unlawful marriage. If you keep free of these, you will be doing what is right. Farewell.' "—The word of the Lord. ℟. **Thanks be to God.** ↓

RESPONSORIAL PSALM Ps 67   [Praise of God]

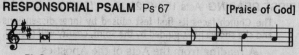

℟. **O   God,   let   all   the   na - tions praise you!**
Or: ℟. **Alleluia.**

May God have pity on us and bless us;
 may he let his face shine upon us.
So may your way be known upon earth;
 among all nations, your salvation.

℟. **O God, let all the nations praise you!**

Or: ℟. **Alleluia.**

May the nations be glad and exult
 because you rule the peoples in equity;
 the nations on the earth you guide.

℟. **O God, let all the nations praise you!**

Or: ℟. **Alleluia.**

May the peoples praise you, O God;
 may all the peoples praise you!
May God bless us,
 and may all the ends of the earth fear him!

℟. **O God, let all the nations praise you!** ↓

Or: ℟. **Alleluia.** ↓

SECOND READING Rv 21:10-14, 22-23   [The City of God]

In symbolic language the Church is depicted as a wonderful glorious city, repenting and caught up in the glory of God.

A reading from the Book of Revelation

THE angel took me in spirit to a great, high mountain and showed me the holy city Jerusalem coming down out of heaven from God. It gleamed with the splendor of God. Its radiance was like that of a precious stone, like jasper, clear as crystal. It had a massive, high wall, with twelve gates where twelve angels were stationed and on which names were inscribed, the names of the twelve tribes of the Israelites. There were three gates facing east, three north, three south, and three west. The wall of the city had twelve courses of stones as its foundation, on which were inscribed the twelve names of the twelve apostles of the Lamb.

I saw no temple in the city for its temple is the Lord God almighty and the Lamb. The city had no need of sun or moon to shine on it, for the glory of God gave it light, and its lamp was the Lamb.—The word of the Lord. ℟. **Thanks be to God.** ↓

ALLELUIA Jn 14:23   [Divine Love]

℟. **Alleluia, alleluia.**
Whoever loves me will keep my word, says the Lord, and my Father will love him and we will come to him. ℟. **Alleluia, alleluia.** ↓

GOSPEL Jn 14:23-29   [The Gift of Peace]

In saying farewell Jesus has not deserted us. In his name the Father sends the Holy Spirit that we may drink in his power.

℣. The Lord be with you. ℟. And with your spirit.
✚ A reading from the holy Gospel according to John.
℟. **Glory to you, O Lord.**

JESUS said to his disciples: "Whoever loves me will keep my word, and my Father will love him, and we will come to him and make our dwelling with him. Whoever does not love me does not keep my words;

yet the word you hear is not mine but that of the Father who sent me.

"I have told you this while I am with you. The Advocate, the Holy Spirit, whom the Father will send in my name, will teach you everything and remind you of all that I told you. Peace I leave with you; my peace I give to you. Not as the world gives do I give it to you. Do not let your hearts be troubled or afraid. You heard me tell you, 'I am going away and I will come back to you.' If you loved me, you would rejoice that I am going to the Father; for the Father is greater than I. And now I have told you this before it happens, so that when it happens you may believe."—The Gospel of the Lord. ℟.
Praise to you, Lord Jesus Christ.   → No. 15, p. 18

PRAYER OVER THE OFFERINGS   [God's Mighty Love]

May our prayers rise up to you, O Lord,
together with the sacrificial offerings,
so that, purified by your graciousness,
we may be conformed to the mysteries of your mighty
     love.
Through Christ our Lord.
℟. **Amen.**   → No. 21, p. 22 (Pref. P 21-25)

COMMUNION ANT. Jn 14:15-16   [Role of the Paraclete]

If you love me, keep my commandments, says the Lord, and I will ask the Father and he will send you another Paraclete, to abide with you for ever, alleluia. ↓

PRAYER AFTER COMMUNION   [Eucharistic Strength]

Almighty ever-living God,
who restore us to eternal life in the Resurrection of
     Christ,
increase in us, we pray, the fruits of this paschal
     Sacrament
and pour into our hearts the strength of this saving food.

Through Christ our Lord.
℟. **Amen.**   → No. 30, p. 77

Optional Solemn Blessings, p. 97, and Prayers over the People, p. 105

"And behold I am sending the promise of my Father upon you."

In those dioceses in which the Ascension is celebrated on Sunday, the Mass of the Ascension (Vigil Mass, below, or Mass during the Day, p. 409) is celebrated in place of the Mass of the 7th Sunday of Easter that appears on p. 411.

MAY 5

THE ASCENSION OF THE LORD

Solemnity

AT THE VIGIL MASS (May 4)

ENTRANCE ANT. Ps 68 (67): 33, 35   [Praise the Lord]
You kingdoms of the earth, sing to God; praise the Lord, who ascends above the highest heavens; his majesty and might are in the skies, alleluia.   → No. 2, p. 10

COLLECT   [Jesus' Promise]

O God, whose Son today ascended to the heavens
as the Apostles looked on,

grant, we pray, that, in accordance with his promise,
we may be worthy for him to live with us always on
   earth,
and we with him in heaven.
Who lives and reigns with you in the unity of the Holy
   Spirit,
one God, for ever and ever. ℟. **Amen.** ↓

FIRST READING Acts 1:1-11   **[Christ's Ascension]**

   **Christ is divine! He will come again! Our faith affirms this
   for us. We live in the era of the Holy Spirit.**

A reading from the Acts of the Apostles

IN the first book, Theophilus, I dealt with all that
Jesus did and taught until the day he was taken up,
after giving instructions through the Holy Spirit to the
apostles whom he had chosen. He presented himself
alive to them by many proofs after he had suffered,
appearing to them during forty days and speaking about
the kingdom of God. While meeting with them, he
enjoined them not to depart from Jerusalem, but to wait
for "the promise of the Father about which you have
heard me speak; for John baptized with water, but in a
few days you will be baptized with the Holy Spirit."

When they had gathered together they asked him,
"Lord, are you at this time going to restore the kingdom to Israel?" He answered them, "It is not for you to
know the times or seasons that the Father has established by his own authority. But you will receive power
when the Holy Spirit comes upon you, and you will be
my witnesses in Jerusalem, throughout Judea and
Samaria, and to the ends of the earth."

When he had said this, as they were looking on, he
was lifted up, and a cloud took him from their sight.
While they were looking intently at the sky as he was
going, suddenly two men dressed in white garments
stood beside them. They said, "Men of Galilee, why are

you standing there looking at the sky? This Jesus who has been taken up from you into heaven will return in the same way as you have seen him going into heaven."—The word of the Lord. ℟. **Thanks be to God.** ↓

RESPONSORIAL PSALM Ps 47   [Praise to the Lord]

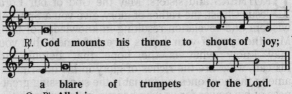

℟. God mounts his throne to shouts of joy; a blare of trumpets for the Lord.
Or: ℟. Alleluia.

All you peoples, clap your hands,
   shout to God with cries of gladness.
For the LORD, the Most High, the awesome,
   is the great king over all the earth.

℟. **God mounts his throne to shouts of joy: a blare of trumpets for the Lord.**

Or: ℟. **Alleluia.**

God mounts his throne amid shouts of joy;
   the LORD, amid trumpet blasts.
Sing praise to God, sing praise;
   sing praise to our king, sing praise.

℟. **God mounts his throne to shouts of joy: a blare of trumpets for the Lord.**

Or: ℟. **Alleluia.**

For king of all the earth is God;
   sing hymns of praise.
God reigns over the nations,
   God sits upon his holy throne.

℟. **God mounts his throne to shouts of joy: a blare of trumpets for the Lord.** ↓

Or: ℟. **Alleluia.** ↓

SECOND READING Eph 1:17-23   [Glorification of Jesus]

Our hope is in God. He is our strength. With Christ our head, we his people will receive the gift of wisdom and insight.

A reading from the Letter of Saint Paul to the Ephesians

BROTHERS and sisters: May the God of our Lord Jesus Christ, the Father of glory, give you a Spirit of wisdom and revelation resulting in knowledge of him. May the eyes of your hearts be enlightened, that you may know what is the hope that belongs to his call, what are the riches of glory in his inheritance among the holy ones, and what is the surpassing greatness of his power for us who believe, in accord with the exercise of his great might, which he worked in Christ, raising him from the dead and seating him at his right hand in the heavens, far above every principality, authority, power, and dominion, and every name that is named not only in this age but also in the one to come. And he put all things beneath his feet and gave him as head over all things to the church, which is his body, the fullness of the one who fills all things in every way.—The word of the Lord. ℟. **Thanks be to God.** ↓

OR

SECOND READING Heb 9:24-28; 10:19-23

[The Ascension and Us]

Christ's Ascension gives us hope. He who made the promise is trustworthy.

A reading from the Letter to the Hebrews

CHRIST did not enter into a sanctuary made by hands, a copy of the true one, but heaven itself, that he might now appear before God on our behalf. Not that he might offer himself repeatedly, as the high priest enters each year into the sanctuary with blood that is not his own; if that were so, he would have had to suffer repeatedly from the foundation of the world. But now once for all he has appeared at the end of the ages to take away sin by his sacrifice. Just as it is appointed that men and women die once, and after this the judgment, so also Christ, offered once to take away the sins of many, will appear a second time, not to take away sin but to bring salvation to those who eagerly await him.

Therefore, brothers and sisters, since through the blood of Jesus we have confidence of entrance into the sanctuary by the new and living way he opened for us through the veil, that is, his flesh, and since we have "a great priest over the house of God," let us approach with a sincere heart and in absolute trust, with our hearts sprinkled clean from an evil conscience and our bodies washed in pure water. Let us hold unwaveringly to our confession that gives us hope, for he who made the promise is trustworthy.—The word of the Lord. ℟. **Thanks be to God.** ↓

ALLELUIA Mt 28:19a, 20b   [Christ's Abiding Presence]

℟. **Alleluia, alleluia.**
Go and teach all nations, says the Lord;
I am with you always, until the end of the world.
℟. **Alleluia, alleluia.** ↓

GOSPEL Lk 24:46-53   [The Ascension]
  We are called to penance for the remission of sins.

℣. The Lord be with you. ℟. **And with your spirit.**
✝ A reading from the holy Gospel according to Luke.
℟. **Glory to you, O Lord.**

JESUS said to his disciples: "Thus it is written that the Christ would suffer and rise from the dead on the third day and that repentance, for the forgiveness of sins, would be preached in his name to all the nations, beginning from Jerusalem. You are witnesses of these things. And behold I am sending the promise of my Father upon you; but stay in the city until you are clothed with power from on high."

Then he led them out as far as Bethany, raised his hands, and blessed them. As he blessed them he parted from them and was taken up to heaven. They did him homage and then returned to Jerusalem with great joy, and they were continually in the temple praising God.—The Gospel of the Lord. ℟. **Praise to you, Lord Jesus Christ.** → No. 15, p. 18

PRAYER OVER THE OFFERINGS [Obtain Mercy]

O God, whose Only Begotten Son, our High Priest,
is seated ever-living at your right hand to intercede for
   us,
grant that we may approach with confidence the
   throne of grace
and there obtain your mercy.
Through Christ our Lord.
℟. **Amen.** → No. 21, p. 22 (Pref. P 26-27)

When the Roman Canon is used, the proper form of the Communicantes (In communion with those) *is said.*

COMMUNION ANT. Cf. Heb 10:12

[Christ at God's Right Hand]

Christ, offering a single sacrifice for sins, is seated for ever at God's right hand, alleluia. ↓

PRAYER AFTER COMMUNION [Longing for Heaven]

May the gifts we have received from your altar, Lord,
kindle in our hearts a longing for the heavenly
   homeland
and cause us to press forward, following in the
   Savior's footsteps,

to the place where for our sake he entered before us.
Who lives and reigns for ever and ever.
℟. **Amen.**   → No. 30, p. 77

Optional Solemn Blessings, p. 97, and Prayers over the People, p. 105

AT THE MASS DURING THE DAY

ENTRANCE ANT. Acts 1:11   [The Lord Will Return]

**Men of Galilee, why gaze in wonder at the heavens?
This Jesus whom you saw ascending into heaven will
return as you saw him go, alleluia.**   → No. 2, p. 10

COLLECT   [Thankful for the Ascension]

Gladden us with holy joys, almighty God,
and make us rejoice with devout thanksgiving,
for the Ascension of Christ your Son
is our exaltation,
and, where the Head has gone before in glory,
the Body is called to follow in hope.
Through our Lord Jesus Christ, your Son,
who lives and reigns with you in the unity of the Holy
    Spirit,
one God, for ever and ever. ℟. **Amen.** ↓

OR   [Belief in the Ascension]

Grant, we pray, almighty God,
that we, who believe that your Only Begotten Son, our
    Redeemer,
ascended this day to the heavens,
may in spirit dwell already in heavenly realms.
Who lives and reigns with you in the unity of the Holy
    Spirit,
one God, for ever and ever. ℟. **Amen.** ↓

The readings for this Mass can be found beginning on p. 404.

PRAYER OVER THE OFFERINGS

[Rise to Heavenly Realms]

We offer sacrifice now in supplication, O Lord,
to honor the wondrous Ascension of your Son:
grant, we pray,
that through this most holy exchange
we, too, may rise up to the heavenly realms.
Through Christ our Lord.
℟. **Amen.**   → No. 21, p. 22 (Pref. P 26-27)

When the Roman Canon is used, the proper form of the
Communicantes (In communion with those) *is said.*

COMMUNION ANT. Mt 28:20   **[Christ's Presence]**

**Behold, I am with you always, even to the end of the
age, alleluia.** ↓

PRAYER AFTER COMMUNION   **[United with Christ]**

Almighty ever-living God,
who allow those on earth to celebrate divine mysteries,
grant, we pray,
that Christian hope may draw us onward
to where our nature is united with you.
Through Christ our Lord.
℟. **Amen.**   → No. 30, p. 77

Optional Solemn Blessings, p. 97, and Prayers over the People, p. 105

"Righteous Father, the world also does not know you, but I know you."

In those dioceses in which the Ascension is celebrated on Sunday, the Mass of the Ascension (Vigil Mass, p. 403, or Mass during the Day, p. 409) is celebrated in place of the following Mass of the 7th Sunday of Easter.

MAY 8

7th SUNDAY OF EASTER

ENTRANCE ANT. Cf. Ps 27 (26):7-9   [Seek the Lord]

O Lord, hear my voice, for I have called to you; of you my heart has spoken: Seek his face; hide not your face from me, alleluia.   → No. 2, p. 10

COLLECT   [Experience Christ among Us]

Graciously hear our supplications, O Lord,
so that we, who believe that the Savior of the human race
is with you in your glory,
may experience, as he promised,
until the end of the world,
his abiding presence among us.
Who lives and reigns with you in the unity of the Holy
   Spirit,
one God, for ever and ever. ℞. **Amen.** ↓

FIRST READING Acts 7:55-60   [Stephen's Martyrdom]

Deacon Stephen, the first martyr, proclaims the glory of Jesus.

A reading from the Acts of the Apostles

STEPHEN, filled with the Holy Spirit, looked up intently to heaven and saw the glory of God and Jesus standing at the right hand of God, and Stephen said, "Behold, I see the heavens opened and the Son of Man standing at the right hand of God." But they cried out in a loud voice, covered their ears, and rushed upon him together. They threw him out of the city, and began to stone him. The witnesses laid down their cloaks at the feet of a young man named Saul. As they were stoning Stephen, he called out, "Lord Jesus, receive my spirit." Then he fell to his knees and cried out in a loud voice, "Lord, do not hold this sin against them"; and when he said this, he fell asleep.—The word of the Lord. ℟. **Thanks be to God.** ↓

RESPONSORIAL PSALM Ps 97   [The Glory of God]

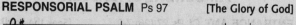

℟. The Lord is king,   the most high over all   the earth.
Or: ℟. **Alleluia.**

The LORD is king; let the earth rejoice;
  let the many isles be glad.
Justice and judgment are the foundation of his throne.

℟. **The Lord is king, the most high over all the earth.**
Or: ℟. **Alleluia.**

The heavens proclaim his justice,
  and all peoples see his glory.
All gods are prostrate before him.

℟. **The Lord is king, the most high over all the earth.**
Or: ℟. **Alleluia.**

You, O LORD, are the Most High over all the earth,
  exalted far above all gods.

℞. **The Lord is king, the most high over all the earth.** ↓

Or: ℞. **Alleluia.** ↓

SECOND READING Rv 22:12-14, 16-17, 20 [Come, Lord Jesus]
   He will come soon to judge each one of us. Now is the time to repent (symbolically wash our robes).

A reading from the Book of Revelation

I, JOHN, heard a voice saying to me: "Behold, I am coming soon. I bring with me the recompense I will give to each according to his deeds. I am the Alpha and the Omega, the first and the last, the beginning and the end."

Blessed are they who wash their robes so as to have the right to the tree of life and enter the city through its gates.

"I, Jesus, sent my angel to give you this testimony for the churches. I am the root and offspring of David, the bright morning star."

The Spirit and the bride say, "Come." Let the hearer say, "Come." Let the one who thirsts come forward, and the one who wants it receive the gift of life-giving water.

The one who gives this testimony says, "Yes, I am coming soon." Amen! Come, Lord Jesus!—The word of the Lord. ℞. **Thanks be to God.** ↓

ALLELUIA Cf. Jn 14:18   [Joyous Return]
℞. **Alleluia, alleluia.**
I will not leave you orphans, says the Lord.
I will come back to you, and your hearts will rejoice.
℞. **Alleluia, alleluia.** ↓

GOSPEL Jn 17:20-26   [One in the Lord]
   Jesus prays for us—who believe in him—that our faith will unite us to each other, to him, and in him to the Father.

℣. The Lord be with you. ℟. **And with your spirit.**

✠ A reading from the holy Gospel according to John.
℟. **Glory to you, O Lord.**

L IFTING up his eyes to heaven, Jesus prayed, saying: "Holy Father, I pray not only for them, but also for those who will believe in me through their word, so that they may all be one, as you, Father, are in me and I in you, that they also may be in us, that the world may believe that you sent me. And I have given them the glory you gave me, so that they may be one, as we are one, I in them and you in me, that they may be brought to perfection as one, that the world may know that you sent me, and that you loved them even as you loved me. Father, they are your gift to me. I wish that where I am they also may be with me, that they may see my glory that you gave me, because you loved me before the foundation of the world. Righteous Father, the world also does not know you, but I know you, and they know that you sent me. I made known to them your name and I will make it known, that the love with which you loved me may be in them and I in them."—The Gospel of the Lord. ℟. **Praise to you, Lord Jesus Christ.**

➜ No. 15, p. 18

PRAYER OVER THE OFFERINGS   [Glory of Heaven]

Accept, O Lord, the prayers of your faithful
with the sacrificial offerings,
that through these acts of devotedness
we may pass over to the glory of heaven.
Through Christ our Lord.
℟. **Amen.**   ➜   No. 21, p. 22 (Pref. P 21-25 or P 26-27)

COMMUNION ANT. Jn 17:22   [Christian Unity]
Father, I pray that they may be one as we also are one, alleluia. ↓

PRAYER AFTER COMMUNION   [Grant Us Confidence]

Hear us, O God our Savior,
and grant us confidence,
that through these sacred mysteries
there will be accomplished in the body of the whole
  Church
what has already come to pass in Christ her Head.
Who lives and reigns for ever and ever.
℟. **Amen.**   → No. 30, p. 77

Optional Solemn Blessings, p. 97, and Prayers over the People, p. 105

"They were all filled with the Holy Spirit."

MAY 15

PENTECOST SUNDAY

Solemnity

AT THE VIGIL MASS (May 14)

ENTRANCE ANT. Rom 5:5; cf. 8:11   [Love-Imparting Spirit]
**The love of God has been poured into our hearts
through the Spirit of God dwelling within us, alleluia.**
       → No. 2, p. 10

COLLECT   [Heavenly Grace]

Almighty ever-living God,
who willed the Paschal Mystery
to be encompassed as a sign in fifty days,
grant that from out of the scattered nations
the confusion of many tongues
may be gathered by heavenly grace
into one great confession of your name.
Through our Lord Jesus Christ, your Son,
who lives and reigns with you in the unity of the Holy
    Spirit,
one God, for ever and ever. ℟. **Amen.** ↓

OR   [New Birth in the Spirit]

Grant, we pray, almighty God,
that the splendor of your glory
may shine forth upon us
and that, by the bright rays of the Holy Spirit,
the light of your light may confirm the hearts
of those born again by your grace.
Through our Lord Jesus Christ, your Son,
who lives and reigns with you in the unity of the Holy
    Spirit,
one God, for ever and ever. ℟. **Amen.** ↓

FIRST READING

 Gn 11:1-9   [Dangers of Human Pride]

**Those who put their trust in pride, and human ability, are
bound to fail.**

A reading from the Book of Genesis

THE whole world spoke the same language, using
the same words. While the people were migrating
in the east, they came upon a valley in the land of
Shinar and settled there. They said to one another,
"Come, let us mold bricks and harden them with fire."

They used bricks for stone, and bitumen for mortar. Then they said, "Come, let us build ourselves a city and a tower with its top in the sky, and so make a name for ourselves; otherwise we shall be scattered all over the earth."

The LORD came down to see the city and the tower that the people had built. Then the LORD said: "If now, while they are one people, all speaking the same language, they have started to do this, nothing will later stop them from doing whatever they presume to do. Let us then go down there and confuse their language, so that one will not understand what another says." Thus the LORD scattered them from there all over the earth, and they stopped building the city. That is why it was called Babel, because there the LORD confused the speech of all the world. It was from that place that he scattered them all over the earth.—The word of the Lord. ℟. **Thanks be to God.** ↓

OR

B Ex 19:3-8a, 16-20b   [The Lord on Mount Sinai]
The Lord God covenants with the Israelites—they are to be a holy nation, a princely Kingdom.

A reading from the Book of Exodus

MOSES went up the mountain to God. Then the LORD called to him and said, "Thus shall you say to the house of Jacob; tell the Israelites: You have seen for yourselves how I treated the Egyptians and how I bore you up on eagle wings and brought you here to myself. Therefore, if you hearken to my voice and keep my covenant, you shall be my special possession, dearer to me than all other people, though all the earth is mine. You shall be to me a kingdom of priests, a holy nation. That is what you must tell the Israelites." So Moses went and summoned the elders of the people. When he set before them all that the LORD had ordered him to tell them, the people all answered together, "Everything the LORD has said, we will do."

On the morning of the third day there were peals of thunder and lightning, and a heavy cloud over the mountain, and a very loud trumpet blast, so that all the people in the camp trembled. But Moses led the people out of the camp to meet God, and they stationed themselves at the foot of the mountain. Mount Sinai was all wrapped in smoke, for the LORD came down upon it in fire. The smoke rose from it as though from a furnace, and the whole mountain trembled violently. The trumpet blast grew louder and louder, while Moses was speaking and God answering him with thunder.

When the LORD came down to the top of Mount Sinai, he summoned Moses to the top of the mountain.—The word of the Lord. ℞. **Thanks be to God.** ↓

OR

C Ez 37:1-14   [Life-Giving Spirit]

The prophet, in a vision, sees the power of God—the band of the living and the dead, as he describes the resurrection of the dead.

A reading from the Book of the Prophet Ezekiel

THE hand of the LORD came upon me, and he led me out in the spirit of the LORD and set me in the center of the plain, which was now filled with bones. He made me walk among the bones in every direction so that I saw how many they were on the surface of the plain. How dry they were! He asked me: Son of man, can these bones come to life? I answered, "LORD God, you alone know that." Then he said to me: Prophesy over these bones, and say to them: Dry bones, hear the word of the LORD! Thus says the Lord GOD to these bones: See! I will bring spirit into you, that you may come to life. I will put sinews upon you, make flesh grow over you, cover you with skin, and put spirit in you so that you may come to life and know that I am the LORD. I, Ezekiel, prophesied as I had been told, and even as I was prophesying I heard a noise; it was a rattling as the bones came together, bone joining bone. I saw the sinews and the flesh come upon them, and the skin cover them, but there was no spirit in them. Then the LORD said to me: Prophesy to the spirit, prophesy, son of man, and say to the spirit: Thus says the Lord GOD: From the four winds come, O spirit, and breathe into these slain that they may come to life. I prophesied as he told me, and the spirit came into them; they came alive and stood upright, a vast army. Then he said to me: Son of man, these bones are the whole house of Israel. They have been saying, "Our bones are dried up, our hope is lost, and we are cut off." Therefore, prophesy and say to them: Thus says the Lord GOD: O my people, I will open your graves and have you rise from them, and bring you back to the land of Israel. Then you shall know that I am the LORD, when I open your graves and have you rise from them, O my people! I will put my spirit in you that you may live, and I will settle you upon your land; thus you shall know that I am the LORD. I have promised, and I will do it, says the LORD.—The word of the Lord. ℟. **Thanks be to God.** ↓

OR

D Jl 3:1-5   **[Signs of the Spirit]**

At the end of time, the Day of the Lord, Judgment Day, those who persevere in faith will be saved.

A reading from the Book of the Prophet Joel

THUS says the LORD:
    I will pour out my spirit upon all flesh.
Your sons and daughters shall prophesy,
    your old men shall dream dreams,
    your young men shall see visions;

even upon the servants and the handmaids,
    in those days, I will pour out my spirit.
And I will work wonders in the heavens and on the
    earth,
    blood, fire, and columns of smoke;
the sun will be turned to darkness,
    and the moon to blood,
at the coming of the day of the LORD,
    the great and terrible day.
Then everyone shall be rescued
    who calls on the name of the LORD;
for on Mount Zion there shall be a remnant,
    as the LORD has said,
and in Jerusalem survivors
    whom the LORD shall call.
The word of the Lord. ℟. **Thanks be to God.** ↓

RESPONSORIAL PSALM Ps 104   [Send Out Your Spirit]

℟. Lord, send out your Spir - it, and re-new the face of the earth.
Or: ℟. **Alleluia.**

Bless the LORD, O my soul!
    O LORD, my God, you are great indeed!
You are clothed with majesty and glory,
    robed in light as with a cloak.—℟.

How manifold are your works, O LORD!
    In wisdom you have wrought them all—
the earth is full of your creatures;
    bless the LORD, O my soul! Alleluia.—℟.

Creatures all look to you
    to give them food in due time.
When you give it to them, they gather it;
    when you open your hand, they are filled with good
        things.—℟.

If you take away their breath, they perish
   and return to their dust.
When you send forth your spirit, they are created,
   and you renew the face of the earth.—℟. ↓

SECOND READING Rom 8:22-27   [The Spirit Our Helper]

Be patient and have hope. The Spirit intercedes for us.

A reading from the Letter of Saint Paul to the Romans

B ROTHERS and sisters: We know that all creation is
   groaning in labor pains even until now; and not
only that, but we ourselves, who have the firstfruits of
the Spirit, we also groan within ourselves as we wait
for adoption, the redemption of our bodies. For in hope
we were saved. Now hope that sees is not hope. For
who hopes for what one sees? But if we hope for what
we do not see, we wait with endurance.

   In the same way, the Spirit too comes to the aid of
our weakness; for we do not know how to pray as we
ought, but the Spirit himself intercedes with inexpress-
ible groanings. And the one who searches hearts
knows what is the intention of the Spirit, because he
intercedes for the holy ones according to God's will.—
The word of the Lord. ℟. **Thanks be to God.** ↓

ALLELUIA   [Fire of God's Love]

℟. **Alleluia, alleluia.**
Come, Holy Spirit, fill the hearts of the faithful
and kindle in them the fire of your love.
℟. **Alleluia, alleluia.** ↓

GOSPEL Jn 7:37-39   [Prediction of the Spirit]

**The Spirit is the source of life for those who have faith and
   believe.**

℣. The Lord be with you. ℟. **And with your spirit.**

✣ A reading from the holy Gospel according to John.

℟. **Glory to you, O Lord.**

O N the last and greatest day of the feast, Jesus stood
up and exclaimed, "Let anyone who thirsts come to
me and drink. As scripture says:

 Rivers of living water will flow from within him
  who believes in me."

He said this in reference to the Spirit that those who
came to believe in him were to receive. There was, of
course, no Spirit yet, because Jesus had not yet been
glorified.—The Gospel of the Lord. ℟. **Praise to you,
Lord Jesus Christ.**   ➜ No. 15, p. 18

PRAYER OVER THE OFFERINGS [Manifestation of Salvation]

Pour out upon these gifts the blessing of your Spirit,
we pray, O Lord,
so that through them your Church may be imbued
  with such love
that the truth of your saving mystery
may shine forth for the whole world.
Through Christ our Lord.
℟. **Amen.**   ➜ Pref. P 28, p. 429

When the Roman Canon is used, the proper form of the
Communicantes (In communion with those) *is said.*

COMMUNION ANT. Jn 7:37   [Thirst for the Spirit]

**On the last day of the festival, Jesus stood and cried
out: If anyone is thirsty, let him come to me and drink,
alleluia.** ↓

PRAYER AFTER COMMUNION   [Aflame with the Spirit]

May these gifts we have consumed
benefit us, O Lord,
that we may always be aflame with the same Spirit,
whom you wondrously poured out on your Apostles.
Through Christ our Lord.
℟. **Amen.**   ➜ No. 30, p. 77

Optional Solemn Blessings, p. 97, and Prayers over the People, p. 105

(At the end of the Dismissal the people respond: **"Thanks be
to God, alleluia, alleluia."***)*

AT THE MASS DURING THE DAY

ENTRANCE ANT. Wis 1:7   [The Spirit in the World]

The Spirit of the Lord has filled the whole world and that which contains all things understands what is said, alleluia.   ➜ No. 2, p. 10

OR Rom 5:5; cf. 8:11   [God's Love for Us]

The love of God has been poured into our hearts through the Spirit of God dwelling within us, alleluia.
          ➜ No. 2, p. 10

COLLECT   [Gifts of the Spirit]

O God, who by the mystery of today's great feast
sanctify your whole Church in every people and
    nation,
pour out, we pray, the gifts of the Holy Spirit
across the face of the earth
and, with the divine grace that was at work
when the Gospel was first proclaimed,
fill now once more the hearts of believers.
Through our Lord Jesus Christ, your Son,
who lives and reigns with you in the unity of the Holy
    Spirit,
one God, for ever and ever. ℟. **Amen.** ↓

FIRST READING Acts 2:1-11   [Coming of the Spirit]

On this day the Holy Spirit in fiery tongues descended upon the apostles and the Mother of Jesus. Today the law of grace and purification from sin was announced. Three thousand were baptized.

A reading from the Acts of the Apostles

W HEN the time for Pentecost was fulfilled, they were all in one place together. And suddenly there came from the sky a noise like a strong driving wind, and it filled the entire house in which they were. Then there appeared to them tongues as of fire, which parted and came to rest on each of them. And they were all filled with the Holy Spirit and began to speak in different tongues, as the Spirit enabled them to proclaim.

Now there were devout Jews from every nation under heaven staying in Jerusalem. At this sound, they gathered in a large crowd, but they were confused because each one heard them speaking in his own language. They were astounded, and in amazement they asked, "Are not all these people who are speaking Galileans? Then how does each of us hear them in his native language? We are Parthians, Medes, and Elamites, inhabitants of Mesopotamia, Judea and Cappadocia, Pontus and Asia, Phrygia and Pamphylia, Egypt, and the districts of Libya near Cyrene, as well as travelers from Rome, both Jews and converts to Judaism, Cretans and Arabs, yet we hear them speaking in our own tongues of the mighty acts of God."—The word of the Lord. ℟. **Thanks be to God.** ↓

RESPONSORIAL PSALM Ps 104   [Renewal by the Spirit]

℟.   Lord, send out your Spir - it,   and re-new the face of the earth.

Or: ℟. **Alleluia.**

Bless the LORD, O my soul!
    O LORD, my God, you are great indeed!
How manifold are your works, O LORD!
    the earth is full of your creatures.

℟. **Lord, send out your Spirit, and renew the face of the earth.**

Or: ℟. **Alleluia.**

May the glory of the LORD endure forever;
    may the LORD be glad in his works!
Pleasing to him be my theme;
    I will be glad in the LORD.

℟. **Lord, send out your Spirit, and renew the face of the earth.**

Or: ℟. **Alleluia.**

If you take away their breath, they perish
  and return to their dust.
When you send forth your spirit, they are created,
  and you renew the face of the earth.

℟. **Lord, send out your Spirit, and renew the face of the earth.** ↓

Or: ℟. **Alleluia.** ↓

SECOND READING 1 Cor 12:3b-7, 12-13 [Grace of the Spirit]

No one can confess the divinity and sovereignty of Jesus unless inspired by the Holy Spirit. Different gifts and ministries are given but all for the one body with Jesus.

A reading from the first Letter of Saint Paul
to the Corinthians

BROTHERS and sisters: No one can say: "Jesus is Lord," except by the Holy Spirit.

There are different kinds of spiritual gifts but the same Spirit; there are different forms of service but the same Lord; there are different workings but the same God who produces all of them in everyone. To each individual the manifestation of the Spirit is given for some benefit.

As a body is one though it has many parts, and all the parts of the body, though many, are one body, so also Christ. For in one Spirit we were all baptized into one body, whether Jews or Greeks, slaves or free persons, and we are all given to drink of one Spirit.—The word of the Lord. ℟. **Thanks be to God.** ↓

OR

SECOND READING Rom 8:8-17   [Living with Christ]

The Spirit places us in a filial relationship with God enabling us to invoke him, as Jesus did, with the name of Father.

A reading from the Letter of Saint Paul to the Romans

BROTHERS and sisters: Those who are in the flesh cannot please God. But you are not in the flesh; on the contrary, you are in the spirit, if only the Spirit of God dwells in you. Whoever does not have the Spirit of Christ does not belong to him. But if Christ is in you, although the body is dead because of sin, the spirit is alive because of righteousness. If the Spirit of the one who raised Jesus from the dead dwells in you, the one who raised Christ from the dead will give life to your mortal bodies also, through his Spirit that dwells in you. Consequently, brothers and sisters, we are not debtors to the flesh, to live according to the flesh. For if you live according to the flesh, you will die, but if by the Spirit you put to death the deeds of the body, you will live.

For those who are led by the Spirit of God are sons of God. For you did not receive a spirit of slavery to fall back into fear, but you received a Spirit of adoption, through whom we cry, "Abba, Father!" The Spirit himself bears witness with our spirit that we are children of God, and if children, then heirs, heirs of God and joint heirs with Christ, if only we suffer with him so that we may also be glorified with him.—The word of the Lord. ℟. **Thanks be to God.** ↓

SEQUENCE *(Veni, Sancte Spiritus)*   [Come, Holy Spirit]
   Come, Holy Spirit, come!
   And from your celestial home
      Shed a ray of light divine!
   Come, Father of the poor!
   Come, source of all our store!
      Come, within our bosoms shine!
   You, of comforters the best;
   You, the soul's most welcome guest;
      Sweet refreshment here below;

In our labor, rest most sweet;
Grateful coolness in the heat;
  Solace in the midst of woe.
O most blessed Light divine,
Shine within these hearts of yours,
  And our inmost being fill!
Where you are not, we have naught,
Nothing good in deed or thought,
  Nothing free from taint of ill.
Heal our wounds, our strength renew;
On our dryness pour your dew;
  Wash the stains of guilt away:
Bend the stubborn heart and will;
Melt the frozen, warm the chill;
  Guide the steps that go astray.
On the faithful, who adore
And confess you, evermore
  In your sevenfold gift descend;
Give them virtue's sure reward;
Give them your salvation, Lord;
  Give them joys that never end. Amen.
  Alleluia. ↓

ALLELUIA   [Fire of God's Love]

℟. Alleluia, alleluia.
Come, Holy Spirit, fill the hearts of your faithful
and kindle in them the fire of your love.
℟. Alleluia, alleluia. ↓

GOSPEL Jn 20:19-23   [Christ Imparts the Spirit]

Jesus breathes on the disciples to indicate the conferring
of the Holy Spirit. Here we see the origin of power over
sin, the Sacrament of Penance. This shows the power of
the Holy Spirit in the hearts of human beings.

℣. The Lord be with you. ℟. **And with your spirit.**
✜ A reading from the holy Gospel according to John.
℟. **Glory to you, O Lord.**

O N the evening of that first day of the week, when
the doors were locked, where the disciples were,
for fear of the Jews, Jesus came and stood in their
midst and said to them, "Peace be with you." When he
had said this, he showed them his hands and
his side. The disciples rejoiced when they saw the
Lord. Jesus said to them again, "Peace be with you. As
the Father has sent me, so I send you." And when he
had said this, he breathed on them and said
to them, "Receive the Holy Spirit. Whose sins you forgive are forgiven them, and whose sins you retain are
retained."—The Gospel of the Lord. ℟. **Praise to you,
Lord Jesus Christ.**   → No. 15, p. 18

OR

GOSPEL Jn 14:15-16, 23b-26   **[Fruits of the Spirit]**
Jesus tells his disciples that the Holy Spirit, the Spirit of
truth, will reveal everything to them. The Holy Spirit will
be their new Advocate.

℣. The Lord be with you. ℟. **And with your spirit.**
✜ A reading from the holy Gospel according to John.
℟. **Glory to you, O Lord.**

J ESUS said to his disciples: "If you love me, you will
keep my commandments. And I will ask the Father,
and he will give you another Advocate to be with you
always.

"Whoever loves me will keep my word, and my
Father will love him, and we will come to him and
make our dwelling with him. Those who do not love me
do not keep my words; yet the word you hear is not
mine but that of the Father who sent me.

"I have told you this while I am with you. The Advocate, the Holy Spirit whom the Father will send in my name, will teach you everything and remind you of all that I told you."—The Gospel of the Lord. ℟. **Praise to you, Lord Jesus Christ.**   ➔ No. 15, p. 18

PRAYER OVER THE OFFERINGS   [All Truth]

Grant, we pray, O Lord,
that, as promised by your Son,
the Holy Spirit may reveal to us more abundantly
the hidden mystery of this sacrifice
and graciously lead us into all truth.
Through Christ our Lord. ℟. **Amen.** ↓

PREFACE (P 28)   [Coming of the Spirit]

℣. The Lord be with you. ℟. **And with your spirit.**
℣. Lift up your hearts. ℟. **We lift them up to the Lord.**
℣. Let us give thanks to the Lord our God. ℟. **It is right and just.**

It is truly right and just, our duty and our salvation,
always and everywhere to give you thanks,
Lord, holy Father, almighty and eternal God.

For, bringing your Paschal Mystery to completion,
you bestowed the Holy Spirit today
on those you made your adopted children
by uniting them to your Only Begotten Son.
This same Spirit, as the Church came to birth,
opened to all peoples the knowledge of God
and brought together the many languages of the earth
in profession of the one faith.

Therefore, overcome with paschal joy,
every land, every people exults in your praise
and even the heavenly Powers, with the angelic hosts,
sing together the unending hymn of your glory,
as they acclaim: ➔ No. 23, p. 23

When the Roman Canon is used, the proper form of the Communicantes (In communion with those) *is said.*

COMMUNION ANT. Acts 2:4, 11   **[Filled with the Spirit]**

They were all filled with the Holy Spirit and spoke of the marvels of God, alleluia. ↓

PRAYER AFTER COMMUNION   **[Safeguard Grace]**

O God, who bestow heavenly gifts upon your Church,
safeguard, we pray, the grace you have given,
that the gift of the Holy Spirit poured out upon her
may retain all its force
and that this spiritual food
may gain her abundance of eternal redemption.
Through Christ our Lord.
℞. **Amen.**   ➜ No. 30, p. 77

Optional Solemn Blessings, p. 97, and Prayers over the People, p. 105

(At the end of the Dismissal the people respond: **"Thanks be to God, alleluia, alleluia."**)

"Glory to the Father, the Son, and the Holy Spirit."

MAY 22

THE MOST HOLY TRINITY

Solemnity

ENTRANCE ANT. [Blessed Trinity]

Blest be God the Father, and the Only Begotten Son of God, and also the Holy Spirit, for he has shown us his merciful love. → No. 2, p. 10

COLLECT [Witnessing to the Trinity]

God our Father, who by sending into the world
the Word of truth and the Spirit of sanctification
made known to the human race your wondrous
   mystery,
grant us, we pray, that in professing the true faith,
we may acknowledge the Trinity of eternal glory
and adore your Unity, powerful in majesty.
Through our Lord Jesus Christ, your Son,
who lives and reigns with you in the unity of the Holy
   Spirit,
one God, for ever and ever.
℟. **Amen.** ↓

FIRST READING Prv 8:22-31   [God's Wisdom]

> In a messianic application the "Wisdom of God" who
> speaks in this reading foreshadowed the revelation of the
> Second Person of the Trinity.

A reading from the Book of Proverbs

THUS says the wisdom of God:
  "The LORD possessed me, the beginning of his ways,
    the forerunner of his prodigies of long ago;
from of old I was poured forth,
    at the first, before the earth.
When there were no depths I was brought forth,
    when there were no fountains or springs of water;
before the mountains were settled into place,
    before the hills, I was brought forth;
while as yet the earth and fields were not made,
    nor the first clods of the world.

"When the Lord established the heavens I was there,
    when he marked out the vault over the face of the
      deep;
when he made firm the skies above,
    when he fixed fast the foundations of the earth;
when he set for the sea its limit,
    so that the waters should not transgress his
      command;
then was I beside him as his craftsman,
    and I was his delight day by day,
playing before him all the while,
    playing on the surface of his earth;
    and I found delight in the human race."
The word of the Lord. ℟. **Thanks be to God.** ↓

RESPONSORIAL PSALM Ps 8   [The Power of God]

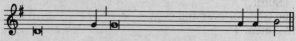

℟. O Lord, our God, how wonderful your name in all the earth!

When I behold your heavens, the work of your
    fingers,
  the moon and the stars which you set in place—
what is man that you should be mindful of him,
  or the son of man that you should care for him?

℟. **O Lord, our God, how wonderful your name in all
    the earth!**

You have made him little less than the angels,
  and crowned him with glory and honor.
You have given him rule over the works of your hands,
  putting all things under his feet:

℟. **O Lord, our God, how wonderful your name in all
    the earth!**

All sheep and oxen,
  yes, and the beasts of the field,
the birds of the air, the fishes of the sea,
  and whatever swims the paths of the seas.

℟. **O Lord, our God, how wonderful your name in all
    the earth!** ↓

SECOND READING Rom 5:1-5 [Justification by Faith]
  **Our hope, our faith, will be fulfilled because the Holy
  Spirit has been given to us.**

A reading from the Letter of Saint Paul to the Romans

BROTHERS and sisters: Therefore, since we have
been justified by faith, we have peace with God
through our Lord Jesus Christ, through whom we have
gained access by faith to this grace in which we stand,
and we boast in hope of the glory of God. Not only
that, but we even boast of our afflictions, knowing that
affliction produces endurance, and endurance, proven
character, and proven character, hope, and hope does
not disappoint, because the love of God has been

poured out into our hearts through the Holy Spirit that has been given to us.—The word of the Lord. ℟. **Thanks be to God.** ↓

ALLELUIA Cf. Rv 1:8   [Triune God]

℟. **Alleluia, alleluia.**
Glory to the Father, the Son, and the Holy Spirit;
to God who is, who was, and who is to come.
℟. **Alleluia, alleluia.** ↓

GOSPEL Jn 16:12-15   [The Spirit of Truth]

All that the Father has belongs to Jesus. The Spirit of truth will guide us and announce to us the things to come. The apostles lived in the time of Christ, and lead us into the era of the Spirit.

℣. The Lord be with you. ℟. **And with your spirit.**
✤ A reading from the holy Gospel according to John.
℟. **Glory to you, O Lord.**

JESUS said to his disciples: "I have much more to tell you, but you cannot bear it now. But when he comes, the Spirit of truth, he will guide you to all truth. He will not speak on his own, but he will speak what he hears, and will declare to you the things that are coming. He will glorify me, because he will take from what is mine and declare it to you. Everything that the Father has is mine; for this reason I told you that he will take from what is mine and declare it to you."— The Gospel of the Lord. ℟. **Praise to you, Lord Jesus Christ.**   → No. 15, p. 18

PRAYER OVER THE OFFERINGS   [Eternal Offering]

Sanctify by the invocation of your name,
we pray, O Lord our God,
this oblation of our service,
and by it make of us an eternal offering to you.

Through Christ our Lord.
℟. **Amen.** ↓

PREFACE (P 43)   [Mystery of the One Godhead]

℣. The Lord be with you. ℟. **And with your spirit.**
℣. Lift up your hearts. ℟. **We lift them up to the Lord.**
℣. Let us give thanks to the Lord our God. ℟. **It is right and just.**

It is truly right and just, our duty and our salvation,
always and everywhere to give you thanks,
Lord, holy Father, almighty and eternal God.

For with your Only Begotten Son and the Holy Spirit
you are one God, one Lord:
not in the unity of a single person,
but in a Trinity of one substance.

For what you have revealed to us of your glory
we believe equally of your Son
and of the Holy Spirit,
so that, in the confessing of the true and eternal
   Godhead,
you might be adored in what is proper to each Person,
their unity in substance,
and their equality in majesty.

For this is praised by Angels and Archangels,
Cherubim, too, and Seraphim,
who never cease to cry out each day,
as with one voice they acclaim: → No. 23, p. 23

COMMUNION ANT. Gal 4:6   [Abba, Father]
**Since you are children of God, God has sent into your
hearts the Spirit of his Son, the Spirit who cries out:
Abba, Father.** ↓

PRAYER AFTER COMMUNION   [Eternal Trinity]

May receiving this Sacrament, O Lord our God,
bring us health of body and soul,

as we confess your eternal holy Trinity and undivided
 Unity.
Through Christ our Lord.
℟. **Amen.** → No. 30, p. 77

Optional Solemn Blessings, p. 97, and Prayers over the People, p. 105

*"[Jesus] said the blessing [over the loaves and fish],
 and gave them to the disciples to set before the crowd."*

[In the Dioceses of the United States]

MAY 29

THE MOST HOLY
BODY AND BLOOD OF CHRIST
(CORPUS CHRISTI)

Solemnity

ENTRANCE ANT. Cf. Ps 81 (80):17 [Finest Wheat and Honey]
**He fed them with the finest wheat and satisfied them
with honey from the rock.** → No. 2, p. 10

COLLECT [Memorial of Christ's Passion]
O God, who in this wonderful Sacrament
have left us a memorial of your Passion,

grant us, we pray,
so to revere the sacred mysteries of your Body and
   Blood
that we may always experience in ourselves
the fruits of your redemption.
Who live and reign with God the Father
in the unity of the Holy Spirit,
one God, for ever and ever. ℟. **Amen.** ↓

FIRST READING Gn 14:18-20   [Blessing of Melchizedek]

> Sharing bread and wine, a foreshadowing of the eucharis-
> tic elements, Abram is blessed and God is praised.

A reading from the Book of Genesis

IN those days, Melchizedek, king of Salem, brought
out bread and wine, and being a priest of God Most
High, he blessed Abram with these words:
   "Blessed be Abram by God Most High,
      the creator of heaven and earth;
   and blessed be God Most High,
      who delivered your foes into your hand."
Then Abram gave him a tenth of everything.—The
word of the Lord. ℟. **Thanks be to God.** ↓

RESPONSORIAL PSALM Ps 110   [Eternal Priesthood]

℟. You are a priest for ev - er, in the line of Mel-chi-ze-dek.

The LORD said to my Lord: "Sit at my right hand
   till I make your enemies your footstool."
℟. **You are a priest for ever,**
   in the line of Melchizedek.
The scepter of your power the LORD will stretch forth
      from Zion:
   "Rule in the midst of your enemies."

℟. **You are a priest for ever, in the line of Melchizedek.**

"Yours is princely power in the day of your birth, in holy
    splendor;
  before the daystar, like the dew, I have begotten you."

℟. **You are a priest for ever, in the line of Melchizedek.**

The LORD has sworn, and he will not repent:
  "You are a priest forever, according to the order of
    Melchizedek."

℟. **You are a priest for ever, in the line of Melchizedek.** ↓

SECOND READING 1 Cor 11:23-26   [The First Eucharist]

When we eat this bread and drink this cup, we proclaim
your glory, Lord Jesus, until you come again.

A reading from the first Letter of Saint Paul
to the Corinthians

B ROTHERS and sisters: I received from the Lord
   what I also handed on to you, that the Lord Jesus,
on the night he was handed over, took bread, and, after
he had given thanks, broke it and said, "This is my
body that is for you. Do this in remembrance of me." In
the same way also the cup, after supper, saying, "This
cup is the new covenant in my blood. Do this, as often
as you drink it, in remembrance of me." For as often as
you eat this bread and drink the cup, you proclaim the
death of the Lord until he comes.—The word of the
Lord. ℟. **Thanks be to God.** ↓

SEQUENCE (*Lauda Sion*)   [Praise of the Eucharist]

The Sequence Laud, O Zion (Lauda Sion), *or the Shorter
Form beginning with the verse* Lo! the angel's food is given,
may be sung optionally before the Alleluia.

Laud, O Zion, your salvation,
Laud with hymns of exultation,
  Christ, your king and shepherd true:

Bring him all the praise you know,
He is more than you bestow,
  Never can you reach his due.

Special theme for glad thanksgiving
Is the quick'ning and the living
  Bread today before you set:

From his hands of old partaken,
As we know, by faith unshaken,
  Where the Twelve at supper met.

Full and clear ring out your chanting,
Joy nor sweetest grace be wanting,
  From your heart let praises burst:

For today the feast is holden,
When the institution olden
  Of that supper was rehearsed.

Here the new law's new oblation,
By the new king's revelation,
  Ends the form of ancient rite:

Now the new the old effaces,
Truth away the shadow chases,
  Light dispels the gloom of night.

What he did at supper seated,
Christ ordained to be repeated,
  His memorial ne'er to cease:

And his rule for guidance taking,
Bread and wine we hallow, making
  Thus our sacrifice of peace.

This the truth each Christian learns,
Bread into his flesh he turns,
  To his precious blood the wine:

Sight has fail'd, nor thought conceives,
But a dauntless faith believes,
  Resting on a pow'r divine.

Here beneath these signs are hidden
Priceless things to sense forbidden;
  Signs, not things are all we see:

Blood is poured and flesh is broken,
Yet in either wondrous token
  Christ entire we know to be.

Whoso of this food partakes,
Does not rend the Lord nor breaks;
  Christ is whole to all that taste:

Thousands are, as one, receivers,
One, as thousands of believers,
  Eats of him who cannot waste.

Bad and good the feast are sharing,

Of what divers dooms preparing,
 Endless death, or endless life.

Life to these, to those damna-
tion,
See how like participation
 Is with unlike issues rife.

When the sacrament is broken,
Doubt not, but believe 'tis spoken,

That each sever'd outward
token
 doth the very whole contain.

Nought the precious gift di-
vides,
Breaking but the sign betides,
 Jesus still the same abides,
 still unbroken does remain.

The Shorter Form of the Sequence begins here.

Lo! the angel's food is given
To the pilgrim who has
striven;
 See the children's bread
from heaven,
 which on dogs may not be
spent.

Truth the ancient types fulfilling,
Isaac bound, a victim willing,
 Paschal lamb, its life blood
spilling,
 manna to the fathers sent.

Very bread, good shepherd,
tend us,

Jesu, of your love befriend us,
 You refresh us, you defend
us,
 Your eternal goodness send
us
In the land of life to see.

You who all things can and
know,
Who on earth such food
bestow,
 Grant us with your saints,
though lowest,
 Where the heav'nly feast
you show,
Fellow heirs and guests to be.
 Amen. Alleluia. ↓

ALLELUIA Jn 6:51   [Living Bread]

℞. **Alleluia, alleluia.**
I am the living bread that came down from heaven,
 says the Lord;
whoever eats this bread will live forever.
℞. **Alleluia, alleluia.** ↓

GOSPEL Lk 9:11b-17   [Loaves and Fishes]
 Jesus feeds the people through the apostles. It all foreshadows the Eucharist.

℣. The Lord be with you. ℟. **And with your spirit.**

✠ A reading from the holy Gospel according to Luke.

℟. **Glory to you, O Lord.**

JESUS spoke to the crowds about the kingdom of God, and he healed those who needed to be cured. As the day was drawing to a close, the Twelve approached him and said, "Dismiss the crowd so that they can go to the surrounding villages and farms and find lodging and provisions; for we are in a deserted place here." He said to them, "Give them some food yourselves." They replied, "Five loaves and two fish are all we have, unless we ourselves go and buy food for all these people." Now the men there numbered about five thousand. Then he said to his disciples, "Have them sit down in groups of about fifty." They did so and made them all sit down. Then taking the five loaves and the two fish, and looking up to heaven, he said the blessing over them, broke them, and gave them to the disciples to set before the crowd. They all ate and were satisfied. And when the leftover fragments were picked up, they filled twelve wicker baskets.—The Gospel of the Lord. ℟. **Praise to you, Lord Jesus Christ.**

→ No. 15, p. 18

PRAYER OVER THE OFFERINGS   [Unity and Peace]

Grant your Church, O Lord, we pray,
the gifts of unity and peace,
whose signs are to be seen in mystery
in the offerings we here present.
Through Christ our Lord.

℟. **Amen.**   → No. 21, p. 22 (Pref. P 47-48)

COMMUNION ANT. Jn 6:57   [Eucharistic Life]

Whoever eats my flesh and drinks my blood remains in me and I in him, says the Lord. ↓

PRAYER AFTER COMMUNION   [Divine Life]

Grant, O Lord, we pray,
that we may delight for all eternity
in that share in your divine life,
which is foreshadowed in the present age
by our reception of your precious Body and Blood.
Who live and reign for ever and ever.
℟. **Amen.**   → No. 30, p. 77

Optional Solemn Blessings, p. 97, and Prayers over the People, p. 105

"The dead man got up and began to speak."

JUNE 5

10th SUNDAY IN ORDINARY TIME

ENTRANCE ANT. Cf. Ps 27 (26):1-2   [My Salvation]
**The Lord is my light and my salvation; whom shall I
fear? The Lord is the stronghold of my life; whom
should I dread? When those who do evil draw near,
they stumble and fall.**   → No. 2, p. 10

COLLECT [Guided by God]

O God, from whom all good things come,
grant that we, who call on you in our need,
may at your prompting discern what is right,
and by your guidance do it.
Through our Lord Jesus Christ, your Son,
who lives and reigns with you in the unity of the Holy
   Spirit,
one God, for ever and ever. ℟. **Amen.** ↓

FIRST READING 1 Kgs 17:17-24   [God, Lord of Life]

Elijah shows that the prophetic word manifests the power
of God. It can raise the dead, for God is the true source of
life.

A reading from the first Book of Kings

ELIJAH went to Zarephath of Sidon to the house of
a widow. The son of the mistress of the house fell
sick, and his sickness grew more severe until he
stopped breathing. So she said to Elijah, "Why have
you done this to me, O man of God? Have you come to
me to call attention to my guilt and to kill my son?"
Elijah said to her, "Give me your son." Taking him from
her lap, he carried the son to the upper room where he
was staying, and put him on his bed. Elijah called out
to the LORD: "O LORD, my God, will you afflict even the
widow with whom I am staying by killing her son?"
Then he stretched himself out upon the child three
times and called out to the LORD: "O LORD, my God, let
the life breath return to the body of this child." The
LORD heard the prayer of Elijah; the life breath
returned to the child's body and he revived. Taking the
child, Elijah brought him down into the house from the
upper room and gave him to his mother. Elijah said to
her, "See! Your son is alive." The woman replied to
Elijah, "Now indeed I know that you are a man of God.

The word of the LORD comes truly from your mouth."—
The word of the Lord. ℟. **Thanks be to God.** ↓

RESPONSORIAL PSALM Ps 50   [God Our Savior]

℟. I will praise you, Lord, for you have res-cued me.

I will extol you, O LORD, for you drew me clear
   and did not let my enemies rejoice over me.
O LORD, you brought me up from the netherworld;
   you preserved me from among those going down
     into the pit.

℟. **I will praise you, Lord, for you have rescued me.**

Sing praise to the LORD, you his faithful ones,
   and give thanks to his holy name.
For his anger lasts but a moment;
   a lifetime, his good will.
At nightfall, weeping enters in,
   but with the dawn, rejoicing.

℟. **I will praise you, Lord, for you have rescued me.**

Hear, O LORD, and have pity on me;
   O LORD, be my helper.
You changed my mourning into dancing;
   O LORD, my God, forever will I give you thanks.

℟. **I will praise you, Lord, for you have rescued me.** ↓

SECOND READING Gal 1:11-19   [Paul's Conversion]

**Paul reminds us that the proclamation of the Gospel is
authentic only if it clearly acknowledges God's saving ini-
tiative.**

A reading from the Letter of Saint Paul to the Galatians

I WANT you to know, brothers and sisters, that the
gospel preached by me is not of human origin. For
I did not receive it from a human being, nor was I

taught it, but it came through a revelation of Jesus Christ.

For you heard of my former way of life in Judaism, how I persecuted the church of God beyond measure and tried to destroy it, and progressed in Judaism beyond many of my contemporaries among my race, since I was even more a zealot for my ancestral traditions. But when God, who from my mother's womb had set me apart and called me through his grace, was pleased to reveal his Son to me, so that I might proclaim him to the Gentiles, I did not immediately consult flesh and blood, nor did I go up to Jerusalem to those who were apostles before me; rather, I went into Arabia and then returned to Damascus.

Then after three years I went up to Jerusalem to confer with Cephas and remained with him for fifteen days. But I did not see any other of the apostles, only James the brother of the Lord.—The word of the Lord. ℟. **Thanks be to God.** ↓

ALLELUIA Lk 7:16   [A Great Prophet]

℟. **Alleluia, alleluia.**
A great prophet has risen in our midst;
God has visited his people.
℟. **Alleluia, alleluia.** ↓

GOSPEL Lk 7:11-17   [Christ, Lord of Life]

   In raising the dead son of a widow, Jesus manifests the hidden reality of God's kingdom, which entails victory over sin and death. He holds it out to all of us.

℣. The Lord be with you. ℟. **And with your spirit.**
✛ A reading from the holy Gospel according to Luke.
℟. **Glory to you, O Lord.**

JESUS journeyed to a city called Nain, and his disciples and a large crowd accompanied him. As he drew near to the gate of the city, a man who had died

was being carried out, the only son of his mother, and she was a widow. A large crowd from the city was with her. When the Lord saw her, he was moved with pity for her and said to her, "Do not weep." He stepped forward and touched the coffin; at this the bearers halted, and he said, "Young man, I tell you, arise!" The dead man sat up and began to speak, and Jesus gave him to his mother. Fear seized them all, and they glorified God, exclaiming, "A great prophet has arisen in our midst," and "God has visited his people." This report about him spread through the whole of Judea and in all the surrounding region.—The Gospel of the Lord.
℟. **Praise to you, Lord Jesus Christ.**   → No. 15, p. 18

PRAYER OVER THE OFFERINGS   [Growth in Charity]

Look kindly upon our service, O Lord, we pray,
that what we offer
may be an acceptable oblation to you
and lead us to grow in charity.
Through Christ our Lord.
℟. **Amen.**   → No. 21, p. 22 (Pref. P 29-36)

COMMUNION ANT. Ps 18 (17):3   [God Our Helper]

The Lord is my rock, my fortress, and my deliverer; my God is my saving strength. ↓

OR 1 Jn 4:16   [Abide in Love]

God is love, and whoever abides in love abides in God, and God in him. ↓

PRAYER AFTER COMMUNION   [Healing Work]

May your healing work, O Lord,
free us, we pray, from doing evil
and lead us to what is right.
Through Christ our Lord.
℟. **Amen.**   → No. 30, p. 77

Optional Solemn Blessings, p. 97, and Prayers over the People, p. 105

"Your faith has has saved you; go in peace."

JUNE 12

11th SUNDAY IN ORDINARY TIME

ENTRANCE ANT. Cf. Ps 27 (26):7, 9   [Hear My Voice]

O Lord, hear my voice, for I have called to you; be my help. Do not abandon or forsake me, O God, my Savior!   → No. 2, p. 10

COLLECT   [Following God's Commands]

O God, strength of those who hope in you,
graciously hear our pleas,
and, since without you mortal frailty can do nothing,
grant us always the help of your grace,
that in following your commands
we may please you by our resolve and our deeds.
Through our Lord Jesus Christ, your Son,
who lives and reigns with you in the unity of the Holy
    Spirit,
one God, for ever and ever. ℞. **Amen.** ↓

447

FIRST READING 2 Sm 12:7-10, 13   [David's Repentance]

The prophet Nathan rebukes King David for having sinned grievously after God had been so good to him. Whenever we have been weak, we should repent and ask God for forgiveness.

A reading from the second Book of Samuel

NATHAN said to David: "Thus says the LORD God of Israel: 'I anointed you king of Israel. I rescued you from the hand of Saul. I gave you your lord's house and your lord's wives for your own. I gave you the house of Israel and of Judah. And if this were not enough, I could count up for you still more. Why have you spurned the Lord and done evil in his sight? You have cut down Uriah the Hittite with the sword; you took his wife as your own, and him you killed with the sword of the Ammonites. Now, therefore, the sword shall never depart from your house, because you have despised me and have taken the wife of Uriah to be your wife.'" Then David said to Nathan, "I have sinned against the LORD." Nathan answered David: "The LORD on his part has forgiven your sin: you shall not die."—The word of the Lord. ℟. **Thanks be to God.** ↓

RESPONSORIAL PSALM Ps 32   [God's Kindness]

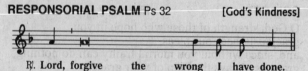

℟. Lord, forgive   the   wrong   I have done.

Blessed is the one whose fault is taken away,
    whose sin is covered.
Blessed the man to whom the LORD imputes not guilt,
    in whose spirit there is no guile.

℟. **Lord, forgive the wrong I have done.**

I acknowledged my sin to you,
    my guilt I covered not.

I said, "I confess my faults to the LORD,"
  and you took away the guilt of my sin.

℟. **Lord, forgive the wrong I have done.**

You are my shelter; from distress you will preserve me;
  with glad cries of freedom you will ring me round.

℟. **Lord, forgive the wrong I have done.**

Be glad in the LORD and rejoice, you just;
  exult, all you upright of heart.

℟. **Lord, forgive the wrong I have done.** ↓

SECOND READING Gal 2:16, 19-21 [Justification by Faith]
   Human endeavor alone cannot justify us. Rather it is faith, total dedication of self to God in the Lord Jesus, that leads us to salvation.

A reading from the Letter of Saint Paul
to the Galatians

BROTHERS and sisters: We who know that a person is not justified by works of the law but through faith in Jesus Christ, even we have believed in Christ Jesus that we may be justified by faith in Christ and not by works of the law, because by works of the law no one will be justified. For through the law I died to the law, that I might live for God. I have been crucified with Christ; yet I live, no longer I, but Christ lives in me; insofar as I now live in the flesh, I live by faith in the Son of God who has loved me and given himself up for me. I do not nullify the grace of God; for if justification comes through the law, then Christ died for nothing.—The word of the Lord. ℟. **Thanks be to God.** ↓

ALLELUIA 1 Jn 4:10b   [God's Forgiving Love]
℟. **Alleluia, alleluia.**
God loved us and sent his Son
as expiation for our sins.
℟. **Alleluia, alleluia.** ↓

GOSPEL Lk 7:36—8:3 or 7:36-50   [Unselfish Love]

Jesus rebukes Simon for his ungracious and self-satisfied behavior, but grants forgiveness to the sinner who sincerely repents for her sins. He is always ready to grant pardon for true repentance.

[If the "Shorter Form" is used, the indented text in brackets is omitted.]

℣. The Lord be with you. ℟. **And with your spirit.**
✛ A reading from the holy Gospel according to Luke.
℟. **Glory to you, O Lord.**

A PHARISEE invited Jesus to dine with him, and he entered the Pharisee's house and reclined at table. Now there was a sinful woman in the city who learned that he was at table in the house of the Pharisee. Bringing an alabaster flask of ointment, she stood behind him at his feet weeping and began to bathe his feet with her tears. Then she wiped them with her hair, kissed them, and anointed them with the ointment. When the Pharisee who had invited him saw this he said to himself, "If this man were a prophet, he would know who and what sort of woman this is who is touching him, that she is a sinner." Jesus said to him in reply, "Simon, I have something to say to you." "Tell me, teacher," he said. "Two people were in debt to a certain creditor; one owed five hundred days' wages and the other owed fifty. Since they were unable to repay the debt, he forgave it for both. Which of them will love him more?" Simon said in reply, "The one, I suppose, whose larger debt was forgiven." He said to him, "You have judged rightly."

Then he turned to the woman and said to Simon, "Do you see this woman? When I entered your house, you did not give me water for my feet, but she has bathed them with her tears and wiped them with her hair. You did not give me a kiss, but she has not ceased kissing my feet since the time I entered. You did not anoint my head with oil, but she anointed my feet with ointment. So I tell you, her many sins have been forgiven because she has shown great love. But the one to whom little is forgiven, loves little." He said to her, "Your sins are forgiven." The others at table said to themselves, "Who is this who even forgives sins?" But he said to the woman, "Your faith has saved you; go in peace."

[Afterward he journeyed from one town and village to another, preaching and proclaiming the good news of the kingdom of God. Accompanying him were the Twelve and some women who had been cured of evil spirits and infirmities, Mary, called Magdalene, from whom seven demons had gone out, Joanna, the wife of Herod's steward Chuza, Susanna, and many others who provided for them out of their resources.]

The Gospel of the Lord. ℟. **Praise to you, Lord Jesus Christ.**   → No. 15, p. 18

PRAYER OVER THE OFFERINGS [Needs of Human Nature]

O God, who in the offerings presented here
provide for the twofold needs of human nature,
nourishing us with food
and renewing us with your Sacrament,
grant, we pray,
that the sustenance they provide
may not fail us in body or in spirit.
Through Christ our Lord.
℟. **Amen.**   → No. 21, p. 22 (Pref. P 29-36)

COMMUNION ANT. Ps 27 (26):4   [Living with the Lord]
There is one thing I ask of the Lord, only this do I seek: to live in the house of the Lord all the days of my life. ↓

OR Jn 17:11   [One with God]

Holy Father, keep in your name those you have given me,
that they may be one as we are one, says the Lord. ↓

PRAYER AFTER COMMUNION   [Church Unity]

As this reception of your Holy Communion, O Lord,
foreshadows the union of the faithful in you,
so may it bring about unity in your Church.
Through Christ our Lord.

℟. **Amen.**

→ No. 30, p. 77

Optional Solemn Blessings, p. 97, and Prayers over the People, p. 105

*"If anyone wishes to come after me, he must deny himself
and take up his cross daily and follow me."*

JUNE 19

12th SUNDAY IN ORDINARY TIME

ENTRANCE ANT. Cf. Ps 28 (27):8-9   [Saving Refuge]

**The Lord is the strength of his people, a saving refuge
for the one he has anointed. Save your people, Lord,
and bless your heritage, and govern them for ever.**

→ No. 2, p. 10

COLLECT   [Foundation of God's Love]

Grant, O Lord,
that we may always revere and love your holy name,
for you never deprive of your guidance
those you set firm on the foundation of your love.
Through our Lord Jesus Christ, your Son,
who lives and reigns with you in the unity of the Holy
    Spirit,
one God, for ever and ever. ℟. **Amen.** ↓

FIRST READING Zec 12:10-11; 13:1   [A Suffering Messiah]

In a messianic vision the prophet evokes for us the memory of Christ's body being pierced by the lance.

A reading from the Book of the Prophet Zechariah

T HUS says the LORD: I will pour out on the house of
  David and on the inhabitants of Jerusalem a spirit
of grace and petition; and they shall look on him
whom they have pierced; and they shall mourn for him
as one mourns for an only son, and they shall grieve
over him as one grieves over a firstborn.

On that day the mourning in Jerusalem shall be as
great as the mourning of Hadadrimmon in the plain of
Megiddo.

On that day there shall be open to the house of
David and to the inhabitants of Jerusalem, a fountain
to purify from sin and uncleanness.—The word of the
Lord. ℟. **Thanks be to God.** ↓

RESPONSORIAL PSALM Ps 63   [Seeking the Lord]

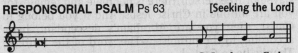

℟. **My soul is thirsting for you, O Lord my God.**

O God, you are my God whom I seek;
    for you my flesh pines and my soul thirsts
    like the earth, parched, lifeless and without water.

℟. **My soul is thirsting for you, O Lord my God.**

Thus have I gazed toward you in the sanctuary
    to see your power and your glory,
for your kindness is a greater good than life;
    my lips shall glorify you.

℟. **My soul is thirsting for you, O Lord my God.**

Thus will I bless you while I live;
    lifting up my hands, I will call upon your name.
As with the riches of a banquet shall my soul be satis-
    fied,
    and with exultant lips my mouth shall praise you.

℟. **My soul is thirsting for you, O Lord my God.**

You are my help,
    and in the shadow of your wings I shout for joy.
My soul clings fast to you;
    your right hand upholds me.

℟. **My soul is thirsting for you, O Lord my God.** ↓

SECOND READING Gal 3:26-29   [One in Christ]

In faith we are united and distinctions are transcended. We look upon Abraham as our father in faith.

A reading from the Letter of Saint Paul to the Galatians

BROTHERS and sisters: Through faith you are all children of God in Christ Jesus. For all of you who were baptized into Christ have clothed yourselves with Christ. There is neither Jew nor Greek, there is neither slave nor free person, there is not male and female; for you are all one in Christ Jesus. And if you belong to Christ, then you are Abraham's descendant, heirs according to the promise.—The word of the Lord. ℟. **Thanks be to God.** ↓

ALLELUIA Jn 10:27   [Christ's Sheep]

℟. **Alleluia, alleluia.**
My sheep hear my voice, says the Lord;

I know them, and they follow me.
℟. **Alleluia, alleluia.** ↓

GOSPEL Lk 9:18-24   [Taking Up One's Cross]

Jesus calls us to bear our cross, to lose our life for his sake so that we may have the fullness of life.

℣. The Lord be with you. ℟. **And with your spirit.**

✠ A reading from the holy Gospel according to Luke.
℟. **Glory to you, O Lord.**

ONCE when Jesus was praying in solitude, and the disciples were with him, he asked them, "Who do the crowds say that I am?" They said in reply, "John the Baptist; others, Elijah; still others, 'One of the ancient prophets has arisen.'" Then he said to them, "But who do you say that I am?" Peter said in reply, "The Christ of God." He rebuked them and directed them not to tell this to anyone.

He said, "The Son of Man must suffer greatly and be rejected by the elders, the chief priests, and the scribes, and be killed and on the third day be raised." Then he said to all, "If anyone wishes to come after me, he must deny himself and take up his cross daily and follow me. For whoever wishes to save his life will lose it, but whoever loses his life for my sake will save it."— The Gospel of the Lord. ℟. **Praise to you, Lord Jesus Christ.**   → No. 15, p. 18

PRAYER OVER THE OFFERINGS   [Pleasing Offering]

Receive, O Lord, the sacrifice of conciliation and praise
and grant that, cleansed by its action,
we may make offering of a heart pleasing to you.
Through Christ our Lord.
℟. **Amen.**   → No. 21, p. 22 (Pref. P 29-36)

COMMUNION ANT. Ps 145 (144):15   [Divine Food]

The eyes of all look to you, Lord, and you give them their food in due season. ↓

OR Jn 10:11, 15   [The Good Shepherd]

I am the Good Shepherd, and I lay down my life for my sheep, says the Lord. ↓

PRAYER AFTER COMMUNION   [Pledge of Redemption]

Renewed and nourished
by the Sacred Body and Precious Blood of your Son,
we ask of your mercy, O Lord,
that what we celebrate with constant devotion
may be our sure pledge of redemption.
Through Christ our Lord.
℟. **Amen.**   → No. 30, p. 77

Optional Solemn Blessings, p. 97, and Prayers over the People, p. 105

"No one who sets a hand to the plow and looks to what was left behind is fit for the kingdom of God."

JUNE 26

13th SUNDAY IN ORDINARY TIME

ENTRANCE ANT. Ps 47 (46):2   [Shouts of Joy]

All peoples, clap your hands. Cry to God with shouts
of joy!   → No. 2, p. 10

COLLECT   [Children of Light]

O God, who through the grace of adoption
chose us to be children of light,
grant, we pray,
that we may not be wrapped in the darkness of error
but always be seen to stand in the bright light of truth.
Through our Lord Jesus Christ, your Son,
who lives and reigns with you in the unity of the Holy
    Spirit,
one God, for ever and ever. ℟. **Amen.** ↓

FIRST READING 1 Kgs 19:16b, 19-21   [Call of Elisha]

    Elisha receives the divine call and leaves all his posses-
sions. Our dedication should also be total.

A reading from the first Book of Kings

THE LORD said to Elijah: "You shall anoint Elisha, son of Shaphat of Abel-meholah, as prophet to succeed you."

Elijah set out and came upon Elisha, son of Shaphat, as he was plowing with twelve yoke of oxen; he was following the twelfth. Elijah went over to him and threw his cloak over him. Elisha left the oxen, ran after Elijah, and said, "Please, let me kiss my father and mother goodbye, and I will follow you." Elijah answered, "Go back! Have I done anything to you?" Elisha left him and, taking the yoke of oxen, slaughtered them; he used the plowing equipment for fuel to boil their flesh, and gave it to his people to eat. Then Elisha left and followed Elijah as his attendant.—The word of the Lord. ℟. **Thanks be to God.** ↓

RESPONSORIAL PSALM Ps 16   [Refuge in the Lord]

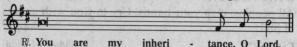

℟. You are my inheri - tance, O Lord.

Keep me, O God, for in you I take refuge;
  I say to the LORD, "My Lord are you."
O LORD, my allotted portion and my cup,
  you it is who hold fast my lot.

℟. **You are my inheritance, O Lord.**

I bless the LORD who counsels me;
  even in the night my heart exhorts me.
I set the LORD ever before me;
  with him at my right hand I shall not be disturbed.

℟. **You are my inheritance, O Lord.**

Therefore my heart is glad and my soul rejoices,
  my body, too, abides in confidence
because you will not abandon my soul to the netherworld,

nor will you suffer your faithful one to undergo corruption.

℟. **You are my inheritance, O Lord.**

You will show me the path to life,
    fullness of joys in your presence,
    the delights at your right hand forever.

℟. **You are my inheritance, O Lord.** ↓

SECOND READING Gal 5:1, 13-18   [Freedom in Christ]

We are called to be at one another's service and to love our fellow men as we love ourselves.

A reading from the Letter of Saint Paul to the Galatians

B‌ROTHERS and sisters: For freedom Christ set us free; so stand firm and do not submit again to the yoke of slavery.

For you were called for freedom, brothers and sisters. But do not use this freedom as an opportunity for the flesh; rather, serve one another through love. For the whole law is fulfilled in one statement, namely, *You shall love your neighbor as yourself.* But if you go on biting and devouring one another, beware that you are not consumed by one another.

I say, then: live by the Spirit and you will certainly not gratify the desire of the flesh. For the flesh has desires against the Spirit, and the Spirit against the flesh; these are opposed to each other, so that you may not do what you want. But if you are guided by the Spirit, you are not under the law.—The word of the Lord. ℟. **Thanks be to God.** ↓

ALLELUIA 1 Sm 3:9; Jn 6:68c   [Listening to God]

℟. **Alleluia, alleluia.**

Speak, O Lord, your servant is listening;
you have the words of everlasting life.

℟. **Alleluia, alleluia.** ↓

GOSPEL Lk 9:51-62   [Following Christ]

To follow Jesus we must be ready to give of ourselves totally.

℣. The Lord be with you. ℟. **And with your spirit.**

✠ A reading from the holy Gospel according to Luke.
℟. **Glory to you, O Lord.**

WHEN the days for Jesus' being taken up were ful-filled, he resolutely determined to journey to Jerusalem, and he sent messengers ahead of him. On the way they entered a Samaritan village to prepare for his reception there, but they would not welcome him because the destination of his journey was Jerusalem. When the disciples James and John saw this they asked, "Lord, do you want us to call down fire from heaven to consume them?" Jesus turned and rebuked them, and they journeyed to another village.

As they were proceeding on their journey someone said to him, "I will follow you wherever you go." Jesus answered him, "Foxes have dens and birds of the sky have nests, but the Son of Man has nowhere to rest his head."

And to another he said, "Follow me." But he replied, "Lord, let me go first and bury my father." But he answered him, "Let the dead bury their dead. But you, go and proclaim the kingdom of God." And another said, "I will follow you, Lord, but first let me say farewell to my family at home." To him Jesus said, "No one who sets a hand to the plow and looks to what was left behind is fit for the kingdom of God."—The Gospel of the Lord. ℟.
Praise to you, Lord Jesus Christ.   ➔ No. 15, p. 18

PRAYER OVER THE OFFERINGS   [Serving God]

O God, who graciously accomplish
the effects of your mysteries,
grant, we pray,
that the deeds by which we serve you

may be worthy of these sacred gifts.
Through Christ our Lord.
℞. **Amen.**   ➔   No. 21, p. 22 (Pref. P 29-36)

COMMUNION ANT. Cf. Ps 103 (102):1   [Bless the Lord]
**Bless the Lord, O my soul, and all within me, his holy
name. ↓**

OR Jn 17:20-21   [One in God]
**O Father, I pray for them, that they may be one in us,
that the world may believe that you have sent me, says
the Lord. ↓**

PRAYER AFTER COMMUNION   [Lasting Charity]
May this divine sacrifice we have offered and received
fill us with life, O Lord, we pray,
so that, bound to you in lasting charity,
we may bear fruit that lasts for ever.
Through Christ our Lord.
℞. **Amen.**   ➔   No. 30, p. 77

Optional Solemn Blessings, p. 97, and Prayers over the People, p. 105

"The harvest is abundant but the laborers are few."

JULY 3

14th SUNDAY IN ORDINARY TIME

ENTRANCE ANT. Cf. Ps 48 (47):10-11 **[God's Love and Justice]**
Your merciful love, O God, we have received in the
midst of your temple. Your praise, O God, like your
name, reaches the ends of the earth; your right hand
is filled with saving justice. → No. 2, p. 10

COLLECT **[Holy Joy]**
O God, who in the abasement of your Son
have raised up a fallen world,
fill your faithful with holy joy,
for on those you have rescued from slavery to sin
you bestow eternal gladness.
Through our Lord Jesus Christ, your Son,
who lives and reigns with you in the unity of the Holy
 Spirit,
one God, for ever and ever. ℟. **Amen.** ↓

FIRST READING Is 66:10-14c   [God's Goodness]

We may apply this reading to the Church. The Church is Jerusalem, a loving, protecting mother, who receives the blessing of God.

A reading from the Book of the Prophet Isaiah

THUS says the LORD:
Rejoice with Jerusalem and be glad because of her,
   all you who love her;
exult, exult with her,
   all you who were mourning over her!
Oh, that you may suck fully
   of the milk of her comfort,
that you may nurse with delight
   at her abundant breasts!
   For thus says the LORD:
Lo, I will spread prosperity over Jerusalem like a river,
   and the wealth of the nations like an overflowing
      torrent.
As nurslings, you shall be carried in her arms,
   and fondled in her lap;
as a mother comforts her child,
   so will I comfort you;
   in Jerusalem you shall find your comfort.

When you see this, your heart shall rejoice
   and your bodies flourish like the grass;
the LORD's power shall be known to his servants.
The word of the Lord. ℟. **Thanks be to God.** ↓

RESPONSORIAL PSALM Ps 66   [Praise of God]

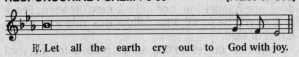

℟. Let all the earth cry out to God with joy.

Shout joyfully to God, all the earth,
  sing praise to the glory of his name;
  proclaim his glorious praise.
Say to God, "How tremendous are your deeds!"

℞. **Let all the earth cry out to God with joy.**

"Let all on earth worship and sing praise to you,
  sing praise to your name!"
Come and see the works of God,
  his tremendous deeds among the children of Adam.

℞. **Let all the earth cry out to God with joy.**

He has changed the sea into dry land;
  through the river they passed on foot;
  therefore let us rejoice in him.
He rules by his might forever.

℞. **Let all the earth cry out to God with joy.**

Hear now, all you who fear God,
  while I declare what he has done for me.
Blessed be God who refused me not
  my prayer or his kindness!

℞. **Let all the earth cry out to God with joy.** ↓

SECOND READING Gal 6:14-18   [Boasting in the Lord]

Through the cross of Christ we are created anew. This is all that really matters.

A reading from the Letter of Saint Paul to the Galatians

BROTHERS and sisters: May I never boast except in the cross of our Lord Jesus Christ, through which the world has been crucified to me, and I to the world. For neither does circumcision mean anything, nor does uncircumcision, but only a new creation. Peace and mercy be to all who follow this rule and to the Israel of God.

From now on, let no one make troubles for me; for I bear the marks of Jesus on my body.

The grace of our Lord Jesus Christ be with your spirit, brothers and sisters. Amen.—The word of the Lord. ℞. **Thanks be to God.** ↓

ALLELUIA Col 3:15a, 16a   [Peace of Christ]

℞. **Alleluia, alleluia.**
Let the peace of Christ control your hearts;
let the word of Christ dwell in you richly.
℞. **Alleluia, alleluia.** ↓

GOSPEL Lk 10:1-12, 17-20 or 10:1-9 [Spreading the Good News]

Even though our good works may be fruitful, we rejoice not in them but in our perseverance in grace.

[If the "Shorter Form" is used, the indented text in brackets is omitted.]

℣. The Lord be with you. ℞. **And with your spirit.**
✠ A reading from the holy Gospel according to Luke.
℞. **Glory to you, O Lord.**

AT that time the Lord appointed seventy-two others whom he sent ahead of him in pairs to every town and place he intended to visit. He said to them, "The harvest is abundant but the laborers are few; so ask the master of the harvest to send out laborers for his harvest. Go on your way; behold, I am sending you like lambs among wolves. Carry no money bag, no sack, no sandals; and greet no one along the way. Into whatever house you enter, first say, 'Peace to this household.' If a peaceful person lives there, your peace will rest on him; but if not, it will return to you. Stay in the same house and eat and drink what is offered to you, for the laborer deserves his payment. Do not move about from one house to another. Whatever town you enter and they welcome you, eat what is set before you, cure the sick in it and say to them, 'The kingdom of God is at hand for you.'

[Whatever town you enter and they do not receive you, go out into the streets and say, 'The dust of your town that clings to our feet, even that we shake off against you.' Yet know this: the kingdom of God is at hand. I tell you, it will be more tolerable for Sodom on that day than for that town."

The seventy-two returned rejoicing, and said, "Lord, even the demons are subject to us because of your name." Jesus said, "I have observed Satan fall like lightning from the sky. Behold, I have given you the power to 'tread upon serpents' and scorpions and upon the full force of the enemy and nothing will harm you. Nevertheless, do not rejoice because the spirits are subject to you, but rejoice because your names are written in heaven."]

The Gospel of the Lord. ℟. **Praise to you, Lord Jesus Christ.**

→ No. 15, p. 18

PRAYER OVER THE OFFERINGS   [Purify Us]

May this oblation dedicated to your name
purify us, O Lord,
and day by day bring our conduct
closer to the life of heaven.
Through Christ our Lord.

℟. **Amen.**   → No. 21, p. 22 (Pref. P 29-36)

COMMUNION ANT. Ps 34 (33):9   [The Lord's Goodness]

Taste and see that the Lord is good; blessed the man who seeks refuge in him. ↓

OR Mt 11:28   [God Refreshes]

Come to me, all who labor and are burdened, and I will refresh you, says the Lord. ↓

PRAYER AFTER COMMUNION   [Salvation and Praise]

Grant, we pray, O Lord,
that, having been replenished by such great gifts,

we may gain the prize of salvation
and never cease to praise you.
Through Christ our Lord.
R/. **Amen.**   ➔ No. 30, p. 77

Optional Solemn Blessings, p. 97, and Prayers over the People, p. 105

*"He approached the victim, poured oil and wine over his
wounds and bandaged them."*

JULY 10

15th SUNDAY IN ORDINARY TIME

ENTRANCE ANT. Cf. Ps 17 (16):15   [God's Face]

**As for me, in justice I shall behold your face; I shall be
filled with the vision of your glory.**   ➔ No. 2, p. 10

COLLECT   [Right Path]

O God, who show the light of your truth
to those who go astray,
so that they may return to the right path,
give all who for the faith they profess
are accounted Christians
the grace to reject whatever is contrary to the name of
   Christ

and to strive after all that does it honor.
Through our Lord Jesus Christ, your Son,
who lives and reigns with you in the unity of the Holy
  Spirit,
one God, for ever and ever. ℟. **Amen.** ↓

FIRST READING Dt 30:10-14   [Obeying the Law]

**We heed the word of the Lord by living his command-
ments. His word is not foreign to us.**

A reading from the Book of Deuteronomy

Moses said to the people: "If only you would heed
the voice of the Lord, your God, and keep his
commandments and statutes that are written in this
book of the law, when you return to the Lord, your
God, with all your heart and all your soul.

"For this command that I enjoin on you today is not
too mysterious and remote for you. It is not up in the
sky, that you should say, 'Who will go up in the sky to
get it for us and tell us of it, that we may carry it out?'
Nor is it across the sea, that you should say, 'Who will
cross the sea to get it for us and tell us of it, that we
may carry it out?' No, it is something very near to you,
already in your mouths and in your hearts; you have
only to carry it out."—The word of the Lord. ℟. **Thanks
be to God.** ↓

RESPONSORIAL PSALM Ps 69   [The Lord's Salvation]

℟. Turn to the Lord in your need, and you will live.

I pray to you, O Lord,
  for the time of your favor, O God!
In your great kindness answer me
  with your constant help.
Answer me, O Lord, for bounteous is your kindness:
  in your great mercy turn toward me.

℟. **Turn to the Lord in your need, and you will live.**

I am afflicted and in pain;
  let your saving help, O God, protect me.
I will praise the name of God in song,
  and I will glorify him with thanksgiving.

℟. **Turn to the Lord in your need, and you will live.**

"See, you lowly ones, and be glad;
  you who seek God, may your hearts revive!
For the LORD hears the poor,
  and his own who are in bonds he spurns not."

℟. **Turn to the Lord in your need, and you will live.**

For God will save Zion
  and rebuild the cities of Judah.
The descendants of his servants shall inherit it,
  and those who love his name shall inhabit it.

℟. **Turn to the Lord in your need, and you will live.** ↓

OR

RESPONSORIAL PSALM Ps 19   **[Word of Life]**

℟. Your words, Lord, are Spirit and life.

The law of the LORD is perfect,
  refreshing the soul;
the decree of the LORD is trustworthy,
  giving wisdom to the simple.

℟. **Your words, Lord, are Spirit and life.**

The precepts of the LORD are right,
  rejoicing the heart;
the command of the LORD is clear,
  enlightening the eye.

℟. **Your words, Lord, are Spirit and life.**

The fear of the LORD is pure,
  enduring forever;

the ordinances of the L̲ORD̲ are true,
 all of them just.

R̪. **Your words, Lord, are Spirit and life.**

They are more precious than gold,
 than a heap of purest gold;
sweeter also than syrup
 or honey from the comb.

R̪. **Your words, Lord, are Spirit and life.** ↓

SECOND READING Col 1:15-20   [The Primacy of Christ]
 The glory of Christ is proclaimed for all to know.

A reading from the Letter of Saint Paul to the Colossians

CHRIST Jesus is the image of the invisible God,
 the firstborn of all creation.
For in him were created all things in heaven and on
   earth,
   the visible and the invisible,
   whether thrones or dominions or principalities or
     powers;
   all things were created through him and for him.
He is before all things,
   and in him all things hold together.
He is the head of the body, the church.
He is the beginning, the firstborn from the dead,
   that in all things he himself might be preeminent.
For in him all the fullness was pleased to dwell,
   and through him to reconcile all things for him,
   making peace by the blood of his cross
   through him, whether those on earth or those in
     heaven.
The word of the Lord. R̪. **Thanks be to God.** ↓

ALLELUIA Cf. Jn 6:63c, 68c   [Spirit and Life]
R̪. **Alleluia, alleluia.**
Your words, Lord, are Spirit and life;

you have the words of everlasting life.

℟. **Alleluia, alleluia.** ↓

GOSPEL Lk 10:25-37   [The Good Samaritan]

> **A man is mugged. Who cares? How do we love others as we love ourself?**

℣. The Lord be with you. ℟. **And with your spirit.**

✟ A reading from the holy Gospel according to Luke.

℟. **Glory to you, O Lord.**

THERE was a scholar of the law who stood up to test Jesus and said, "Teacher, what must I do to inherit eternal life?" Jesus said to him, "What is written in the law? How do you read it?" He said in reply, "*You shall love the Lord, your God, with all your heart, with all your being, with all your strength, and with all your mind, and your neighbor as yourself.*" He replied to him, "You have answered correctly; do this and you will live."

But because he wished to justify himself, he said to Jesus, "And who is my neighbor?" Jesus replied, "A man fell victim to robbers as he went down from Jerusalem to Jericho. They stripped and beat him and went off leaving him half-dead. A priest happened to be going down that road, but when he saw him, he passed by on the opposite side. Likewise a Levite came to the place, and when he saw him, he passed by on the opposite side. But a Samaritan traveler who came upon him was moved with compassion at the sight. He approached the victim, poured oil and wine over his wounds and bandaged them. Then he lifted him up on his own animal, took him to an inn, and cared for him. The next day he took out two silver coins and gave them to the innkeeper with the instruction, 'Take care of him. If you spend more than what I have given you, I shall repay you on my way back.' Which of these three, in your opinion, was neighbor to the robbers' victim?" He answered, "The one who treated him with mercy." Jesus said to him, "Go and do likewise."—The Gospel of the Lord. ℟. **Praise to you, Lord Jesus Christ.**

→ No. 15, p. 18

PRAYER OVER THE OFFERINGS   [Greater Holiness]

Look upon the offerings of the Church, O Lord,
as she makes her prayer to you,
and grant that, when consumed by those who believe,
they may bring ever greater holiness.
Through Christ our Lord.
℟. **Amen.**

→ No. 21, p. 22 (Pref. P 29-36)

COMMUNION ANT. Cf. Ps 84 (83):4-5   [The Lord's House]

The sparrow finds a home, and the swallow a nest for her young: by your altars, O Lord of hosts, my King and my God. Blessed are they who dwell in your house, for ever singing your praise. ↓

OR Jn 6:57   [Remain in Jesus]

Whoever eats my flesh and drinks my blood remains in me and I in him, says the Lord. ↓

PRAYER AFTER COMMUNION   [Saving Effects]

Having consumed these gifts, we pray, O Lord,
that, by our participation in this mystery,
its saving effects upon us may grow.
Through Christ our Lord.
℟. **Amen.**

→ No. 30, p. 77

Optional Solemn Blessings, p. 97, and Prayers over the People, p. 105

"Mary has chosen the better part and it will not be taken from her."

JULY 17

16th SUNDAY IN ORDINARY TIME

ENTRANCE ANT. Ps 54 (53):6, 8   **[God Our Help]**

See, I have God for my help. The Lord sustains my soul. I will sacrifice to you with willing heart, and praise your name, O Lord, for it is good.   ➔ No. 2, p. 10

COLLECT   **[Keeping God's Commands]**

Show favor, O Lord, to your servants
and mercifully increase the gifts of your grace,
that, made fervent in hope, faith and charity,
they may be ever watchful in keeping your commands.
Through our Lord Jesus Christ, your Son,
who lives and reigns with you in the unity of the Holy
    Spirit,
one God, for ever and ever. ℟. **Amen.** ↓

FIRST READING Gn 18:1-10a   **[Hospitality]**

Abraham extends hospitality and the Lord reveals that his promise to Abraham will be fulfilled.

A reading from the Book of Genesis

THE LORD appeared to Abraham by the terebinth of
Mamre, as he sat in the entrance of his tent, while the
day was growing hot. Looking up, Abraham saw three
men standing nearby. When he saw them, he ran from
the entrance of the tent to greet them; and bowing to the
ground, he said: "Sir, if I may ask you this favor, please do
not go on past your servant. Let some water be brought,
that you may bathe your feet, and then rest yourselves
under the tree. Now that you have come this close to your
servant, let me bring you a little food, that you may
refresh yourselves; and afterward you may go on your
way." The men replied, "Very well, do as you have said."

Abraham hastened into the tent and told Sarah,
"Quick, three measures of fine flour! Knead it and
make rolls." He ran to the herd, picked out a tender,
choice steer, and gave it to a servant, who quickly prepared it. Then Abraham got some curds and milk, as
well as the steer that had been prepared, and set these
before the three men; and he waited on them under the
tree while they ate.

They asked Abraham, "Where is your wife Sarah?"
He replied, "There in the tent." One of them said, "I will
surely return to you about this time next year, and
Sarah will then have a son."—The word of the Lord. ℟.
Thanks be to God. ↓

RESPONSORIAL PSALM Ps 15   [The Just Man]

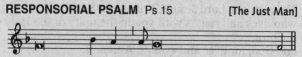

℟. He who does just - tice will live in the presence of the Lord.

One who walks blamelessly and does justice;
  who thinks the truth in his heart
  and slanders not with his tongue.

℟. **He who does justice will live in the presence of the Lord.**

Who harms not his fellow man,
    nor takes up a reproach against his neighbor;
by whom the reprobate is despised,
    while he honors those who fear the LORD.

℟. **He who does justice will live in the presence of the Lord.**

Who lends not his money at usury
    and accepts no bribe against the innocent.
One who does these things
    shall never be disturbed.

℟. **He who does justice will live in the presence of the Lord.** ↓

SECOND READING Col 1:24-28   [The Mystery of Christ]
    The word of God in its fullness is then revealed in the mystery of Christ.

A reading from the Letter of Saint Paul to the Colossians

BROTHERS and sisters: Now I rejoice in my sufferings for your sake, and in my flesh I am filling up what is lacking in the afflictions of Christ on behalf of his body, which is the church, of which I am a minister in accordance with God's stewardship given to me to bring to completion for you the word of God, the mystery hidden from ages and from generations past. But now it has been manifested to his holy ones, to whom God chose to make known the riches of the glory of this mystery among the Gentiles; it is Christ in you, the hope for glory. It is he whom we proclaim, admonishing everyone and teaching everyone with all wisdom, that we may present everyone perfect in Christ.—The word of the Lord. ℟. **Thanks be to God.** ↓

ALLELUIA Cf. Lk 8:15   [Perseverance]

℟. **Alleluia, alleluia.**
Blessed are they who have kept the word with a
  generous heart
and yield a harvest through perseverance.
℟. **Alleluia, alleluia.** ↓

GOSPEL Lk 10:38-42   [Martha and Mary]

> Strive for a sense of proportion—maintain a balance in all
> things.

℣. The Lord be with you. ℟. **And with your spirit.**
✤ A reading from the holy Gospel according to Luke.
℟. **Glory to you, O Lord.**

JESUS entered a village where a woman whose
  name was Martha welcomed him. She had a sister
named Mary who sat beside the Lord at his feet listening to him speak. Martha, burdened with much serving, came to him and said, "Lord, do you not care that
my sister has left me by myself to do the serving? Tell
her to help me." The Lord said to her in reply, "Martha,
Martha, you are anxious and worried about many
things. There is need of only one thing. Mary has chosen the better part and it will not be taken from her."—
The Gospel of the Lord. ℟. **Praise to you, Lord Jesus
Christ.**   → No. 15, p. 18

PRAYER OVER THE OFFERINGS   [Saving Offerings]

O God, who in the one perfect sacrifice
brought to completion varied offerings of the law,
accept, we pray, this sacrifice from your faithful
  servants
and make it holy, as you blessed the gifts of Abel,
so that what each has offered to the honor of your
  majesty
may benefit the salvation of all.

Through Christ our Lord.
℞. **Amen.**   ➔ No. 21, p. 22 (Pref. P 29-36)

COMMUNION ANT. Ps 111 (110):4-5   [Jesus Gives]

The Lord, the gracious, the merciful, has made a memorial of his wonders; he gives food to those who fear him. ↓

OR Rv 3:20   [Jesus Knocks]

Behold, I stand at the door and knock, says the Lord. If anyone hears my voice and opens the door to me, I will enter his house and dine with him, and he with me. ↓

PRAYER AFTER COMMUNION   [New Life]

Graciously be present to your people, we pray, O Lord, and lead those you have imbued with heavenly mysteries
to pass from former ways to newness of life.
Through Christ our Lord.
℞. **Amen.**   ➔ No. 30, p. 77

Optional Solemn Blessings, p. 97, and Prayers over the People, p. 105

"Lord, teach us to pray just as John taught his disciples."

JULY 24

17th SUNDAY IN ORDINARY TIME

ENTRANCE ANT. Cf. Ps 68 (67):6-7, 36 [God Our Strength]

God is in his holy place, God who unites those who dwell in his house; he himself gives might and strength to his people. → No. 2, p. 10

COLLECT [Enduring Things]

O God, protector of those who hope in you,
without whom nothing has firm foundation, nothing is
    holy,
bestow in abundance your mercy upon us
and grant that, with you as our ruler and guide,
we may use the good things that pass
in such a way as to hold fast even now
to those that ever endure.
Through our Lord Jesus Christ, your Son,
who lives and reigns with you in the unity of the Holy
    Spirit,
one God, for ever and ever. ℟. **Amen.** ↓

FIRST READING Gn 18:20-32   [Praying with Perseverance]
The Lord is just and merciful.

A reading from the Book of Genesis

IN those days, the LORD said: "The outcry against
Sodom and Gomorrah is so great, and their sin so
grave, that I must go down and see whether or not
their actions fully correspond to the cry against them
that comes to me. I mean to find out."

While Abraham's visitors walked on farther toward
Sodom, the LORD remained standing before Abraham.
Then Abraham drew nearer and said: "Will you sweep
away the innocent with the guilty? Suppose there were
fifty innocent people in the city; would you wipe out the
place, rather than spare it for the sake of the fifty innocent people within it? Far be it from you to do such a
thing, to make the innocent die with the guilty so that
the innocent and the guilty would be treated alike!
Should not the judge of all the world act with justice?"
The LORD replied, "If I find fifty innocent people in the
city of Sodom, I will spare the whole place for their
sake." Abraham spoke up again: "See how I am presuming to speak to my Lord, though I am but dust and
ashes! What if there are five less than fifty innocent
people? Will you destroy the whole city because of those
five?" He answered, "I will not destroy it, if I find forty-
five there." But Abraham persisted, saying, "What if only
forty are found there?" He replied, "I will forbear doing it
for the sake of the forty." Then Abraham said, "Let not
my Lord grow impatient if I go on. What if only thirty are
found there?" He replied, "I will forbear doing it if I can
find but thirty there." Still Abraham went on, "Since I
have thus dared to speak to my Lord, what if there are
no more than twenty?" The LORD answered, "I will not
destroy it, for the sake of the twenty." But he still persisted: "Please, let not my Lord grow angry if I speak up this
last time. What if there are at least ten there?" He replied,

"For the sake of those ten, I will not destroy it."—The word of the Lord. ℟. **Thanks be to God.** ↓

RESPONSORIAL PSALM Ps 138   [The Lord's Help]

℟. Lord, on the day I called for help,   you an - swered me.

I will give thanks to you, O LORD, with all my heart,
  for you have heard the words of my mouth;
    in the presence of the angels I will sing your praise;
I will worship at your holy temple
  and give thanks to your name.

℟. **Lord, on the day I called for help, you answered me.**

Because of your kindness and your truth;
  for you have made great above all things
    your name and your promise.
When I called you answered me;
  you built up strength within me.

℟. **Lord, on the day I called for help, you answered me.**

The LORD is exalted, yet the lowly he sees,
  and the proud he knows from afar.
Though I walk amid distress, you preserve me;
  against the anger of my enemies you raise your
    hand.

℟. **Lord, on the day I called for help, you answered me.**

Your right hand saves me.
  The LORD will complete what he has done for me;
your kindness, O LORD, endures forever;
  forsake not the work of your hands.

℟. **Lord, on the day I called for help, you answered me.** ↓

SECOND READING Col 2:12-14   [New Life from God]
The merciful Lord cancels our debt, pardons all our sins.

A reading from the Letter of Saint Paul
to the Colossians

Brothers and sisters: You were buried with him in baptism, in which you were also raised with him through faith in the power of God, who raised him from the dead. And even when you were dead in transgressions and the uncircumcision of your flesh, he brought you to life along with him, having forgiven us all our transgressions; obliterating the bond against us, with its legal claims, which was opposed to us, he also removed it from our midst, nailing it to the cross.—The word of the Lord. ℟. **Thanks be to God.** ↓

ALLELUIA Rom 8:15bc   [Children of God]
℟. **Alleluia, alleluia.**
You have received a Spirit of adoption,
through which we cry, Abba, Father.
℟. **Alleluia, alleluia.** ↓

GOSPEL Lk 11:1-13   [The Lord's Prayer]
   In the Lord's Prayer Jesus urges us to persevere in prayer
   and trust in the goodness of our loving Father.

℣. The Lord be with you. ℟. **And with your spirit.**
✝ A reading from the holy Gospel according to Luke.
℟. **Glory to you, O Lord.**

Jesus was praying in a certain place, and when he had finished, one of his disciples said to him, "Lord, teach us to pray just as John taught his disciples." He said to them, "When you pray, say:

   Father, hallowed be your name,
      your kingdom come.
      Give us each day our daily bread
      and forgive us our sins
      for we ourselves forgive everyone in debt to us,
      and do not subject us to the final test."

And he said to them, "Suppose one of you has a friend to whom he goes at midnight and says, 'Friend, lend me three loaves of bread, for a friend of mine has arrived at my house from a journey and I have nothing to offer him,' and he says in reply from within, 'Do not bother me; the door has already been locked and my children and I are already in bed. I cannot get up to give you anything.' I tell you, if he does not get up to give the visitor the loaves because of their friendship, he will get up to give him whatever he needs because of his persistence.

"And I tell you, ask and you will receive; seek and you will find; knock and the door will be opened to you. For everyone who asks, receives; and the one who seeks, finds; and to the one who knocks, the door will be opened. What father among you would hand his son a snake when he asks for a fish? Or hand him a scorpion when he asks for an egg? If you then, who are wicked, know how to give good gifts to your children, how much more will the Father in heaven give the Holy Spirit to those who ask him?"—The Gospel of the Lord. ℟. **Praise to you, Lord Jesus Christ.**   → No. 15, p. 18

PRAYER OVER THE OFFERINGS   [Sanctifying Mysteries]

Accept, O Lord, we pray, the offerings
which we bring from the abundance of your gifts,
that through the powerful working of your grace
these most sacred mysteries may sanctify our present
    way of life
and lead us to eternal gladness.
Through Christ our Lord.
℟. **Amen.**   → No. 21, p. 22 (Pref. P 29-36)

COMMUNION ANT. Ps 103 (102):2   [Bless the Lord]
Bless the Lord, O my soul, and never forget all his benefits. ↓

OR Mt 5:7-8   [Blessed the Clean of Heart]

Blessed are the merciful, for they shall receive mercy.
Blessed are the clean of heart, for they shall see God. ↓

PRAYER AFTER COMMUNION   [Memorial of Christ]

We have consumed, O Lord, this divine Sacrament,
the perpetual memorial of the Passion of your Son;
grant, we pray, that this gift,
which he himself gave us with love beyond all telling,
may profit us for salvation.
Through Christ our Lord.
℞. **Amen.**   → No. 30, p. 77

Optional Solemn Blessings, p. 97, and Prayers over the People, p. 105

*"There was a rich man whose land produced
a bountiful harvest."*

JULY 31

18th SUNDAY IN ORDINARY TIME

ENTRANCE ANT. Ps 70 (69):2, 6   [God's Help]

O God, come to my assistance; O Lord, make haste to
help me! You are my rescuer, my help; O Lord, do not
delay.   → No. 2, p. 10

COLLECT   [God's Unceasing Kindness]

Draw near to your servants, O Lord,
and answer their prayers with unceasing kindness,
that, for those who glory in you as their Creator and
   guide,
you may restore what you have created
and keep safe what you have restored.
Through our Lord Jesus Christ, your Son,
who lives and reigns with you in the unity of the Holy
   Spirit,
one God, for ever and ever. ℟. **Amen.** ↓

FIRST READING Eccl 1:2; 2:21-23   [The Folly of Vanity]
Without our faith all our strivings lead to nothing.

A reading from the Book of Ecclesiastes

V ANITY of vanities, says Qoheleth,
  vanity of vanities! All things are vanity!
   Here is one who has labored with wisdom and
knowledge and skill, and yet to another who has not
labored over it, he must leave property. This also is
vanity and a great misfortune. For what profit comes
to man from all the toil and anxiety of heart with
which he has labored under the sun? All his days sorrow and grief are his occupation; even at night his
mind is not at rest. This also is vanity.—The word of the
Lord. ℟. **Thanks be to God.** ↓

RESPONSORIAL PSALM Ps 90   [Worship the Lord]

℟. **If today you hear his voice, harden not your hearts.**

You turn man back to dust,
   saying, "Return, O children of men."
For a thousand years in your sight
   are as yesterday, now that it is past,
   or as a watch of the night.

℟. **If today you hear his voice, harden not your hearts.**

You make an end of them in their sleep;
  the next morning they are like the changing grass,
which at dawn springs up anew,
  but by evening wilts and fades.

℟. **If today you hear his voice, harden not your hearts.**

Teach us to number our days aright,
  that we may gain wisdom of heart.
Return, O LORD! How long?
  Have pity on your servants!

℟. **If today you hear his voice, harden not your hearts.**

Fill us at daybreak with your kindness,
  that we may shout for joy and gladness all our days.
And may the gracious care of the LORD our God be
    ours;
  prosper the work of our hands for us!
  Prosper the work of our hands!

℟. **If today you hear his voice, harden not your hearts.** ↓

SECOND READING Col 3:1-5, 9-11   [Christ Our Life]
A life worthy of the Lord consists of selflessness, gentleness, patience, and bearing love for one another.

A reading from the Letter of Saint Paul to the Colossians

BROTHERS and sisters: If you were raised with Christ, seek what is above, where Christ is seated at the right hand of God. Think of what is above, not of what is on earth. For you have died, and your life is hidden with Christ in God. When Christ your life appears, then you too will appear with him in glory.

Put to death, then, the parts of you that are earthly: immorality, impurity, passion, evil desire, and the greed that is idolatry. Stop lying to one another, since you have taken off the old self with its practices and have put on the new self, which is being renewed, for knowledge, in the image of its creator. Here there is not Greek and Jew, circumcision and uncircumcision, barbarian, Scythian, slave, free; but Christ is all and in all.—The word of the Lord. ℟. **Thanks be to God.** ↓

ALLELUIA Mt 5:3   [Heirs of Heaven]

℟. **Alleluia, alleluia.**
Blessed are the poor in spirit,
for theirs is the kingdom of heaven.
℟. **Alleluia, alleluia.** ↓

GOSPEL Lk 12:13-21   [True Wealth in God]

How foolish and vain are those who put all their trust in their own devices.

℣. The Lord be with you. ℟. **And with your spirit.**
✚ A reading from the holy Gospel according to Luke.
℟. **Glory to you, O Lord.**

SOMEONE in the crowd said to Jesus, "Teacher, tell my brother to share the inheritance with me." He replied to him, "Friend, who appointed me as your judge and arbitrator?" Then he said to the crowd, "Take care to guard against all greed, for though one may be rich, one's life does not consist of possessions."

Then he told them a parable. "There was a rich man whose land produced a bountiful harvest. He asked himself, 'What shall I do, for I do not have space to store my harvest?' And he said, 'This is what I shall do: I shall tear down my barns and build larger ones. There I shall store all my grain and other goods and I shall say to myself, "Now as for you, you have so many good things stored up for many years, rest, eat, drink, be merry!"' But God

said to him, 'You fool, this night your life will be demanded of you; and the things you have prepared, to whom
will they belong?' Thus will it be for all who store up
treasure for themselves but are not rich in what matters
to God."—The Gospel of the Lord. ℟. **Praise to you, Lord
Jesus Christ.**   ➙ No. 15, p. 18

PRAYER OVER THE OFFERINGS   [Spiritual Sacrifice]

Graciously sanctify these gifts, O Lord, we pray,
and, accepting the oblation of this spiritual sacrifice,
make of us an eternal offering to you.
Through Christ our Lord.
℟. **Amen.**   ➙ No. 21, p. 22 (Pref. P 29-36)

COMMUNION ANT. Wis 16:20   [Bread from Heaven]
**You have given us, O Lord, bread from heaven, endowed
with all delights and sweetness in every taste.** ↓

OR Jn 6:35   [Bread of Life]
**I am the bread of life, says the Lord; whoever comes
to me will not hunger and whoever believes in me will
not thirst.** ↓

PRAYER AFTER COMMUNION   [Heavenly Gifts]

Accompany with constant protection, O Lord,
those you renew with these heavenly gifts
and, in your never-failing care for them,
make them worthy of eternal redemption.
Through Christ our Lord.
℟. **Amen.**   ➙ No. 30, p. 77

Optional Solemn Blessings, p. 97, and Prayers over the People, p. 105

"Gird your loins and light your lamps."

AUGUST 7

19th SUNDAY IN ORDINARY TIME

ENTRANCE ANT. Cf. Ps 74 (73):20, 19, 22, 23

[Arise, O God]

Look to your covenant, O Lord, and forget not the life of your poor ones for ever. Arise, O God, and defend your cause, and forget not the cries of those who seek you.

→ No. 2, p. 10

COLLECT [Spirit of Adoption]

Almighty ever-living God,
whom, taught by the Holy Spirit,
we dare to call our Father,
bring, we pray, to perfection in our hearts
the spirit of adoption as your sons and daughters,
that we may merit to enter into the inheritance
which you have promised.
Through our Lord Jesus Christ, your Son,
who lives and reigns with you in the unity of the Holy
Spirit,
one God, for ever and ever. ℟. **Amen.** ↓

FIRST READING Wis 18:6-9   [Salvation of the Just]

The first Passover is recalled, when the faithful people of God prayed behind closed doors, and the angel of death struck at the firstborn of Egypt.

A reading from the Book of Wisdom

THE night of the passover was known beforehand to our fathers,

that, with sure knowledge of the oaths in which they put their faith,

they might have courage.

Your people awaited the salvation of the just

and the destruction of their foes.

For when you punished our adversaries,

in this you glorified us whom you had summoned.

For in secret the holy children of the good were offering sacrifice

and putting into effect with one accord the divine institution.

The word of the Lord. ℟. **Thanks be to God.** ↓

RESPONSORIAL PSALM Ps 33   [Refuge in God]

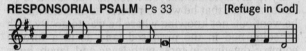

℟. **Bles - sed the peo - ple   the Lord has chosen to be his own.**

Exult, you just, in the LORD;

praise from the upright is fitting.

Blessed the nation whose God is the LORD,

the people he has chosen for his own inheritance.

℟. **Blessed the people the Lord has chosen to be his own.**

See, the eyes of the LORD are upon those who fear him,

upon those who hope for his kindness,

to deliver them from death

and preserve them in spite of famine.

℟. **Blessed the people the Lord has chosen to be his own.**

Our soul waits for the LORD,
  who is our help and our shield.
May your kindness, O LORD, be upon us
  who have put our hope in you.

℟. **Blessed the people the Lord has chosen to be his own.** ↓

SECOND READING Heb 11:1-2, 8-19 or 11:1-2, 8-12 [Faith]

  Abraham, our father in faith, relies on the confident assurance of what he hopes for. May we take courage from his example.

[If the "Shorter Form" is used, the indented text in brackets is omitted.]

A reading from the Letter to the Hebrews

BROTHERS and sisters: Faith is the realization of what is hoped for and evidence of things not seen. Because of it the ancients were well attested.

By faith Abraham obeyed when he was called to go out to a place that he was to receive as an inheritance; he went out, not knowing where he was to go. By faith he sojourned in the promised land as in a foreign country, dwelling in tents with Isaac and Jacob, heirs of the same promise; for he was looking forward to the city with foundations, whose architect and maker is God. By faith he received power to generate, even though he was past the normal age—and Sarah herself was sterile—for he thought that the one who had made the promise was trustworthy. So it was that there came forth from one man, himself as good as dead, descendants as numerous as the stars in the sky and as countless as the sands on the seashore.

  [All these died in faith. They did not receive what had been promised but saw it and greeted it from afar and acknowledged themselves to be strangers and aliens on earth, for those who speak thus show that they are seeking a homeland. If they had been thinking of the land from which they had come, they would have had opportunity to return. But now they desire a better homeland, a heavenly one. Therefore, God is not ashamed to be called their God, for he has prepared a city for them.

By faith Abraham, when put to the test, offered up Isaac, and he who had received the promises was ready to offer his only son, of whom it was said, "Through Isaac descendants shall bear your name." He reasoned that God was able to raise even from the dead, and he received Isaac back as a symbol.]

The word of the Lord. ℟. **Thanks be to God.** ↓

ALLELUIA Mt 24:42a, 44   [Be Ready]
℟. **Alleluia, alleluia.**
Stay awake and be ready!
For you do not know on what day your Lord will come.
℟. **Alleluia, alleluia.** ↓

GOSPEL Lk 12:32-48 or 12:35-40   [Awaiting the Lord]
As the faithful people of God, we must act in accordance with our faith. We must be constant.

[If the "Shorter Form" is used, the indented text in brackets is omitted.]

℣. The Lord be with you. ℟. **And with your spirit.**
✝ A reading from the holy Gospel according to Luke.
℟. **Glory to you, O Lord.**

JESUS said to his disciples:
["Do not be afraid any longer, little flock, for your Father is pleased to give you the kingdom. Sell your belongings and give alms. Provide money

bags for yourselves that do not wear out, an inexhaustible treasure in heaven that no thief can reach nor moth destroy. For where your treasure is, there also will your heart be.]

"Gird your loins and light your lamps and be like servants who await their master's return from a wedding, ready to open immediately when he comes and knocks. Blessed are those servants whom the master finds vigilant on his arrival. Amen, I say to you, he will gird himself, have them recline at table, and proceed to wait on them. And should he come in the second or third watch and find them prepared in this way, blessed are those servants. Be sure of this: if the master of the house had known the hour when the thief was coming, he would not have let his house be broken into. You also must be prepared, for at an hour you do not expect, the Son of Man will come."

[Then Peter said, "Lord, is this parable meant for us or for everyone?" And the Lord replied, "Who, then, is the faithful and prudent steward whom the master will put in charge of his servants to distribute the food allowance at the proper time? Blessed is that servant whom his master on arrival finds doing so. Truly, I say to you, the master will put the servant in charge of all his property. But if that servant says to himself, 'My master is delayed in coming,' and begins to beat the menservants and the maidservants, to eat and drink and get drunk, then that servant's master will come on an unexpected day and at an unknown hour and will punish the servant severely and assign him a place with the unfaithful. That servant who knew his master's will but did not make preparations nor act in accord with his will shall be beaten severely; and the servant who was ignorant of his master's will but acted in a way deserving of a severe beating shall be beaten only lightly. Much will be required of the person entrusted with much, and still more will be demanded of the person entrusted with more."]

The Gospel of the Lord. ℟. **Praise to you, Lord Jesus Christ.**   ➔ No. 15, p. 18

PRAYER OVER THE OFFERINGS   [Mystery of Salvation]

Be pleased, O Lord, to accept the offerings of your Church,
for in your mercy you have given them to be offered
and by your power you transform them
into the mystery of our salvation.
Through Christ our Lord.
℟. **Amen.**   ➔ No. 21, p. 22 (Pref. P 29-36)

COMMUNION ANT. Ps 147 (146):12, 14   [Glorify the Lord]

O Jerusalem, glorify the Lord, who gives you your fill of finest wheat. ↓

OR Cf. Jn 6:51   [The Flesh of Jesus]

The bread that I will give, says the Lord, is my flesh for the life of the world. ↓

PRAYER AFTER COMMUNION [Confirm Us in God's Truth]

May the communion in your Sacrament
that we have consumed, save us, O Lord,
and confirm us in the light of your truth.
Through Christ our Lord.
℟. **Amen.**   ➔ No. 30, p. 77

Optional Solemn Blessings, p. 97, and Prayers over the People, p. 105

"I have come to set the earth on fire."

AUGUST 14

20th SUNDAY IN ORDINARY TIME

ENTRANCE ANT. Ps 84 (83):10-11   [God Our Shield]

Turn your eyes, O God, our shield; and look on the face of your anointed one; one day within your courts is better than a thousand elsewhere.   → No. 2, p. 10

COLLECT   [Attaining God's Promises]

O God, who have prepared for those who love you
good things which no eye can see,
fill our hearts, we pray, with the warmth of your love,
so that, loving you in all things and above all things,
we may attain your promises,
which surpass every human desire.
Through our Lord Jesus Christ, your Son,
who lives and reigns with you in the unity of the Holy
   Spirit,
one God, for ever and ever. ℟. **Amen.** ↓

FIRST READING Jer 38:4-6, 8-10 [Imprisonment of Jeremiah]

In a symbolic way the prophet's experience is a resurrection. He is buried in the cistern and later drawn up from it.

A reading from the Book of the Prophet Jeremiah

IN those days, the princes said to the king: "Jeremiah ought to be put to death; he is demoralizing the soldiers who are left in this city, and all the people, by speaking such things to them; he is not interested in the welfare of our people, but in their ruin." King Zedekiah answered: "He is in your power"; for the king could do nothing with them. And so they took Jeremiah and threw him into the cistern of Prince Malchiah, which was in the quarters of the guard, letting him down with ropes. There was no water in the cistern, only mud, and Jeremiah sank into the mud.

Ebed-melech, a court official, went there from the palace and said to him: "My lord king, these men have been at fault in all they have done to the prophet Jeremiah, casting him into the cistern. He will die of famine on the spot, for there is no more food in the city." Then the king ordered Ebed-melech the Cushite to take three men along with him, and draw the prophet Jeremiah out of the cistern before he should die.—The word of the Lord. ℟. **Thanks be to God.** ↓

RESPONSORIAL PSALM Ps 40   [The Lord Our Help]

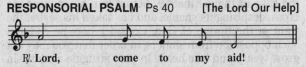

℟. **Lord,   come   to   my   aid!**

I have waited, waited for the LORD,
    and he stooped toward me.

℟. **Lord, come to my aid!**

The LORD heard my cry.
He drew me out of the pit of destruction,
    out of the mud of the swamp;

he set my feet upon a crag;
 he made firm my steps.

℞. **Lord, come to my aid!**

And he put a new song into my mouth,
 a hymn to our God.
Many shall look on in awe
 and trust in the LORD.

℞. **Lord, come to my aid!**

Though I am afflicted and poor,
 yet the LORD thinks of me.
You are my help and my deliverer;
 O my God, hold not back!

℞. **Lord, come to my aid!** ↓

SECOND READING Heb 12:1-4 [Perseverance]

Take courage from the example of Christ. Do not lose sight of the eternal reward.

A reading from the Letter to the Hebrews

BROTHERS and sisters: Since we are surrounded by so great a cloud of witnesses, let us rid ourselves of every burden and sin that clings to us and persevere in running the race that lies before us while keeping our eyes fixed on Jesus, the leader and perfecter of faith. For the sake of the joy that lay before him he endured the cross, despising its shame, and has taken his seat at the right of the throne of God. Consider how he endured such opposition from sinners, in order that you may not grow weary and lose heart. In your struggle against sin you have not yet resisted to the point of shedding blood.—The word of the Lord. ℞. **Thanks be to God.** ↓

ALLELUIA Jn 10:27 [Christ's Sheep]

℞. **Alleluia, alleluia.**
My sheep hear my voice, says the Lord;

I know them, and they follow me.
℟. **Alleluia, alleluia.** ↓

GOSPEL Lk 12:49-53   [A Divided Household]

> Many cannot find peace because they do not accept Christ.
> To them his coming is the cause of division.

℣. The Lord be with you. ℟. **And with your spirit.**
✠ A reading from the holy Gospel according to Luke.
℟. **Glory to you, O Lord.**

JESUS said to his disciples: "I have come to set the earth on fire, and how I wish it were already blazing! There is a baptism with which I must be baptized, and how great is my anguish until it is accomplished! Do you think that I have come to establish peace on the earth? No, I tell you, but rather division. From now on a household of five will be divided, three against two and two against three; a father will be divided against his son and a son against his father, a mother against her daughter and a daughter against her mother, a mother-in-law against her daughter-in-law and a daughter-in-law against her mother-in-law."—The Gospel of the Lord. ℟. **Praise to you, Lord Jesus Christ.**   → No. 15, p. 18

PRAYER OVER THE OFFERINGS   [Glorious Exchange]

Receive our oblation, O Lord,
by which is brought about a glorious exchange,
that, by offering what you have given,
we may merit to receive your very self.
Through Christ our Lord.
℟. **Amen.**   → No. 21, p. 22 (Pref. P 29-36)

COMMUNION ANT. Ps 130 (129):7   [Plentiful Redemption]
With the Lord there is mercy; in him is plentiful redemption. ↓

OR Jn 6:51   [Eternal Life]

**I am the living bread that came down from heaven,
says the Lord. Whoever eats of this bread will live for
ever.** ↓

PRAYER AFTER COMMUNION   [Coheirs in Heaven]

Made partakers of Christ through these Sacraments,
we humbly implore your mercy, Lord,
that, conformed to his image on earth,
we may merit also to be his coheirs in heaven.
Who lives and reigns for ever and ever.
℞. **Amen.**   → No. 30, p. 77

Optional Solemn Blessings, p. 97, and Prayers over the People, p. 105

"Alleluia. Mary is taken up to heaven."

AUGUST 15

THE ASSUMPTION OF THE BLESSED VIRGIN MARY

Solemnity

AT THE VIGIL MASS (August 14)

ENTRANCE ANT. [Mary Exalted]

Glorious things are spoken of you, O Mary, who today were exalted above the choirs of Angels into eternal triumph with Christ. → No. 2, p. 10

COLLECT [Crowed with Glory]

O God, who, looking on the lowliness of the Blessed
    Virgin Mary,
raised her to this grace,
that your Only Begotten Son was born of her according
    to the flesh
and that she was crowned this day with surpassing glory,
grant through her prayers,
that, saved by the mystery of your redemption,
we may merit to be exalted by you on high.
Through our Lord Jesus Christ, your Son,

499

who lives and reigns with you in the unity of the Holy
  Spirit,
one God, for ever and ever. ℟. **Amen.** ↓

FIRST READING 1 Chr 15:3-4, 15-16; 16:1-2

[Procession of Glory]

**Under David's direction the Israelites brought the ark of
the Lord to the tent prepared for it. They showed great
respect for it. They offered holocausts and peace offerings.
This becomes a figure of Mary who bore the Son of God.**

A reading from the first Book of Chronicles

D AVID assembled all Israel in Jerusalem to bring
  the ark of the LORD to the place which he had prepared for it. David also called together the sons of
Aaron and the Levites.

The Levites bore the ark of God on their shoulders
with poles, as Moses had ordained according to the
word of the LORD.

David commanded the chiefs of the Levites to
appoint their kinsmen as chanters, to play on musical
instruments, harps, lyres, and cymbals, to make a loud
sound of rejoicing.

They brought in the ark of God and set it within the
tent which David had pitched for it. Then they offered up
burnt offerings and peace offerings to God. When David
had finished offering up the burnt offerings and peace
offerings, he blessed the people in the name of the
LORD.—The word of the Lord. ℟. **Thanks be to God.** ↓

RESPONSORIAL PSALM Ps 132   [Mary, Ark of God]

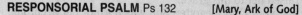

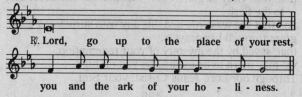

℟. Lord, go up to the place of your rest,
you and the ark of your ho - li - ness.

Behold, we heard of it in Ephrathah;
  we found it in the fields of Jaar.
Let us enter into his dwelling,
  let us worship at his footstool.

℞. **Lord, go up to the place of your rest, you and the ark of your holiness.**

May your priests be clothed with justice;
  let your faithful ones shout merrily for joy.
For the sake of David your servant,
  reject not the plea of your anointed.

℞. **Lord, go up to the place of your rest, you and the ark of your holiness.**

For the LORD has chosen Zion;
  he prefers her for his dwelling.
"Zion is my resting place forever;
  in her will I dwell, for I prefer her."

℞. **Lord, go up to the place of your rest, you and the ark of your holiness.** ↓

SECOND READING 1 Cor 15:54b-57   [Victory over Death]

Paul reminds the Corinthians that in life after death there is victory. Through his love for us, God has given victory over sin and death in Jesus, his Son.

A reading from the first Letter of Saint Paul
to the Corinthians

BROTHERS and sisters: When that which is mortal clothes itself with immortality, then the word that is written shall come about:
  Death is swallowed up in victory.
  Where, O death, is your victory?
  Where, O death, is your sting?
The sting of death is sin, and the power of sin is the law. But thanks be to God who gives us the victory through our Lord Jesus Christ.—The word of the Lord.
℞. **Thanks be to God.** ↓

ALLELUIA Lk 11:28   [Doers of God's Word]

℟. **Alleluia, alleluia.**
Blessed are they who hear the word of God
and observe it.
℟. **Alleluia, alleluia.** ↓

GOSPEL Lk 11:27-28   [Keeping God's Word]

Mary's relationship as the mother of Jesus is unique in all of
history. But Jesus reminds us that those who keep his word
are most pleasing to God. In this Mary has set an example.

℣. The Lord be with you. ℟. **And with your spirit.**
✣ A reading from the holy Gospel according to Luke.
℟. **Glory to you, O Lord.**

WHILE Jesus was speaking, a woman from the
crowd called out and said to him, "Blessed is the
womb that carried you and the breasts at which you
nursed." He replied, "Rather, blessed are those who hear
the word of God and observe it."—The Gospel of the
Lord. ℟. **Praise to you, Lord Jesus Christ.** → No. 15, p. 18

PRAYER OVER THE OFFERINGS   [Sacrifice of Praise]

Receive, we pray, O Lord,
the sacrifice of conciliation and praise,
which we celebrate on the Assumption of the holy
   Mother of God,
that it may lead us to your pardon
and confirm us in perpetual thanksgiving.
Through Christ our Lord. ℟. **Amen.** → Pref. P 59, p. 507

COMMUNION ANT. Cf. Lk 11:27   [Mary Carried Christ]

**Blessed is the womb of the Virgin Mary, which bore the
Son of the eternal Father.** ↓

PRAYER AFTER COMMUNION   [Beseech God's Mercy]

Having partaken of this heavenly table,
we beseech your mercy, Lord our God,

that we, who honor the Assumption of the Mother of
  God,
may be freed from every threat of harm.
Through Christ our Lord.
℟. **Amen.**   ➜ No. 30, p. 77

Optional Solemn Blessings, p. 97, and Prayers over the People, p. 105

AT THE MASS DURING THE DAY

ENTRANCE ANT. Cf. Rv 12:1   [Mary's Glory]
**A great sign appeared in heaven: a woman clothed
with the sun, and the moon beneath her feet, and on
her head a crown of twelve stars.**   ➜ No. 2, p. 10

OR   [Joy in Heaven]
**Let us all rejoice in the Lord, as we celebrate the feast
day in honor of the Virgin Mary, at whose Assumption
the Angels rejoice and praise the Son of God.**
                                                ➜ No. 2, p. 10

COLLECT   [Sharing Mary's Glory]
Almighty ever-living God,
who assumed the Immaculate Virgin Mary, the Mother
  of your Son,
body and soul into heavenly glory,
grant, we pray,
that, always attentive to the things that are above,
we may merit to be sharers of her glory.
Through our Lord Jesus Christ, your Son,
who lives and reigns with you in the unity of the Holy
  Spirit,
one God, for ever and ever. ℟. **Amen.** ↓

FIRST READING Rv 11:19a; 12:1-6a, 10ab [Mary, the Ark]
    The appearance of the Ark in this time of retribution indi-
    cates that God is now accessible—no longer hidden, but

present in the midst of his people. Filled with hatred, the devil spares no pains to destroy Christ and his Church. The dragon seeks to destroy the celestial woman and her Son. Its hatred is futile.

A reading from the Book of Revelation

GOD'S temple in heaven was opened, and the ark of his covenant could be seen in the temple.

A great sign appeared in the sky, a woman clothed with the sun, with the moon beneath her feet, and on her head a crown of twelve stars. She was with child and wailed aloud in pain as she labored to give birth. Then another sign appeared in the sky; it was a huge red dragon, with seven heads and ten horns, and on its heads were seven diadems. Its tail swept away a third of the stars in the sky and hurled them down to the earth. Then the dragon stood before the woman about to give birth, to devour her child when she gave birth. She gave birth to a son, a male child, destined to rule all the nations with an iron rod. Her child was caught up to God and his throne. The woman herself fled into the desert where she had a place prepared by God.

Then I heard a loud voice in heaven say:

"Now have salvation and power come,
    and the Kingdom of our God
    and the authority of his Anointed One."
The word of the Lord. ℟. **Thanks be to God.** ↓

RESPONSORIAL PSALM Ps 45   [Mary the Queen]

℟. The queen stands at your right hand, ar-rayed in gold.

The queen takes her place at your right hand in gold
    of Ophir.

℟. **The queen stands at your right hand, arrayed in
    gold.**

Hear, O daughter, and see; turn your ear,
  forget your people and your father's house.

℞. **The queen stands at your right hand, arrayed in gold.**

So shall the king desire your beauty;
  for he is your lord.

℞. **The queen stands at your right hand, arrayed in gold.**

They are borne in with gladness and joy;
  they enter the palace of the king.

℞. **The queen stands at your right hand, arrayed in gold.** ↓

SECOND READING 1 Cor 15:20-27   [Christ the King]

The offering of the firstfruits was the symbol of the dedication of the entire harvest to God. So the Resurrection of Christ involves the resurrection of all who are in him. Since his glorious Resurrection, Christ reigns in glory; he is the Lord.

A reading from the first Letter of Saint Paul
to the Corinthians

BROTHERS and sisters: Christ has been raised from the dead, the firstfruits of those who have fallen asleep. For since death came through man, the resurrection of the dead came also through man. For just as in Adam all die, so too in Christ shall all be brought to life, but each one in proper order: Christ the firstfruits; then, at his coming, those who belong to Christ; then comes the end, when he hands over the Kingdom to his God and Father, when he has destroyed every sovereignty and every authority and power. For he must reign until he has put all his enemies under his feet. The last enemy to be destroyed is death, for "he subjected everything under his feet."—The word of the Lord. ℞. **Thanks be to God.** ↓

ALLELUIA   [Mary in Heaven]
℟. **Alleluia, alleluia.**
Mary is taken up to heaven;
a chorus of angels exults.
℟. **Alleluia, alleluia.** ↓

GOSPEL Lk 1:39-56   [Blessed among Women]
   Mary visits her kinswoman, Elizabeth. Mary's song of
   thanksgiving, often called the "Magnificat," has been put
   together from many Old Testament phrases.

℣. The Lord be with you. ℟. **And with your spirit.**
✛ A reading from the holy Gospel according to Luke.
℟. **Glory to you, O Lord.**

MARY set out and traveled to the hill country in
haste to a town of Judah, where she entered the
house of Zechariah and greeted Elizabeth. When
Elizabeth heard Mary's greeting, the infant leaped in her
womb, and Elizabeth, filled with the Holy Spirit, cried
out in a loud voice and said, "Blessed are you among
women, and blessed is the fruit of your womb. And how
does this happen to me, that the mother of my Lord
should come to me? For at the moment the sound of your
greeting reached my ears, the infant in my womb leaped
for joy. Blessed are you who believed that what was spoken to you by the Lord would be fulfilled."

   And Mary said:
   "My soul proclaims the greatness of the Lord;
      my spirit rejoices in God my Savior
      for he has looked upon his lowly servant.
   From this day all generations will call me blessed:
      the Almighty has done great things for me,
      and holy is his Name.
   He has mercy on those who fear him
      in every generation.
   He has shown the strength of his arm,
      and has scattered the proud in their conceit.

He has cast down the mighty from their thrones,
    and has lifted up the lowly.
He has filled the hungry with good things,
    and the rich he has sent away empty.
He has come to the help of his servant Israel
    for he has remembered his promise of mercy,
    the promise he made to our fathers,
        to Abraham and his children for ever."

Mary remained with her about three months and then returned to her home.—The Gospel of the Lord.
℞. **Praise to you, Lord Jesus Christ.**   ➜ No. 15, p. 18

PRAYER OVER THE OFFERINGS   [Longing for God]

May this oblation, our tribute of homage,
rise up to you, O Lord,
and, through the intercession of the most Blessed
    Virgin Mary,
whom you assumed into heaven,
may our hearts, aflame with the fire of love,
constantly long for you.
Through Christ our Lord.
℞. **Amen.** ↓

PREFACE (P 59)   [Assumption—Sign of Hope]

℣. The Lord be with you. ℞. **And with your spirit.**
℣. Lift up your hearts. ℞. **We lift them up to the Lord.**
℣. Let us give thanks to the Lord our God. ℞. **It is right and just.**

It is truly right and just, our duty and our salvation,
always and everywhere to give you thanks,
Lord, holy Father, almighty and eternal God,
through Christ our Lord.

For today the Virgin Mother of God
was assumed into heaven
as the beginning and image
of your Church's coming to perfection

and a sign of sure hope and comfort to your pilgrim
 people;
rightly you would not allow her
to see the corruption of the tomb
since from her own body she marvelously brought forth
your incarnate Son, the Author of all life.

And so, in company with the choirs of Angels,
we praise you, and with joy we proclaim:

➜ No. 23, p. 23

COMMUNION ANT. Lk 1:48-49   [Blessed Is Mary]
**All generations will call me blessed, for he who is
mighty has done great things for me.** ↓

PRAYER AFTER COMMUNION   [Mary's Intercession]
Having received the Sacrament of salvation,
we ask you to grant, O Lord,
that, through the intercession of the Blessed Virgin
 Mary,
whom you assumed into heaven,
we may be brought to the glory of the resurrection.
Through Christ our Lord.
℞. **Amen.**

➜ No. 30, p. 77

Optional Solemn Blessings, p. 97, and Prayers over the People, p. 105

"Strive to enter through the narrow gate."

AUGUST 21

21st SUNDAY IN ORDINARY TIME

ENTRANCE ANT. Cf. Ps 86 (85):1-3   **[Save Us]**

Turn your ear, O Lord, and answer me; save the servant who trusts in you, my God. Have mercy on me, O Lord, for I cry to you all the day long.   → No. 2, p. 10

COLLECT   **[One in Mind and Heart]**

O God, who cause the minds of the faithful
to unite in a single purpose,
grant your people to love what you command
and to desire what you promise,
that, amid the uncertainties of this world,
our hearts may be fixed on that place
where true gladness is found.
Through our Lord Jesus Christ, your Son,
who lives and reigns with you in the unity of the Holy
   Spirit,
one God, for ever and ever.
℟. **Amen.** ↓

FIRST READING Is 66:18-21 [Salvation Offered to All]

> Salvation is offered to all and will embrace all, even the alien, some of whom will receive the sacred duty to minister the Holy Mysteries.

A reading from the Book of the Prophet Isaiah

THUS says the LORD: I know their works and their thoughts, and I come to gather nations of every language; they shall come and see my glory. I will set a sign among them; from them I will send fugitives to the nations: to Tarshish, Put and Lud, Mosoch, Tubal and Javan, to the distant coastlands that have never heard of my fame, or seen my glory; and they shall proclaim my glory among the nations. They shall bring all your brothers and sisters from all the nations as an offering to the LORD, on horses and in chariots, in carts, upon mules and dromedaries, to Jerusalem, my holy mountain, says the LORD, just as the Israelites bring their offering to the house of the LORD in clean vessels. Some of these I will take as priests and Levites, says the LORD.—The word of the Lord. ℟. **Thanks be to God.** ↓

RESPONSORIAL PSALM Ps 117 [God's Kindness]

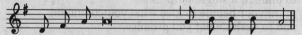

℟. **Go out to all the world and tell the Good News.**
Or: ℟. **Alleluia.**

Praise the LORD, all you nations;
   glorify him, all you peoples!
℟. **Go out to all the world and tell the Good News.**
Or: ℟. **Alleluia.**

For steadfast is his kindness toward us,
   and the fidelity of the LORD endures forever.

℟. **Go out to all the world and tell the Good News.** ↓
Or: ℟. **Alleluia.** ↓

SECOND READING Heb 12:5-7, 11-13   [Discipline]
   **Look beyond trials and tribulations, remain steadfast in
   faith, and rely on the goodness and love of God.**

   A reading from the Letter to the Hebrews

Brothers and sisters, You have forgotten the
exhortation addressed to you as children:"My son,
do not disdain the discipline of the Lord or lose heart
when reproved by him; for whom the Lord loves, he
disciplines; he scourges every son he acknowledges."
Endure your trials as "discipline"; God treats you as
sons. For what "son" is there whom his father does not
discipline? At the time, all discipline seems a cause not
for joy but for pain, yet later it brings the peaceful fruit
of righteousness to those who are trained by it.
   So strengthen your drooping hands and your weak
knees. Make straight paths for your feet, that what is
lame may not be disjointed but healed.—The word of
the Lord. ℟. **Thanks be to God.** ↓

ALLELUIA Jn 14:6   [Through Christ]
℟. **Alleluia, alleluia.**
I am the way, the truth and the life, says the Lord;
no one comes to the Father, except through me.
℟. **Alleluia, alleluia.** ↓

GOSPEL Lk 13:22-30   [Saved Through Repentance]
   **The Kingdom of God will extend to people from all over,
   and some who have rejected the Word will find themselves as outcasts.**

℣. The Lord be with you. ℟. **And with your spirit.**
✚ A reading from the holy Gospel according to Luke.
℟. **Glory to you, O Lord.**

J ESUS passed through towns and villages, teaching as he went and making his way to Jerusalem. Someone asked him, "Lord, will only a few people be saved?" He answered them, "Strive to enter through the narrow gate, for many, I tell you, will attempt to enter but will not be strong enough. After the master of the house has arisen and locked the door, then will you stand outside knocking and saying, 'Lord, open the door for us.' He will say to you in reply, 'I do not know where you are from.' And you will say, 'We ate and drank in your company and you taught in our streets.' Then he will say to you, 'I do not know where you are from. Depart from me, all you evildoers!' And there will be wailing and grinding of teeth when you see Abraham, Isaac, and Jacob and all the prophets in the kingdom of God and you yourselves cast out. And people will come from the east and the west and from the north and the south and will recline at table in the kingdom of God. For behold, some are last who will be first, and some are first who will be last."—The Gospel of the Lord. ℟. **Praise to you, Lord Jesus Christ.**

→ No. 15, p. 18

PRAYER OVER THE OFFERINGS   [Unity and Peace]

O Lord, who gained for yourself a people by adoption through the one sacrifice offered once for all,
bestow graciously on us, we pray,
the gifts of unity and peace in your Church.
Through Christ our Lord.
℟. **Amen.**   → No. 21, p. 22 (Pref. P 29-36)

COMMUNION ANT. Cf. Ps 104 (103):13-15

[Sacred Bread and Wine]

The earth is replete with the fruits of your work, O Lord; you bring forth bread from the earth and wine to cheer the heart. ↓

OR Cf. Jn 6:54   [Eternal Life]

Whoever eats my flesh and drinks my blood has eternal life, says the Lord, and I will raise him up on the last day. ↓

PRAYER AFTER COMMUNION   [Pleasing God]

Complete within us, O Lord, we pray,
the healing work of your mercy
and graciously perfect and sustain us,
so that in all things we may please you.
Through Christ our Lord.
℟. **Amen.**   ➔ No. 30, p. 77

Optional Solemn Blessings, p. 97, and Prayers over the People, p. 105

"Everyone who exalts himself will be humbled. . . ."

AUGUST 28

22nd SUNDAY IN ORDINARY TIME

ENTRANCE ANT. Cf. Ps 86 (85):3, 5   [Call Upon God]
Have mercy on me, O Lord, for I cry to you all the day long. O Lord, you are good and forgiving, full of mercy to all who call to you.   ➔ No. 2, p. 10

COLLECT   **[God's Watchful Care]**

God of might, giver of every good gift,
put into our hearts the love of your name,
so that, by deepening our sense of reverence,
you may nurture in us what is good
and, by your watchful care,
keep safe what you have nurtured.
Through our Lord Jesus Christ, your Son,
who lives and reigns with you in the unity of the Holy
    Spirit,
one God, for ever and ever. ℟. **Amen.** ↓

FIRST READING Sir 3:17-18, 20, 28-29   **[Humility]**
  Know your own limitations. Live within your own capabilities.

A reading from the Book of Sirach

M Y child, conduct your affairs with humility,
    and you will be loved more than a giver of gifts.
Humble yourself the more, the greater you are,
    and you will find favor with God.
What is too sublime for you, seek not,
    into things beyond your strength search not.
The mind of a sage appreciates proverbs,
    and an attentive ear is the wise man's joy.
Water quenches a flaming fire,
    and alms atone for sins.
The word of the Lord. ℟. **Thanks be to God.** ↓

RESPONSORIAL PSALM Ps 68   **[Defender of the Poor]**

  ℟. God, in your good-ness, you have made a home for the poor.

The just rejoice and exult before God;
    they are glad and rejoice.
Sing to God, chant praise to his name;
    whose name is the LORD.

℟. **God, in your goodness, you have made a home for the poor.**

The father of orphans and the defender of widows
  is God in his holy dwelling.
God gives a home to the forsaken;
  he leads forth prisoners to prosperity.

℟. **God, in your goodness, you have made a home for the poor.**

A bountiful rain you showered down, O God, upon
    your inheritance;
  you restored the land when it languished;
your flock settled in it;
  in your goodness, O God, you provided it for the
    needy.

℟. **God, in your goodness, you have made a home for the poor.** ↓

SECOND READING Heb 12:18-19, 22-24a

[The Heavenly Jerusalem]

We are drawn to God because of his love and his gift of faith. We are not driven to him out of fear.

A reading from the Letter to the Hebrews

BROTHERS and sisters: You have not approached that which could be touched and a blazing fire and gloomy darkness and storm and a trumpet blast and a voice speaking words such that those who heard begged that no message be further addressed to them. No, you have approached Mount Zion and the city of the living God, the heavenly Jerusalem, and countless angels in festal gathering, and the assembly of the firstborn enrolled in heaven, and God the judge of all, and the spirits of the just made perfect, and Jesus, the mediator of a new covenant, and the sprinkled blood that speaks more eloquently than that of Abel.—The word of the Lord. ℟. **Thanks be to God.** ↓

ALLELUIA Mt 11:29ab [Christ's Yoke]

℟. **Alleluia, alleluia.**

Take my yoke upon you, says the Lord,

and learn from me, for I am meek and humble of heart.

℟. **Alleluia, alleluia.** ↓

GOSPEL Lk 14:1, 7-14 [The Reward of Humility]

Act in true humility. Do not be frustrated by trying to just create an "image" for yourself.

℣. The Lord be with you. ℟. **And with your spirit.**

✝ A reading from the holy Gospel according to Luke.

℟. **Glory to you, O Lord.**

ON a sabbath Jesus went to dine at the home of one of the leading Pharisees, and the people there were observing him carefully.

He told a parable to those who had been invited, noticing how they were choosing the places of honor at the table. "When you are invited by someone to a wedding banquet, do not recline at table in the place of honor. A more distinguished guest than you may have been invited by him, and the host who invited both of you may approach you and say, 'Give your place to this man,' and then you would proceed with embarrassment to take the lowest place. Rather, when you are invited, go and take the lowest place so that when the host comes to you he may say, 'My friend, move up to a higher position.' Then you will enjoy the esteem of your companions at the table. For everyone who exalts himself will be humbled, but the one who humbles himself will be exalted." Then he said to the host who invited him, "When you hold a lunch or a dinner, do not invite your friends or your brothers or your relatives or your wealthy neighbors, in case they may invite you back and you have repayment. Rather, when you hold

a banquet, invite the poor, the crippled, the lame, the blind; blessed indeed will you be because of their inability to repay you. For you will be repaid at the resurrection of the righteous."—The Gospel of the Lord.
℟. **Praise to you, Lord Jesus Christ.**   → No. 15, p. 18

PRAYER OVER THE OFFERINGS   [Blessing of Salvation]

May this sacred offering, O Lord,
confer on us always the blessing of salvation,
that what it celebrates in mystery
it may accomplish in power.
Through Christ our Lord.
℟. **Amen.**   → No. 21, p. 22 (Pref. P 29-36)

COMMUNION ANT. Ps 31 (30):20   [God's Goodness]

How great is the goodness, Lord, that you keep for those who fear you. ↓

OR Mt 5:9-10   [Blessed the Peacemakers]

Blessed are the peacemakers, for they shall be called children of God. Blessed are they who are persecuted for the sake of righteousness, for theirs is the Kingdom of Heaven. ↓

PRAYER AFTER COMMUNION   [Serving God in Neighbor]

Renewed by this bread from the heavenly table,
we beseech you, Lord,
that, being the food of charity,
it may confirm our hearts
and stir us to serve you in our neighbor.
Through Christ our Lord.
℟. **Amen.**   → No. 30, p. 77

Optional Solemn Blessings, p. 97, and Prayers over the People, p. 105

"Whoever does not carry his own cross and come after me cannot be my disciple."

SEPTEMBER 4

23rd SUNDAY IN ORDINARY TIME

ENTRANCE ANT. Ps 119 (118):137, 124   **[Plea for Mercy]**

You are just, O Lord, and your judgment is right; treat your servant in accord with your merciful love.

→ No. 2, p. 10

COLLECT   **[Christian Freedom]**

O God, by whom we are redeemed and receive adoption,
look graciously upon your beloved sons and daughters,
that those who believe in Christ
may receive true freedom
and an everlasting inheritance.
Through our Lord Jesus Christ, your Son,
who lives and reigns with you in the unity of the Holy
   Spirit,
one God, for ever and ever. ℟. **Amen.** ↓

FIRST READING Wis 9:13-18b   **[God's Counsel]**

   Our human knowledge (science) alone cannot reach the
   heights attained by faith.

A reading from the Book of Wisdom

WHO can know God's counsel,
or who can conceive what the LORD intends?
For the deliberations of mortals are timid,
and unsure are our plans.
For the corruptible body burdens the soul
and the earthen shelter weighs down the mind
that has many concerns.
And scarce do we guess the things on earth,
and what is within our grasp we find with difficulty;
but when things are in heaven, who can search
them out?
Or who ever knew your counsel, except you had
given Wisdom
and sent your holy spirit from on high?
And thus were the paths of those on earth made
straight.
The word of the Lord. ℟. **Thanks be to God.** ↓

RESPONSORIAL PSALM Ps 90   [The Lord Our Refuge]

℟. In ev - ery age, O Lord, you have been our ref-uge.

You turn man back to dust,
saying, "Return, O children of men."
For a thousand years in your sight,
are as yesterday, now that it is past,
or as a watch of the night.

℟. **In every age, O Lord, you have been our refuge.**

You make an end of them in their sleep;
the next morning they are like the changing grass,
which at dawn springs up anew,
but by evening wilts and fades.

℟. **In every age, O Lord, you have been our refuge.**

Teach us to number our days aright,
　that we may gain wisdom of heart.
Return, O LORD! How long?
　Have pity on your servants!

℟. **In every age, O Lord, you have been our refuge.**

Fill us at daybreak with your kindness,
　that we may shout for joy and gladness all our days.
And may the gracious care of the LORD our God be ours;
　prosper the work of our hands for us!
　Prosper the work of our hands!

℟. **In every age, O Lord, you have been our refuge.** ↓

SECOND READING Phlm 9-10, 12-17   [Brothers in Christ]
　Paul has converted a runaway slave, and he asks the slave's master to forgive the man.

A reading from the Letter of Saint Paul to Philemon

I, PAUL, an old man, and now also a prisoner for Christ Jesus, urge you on behalf of my child Onesimus, whose father I have become in my imprisonment; I am sending him, that is, my own heart, back to you. I should have liked to retain him for myself, so that he might serve me on your behalf in my imprisonment for the gospel, but I did not want to do anything without your consent, so that the good you do might not be forced but voluntary. Perhaps this is why he was away from you for a while, that you might have him back forever, no longer as a slave but more than a slave, a brother, beloved especially to me, but even more so to you, as a man and in the Lord. So if you regard me as a partner, welcome him as you would me.—The word of the Lord. ℟. **Thanks be to God.** ↓

ALLELUIA Ps 119:135   [Teach Us]
℟. **Alleluia, alleluia.**
Let your face shine upon your servant;

and teach me your laws.
℟. **Alleluia, alleluia.** ↓

GOSPEL Lk 14:25-33   [Following Christ]

We are all careful to estimate the cost of worldly ventures.
We must also be willing to sacrifice whatever is necessary
to preserve our faith.

℣. The Lord be with you. ℟. **And with your spirit.**
✛ A reading from the holy Gospel according to Luke.
℟. **Glory to you, O Lord.**

GREAT crowds were traveling with Jesus, and he
turned and addressed them, "If anyone comes to me
without hating his father and mother, wife and children,
brothers and sisters, and even his own life, he cannot be
my disciple. Whoever does not carry his own cross and
come after me cannot be my disciple. Which of you wishing to construct a tower does not first sit down and cal-
culate the cost to see if there is enough for its completion? Otherwise, after laying the foundation and finding
himself unable to finish the work the onlookers should
laugh at him and say, 'This one began to build but did not
have the resources to finish.' Or what king marching into
battle would not first sit down and decide whether with
ten thousand troops he can successfully oppose another
king advancing upon him with twenty thousand troops?
But if not, while he is still far away, he will send a delegation to ask for peace terms. In the same way, anyone
of you who does not renounce all his possessions cannot
be my disciple."—The Gospel of the Lord. ℟. **Praise to
you, Lord Jesus Christ.**   ➜ No. 15, p. 18

PRAYER OVER THE OFFERINGS [True Prayer and Peace]

O God, who give us the gift of true prayer and of peace,
graciously grant that, through this offering,
we may do fitting homage to your divine majesty
and, by partaking of the sacred mystery,

we may be faithfully united in mind and heart.
Through Christ our Lord.
℞. **Amen.**   ➜   No. 21, p. 22 (Pref. P 29-36)

COMMUNION ANT. Cf. Ps 42 (41):2-3   [Yearning for God]
**Like the deer that yearns for running streams, so my
soul is yearning for you, my God; my soul is thirsting
for God, the living God.** ↓

OR Jn 8:12   [The Light of Life]
**I am the light of the world, says the Lord; whoever fol-
lows me will not walk in darkness, but will have the
light of life.** ↓

PRAYER AFTER COMMUNION   [Word and Sacrament]
Grant that your faithful, O Lord,
whom you nourish and endow with life
through the food of your Word and heavenly
  Sacrament,
may so benefit from your beloved Son's great gifts
that we may merit an eternal share in his life.
Who lives and reigns for ever and ever.
℞. **Amen.**   ➜   No. 30, p. 77

Optional Solemn Blessings, p. 97, and Prayers over the People, p. 105

"Rejoice with me because I have found my lost sheep."

SEPTEMBER 11

24th SUNDAY IN ORDINARY TIME

ENTRANCE ANT. Cf. Sir 36:18   [God's Peace]

Give peace, O Lord, to those who wait for you, that your prophets be found true. Hear the prayers of your servant, and of your people Israel.   → No. 2, p. 10

COLLECT   [Serving God]

Look upon us, O God,
Creator and ruler of all things,
and, that we may feel the working of your mercy,
grant that we may serve you with all our heart.
Through our Lord Jesus Christ, your Son,
who lives and reigns with you in the unity of the Holy
   Spirit,
one God, for ever and ever. ℟. **Amen.** ↓

FIRST READING Ex 32:7-11, 13-14   [The Plea of Moses]

   Despite the unfaithfulness of his people, the Lord remains
   true to his covenant.

A reading from the Book of Exodus

THE LORD said to Moses, "Go down at once to your people, whom you brought out of the land of Egypt, for they have become depraved. They have soon turned aside from the way I pointed out to them, making for themselves a molten calf and worshiping it, sacrificing to it and crying out, 'This is your God, O Israel, who brought you out of the land of Egypt!' I see how stiff-necked this people is," continued the LORD to Moses. "Let me alone, then, that my wrath may blaze up against them to consume them. Then I will make of you a great nation."

But Moses implored the LORD, his God, saying, "Why, O LORD, should your wrath blaze up against your own people, whom you brought out of the land of Egypt with such great power and with so strong a hand? Remember your servants Abraham, Isaac, and Israel, and how you swore to them by your own self, saying, 'I will make your descendants as numerous as the stars in the sky; and all this land that I promised, I will give your descendants as their perpetual heritage.'" So the LORD relented in the punishment he had threatened to inflict on his people.—The word of the Lord. ℞. **Thanks be to God.** ↓

RESPONSORIAL PSALM Ps 51   [A Contrite Heart]

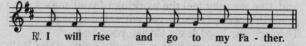

℞. I will rise and go to my Fa - ther.

Have mercy on me, O God, in your goodness;
  in the greatness of your compassion wipe out my
    offense.
Thoroughly wash me from my guilt
  and of my sin cleanse me.

℞. **I will rise and go to my Father.**

A clean heart create for me, O God,
  and a steadfast spirit renew within me.

Cast me not out from your presence,
  and your Holy Spirit take not from me.

℟. **I will rise and go to my Father.**

O Lord, open my lips,
  and my mouth shall proclaim your praise.
My sacrifice, O God, is a contrite spirit;
  a heart contrite and humbled, O God, you will not
  spurn.

℟. **I will rise and go to my Father.** ↓

SECOND READING 1 Tm 1:12-17   [God's Mercy]

**Christ has come to bring salvation to sinners. We have but
to turn to him and we will receive grace in overflowing
measure.**

A reading from the first Letter of Saint Paul to Timothy

BELOVED: I am grateful to him who has strengthened me, Christ Jesus our Lord, because he considered me trustworthy in appointing me to the ministry.
I was once a blasphemer and a persecutor and arrogant, but I have been mercifully treated because I
acted out of ignorance in my unbelief. Indeed, the
grace of our Lord has been abundant, along with the
faith and love that are in Christ Jesus. This saying is
trustworthy and deserves full acceptance: Christ Jesus
came into the world to save sinners. Of these I am the
foremost. But for that reason I was mercifully treated,
so that in me, as the foremost, Christ Jesus might display all his patience as an example for those who
would come to believe in him for everlasting life. To the
king of ages, incorruptible, invisible, the only God,
honor and glory forever and ever. Amen.—The word of
the Lord. ℟. **Thanks be to God.** ↓

ALLELUIA 2 Cor 5:19   [Reconciliation]

℟. **Alleluia, alleluia.**
God was reconciling the world to himself in Christ

and entrusting to us the message of reconciliation.
℟. **Alleluia, alleluia.** ↓

GOSPEL Lk 15:1-32, or 15:1-10   **[The Prodigal Son]**

Repentance, turning away from sin, brings joy to all. Not only the one who repents, but all who love and care.

[If the "Shorter Form" is used, the indented text in brackets is omitted.]

℣. The Lord be with you. ℟. **And with your spirit.**
✛ A reading from the holy Gospel according to Luke.
℟. **Glory to you, O Lord.**

TAX collectors and sinners were all drawing near to listen to Jesus, but the Pharisees and scribes began to complain, saying, "This man welcomes sinners and eats with them." So to them he addressed this parable. "What man among you having a hundred sheep and losing one of them would not leave the ninety-nine in the desert and go after the lost one until he finds it? And when he does find it, he sets it on his shoulders with great joy and, upon his arrival home, he calls together his friends and neighbors and says to them, 'Rejoice with me because I have found my lost sheep.' I tell you, in just the same way there will be more joy in heaven over one sinner who repents than over ninety-nine righteous people who have no need of repentance.

"Or what woman having ten coins and losing one would not light a lamp and sweep the house, searching carefully until she finds it? And when she does find it, she calls together her friends and neighbors and says to them, 'Rejoice with me because I have found the coin that I lost.' In just the same way, I tell you, there will be rejoicing among the angels of God over one sinner who repents."

[Then he said, "A man had two sons, and the younger son said to his father, 'Father, give me the share of your estate that should come to me.' So the father divided the property between them. After a few days, the younger son collected all his belongings and set off to a distant country where he squandered his inheritance on a life of dissipation. When he had freely spent everything, a severe famine struck that country, and he found himself in dire need. So he hired himself out to one of the local citizens who sent him to his farm to tend the swine. And he longed to eat his fill of the pods on which the swine fed, but nobody gave him any. Coming to his senses he thought, 'How many of my father's hired workers have more than enough food to eat, but here am I, dying from hunger. I shall get up and go to my father and I shall say to him, "Father, I have sinned against heaven and against you. I no longer deserve to be called your son; treat me as you would treat one of your hired workers."' So he got up and went back to his father. While he was still a long way off, his father caught sight of him, and was filled with compassion. He ran to his son, embraced him and kissed him. His son said to him, 'Father, I have sinned against heaven and against you; I no longer deserve to be called your son.' But his father ordered his servants, 'Quickly bring the finest robe and put it on him; put a ring on his finger and sandals on his feet. Take the fattened calf and slaughter it. Then let us celebrate with a feast, because this son of mine was dead, and has come to life again; he was lost, and has been found.' Then the celebration began. Now the older son had been out in the field and, on his way back, as he neared the house, he heard the sound of music and dancing. He called one of the servants and asked what this might mean. The servant said to him, 'Your brother has returned and your father has slaughtered the fattened calf because he has him back safe and sound.' He became angry, and when he refused to enter the house, his father came out and pleaded with him. He said to his father in reply, 'Look, all these years I served you and not once did I disobey your orders; yet you never gave me even a young goat to feast on with my friends. But when your son returns, who swallowed up your property with prostitutes, for him you slaughter the fattened calf.' He said to him, 'My son, you are here with me always; everything I have is yours. But now we must celebrate and rejoice, because your brother was dead and has come to life again; he was lost and has been found.' "]

The Gospel of the Lord. ℟. **Praise to you, Lord Jesus Christ.**
→ No. 15, p. 18

PRAYER OVER THE OFFERINGS   [Accept Our Offerings]

Look with favor on our supplications, O Lord,
and in your kindness accept these, your servants' offerings,
that what each has offered to the honor of your name
may serve the salvation of all.
Through Christ our Lord.
℟. **Amen.**   → No. 21, p. 22 (Pref. P 29-36)

COMMUNION ANT. Cf. Ps 36 (35):8   [God's Mercy]
How precious is your mercy, O God! The children of men seek shelter in the shadow of your wings. ↓

OR Cf. 1 Cor 10:16   [Share of Christ]
The chalice of blessing that we bless is a communion in the Blood of Christ; and the bread that we break is a sharing in the Body of the Lord. ↓

PRAYER AFTER COMMUNION   [Heavenly Gift]

May the working of this heavenly gift, O Lord, we pray,
take possession of our minds and bodies,
so that its effects, and not our own desires,
may always prevail in us.
Through Christ our Lord.
℟. **Amen.**   → No. 30, p. 77

Optional Solemn Blessings, p. 97, and Prayers over the People, p. 105

"Prepare a full account of your stewardship. . . ."

SEPTEMBER 18

25th SUNDAY IN ORDINARY TIME

ENTRANCE ANT.   [Salvation of People]

I am the salvation of the people, says the Lord. Should
they cry to me in any distress, I will hear them, and I
will be their Lord for ever.   → No. 2, p. 10

COLLECT   [Attaining Eternal Life]

O God, who founded all the commands of your sacred
    Law
upon love of you and of our neighbor,

grant that, by keeping your precepts,
we may merit to attain eternal life.
Through our Lord Jesus Christ, your Son,
who lives and reigns with you in the unity of the Holy
   Spirit,
one God, for ever and ever. ℞. **Amen.** ↓

FIRST READING Am 8:4-7   **[The Just Are Persecuted]**

**The Lord will punish those who cheat and oppress the
poor. There is no place for the gouger, the con-artist, the
greedy.**

A reading from the Book of the Prophet Amos

HEAR this, you who trample upon the needy
   and destroy the poor of the land!
"When will the new moon be over," you ask,
   "that we may sell our grain,
   and the sabbath, that we may display the wheat?
We will diminish the ephah,
   add to the shekel,
   and fix our scales for cheating!
We will buy the lowly for silver,
   and the poor for a pair of sandals;
   even the refuse of the wheat we will sell!"
The LORD has sworn by the pride of Jacob:
   Never will I forget a thing they have done!
The word of the Lord. ℞. **Thanks be to God.** ↓

RESPONSORIAL PSALM Ps 113   **[Praise the Lord]**

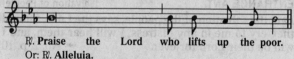

℞. **Praise the Lord who lifts up the poor.**
Or: ℞. **Alleluia.**

Praise, you servants of the LORD,
   praise the name of the LORD.
Blessed be the name of the LORD
   both now and forever.

℟. **Praise the Lord who lifts up the poor.**
Or: ℟. **Alleluia.**

High above all nations is the LORD;
  above the heavens is his glory.
Who is like the LORD, our God, who is enthroned on high
  and looks upon the heavens and the earth below?

℟. **Praise the Lord who lifts up the poor.**
Or: ℟. **Alleluia.**

He raises up the lowly from the dust;
  from the dunghill he lifts up the poor
to seat them with princes,
  with the princes of his own people.

℟. **Praise the Lord who lifts up the poor.** ↓
Or: ℟. **Alleluia.** ↓

SECOND READING 1 Tm 2:1-8   [Christ Our Mediator]

**We should pray with a pure heart and blameless hands.
Our penitential act in the liturgy must be sincere if our
prayers are to meet this demand.**

A reading from the first Letter of Saint Paul to Timothy

BELOVED: First of all, I ask that supplications,
prayers, petitions, and thanksgivings be offered for
everyone, for kings and for all in authority, that we
may lead a quiet and tranquil life in all devotion and
dignity. This is good and pleasing to God our savior,
who wills everyone to be saved and to come to knowledge of the truth.
  For there is one God.
  There is also one mediator between God and men,
  the man Christ Jesus,
  who gave himself as ransom for all.
This was the testimony at the proper time. For this I
was appointed preacher and apostle—I am speaking
the truth, I am not lying—, teacher of the Gentiles in
faith and truth.

It is my wish, then, that in every place the men should pray, lifting up holy hands, without anger or argument.—The word of the Lord. ℟. **Thanks be to God.** ↓

ALLELUIA Cf. 2 Cor 8:9   [Poor But Rich]

℟. **Alleluia, alleluia.**
Though our Lord Jesus Christ was rich, he became poor,
so that by his poverty you might become rich.
℟. **Alleluia, alleluia.** ↓

GOSPEL Lk 16:1-13 or 16:10-13   [The Wily Manager]

If we are shrewd in an evil way, we may be admired by other evil people for our cleverness. But we cannot win in the long run. We cannot divide ourselves between God and worldly gain.

[If the "Shorter Form" is used, the indented text in brackets is omitted.]

℣. The Lord be with you. ℟. **And with your spirit.**
✠ A reading from the holy Gospel according to Luke.
℟. **Glory to you, O Lord.**

JESUS said to his disciples,
["A rich man had a steward who was reported to him for squandering his property. He summoned him and said, 'What is this I hear about you? Prepare a full account of your stewardship, because you can no longer be my steward.' The steward said to himself, 'What shall I do, now that my master is taking the position of steward away from me? I am not strong enough to dig and I am ashamed to beg. I know what I shall do so that, when I am removed from the stewardship, they may welcome me into their homes.' He called in his master's debtors one by one. To the first he said, 'How much do you owe my master?' He replied, 'One hundred measures of olive oil.' He said to him, 'Here is your promissory note. Sit down and quickly write one for fifty.' Then

to another the steward said, 'And you, how much do you owe?' He replied, 'One hundred kors of wheat.' The steward said to him, 'Here is your promissory note; write one for eighty.' And the master commended that dishonest steward for acting prudently.

"For the children of this world are more prudent in dealing with their own generation than are the children of light. I tell you, make friends for yourselves with dishonest wealth, so that when it fails, you will be welcomed into eternal dwellings.]

"The person who is trustworthy in very small matters is also trustworthy in great ones; and the person who is dishonest in very small matters is also dishonest in great ones. If, therefore, you are not trustworthy with dishonest wealth, who will trust you with true wealth? If you are not trustworthy with what belongs to another, who will give you what is yours? No servant can serve two masters. He will either hate one and love the other, or be devoted to one and despise the other. You cannot serve both God and mammon."—The Gospel of the Lord. ℟. **Praise to you, Lord Jesus Christ.**

➡ No. 15, p. 18

PRAYER OVER THE OFFERINGS   [Devotion and Faith]

Receive with favor, O Lord, we pray,
the offerings of your people,
that what they profess with devotion and faith
may be theirs through these heavenly mysteries.
Through Christ our Lord.
℟. **Amen.**   ➡ No. 21, p. 22 (Pref. P 29-36)

COMMUNION ANT. Ps 119 (118):4-5

[Keeping God's Statutes]

You have laid down your precepts to be carefully kept; may my ways be firm in keeping your statutes. ↓

OR Jn 10:14　　　　　　　　　　[The Good Shepherd]

**I am the Good Shepherd, says the Lord; I know my
sheep, and mine know me.** ↓

PRAYER AFTER COMMUNION　　[Possessing Redemption]

Graciously raise up, O Lord,
those you renew with this Sacrament,
that we may come to possess your redemption
both in mystery and in the manner of our life.
Through Christ our Lord.
℟. **Amen.**　　　　　　　　　　→　No. 30, p. 77

Optional Solemn Blessings, p. 97, and Prayers over the People, p. 105

"From the netherworld [he] . . . saw Abraham far off and Lazarus at his side."

SEPTEMBER 25

26th SUNDAY IN ORDINARY TIME

ENTRANCE ANT. Dn 3:31, 29, 30, 43, 42   [God's Mercy]

All that you have done to us, O Lord, you have done with true judgment, for we have sinned against you and not obeyed your commandments. But give glory to your name and deal with us according to the bounty of your mercy.   ➡ No. 2, p. 10

COLLECT   [God's Pardon]

O God, who manifest your almighty power
above all by pardoning and showing mercy,
bestow, we pray, your grace abundantly upon us
and make those hastening to attain your promises
heirs to the treasures of heaven.
Through our Lord Jesus Christ, your Son,
who lives and reigns with you in the unity of the Holy
    Spirit,
one God, for ever and ever. ℟. **Amen.** ↓

FIRST READING Am 6:1a, 4-7   [Lack of Compassion]

There is no security in wealth. Those who seek only pleasure will not find peace and happiness.

A reading from the Book of the Prophet Amos

THUS says the LORD the God of hosts:
Woe to the complacent in Zion!
Lying upon beds of ivory,
    stretched comfortably on their couches,
they eat lambs taken from the flock,
    and calves from the stall!
Improvising to the music of the harp,
    like David, they devise their own accompaniment.
They drink wine from bowls
    and anoint themselves with the best oils;
        yet they are not made ill by the collapse of Joseph!
Therefore, now they shall be the first to go into exile,
    and their wanton revelry shall be done away with.
The word of the Lord. ℟. **Thanks be to God.** ↓

RESPONSORIAL PSALM Ps 146   [Praise the Lord]

℟. **Praise   the   Lord,   my   soul!**
Or: ℟. **Alleluia.**

Blessed is he who keeps faith forever,
    secures justice for the oppressed,
        gives food to the hungry.
The LORD sets captives free.
℟. **Praise the Lord, my soul!**
Or: ℟. **Alleluia.**
The LORD gives sight to the blind;
    the LORD raises up those who were bowed down.
The LORD loves the just;
    the LORD protects strangers.

℟. **Praise the Lord, my soul!**

Or: ℟. **Alleluia.**

The fatherless and the widow he sustains,
   but the way of the wicked he thwarts.
The LORD shall reign forever;
   your God, O Zion, through all generations. Alleluia.

℟. **Praise the Lord, my soul!** ↓

Or: ℟. **Alleluia.** ↓

SECOND READING 1 Tm 6:11-16   [A Virtuous Life]

> **In faith is salvation. Be positive and steadfast; hold firm for the Lord Jesus will come again.**

A reading from the first Letter of Saint Paul to Timothy

BUT you, man of God, pursue righteousness, devotion, faith, love, patience, and gentleness. Compete well for the faith. Lay hold of eternal life, to which you were called when you made the noble confession in the presence of many witnesses. I charge you before God, who gives life to all things, and before Christ Jesus, who gave testimony under Pontius Pilate for the noble confession, to keep the commandment without stain or reproach until the appearance of our Lord Jesus Christ that the blessed and only ruler will make manifest at the proper time, the King of kings and Lord of lords, who alone has immortality, who dwells in unapproachable light, and whom no human being has seen or can see. To him be honor and eternal power. Amen.—The word of the Lord.

℟. **Thanks be to God.** ↓

ALLELUIA Cf. 2 Cor 8:9   [Rich in Christ]

℟. **Alleluia, alleluia.**

Though our Lord Jesus Christ was rich, he became
   poor,
so that by his poverty you might become rich.

℟. **Alleluia, alleluia.** ↓

GOSPEL Lk 16:19-31   [Eternal Consolation]

Even the richest person cannot buy salvation. This comes from being faithful to the Word of God.

℣. The Lord be with you. ℟. **And with your spirit.**

✠ A reading from the holy Gospel according to Luke.

℟. **Glory to you, O Lord.**

JESUS said to the Pharisees: "There was a rich man who dressed in purple garments and fine linen and dined sumptuously each day. And lying at his door was a poor man named Lazarus, covered with sores, who would gladly have eaten his fill of the scraps that fell from the rich man's table. Dogs even used to come and lick his sores. When the poor man died, he was carried away by angels to the bosom of Abraham. The rich man also died and was buried, and from the netherworld, where he was in torment, he raised his eyes and saw Abraham far off and Lazarus at his side. And he cried out, 'Father Abraham, have pity on me. Send Lazarus to dip the tip of his finger in water and cool my tongue, for I am suffering torment in these flames.' Abraham replied, 'My child, remember that you received what was good during your lifetime while Lazarus likewise received what was bad; but now he is comforted here, whereas you are tormented. Moreover, between us and you a great chasm is established to prevent anyone from crossing who might wish to go from our side to yours or from your side to ours.' He said, 'Then I beg you, father, send him to my father's house, for I have five brothers, so that he may warn them, lest they too come to this place of torment.' But Abraham replied, 'They have Moses and the prophets. Let them listen to them.' He said, 'Oh no, father Abraham, but if someone from the dead goes to them, they will repent.' Then Abraham said, 'If they will not listen to Moses and the prophets, neither will they be

persuaded if someone should rise from the dead.' "—
The Gospel of the Lord. ℟. **Praise to you, Lord Jesus Christ.**   ➜ No. 15, p. 18

PRAYER OVER THE OFFERINGS   [Offering as a Blessing]

Grant us, O merciful God,
that this our offering may find acceptance with you
and that through it the wellspring of all blessing
may be laid open before us.
Through Christ our Lord.
℟. **Amen.**   ➜ No. 21, p. 22 (Pref. P 29-36)

COMMUNION ANT. Cf. Ps 119 (118):49-50 [Words of Hope]

Remember your word to your servant, O Lord, by which you have given me hope. This is my comfort when I am brought low. ↓

OR 1 Jn 3:16   [Offering of Self]

By this we came to know the love of God: that Christ laid down his life for us; so we ought to lay down our lives for one another. ↓

PRAYER AFTER COMMUNION   [Coheirs with Christ]

May this heavenly mystery, O Lord,
restore us in mind and body,
that we may be coheirs in glory with Christ,
to whose suffering we are united
whenever we proclaim his Death.
Who lives and reigns for ever and ever.
℟. **Amen.**   ➜ No. 30, p. 77

Optional Solemn Blessings, p. 97, and Prayers over the People, p. 105

"If you have faith the size of a mustard seed, you would say to this mulberry tree, 'Be uprooted....'"

OCTOBER 2

27th SUNDAY IN ORDINARY TIME

ENTRANCE ANT. Cf. Est 4:17   **[Lord of All]**

Within your will, O Lord, all things are established, and there is none that can resist your will. For you have made all things, the heaven and the earth, and all that is held within the circle of heaven; you are the Lord of all.
→ No. 2, p. 10

COLLECT   **[Mercy and Pardon]**

Almighty ever-living God,
who in the abundance of your kindness
surpass the merits and the desires of those who
    entreat you,
pour out your mercy upon us
to pardon what conscience dreads
and to give what prayer does not dare to ask.
Through our Lord Jesus Christ, your Son,
who lives and reigns with you in the unity of the Holy
    Spirit,
one God, for ever and ever. ℟. **Amen.** ↓

540

FIRST READING Hb 1:2-3; 2:2-4   [Reward of the Just]

We might become discouraged. But let us take heart; in his own time the Lord will save us.

A reading from the Book of the Prophet Habakkuk

HOW long, O LORD? I cry for help
but you do not listen!
I cry out to you, "Violence!"
  but you do not intervene.
Why do you let me see ruin;
  why must I look at misery?
Destruction and violence are before me;
  there is strife, and clamorous discord.
Then the LORD answered me and said:
  Write down the vision clearly upon the tablets,
  so that one can read it readily.
For the vision still has its time,
  presses on to fulfillment, and will not disappoint;
if it delays, wait for it,
  it will surely come, it will not be late.
The rash one has no integrity;
  but the just one, because of his faith, shall live.
The word of the Lord. ℟. **Thanks be to God.** ↓

RESPONSORIAL PSALM Ps 95   [Worship the Lord]

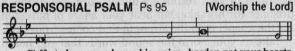

℟. If today you hear his voice, harden not your hearts.

Come, let us sing joyfully to the LORD;
  let us acclaim the Rock of our salvation.
Let us come into his presence with thanksgiving;
  let us joyfully sing psalms to him.
℟. **If today you hear his voice, harden not your hearts.**
Come, let us bow down in worship;
  let us kneel before the LORD who made us.

For he is our God,
    and we are the people he shepherds, the flock he
      guides.

℟. **If today you hear his voice, harden not your
hearts.**

Oh, that today you would hear his voice:
    "Harden not your hearts as at Meribah,
      as in the day of Massah in the desert,
where your fathers tempted me;
    they tested me though they had seen my works."

℟. **If today you hear his voice, harden not your
hearts.** ↓

SECOND READING 2 Tm 1:6-8, 13-14   **[Gift of the Spirit]**

**Be firm in faith despite all adversity. The Holy Spirit dwells
in us—he is the spirit of strength.**

A reading from the second Letter of Saint Paul
to Timothy

B ELOVED: I remind you to stir into flame the gift of
God that you have through the imposition of my
hands. For God did not give us a spirit of cowardice but
rather of power and love and self-control. So do not be
ashamed of your testimony to our Lord, nor of me, a
prisoner for his sake; but bear your share of hardship
for the gospel with the strength that comes from God.

Take as your norm the sound words that you heard
from me, in the faith and love that are in Christ Jesus.
Guard this rich trust with the help of the Holy Spirit
that dwells within us.—The word of the Lord. ℟.
Thanks be to God. ↓

ALLELUIA 1 Pt 1:25   **[Eternal Word]**

℟. **Alleluia, alleluia.**
The word of the Lord remains for ever.
This is the word that has been proclaimed to you.
℟. **Alleluia, alleluia.** ↓

GOSPEL Lk 17:5-10   [The Power of Faith]

> Our faith is to be lived. We cannot be satisfied with mere-
> ly doing no more than our duty. We must strive to excel.

℣. The Lord be with you. ℟. **And with your spirit.**

✚ A reading from the holy Gospel according to Luke.

℟. **Glory to you, O Lord.**

THE apostles said to the Lord, "Increase our faith." The
Lord replied, "If you have faith the size of a mustard
seed, you would say to this mulberry tree, 'Be uprooted
and planted in the sea,' and it would obey you.

"Who among you would say to your servant who has
just come in from plowing or tending sheep in the
field, 'Come here immediately and take your place at
table'? Would he not rather say to him, 'Prepare something for me to eat. Put on your apron and wait on me
while I eat and drink. You may eat and drink when I am
finished'? Is he grateful to that servant because he did
what was commanded? So should it be with you. When
you have done all you have been commanded, say, 'We
are unprofitable servants; we have done what we were
obliged to do.' "—The Gospel of the Lord. ℟. **Praise to
you, Lord Jesus Christ.**   → No. 15, p. 18

PRAYER OVER THE OFFERINGS   [Sanctifying Work]

Accept, O Lord, we pray,
the sacrifices instituted by your commands
and, through the sacred mysteries,
which we celebrate with dutiful service,
graciously complete the sanctifying work
by which you are pleased to redeem us.
Through Christ our Lord.

℟. **Amen.**   → No. 21, p. 22 (Pref. P 29-36)

COMMUNION ANT. Lam 3:25   [Hope in the Lord]

**The Lord is good to those who hope in him, to the soul
that seeks him.** ↓

OR Cf. 1 Cor 10:17   [One Bread, One Body]

Though many, we are one bread, one body, for we all partake of the one Bread and one Chalice. ↓

PRAYER AFTER COMMUNION   [Nourished by Sacrament]

Grant us, almighty God,
that we may be refreshed and nourished
by the Sacrament which we have received,
so as to be transformed into what we consume.
Through Christ our Lord.
℟. **Amen.**   → No. 30, p. 77

Optional Solemn Blessings, p. 97, and Prayers over the People, p. 105

"Stand up and go; your faith has saved you."

OCTOBER 9

28th SUNDAY IN ORDINARY TIME

ENTRANCE ANT. Ps 130 (129):3-4   [A Forgiving God]

If you, O Lord, should mark iniquities, Lord, who could stand? But with you is found forgiveness, O God of Israel.   → No. 2, p. 10

COLLECT   [Good Works]

May your grace, O Lord, we pray,
at all times go before us and follow after
and make us always determined
to carry out good works.
Through our Lord Jesus Christ, your Son,
who lives and reigns with you in the unity of the Holy
    Spirit,
one God, for ever and ever. ℟. **Amen.** ↓

FIRST READING 2 Kgs 5:14-17   [Gratitude to God]

> The healing power of God comes to a man who does not
> belong to the chosen people, and he proclaims his faith in
> the Lord.

A reading from the second Book of Kings

NAAMAN went down and plunged into the Jordan
seven times at the word of Elisha, the man of God.
His flesh became again like the flesh of a little child,
and he was clean of his leprosy.

Naaman returned with his whole retinue to the man of
God. On his arrival he stood before Elisha and said,
"Now I know that there is no God in all the earth, except
in Israel. Please accept a gift from your servant."

Elisha replied, "As the LORD lives whom I serve, I will
not take it"; and despite Naaman's urging, he still
refused. Naaman said: "If you will not accept, please let
me, your servant, have two mule-loads of earth, for I
will no longer offer holocaust or sacrifice to any other
god except to the LORD."—The word of the Lord. ℟.
Thanks be to God. ↓

RESPONSORIAL PSALM Ps 98   [Wondrous Deeds]

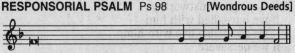

℟. **The Lord has revealed to the na-tions his   sav-ing pow'r.**

Sing to the Lord a new song,
  for he has done wondrous deeds;
his right hand has won victory for him,
  his holy arm.

℟. **The Lord has revealed to the nations his saving power.**

The Lord has made his salvation known:
  in the sight of the nations he has revealed his justice.
He has remembered his kindness and his faithfulness
  toward the house of Israel.

℟. **The Lord has revealed to the nations his saving power.**

All the ends of the earth have seen
  the salvation by our God.
Sing joyfully to the Lord, all you lands:
  break into song; sing praise.

℟. **The Lord has revealed to the nations his saving power.** ↓

SECOND READING 2 Tm 2:8-13   [Life in Christ]

  In Christ we have died. Through Christ we are to rise, and
  with him we shall reign.

A reading from the second Letter of Saint Paul
to Timothy

BELOVED: Remember Jesus Christ, raised from the
dead, a descendant of David: such is my gospel, for
which I am suffering, even to the point of chains, like
a criminal. But the word of God is not chained.
Therefore, I bear with everything for the sake of those
who are chosen, so that they too may obtain the salvation that is in Christ Jesus, together with eternal glory.
This saying is trustworthy:
  If we have died with him
    we shall also live with him;
  if we persevere
    we shall also reign with him.

But if we deny him
  he will deny us.
If we are unfaithful
  he remains faithful,
    for he cannot deny himself.
The word of the Lord. ℞. **Thanks be to God.** ↓

ALLELUIA 1 Thes 5:18   [Give Thanks]

℞. **Alleluia, alleluia.**
In all circumstances, give thanks,
for this is the will of God for you in Christ Jesus.
℞. **Alleluia, alleluia.** ↓

GOSPEL Lk 17:11-19   [Salvation Through Faith]
The healing power of God comes through Christ, even to a man who does not belong to the chosen people. This man's faith prompts his thankfulness.

℣. The Lord be with you. ℞. **And with your spirit.**
✣ A reading from the holy Gospel according to Luke.
℞. **Glory to you, O Lord.**

A S Jesus continued his journey to Jerusalem, he traveled through Samaria and Galilee. As he was entering a village, ten lepers met him. They stood at a distance from him and raised their voices, saying, "Jesus, Master! Have pity on us!" And when he saw them, he said, "Go show yourselves to the priests." As they were going they were cleansed. And one of them, realizing he had been healed, returned, glorifying God in a loud voice; and he fell at the feet of Jesus and thanked him. He was a Samaritan. Jesus said in reply, "Ten were cleansed, were they not? Where are the other nine? Has none but this foreigner returned to give thanks to God?" Then he said to him, "Stand up and go; your faith has saved you."—The Gospel of the Lord. ℞. **Praise to you, Lord Jesus Christ.**

➔ No. 15, p. 18

PRAYER OVER THE OFFERINGS   [Devotedness]

Accept, O Lord, the prayers of your faithful
with the sacrificial offerings,
that, through these acts of devotedness,
we may pass over to the glory of heaven.
Through Christ our Lord.
℟. **Amen.**   ➡ No. 21, p. 22 (Pref. P 29-36)

COMMUNION ANT. Cf. Ps 34 (33):11   [God's Providence]

**The rich suffer want and go hungry, but those who
seek the Lord lack no blessing.** ↓

OR 1 Jn 3:2   [Vision of God]

**When the Lord appears, we shall be like him, for we
shall see him as he is.** ↓

PRAYER AFTER COMMUNION   [Christ's Divine Nature]

We entreat your majesty most humbly, O Lord,
that, as you feed us with the nourishment
which comes from the most holy Body and Blood of
    your Son,
so you may make us sharers of his divine nature.
Who lives and reigns for ever and ever.
℟. **Amen.**   ➡ No. 30, p. 77

Optional Solemn Blessings, p. 97, and Prayers over the People, p. 105

God will "secure the rights of his chosen ones who call out to him day and night."

OCTOBER 16

29th SUNDAY IN ORDINARY TIME

ENTRANCE ANT. Cf. Ps 17 (16):6, 8   **[Refuge in God]**

To you I call; for you will surely heed me, O God; turn your ear to me; hear my words. Guard me as the apple of your eye; in the shadow of your wings protect me.

→ No. 2, p. 10

COLLECT   **[Sincerity of Heart]**

Almighty ever-living God,
grant that we may always conform our will to yours
and serve your majesty in sincerity of heart.
Through our Lord Jesus Christ, your Son,
who lives and reigns with you in the unity of the Holy
   Spirit,
one God, for ever and ever. ℟. **Amen.** ↓

FIRST READING Ex 17:8-13   **[God Our Warrior]**

    Moses prays without ceasing, not losing heart despite physical fatigue.

A reading from the Book of Exodus

IN those days, Amalek came and waged war against Israel. Moses, therefore, said to Joshua, "Pick out certain men, and tomorrow go out and engage Amalek in battle. I will be standing on top of the hill with the staff of God in my hand." So Joshua did as Moses told him: he engaged Amalek in battle after Moses had climbed to the top of the hill with Aaron and Hur. As long as Moses kept his hands raised up, Israel had the better of the fight, but when he let his hands rest, Amalek had the better of the fight. Moses' hands, however, grew tired; so they put a rock in place for him to sit on. Meanwhile Aaron and Hur supported his hands, one on one side and one on the other, so that his hands remained steady till sunset. And Joshua mowed down Amalek and his people with the edge of the sword.— The word of the Lord. ℟. **Thanks be to God.** ↓

RESPONSORIAL PSALM Ps 121   [God Our Guardian]

℟. **Our help is from the Lord, who made heav'n and earth.**

I lift up my eyes toward the mountains;
   whence shall help come to me?
My help is from the LORD,
   who made heaven and earth.

℟. **Our help is from the Lord, who made heaven and earth.**

May he not suffer your foot to slip;
   may he slumber not who guards you:
indeed he neither slumbers nor sleeps,
   the guardian of Israel.

℟. **Our help is from the Lord, who made heaven and earth.**

The LORD is your guardian; the LORD is your shade;
  he is beside you at your right hand.
The sun shall not harm you by day,
  nor the moon by night.

℞. **Our help is from the Lord, who made heaven and
  earth.**

The LORD will guard you from all evil;
  he will guard your life.
The LORD will guard your coming and your going,
  both now and forever.

℞. **Our help is from the Lord, who made heaven and
  earth.** ↓

SECOND READING 2 Tm 3:14—4:2 [Inspiration of Scripture]
  The Bible is the source of teaching, the safe guide for the
  man of God in every good work.

A reading from the second Letter of Saint Paul
to Timothy

BELOVED: Remain faithful to what you have
learned and believed, because you know from
whom you learned it, and that from infancy you have
known the sacred Scriptures, which are capable of
giving you wisdom for salvation through faith in
Christ Jesus. All Scripture is inspired by God and is
useful for teaching, for refutation, for correction, and
for training in righteousness, so that one who belongs
to God may be competent, equipped for every good
work.

  I charge you in the presence of God and of Christ
Jesus, who will judge the living and the dead, and by
his appearing and his kingly power: proclaim the
word; be persistent whether it is convenient or incon-
venient; convince, reprimand, encourage through all
patience and teaching.—The word of the Lord. ℞.
Thanks be to God. ↓

ALLELUIA Heb 4:12   [Living Word]

℟. **Alleluia, alleluia.**

The word of God is living and effective,
discerning reflections and thoughts of the heart.

℟. **Alleluia, alleluia.** ↓

GOSPEL Lk 18:1-8   [The Justice of God]

**Jesus urges us to pray without ceasing and to have faith in
the goodness of God.**

℣. The Lord be with you. ℟. **And with your spirit.**

✣ A reading from the holy Gospel according to Luke.

℟. **Glory to you, O Lord.**

JESUS told his disciples a parable about the necessity for them to pray always without becoming weary.
He said, "There was a judge in a certain town who neither feared God nor respected any human being. And
a widow in that town used to come to him and say,
'Render a just decision for me against my adversary.'
For a long time the judge was unwilling, but eventually he thought, 'While it is true that I neither fear God
nor respect any human being, because this widow
keeps bothering me I shall deliver a just decision for
her lest she finally come and strike me.' " The Lord
said, "Pay attention to what the dishonest judge says.
Will not God then secure the rights of his chosen ones
who call out to him day and night? Will he be slow to
answer them? I tell you, he will see to it that justice is
done for them speedily. But when the Son of Man
comes, will he find faith on earth?"—The Gospel of the
Lord. ℟. **Praise to you, Lord Jesus Christ.**

➜ No. 15, p. 18

PRAYER OVER THE OFFERINGS   [Respect Gifts]

Grant us, Lord, we pray,
a sincere respect for your gifts,

that, through the purifying action of your grace,
we may be cleansed by the very mysteries we serve.
Through Christ our Lord.
℟. **Amen.**   ➙ No. 21, p. 22 (Pref. P 29-36)

COMMUNION ANT. Cf. Ps 33 (32):18-19 [Divine Protection]
**Behold, the eyes of the Lord are on those who fear
him, who hope in his merciful love, to rescue their
souls from death, to keep them alive in famine.** ↓

OR Mk 10:45   [Christ Our Ransom]
**The Son of Man has come to give his life as a ransom
for many.** ↓

PRAYER AFTER COMMUNION   [Eternal Gifts]
Grant, O Lord, we pray,
that, benefiting from participation in heavenly things,
we may be helped by what you give in this present age
and prepared for the gifts that are eternal.
Through Christ our Lord.
℟. **Amen.**   ➙ No. 30, p. 77

Optional Solemn Blessings, p. 97, and Prayers over the People, p. 105

"O God, I thank you that I am not like the rest of humanity."

OCTOBER 23

30th SUNDAY IN ORDINARY TIME

ENTRANCE ANT. Cf. Ps 105 (104):3-4   [Seek the Lord]

Let the hearts that seek the Lord rejoice; turn to the Lord and his strength; constantly seek his face.

➜ No. 2, p. 10

COLLECT   [Increase Virtues]

Almighty ever-living God,
increase our faith, hope and charity,
and make us love what you command,
so that we may merit what you promise.
Through our Lord Jesus Christ, your Son,
who lives and reigns with you in the unity of the Holy
  Spirit,
one God, for ever and ever. ℟. **Amen.** ↓

FIRST READING Sir 35:12-14, 16-18   [A God of Justice]

No one is unimportant in the sight of God. If we serve God
willingly he will receive our prayers.

A reading from the Book of Sirach

THE LORD is a God of justice,
who knows no favorites.
Though not unduly partial toward the weak,
　yet he hears the cry of the oppressed.
The Lord is not deaf to the wail of the orphan,
　nor to the widow when she pours out her complaint.
He who serves God willingly is heard;
　his petition reaches the heavens.
The prayer of the lowly pierces the clouds;
　it does not rest till it reaches its goal,
nor will it withdraw till the Most High responds,
　judges justly and affirms the right,
and the Lord will not delay.
The word of the Lord. ℟. **Thanks be to God.** ↓

RESPONSORIAL PSALM Ps 34   [Refuge in the Lord]

℟. The　Lord　hears　the　cry　of　the poor.

I will bless the LORD at all times;
　his praise shall be ever in my mouth.
Let my soul glory in the LORD;
　the lowly will hear me and be glad.

℟. **The Lord hears the cry of the poor.**

The LORD confronts the evildoers,
　to destroy remembrance of them from the earth.
When the just cry out, the LORD hears them,
　and from all their distress he rescues them.

℟. **The Lord hears the cry of the poor.**

The LORD is close to the brokenhearted;
　and those who are crushed in spirit he saves.
The LORD redeems the lives of his servants;
　no one incurs guilt who takes refuge in him.

℟. **The Lord hears the cry of the poor.** ↓

SECOND READING 2 Tm 4:6-8, 16-18   [A Merited Crown]

Paul sees time running out and his life drawing to a close. He is comforted by faith in God's just judgment.

A reading from the second Letter of Saint Paul
to Timothy

BELOVED: I am already being poured out like a libation, and the time of my departure is at hand. I have competed well; I have finished the race; I have kept the faith. From now on the crown of righteousness awaits me, which the Lord, the just judge, will award to me on that day, and not only to me, but to all who have longed for his appearance.

At my first defense no one appeared on my behalf, but everyone deserted me. May it not be held against them! But the Lord stood by me and gave me strength, so that through me the proclamation might be completed and all the Gentiles might hear it. And I was rescued from the lion's mouth. The Lord will rescue me from every evil threat and will bring me safe to his heavenly kingdom. To him be glory forever and ever. Amen.— The word of the Lord. ℟. **Thanks be to God.** ↓

ALLELUIA 2 Cor 5:19   [Reconciliation in Christ]

℟. **Alleluia, alleluia.**
God was reconciling the world to himself in Christ,
and entrusting to us the message of salvation.
℟. **Alleluia, alleluia.** ↓

GOSPEL Lk 18:9-14   [Humility]

Pride brings no true reward but only projects an "image." In humility true values are seen.

℣. The Lord be with you. ℟. **And with your spirit.**
✣ A reading from the holy Gospel according to Luke.
℟. **Glory to you, O Lord.**

JESUS addressed this parable to those who were convinced of their own righteousness and despised

everyone else. "Two people went up to the temple area to pray; one was a Pharisee and the other was a tax collector. The Pharisee took up his position and spoke this prayer to himself, 'O God, I thank you that I am not like the rest of humanity—greedy, dishonest, adulterous—or even like this tax collector. I fast twice a week, and I pay tithes on my whole income.' But the tax collector stood off at a distance and would not even raise his eyes to heaven but beat his breast and prayed, 'O God, be merciful to me a sinner.' I tell you, the latter went home justified, not the former; for whoever exalts himself will be humbled, and the one who humbles himself will be exalted."—The Gospel of the Lord.
℟. **Praise to you, Lord Jesus Christ.**   ➜ No. 15, p. 18

PRAYER OVER THE OFFERINGS   [Glorifying God]

Look, we pray, O Lord,
on the offerings we make to your majesty,
that whatever is done by us in your service
may be directed above all to your glory.
Through Christ our Lord.
℟. **Amen.**   ➜ No. 21, p. 22 (Pref. P 29-36)

COMMUNION ANT. Cf. Ps 20 (19):6   [Saving Help]

We will ring out our joy at your saving help and exult in the name of our God. ↓

OR Eph 5:2   [Christ's Offering for Us]

Christ loved us and gave himself up for us, as a fragrant offering to God. ↓

PRAYER AFTER COMMUNION   [Celebrate in Signs]

May your Sacraments, O Lord, we pray,
perfect in us what lies within them,
that what we now celebrate in signs
we may one day possess in truth.

Through Christ our Lord.
℟. **Amen.**   ➜ No. 30, p. 77

Optional Solemn Blessings, p. 97, and Prayers over the People, p. 105

"Zacchaeus, come down quickly, for today I must stay at your house."

OCTOBER 30

31st SUNDAY IN ORDINARY TIME

ENTRANCE ANT. Cf. Ps 38 (37):22-23

[Call for God's Help]

**Forsake me not, O Lord, my God; be not far from me!
Make haste and come to my help, O Lord, my strong
salvation!**   ➜ No. 2, p. 10

COLLECT   [Praiseworthy Service]

Almighty and merciful God,
by whose gift your faithful offer you
right and praiseworthy service,
grant, we pray,
that we may hasten without stumbling
to receive the things you have promised.

Through our Lord Jesus Christ, your Son,
who lives and reigns with you in the unity of the Holy
   Spirit,
one God, for ever and ever. ℟. **Amen**. ↓

FIRST READING Wis 11:22—12:2   [Imperishable Spirit]

**The Lord is the most. Everything else is insignificant;
everything else depends on him.**

A reading from the Book of Wisdom

B EFORE the L ORD the whole universe is as a
   grain from a balance
   or a drop of morning dew come down upon the earth.
But you have mercy on all, because you can do all
      things;
   and you overlook people's sins that they may
      repent.
For you love all things that are
   and loathe nothing that you have made;
   for what you hated, you would not have fashioned.
And how could a thing remain, unless you willed it;
   or be preserved, had it not been called forth by you?
But you spare all things, because they are yours,
   O L ORD and lover of souls,
   for your imperishable spirit is in all things!
Therefore you rebuke offenders little by little,
   warn them and remind them of the sins they are
      committing,
   that they may abandon their wickedness and be-
      lieve in you, O L ORD!
The word of the Lord. ℟. **Thanks be to God.** ↓

RESPONSORIAL PSALM Ps 145   [Praise the Lord]

℟. I will praise your name for ev - er my king and my God.

I will extol you, O my God and King,
  and I will bless your name forever and ever.
Every day will I bless you,
  and I will praise your name forever and ever.

℟. **I will praise your name for ever, my king and my God.**

The Lord is gracious and merciful,
  slow to anger and of great kindness.
The Lord is good to all
  and compassionate toward all his works.

℟. **I will praise your name for ever, my king and my God.**

Let all your works give you thanks, O Lord,
  and let your faithful ones bless you.
Let them discourse of the glory of your kingdom
  and speak of your might.

℟. **I will praise your name for ever, my king and my God.**

The Lord is faithful in all his words
  and holy in all his works.
The Lord lifts up all who are falling
  and raises up all who are bowed down.

℟. **I will praise your name for ever, my king and my God.** ↓

SECOND READING 2 Thes 1:11—2:2   [The Day of the Lord]

> The Lord will come again. Do not be misled by false pre-
> dictions; rather strive to be worthy of his call.

A reading from the second Letter of Saint Paul
to the Thessalonians

BROTHERS and sisters: We always pray for you,
that our God may make you worthy of his calling
and powerfully bring to fulfillment every good purpose
and every effort of faith, that the name of our Lord Jesus
may be glorified in you, and you in him, in accord with
the grace of our God and Lord Jesus Christ.

We ask you, brothers and sisters, with regard to the
coming of our Lord Jesus Christ and our assembling

with him, not to be shaken out of your minds suddenly, or to be alarmed either by a "spirit," or by an oral
statement, or by a letter allegedly from us to the effect
that the day of the Lord is at hand.—The word of the
Lord. ℟. **Thanks be to God.** ↓

ALLELUIA Jn 3:16   [Eternal Life]

℟. **Alleluia, alleluia.**
God so loved the world that he gave his only Son,
so that everyone who believes in him might have
    eternal life.
℟. **Alleluia, alleluia.** ↓

GOSPEL Lk 19:1-10   [Salvation]

  No one is so evil, so bad, that he cannot be saved. God's
  love will bring his forgiveness and reunite all who repent.

℣. The Lord be with you. ℟. **And with your spirit.**
✠ A reading from the holy Gospel according to Luke.
℟. **Glory to you, O Lord.**

A T that time, Jesus came to Jericho and intended to
    pass through the town. Now a man there named
Zacchaeus, who was a chief tax collector and also a
wealthy man, was seeking to see who Jesus was; but
he could not see him because of the crowd, for he was
short in stature. So he ran ahead and climbed a
sycamore tree in order to see Jesus, who was about to
pass that way. When he reached the place, Jesus
looked up and said, "Zacchaeus, come down quickly,
for today I must stay at your house." And he came
down quickly and received him with joy. When they all
saw this, they began to grumble, saying, "He has gone
to stay at the house of a sinner." But Zacchaeus stood
there and said to the Lord, "Behold, half of my possessions, Lord, I shall give to the poor, and if I have extorted anything from anyone I shall repay it four times

over." And Jesus said to him, "Today salvation has come to this house because this man too is a descendant of Abraham. For the Son of Man has come to seek and to save what was lost."—The Gospel of the Lord. ℟. **Praise to you, Lord Jesus Christ.**   → No. 15, p. 18

PRAYER OVER THE OFFERINGS   [God's Mercy]

May these sacrificial offerings, O Lord,
become for you a pure oblation,
and for us a holy outpouring of your mercy.
Through Christ our Lord.
℟. **Amen.**   → No. 21, p. 22 (Pref. P 29-36)

COMMUNION ANT. Cf. Ps 16 (15):11   [Joy]

You will show me the path of life, the fullness of joy in your presence, O Lord. ↓

OR Jn 6:58   [Life]

Just as the living Father sent me and I have life because of the Father, so whoever feeds on me shall have life because of me, says the Lord. ↓

PRAYER AFTER COMMUNION   [Renewal]

May the working of your power, O Lord,
increase in us, we pray,
so that, renewed by these heavenly Sacraments,
we may be prepared by your gift
for receiving what they promise.
Through Christ our Lord.
℟. **Amen.**   → No. 30, p. 77

Optional Solemn Blessings, p. 97, and Prayers over the People, p. 105

"Blessed are the clean of heart, for they will see God."

NOVEMBER 1

ALL SAINTS

Solemnity

ENTRANCE ANT. [Honoring All the Saints]

Let us all rejoice in the Lord, as we celebrate the feast day in honor of all the Saints, at whose festival the Angels rejoice and praise the Son of God. → No. 2, p. 10

COLLECT [Reconciliation]

Almighty ever-living God,
by whose gift we venerate in one celebration
the merits of all the Saints,
bestow on us, we pray,
through the prayers of so many intercessors,
an abundance of the reconciliation with you
for which we earnestly long.
Through our Lord Jesus Christ, your Son,
who lives and reigns with you in the unity of the Holy
    Spirit,
one God, for ever and ever. ℟. **Amen.** ↓

FIRST READING Rv 7:2-4, 9-14   [A Huge Crowd of Saints]

> The elect give thanks to God and the Lamb who saved them. The whole court of heaven joins the acclamation of the saints.

A reading from the Book of Revelation

I, JOHN, saw another angel come up from the East, holding the seal of the living God. He cried out in a loud voice to the four angels who were given power to damage the land and the sea, "Do not damage the land or the sea or the trees until we put the seal on the foreheads of the servants of our God." I heard the number of those who had been marked with the seal, one hundred and forty-four thousand marked from every tribe of the children of Israel.

After this I had a vision of a great multitude, which no one could count, from every nation, race, people, and tongue. They stood before the throne and before the Lamb, wearing white robes and holding palm branches in their hands. They cried out in a loud voice:

"Salvation comes from our God, who is seated on the throne,
and from the Lamb."

All the angels stood around the throne and around the elders and the four living creatures. They prostrated themselves before the throne, worshiped God, and exclaimed:

"Amen. Blessing and glory, wisdom and thanksgiving,
honor, power, and might
be to our God forever and ever. Amen."

Then one of the elders spoke up and said to me, "Who are these wearing white robes, and where did they come from?" I said to him, "My lord, you are the one who knows." He said to me, "These are the ones who have survived the time of great distress; they have washed their robes and made them white in the Blood of the Lamb."—The word of the Lord. ℟. **Thanks be to God.** ↓

RESPONSORIAL PSALM Ps 24   [Longing To See God]

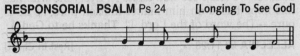

℟. Lord, this is the peo-ple that longs to see your face.

The LORD's are the earth and its fullness;
  the world and those who dwell in it.
For he founded it upon the seas
  and established it upon the rivers.

℟. **Lord, this is the people that longs to see your face.**

Who can ascend the mountain of the LORD?
  or who may stand in his holy place?
One whose hands are sinless, whose heart is clean,
  who desires not what is vain.

℟. **Lord, this is the people that longs to see your face.**

He shall receive a blessing from the LORD,
  a reward from God his savior.
Such is the race that seeks for him,
  that seeks the face of the God of Jacob.

℟. **Lord, this is the people that longs to see your face.** ↓

SECOND READING 1 Jn 3:1-3   [We Shall See God]

God's gift of love has been the gift of His only Son as Savior of the world. It is this gift that has made it possible for us to be called the children of God.

A reading from the first Letter of Saint John

BELOVED: See what love the Father has bestowed on us that we may be called the children of God. Yet so we are. The reason the world does not know us is that it did not know him. Beloved, we are God's chil-

dren now; what we shall be has not yet been revealed.
We do know that when it is revealed we shall be like
him, for we shall see him as he is. Everyone who has
this hope based on him makes himself pure, as he is
pure.—The word of the Lord. ℟. **Thanks be to God.** ↓

ALLELUIA Mt 11:28   [Rest in Christ]

℟. **Alleluia, alleluia.**
Come to me, all you who labor and are burdened,
and I will give you rest, says the Lord.
℟. **Alleluia, alleluia.** ↓

GOSPEL Mt 5:1-12a   [The Beatitudes]

Jesus is meant to be the new Moses proclaiming the new
revelation on a new Mount Sinai. This is the proclamation of
the kingdom, or the "Good News." Blessings are pronounced on those who do not share the values of the world.

℣. The Lord be with you. ℟. **And with your spirit.**
✠ A reading from the holy Gospel according to
Matthew. ℟. **Glory to you, O Lord.**

WHEN Jesus saw the crowds, he went up the
mountain, and after he had sat down, his disciples came to him. He began to teach them, saying:
 "Blessed are the poor in spirit,
  for theirs is the Kingdom of heaven.
Blessed are they who mourn,
 for they will be comforted.
Blessed are the meek,
 for they will inherit the land.
Blessed are they who hunger and thirst for
  righteousness,
 for they will be satisfied.
Blessed are the merciful,
 for they will be shown mercy.
Blessed are the clean of heart,
 for they will see God.

Blessed are the peacemakers,
for they will be called children of God.
Blessed are they who are persecuted for the sake of
righteousness,
for theirs is the Kingdom of heaven.
Blessed are you when they insult you and persecute
you and utter every kind of evil against you falsely
because of me. Rejoice and be glad, for your reward
will be great in heaven."—The Gospel of the Lord. ℟.
Praise to you, Lord Jesus Christ.   ➜ No. 15, p. 18

PRAYER OVER THE OFFERINGS
[The Saints' Concern for Us]

May these offerings we bring in honor of all the Saints
be pleasing to you, O Lord,
and grant that, just as we believe the Saints
to be already assured of immortality,
so we may experience their concern for our salvation.
Through Christ our Lord. ℟. **Amen.** ↓

PREFACE (P 71)   [Saints Give Us Strength and Example]

℣. The Lord be with you. ℟. **And with your spirit.**
℣. Lift up your hearts. ℟. **We lift them up to the Lord.**
℣. Let us give thanks to the Lord our God. ℟. **It is right
and just.**

It is truly right and just, our duty and our salvation,
always and everywhere to give you thanks,
Lord, holy Father, almighty and eternal God.

For today by your gift we celebrate the festival of your
city,
the heavenly Jerusalem, our mother,
where the great array of our brothers and sisters
already gives you eternal praise.

Towards her, we eagerly hasten
as pilgrims advancing by faith,

rejoicing in the glory bestowed upon those exalted
members of the Church
through whom you give us, in our frailty, both strength
and good example.

And so, we glorify you with the multitude of Saints
and Angels,
as with one voice of praise we acclaim: → No. 23, p. 23

COMMUNION ANT. Mt 5:8-10 [The Saints: Children of God]
**Blessed are the clean of heart, for they shall see God.
Blessed are the peacemakers, for they shall be called
children of God. Blessed are they who are persecuted
for the sake of righteousness, for theirs is the
Kingdom of Heaven.** ↓

PRAYER AFTER COMMUNION [Heavenly Homeland]
As we adore you, O God, who alone are holy
and wonderful in all your Saints,
we implore your grace,
so that, coming to perfect holiness in the fullness of
your love,
we may pass from this pilgrim table
to the banquet of our heavenly homeland.
Through Christ our Lord.
℟. **Amen.** → No. 30, p. 77

Optional Solemn Blessings, p. 97, and Prayers over the People, p. 105

"He is not God of the dead, but of the living."

NOVEMBER 6

32nd SUNDAY IN ORDINARY TIME

ENTRANCE ANT. Cf. Ps 88 (87):3   [Answer to Prayer]

Let my prayer come into your presence. Incline your ear to my cry for help, O Lord.   ➜ No. 2, p. 10

COLLECT   [Freedom of Heart]

Almighty and merciful God,
graciously keep from us all adversity,
so that, unhindered in mind and body alike,
we may pursue in freedom of heart
the things that are yours.
Through our Lord Jesus Christ, your Son,
who lives and reigns with you in the unity of the Holy
   Spirit,
one God, for ever and ever.
℟. **Amen.** ↓

FIRST READING 2 Mc 7:1-2, 9-14   [Martyrdom]

    Faith in the resurrection, a belief held even before the coming of Christ, gives strength to endure all trials.

569

A reading from the second Book of Maccabees

IT happened that seven brothers with their mother were arrested and tortured with whips and scourges by the king, to force them to eat pork in violation of God's law. One of the brothers, speaking for the others, said: "What do you expect to achieve by questioning us? We are ready to die rather than transgress the laws of our ancestors."

At the point of death he said: "You accursed fiend, you are depriving us of this present life, but the King of the world will raise us up to live again forever. It is for his laws that we are dying."

After him the third suffered their cruel sport. He put out his tongue at once when told to do so, and bravely held out his hands, as he spoke these noble words: "It was from Heaven that I received these; for the sake of his laws I disdain them; from him I hope to receive them again." Even the king and his attendants marveled at the young man's courage, because he regarded his sufferings as nothing.

After he had died, they tortured and maltreated the fourth brother in the same way. When he was near death, he said, "It is my choice to die at the hands of men with the hope God gives of being raised up by him; but for you, there will be no resurrection to life."—The word of the Lord. ℟. **Thanks be to God.** ↓

RESPONSORIAL PSALM Ps 17   [Joy in the Lord]

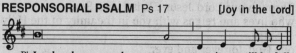

℟. Lord, when your glory ap-pears, my joy will be full.

Hear, O LORD, a just suit;
    attend to my outcry;
    hearken to my prayer from lips without deceit.

℟. **Lord, when your glory appears, my joy will be full.**

My steps have been steadfast in your paths,
  my feet have not faltered.
I call upon you, for you will answer me, O God;
  incline your ear to me; hear my word.
℟. **Lord, when your glory appears, my joy will be
  full.**

Keep me as the apple of your eye,
  hide me in the shadow of your wings.
But I in justice shall behold your face;
  on waking I shall be content in your presence.
℟. **Lord, when your glory appears, my joy will be
  full.** ↓

SECOND READING   2 Thes 2:16—3:5

[Consolation and Strength]

**Have faith, fear no evil, the Lord is constant. He is our
strength.**

A reading from the second Letter of Saint Paul
to the Thessalonians

BROTHERS and sisters: May our Lord Jesus Christ
himself and God our Father, who has loved us and
given us everlasting encouragement and good hope
through his grace, encourage your hearts and
strengthen them in every good deed and word.

Finally, brothers and sisters, pray for us, so that the
word of the Lord may speed forward and be glorified,
as it did among you, and that we may be delivered from
perverse and wicked people, for not all have faith. But
the Lord is faithful; he will strengthen you and guard
you from the evil one. We are confident of you in the
Lord that what we instruct you, you are doing and will
continue to do. May the Lord direct your hearts to the
love of God and to the endurance of Christ.—The word
of the Lord. ℟. **Thanks be to God.** ↓

ALLELUIA Rv 1:5a, 6b   [Firstborn of the Dead]

℟. **Alleluia, alleluia.**

Jesus Christ is the firstborn of the dead;

to him be glory and power, forever and ever.

℟. **Alleluia, alleluia.** ↓

GOSPEL Lk 20:27-38 or 20:27, 34-38   [Alive for God]

Our God is God of the living who reveals the mystery of resurrection.

[If the "Shorter Form" is used, the indented text in brackets is omitted.]

℣. The Lord be with you. ℟. **And with your spirit.**

✜ A reading from the holy Gospel according to Luke.

℟. **Glory to you, O Lord.**

SOME Sadducees, those who deny that there is a resurrection, came forward
[and put this question to Jesus, saying, "Teacher, Moses wrote for us, *If someone's brother dies leaving a wife but no child, his brother must take the wife and raise up descendants for his brother.* Now there were seven brothers; the first married a woman but died childless. Then the second and the third married her, and likewise all the seven died childless. Finally the woman also died. Now at the resurrection whose wife will that woman be? For all seven had been married to her."]
Jesus said to them, "The children of this age marry and remarry; but those who are deemed worthy to attain to the coming age and to the resurrection of the dead neither marry nor are given in marriage. They can no longer die, for they are like angels; and they are the children of God because they are the ones who will rise. That the dead will rise even Moses made known in the passage about the bush, when he called out 'Lord,' the God of Abraham, the God of Isaac, and the God of Jacob; and he is not God of the dead, but of the living, for to him all

are alive." —The Gospel of the Lord. ℞. **Praise to you,
Lord Jesus Christ.**   ➜ No. 15, p. 18

PRAYER OVER THE OFFERINGS   [Celebrating the Passion]

Look with favor, we pray, O Lord,
upon the sacrificial gifts offered here,
that, celebrating in mystery the Passion of your Son,
we may honor it with loving devotion.
Through Christ our Lord.
℞. **Amen.**   ➜ No. 21, p. 22 (Pref. P 29-36)

COMMUNION ANT. Cf. Ps 23 (22):1-2 [The Lord Our Shepherd]

**The Lord is my shepherd; there is nothing I shall
want. Fresh and green are the pastures where he gives
me repose, near restful waters he leads me.** ↓

OR Cf. Lk 24:35   [Jesus in the Eucharist]

**The disciples recognized the Lord Jesus in the break-
ing of bread.** ↓

PRAYER AFTER COMMUNION   [Outpouring of the Spirit]

Nourished by this sacred gift, O Lord,
we give you thanks and beseech your mercy,
that, by the pouring forth of your Spirit,
the grace of integrity may endure
in those your heavenly power has entered.
Through Christ our Lord.
℞. **Amen.**   ➜ No. 30, p. 77

Optional Solemn Blessings, p. 97, and Prayers over the People, p. 105

"The days will come when there will not be left a stone upon another stone that will not be thrown down."

NOVEMBER 13

33rd SUNDAY IN ORDINARY TIME

ENTRANCE ANT. Jer 29:11, 12, 14   **[God Hears Us]**
The Lord said: I think thoughts of peace and not of affliction. You will call upon me, and I will answer you, and I will lead back your captives from every place.

➜ No. 2, p. 10

COLLECT   **[Glad Devotion]**
Grant us, we pray, O Lord our God,
the constant gladness of being devoted to you,
for it is full and lasting happiness
to serve with constancy
the author of all that is good.
Through our Lord Jesus Christ, your Son,
who lives and reigns with you in the unity of the Holy
   Spirit,
one God, for ever and ever.
℞. **Amen.** ↓

FIRST READING Mal 3:19-20a   [The Sun of Justice]

The time of judgment is coming. For the faithful it will be a day of glory.

A reading from the Book of the Prophet Malachi

LO, the day is coming, blazing like an oven,
  when all the proud and all evildoers will be stubble,
and the day that is coming will set them on fire,
    leaving them neither root nor branch,
      says the LORD of hosts.
But for you who fear my name, there will arise
    the sun of justice with its healing rays.
The word of the Lord. ℟. **Thanks be to God.** ↓

RESPONSORIAL PSALM Ps 98   [Rule with Justice]

℟. The Lord comes to   rule the earth with   jus - tice.

Sing praise to the LORD with the harp,
  with the harp and melodious song.
With trumpets and the sound of the horn
  sing joyfully before the King, the LORD.

℟. **The Lord comes to rule the earth with justice.**

Let the sea and what fills it resound,
  the world and those who dwell in it;
let the rivers clap their hands,
  the mountains shout with them for joy.

℟. **The Lord comes to rule the earth with justice.**

Before the LORD, for he comes,
  for he comes to rule the earth;
he will rule the world with justice
  and the peoples with equity.

℟. **The Lord comes to rule the earth with justice.** ↓

SECOND READING 2 Thes 3:7-12   [Models for Imitation]

> We must all work together and cooperate with one anoth-er. No one can sit back and enjoy the fruits of another's labor.

A reading from the second Letter of Saint Paul
to the Thessalonians

BROTHERS and sisters: You know how one must imitate us. For we did not act in a disorderly way among you, nor did we eat food received free from anyone. On the contrary, in toil and drudgery, night and day we worked, so as not to burden any of you. Not that we do not have the right. Rather, we wanted to present ourselves as a model for you, so that you might imitate us. In fact, when we were with you, we instructed you that if anyone was unwilling to work, neither should that one eat. We hear that some are con-ducting themselves among you in a disorderly way, by not keeping busy but minding the business of others. Such people we instruct and urge in the Lord Jesus Christ to work quietly and to eat their own food.—The word of the Lord. ℟. **Thanks be to God.** ↓

ALLELUIA Lk 21:28   [Redemption]

℟. **Alleluia, alleluia.**
Stand erect and raise your heads
because your redemption is at hand.
℟. **Alleluia, alleluia.** ↓

GOSPEL Lk 21:5-19   [Salvation in Christ]

> Nothing in this world will last forever and we can be sure of trials and tribulations. But if we put our trust and hope in Christ, we will find life.

℣. The Lord be with you. ℟. **And with your spirit.**
✚ A reading from the holy Gospel according to Luke.
℟. **Glory to you, O Lord.**

WHILE some people were speaking about how the temple was adorned with costly stones and votive offerings, Jesus said, "All that you see here—the days will come when there will not be left a stone upon another stone that will not be thrown down."

Then they asked him, "Teacher, when will this happen? And what sign will there be when all these things are about to happen?" He answered, "See that you not be deceived, for many will come in my name, saying, 'I am he,' and 'The time has come.' Do not follow them! When you hear of wars and insurrections, do not be terrified; for such things must happen first, but it will not immediately be the end." Then he said to them, "Nation will rise against nation, and kingdom against kingdom. There will be powerful earthquakes, famines, and plagues from place to place; and awesome sights and mighty signs will come from the sky.

"Before all this happens, however, they will seize and persecute you, they will hand you over to the synagogues and to prisons, and they will have you led before kings and governors because of my name. It will lead to your giving testimony. Remember, you are not to prepare your defense beforehand, for I myself shall give you a wisdom in speaking that all your adversaries will be powerless to resist or refute. You will even be handed over by parents, brothers, relatives, and friends, and they will put some of you to death. You will be hated by all because of my name, but not a hair on your head will be destroyed. By your perseverance you will secure your lives."—The Gospel of the Lord. ℟. **Praise to you, Lord Jesus Christ.**

→ No. 15, p. 18

PRAYER OVER THE OFFERINGS   [Everlasting Happiness]

Grant, O Lord, we pray,
that what we offer in the sight of your majesty

may obtain for us the grace of being devoted to you
and gain us the prize of everlasting happiness.
Through Christ our Lord.
℞. **Amen.**   ➜ No. 21, p. 22 (Pref. P 29-36)

COMMUNION ANT. Ps 73 (72):28   [Hope in God]
**To be near God is my happiness, to place my hope in
God the Lord.** ↓

OR Mk 11:23-24   [Believing Prayer]
**Amen, I say to you: Whatever you ask in prayer,
believe that you will receive, and it shall be given to
you, says the Lord.** ↓

PRAYER AFTER COMMUNION   [Growth in Charity]
We have partaken of the gifts of this sacred mystery,
humbly imploring, O Lord,
that what your Son commanded us to do
in memory of him
may bring us growth in charity.
Through Christ our Lord.
℞. **Amen.**   ➜ No. 30, p. 77

Optional Solemn Blessings, p. 97, and Prayers over the People, p. 105

"The Lord will reign for ever."

NOVEMBER 20

Last Sunday in Ordinary Time

OUR LORD JESUS CHRIST, KING OF THE UNIVERSE

Solemnity

ENTRANCE ANT. Rv 5:12; 1:6   [Christ's Glory]

How worthy is the Lamb who was slain, to receive power and divinity, and wisdom and strength and honor. To him belong glory and power for ever and ever. ➜ No. 2, p. 10

COLLECT   [King of the Universe]

Almighty ever-living God,
whose will is to restore all things
in your beloved Son, the King of the universe,
grant, we pray,
that the whole creation, set free from slavery,
may render your majesty service
and ceaselessly proclaim your praise.
Through our Lord Jesus Christ, your Son,

579

who lives and reigns with you in the unity of the Holy
   Spirit,
one God, for ever and ever. ℟. **Amen.** ↓

FIRST READING 2 Sm 5:1-3   [Shepherd My People]
   David is anointed to be king in fulfillment of the promise
   of the Lord.

A reading from the second Book of Samuel

IN those days, all the tribes of Israel came to David in
Hebron and said: "Here we are, your bone and your
flesh. In days past, when Saul was our king, it was you
who led the Israelites out and brought them back. And
the LORD said to you, 'You shall shepherd my people
Israel and shall be commander of Israel.'" When all
the elders of Israel came to David in Hebron, King
David made an agreement with them there before the
LORD, and they anointed him king of Israel.—The word
of the Lord. ℟. **Thanks be to God.** ↓

RESPONSORIAL PSALM Ps 122 [The House of the Lord]

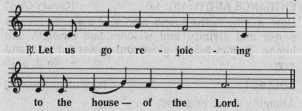

℟. Let us go re - joic - ing
to the house — of the Lord.

I rejoiced because they said to me,
   "We will go up to the house of the LORD."
And now we have set foot
   within your gates, O Jerusalem.

℟. **Let us go rejoicing to the house of the Lord.**

Jerusalem, built as a city
   with compact unity.

To it the tribes go up,
   the tribes of the LORD.

℟. **Let us go rejoicing to the house of the Lord.**

According to the decree for Israel,
   to give thanks to the name of the LORD.
In it are set up judgment seats,
   seats for the house of David.

℟. **Let us go rejoicing to the house of the Lord.** ↓

SECOND READING Col 1:12-20   [Primacy of Christ]

We belong to the Kingdom of God through his Son who has dominion over all creation.

A reading from the Letter of Saint Paul to the Colossians

BROTHERS and sisters: Let us give thanks to the Father, who has made you fit to share in the inheritance of the holy ones in light. He delivered us from the power of darkness and transferred us to the kingdom of his beloved Son, in whom we have redemption, the forgiveness of sins.

He is the image of the invisible God,
   the firstborn of all creation.
For in him were created all things in heaven and on earth,
   the visible and the invisible,
   whether thrones or dominions or principalities or powers;
   all things were created through him and for him.
He is before all things,
   and in him all things hold together.
He is the head of the body, the church.
He is the beginning, the firstborn from the dead,
   that in all things he himself might be preeminent.
For in him all the fullness was pleased to dwell,
   and through him to reconcile all things for him,
   making peace by the blood of his cross

through him, whether those on earth or those in heaven.

The word of the Lord. ℟. **Thanks be to God.** ↓

ALLELUIA Mk 11:9, 10   [Son of David]

℟. **Alleluia, alleluia.**

Blessed is he who comes in the name of the Lord!
Blessed is the kingdom of our father David that is to come!

℟. **Alleluia, alleluia.** ↓

GOSPEL Lk 23:35-43   [The Crucifixion]

The son of David, King of the Jews, the crucified Savior, reigns—he is King of paradise.

℣. The Lord be with you. ℟. **And with your spirit.**

✣ A reading from the holy Gospel according to Luke.

℟. **Glory to you, O Lord.**

THE rulers sneered at Jesus and said, "He saved others, let him save himself if he is the chosen one, the Christ of God." Even the soldiers jeered at him. As they approached to offer him wine they called out, "If you are King of the Jews, save yourself." Above him there was an inscription that read, "This is the King of the Jews."

Now one of the criminals hanging there reviled Jesus, saying, "Are you not the Christ? Save yourself and us." The other, however, rebuking him, said in reply, "Have you no fear of God, for you are subject to the same condemnation? And indeed, we have been condemned justly, for the sentence we received corresponds to our crimes, but this man has done nothing criminal." Then he said, "Jesus, remember me when you come into your kingdom." He replied to him, "Amen, I say to you, today you will be with me in Paradise."—The Gospel of the Lord. ℟. **Praise to you, Lord Jesus Christ.**   → No. 15, p. 18

PRAYER OVER THE OFFERINGS   [Unity and Peace]

As we offer you, O Lord, the sacrifice
by which the human race is reconciled to you,
we humbly pray
that your Son himself may bestow on all nations
the gifts of unity and peace.
Through Christ our Lord.
℟. **Amen.** ↓

PREFACE (P 51)   [Marks of Christ's Kingdom]

℣. The Lord be with you. ℟. **And with your spirit.**
℣. Lift up your hearts. ℟. **We lift them up to the Lord.**
℣. Let us give thanks to the Lord our God. ℟. **It is right and just.**

It is truly right and just, our duty and our salvation,
always and everywhere to give you thanks,
Lord, holy Father, almighty and eternal God.

For you anointed your Only Begotten Son,
our Lord Jesus Christ, with the oil of gladness
as eternal Priest and King of all creation,
so that, by offering himself on the altar of the Cross
as a spotless sacrifice to bring us peace,
he might accomplish the mysteries of human
    redemption
and, making all created things subject to his rule,
he might present to the immensity of your majesty
an eternal and universal kingdom,
a kingdom of truth and life,
a kingdom of holiness and grace,
a kingdom of justice, love and peace.

And so, with Angels and Archangels,
with Thrones and Dominions,
and with all the hosts and Powers of heaven,
we sing the hymn of your glory,
as without end we acclaim: → No. 23, p. 23

COMMUNION ANT. Ps 29 (28):10-11   [Blessing of Peace]

The Lord sits as King for ever. The Lord will bless his people with peace.↓

PRAYER AFTER COMMUNION [Christ's Heavenly Kingdom]

Having received the food of immortality,
we ask, O Lord,
that, glorying in obedience
to the commands of Christ, the King of the universe,
we may live with him eternally in his heavenly
   Kingdom.
Who lives and reigns for ever and ever.
℟. **Amen.**   ➜ No. 30, p. 77

Optional Solemn Blessings, p. 97, and Prayers over the People, p. 105

Saint Joseph

HYMNAL

Praise My Soul, The King of Heaven 1

F. Lyte

John Goss

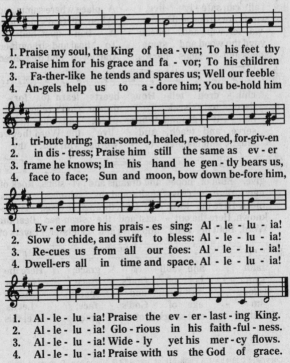

1. Praise my soul, the King of hea - ven; To his feet thy
2. Praise him for his grace and fa - vor; To his children
3.   Fa-ther-like he tends and spares us; Well our feeble
4. An-gels help us to a - dore him; You be-hold him

1.   tri-bute bring; Ran-somed, healed, re-stored, for-giv-en
2.   in dis - tress; Praise him still the same as ev - er
3. frame he knows; In his hand he gen - tly bears us,
4. face to face; Sun and moon, bow down be-fore him,

1.   Ev - er more his prais - es sing: Al - le - lu - ia!
2. Slow to chide, and swift to bless: Al - le - lu - ia!
3. Re-cues us from all our foes: Al - le - lu - ia!
4. Dwell-ers all in time and space. Al - le - lu - ia!

1. Al - le - lu - ia! Praise the ev - er - last - ing King.
2. Al - le - lu - ia! Glo - rious in his faith -ful - ness.
3. Al - le - lu - ia! Wide - ly yet his mer - cy flows.
4. Al - le - lu - ia! Praise with us the God of grace.

2

All Are Welcome

Tune: TWO OAKS 9 6 8 6 8 7 10
with refrain; Marty Haugen, b. 1950

Text: Marty Haugen, b. 1950

1. Let us build   a house where   love can dwell   And
2. Let us build   a house where   proph-ets speak,   And
3. Let us build   a house where   love   is found   In
4. Let us build   a house where   hands will reach   Be -
5. Let us build   a house where   all   are named,   Their

all can safe - ly   live,   A place where saints and
words are strong and   true,   Where all God's chil-dren
wa - ter, wine and   wheat: A ban - quet hall on
yond the wood and   stone   To   heal and strength-en,
songs and vi - sions   heard   And loved and treas-ured,

chil - dren   tell   How   hearts   learn to   for -
dare   to   seek   To   dream   God's reign a -
ho - ly   ground, Where   peace   and jus - tice
serve   and teach,   And   live   the Word they've
taught and claimed   As   words   with - in   the

give.   Built of   hopes and dreams and vi - sions,   Rock of
new.   Here the   cross   shall stand   as   wit - ness   And as
meet.   Here the   love   of God, through Je - sus,   Is re-
known.   Here the   out - cast and   the stran - ger   Bear the
Word.   Built of   tears   and cries and   laugh - ter,   Prayers of

faith   and vault   of   grace;   Here the
sym - bol   of   God's   grace;   Here as
vealed   in   time   and   space;   As we
im - age   of   God's   face;   Let us
faith   and songs   of   grace,   Let this

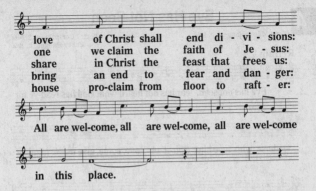

love of Christ shall end di - vi - sions:
one we claim the faith of Je - sus:
share in Christ the feast that frees us:
bring an end to fear and dan - ger:
house pro-claim from floor to raft - er:

All are wel-come, all are wel-come, all are wel-come

in this place.

Praise to the Lord

3

1. Praise to the Lord,
   The almighty, the King of creation;
   O my soul, praise him,
   For he is our health and salvation;
   Hear the great throng,
   Joyous with praises and song,
   Sounding in glad adoration.

2. Praise to the Lord,
   Who doth prosper thy way and defend thee;
   Surely his goodness
   And mercy shall ever attend thee;
   Ponder anew
   What the almighty can do,
   Who with his love doth befriend thee.

3. Praise to the Lord,
   O let all that is in me adore him!
   All that hath breath join
   In our praises now to adore him!
   Let the "Amen"
   Sung by all people again
   Sound as we worship before him. Amen.

4 Eye Has Not Seen

Tune: Marty Haugen, b. 1950

Text: 1 Corinthians 2:9-10;
Marty Haugen, b. 1950

Refrain

Eye has not seen, ear has not heard what God has read-y for those who love him; Spir-it of love, come, give us the mind of Je - sus, teach us the wis-dom of God.

Verses 1-3

1. When pain and sor-row weigh us down, be near to us, O
2. Our lives are but a sin-gle breath, we flow-er and we
3. To those who see with eyes of faith, the Lord is ev - er

Lord, for - give the weak - ness of our faith, and
fade, yet all our days are in your hands, so
near, re - flect-ed in the fac - es of

D.C.

bear us up with-in your peace-ful word.
we re-turn in love what love has made.
all the poor and low-ly of the world.

Verse 4

4. We sing a mys-t'ry from the past in halls where saints have

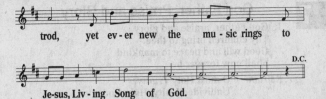

trod,   yet ev - er new   the   mu - sic rings   to

Je-sus, Liv - ing Song of   God.

Praise God from Whom All Blessings Flow 5

1. Praise God, from whom all blessings flow;
   Praise him, all creatures here below;
   Praise him above, ye heav'nly host:
   Praise Father, Son, and Holy Ghost.

2. All people that on earth do dwell,
   Sing to the Lord with cheerful voice;
   Him serve with mirth, his praise forth tell,
   Come ye before him and rejoice.

3. Know that the Lord is God indeed;
   Without our aid he did us make;
   We are his flock, he doth us feed,
   And for his sheep he doth us take.

4. O enter then his gates with praise,
   Approach with joy his courts unto;
   Praise, laud, and bless his name always,
   For it is seemly so to do. Amen.

Faith of Our Fathers 6

1. Faith of our fathers! living still,
   In spite of dungeon, fire, and sword;
   O how our hearts beat high with joy,
   Whene'er we hear that glorious word!

   Refrain: Faith of our fathers holy faith,
              We will be true to thee till death.

2. Faith of our fathers! We will love
   Both friend and foe in all our strife,
   And preach thee too, as love knows how,
   By kindly words and virtuous life.

3. Faith of our fathers! Mary's prayers
   Shall keep our country close to thee;
   And through the truth that comes from God,
   O we shall prosper and be free.

589

7 God Father, Praise and Glory

1. God Father, praise and glory
   Thy children bring to thee.
   Good will and peace to mankind
   Shall now forever be.

Refrain: O most Holy Trinity,
   Undivided Unity; Holy God,
   Mighty God, God immortal be adored.

2. And thou, Lord Coeternal.
   God's sole begotten Son;
   O Jesus, King anointed,
   Who hast redemption won.—*Refrain*

3. O Holy Ghost, Creator.
   Thou gift of God most high;
   Life, love and sacred Unction
   Our weakness thou supply.—*Refrain*

8 Praise the Lord of Heaven

Praise the Lord of Heaven,
Praise Him in the height.
Praise Him all ye angels,
Praise Him stars and light;
Praise Him skies and waters
   which above the skies
When His word commanded,
Mighty did arise,

Praise Him man and maiden,
Princes and all kings,
Praise Him hills and mountains,
All created things;
Heav'n and earth He fashioned
   mighty oceans raised;
This day and forever
His name shall be praised.

9 Holy, Holy, Holy

1. Holy, holy, holy! Lord God almighty.
   Early in the morning our song shall rise to thee:
   Holy, holy, holy! Merciful and mighty,
   God in three persons, blessed Trinity.

2. Holy, holy, holy! Lord God almighty.
   All thy works shall praise thy name in earth and sky
      and sea;
   Holy, holy, holy! Merciful and mighty,
   God in three persons, blessed Trinity.

3. Holy, holy, holy! All thy saints adore thee,
   Praising thee in glory, with thee to ever be;
   Cherubim and Seraphim, falling down before thee,
   Which wert and art and evermore shall be.

Now Thank We All Our God

1. Now thank we all our God,
   With heart and hands and voices,
   Who wondrous things hath done,
   In whom the world rejoices;
   Who from our mother's arms
   Hath blessed us on our way
   With countless gifts of love,
   And still is ours today.

2. All praise and thanks to God,
   The Father now be given,
   The Son, and him who reigns
   With them in highest heaven,
   The one eternal God
   Whom earth and heav'n adore;
   For thus it was, is now,
   And shall be ever more.

The Church's One Foundation

1

The Church's one foundation
Is Jesus Christ her Lord.
She is his new creation,
By water and the Word;
From heav'n he came and sought her,
To be his holy bride;
With his own blood he bought her,
And for her life he died.

2

Elect from ev'ry nation,
Yet one o'er all the earth.
Her charter of salvation,
One Lord, one faith, one birth;
One holy Name she blesses,
Partakes one holy food;
And to one hope she presses,
With ev'ry grace endued.

3

Mid toil and tribulation,
And tumult of her war.
She waits the consummation
Of peace for evermore;
Till with the vision glorious
Her loving eyes are blest,
And the great Church victorious
Shall be the Church at rest.

12 Awake, Awake and Greet the New Morn

Tune: REJOICE, REJOICE, 98988789;
Marty Haugen, b. 1950

Text: Marty Haugen, b. 1950

1. A - wake! a - wake, and greet the new morn, For
2. To us, to all in sor - row and fear, Em -
3. In dark - est night his com - ing shall be, When
4. Re - joice, re - joice, take heart in the night, Though

an - gels her - ald its dawn - ing, Sing out your joy, for
man - u - el comes a - sing - ing, His hum - ble song is
all the world is de - spair - ing, As morn - ing light so
dark the win - ter and cheer - less, The ris - ing sun shall

now* he is born, Be - hold! the Child of our long - ing.
qui - et and near, Yet fills the earth with its ring - ing;
qui - et and free, So warm and gen - tle and car - ing.
crown you with light, Be strong and lov - ing and fear - less;

Come as a ba - by weak and poor, To bring all hearts to -
Mu - sic to heal the bro - ken soul And hymns of lov - ing
Then shall the music break forth in song, The lame shall leap in
Love be our song and love our prayer, And love our end - less

geth - er, He o - pens wide the heav'n - ly door And
kind - ness, The thun - der of his an - thems roll To
won - der, The weak be raised a - bove the strong, And
sto - ry, May God fill ev - 'ry day we share, And

lives now in - side us for ev - er.
shat - ter all ha - tred and blind - ness.
weap - ons be bro - ken a - sun - der.
bring us at last in - to glo - ry.

* During Advent: "soon"

Canticle of the Sun

Tune: Marty Haugen, b. 1950

Text: Marty Haugen, b. 1950

Refrain

The heav-ens are tell-ing the glo-ry of God,

and all cre - a-tion is shout-ing for joy. Come,

dance in the for-est, come, play in the field, and

sing, sing to the glo-ry of the Lord.

Verses

1. Praise for the sun, the bring - er of day, He car - ries the
2. Praise for the wind that blows through the trees, The seas' might-y
3. Praise for the rain that wa - ters our fields, And bless - es our
4. Praise for the fire who gives us his light, The warmth of the
5. Praise for the earth who makes life to grow, The crea-tures you

light of the Lord in his rays; The moon and the stars who
storms ⅞ the gen - tl - est breeze; They blow where they will, they
crops ⅞ so all the earth yields; From death un - to life her
sun ⅞ to bright-en our night; He danc - es with joy, his
made ⅞ to let your life show; The flow-ers and trees that

D.C.

light up the way Un - to your throne.
blow where they please To please the Lord.
mys- 'try re-vealed Springs forth in joy.
help us to know The heart of love.
pres - ence re - vealed To lead us home.

14 We Praise Thee, O God, Our Redeemer

Ps 26:12
Tr. Julia B. Cady

E. Kremser

1. We praise Thee, O God, our Re-deem-er, Cre-a-tor, In grate-ful de-vo-tion our trib-ute we bring; We lay it be-fore Thee, we kneel and a-dore Thee, We bless Thy ho-ly name, glad prais-es we sing.

2. We wor-ship Thee, God of our fa-thers, we bless Thee; Thro' trou-ble and tem-pest our Guide hast Thou been; When per-ils o'er-take us, es-cape Thou wilt make us, And with Thy help, O Lord, our bat-tles we win.

3. With voic-es u-nit-ed our prais-es we of-fer, To Thee, great Je-ho-vah, glad an-thems we raise. Thy strong arm will guide us, our God is be-side us, To Thee, our great Re-deem-er for-ev-er be praise. A-men.

594

Rejoice, the Lord Is King

15

C. Wesley, alt.

J. Darwall, 1770

1. Re - joice, the Lord is King! Your Lord and King a-
2. The Lord, the Sav - ior reigns, The God of truth and
3. His king-dom can - not fail; He rules o'er earth and

1. dore! Let all give thanks and sing, And tri-umph
2. love, When he had purged our stains, He took his
3. heav'n; The King of vic - t'ry hail, all praise to

Refrain

1. ev - er more. Lift up your heart! Lift
2. seat a - bove.
3. Christ be giv'n.

up your voice! Re - joice! a-gain I say re - joice!

We Gather Together

16

(Same Melody as Hymn No. 14)

1. We gather together to ask the Lord's blessing;
   He chastens and hastens his will to make known;
   The wicked oppressing now cease from distressing;
   Sing praises to his name; he forgets not his own.

2. Beside us to guide us, our God with us joining,
   Ordaining, maintaining his kingdom divine;
   So from the beginning the fight we were winning;
   Thou Lord, wast at our side: all glory be thine.

3. We all do extol thee, thou leader triumphant,
   And pray that thou still our defender wilt be.
   Let thy congregation escape tribulation:
   Thy name be ever praised! O Lord, make us free!

17 Come All You People

Tune: Alexander Gondo;
arr. by John L. Bell, b. 1949

Text: Alexander Gondo

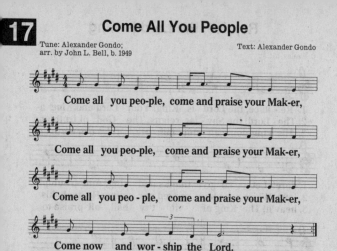

Come all you peo-ple, come and praise your Mak-er,

Come all you peo-ple, come and praise your Mak-er,

Come all you peo - ple, come and praise your Mak-er,

Come now and wor - ship the Lord.

18 To Jesus Christ, Our Sovereign King

1. To Jesus Christ, our sov'reign King,
   Who is the world's Salvation,
   All praise and homage do we bring
   And thanks and adoration.

2. Your reign extend, O King benign,
   To ev'ry land and nation;
   For in your kingdom, Lord divine,
   Alone we find salvation.

3. To you and to your Church, great King,
   We pledge our heart's oblation;
   Until before your throne we sing
   In endless jubilation.

   Refrain:
   Christ Jesus, Victor! Christ Jesus, Ruler!
   Christ Jesus, Lord and Redeemer!

596

Crown Him with Many Crowns

1. Crown him with many crowns,
   The Lamb upon his throne;
   Hark how the heav'nly anthem drowns
   All music but its own;

   Awake my soul, and sing
   Of him who died for thee,
   And hail him as thy matchless King
   Through all eternity.

2. Crown him of lords the Lord,
   Who over all doth reign,
   Who once on earth, the incarnate Word,
   For ransomed sinners slain.

   Now lives in realms of light,
   Where saints with angels sing
   Their songs before him day and night,
   Their God, Redeemer, King.

O Perfect Love

1. O perfect Love, all human thought transcending.
   Lowly we kneel in prayer before thy throne,
   That theirs may be the love that knows no ending,
   Whom thou for evermore dost join in one.

2. O perfect Life, be thou their full assurance
   Of tender charity and steadfast faith,
   Of patient hope, and quiet, brave endurance,
   With child-like trust that fears not pain nor death.

On Jordan's Bank

1. On Jordan's bank the Baptist's cry
   Announces that the Lord is nigh,
   Awake and hearken, for he brings
   Glad tidings of the King of Kings.

2. Then cleansed be ev'ry breast from sin;
   Make straight the way of God within,
   Oh, let us all our hearts prepare
   For Christ to come and enter there.

22 Gather Us In

Tune: GATHER US IN, Irreg.,
Marty Haugen, b. 1950

Text: Marty Haugen, b. 1950

1. Here in this place new light is stream-ing,
2. We are the young—our lives are a mys-t'ry,
3. Here we will take the wine and the wa - ter,
4. Not in the dark of build-ings con - fin -ing,

Now is the dark - ness van-ished a - way,
We are the old— who yearn for your face,
Here we will take the bread of new birth,
Not in some heav - en, light-years a - way, But

See in this space our fears and our dream-ings,
We have been sung through-out all of his - t'ry,
Here you shall call your sons and your daugh-ters,
here in this place the new light is shin-ing,

Brought here to you in the light of this day,
Called to be light to the whole hu-man race.
Call us a - new to be salt for the earth.
Now is the King-dom, now is the day.

Gath - er us in— the lost and for - sak - en,
Gath - er us in— the rich and the haugh-ty,
Give us to drink the wine of com - pas-sion,
Gath - er us in and hold us for ev - er,

Gath-er us in— the blind and the lame;
Gath-er us in— the proud and the strong;
Give us to eat the bread that is you;
Gath-er us in and make us your own;

Call to us now, and we shall a-wak-en,
Give us a heart so meek and so low-ly,
Nour-ish us well, and teach us to fash-ion
Gath-er us in— all peo-ples to-geth-er,

We shall a-rise at the sound of our name.
Give us the cour-age to en-ter the song.
Lives that are ho-ly and hearts that are true.
Fire of love in our flesh and our bone.

Confitemini Domino / Come and Fill

Tune: Jacques Berthier, 1923-1994

23

Text: Psalm 137,
Give thanks to the Lord for he is good;
Taizé Community, 1982

Ostinato Refrain

Con - fi - te - mi - ni   Do - mi - no
Come and fill our hearts   with your peace.

quo - ni - am   bo - nus. Con - fi - te - mi - ni
You a - lone, O Lord, are   ho - ly. Come and fill our hearts

Do - mi - no,   Al - le - lu   -   ia!
with your peace,   Al - le - lu   -   ia!

24 ## O Come, O Come, Emmanuel

John M. Neal, Tr.   Melody adapted by T. Helmore

O come, O come, Emmanuel,
And ransom captive Israel,
That mourns in lowly exile here,
Until the Son of God appear.

Refrain: Rejoice! Rejoice! O Israel,
              To thee shall come Emmanuel.

25 ## Come, Thou Long Expected Jesus

1. Come, thou long expected Jesus,
   Born to set thy people free;
   From our sins and fears release us,
   Let us find our rest in thee.

2. Israel's strength and consolation,
   Hope of all the earth thou art;
   Dear desire of every nation,
   Joy of every longing heart.

3. Born thy people to deliver,
   Born a child and yet a king.
   Born to reign in us for ever,
   Now thy gracious kingdom bring.

26 ## O Come Little Children

O come little children, O come one and all
Draw near to the crib here in Bethlehem's stall
And see what a bright ray of heaven's delight,
Our Father has sent on this thrice holy night.

He lies there, O children, on hay and straw,
Dear Mary and Joseph regard HIm with awe,
The shepherds, adoring, how humbly in pray'r
Angelical choirs with song rend the air.

O children bend low and adore Him today,
O lift up your hands like the shepherds, and pray
Sing joyfully children, with hearts full of love
In jubilant song join the angels above.

O Come, All Ye Faithful

1. O come, all ye faithful, joyful and triumphant,
   O come ye, O come ye to Bethlehem;
   Come and behold Him born, the King of angels.

   Refrain:
   O come, let us adore Him,
   O come, let us adore Him,
   O come, let us adore Him, Christ the Lord.

2. Sing choirs of angels, Sing in exultation.
   Sing all ye citizens of Heav'n above;
   Glory to God, Glory to the highest.—*Refrain*

3. Yea, Lord, we greet thee, born this happy morning,
   Jesus to thee be all glory giv'n;
   Word of the Father, now in flesh appearing.—*Refrain*

The First Noel

28

1. The first Noel the angel did say,
   Was to certain poor shepherds in fields as they lay;
   In fields where they lay keeping their sheep
   On a cold winter's night that was so deep.

   Refrain:
   Noel, Noel, Noel, Noel,
   Born is the King of Israel.

2. They looked up and saw a star,
   Shining in the east, beyond them far,
   And to the earth it gave great light,
   And so it continued both day and night.—*Refrain*

3. This star drew nigh to the northwest,
   O'er Bethlehem it took its rest,
   And there it did stop and stay,
   Right over the place where Jesus lay.—*Refrain*

4. Then entered in those wise men three,
   Full reverently upon their knee,
   And offered there, in his presence,
   Their gold and myrrh and frankincense.—*Refrain*

A Child Is Born in Bethlehem
Three Magi Kings

Carlton

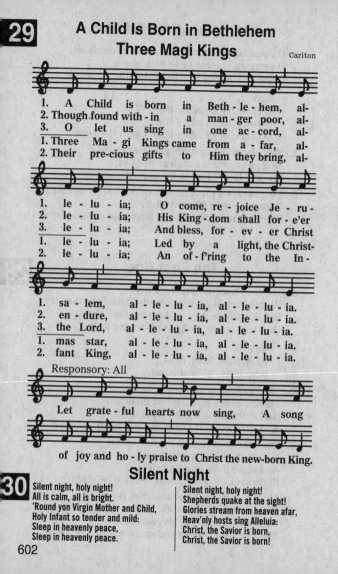

1. A Child is born in Beth-le-hem, al-
2. Though found with-in a man-ger poor, al-
3. O let us sing in one ac-cord, al-
1. Three Ma-gi Kings came from a-far, al-
2. Their pre-cious gifts to Him they bring, al-

1. le-lu-ia; O come, re-joice Je-ru-
2. le-lu-ia; His King-dom shall for-e'er
3. le-lu-ia; And bless, for-ev-er Christ
1. le-lu-ia; Led by a light, the Christ-
2. le-lu-ia; An of-f'ring to the In-

1. sa-lem, al-le-lu-ia, al-le-lu-ia.
2. en-dure, al-le-lu-ia, al-le-lu-ia.
3. the Lord, al-le-lu-ia, al-le-lu-ia.
1. mas star, al-le-lu-ia, al-le-lu-ia.
2. fant King, al-le-lu-ia, al-le-lu-ia.

Responsory: All

Let grate-ful hearts now sing, A song

of joy and ho-ly praise to Christ the new-born King.

Silent Night

Silent night, holy night!
All is calm, all is bright.
'Round yon Virgin Mother and Child,
Holy Infant so tender and mild:
Sleep in heavenly peace,
Sleep in heavenly peace.

Silent night, holy night!
Shepherds quake at the sight!
Glories stream from heaven afar,
Heav'nly hosts sing Alleluia:
Christ, the Savior is born,
Christ, the Savior is born!

3. Silent night, holy night!
   Son of God, love's pure light.
   Radiant beams from thy holy face,
   With the dawn of redeeming grace,
   Jesus, Lord, at thy birth,
   Jesus, Lord, at thy birth.

Hark! The Herald Angels Sing

31

1. Hark! The herald angels sing.
   "Glory to the new-born King.
   Peace on earth, and mercy mild
   God and sinners reconciled."
   Joyful all ye nations rise,
   Join the triumph of the skies.
   With th' angelic host proclaim,
   "Christ is born in Bethlehem."

   Refrain:
   Hark! The herald angels sing,
   "Glory to the new-born King."

2. Christ, by highest heaven adored,
   Christ, the everlasting Lord.
   Late in time behold Him come,
   Off-spring of a virgin's womb.
   Veiled in flesh, the God-head see;
   Hail th' incarnate Deity!
   Pleased as Man with men to appear,
   Jesus, our Immanuel here!—*Refrain*

O Sing a Joyous Carol

32

1. O sing a joyous carol
   Unto the Holy Child,
   And praise with gladsome
       voices
   His mother undefiled.
   Our gladsome voices greeting
   Shall hail our Infant King;
   And our sweet Lady listens
   When joyful voices sing.

2. Who is there meekly lying
   In yonder stable poor?
   Dear children, it is Jesus;
   He bids you now adore.
   Who is there kneeling by him
   In virgin beauty fair?
   It is our Mother Mary,
   She bids you all draw near.

33 Good Christian Men Rejoice

Tr. John Mason Neale

1. Good Chris - tian men, re - joice ——— With
2. Good Chris - tian men, re - joice ——— With
3. Good Chris - tian men, re - joice ——— With

1. heart and soul and voice; ——— Give ye heed to
2. heart and soul and voice; ——— Now ye hear of
3. heart and soul and voice; ——— Now ye need not

1. what we say: Je - sus Christ is born to - day!
2. end-less bliss: Je - sus Christ was born for this!
3. fear the grave: Je - sus Christ was born to save!

1. Ox and ass be - fore him bow, And he is
2. He has oped the heav - n'ly door, And man is
3. Calls you one and calls you all To gain his

1. in the man - ger now. Christ is born
2. bless - ed ev - er - more. Christ was born
3. Ev - er - last - ing hall. Christ was born

1. to - day! ——— Christ is born to - day!
2. for this! ——— Christ was born for this!
3. to save! ——— Christ was born to save!

604

Angels We Have Heard on High

1. Angels we have heard on high,
   Sweetly singing o'er the plains,
   And the mountains in reply
   Echoing their joyous strains.

   Refrain: Gloria in excelsis Deo. (Repeat)

2. Shepherds, why this jubilee,
   Why your rapturous song prolong?
   What the gladsome tidings be
   Which inspire your heav'nly song?—*Refrain*

3. Come to Bethlehem and see
   Him whose birth the angels sing;
   Come, adore on bended knee
   Christ the Lord, the new-born King.—*Refrain*

Away in a Manger

1. Away in a manger, no crib for his bed,
   The little Lord Jesus laid down his sweet head.
   The stars in the bright sky looked down where he lay,
   The little Lord Jesus asleep on the hay.

2. The cattle are lowing, the baby awakes,
   But little Lord Jesus no crying he makes.
   I love thee, Lord Jesus! Look down from the sky,
   And stay by my side until morning is nigh.

3. Be near me Lord Jesus, I ask thee to stay
   Close by me forever, and love me I pray.
   Bless all the dear children in thy tender care,
   And fit us for heaven to live with thee there.

O Little Town of Bethlehem

O little town of Bethlehem,
How still we see thee lie!
Above the deep and dreamless sleep
The silent stars go by;
Yet in the dark streets shineth
The everlasting Light;
The hopes and fears of all the years
Are met in thee tonight.

For Christ is born of Mary,
And gathered all above,
While mortals sleep, the angels keep
Their watch of wondering love.
O morning stars, together
Proclaim the holy birth!
And praising sing to God the King
And peace to men on earth.

O holy Child of Bethlehem!
Descend on us we pray;
Cast out our sin, and enter in,
Be born in us today.
We hear the Christmas angels,
The great glad tidings tell;
O come to us, abide with us,
Our Lord Emmanuel.

37 What Child Is This?

What child is this, who laid to rest,
On Mary's lap is sleeping?
Whom angels greet with anthems sweet,
While shepherds watch are keeping?

Refrain:
This, this is Christ the King,
Whom shepherds guard and angels sing;
Haste, haste to bring him laud,
The Babe, the Son of Mary.

Why lies he in such mean estate
Where ox and ass are feeding?
Good Christian fear, for sinners here
The silent Word is pleading.—*Refrain*

So bring him incense, gold, and myrrh,
Come peasant, king to own him,
The King of kings salvation brings,
Let loving hearts enthrone him.—*Refrain*

We Three Kings

1. We three kings of Orient are
   Bearing gifts we traverse afar,
   Field and fountain, moor and mountain,
   Following yonder star.

   Refrain:
   O Star of wonder, Star of night,
   Star with royal beauty bright,
   Westward leading, still proceeding,
   Guide us to thy perfect light.

2. Born a king on Bethlehem's plain,
   Gold I bring to crown Him again,
   King forever, ceasing never,
   Over us all to reign.—*Refrain*

3. Frankincense to offer have I
   Incense owns a Deity high,
   Prayer and praising, all men raising,
   Worship Him, God most High.—*Refrain*

4. Myrrh is mine, its bitter perfume
   Breathes a life of gathering gloom:
   Sorrowing, sighing, bleeding, dying,
   Sealed in the stone-cold tomb.—*Refrain*

5. Glorious now behold Him arise,
   King and God and Sacrifice,
   Alleluia, Alleluia,
   Earth to the heavens replies.—*Refrain*

Holy God, We Praise Thy Name

1. Holy God, we praise Thy Name!
   Lord of all, we bow before Thee!
   All on earth Thy sceptre claim,
   All in heaven above adore Thee.
   Infinite Thy vast domain,
   Everlasting is Thy reign. *Repeat last two lines*

2. Hark! the loud celestial hymn,
   Angel choirs above are raising;
   Cherubim and seraphim,
   In unceasing chorus praising,
   Fill the heavens with sweet accord;
   Holy, holy, holy Lord! *Repeat last two lines*

Lord, Who throughout These 40 Days

1. Lord, who throughout these forty days
   For us did fast and pray,
   Teach us with you to mourn our sins,
   And close by you to stay.

2. And through these days of penitence,
   And through your Passiontide,
   Yea, evermore, in life and death,
   Jesus! with us abide.

3. Abide with us, that so, this life
   Of suff'ring over past,
   An Easter of unending joy
   We may attain at last. Amen.

When I Behold the Wondrous Cross

1. When I____ be - hold the won-drous cross
2. For - bid__ it, Lord, that I should boast,
3. See from__ his head, his hands, his feet,
4. Were all____ the realms of na - ture mine,

1. On which the prince of glo - ry died,_
2. Save in the death of Christ, my God;_
3. What grief and love flow min - gled down;_
4. It would be off - 'ring far__ too small;_

1. My rich - est gain I count_ but loss,
2. The vain things that at - tract__ me most,
3. Did e'er such love that sor - row meet,
4. Love so a - maz - ing, so____ di - vine,

1. And pour con - tempt on all___ my pride.
2. I sac - ri - fice them to__ his blood.
3. Or thorns com - pose so rich__ a crown?
4. De - mands my soul, my life,__ my all.

Jesus, Remember Me

Tune: Jacques Berthier, 1923-1994

Text: Luke 23:42
Taizé Community, 1981

Ostinato Refrain

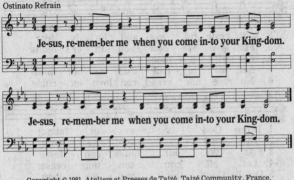

Je-sus, re-mem-ber me when you come in-to your King-dom.

Je-sus, re-mem-ber me when you come in-to your King-dom.

O Sacred Head Surrounded

1. O sacred Head surrounded
   By crown of piercing thorn!
   O bleeding Head, so wounded,
   Reviled, and put to scorn!
   Death's pallid hue comes ov'r you,
   The glow of life decays,
   Yet angel hosts adore you,
   And tremble as they gaze.

2. I see your strength and vigor
   All fading in the strife,
   And death with cruel rigor,
   Bereaving you of life.
   O agony and dying!
   O love to sinners free!
   Jesus, all grace supplying,
   O turn your face on me.

Where Charity and Love Prevail

1. Where char - i - ty and love pre - vail
2. With grate - ful joy and ho - ly fear
3. For - give we now each oth - er's faults
4. Let strife a - mong us be un - known,
5. Let us re - call that in our midst
6. No race nor creed can love ex - clude

1. There God is ev - er found;
2. His char - i - ty we learn;
3. As we our faults con - fess;
4. Let all con - ten - tion cease;
5. Dwells God's be - got - ten Son;
6. If hon - ored be God's Name;

1. Brought here to - geth - er by Christ's love
2. Let us with heart and mind and soul
3. And let us love each oth - er well
4. Be his the glo - ry that we seek,
5. As mem - bers of his Bod - y joined
6. Our broth - er - hood em - brac - es all

1. By love are we thus bound.
2. Now love him in re - turn.
3. In Chris - tian ho - li - ness.
4. Be ours his ho - ly peace.
5. We are in him made one.
6. Whose Fa - ther is the same.

610

O Faithful Cross

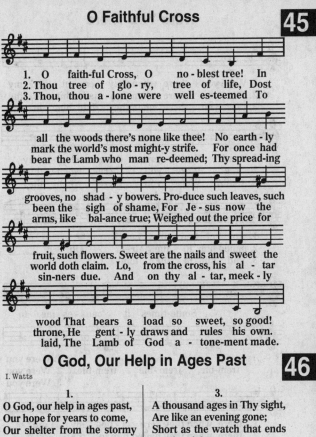

1. O faith-ful Cross, O no - blest tree! In
2. Thou tree of glo - ry, tree of life, Dost
3. Thou, thou a - lone were well es-teemed To

all the woods there's none like thee! No earth - ly
mark the world's most might-y strife. For once had
bear the Lamb who man re-deemed; Thy spread-ing

grooves, no shad - y bowers. Pro-duce such leaves, such
been the sigh of shame, For Je - sus now the
arms, like bal-ance true; Weighed out the price for

fruit, such flowers. Sweet are the nails and sweet the
world doth claim. Lo, from the cross, his al - tar
sin-ners due. And on thy al - tar, meek - ly

wood That bears a load so sweet, so good!
throne, He gent - ly draws and rules his own.
laid, The Lamb of God a - tone-ment made.

O God, Our Help in Ages Past

I. Watts

1.

O God, our help in ages past,
Our hope for years to come,
Our shelter from the stormy blast,
And our eternal home.

2.

Under the shadow of Thy throne,
Thy saints have dwelt secure.
Sufficient is Thine arm alone,
And our defense is sure.

3.

A thousand ages in Thy sight,
Are like an evening gone;
Short as the watch that ends the night,
Before the rising sun.

4.

O God, our help in ages past,
Our hope for years to come,
Be Thou our guide while troubles last,
And our eternal home.

Were You There

1. Were you there when they cru - ci - fied my
2. Were you there when they nailed him to the
3. Were you there when they laid him in the

1. Lord? Were you there when they
2. tree? Were you there when they
3. tomb? Were you there when they

1. cru - ci - fied my Lord?
2. nailed him to the tree?
3. laid him in the tomb? } Oh_____

Some-times it caus - es me to

trem-ble, trem - ble trem-ble. {
1. Were you
2. Were you
3. Were you

1. there when they cru - ci - fied my Lord?
2. there when they nailed him to the tree?
3. there when they laid him in the tomb?

612

At the Cross Her Station Keeping

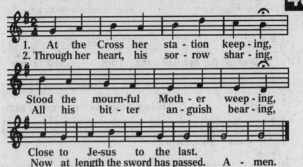

1. At the Cross her sta-tion keep-ing,
2. Through her heart, his sor-row shar-ing,

Stood the mourn-ful Moth-er weep-ing,
All his bit-ter an-guish bear-ing,

Close to Je-sus to the last.
Now at length the sword has passed. A - men.

3. Oh, how sad and sore distressed
Was that Mother highly blessed
Of the sole begotten One!

4. Christ above in torment hangs,
She beneath beholds the pangs
Of her dying, glorious Son.

5. Is there one who would not weep
'Whelmed in miseries so deep
Christ's dear Mother to behold?

6. Can the human heart refrain
From partaking in her pain,
In that mother's pain untold?

7. Bruised, derided, cursed, defiled,
She beheld her tender Child,
All with bloody scourges rent.

8. For the sins of His own nation
Saw Him hang in desolation
Till His spirit forth He sent.

9. O sweet Mother! fount of love,
Touch my spirit from above,
Make my heart with yours accord.

10. Make me feel as you have felt.
Make my soul to glow and melt
With the love of Christ, my Lord.

11. Holy Mother, pierce me through,
In my heart each wound renew
Of my Savior crucified.

12. Let me share with you His pain,
Who for all our sins was slain,
Who for me in torments died.

13. Let me mingle tears with you
Mourning Him Who mourned for me,
All the days that I may live.

14. By the Cross with you to stay,
There with you to weep and pray,
Is all I ask of you to give.

15. Virgin of all virgins blest!
Listen to my fond request.
Let me share your grief divine.

16. Let me, to my latest breath
In my body bear the death
Of that dying Son of yours.

17. Wounded with His every wound,
Steep my soul till it has swooned
In His very blood away.

18. Be to me, O Virgin, nigh,
Lest in flames I burn and die,
In His awful judgment day.

19. Christ, when You shall call me hence
Be Your Mother my defense.
Be Your Cross my victory.

20. While my body here decays,
May my soul Your goodness praise
Safe in heaven eternally.
Amen. Alleluia.

49   Now We Remain

Tune: David Haas, b. 1957

Text: Corinthians, 1 John, 2 Timothy;
David Haas, b. 1957

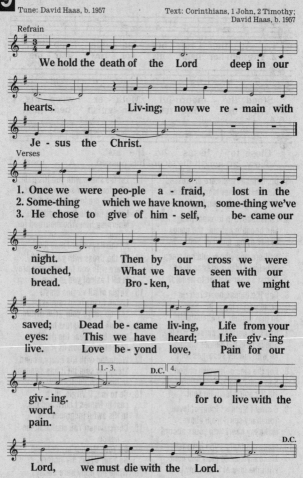

Refrain
We hold the death of the Lord deep in our hearts. Liv-ing; now we re-main with Je-sus the Christ.

Verses

1. Once we were peo-ple a-fraid, lost in the night. Then by our cross we were saved; Dead be-came liv-ing, Life from your giv-ing.
2. Some-thing which we have known, some-thing we've touched, What we have seen with our eyes: This we have heard; Life giv-ing word.
3. He chose to give of him-self, be-came our bread. Bro-ken, that we might live. Love be-yond love, Pain for our pain.

D.C. *4.* for to live with the Lord,

D.C. we must die with the Lord.

O Lord, Hear My Prayer

Tune: Jacques Berthier, 1923-1994

Text: Psalm 102
Taizé Community, 1982

Ostinato Chorale

O Lord, hear my prayer, O Lord, hear my prayer:

when I call an-swer me. O Lord, hear my prayer, O

Lord, hear my prayer. Come and lis-ten to me. O

Stay Here and Keep Watch

Tune: Jacques Berthier, 1923-1994

Text: from Matthew 26;
Taizé Community

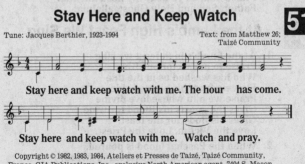

Stay here and keep watch with me. The hour has come.

Stay here and keep watch with me. Watch and pray.

52 Prepare the Way of the Lord

Tune: Jaques Berthier, 1923-1994

Text: Luke 3:4, 6;
Taizé Community

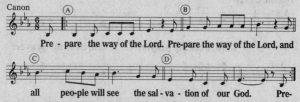

Canon

Pre - pare the way of the Lord. Pre-pare the way of the Lord, and
all peo-ple will see the sal - va - tion of our God. Pre-

53 Jesus Christ Is Risen Today

1. Jesus Christ is ris'n today, alleluia!
   Our triumphant holy day, alleluia!
   Who did once upon the cross, alleluia!
   Suffer to redeem our loss, alleluia!

2. Hymns of praise then let us sing, alleluia!
   Unto Christ our heav'nly King, alleluia!
   Who endured the cross and grave, alleluia!
   Sinners to redeem and save, alleluia!

3. Sing we to our God above, alleluia!
   Praise eternal as his love, alleluia!
   Praise him, all ye heav'nly host, alleluia!
   Father, Son and Holy Ghost, alleluia!

54 At the Lamb's High Feast We Sing

1. At the Lamb's high feast we sing
   Praise to our victor'ous King,
   Who has washed us in the tide
   Flowing from his pierced side;
   Praise we him whose love divine
   Gives the guests his Blood for wine,
   Gives his Body for the feast,
   Love the Victim, Love the Priest.

2. When the Paschal blood is poured,
   Death's dark Angel sheathes his sword;
   Israel's hosts triumphant go
   Through the wave that drowns the foe.

Christ, the Lamb whose Blood was shed,
Paschal victim, Paschal bread;
With sincerity and love
Eat we Manna from above.

Christ the Lord Is Risen Today

55

Tr. Jane E. Leeson, 1807-1882

Traditional

1. Christ, the Lord is risn' to-day,
2. Christ, the Vic-tim un-de-filed,
3. Christ, Who once for sin-ners bled,

Chris-tians, haste your vows to pay; Of-fer ye your
Man to God hath re-con-ciled; When in strange and
Now the first born of the dead, Thron'd in end-less

prais-es meet At the Pas-chal Vic-tim's feet.
aw-ful strife Met to-geth-er death and life;
might and pow'r, Lives and reigns for-ev-er more.

For the sheep the Lamb hath bled; Sin-less in the
Chris-tians on this hap-py day Haste with joy your
Hail, e-ter-nal Hope on high! Hail, Thou King of

sin-ner's stead; Christ, the Lord, is ris'n on high,
vows to pay. Christ, the Lord, is ris'n on high,
Vic-to-ry! Hail, Thou Prince of Life a-dored!

Now He lives no— more to die!
Now He lives no— more to die!
Help and save us— gra-cious Lord. 617

56 All Glory, Laud, and Honor

Tr. John Mason Neale, 1851

Melchior Teschner, pub. 1615

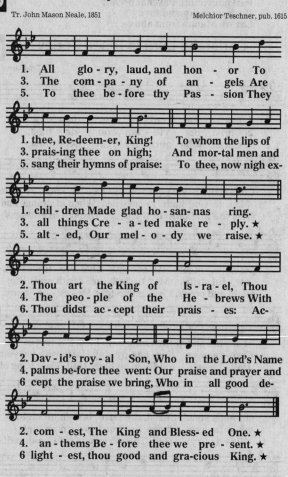

1. All glo-ry, laud, and hon-or To
3. The com-pa-ny of an-gels Are
5. To thee be-fore thy Pas-sion They

1. thee, Re-deem-er, King!   To whom the lips of
3. prais-ing thee on high;   And mor-tal men and
5. sang their hymns of praise: To thee, now nigh ex-

1. chil-dren Made glad ho-san-nas   ring.
3. all things Cre-a-ted make re-ply. ★
5. alt-ed, Our mel-o-dy we   raise. ★

2. Thou art the King of   Is-ra-el, Thou
4. The peo-ple of the   He-brews With
6. Thou didst ac-cept their prais-es: Ac-

2. Dav-id's roy-al Son, Who in the Lord's Name
4. palms be-fore thee went: Our praise and prayer and
6 cept the praise we bring, Who in all good de-

2. com-est, The King and Bless-ed One. ★
4. an-thems Be-fore thee we pre-sent. ★
6 light-est, thou good and gra-cious King. ★

★ *Refrain:* after each stanza except the first.

618

The Strife Is O'er

Alleluia! Alleluia! Alleluia!

1. The strife is o'er, the battle done!
   The victory of life is won!
   The song of triumph has begun! Alleluia!

2. The powers of death have done their worst,
   But Christ their legions has dispersed;
   Let shouts of holy joy outburst! Alleluia!

3. The three sad days are quickly sped,
   He rises glor'ous from the dead;
   All glory to our risen Head! Alleluia!

4. He closed the yawning gates of hell;
   The bars from heaven's high portals fell;
   Let hymns of praise His triumph tell! Alleluia!

O Sons and Daughters, Let Us Sing!

Alleluia! Alleluia! Alleluia!

1. O sons and daughters, let us sing!
   The King of heav'n, the glorious King,
   Today is ris'n and triumphing. Alleluia!

2. On Easter morn, at break of day,
   The faithful women went their way
   To seek the tomb where Jesus lay. Alleluia!

3. An angel clad in white they see,
   Who sat and spoke unto the three,
   "Your Lord doth go to Galilee." Alleluia!

4. On this most holy day of days,
   To you our hearts and voice we raise,
   In laud and jubilee and praise. Alleluia!

5. Glory to Father and to Son,
   Who has for us the vict'ry won
   And Holy Ghost; blest Three in One. Alleluia!

Christt the Lord Is Risen Again

1. Christ the Lord is ris'n a-gain!
2. He who gave for us his life,
3. He who bore all pain and loss

Christ has bro-ken ev-'ry chain!
Who for us en-dured the strife,
Com-fort-less up-on the Cross,

Hark, the an-gels shout for joy,
Is our Pas-chal Lamb to-day!
Lives in glo-ry now on high,

Sing-ing ev-er more on high,
We too sing for joy and say,__
Pleads for us and hears our cry,__

Al-le-lu - ia. Al - le - lu-

ia. Al - le - lu - ia.

Creator Spirit, Lord of Grace

Creator Spirit, Lord of Grace,
Make thou our hearts thy dwelling place;
And, with thy might celestial, aid
The souls of those whom thou hast made.

O to our souls thy light impart,
And give thy love to every heart;
Turn all our weakness into might,
O thou the source of life and light.

Send Us Your Spirit

61

Tune: David Haas, b. 1957
acc. by Jeanne Cotter, b. 1964

Text: David Haas, b. 1957

Refrain

*1. 2.

Come Lord Je-sus, send us your Spir-it, re-new the face of the earth. Come Lord Je-sus, send us your Spir-it, re-new the face of the earth.

Verses

1. Come to us, Spir-it of God, breathe in us now, we sing to-geth-er. Spir-it of hope and of light, fill our lives, come to us, Spir-it of God.

2. Fill us with the fire of your love, burn in us now, bring us to-geth-er. Come to us, dwell in us, change our lives, O Lord, come to us, Spir-it of God.

3. Send us the wings of new birth, fill all the earth with the love you have taught us. Let all cre-a-tion now be shak-en with love, come to us, Spir-it of God.

D.C.

* May be sung in canon.

Come Down, O Love Divine

1. Come down, O Love di - vine,
2. O let it free - ly burn,
3. And so the yearn - ing strong,

1. Seek thou this soul_ of mine, And
2. Till earth - ly pas - sions turn To
3. With which the soul_ will long, Shall

1. vis - it it with thine own ar - dor glow - ing;
2. dust and ash - es in its heat con - sum - ing;
3. far out - pass the pow'r of hu - man tell - ing;

1. O Com - fort - er, draw near, With - in my
2. And let thy glo - rious light Shine ev - er
3. For none can guess its grace, Till he be-

1. heart ap - pear, And kin - dle it, thy
2. on my sight, And clothe me round, the
3. come the place Where - in the Ho - ly

1. ho - ly flame be - stow - ing.
2. while my path il - lum - ing.
3. Spir - it makes his dwell - ing.

Come, Holy Ghost, Creator Blest

1. Come, Holy Ghost, Creator blest,
   And in our hearts take up thy rest;
   Come with thy grace and heav'nly aid
   To fill the hearts which thou hast made,
   To fill the hearts which thou hast made.

2. O Comforter, to thee we cry,
   Thou heav'nly gift of God most high;
   Thou fount of life and fire of love
   And sweet anointing from above,
   And sweet anointing from above.

3. Praise we the Father, and the Son,
   And the blest Spirit with them one;
   And may the Son on us bestow
   The gifts that from the Spirit flow,
   The gifts that from the Spirit flow.

O God of Loveliness

1. O God of loveliness, O Lord of Heav'n above,
   How worthy to possess my heart's devoted love!
   So sweet Thy Countenance, so gracious to behold,
   That one, and only glance to me were bliss untold.

2. Thou are blest Three in One, yet undivided still;
   Thou art that One alone whose love my heart can fill,
   The heav'ns and earth below, were fashioned by Thy
       Word;
   How amiable art Thou, my ever dearest Lord!

3. O loveliness supreme, and beauty infinite
   O everflowing Stream, and Ocean of delight;
   O life by which I live, my truest life above,
   To You alone I give my undivided love.

65   Psalm 23: Shepherd Me, O God

Music: Marty Haugen

Text: Psalm 23; Marty Haugen

Refrain

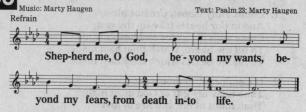

Shep-herd me, O God, be-yond my wants, be-

yond my fears, from death in-to life.

Verses

1. God is my shepherd, so nothing shall I want,
   I rest in the meadows of faithfulness and love,
   I walk by the quiet waters of peace.

2. Gently you raise me and heal my weary soul,
   you lead me by pathways of righteousness and truth,
   my spirit shall sing the music of your name.

3. Though I should wander the valley of death,
   I fear no evil, for you are at my side, your rod and your
      staff,
   my comfort and my hope.

4. Surely your kindness and mercy follow me all the days
      of my life;
   I will dwell in the house of my God for evermore.

66   Eat This Bread

Tune: Jacques Berthier, 1923-1994   Text: John 6; adapt. by Robert J. Batastini, b. 1942
and the Taizé Community

Refrain

Eat this bread, drink this cup, come to him and nev-er be hun-gry.

Eat this bread, drink this cup, trust in him and you will not thirst.

When Morning Gilds the Skies

E. Caswall, Tr.   Traditional

1. When morn-ing gilds the skies   My
2. Be this, while life is mine,   My
3. To God, the Word, on high   The
4. Let earth's wide cir-cle round   In

1. heart a-wak-ing cries;   May Je-sus Christ be
2. cant-i-cle di-vine;   May Je-sus Christ be
3. hosts of an-gels cry;   May Je-sus Christ be
4. joy-ful song re-sound;   May Je-sus Christ be

1. praised!   A-like at work and   prayer   To
2. praised!   Be our e-ter-nal   song, Through
3. praised!   Let na-tions too up-raise   Their
4. praised!   Let air, and sea, and   sky, Through

1. Je-sus I re-pair: May Je-sus Christ be
2. all the a-ges long.   May Je-sus Christ be
3. voice in hymns of praise: May Je-sus Christ be
4. depth and height re-ply   May Je-sus Christ be

1. praised!   May Je-sus Christ be   praised!
2. praised!   May Je-sus Christ be   praised!
3. praised!   May Je-sus Christ be   praised!
4. praised!   May Je-sus Christ be   praised!

68. Loving Shepherd of Your Sheep

1. Lov - ing Shep - herd of your sheep,
2. Lov - ing Shep - herd you did give,
3. Lov - ing Shep - herd ev - er near,

Keep us Lord in safe - ty keep;
Your own life that we might live;
Teach us still your voice to hear;

Noth - ing can your pow'r with - stand,
May we love you day by day,
Suf - fer not our steps to stray

None can pluck us from your hand.
Glad - ly your sweet Will o - bey.
From the straight and nar - row way.

Good Shep - herd, shield us.
Good Shep - herd, shield us.
Good Shep - herd, shield us.

69. In the Lord's Atoning Grief

1. In the Lord's atoning grief
   Be our rest and sweet relief;
   Deep within our hearts we'll store
   Those dear pains and wrongs he bore.

2. Thorns and cross and nail and spear,
   Wounds that faithful hearts revere,
   Vinegar and gall and reed
   And the pang his soul that freed.

3. Crucified we thee adore,
   Thee with all our hearts implore;
   With the saints our soul unite,
   In the realms of heav'nly light.

626

Taste and See

Tune: James E. Moore, Jr., b. 1951

Text: Psalm 34;
James E. Moore, Jr., b. 1951

Refrain

Taste and see, taste and see the good-ness of the

Lord.   O   taste and see,   taste and see the

good - ness of   the Lord,   of the Lord.

Verses

1. I will bless   the Lord   at all   times.
2. Glo - ri - fy   the Lord   with   me,
3. Wor-ship   the Lord,   all you   peo-ple.

Praise   shall al-ways be   on my lips;
To-geth-er   let us all   praise God's name.
You'll   want for noth-ing   if you ask.

my soul   shall glo-ry   in the Lord
I called   the Lord   who an - swered me;
Taste   and see   that the Lord is   good;

D.C.

for God   has been   so good to   me.
from all   my trou-bles   I was set   free.
in God   we need   put all our   trust.

Song of the Body of Christ /
Canción del Cuerpo de Cristo

Tune: NO KE ANO' AHI, Irreg.,
Hawaiian traditional,
arr. by David Haas, b. 1957

Text: David Haas, b. 1957,
Spanish translation by Donna Peña, b. 1955,
and Ronald F. Krisman, b. 1946

Refrain

We come to share our sto-ry we
Hoy ve-ni-mos a con-tar nues-tra_his-to-ria, com-par-

come to break the bread, We come to
tien-do_el pan ce-les-tial. Hoy ve-ni-mos jun-tos

know our ris-ing from the dead.
a ce-le-brar tu mis-te-rio pas-cual.

Verses

1. We come as your peo-ple, we
2. We are called to heal the bro-ken, to be
3. Bread of life and cup of prom-ise, in this
4. You will lead and we shall fol-low, you will
5. We will live and sing: your prais-es, "Al le-

come as your own, u-nit-ed with each
hope for the poor, we are called to feed the
meal we all are one. In our dy-ing and our
be the breath of life; liv-ing wa-ter, we are
lu-ia" is our song. May we live in love and

D.C.

oth-er, love finds a home.
hun-gry at our door.
ris-ing, may your king-dom come.
thirst-ing for your light.
peace our whole life long.

1. Hoy ve - ni-mos por-que so - mos tu pue - blo, re - na -
2. A sa-nar al en - fer - mo nos lla - mas, al an -
3. Pan de vi - da y san-gre de la_a-lian - za, haz - nos
4. Nos guia-rás y te se-gui - re - mos. Nues-tro_a -
5. Vi - vi - re - mos can-tan - do "A - lo - ja." "A - le -

ci - dos por tu per - dón, re - u - ni - dos
sio-so, tu_es-pe-ran - za tra - er, y al ham - brien - to,
u - no_en es-ta co-mu - nión. Que tu rei - no
lien - to vi-tal tú se - rás. Nuse-tra luz en el
lu - ya" es nues-tra can-ción. Que vi - va - mos por

D.C.

en tu_a - mor, y de un co-ra - zón.
nues - tro_a-li - men-to o - fre - cer.
ven - ga en nues - tra trans-for-ma - ción.
dí - a y_en la no - che bri - lla - rás.
siem - pre en paz y fra-ter - na u - nión.

Ubi Caritas

Tune: Jacques Berthier 1923-1994   Text: 1 Corinthians 13:2-8

Refrain

U - bi ca - ri - tas et a - mor,
Live in char-i - ty and stead-fast love,

u - bi ca - ri - tas De - us i - bi est.
live in char-i - ty; God will dwell with you.

I Am the Bread of Life

Tune: BREAD OF LIFE, Irreg with refrain;
Suzanne Toolan, SM, b. 1927.

Text: John 6;
Suzanne Toolan, SM, b. 1927

1. ___ I am the Bread of life. You who
2. The bread that ___ I will give is my
3. Un - less _____ you ___ eat of the
4. ___ I am the Res - ur - rec - tion, _____
5. Yes, Lord, _____ I be - lieve that ___

1. ___ Yo soy el pan de vi - da. El que
2. El pan que ___ yo da - ré ____ es mi
3. ___ Mien - tras no co-mas el ___
4. ___ Yo soy la re - su - rrec - ción. _____
5. ___ Sí, Se - ñor, yo cre - o que ___

come to me shall not hun - ger; ___ and who be-
flesh for the life of the world, _____ and if you
flesh of the Son of Man _____ and ___
I _____ am the life. If you be-
you _____ are the Christ, _____ the ___

vie - ne_a mí no ten-drá ham - bre. _____ El que
cuer - po ___ vi - da del mun - do, ___ y el que
cuer-po del hi-jo del hom-bre, ___ y ___
Yo _____ soy la vi - da. _____ El que
tú e - res el Cris - to, _____ El ___

lieve in me shall not thirst. _____ No one can come to
eat _____ of this bread, _____ you shall ___ live for
drink _____ of his blood, ___ and drink ___ of his
lieve ___ in ___ me, _____ e-ven_ though you
Son of ___ God, ___ Who ___ has ___

cree_en mí no ten-drá sed. _____ Na - die ___ vie - ne_a
co - ma ___ de mi car-ne _____ ten-drá ___ vi - da_e-
be - bas ___ de su san-gre y ___ be-bas ___ de su
cree _____ en ___ mí, _____ aun-que ___ mu - rie-
Hi - jo de Dios, ___ que vi - no al

me un-less the__ Fa-ther beck-ons.
ev - er,_____ you shall__ live for ev - er.
blood,_____ you shall not have life with - in you.
die,_____ you shall__ live for ev - er.
come in - to the_____ world.
mí_____ mien-tras el Pa-dre lla-me.
ter - na,_____ ten-drá__ vi-da e ter-na.
san - gre, no ten-drá__ vi-da en ti.
ra,_____ ten-drá vi-da e ter-na.
mun-do_____ pa-ra sal-var-nos.

And I will raise you up, and I will
Yo le re - su - ci - ta - ré, Yo lo re-

raise you up, and I will raise you
su - ci - ta - ré, Yo lo re - su - ci - ta-

up on the last day.
ré el di - a de_El.

O Lord, I Am Not Worthy

74

1. O Lord, I am not worthy,
   That thou should come to me,
   But speak the word of comfort
   My spirit healed shall be.

2. And humbly I'll receive thee,
   The bridegroom of my soul,
   No more by sin to grieve thee
   Or fly thy sweet control.

3. O Sacrament most holy,
   O Sacrament divine,
   All praise and all thanksgiving
   Be every moment thine.

75 The Summons

Tune: KELVINGROVE, 7 6 7 6 777 6;
Scottish traditional; arr. by John L. Bell, b. 1949

Text: John L. Bell, b. 1949;

1. Will you come and fol - low me If I but call your name? Will you go where you don't know And nev - er be the same? Will you let my love be shown, Will you let my name be known, Will you let my life be grown In you and you in me?

2. Will you leave your - self be - hind If I but call your name? Will you care for cruel and kind And nev - er be the same? Will you risk the hos - tile stare Should your life at - tract or scare? Will you let me an - swer prayer In you and you in me?

3. Will you let the blind - ed see If I but call your name? Will you set the pris - 'ners free And nev - er be the same? Will you kiss the lep - er clean, And do such as this un - seen, And ad - mit to what I mean In you and you in me?

4. Will you love the 'you' you hide If I but call your name? Will you quell the fear in - side And nev - er be the same? Will you use the faith you've found To re - shape the world a - round, Through my sight and touch and sound In you and you in me?

You Are Mine

Tune: David Haas, b. 1957

Text: David Haas, b. 1957

Verses

1. I will come to you in the si - lence,
2. I am hope for all who are hope-less,
3. I am strength for all the de - spair-ing,
4. am the Word that leads all to free-dom, I

I will lift you from all your fear.
I am eyes for all who long to see. In the
heal-ing for the ones who dwell in shame.
am the peace the world can-not give.

You will hear my voice, I claim you as my choice, be
shad-ows of the night, I will be your light,
All the blind will see, the lame will all run free, and
I will call your name, em - brac-ing all your pain, stand

still and know I am here. (To verse 2)
come and rest in me. (To refrain)
all will know my name. (To refrain)
up now walk, and live! (To refrain)

Refrain

Do not be a-fraid, I am with you. I have called you

each by name. Come and fol-low me, I will bring you

D.C.

home; I love you and you are mine.

4. I

77 God of Day and God of Darkness

Tune: BEACH SPRING, 8 7 8 7 D;
The Sacred Harp, 1844;
harm. by Marty Haugen, b. 1950

Text: Marty Haugen, b. 1950;

1. God of day and God of dark - ness, Now we
2. Still the na - tions curse the dark - ness, Still the
3. Show us Christ in one an - oth - er, Make us
4. You shall be the path that guides us, You the

stand be - fore the night; As the shad - ows stretch and
rich op - press the poor; Still the earth is bruised and
ser - vants strong and true; Give us all your love of
light that in us burns; Shin - ing deep with - in all

deep - en, Come and make our dark-ness bright. All cre-
brok - en By the ones who still want more. Come and
jus - tice So we do what you would do. Let us
peo - ple, Yours the love that we must learn, For our

a - tion still is groan-ing For the dawn-ing of your
wake us from our sleep-ing, So our hearts can - not ig -
call all peo-ple ho - ly, Let us pledge our lives a -
hearts shall wan-der rest-less 'Til they safe to you re -

might, When the Sun of peace and jus - tice
nore all your peo - ple lost and bro - ken,
new, Make us one with all the low - ly,
turn; Find - ing you in one an - oth - er,

Fills the earth with ra-diant light.
All your chil - dren at our door.
Let us all be one in you.
We shall all your face dis - cern.

We Walk by Faith

Tune: SHANTI, CM;
Marty Haugen, b. 1950

Text: Henry Alford, 1810-1871, alt.

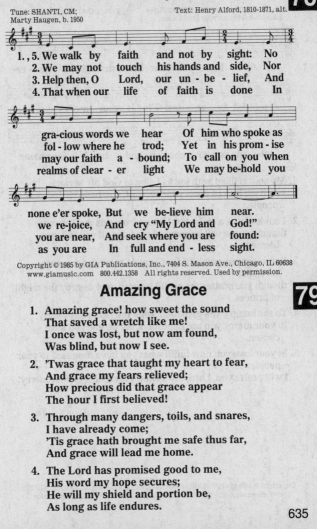

1., 5. We walk by faith and not by sight: No
2. We may not touch his hands and side, Nor
3. Help then, O Lord, our un-be-lief, And
4. That when our life of faith is done In

gra-cious words we hear Of him who spoke as
fol-low where he trod; Yet in his prom-ise
may our faith a-bound; To call on you when
realms of clear-er light We may be-hold you

none e'er spoke, But we be-lieve him near.
we re-joice, And cry "My Lord and God!"
you are near, And seek where you are found:
as you are In full and end-less sight.

Amazing Grace

1. Amazing grace! how sweet the sound
   That saved a wretch like me!
   I once was lost, but now am found,
   Was blind, but now I see.

2. 'Twas grace that taught my heart to fear,
   And grace my fears relieved;
   How precious did that grace appear
   The hour I first believed!

3. Through many dangers, toils, and snares,
   I have already come;
   'Tis grace hath brought me safe thus far,
   And grace will lead me home.

4. The Lord has promised good to me,
   His word my hope secures;
   He will my shield and portion be,
   As long as life endures.

80 Holy Is Your Name / Luke 1:46-55

Music: WILD MOUNTAIN THYME, Irreg. Text: Luke 1:46-55, David Haas
Irish traditional; arr. by David Haas

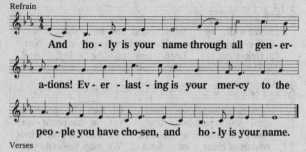

Refrain

And ho - ly is your name through all gen - er-
a - tions! Ev - er - last - ing is your mer - cy to the
peo - ple you have cho - sen, and ho - ly is your name.

Verses

1. My soul is filled with joy as I sing to God my savior:
   you have looked upon your servant, you have visited your
   people.

2. I am lowly as a child, but I know from this day forward
   that my name will be remembered, for all will call me
   blessed.

3. I proclaim the pow'r of God, you do marvels for your
   servants;
   though you scatter the proud hearted, and destroy the might
   of princes.

4. To the hungry you give food, send the rich away empty.
   In your mercy you are mindful of the people you have
   chosen.

5. In your love you now fulfill what you have promised to your
   people.
   I will praise you, Lord, my savior, everlasting is your mercy.

Sing My Tongue the Savior's Glory

1. Sing my tongue, the Savior's glory,
   Of his flesh the mystr'y sing;
   Of the Blood all price exceeding,
   Shed by our immortal King,
   Destined for the world's redemption,
   From a noble womb to spring.

2. Of a pure and spotless Virgin
   Born for us on earth below,
   He, as Man, with man conversing,
   Stayed, the seeds of truth to sow;
   Then he closed in solemn order
   Wondrously his life of woe.

3. On the night of that Last Supper,
   Seated with his chosen band,
   He the Paschal victim eating,
   First fulfills the Law's command;
   Then as food to his Apostles
   Gives himself with his own hand.

4. Word made flesh the bread of nature
   By his word to Flesh he turns;
   Wine into his blood he changes
   What though sense no change discerns?
   Only be the heart in earnest,
   Faith her lesson quickly learns.

   (Tantum ergo)

5. Down in adoration falling
   Lo! the sacred Host we hail,
   Lo! o'er ancient forms departing,
   Newer rites of grace prevail;
   Faith for all defects supplying,
   Where the feeble senses fail.

6. To the Everlasting Father,
   And the Son who reigns on high,
   With the Holy Ghost proceeding
   Forth from each eternally
   Be salvation, honor, blessing,
   Might, and endless majesty. Amen.

Immaculate Mary

82

1. Immaculate Mary, thy praises we sing,
   Who reignest in splendor with Jesus, our King.

   Refrain:
   Ave, ave, ave, Maria! Ave, ave, Maria!

2. In heaven, the blessed thy glory proclaim,
   On earth, we thy children invoke thy fair name.
   —*Refrain*

3. Thy name is our power, thy virtues our light,
   Thy love is our comfort, thy pleading our might.
   —*Refrain*

4. We pray for our mother, the Church upon earth,
   And bless, dearest Lady, the land of our birth.
   —*Refrain*

Hail, Holy Queen Enthroned Above

83

1. Hail, holy Queen enthroned above, O Maria!
   Hail, Mother of mercy and of love, O Maria!

   Refrain:
   Triumph, ail ye cherubim,
   Sing with us, ye seraphim,
   Heav'n and earth resound the hymn.
   Salve; salve, salve Regina.

2. Our life, our sweetness here below, O Maria!
   Our hope in sorrow and in woe, O Maria!
   —*Refrain*

3. To thee we cry, poor sons of Eve, O Maria!
   To thee we sigh, we mourn, we grieve, O Maria!
   —*Refrain*

4. Turn, then, most gracious Advocate, O Maria!
   Toward us thine eyes compassionate, O Maria!
   —*Refrain*

5. When this our exile's time is o'er, O Maria!
   Show us thy Son for evermore, O Maria!
   —*Refrain*

For All the Saints

William W. How
Moderately, in unison

R. Vaughan Williams, 1872-1958

1. For all the saints,
who from their labors
rest,
Who Thee by faith
before the world con-
fessed,
Thy Name, O Jesus, be
for ever blest.
Alleluia, alleluia!

2. O blest communion!
fellowship divine!
We feebly struggle,
they in glory shine;
Yet all are one in Thee,
for all are Thine.
Alleluia, alleluia!

3. From earth's wide
bounds,
from ocean's farthest
coast,
Through gates of pearl
streams
in the countless host,
Singing to Father, Son
and Holy Ghost.
Alleluia, alleluia!

America

1.
My country, 'tis of thee,
Sweet land of liberty,
Of thee I sing;
Land where my fathers died,
Land of the pilgrim's pride
From ev'ry mountainside
Let freedom ring.

2.
My native country, thee,
Land of the noble free,
Thy name I love;
I love thy rocks and rills,
Thy woods and templed hills;
My heart with rapture thrills
Like that above.

America the Beautiful

1. O beautiful for spacious skies,
For amber wave of grain,
For purple mountain majesties
Above the fruited plain.
America! America! God shed his grace on thee.
And crown thy good with brotherhood
From sea to shining sea.

2. O beautiful for pilgrim feet
Whose stern impassioned stress
A thoroughfare for freedom beat
Across the wilderness.
America! America! God mend thy ev'ry flaw,
Confirm thy soul in self control,
Thy liberty in law.

Ye Watchers and Ye Holy Ones

Athelstan Riley, 1858-1945

Cologne, 1623

1. Ye watch - ers and ye ho - ly ones, Bright
2. Re - spond, ye souls in end - less rest, Ye
3. O friends, in glad - ness let us sing, All

ser - aphs, cher - u - bim; and thrones, Raise the
pa - tri - archs and proph - ets blest, Al - le -
heav - en's an - thems ech - o - ing, Al - le -

glad strain, al - le - lu - ia! Cry out, do - min - ions,
lu - ia, al - le - lu - ia! Ye ho - ly twelve, ye
lu - ia, al - le - lu - ia! To God the Fa - ther,

prince - doms, powers, Vir - tues, arch - an - gels,
mar - tyrs strong, All saints, tri - umph - ant,
God the Son, And God the Spir - it,

an - gels' choirs,
raise the song: Al - le - lu - ia,
Three in one,

al - le - lu - ia, al - le - lu - ia,

al - le - lu - ia, al - le - lu - ia!

HYMN INDEX

TREASURY OF PRAYERS

MORNING PRAYERS

Most holy and adorable Trinity, one God in three Persons, I praise you and give you thanks for all the favors you have bestowed upon me. Your goodness has preserved me until now. I offer you my whole being and in particular all my thoughts, words and deeds, together with all the trials I may undergo this day. Give them your blessing. May your Divine Love animate them and may they serve your greater glory.

I make this morning offering in union with the Divine intentions of Jesus Christ who offers himself daily in the holy Sacrifice of the Mass, and in union with Mary, his Virgin Mother and our Mother, who was always the faithful handmaid of the Lord.

Glory be to the Father, and to the Son, and to the Holy Spirit. Amen.

Prayer for Divine Guidance through the Day

Partial indulgence (No. 21) *

Lord, God Almighty, you have brought us safely to the beginning of this day. Defend us today by your mighty power, that we may not fall into any sin, but that all our words may so proceed and all our thoughts and actions be so directed, as to be always just in your sight. Through Christ our Lord. Amen.

* The indulgences quoted in this Missal are taken from the 1968 Vatican edition of the "Enchiridion Indulgentiarum" (published by Catholic Book Publishing Corp.).

Partial indulgence (No. 1)

Direct, we beg you, O Lord, our actions by your holy inspirations, and carry them on by your gracious assistance, that every prayer and work of ours may begin always with you, and through you be happily ended. Amen.

NIGHT PRAYERS

I adore you, my God, and thank you for having created me, for having made me a Christian and preserved me this day. I love you with all my heart and I am sorry for having sinned against you, because you are infinite Love and infinite Goodness. Protect me during my rest and may your love be always with me. Amen.

Eternal Father, I offer you the Precious Blood of Jesus Christ in atonement for my sins and for all the intentions of our Holy Church.

Holy Spirit, Love of the Father and the Son, purify my heart and fill it with the fire of your Love, so that I may be a chaste Temple of the Holy Trinity and be always pleasing to you in all things. Amen.

Plea for Divine Help

Partial indulgence (No. 24)

Hear us, Lord, holy Father, almighty and eternal God; and graciously send your holy angel from heaven to watch over, to cherish, to protect, to abide with, and to defend all who dwell in this house. Through Christ our Lord. Amen.

PRAYERS BEFORE HOLY COMMUNION

Act of Faith

Lord Jesus Christ, I firmly believe that you are present in this Blessed Sacrament as true God and true Man, with your Body and Blood, Soul and Divinity. My Redeemer and my Judge, I adore your Divine Majesty together with the angels and saints. I believe, O Lord; increase my faith.

Act of Hope

Good Jesus, in you alone I place all my hope. You are my salvation and my strength, the Source of all good. Through your mercy, through your Passion and Death, I hope to obtain the pardon of my sins, the grace of final perseverance and a happy eternity.

Act of Love

Jesus, my God, I love you with my whole heart and above all things, because you are the one supreme Good and an infinitely perfect Being. You have given your life for me, a poor sinner, and in your mercy you have even offered yourself as food for my soul. My God, I love you. Inflame my heart so that I may love you more.

Act of Contrition

O my Savior, I am truly sorry for having offended you because you are infinitely good and sin displeases you. I detest all the sins of my life and I desire to atone for them. Through the merits of your Precious Blood, wash from my soul all stain of sin, so that, cleansed in body and soul, I may worthily approach the Most Holy Sacrament of the Altar.

PRAYERS AFTER HOLY COMMUNION

Act of Faith

Jesus, I firmly believe that you are present within me as God and Man, to enrich my soul with graces and to fill my heart with the happiness of the blessed. I believe that you are Christ, the Son of the living God!

Act of Adoration

With deepest humility, I adore you, my Lord and God; you have made my soul your dwelling place. I adore you as my Creator from whose hands I came and with whom I am to be happy forever.

Act of Love

Dear Jesus, I love you with my whole heart, my whole soul, and with all my strength. May the love of your own Sacred Heart fill my soul and purify it so that I may die to the world for love of you, as you died on the Cross for love of me. My God, you are all mine; grant that I may be all yours in time and in eternity.

Act of Thanksgiving

From the depths of my heart I thank you, dear Lord, for your infinite kindness in coming to me. How good you are to me! With your most holy Mother and all the angels, I praise your mercy and generosity toward me, a poor sinner. I thank you for nourishing my soul with your Sacred Body and Precious Blood. I will try to show my gratitude to you in the Sacrament of your love, by obedience to your holy commandments, by fidelity to my duties, by kindness to my neighbor and by an earnest endeavor to become more like you in my daily conduct.

Act of Offering

Jesus, you have given yourself to me, now let me give myself to you; I give you my body, that it may be chaste and pure. I give you my soul, that it may be free from sin. I give you my heart, that it may always love you. I give you every thought, word, and deed of my life, and I offer all for your honor and glory.

Prayer to Christ the King

O Christ Jesus, I acknowledge you King of the universe. All that has been created has been made for you. Exercise upon me all your rights. I renew my baptismal promises, renouncing Satan and all his works and pomps. I promise to live a good Christian life and to do all in my power to procure the triumph of the rights of God and your Church.

Divine Heart of Jesus, I offer you my poor actions in order to obtain that all hearts may acknowledge your sacred Royalty, and that thus the reign of your peace may be established throughout the universe. Amen.

Indulgenced Prayer before a Crucifix

Look down upon me, good and gentle Jesus, while before your face I humbly kneel, and with a burning soul pray and beseech you to fix deep in my heart lively sentiments of faith, hope and charity, true contrition for my sins, and a firm purpose of amendment, while I contemplate with great love and tender pity your five wounds, pondering over them within me, calling to mind the words which David, your prophet, said of you, my good Jesus: "They have pierced my hands and my feet; they have numbered all my bones" (Ps 22:17-18).

A *plenary indulgence* is granted on each Friday of Lent and Passiontide to the faithful, who after Communion piously recite the above prayer before an image of Christ crucified; on other days of the year the indulgence is partial. *(No. 22)*

Prayer to Mary

O Jesus living in Mary, come and live in your servants, in the spirit of your holiness, in the fullness of your power, in the perfection of your ways, in the truth of your mysteries. Reign in us over all adverse powers by your Holy Spirit, and for the glory of the Father. Amen.

Anima Christi

Partial indulgence (No. 10)

Soul of Christ, sanctify me.
Body of Christ, save me.
Blood of Christ, inebriate me.
Water from the side of Christ, wash me.
Passion of Christ, strengthen me.
O good Jesus, hear me.
Within your wounds hide me.
Separated from you let me never be.
From the malignant enemy, defend me.
At the hour of death, call me.
And close to you bid me.
That with your saints I may be
Praising you, for all eternity. Amen.

THE SCRIPTURAL WAY OF THE CROSS

The Way of the Cross is a devotion in which we accompany, in spirit, our Blessed Lord in his sorrowful journey to Calvary, and devoutly meditate on his suffering and death.

A plenary indulgence is granted to those who make the Way of the Cross. (No. 63)

1. Jesus Is Condemned to Death—God so loved the world that he gave his only-begotten Son to save it (Jn 3:16).

2. Jesus Bears His Cross—If anyone wishes to come after me, let him deny himself, and take up his cross daily (Lk 9:23).

3. Jesus Falls the First Time—The Lord laid upon him the guilt of us all (Is 53:6).

4. Jesus Meets His Mother—Come, all you who pass by the way, look and see whether there is any suffering like my suffering (Lam 1:13).

5. Jesus Is Helped by Simon—As long as you did it for one of these, the least of my brethren, you did it for me (Mt 25:40).

6. Veronica Wipes the Face of Jesus—He who sees me, sees also the Father (Jn 14:9).

7. Jesus Falls a Second Time—Come to me, all you who labor, and are burdened, and I will give you rest (Mt 11:28).

8. Jesus Speaks to the Women—Daughters of Jerusalem, do not weep for me, but weep for yourselves and for your children (Lk 23:2).

9. Jesus Falls a Third Time—Everyone who exalts himself shall be humbled, and he who humbles himself shall be exalted (Lk 14:11).

10. Jesus Is Stripped of His Garments—Every one of you who does not renounce all that he possesses cannot be my disciple (Lk 14:33).

11. Jesus Is Nailed to the Cross—I have come down from heaven, not to do my own will, but the will of him who sent me (Jn 6:38).

12. Jesus Dies on the Cross—He humbled himself, becoming obedient to death, even to death on a cross. Therefore God has exalted him (Phil 2:8-9).

13. Jesus Is Taken Down from the Cross—Did not the Christ have to suffer those things before entering into his glory? (Lk 24:26).

14. Jesus Is Placed in the Tomb—Unless the grain of wheat falls into the ground and dies, it remains alone. But if it dies, it brings forth much fruit (Jn 12:24-25).

STATIONS
of the
CROSS

1. Jesus Is Condemned to Death

O Jesus, help me to appreciate Your sanctifying grace more and more.

2. Jesus Bears His Cross

O Jesus, You chose to die for me. Help me to love You always with all my heart.

3. Jesus Falls the First Time

O Jesus, make me strong to conquer my wicked passions, and to rise quickly from sin.

4. Jesus Meets His Mother

O Jesus, grant me a tender love for Your Mother, who offered You for love of me.

STATIONS
of the
CROSS

5. Jesus Is Helped by Simon

O Jesus, like Simon lead me ever closer to You through my daily crosses and trials.

6. Jesus and Veronica

O Jesus, imprint Your image on my heart that I may be faithful to You all my life.

7. Jesus Falls a Second Time

O Jesus, I repent for having offended You. Grant me forgiveness of all my sins.

8. Jesus Speaks to the Women

O Jesus, grant me tears of compassion for Your sufferings and of sorrow for my sins.

STATIONS
of the
CROSS

9. Jesus Falls a Third Time

O Jesus, let me never yield to despair. Let me come to You in hardship and spiritual distress.

10. He Is Stripped of His Garments

O Jesus, let me sacrifice all my attachments rather than imperil the divine life of my soul.

11. Jesus Is Nailed to the Cross

O Jesus, strengthen my faith and increase my love for You. Help me to accept my crosses.

12. Jesus Dies on the Cross

O Jesus, I thank You for making me a child of God. Help me to forgive others.

STATIONS
of the
CROSS

13. Jesus Is Taken Down from the Cross

O Jesus, through the intercession of Your holy Mother, let me be pleasing to You.

14. Jesus Is Laid in the Tomb

O Jesus, strengthen my will to live for You on earth and bring me to eternal bliss in heaven.

Prayer after the Stations

JESUS, You became an example of humility, obedience and patience, and preceded me on the way of life bearing Your Cross. Grant that, inflamed with Your love, I may cheerfully take upon myself the sweet yoke of Your Gospel together with the mortification of the Cross and follow You as a true disciple so that I may be united with You in heaven. Amen.

The Five

Joyful

Mysteries

Said on Mondays and Saturdays [except during Lent], and the Sundays from Advent to Lent.

3. The Nativity
For the spirit of poverty.

1. The Annunciation
For the love of humility.

4. The Presentation
For the virtue of obedience.

2. The Visitation
For charity toward my neighbor.

5. Finding in the Temple
For the virtue of piety.

The Five Luminous Mysteries *

Said on Thursdays [except during Lent].

*Added to the Mysteries of the Rosary by Pope John Paul II in his Apostolic Letter of October 16, 2002, entitled *The Rosary of the Virgin Mary.*

1. The Baptism of Jesus
For living my Baptismal Promises.

2. The Wedding at Cana
For doing whatever Jesus says.

4. The Transfiguration
Becoming a New Person in Christ.

3. Proclamation of the Kingdom
For seeking God's forgiveness.

5. Institution of the Eucharist
For active participation at Mass.

The Five Sorrowful Mysteries

Said on Tuesdays and Fridays throughout the year, and every day from Ash Wednesday until Easter.

3. Crowning with Thorns
For moral courage.

1. Agony in the Garden
For true contrition.

4. Carrying of the Cross
For the virtue of patience.

2. Scourging at the Pillar
For the virtue of purity.

5. The Crucifixion
For final perseverance.

The Five Glorious Mysteries

1. The Resurrection
For the virtue of faith.

Said on Wednesdays [except during Lent], and the Sundays from Easter to Advent.

2. The Ascension
For the virtue of hope.

4. Assumption of the BVM
For devotion to Mary.

3. Descent of the Holy Spirit
For love of God.

5. Crowning of the BVM
For eternal happiness.

PRAYER TO ST. JOSEPH

O Blessed St. Joseph, loving father and faithful guardian of Jesus, and devoted spouse of the Mother of God, I beg you to offer God the Father his divine Son, bathed in blood on the Cross. Through the holy Name of Jesus obtain for us from the Father the favor we implore.

FOR THE SICK

Father, your Son accepted our sufferings to teach us the virtue of patience in human illness. Hear the prayers we offer for our sick brothers and sisters. May all who suffer pain, illness or disease realize that they are chosen to be saints, and know that they are joined to Christ in his suffering for the salvation of the world, who lives and reigns with you and the Holy Spirit, one God, for ever and ever.

FOR RELIGIOUS VOCATIONS

Father, you call all who believe in you to grow perfect in love by following in the footsteps of Christ your Son. May those whom you have chosen to serve you as religious provide by their way of life a convincing sign of your kingdom for the Church and the whole world.

PRAYER FOR CIVIL AUTHORITIES

Almighty and everlasting God, You direct the powers and laws of all nations; mercifully regard those who rule over us, that, by Your protecting right hand, the integrity of religion and the security of each country might prevail everywhere on earth. Through Christ our Lord. Amen.

PRAYER FOR HEALTH

O Sacred Heart of Jesus, I come to ask of Your infinite mercy the gift of health and strength that I may serve You more faithfully and love You more sincerely than in the past. I wish to be well and strong if this be Your good pleasure and for Your greater glory. Filled with high resolves and determined to perform my tasks most perfectly for love of You, I wish to be enabled to go back to my duties.

PRAYER FOR PEACE AND JOY

Jesus, I want to rejoice in You always. You are near. Let me have no anxiety, but in every concern by prayer and supplication with thanksgiving I wish to let my petitions be made known in my communing with God.

May the peace of God, which surpasses all understanding, guard my heart and my thoughts in You.

PRAYER TO KNOW GOD'S WILL

God the Father of our Lord Jesus Christ, the Author of glory, grant me spiritual wisdom and revelation. Enlighten the eyes of my mind with a deep knowledge of You and Your holy will. May I understand of what nature is the hope to which You call me, what is the wealth of the splendor of Your inheritance among the Saints, and what is the surpassing greatness of Your power toward me.

PRAYER FOR ETERNAL REST

Eternal rest grant unto them, O Lord, and let perpetual light shine upon them. May the souls of the faithful departed, through the mercy of God, rest in peace. Amen.

MAJOR PRACTICES

THE LITURGICAL YEAR

The Liturgical Year is the succession of Times and Feasts of the Church celebrated annually from Advent to Advent.

As presently constituted, the Liturgical Year has the following Times (divisions):

Advent: Beginning on the Sunday closest to November 30 (the Feast of St. Andrew), this period of preparation for the Nativity of the Lord extends over four Sundays.

Christmas Time: This Time begins with the Vigil Masses for the Solemnity of the Nativity of the Lord [Christmas] and concludes on the Feast of the Baptism of the Lord. The period from the end of Christmas Time until the beginning of Lent is included in Ordinary Time (see below).

Lent: The penitential season of Lent begins on Ash Wednesday and ends on Holy Thursday before the Mass of the Lord's Supper that evening. The final week, Holy Week, concludes with the Sacred Paschal Triduum, which takes place from the evening of Holy Thursday to the evening of Easter Sunday.

Easter Time: This Time spans a 50-day period, from the Solemnity of Easter to Pentecost. Its central theme is the Resurrection of Christ together with our resurrection from sin to the new life of grace.

Ordinary Time: This Time comprises the other 33 or 34 weeks of the Liturgical Year. It includes not only the period between the end of Christmas Time and the beginning of Lent but all Sundays and weekdays after Pentecost until the beginning of Advent. It is "ordinary" only by comparison, because the great Feasts of our Lord are prepared for and specially celebrated other times of the year.

Feasts: The first Christians knew only one Feast, Easter, the Feast of our Lord's Resurrection. But this they celebrated all the time, whenever they gathered for the Eucharist. In the Eucharistic celebration, every day and especially every Sunday became for them a little Easter. Easter, in fact, is the center in which all Mysteries of our Redemption merge.

Eventually, however, the Church began to celebrate many of these mysteries in their own right, with Feasts of their own, especially the Birth of our Lord, His Life and Death as well as His Resurrection and Glorification, and also the sending of the Holy Spirit and His work of grace in the soul. Gradually added were Feasts of the Blessed Mother Mary and the Saints.

The Liturgical Year, therefore, has had a long history of development. As early as the year 700, however, the Roman Liturgical Year was essentially as it is today, with two major cycles, Christmas with its Advent and Easter with its Lent, plus the Sundays in between.

HOLYDAYS OF OBLIGATION
Holydays in the United States

Solemnity of Mary, the Holy Mother
of God... January 1
Ascension of the Lord.................. 40 days after Easter or
Sunday after the 6th Sunday of Easter
Assumption of the Blessed Virgin Mary........... August 15
All Saints .... November 1
Immaculate Conception of the Blessed
Virgin Mary...December 8
Nativity of the Lord [Christmas].................December 25

SPIRITUAL WORKS OF MERCY

1. To admonish the sinner (correct those who need it).
2. To instruct the ignorant (teach the ignorant).
3. To counsel the doubtful (give advice to those who need it).
4. To comfort the sorrowful (comfort those who suffer).
5. To bear wrongs patiently (be patient with others).
6. To forgive all injuries (forgive others who hurt you).
7. To pray for the living and the dead (pray for others).

CORPORAL WORKS OF MERCY

1. To feed the hungry.
2. To give drink to the thirsty.
3. To clothe the naked.
4. To visit the imprisoned.
5. To shelter the homeless.
6. To visit the sick.
7. To bury the dead.

THE TEN COMMANDMENTS

1. I, the Lord, am your God. You shall not have other gods besides Me.
2. You shall not take the name of the Lord, your God, in vain.
3. Remember to keep holy the Sabbath day.
4. Honor your father and your mother.
5. You shall not kill.
6. You shall not commit adultery.
7. You shall not steal.
8. You shall not bear false witness against your neighbor.
9. You shall not covet your neighbor's wife.
10. You shall not covet your neighbor's goods.

PRECEPTS OF THE CHURCH
(Traditional Form)

1. To participate at Mass on all Sundays and Holydays of Obligation.
2. To fast and to abstain on the days appointed.
3. To confess our sins at least once a year.
4. To receive Holy Communion during Easter Time.
5. To contribute to the support of the Church.
6. To observe the laws of the Church concerning marriage.

GUIDELINES FOR THE RECEPTION
OF COMMUNION

For Catholics

As Catholics, we fully participate in the celebration of the Eucharist when we receive Holy Communion. We are encouraged to receive Communion devoutly and frequently. In order to be properly disposed to receive Communion, participants should not be conscious of grave sin and normally should have fasted for one hour. A person who is conscious of grave sin is not to receive the Body and Blood of the Lord without prior sacramental confession except for a grave reason where there is no opportunity for confession. In this case, the person is to be mindful of the obligation to make an act of perfect contrition, including the intention of confessing as soon as possible (*Code of Canon Law, canon 916*). A frequent reception of the Sacrament of Penance is encouraged for all.

For Fellow Christians

We welcome our fellow Christians to this celebration of the Eucharist as our brothers and sisters. We pray that our common baptism and the action of the Holy Spirit in this Eucharist will draw us closer to one another and begin to dispel the sad divisions that separate us. We pray that these will lessen and finally disappear, in keeping with Christ's prayer for us "that they may all be one" (John 17:21).

Because Catholics believe that the celebration of the Eucharist is a sign of the reality of the oneness of faith, life, and worship, members of those churches with whom we are not yet fully united are ordinarily not admitted to Holy Communion. Eucharistic sharing in exceptional circumstances by other Christians requires permission according to the directives of the diocesan bishop and the provisions of canon law (*canon 844 § 4*). Members of the Orthodox Churches, the Assyrian Church of the East, and the Polish National Catholic Church are urged to respect the discipline of their own Churches. According to Roman Catholic discipline, the Code of Canon Law does not object to the reception of Communion by Christians of these Churches (*canon 844 § 3*).

For Those Not Receiving Holy Communion

All who are not receiving Holy Communion are encouraged to express in their hearts a prayerful desire for unity with the Lord Jesus and with one another.

For Non-Christians

We also welcome to this celebration those who do not share our faith in Jesus Christ. While we cannot admit them to Holy Communion, we ask them to offer their prayers for the peace and the unity of the human family.

NEW RITE OF PENANCE

(Extracted from the Rite of Penance)

Texts for the Penitent

The penitent should prepare for the celebration of the sacrament by prayer, reading of Scripture, and silent reflection. The penitent should think over and should regret all sins since the last celebration of the sacrament.

RECEPTION OF THE PENITENT

The penitent enters the confessional or other place set aside for the celebration of the sacrament of penance. After the welcoming of the priest, the penitent makes the sign of the cross saying:

In the name of the Father, and of the Son, and of the Holy Spirit. Amen.

The penitent is invited to have trust in God and replies:

Amen.

READING OF THE WORD OF GOD

The penitent then listens to a text of Scripture which tells about God's mercy and calls man to conversion.

CONFESSION OF SINS AND ACCEPTANCE OF SATISFACTION

The penitent speaks to the priest in a normal, conversational fashion. The penitent tells when he or she last celebrated the sacrament and then confesses his or her sins. The penitent then listens to any advice the priest may give and accepts the satisfaction from the priest. The penitent should ask any appropriate questions.

PRAYER OF THE PENITENT AND ABSOLUTION

Prayer

Before the absolution is given, the penitent expresses sorrow for sins in these or similar words:

**My God,
I am sorry for my sins with all my heart.
In choosing to do wrong
and failing to do good,
I have sinned against you
whom I should love above all things.
I firmly intend, with your help,
to do penance,
to sin no more,
and to avoid whatever leads me to sin.
Our Savior Jesus Christ
suffered and died for us.
In his name, my God, have mercy.**

OR:

Remember that your compassion, O LORD,
and your love are from of old.
In your kindness remember me,
because of your goodness, O LORD.

OR:

Thoroughly wash me from my guilt
and of my sin cleanse me.
For I acknowledge my offense,
and my sin is before me always.

OR:

Father, I have sinned [. . .] against you.
I no longer deserve to be called your son.
Be merciful to me a sinner.

OR:

Father of mercy,
like the prodigal son
I return to you and say:
"I have sinned against you
and am no longer worthy to be called your son."
Christ Jesus, Savior of the world,
I pray with the repentant thief
to whom you promised Paradise:
"Lord, remember me in your kingdom."
Holy Spirit, fountain of love,
I call on you with trust:
"Purify my heart,
and help me to walk as a child of light."

OR:

Lord Jesus,
you opened the eyes of the blind,
healed the sick,
forgave the sinful woman,
and after Peter's denial confirmed him in your love.
Listen to my prayer:
forgive all my sins,
renew your love in my heart,
help me to live in perfect unity with my fellow Christians
that I may proclaim your saving power to all the world.

OR:

Lord Jesus,
you chose to be called the friend of sinners.
By your saving death and resurrection
free me from my sins.
May your peace take root in my heart

and bring forth a harvest
of love, holiness, and truth.

OR:

Lord Jesus Christ,
you are the Lamb of God;
you take away the sins of the world.
Through the grace of the Holy Spirit
restore me to friendship with your Father,
cleanse me from every stain of sin
in the blood you shed for me,
and raise me to new life
for the glory of your name.

OR:

Lord God,
in your goodness have mercy on me:
do not look on my sins,
but take away all my guilt.
Create in me a clean heart
and renew within me an upright spirit.

OR:

Lord Jesus, Son of God,
have mercy on me, a sinner.

ABSOLUTION

*If the penitent is not kneeling, he or she bows his or her head
as the priest extends his hands (or at least extends his right
hand).*

God, the Father of mercies,
through the death and resurrection of his Son
has reconciled the world to himself
and sent the Holy Spirit among us
for the forgiveness of sins;
through the ministry of the Church
may God give you pardon and peace,
and I absolve you from your sins
in the name of the Father, and of the Son, ✠
and of the Holy Spirit. Amen.

PROCLAMATION OF PRAISE OF GOD AND DISMISSAL

Penitent and priest give praise to God.

Priest: Give thanks to the Lord, for he is good.
Penitent: His mercy endures for ever.

Then the penitent is dismissed by the priest.

Form of Examination of Conscience

This suggested form for an examination of conscience should be completed and adapted to meet the needs of different individuals and to follow local usages.

In an examination of conscience, before the sacrament of penance, each individual should ask himself these questions in particular:

1. What is my attitude to the sacrament of penance? Do I sincerely want to be set free from sin, to turn again to God, to begin a new life, and to enter into a deeper friendship with God? Or do I look on it as a burden, to be undertaken as seldom as possible?

2. Did I forget to mention, or deliberately conceal, any grave sins in past confessions?

3. Did I perform the penance I was given? Did I make reparation for any injury to others? Have I tried to put into practice any resolution to lead a better life in keeping with the Gospel?

Each individual should examine his life in the light of God's word.

I. The Lord says: "You shall love the Lord your God with your whole heart."

1. Is my heart set on God, so that I really love him above all things and am faithful to his commandments, as a son loves his father? Or am I more concerned about the things of this world? Have I a right intention in what I do?

2. God spoke to us in his Son. Is my faith in God firm and secure? Am I wholehearted in accepting the Church's teaching? Have I been careful to grow in my understanding of the faith, to hear God's word, to listen to instructions on the faith, to avoid dangers to faith? Have I been always strong and fearless in professing my faith in God and the Church? Have I been willing to be known as a Christian in private and public life?

3. Have I prayed morning and evening? When I pray, do I really raise my mind and heart to God or is it a matter of words only? Do I offer God my difficulties, my joys, and my sorrows? Do I turn to God in time of temptation?

4. Have I love and reverence for God's name? Have I offended him in blasphemy, swearing falsely, or taking his name in vain? Have I shown disrespect for the Blessed Virgin Mary and the saints?

5. Do I keep Sundays and feast days holy by taking a full part, with attention and devotion, in the liturgy, and especially in the Mass? Have I fulfilled the precept of annual confession and of communion during the Easter season?

6. Are there false gods that I worship by giving them greater attention and deeper trust than I give to God: money, superstition, spiritism, or other occult practices?

II. The Lord says: "Love one another as I have loved you."

1. Have I a genuine love for my neighbors? Or do I use them for my own ends, or do to them what I would not want done to myself? Have I given grave scandal by my words or actions?

2. In my family life, have I contributed to the well-being and happiness of the rest of the family by patience and genuine love? Have I been obedient to parents, showing them proper respect and giving them help in their spiritual and material needs? Have I been careful to give a Christian upbringing to my children, and to help them by good example and by exercising authority as a parent? Have I been faithful to my husband/wife in my heart and in my relations with others?

3. Do I share my possessions with the less fortunate? Do I do my best to help the victims of oppression, misfortune, and poverty? Or do I look down on my neighbor, especially the poor, the sick, the elderly, strangers, and people of other races?

4. Does my life reflect the mission I received in confirmation? Do I share in the apostolic and charitable works of the Church and in the life of my parish? Have I helped to meet the needs of the Church and of the world and prayed for them: for unity in the Church, for the spread of the Gospel among the nations, for peace and justice, etc.?

5. Am I concerned for the good and prosperity of the human community in which I live, or do I spend my life caring only for myself? Do I share to the best of my ability in the work of promoting justice, morality, harmony, and love in human relations? Have I done my duty as a citizen? Have I paid my taxes?

6. In my work or profession am I just, hard-working, honest, serving society out of love for others? Have I paid a fair wage to my employees? Have I been faithful to my promises and contracts?

7. Have I obeyed legitimate authority and given it due respect?

8. If I am in a position of responsibility or authority, do I use this for my own advantage or for the good of others, in a spirit of service?

9. Have I been truthful and fair, or have I injured others by deceit, calumny, detraction, rash judgment, or violation of a secret?

10. Have I done violence to others by damage to life or limb, reputation, honor, or material possessions? Have I involved them in loss? Have I been responsible for advising an abortion or procuring one?

Have I kept up hatred for others? Am I estranged from others through quarrels, enmity, insults, anger? Have I been guilty of refusing to testify to the innocence of another because of selfishness?

11. Have I stolen the property of others? Have I desired it unjustly and inordinately? Have I damaged it? Have I made restitution of other people's property and made good their loss?

12. If I have been injured, have I been ready to make peace for the love of Christ and to forgive, or do I harbor hatred and the desire for revenge?

III. Christ our Lord says: "Be perfect as your Father is perfect."

1. Where is my life really leading me? Is the hope of eternal life my inspiration? Have I tried to grow in the life of the Spirit through prayer, reading the word of God and meditating on it, receiving the sacraments, self-denial? Have I been anxious to control my vices, my bad inclinations and passions, e.g., envy, love of food and drink? Have I been proud and boastful, thinking myself better in the sight of God and despising others as less important than myself? Have I imposed my own will on others, without respecting their freedom and rights?

2. What use have I made of time, of health and strength, of the gifts God has given to me to be used like the talents in the Gospel? Do I use them to become more perfect every day? Or have I been lazy and too much given to leisure?

3. Have I been patient in accepting the sorrows and disappointments of life? How have I performed mortification so as to "fill up what is wanting to the sufferings of Christ"? Have I kept the precept of fasting and abstinence?

4. Have I kept my senses and my whole body pure and chaste as a temple of the Holy Spirit consecrated for resurrection and glory, and as a sign of God's faithful love for men and women, a sign that is seen most perfectly in the sacrament of matrimony? Have I dishonored my body by fornication, impurity, unworthy conversation or thoughts, evil desires or actions? Have I given in to sensuality? Have I indulged in reading, conversation, shows, and entertainments that offend against Christian and human decency? Have I encouraged others to sin by my own failure to maintain these standards? Have I been faithful to the moral law in my married life?

5. Have I gone against my conscience out of fear or hypocrisy?

6. Have I always tried to act in the true freedom of the sons of God according to the law of the Spirit, or am I the slave of forces within me?

WHY You should have a MISSAL of Your OWN!

AT MASS . . . for complete participation and understanding

- ✔ TO RECITE or SING your parts with understanding and devotion.
- ✔ TO LISTEN attentively to the Word of God.
- ✔ TO UNITE with the prayers of the Priest.
- ✔ TO HOLD attention and increase your devotion.
- ✔ TO HELP during short periods recommended for personal prayer.

AT HOME . . . to guide your Christian Life and personal spiritual reading

- ✔ TO PREPARE yourself for Mass by reading over the texts and helpful commentary.
- ✔ TO SEE the liturgical year as a whole.
- ✔ TO GUIDE your life in the spirit of the liturgy.
- ✔ TO MODEL your prayers on liturgical sources.
- ✔ TO MEDITATE often on the Word of God.